D1024825

richard north patterson

TWO COMPLETE NOVELS

DEGREE OF GUILT

THE FINAL JUDGMENT

WINGS BOOKS
NEW YORK

This omnibus edition was originally published in two separate volumes, and contains the complete text of each volume.

DEGREE OF GUILT Copyright © 1992 by Richard North Patterson

THE FINAL JUDGMENT Copyright © 1995 by Richard North Patterson

This 2002 edition published by Wings Books®, an imprint of Random House Value Publishing, a division of Random House, Inc., 280 Park Avenue, New York, NY 10017, by arrangement with Alfred A. Knopf Publishers, a division of Random House, Inc.

Wings Books® and colophon are trademarks of Random House, Inc.

Printed in the United States of America

Random House
New York • Toronto • London • Sydney • Auckland
www.randomhouse.com

Library of Congress Cataloging-in-Publication Data

Patterson, Richard North.
    [Degree of guilt]
    Two complete novels / Richard North Patterson.
        p. cm.
    Contents: Degree of guilt -- The final judgment.
    ISBN 0-517-21971-9
        1. Legal stories, American. 2. Trials (Murder)--Fiction. I. Patterson, Richard
North. Final judgment. II. Title: Final judgment. III. Title.

PS3566.A8242 D4 2002
813'.54--dc21
                                                                            2001045508

9 8 7 6 5 4 3 2

CONTENTS

DEGREE OF GUILT

1

THE FINAL JUDGMENT

549

ACKNOWLEDGMENTS

There are a number of people to whom I owe a great deal. Those who contributed important background information include Bill Fazio and Frank Pasaglia of the District Attorney's Office in San Francisco; Homicide Inspector Napoleon Hendricks; County Medical Examiner Dr. Boyd Stephens; defense attorney Jim Collins; and my colleague, Randy Knox. Dr. Norman Mages was a valuable sounding board when I applied my lay psychology to several of the characters. And Al Giannini, also of the District Attorney's Office, not only provided me with stimulating advice before I began writing but gave me important guidance once the manuscript was done. They deserve a goodly share of the credit for verisimilitude on matters such as medical and criminal procedure; any errors or omissions are my own.

There is no greater favor a writer can ask of a friend than to be an objective and critical reader. A book in progress can feel quite fragile; it is of immeasurable assistance to have readers who are supportive but honest. Because my fiancé, Laurie Anderson, my close friend and partner, Philip Rotner, and my great pal and literary agent, Fred Hill, were discerning judges of the strengths and weaknesses of my first draft, *Degree of Guilt* is a far better novel. And there is no finer editor than Sonny Mehta—incisive, patient, and devoted to bringing out the best values of the manuscript from the day that he first read it.

Finally, this book would not have happened the way it did without Alison Porter Thomas. That she typed the manuscript was the least of it: page to page and scene to scene, she was a gifted critic of language, characterization, and dialogue. I cannot ever thank her enough.

DEGREE OF GUILT

FOR LAURIE,
FOR EVERYTHING

PART ONE

THE KILLING

JANUARY 13

ONE

THE WOMAN FROZE in the hallway, staring at the numbered door-plate.

For a moment, she felt uncertain that this was the same suite she had left perhaps a minute before. Then she turned the knob slowly, wincing at its metallic click.

The door cracked ajar, a pallid sliver of light coming from inside. She paused, looking over her shoulder, less from fear of being seen than the desire to stay suspended in time, outside the room.

Time. She glanced at her gold wristwatch. When had it happened? she wondered. No way of telling now. Thirty minutes, she decided arbitrarily. Thirty minutes, and she had not decided what to do. Her mind was sluggish, numb with disbelief. She felt drugged.

Her fingertips were damp, she realized. With every thought, her choices seemed to narrow. She fought the impulse to stop thinking, to run. It took all her will to do nothing.

The chime of an elevator rang.

She flinched. Quickly, she tried to remember arriving in the elevator, how far it was down the hallway. Afraid to turn, unable to recall the corridor right behind her.

She straightened, squaring her shoulders, and pushed open the door.

The rectangle of light from within captured her like a photograph, a slender woman with long black hair, standing motionless in the door frame. The elevator opened. A second chime penetrated her shock.

She stepped inside and shut the door behind her.

Closing, it sounded heavy. Final, she corrected herself. It sounded final.

She turned to face the room.

Her eyes sought out details. Drawn blinds. Her black leather purse on the floor. The gold neck of an empty champagne bottle, above the rim of a silver ice bucket on a glass coffee table. The two crystal glasses. The heavy oil painting of San Francisco Bay she had remarked on, slightingly, when she first entered. Her panty hose on the carpet, ripped in one leg.

She touched her throat, feeling for scratches. She had broken a nail; it was that, oddly, which made her remember her own fragility.

Finally, she looked at him.

There was blood on the carpet now, beneath his chest. His pants were pulled below his knees.

A sudden jumble of images: Legs splayed at crazy angles. Blue argyle socks. A curly shock of red hair. Thin craggy face, turned to chalk. Eyes open as if to stare at the black handgun, lying near his head where she had left it.

For an instant, she was paralyzed.

She breathed in deeply, once, and exhaled. Then she took three steps, standing over him, and stared down at his bare buttocks.

The wave of revulsion hit her again, rose to her throat. She felt sure she would vomit; some cold, distant part of her brain wondered how that would look to them. Perhaps they would see her fear, see how afraid he had made her. Then the hatred ran through her again, hard and deep and raw.

She shut her eyes, remembering. What he had done. What he had wanted to do.

When they opened again, she felt stronger, more ready. More like the woman who had come here. More like the woman she had always been.

The nausea had passed. She sat beside him on the carpet.

There was no hole in his back, she saw; the bullet had not gone through. The flabby skin of his buttocks was turning gray. She could hardly see the scratches she had left there.

In her new resolve, she tried to summon a clinical dispassion. Perhaps forty minutes before, she realized, his heart had stopped pumping blood. The great man, bottom in the air, pale as a fish. It was almost comic.

The smile, small and involuntary, hurt her bruised mouth. The dark mirth vanished.

The rest of her life, she resolved, would not be about him. She would not let him do that to her. She would leave this day behind her.

Starting now.

She looked down at her watch. Too much time had passed. She must think quickly.

She stood with a kind of awkward dignity, preparing herself.

Walking carefully around the dead man, she knelt again on the other side, to pick up her panty hose. She left the gun where it was.

She held the hose dangling in one hand, reflecting. Then she hitched up her skirt, examining her legs. The scratch on her left thigh traced the tear in her panty hose.

They would ask to see her legs, she was certain.

Long, slender from the twenty years of exercise since college—running in the morning, gyms at night. Twenty years of willpower: like everything else in her life, her body was as nearly perfect as she could make it. But today, it had seemed, not perfect enough.

Struggling into the hose, she realized that her shoes were still under the coffee table.

What mattered? she wondered. It was hard to know.

She walked to the coffee table, staring down at the tape recorder.

Small and black, it stood upright near the glasses. Through its plastic window she saw that the tape had played until it stopped. And, with it, the woman's voice. Low and smoky, damning in a monotone a man whom she had never met and yet had believed in. Until now.

It was a moment before she realized that her fists had clenched. Another before she could move again.

As if in her sleep, she straightened her dress, put on her shoes. Looking around the suite, she saw that the bedroom door was shut. Strange, she thought, that he had not shown it to her.

She looked back toward the room.

The desk drawer was still open. She walked across the room, past the body, and closed it.

As she turned, the mirror above the couch caught her face.

It stopped her. With an odd detachment, she realized that the cameras would magnify the bruise beneath her eye.

She found nothing else. Neither the years since Washington, nor the past hour, had changed her much. No matter what he had said or done, or could not do.

She studied her reflection.

A face that photographed well, filmed well. A strong face, high cheekbones, clear brown eyes. It had always helped her, whether or not she had wanted that kind of help. She did not know whether it could help her now.

Turning, she took one final look at him, then at the room around her. To remember. Simply to remember. It would be a long day, she knew, a long night without sleep. Perhaps many nights until she slept. But she would need to remember, not forget.

Briefly, she thought again of the boy, and was ready.

The telephone was on an end table, next to the couch. She picked it up, standing stiffly, listening to the dial tone. Then her gaze caught the tape recorder.

They would record her, she knew. Listen to her words over and over. Listen to her tone of voice.

She swallowed once, clearing her throat. Her mouth tasted bitter.

Willfully, she stabbed the numbers.

The dial tone broke, became a ringing on the other end. She listened, steeling herself for the answering voice. But the man's brusque tone startled her. How foolish, she thought, to have wished for a woman.

"San Francisco Emergency," the male voice snapped again.

She found herself staring at the man on the floor, fixated on the black gun by his head. A foreign object, she thought. Foreign in her life. Foreign in her hand.

"There's been an accident," she said simply.

Teresa Peralta glanced at her watch. It was close to five, and he still had not sprung the trap.

The deposition had been going for seven hours. It was like watching a cat-and-mouse game where the cat had his eye on a second mouse; what lent the game its fascination was the smugness of the second mouse, who sat watching the cat toy with the first mouse, secure in his delusion that the cat had not seen him.

"Perhaps I can refresh your memory," Christopher Paget said pleasantly, and handed the first mouse a document. "Can you identify Defendant's Exhibit 13?"

This particular cat wore a navy double-breasted pinstripe of soft

Italian wool. With that came a silk floral tie; a white cotton shirt; square gold cuff links. As with other things about Christopher Paget, Terri wondered whether the careful dress was a form of camouflage, meant to deflect attention from who he really was.

They sat in a large conference room with a view of San Francisco Bay. Two lawyers on each side of the table, a witness and a court reporter. Terri was next to Paget, watching. The document—which seemed to have transfixed the witness—was his last.

"Please take your time," Paget suggested calmly.

Time, Terri thought again. Through the window, dusk was falling across the bay; lights were beginning to glimmer from the city and, across the gray swath of water, from Marin County. Five o'clock; the day care center would close at six. It was on the other side of the Bay Bridge, for Richie's convenience, near where they lived because Richie liked Berkeley better than the city. Next to her was a message, brought in at four-thirty. Richie was having dinner with some "business associates," to work on his new software "deal"; Terri must pick up Elena.

Forget it for a moment, she told herself. Learn something. Watch him do this.

Her metaphor, she decided, was better than she had thought. Paget had a cat's patience, a cat's still blue eyes. And there was a look of fineness to him, the result of great self-discipline and much exercise. The copper hair, ridged nose, and clean angles of his face seemed little different from the classic photograph, taken fifteen years before.

Christopher Paget had been famous so young, she knew, that some saw his career since then as an afterthought; the picture had been on the cover of *Time*, when he was twenty-nine.

She had found it in the library, as she was about to interview for a job as his associate. It was a well-known cover: a young lawyer testifying before Congress, the portrait of idealism and risk. Curiosity had led her from one article to another, relearning things she had heard about but had been too young to remember clearly.

The case had involved William Lasko, a close friend and financial supporter of the President. Paget was an investigator for the Economic Crimes Commission, assigned to check out Lasko's stock transactions. A key witness—one of Lasko's employees—had died in a hit-and-run "accident," leaving behind one ambiguous memo and the suspicion in Paget that someone within the ECC was betraying his inquiry.

Slowly, Paget had begun to uncover corruption within the ECC, which, he came to suspect, reached all the way to the White House. Then a second witness was kidnapped. When Paget persisted, someone had tried to kill him, just before he pieced together the meaning of Lasko's transactions.

The transactions, it turned out, were meant to funnel one and one-half million dollars to the President's campaign. And the man who had been leaking information about the investigation to Lasko was the chairman of Paget's agency. A man named Jack Woods.

It was never clear, Terri had found, whether Paget had entirely uncovered the corruption within the ECC itself. But he had taken the story to the Washington *Post* and then to Congress. A second witness had come forward—a young woman lawyer who was Woods's chief assistant. The results were prison sentences for Woods and Lasko, and political ruin for the President.

Christopher Paget was the first twenty-nine-year-old, a columnist wrote sourly, to bring down a President without using sex. The columnist seemed slightly nettled; Paget refused all requests for interviews.

As far as Terri could tell, he had never spoken of the Lasko case again.

The strain must have been enormous; everyone wanted a piece of him. The young woman witness, Terri knew, had become a television journalist. But Paget seemed to want no part of it. And, much more than the woman, he had earned the undying enmity of partisans of the President, who felt that he had tampered with the scales of history. He had left Washington and returned to California for good.

He had started his own firm, turned down requests to enter politics, made a specialty of white-collar crime. Within the office, Paget's time in Washington was treated like some private trauma, which people were too tactful to mention. In six months, she had learned almost nothing about him except that he was very good at his job.

"Mr. Gepfer?" he asked politely.

Across the table, the witness was staring at several pages of handwritten figures, seemingly unable to move or speak. He *looked* like a mouse, Terri decided: thin, sharp face, sandy hair combed to cover a bald spot, small eyes that shifted between avarice and fear. Had he not been so dishonest, and the moment so sublime, she would have felt sorry for him.

"I don't recall this document," opposing counsel broke in. "I'd like to know what this is and where you got it."

It was with Starr that Terri's conceit of cats and mice broke down. He had a basilisk face, slicked-back gray hair, and an air of deliberate shrewdness; it had not surprised her to learn from the skinny associate who sat next to Starr that he treated his staff like serfs.

Ignoring him, Paget turned to the court reporter, a young woman who sat watching from the end of the table, fingers poised over her machine. "In Mr. Starr's excitement," he said, "the witness may have forgotten the question. Perhaps you should read it back."

Starr leaned across the table. Terri scrutinized him, trying to figure out how much he understood. Not quite enough, she concluded; he looked like a man who was prepared for a setback but not for a disaster.

"Oh, go ahead."

"Thank you." Paget's tone held the barest trace of irony. He nodded to the reporter.

"Can you identify Defendant's Exhibit 13?" the reporter read out.

Almost inaudibly, Gepfer answered, "Yes."

Paget took up the questioning. "And is that document in your handwriting?"

"Yes."

"Could you read the heading at the top center, please."

Gepfer's eyes shut. "Liberal Accounting Adjustments," he said in a monotone.

"How did you come to call it that?"

"David Frank suggested it."

"When he was still chairman of Lyon Industries?"

"Yes."

"Did you also get the figures under that heading from Mr. Frank?"

Starr watched the questioning without changing expression. What Terri noticed was how intent he was.

"He set the direction," Gepfer answered miserably. "I came up with the numbers for him."

"And what do these numbers represent?"

"The amount of additional income Lyon needed to show a profit in fiscal 1991."

"Additional, or imaginary?"

Gepfer frowned, as if pondering a complex thought. "We didn't make the money," he finally answered, "if that's what you meant."

"But the figures on the document," Paget said, "became the figures on Lyon's financial statements, correct?"

"Correct."

"And were used to raise $53 million in the public offering?"

"Yes."

"Mr. Frank sold stock in that offering, correct?"

"Yes."

"And made several million dollars."

"Yes."

"And you also sold stock in the offering?"

"Yes."

"And made roughly $670,000."

"Yes," Gepfer said again.

Paget had him in a rhythm now. "Whose idea was it to change the books?"

Gepfer's voice turned accusatory. "Mr. Frank's."

"And you just went along."

"Yes."

"Did my client, Steve Rudin, know about this?"

"Objection," Starr cut in. "Calls for speculation."

Paget's eyes widened. "Really, Mr. Starr, I'm proving your entire case. I'd think you'd be more grateful. . . ."

"Come off it. Frank killed himself. How can this man know who Frank talked to?"

Paget looked at him a moment. Not for the first time, Terri had the sense that nothing surprised him; that something had taught him not to show what he felt; that he expected very little from anyone. "You mean you haven't asked him?" he asked Starr softly. "You're prosecuting this case against my client, this man's cooperating with you, and you haven't asked him yet?"

Starr leaned back. "I'm not the witness here," he retorted. "I'm not telling you what I've asked or haven't asked. That's work product."

"I'll try another question," Paget said agreeably, turning to the witness. "Before today, when was the last time you saw this document?"

Starr's face said everything; too late, he saw where this was about to go. Could hear the next five questions before they were ever asked.

"July," the witness said. For Gepfer, Terri knew, the worst had already happened; the questions were now worse for someone else.

Paget sat back, looking at both Starr and the witness. "At that time, did you give this document to anyone?"

"Yes."

Paget had stopped looking at Gepfer now. When he asked the next question, his gaze was fixed on Starr.

"And who was that?"

"Objection!" Starr stood up. "That's work product."

The court reporter's head had begun moving back and forth, following the voices.

Paget turned to Gepfer. "You may answer."

"Press on," Starr snapped, "or we're walking out."

"That hardly seems reasonable." Paget had yet to raise his voice. "Let me suggest this, Mr. Starr. Why don't we call a magistrate and get a ruling by telephone."

"Fine." Starr spoke with more assurance. "But the courts close at five—there's no one there to give us a ruling. I'm busy the next few weeks. Maybe sometime in February."

Terri suppressed a smile.

"Curiously," Paget said to Starr, "I anticipated this problem and called Magistrate Riordan's office this morning. He'll be available until six."

Starr stared at him. Paget pointed toward a telephone table. "The telephone is over there," he said. "Just dial nine for an outside line. I believe Ms. Peralta's written the number down for you, if you haven't yet committed it to memory. . . ."

"This is an abuse. You're trying to invade the tactical decisions of opposing counsel. That's the classic definition of work product."

"Hardly. In fact, I'm fascinated to know how the identity of the nameless person with whom Mr. Gepfer shared this document could be *anyone's* work product. Really, Mr. Starr, it seems you have but two choices. The first is to call Magistrate Riordan and present an argument that, quite likely, is without precedent in the annals of Western jurisprudence. That's the option I favor, if only for the sheer interest of listening to it.

"The second and more mundane choice is to take a ten-minute break and see if we can resolve this matter without compelling Mr. Gepfer to answer any more questions."

Starr was impassive. Finally, he waved Gepfer and the court reporter from the room.

"If you have something to say to me," Starr said at length, "I'll give you ten minutes."

Terri could not help but admire the gall that made a trip to the abattoir sound like a concession to good manners.

"Ten minutes," Paget responded, "is all I'm giving you to drop this lawsuit."

"What kind of crap—"

Paget reached beneath the table, pulling a typed agreement from his briefcase. "This is a stipulation of settlement. It recites that you have become aware that your charges against Steve Rudin are mistaken; that Mr. Gepfer has confirmed the error; that you are dismissing this lawsuit; and that your firm is paying Mr. Rudin $250,000 to compensate him for his time and expenses."

"I won't sign that."

"For at least six months," Paget went on, "you've had this document. Which means that you've known for at least six months that my client was innocent of fraud."

"You can't hold me responsible for what Gepfer says now."

Paget looked at his watch. "Why don't we save eight minutes and ask Gepfer what you knew?"

"The man's admitted falsifying documents. Now you want him to give false testimony. Whatever he says, no one will believe it."

"Won't they? Frank was bankrupt when he killed himself. That leaves only two defendants with money. Gepfer has less than a million; but my client is *very* wealthy *and* covered by insurance. So you make a deal with Gepfer: if he doesn't give anyone else the document and doesn't tell anyone what really happened, you let him keep the money he stole and try to extract a settlement from my client by tying him up in an endless lawsuit you know to be a fraud."

Starr folded his arms. "You can never prove that."

"Care to find out? Because if the case against Steve Rudin goes one question longer, you'll find out more than that. Whether we can prove it. Whether we can win a suit for malicious prosecution. Whether the legal press will enjoy watching us try. Whether the Bar Association will let you keep your license. Whether every judge in this district will start looking at you like some evolutionary cul-de-sac. And the only person who will enjoy that more than I is Steve Rudin—the man you charged with fraud." Standing, Paget looked at his watch again. "You have five minutes, it seems."

Terri followed him to his office.

It was sparsely furnished: bright modern prints; two plants; a glass table; a single picture of a dark-haired boy. Paget collected art, she knew; one of the prints was a Miró. She had no idea who the boy was.

Paget stood staring out the window.

"Will they go for it?" Terri asked.

"Yes." He answered without turning. "Starr is driven by sheer self-interest."

"I can hardly believe he knew."

"Oh, he knew. Always expect people to be what they've been in the past. That way, they don't surprise or disappoint you." Paget shoved his hands in his pockets, sounding suddenly weary. "Being surprised is a sin, professionally. But it's the disappointment that can be so soul-wearing."

The remark was uncharacteristic; it was almost, Terri thought, as if he were talking to himself.

"How *did* you get the document?" she asked.

"I promised not to say." He turned, smiling faintly. "But Starr really should treat his employees better."

There was a knock on the door. Starr's associate came in, holding the settlement papers. He paused, glancing at Terri. She wondered if the associate, who seemed a little too interested in her, realized that she was married. It wasn't as though he *knew* her at all, and lately it was harder to believe that men could find her attractive. What could you say about a nose that she thought was a little too sharp, crescent eyes a little too small for her liking, straight brown hair that she shared with fifty million other Hispanic women in the Western Hemisphere alone? You could say what Richie said in that ambiguous tone of voice—that she looked smart.

"He signed them," Starr's associate said, and handed the papers to Terri.

"Thank you," Paget answered civilly. The associate looked at him, then at Terri, and left.

Terri felt a rush of triumph, although the triumph was not hers.

Without really thinking, she said, "I thought maybe the watch trick was overdoing it a bit. At least on top of handing him the agreement."

He shrugged. "Apparently not."

"Did you ever do that before?"

He regarded her a moment. "Once. Years ago."

"Did it work?"

"After a fashion."

There was distance in his tone, perhaps preoccupation. Feeling awkward, she looked at her watch.

"I have to run. A kid emergency."

"I have somewhere to go too. We'll call Steve Rudin in the morning."

The telephone rang. Distractedly, Paget answered it. Terri paused in the doorway, thinking it might be something about the case. But what kept her there, forgetful of herself and time, was the stillness that came over him.

"Where are you?" Paget finally asked.

He listened for another moment.

"Don't talk to anyone," he said. "I'll be right down."

Paget sounded quite calm. Only when he put the telephone down, with almost exaggerated care, did she notice he was pale.

She looked at him quizzically.

Paget seemed surprised to see her. Then he said simply, "Mark Ransom's been killed."

It startled her. She did not know why someone would be calling him or how he was connected to the famous writer. Finally, she asked, "Who was that?"

He paused a moment. "Mary Carelli."

"The TV interviewer?"

The description seemed to surprise him. Suddenly it came to her: the woman in Washington, the second witness against Lasko. Then, as if correcting her, Christopher Paget replied, "My son Carlo's mother."

TWO

CHRISTOPHER PAGET had not imagined that the mother of his only son, a woman for whom he had felt much more passion than trust, would be accused of murder within twenty-four hours of appearing in their lives for the first time in eight years.

They had been in the kitchen of their house in Pacific Heights. It was four o'clock: through the floor-to-ceiling window, the failing sunlight lent the trim Victorians and stucco mansions a pale Florentine pink and white; the bay a slate blue; the Marin headlands beyond a tawny brown. Paget was slicing lemons for chicken piccata. Carlo was sitting on a barstool, slender frame leaning against the counter, complaining about his girlfriend's parents.

"She's *fifteen*," Carlo was saying, "and they're absolutely paranoid. They've done everything but have her tubes tied."

Paget smiled at the hyperbole; he was fairly confident that Carlo did not yet warrant such drastic measures.

"Like what, exactly?" he asked.

"Like they won't even let her out on weekends."

"At all?"

"At all."

Paget began chopping scallions. "That's a bit medieval. Are you sure there isn't some history there?"

"She *has* no history, Dad. They've never let her out of the house at night. They're afraid her morals are going to get corrupted or something, and all *I* want to do is introduce her to my friends and do stuff with everybody."

For the moment, Paget guessed, that was pretty much true; Carlo and his friends hung out in groups, and the easy interchange of boys and girls as friends struck Paget as infinitely saner than the rituals of his own teenage years, when girls were a mystery and dates took place in cars.

"They're afraid of *something*," Paget finally said. "Perhaps from their own lives."

Carlo pondered that a moment. Not for the first time, Paget examined his son with a kind of wonder. To be so uncertain still, he thought, yet so suddenly close to manhood. Paget could recall like yesterday carrying Carlo on his shoulders. Now Carlo was taller than he, a handsome black-haired boy with a crooked grin and startling blue eyes. The eyes were regarding him with that opaque look which, Paget knew, often concealed thoughts too close to home. "They're pretty young," Carlo ventured, "to be parents of a fifteen-year-old."

Paget refocused on the scallions. "And Jennifer is an only child?"

Carlo nodded. "After her, she says, her parents gave up sex."

"Kids always think that." Paget smiled. "The alternative is too grotesque for any teenager to imagine."

"I don't know." Carlo's voice took on a teasing edge. "I've never had much trouble with that."

"I suppose it's that I'm single." Paget took a light tone, trying to decipher the meaning of his son's remark. "I guess that makes my social life a little more conspicuous and makes it somewhat less likely you'll confuse me with Ward Cleaver. Back to Jennifer: is your homework done?"

"Yes—for hours. We've got a basketball game tomorrow, and I want to rest up. Anyhow, what does my homework have to do with Jennifer?"

"If you have time, perhaps we could invite her to dinner this evening. I can make more chicken, and maybe Jennifer's parents will feel better about letting her go somewhere they know there's another parent and perhaps a few house rules."

Carlo grinned. "Like safe sex and a two-drink limit?"

"If I were you, I would keep *that* line in the family." Paget looked over at him. "I sometimes wonder, Carlo, what lessons you've learned from me."

"What do you mean?"

Carlo looked genuinely puzzled. Perhaps, Paget thought, there was less beneath the conversation than he had feared. "There's enough to choose from," Paget finally said. "Your life hasn't precisely been the Disney Channel."

"Did I ever accuse you," Carlo said, deadpan, "of murdering Mickey Mouse?"

Paget put down the knife. "You are absolutely determined to make this hard for me. Okay, the message goes like this: The subject of the moment is sex. It can be wonderful—as long as you treat it with respect, it's part of a friendship, and you're as honest about your feelings as you would be with any friend when the subject truly matters. Sometime, making love will be there for you. When it is, don't lie, don't push, and don't sleep with anyone you won't care for next month. Is that succinct enough?"

Once more, Paget saw the question in Carlo's eyes. But his son let it go unspoken, as he had for eight years. "Maybe," Carlo said simply, "our generation will do better with all that."

"I think you'll do better with everything." How, Paget wondered, to steer the conversation from this precipice. "The most important thing," he added, "is to listen, to be fair with each other, and to speak your heart without attacking your partner. But my own parents could neither show nor tell me, and I've only been able to tell you." And, Paget thought silently, I've been all you had. "Maybe," he finished, "you can show *me*."

When the doorbell rang, his son was still regarding him, as if forming a thought or question. Paget smiled. "Dorothy Parker once asked, when the doorbell rang, 'What fresh hell is this?' But in this case, someone's just saved you from 'Father Knows Best.' "

Carlo raised an eyebrow. "Guess you want me to get that."

"Please."

Paget heard his son head past the dining room, feet padding on the hardwood floor. The living room was large, with a sprawling Persian rug and a ten-foot ceiling that tended to eat up sound, muffling Carlo's footsteps as he moved toward the door. Paget resumed thinking about chicken piccata.

"Dad?"

"Yes," Paget called out.

"There's someone here."

Carlo's voice sounded thin and a little strained. Paget put the knife down and headed for the living room.

She stood with her back to him, looking at the prints as she had that morning in Washington, fifteen years before.

He watched her, silent.

Without haste, she finished her scrutiny of the last print, an exotic African landscape by Jesse Allen, lush trees and surreal birds that existed only in the artist's imagination. Turning, she said, "It's rather like your apartment on East Capitol. Of course, I recognize several of the prints." She smiled almost imperceptibly, pointing out the red-and-blue print of a geometric ball that seemed to roll as one approached it. "That's a Vasarely, I believe you once informed me."

Speak of the devil, Paget thought, looking from the woman to his son. But they had not been speaking of her, not directly, and Paget found himself speechless with surprise and withheld anger.

"Carlo," he finally said, "I believe you recall your mother."

Carlo stood as if caught between them, uncertain of what to do or say. Flashing the boy a warm, almost intimate smile, she moved to him. "Oh, yes," she said dryly to Paget. "We've met."

Paget was struck by how alike they were: dark hair, olive skin, chiseled faces, a slimness that combined strength with a certain delicacy. In Carlo, her grace was still a tentative teenage dignity, which, Paget knew, might well mature into the stylish ease that can capture a room. As she could.

"What brings you here?" he asked.

"Work," she said dismissively. "Perhaps an interview."

If she had any further explanation, her tone said, it would not come in front of Carlo. The boy shifted from foot to foot, like a matchmaker watching a blind date go sour. Paget felt desperately sorry for him.

"Don't worry," Mary said to Carlo, taking his arm. "He's always like that around me—completely mesmerized. When he was twenty-nine, it was all he could do to ask me out. But then it was all *I* could do to accept."

Carlo grinned, still embarrassed, but relieved at her banter. "Then why did you?"

"Oh, I was waiting for Kevin Costner to mature. And your father had a certain indefinable charm."

Paget stood there, grateful that she had put Carlo more at ease, unsettled by the artificiality of it all. "I'm not speechless. Just cooking.

I can either skip this celebrity roast or burn the chicken." He paused at the look in Carlo's eyes. "Can you stay for dinner?"

"I can't, really." Her half smile reflected how tepid he had sounded. "Go cook. Perhaps Carlo can show me the house."

Her voice was different, Paget realized. The trace evidence that she was second-generation Italian—a sort of Mediterranean intensity that underscored certain words—had become the studied diction of a stage actress. Television, he thought: flipping channels, he had seen her once by accident and stopped, bemused by her genesis from lawyer to "personality." Abruptly, he had snapped off the picture; some moments later, he had found himself staring at a blank screen.

"Carlo's room alone," he said now, "should make the tour worthwhile. There's been nothing like it since Chernobyl."

She smiled again. "I'm Carlo's guest," she said. "I'll let him pick his spots."

Awkwardly, Carlo led her upstairs.

Paget walked to the kitchen, still suspended in time.

So much like Washington, she had said. Remembering the Vasarely as Paget remembered her standing in front of it, studying its patterns, wearing nothing at all.

It was the last weekend they had ever made love.

The Lasko case had not yet broken, and Paget had been certain that it never would—that he was at the end of things, that Lasko had killed a witness with impunity, and that Lasko's source within the agency, the one who had monitored Paget's progress, would never be detected. Trapped in a deep and solitary anger, feeling that Mary was opposed to him, Paget had meant to spend the weekend alone. Then Mary had come to his apartment unannounced, as she had come today.

They were both in their late twenties, Paget reflected now, so sure of what they already knew, so disastrously unknowing. Alone in his kitchen, with Mary and their son upstairs, he felt the blindness of the moment as they lived it then.

At first, the sense of things unspoken had hung between them. They played backgammon, drank wine, smoked dope. They did not speak of Lasko.

Finally, gradually, they talked about themselves.

"What do you want in a woman?" she had asked him.

Her voice wasn't intrusive, just curious. Paget felt stoned enough to try to answer; drugs, and defeat, seemed to have lowered his defenses. "A lot of what I look for in anyone, I guess. Curiosity. Dislike for the easy answer. That in a good moment they can imagine what it's like to be an old woman or a small child. That they are more than what they do or what they are."

Mary smiled through the haze. "You don't ask much."

"Not much at all."

They slid down the couch, heads resting on opposite arms, legs parallel on the pillows. The next record fell on the stereo.

The Starship began singing.

Paget's limbs felt numb. The darkened room became images in a field of black, suspended in black: the spotlit Vasarely ball rolling toward them; the two empty glasses; the last roll of the dice faceup on the backgammon board. Her eyes.

He began to feel lost in them. The notes of "Miracles" came to him one at a time, from some great distance. He did not know or care how many moments had passed since anyone had spoken.

Her voice broke the quiet.

"You know, Chris, you've been very lucky. You've never wanted— or needed—anything."

It sounded like someone else, not him. But all he said was, "I keep hearing that."

"No, I mean it. Half the girls I knew growing up were married at eighteen. Sometimes I hate looking back."

Her words seemed to hang in the air. Paget realized that he had forgotten the bitterness she seemed to carry: about being Catholic; about her parents' stillborn emotions and lack of encouragement; about the ex-husband who had wanted her to quit law school and have babies. Forgotten, more surprisingly, how much she needed to succeed. Forgotten her fierce pride at being assistant to the chairman of their agency, the ambition that had caused her to clash with Paget as many nights as they had made love.

Tonight he wanted none of it.

"No need," Paget answered smilingly. "You've done a lot. That's something else I like in a woman."

She smiled back. Paget reached for her then. She looked at him with a clear black gaze. Then her arm rose in a graceful arc and pulled him down.

They undressed each other slowly, mouths and fingertips stopping where they cared to. For a long time, they lay in a cocoon of touching, finding, sounds that were not words. From one thing to another, mouth on her nipple, hand grazing her wetness, her hips rising, body twisting into him. Warm skin, thick clean hair against his face. Moments of suspended time, the absence of haste, the banishment of their ambitions and anything else that mattered in the daylight.

Perhaps an hour passed before he was inside her.

Even that felt different. Especially that.

Her stomach and hips rose, pressing against him as if desperate to pull him inside, to touch as much skin with her skin as she could. When they moved together, it was without hesitance, subtle changes in rhythm passing between them without words, suddenly faster, almost desperate, until she shuddered as their mouths found each other and a half cry rose from her throat and met his.

Afterward, no one spoke.

It was as if, Paget thought, their bodies had learned something their heads did not yet know. Neither of them wanted to spoil that. Neither wanted to ask for anything.

"You wanted to ask me something?" she said now.

He turned from the stove.

She stood in the doorway, without Carlo. Paget sensed that she had been there for some moments and that, unusual for him, he had been too abstracted to sense her presence. He looked past her, toward the living room.

She followed his thoughts. "Carlo's waiting outside," she said in a quiet voice. "I told him I wanted to say goodbye."

"I might have wished," Paget answered with equal quiet, "that you'd bothered saying hello."

"He's my son—"

"A cat's a better mother," Paget cut in. "You performed a storage function, that's all. And we both know whom you did *that* for."

"Do we, Chris?" Her smile was bitter. "Do *we*, really? Because I doubt you'll ever know or understand."

Paget's gaze was cold. "I've come to understand a great many things. About you, and about myself."

"Including why *you* did things? Or are *your* motives as pure as ever?"

Paget stared at her, silent.

"It seems," Mary said with muted irony, "that we're beyond the help of a family counselor."

Paget kept watching her. "What I was going to ask," he said more evenly, "is why you're here."

"As I told you, I'm here to do background for an interview."

"You could have come and gone. As you have a dozen times."

"I wanted to see him." She gave a small, almost helpless shrug; it was sufficiently unlike her to give Paget pause. "Needed to. For reasons of my own."

"What about *him?*"

"Is it really bad," she retorted quietly, "for Carlo to think I care a little?"

"Why now?" Paget shoved his hands in his pockets. "You could have called. I could have prepared him. I wouldn't have stopped you."

"Then call it a moment of weakness, Chris, and trust the good outweighs the bad." She smiled faintly. "We've had those moments before."

Paget looked past her "He's a nice boy," he said finally. "Normal. I think quite happy, for the most part."

"I can see that." She paused, then spoke with more feeling. "It was what I *wanted* to see."

Paget nodded. "Now you have."

She turned to leave. Turning again, she paused in the doorway. "You look well, Chris."

"And you."

She smiled again, as if some private thought amused her, and was gone. Paget stood there, suddenly quite certain that she intended never to see him again.

Now, a day later, she had called.

"If you need me," Terri Peralta was saying, "I can call a neighbor, see if someone can pick up Elena."

They were standing in the elevator on the way down to the parking garage. He had been lost in memory; it took him a moment to respond.

"Thanks," he answered. "Just go home, be a mom." He saw her puzzlement, realized how dismissive he might sound. "She'll want a referral, that's all."

"Are you sure?"

"Positive. It's never good to represent someone you know, and she's far too smart to want that. Plus I haven't done a homicide in years."

Terri was studying him intently. She doesn't miss much, he thought, but this is more than she will ever understand.

The elevator opened. Paget said good night and walked quickly to his car.

THREE

MARY WAITED IN a witness room on the sixth floor of the Hall of Justice.

The room was spare: a bare table, white cinder-block walls, gray linoleum floors. A squat female cop watched through a glass window to ensure that Mary did not harm herself.

She turned her back to the guard.

The monastic simplicity helped her concentrate. He would want to know what happened; unless the years had changed the way he thought, no detail would be too minute.

He would not, she was determined, find her desperate and without resources.

What would help most was to trace what the police had done. To remember, moment by moment, the four hours that had passed since she stood staring at Ransom's body, telephone in her hand.

"What happened?" Emergency had asked.

She had envisioned the tape spinning, capturing her words and tone of voice. "There's been an accident."

"What kind of accident?"

She hesitated. "A gun went off."

"Someone's been shot?"

"Yes." The stain was spreading on the rug. "I think he's dead."

It sounded so foolish that the tremor in her own voice startled her. "Where are you?" Emergency was demanding.

"The Hotel Flood." She went blank. "I can't remember the room."

"Who is this?"

"Wait. . . . It's registered to Mark Ransom. A suite."

"Who is this?" the voice repeated.

"Just come," she said.

When the two police officers and three paramedics burst through the doorway, they found her sitting in front of the tape recorder, legs crossed, staring fixedly across his body at the drawn blinds of a window.

The paramedics ran to the body. They flipped it on its back, opened the bloodstained shirt, placed pads on its chest. To her, their near frenzy seemed close to pantomime, like practice for a paramedic class. It was standard procedure, Mary supposed; only she knew how very dead he was.

"It's a coroner's case," one of them said.

The others nodded. Much more slowly, they turned Ransom on his stomach, as he had been before. When they rose, stepping back from the body, she saw that Ransom's eyes were still open. With a rush of nausea and anger, she remembered how he had looked at her in the moments before he died. Once more, she hated him.

"What happened?" a policeman asked her.

He was a big man, with a creased young-old face and light-blue eyes that looked immensely sad. He seemed to know who she was; for a moment she wanted to talk to him until she had nothing more to say. Then she caught herself; like the 911 tape, everything she said would be sifted by the police, the district attorney, the media.

"He tried to rape me," she answered.

The cop looked her up and down, pausing at the bruise on her cheek. She became aware that the second cop, a small, wiry man with glasses and a brown mustache and a notepad, was staring at the tape recorder. "Did he?" the first cop asked.

"Did he what?"

"Penetrate you?"

"No." She realized that she had folded her arms.

"Do you need a doctor?"

"No. Please. It's the last thing I want—someone touching me."

Slowly, he nodded. "Could you tell us your name, ma'am?"

The respectful "ma'am" carried a certain irony: she did not date the loss of youth from her fortieth birthday but from the first time the salesgirl at the Saks cosmetics counter had called her ma'am.

"Mary Carelli."

"I've seen you on TV." He hesitated. "And *his* name was Ransom?"

"Yes." Her voice was flat. "Mark O'Malley Ransom."

He paused, perhaps in recognition of Ransom's name, perhaps wondering how much he could ask without giving her Miranda warnings. He seemed to be feeling some new hesitancy, a concern about mistakes.

"Whose handgun is that?" he finally asked.

"Mine."

Her interrogator looked briefly at the second cop. "Thank you, ma'am," he said.

She nodded.

He glanced back at the body. "We'll need to keep you here for a while."

The second cop went to the door and stationed himself outside. The first went to the phone.

The next hour was a jumble that Mary struggled to understand. Several men in plainclothes arrived. They videotaped the body, took pictures. Blinking at the flashbulbs, she watched as a slight blond woman she took to be from the coroner's office glanced quickly at her and then bent over Ransom.

The woman flexed Ransom's arms, felt his forehead and beneath his armpits. Then she examined the surface of his shirt where the bullet entered; inspected his hands; slid an instrument under his fingernails; applied some type of swab to his penis. The woman's cool meticulousness made Mary feel sick. Her throat was dry.

Two more men arrived, one white, one black. The black man had short grizzled hair, a shambling frame that half concealed a paunch, gold wire-rimmed glasses, and an impassive face that seemed never to change. He took in Ransom, then the room.

The woman had turned Ransom on his stomach, examining his back. "It didn't go through," she said to the black man.

She sounded faintly disappointed, as if that were a problem. The black man nodded, and she resumed her inspection of the corpse.

She paused at Ransom's buttocks, eyes narrowing. She traced the scratches with her fingertip.

The black man was speaking to Mary. "Inspector Monk," he said. "Homicide."

She looked up at him, startled. He nodded toward the woman. "There are some things we'll need to do." Like everything else around them, his rich baritone seemed too methodical to be human.

How long must I stay here? Mary almost asked, and then caught herself. Much better that she stayed, she realized. She asked simply, "Can I have some water?"

Monk went to the bathroom and returned with a glass of water. As he placed it in her hand, the woman appeared next to him. "This is Dr. Shelton," Monk said. "The medical examiner."

The woman had level blue eyes and wore no makeup. "Elizabeth Shelton," she amended. We're sisters, the clear voice conveyed; I recognize you. As the woman knelt by the couch, Mary felt a moment's gratitude.

"He didn't penetrate you?" her new friend asked.

"No."

Shelton nodded. "Do you care to see a doctor?"

"No. I don't want to be touched."

Shelton paused. "Can *I* look at your neck?" she asked.

Her expression seemed as sympathetic as her voice. Silent, Mary leaned forward.

Gently, the woman raised Mary's chin with her fingertips. "How did this happen?" she asked.

Mary swallowed. "He did it." She hesitated, and then added, "When he was on top of me."

"Are you hurt anywhere else?"

Mary touched her cheek. "Here."

"What happened?"

"He slapped me."

Shelton looked at her. "With his palm open?"

"Yes." Mary's voice fell. "He just kept hitting me."

"How many times?"

"I'm not sure."

Shelton hesitated. "Are there other places?" she asked.

Mary looked down at her legs. "Yes."

"Where?"

"My thigh."

Shelton nodded. "Can you show me?"

Mary said nothing. Shelton glanced up at Monk. Wordless, he retreated to the other side of the room.

Gently, Shelton said, "It will help us."

Mary glanced around her. Monk was pulling up the closed blinds.

Monk's partner—a pale, balding man who reminded Mary of a priest—
was stooped over her black gun. The first uniformed cop watched him
with an expression of infinite melancholy.

Slowly, Mary pulled up her dress.

The welt seemed more raised now, a red jagged line beneath her
panty hose. Shelton tilted her head. "What happened here?"

"He was trying to pull down my panty hose."

Shelton contemplated the welt. "You had them on, then."

"Yes. Of course."

Almost solicitously, Shelton pulled down Mary's dress. Only after
a moment did Mary realize that she was examining the fabric.

"May I look at your hands?"

When Mary nodded, Shelton took each hand in hers. Once more
her tone was cool, gentle. "I'd like to take samples," she said. "From
your fingernails."

She went quickly to a black bag and reached inside. Then she returned and knelt again, holding a slim metal instrument and a small
white envelope. "May I?" she asked.

After a moment, Mary nodded. Shelton slid the instrument under
the forefinger of Mary's right hand. As she did, Mary noticed her gold
hoop earrings.

Mary still said nothing. Finger by finger, the woman took samples.
Suddenly, oddly, Mary felt naked.

"I'm tired," she murmured.

"Just three more." The woman sounded like a pediatrician now,
talking to a child. "I'm almost done."

Mary just sat there. She seemed unable to do anything.

"Thank you," Shelton said.

She paused, glancing at the tape player, an unspoken question forming in her eyes. Mary imagined Shelton's surprise when she listened
to the tape. Then Shelton rose, breaking her thought, and went to
Monk.

Standing beside Ransom's body, they spoke too quietly to be heard.
Mary felt utterly alone.

Monk nodded to Shelton and came back. "We'll need to take you
down to Homicide, go through what happened."

Mary felt herself stiffen. "How long will it be?" she asked.

"A few hours. You'll have to wait while we clean up here."

He never apologized, she noticed, as if she were the grist for some impersonal machine. "He *abused* me," she said.

"You can tell us that." His voice was neither indifferent nor impressed. "You can tell us all about that."

Something in his tone bespoke hour after endless hour. When Mary stood, her legs felt shaky. She was all right, she told herself. It was just that she had been sitting too long.

"Officer DiStefano will take you," Monk was saying.

The sad-faced policeman took her arm. Haltingly, she let him steer her toward the door. How many hours, she wondered, had it been since she had first entered, taken the glass of champagne from his hand? Listened to the woman's voice on tape, telling her what Ransom wanted?

Turning, she half hoped to see an empty room.

The tape recorder still rested on the coffee table.

The second cop was putting the two wineglasses in a bag. To his left, Shelton had turned Ransom on his back again. Ransom stared emptily at the ceiling as Shelton examined his shirt, then his fingers. She slid two glassine bags over Ransom's hands.

Suddenly, irrationally, Mary felt that she could not leave them alone with Ransom.

"Come on, Miss Carelli."

The door closed behind them.

Downstairs, the lobby felt strange. A concierge, a few tourists, a middle-aged man with his arm around someone who looked like an expensive prostitute. No one else. Some watchful part of Mary's mind registered that the media did not yet know.

Outside, it was cool. As they walked to the patrol car, she was only half aware of the city surrounding Nob Hill. Then a car door slammed behind her, and it was cramped and dark.

In the back seat, Mary found herself staring at the metal grille between herself and DiStefano. He started the engine.

"Just stay here for a moment," she said. "And open the windows. Please."

The Hall of Justice was a featureless monolith, longer than a football field. The lobby was as bleak as the emergency room of a city hospital:

dim light; bare walls; green vinyl tile worn by countless footsteps. A few refugees from the urban underclass drifted through the hallways on their way to some business with police. Mary had the surreal feeling of having passed into another life.

They took her to the sixth floor, through a door marked HOMICIDE in forties-style black letters, and put her in an eight-by-eleven room without windows. Someone brought her coffee with powdered cream and a stir stick. She examined the room: a long table, hard wooden chairs, yellow walls, green carpeting. The coffee tasted thin and bitter.

Mary waited for two hours.

What were they doing? she wondered. Staring at the bare walls, she reviewed what Shelton had done: her inch-by-inch examination of the body, her finger tracing the scratches on Ransom's buttocks, her stillness as she studied Ransom's wound. What had she seen?

Reflexively, Mary touched the bruise beneath her eye.

It felt puffy, hurt to the touch. The scratch on her neck made it painful to turn.

Fingernails. Shelton had looked at them. Looked at Ransom's. Looked at the wound again. Sent Mary away.

Monk appeared in the doorway.

"Are you comfortable?" he asked.

"Yes."

"Feel up to talking?"

"Yes." Mary felt new energy. "I want to get this over with."

Monk left, and then he returned holding a tape recorder. He placed it on the table between them.

Mary stared at it. "What's on that tape?" she finally asked.

Monk appraised her. "It's a blank tape," he said. "We record all interviews."

Somehow she had not expected that. Eyes fixed on the tape recorder, she nodded.

He pressed the button. Mary watched the tape begin slowly turning.

"This is an initial homicide investigation." Speaking into the tape, Monk's voice was deliberate, uninflected. "It is January 13 at 4:45 P.M. The victim is Mark Ransom. The interviewee is Mary Carelli. I am Inspector Charles Monk."

Monk took a small white card from the inside pocket of his suit coat. "Miss Carelli, we are obligated to advise you of your rights. I am going to read your rights from this card. Please respond in a clear voice."

"All right."

"You have the right to remain silent. That means you do not have to answer any question I ask. Do you understand that?"

"Yes."

"Anything you say can and will be used against you in a court of law. Do you understand that?"

Mary watched the tape turn one rotation, then another.

"Miss Carelli?"

"Yes. I understand that."

"You have the right to have an attorney present. If you cannot afford an attorney, one will be provided for you. Do you understand that?"

"Yes. Of course."

"Do you want an attorney present?"

"No."

"Do you wish to answer my questions?"

"Yes." Raising her eyes from the tape, Mary sat straighter. "He tried to *rape* me. Does anyone here care about that?"

A moment's hesitation, and then Monk's impassivity returned. "Did you know Mark Ransom?" he asked.

"Only in the way that everyone knows Mark Ransom." She caught herself. "Mark Ransom courted celebrity. But I'd never met him before today."

"How did you come to be in his hotel suite?"

"It was work." She paused, and then asked, "How much about myself do I explain?"

Monk regarded her a moment. "I recognize you," he answered. "But the tape doesn't, and this is *your* story."

"All right." Mary shrugged. "I'm a television journalist, for ABC. Since last fall, I've been doing interview segments for *Deadline.*" Suddenly Mary wanted Monk to confirm her existence outside this room. "You've seen it—on Tuesday nights?"

Monk considered the question, as if it would change the dynamic between them. "My wife watches," he said at last. "Go on."

"That was why I was meeting with him. To discuss a possible interview."

"Who arranged the meeting?"

"It was *his* idea." Mary could hear her own bitterness. "He *called* me."

"Where?"

"He left a message at my office. In Manhattan." She paused. "I called him back from home."

"What did he say?"

"That he thought I'd be interested in the book he'd just finished."

"Did he tell you what the book was about?"

"Laura Chase." Monk did not ask who she was; presumably, Mary thought, the tape recorder was more familiar with dead movie goddesses who had put revolvers in their mouths and pulled the trigger. "Ransom claimed to have new information about her suicide."

Monk looked slightly puzzled. "How long has Laura Chase been dead?"

"Almost twenty years."

"What kind of information did Ransom have?"

Mary paused, keeping her tone level. "About her affair with Senator James Colt."

"James Colt?" Monk said the words softly, as if to himself. For a moment, he seemed to lose the thread of his question.

"James Colt," Mary repeated. "It's part of the whole mystique about her suicide: 'Who Killed Laura Chase?' and all that folklore about the mysterious woman who called the police to say that Laura had killed herself. It never seems to stop: just last month, someone insisted to me at a cocktail party that the Colt family had murdered Laura Chase to save his chances to be President, and that the unknown caller was the senator's wife." Mary's voice turned bitter. "But Ransom said he had something new that no one knew but him. Something he would share with me."

"What was that?"

"Ransom claimed that James Colt met her in Palm Springs about a week before she died. She got drunk, took pills." Mary paused. "After Senator Colt got through with her, Ransom told me, he passed her on to two friends."

Monk's impassivity seemed now to take an effort. "Passed her on?" he repeated quietly.

"Supposedly, Colt watched them do it to her." Mary looked at her lap. "Laura Chase remembered him through some sort of semi-alcoholic haze, sitting in a chair by the bed and sipping a martini while his friends took turns."

Monk was quiet for a time. "I don't understand," he said finally. "How does a dead woman 'remember' anything?"

Mary found herself staring at the tape recorder. "Ransom had a tape of Laura Chase. Talking to her psychiatrist." She paused again. "That was what Mark Ransom called to tell me."

For the first time, Monk's inflection changed. "When you said she *remembered* . . ."

"It's on the tape." Mary hesitated. "The one on the coffee table."

Monk studied the tape recorder, as if newly fascinated by its workings. Mary could see him imagining the tape: the husky voice of a famous actress, describing her abuse by a senator from California—a man who millions wished had become President and whose death in a plane crash was still widely mourned. A man whose son was now poised to become governor.

"You could hurt people," Monk said softly, "with a tape like that."

The words held the resonance of feeling, reminding Mary that Monk lived a life outside this room and that some image of James Colt was surely part of that. Mary had images of her own: James Colt marching with migrant workers; speaking with passion on the Senate floor against the tragedy and waste of Vietnam, yet demanding of college students that they give up their deferments to "fight against a war the less advantaged are fighting in your place." Looking now at Monk, Mary reflected that James Colt occupied a special place for blacks: he had been the last potential President to speak for social justice without apology. The people Ransom's tape would "hurt," as Monk had put it, were not just James Colt's family.

"Yes." Her eyes rose from the tape recorder. "Tapes like that could hurt people."

Monk seemed to settle in his chair; something about him, Mary thought, seemed more tired than before. "Did Ransom say how he got the tape?" he asked finally.

"He bought it." Mary felt the edge in her voice. "From Dr. Steinhardt's daughter. She wanted to keep the house in Beverly Hills."

"Dr. Steinhardt."

"The psychiatrist. He's dead."

"But aren't there rules about that? In this state, we have a psychiatrist-patient privilege."

Mary shrugged again. "Laura Chase and Steinhardt are both dead. Who's left? Only Steinhardt's daughter and . . ." And Ransom, she had been about to say.

"Are you all right?"

"Yes." Mary realized that she had touched her eyes with the fingertips of one hand. "It's just that I saw him for a moment."

"Him?"

"Ransom. When he died, he was staring at me."

"Yes," Monk said. "We'll get to that."

Beneath his voice, she heard the faint whirring of the tape recorder. "Let's do that now," she said. "I'm tired."

"We just need to cover things."

She opened her eyes. "May I have some water?"

"Sure."

He got up, went out, returned with a Styrofoam cup of cold water. The tape kept spinning.

Monk leaned against the wall. "You've mentioned conversations—he called you at work, you called him at home. Before the interview, were there any more?"

"He called again. To tell me where and when he could see me."

"He chose San Francisco."

"Yes."

"Was that convenient for you?"

"No."

"Why did you do it?"

Mary flushed. "He said he might play the tape for me," she said finally. "If I came alone."

Monk's eyes widened, almost imperceptibly. "That was what persuaded you."

Mary sipped water, selecting her words. "I wasn't interested in destroying James Colt's memory—or in Laura Chase's death, for that matter. I was interested in the ethics of it. Buying and selling people's most intimate secrets, things they wouldn't tell you."

"How did you feel about that?"

"That he shouldn't use the tape." Mary paused. "But I'm also a journalist. Ransom told me that truth was more important than privacy or sentiment, for the dead and for the living."

"Did you agree?"

"No." Mary examined her broken nail. "But it was impossible not to see him."

"Did he say why he contacted you?"

"Yes."

"And why was that?"

She felt herself stiffen. "That he liked watching me on television. And that the 'subject matter' might interest me."

"Did he elaborate?"

"No." Her voice cooled again. "Not until I saw him."

Monk sat down and contemplated her across the tape recorder, hand touching his chin. "What happened," he finally asked, "when you came to his suite?"

Mary looked past him at the wall. Think about each detail, she told herself, one sentence at a time.

"I got there at eleven-thirty." Her voice turned cool. "I expected him to have a publicist. But he was alone."

Monk sat back. "Instead of me asking questions, why don't you just go through it. We can go back over any details later."

Mary found herself watching the tape recorder, mute.

"Maybe," Monk prodded, "you can start with what he was like."

Mary raised her eyes, looking straight at Monk. "He was disgusting."

"In what way?"

"*Every* way." She exhaled. "To really understand, you would have to be a woman."

Monk seemed to smile without changing expression. "Try me," he said.

Mary looked down. "To start," she said finally, "he was repellent physically. He was a tall man, and he tried to be so patrician—his Anglo-Irish accent, the way he would stand, as if posing for a portrait. But it was like watching a figure in a wax museum. Even his skin looked cold. He had this soft white stomach . . ." She stopped herself. "That wasn't until later."

Monk's eyes narrowed. "Take it from the beginning."

Slowly, Mary nodded.

"At the beginning, it was the *way* he looked at me. He was Irish, of course, but he had these ice-blue eyes and kind of Slavic features— a face with a lot of surfaces, and eyes that seemed to pull up at the ends, maybe from plastic surgery. And even when he smiled, his eyes never changed." She turned away. "I remember suddenly thinking that he looked less like an intellectual than like a Russian general at a May Day parade. One whose grandfather had raped his grandmother in some peasant uprising . . ." Mary found that she was clasping her wrist. Quietly, she finished: "I thought that before I even sat down, and congratulated myself on what a clever observation it was."

Monk waited, letting her collect herself. "What did he say when you first got there?"

"That I was a beautiful woman." Monk looked up again. "That the camera didn't capture all of me."

"What did you say?"

"I thanked him." Her voice was ironic. "Of course. Then I changed the subject."

"To what?"

"To his writing. What else do you talk about to a writer who has already proposed his own obituary: 'More than anyone, he saw and wrote the truth about his times' . . . ?"

Monk said nothing. He was waiting her out, she realized; she was digressing, trying to avoid the essence of her story. "It was while we were talking," she said, "that I noticed the tape recorder."

"Tell me about that."

Mary nodded again. "It was on the coffee table."

"Yes?"

"At first I didn't understand. When I sat down, I asked him what it was for."

"You didn't know?"

Mary realized that she was staring at the tape recorder. "I thought he might be recording us for some reason."

"What did he say?"

"That it was the tape of Laura Chase. He was going to give me an exclusive opportunity, he said."

"What did he mean?"

"What he *said* he meant was that when the book came out, I could do the first television interview." She paused again. "All about Laura and James Colt."

Monk folded his hands. After a moment, he asked, "Did Ransom say why he'd brought the tape with him?"

"As bait. He said he might let me listen." She stared at her wrist. "The tape seemed to excite him—he kept looking at it."

"What did *you* say?"

"Nothing. He said that he wanted to talk first, about the book. That we should have some champagne."

"Did you?"

"I didn't want to. But it was a story, and I was there, and champagne was part of his pretense of elegance. So I let him order champagne from room service. We sat on the couch, talking, and I had one glass."

Monk raised his eyebrows. "The bottle was empty," he observed.

"He drank the rest." Mary closed her eyes. "While we listened to the tape."

Monk was silent. "You listened to it?" he finally asked.

"Yes. At some point, I realized that was why I was there. He wanted to *share* it." She paused, speaking more slowly. "He needed me to hear what James Colt had done to Laura Chase."

Monk seemed to search for another question. Then he asked simply, "What happened?"

Mary felt cold. "It was horrible. The last time I had heard Laura Chase was at the movies, or perhaps on her early records. It was the same voice, but there weren't any pictures. Instead I was sitting in a hotel suite with Mark Ransom, while an actress who's been dead for twenty years described how a senator I remembered admiring watched two of his friends take turns with her." She found herself staring at the tape recorder again. "I'm not sure, at first, that I even felt his hand on my knee."

"Ransom fondled you while the tape was playing?"

She nodded. "At first, I thought it was a mistake. I mean, it was more like grazing than touching. Then I stopped and looked at him.

"He just stared back at me. When he knew he had my attention, he looked down at his lap. Slowly, to make sure I would follow him."

"And."

"He had an erection. That was what he wanted me to see."

The gold-rimmed glasses seemed to magnify Monk's eyes. "He had his penis out?"

"No. It was obvious enough."

"Did he say anything?"

"He offered me an 'arrangement,' to play the tape on *Deadline*."

"Did he say what kind of arrangement?"

"Are you serious?"

"Just what he said."

"All right. What he said, exactly, was, 'I like fucking women I've seen on film. It's as if I've made them real.' "

Monk touched his chin. "What did *you* do?" he finally asked.

"I told him I was much too smart to fuck him, and took his hand away. Then I said to him, much more calmly, that I was willing to deal with him as a news professional and make some other kind of 'arrangement.' "

"What did he say?"

"That *his* arrangement was the *only* arrangement. That I'd like it." Mary paused again. "All this time, Laura Chase is still talking on the tape, about having sex while James Colt watches."

The room was silent. Mary could hear the whisper of the tape.

"What happened next?" Monk asked.

"I stood up, grabbed my purse off the coffee table . . ." Her voice trailed off.

"Yes?"

"Ransom caught me by the arm."

Monk waited for a moment. "Take your time."

"Can I have more water?"

"Sure." Monk stood again. "Anytime you want something, just tell me."

Mary picked a spot on the wall. Don't think about Monk, she told herself. Concentrate on the words. When Monk returned and handed her the full cup of water, she kept her eyes on the wall.

"Go ahead," Monk said.

She nodded. "Ransom spun me around and clasped both of my arms. It threw me off balance . . ."

"Yes?"

"He pushed me to the floor. It was so sudden—I was still holding my purse. And then he was on top of me." She drank water. "Really, I can't remember all of it."

"Why don't you tell me what he did."

"He was grunting, almost—for me to stay still. That he was going to fuck me, no one would know. His face was against my neck. He was hot and smelled like champagne and men's cologne." She stopped for a moment. "Somehow, he pulled open my legs. That must be when my thigh got scratched."

"Go on."

"It was like the wind had been knocked out of me. I remember feeling sick, the room getting dark for a moment, Laura Chase's smoky voice in the background . . ."

"The tape was still on?"

"Yes." Mary nodded. "For some reason, I could hear it clearly. She was talking about the second man, doing whatever he wanted."

Monk examined his tie clasp. "What happened then?" he asked.

Mary touched her face. Coldly, she said, "That was when I started fighting."

"How?"

"I made fists. Hit his face, arms, anything."

"And then?"

"He put one hand on my chest and leaned on it to pin me to the floor, propping himself over me. His face was red, and his eyes were fixed and full of hate. It stopped—just for a second. I half raised my head to look at him." She paused, took one breath, and finished: "Then he raised his arm, very slowly, and slapped me across the face."

"What happened then?"

"I cried out." Mary paused. "So he hit me again."

"And then?"

She looked away. "I stopped fighting."

"Is that the bruise?"

"Yes." Mary kept staring past him. Her voice had become a monotone. "My head hit the floor. Pain shot through my neck. For a moment, it got dark again. I think maybe he was choking me."

"You're not sure."

"No." She swallowed. "The next thing I remember is that my skirt is around my waist and my legs are spread apart, with the panty hose still on."

"What is Ransom doing?"

"He's kneeling between my legs, staring down at me. His pants are around his knees." She paused. "It's so crazy—somehow it shocks me that his pubic hairs are red. There's a red birthmark on his thigh . . ."

From the corner of her eye, Mary saw Monk pause, absently pushing the gold-rimmed glasses where they touched the bridge of his nose.

"What does he do then?"

"He stops for a moment." Mary's voice grew quieter. "I think he's listening to Laura Chase."

"And then?"

"I feel the strap of my purse in my left hand. It's funny: I've never let it go." Mary spoke more softly still. "And then I remember the gun."

Monk's own voice had become quiet. "Go on," he said.

"All this time, I've never spoken. Now I say, 'You can take me. I'll let you do it, any way you want.' His eyes seem to light up." Mary paused, permitting herself a bitter smile. "Then I tell him, 'But only if you use a rubber.' "

Monk's impassivity had become a stare. "What," he asked at length, "did Ransom say?"

"He laughs—kind of a short bark. 'No,' I say, 'there's one in my purse.' It seems to startle him. Before he can answer, I twist and reach into my purse. . . .

"When he pushes me on my back again, the gun is in my hand.

"When he grabs for it, I knee him. His hands are on my wrists. He gives this cry; his body seems almost to twitch. . . ." Mary closed her eyes. "That's when the gun went off."

"What else do you remember?"

Mary bent forward. "Just his face. He looks softer, almost disappointed, as if I had hurt his feelings. I catch him in both hands, an inch or two from my body. His breath still stinks. All my strength, and I can barely push him off." She paused once more, and finished. "That's when I noticed that Laura had stopped talking."

There was silence. Mary felt herself slump in the chair. Over, she told herself. It's over.

She opened her eyes. "Can I go now?"

Monk watched her. "I'd like to ask you a few more questions. Just about what you've told me."

Mary felt a surge of anger. She sat, irresolute, replaying the tone of Monk's voice. His face showed nothing.

"The gun," he said. "Why do you carry one?"

She sat back, drained. "I've had threatening phone calls, she said finally."

"When did they happen?"

"The past two months . . . I don't know, exactly."

"Male or female?"

"Male."

"At work?"

"No. At home."

"Are you listed?"

"No."

"Did the person seem to know who you were?"

"I don't know."

"Could it have been Ransom?"

Mary hesitated. "I don't think so."

"How many calls?"

"Two, I think."

"What did they say?"

"Not much. Just that they were watching me."

"Did you report them?"

"No."

"Did you tell anyone?"

"No. Not that I remember."

"But you bought a gun."

"Yes." Mary summoned a tone of weary patience. "I'm a public person. Those calls reminded me that there are strange people out there, and that I'm a woman living alone."

"When did you buy the gun?"

Mary shrugged. "About two weeks ago."

"Was that before, or after, you first heard from Ransom?"

Mary stared at him. "After, I think."

Monk leaned slightly forward. "You flew here from New York, correct?"

"Yes."

"When?"

"Sunday morning."

Monk cocked his head, as if to consider her from another angle. "Who made the hotel and plane reservations?"

"I did."

"Did you make them through *Deadline*?"

"No." Mary paused. "I paid for them myself."

"Doesn't ABC pay for business travel?"

"Of course." Mary's voice grew impatient. "Why is this important? They can either pay me in advance or reimburse me."

"Did you tell anyone at ABC about seeing Ransom?"

"No. I wouldn't have to."

"Or about his calls?"

Don't be defensive, Mary told herself. "No," she answered.

"And you brought the gun with you?"

"Yes."

"How did you get it out here?"

"In my luggage."

Monk's eyes seemed never to move. "Did you tell the airport people you had it?"

"No."

Monk paused for a moment. "Today," he said, "did anyone see you in the lobby?"

"I don't know. I went right to his suite."

"Once you were inside, did anyone come to the room?"

"Not that I remember."

"What about room service?"

"Yes . . . that . . ."

"Was the person a man or a woman?"

"A man."

"Can you tell me what he looked like?"

"I don't know . . . short. Hispanic, I think."

Monk leaned back. "When you got to the room," he said, "were the blinds closed?"

"I think so." Once again, Mary paused. "Yes, I'm sure."

"There were scratches on Ransom's buttocks. Do you know how they got there?"

"Of course. When I was struggling with him."

"You'd mentioned your fists being closed, and I don't remember anything about scratching his buttocks."

Mary recalled Dr. Shelton, tracing the scratches with her finger. "I don't know," she said wearily. "Maybe it happened when I was pushing him off me. After the gun went off."

Monk nodded again. "When you were struggling with the gun, were Ransom's hands on it?"

Shelton had inspected the dead man's hands, put them both in glassine bags. . . .

"I don't remember."

"When the gun fired, Miss Carelli, how far was it from Ransom's chest?"

She had touched his wound, the torn cloth around it. . . .

"Very close."

"*How* close? Was it touching him?"

"No." Mary could hear the tape recorder whirring. "Two inches . . ."

Monk leaned forward. "Not two *feet,* or three feet?"

"No."

"The scratch on your throat—it happened after Ransom slapped you?"

She had taken samples from her fingernails, then his. . . .

"Yes."

"And then he pulled his pants down."

"Yes."

"Did he have an erection?"

She had taken swabs from his penis. . . .

"Miss Carelli?"

The tape kept spinning.

"Yes." She reached for the empty cup of water. The tape still coiled, slowly, repeatedly.

"The erection." Monk's voice seemed far away. "What do you remember about it?"

"I don't know. It was an erection, that's all. I didn't have time to think about how special it was."

Monk folded his arms. "After the gun went off, what did you do?"

"I don't know. . . . I was dazed."

"How long did it take for you to call 911?"

She had reached under his armpit, felt his skin. . . .

"I don't know. As soon as I was able."

The tape turned again. Once, twice.

"While you were at the suite, did you leave at any time?"

Mary looked up.

"Miss Carelli?"

"Could you stop the tape a moment? Please."

"I can't do that." Monk said calmly. "It's regulation."

The tape turned again, recording silence.

Mary reached out and pushed a button. The tape clicked off.

"I want to see a lawyer," she said. "Now."

FOUR

THEY TOOK PAGET to the witness room, opened the door, and closed it again, leaving them alone.

The way she looked startled him.

The fluorescent light captured with pitiless clarity the change since the previous day: puffy eyelids; a yellow pallor to her skin; the slack beneath her face. Slumped in the chair, her slender frame looked drained of energy, much older and too thin.

He gazed at the bruise next to her eye, then at her eyes themselves. They had a haunted, fearful look she would hate if she could see it.

It was that—the sense that some essence had been taken from her—which made Paget want to touch her. And then feel, in the next moment, that this was the last thing he should do.

"I'm sorry this happened," he said.

She studied him. "Don't feel sorry, Chris. It happened, and it's done. I just want to get out of here."

"Are you all right?"

"Yes. Please, just help me."

Paget nodded. "The first thing is to persuade the D.A. he doesn't have a case."

"How do I do that?"

"I'll help you find a first-rate criminal lawyer—someone who's tried these cases a lot and whom the D.A. respects. He or she can sit down with the prosecution and tell them why they should drop this."

Mary gazed through him, as if she had not heard.

"If you want," he said, "I can probably get someone here to see you within an hour. Get them started."

Slowly, she shook her head.

Paget sat across from her. "I know you're tired . . ."

"You don't understand, Chris. *You* have to do this."

Paget felt a kind of dull surprise. It was as if, he thought, her own shock was a contagion.

"Look," he said at length, "I know you can't believe what happened, that it doesn't seem real. But it is. You need a real lawyer."

"And you're not one?"

"Not for this. I don't do homicides anymore."

"Do this one."

Paget stared at her. Were it not for what she wanted, her new animation would have made him feel better; some life was back in her face.

"If I were going to resume an old career, Mary, yours would be the last case I'd choose. You don't try cases for someone you know."

"Is that what I am?" she said with irony. "Someone you know?"

Paget leaned back. "I would have a very hard time defining," he said at length, "all the things you are to me. You know as well as I do the reasons I can't take this."

Mary seemed to gauge his strength of will. "They're the very same reasons," she said finally, "that you have no choice."

Paget felt a rush of anger. "You're in no position—"

"No choice at all," she interrupted. "As you know all too well." The irony stole back into her voice. "After all, there is so very much that binds us."

Paget fought for self-control. In a lower key, he said, "Carlo, you mean."

She looked away. "Choose whatever reason you like, Chris. The one that makes you feel best. Just do this."

"Damn you," Paget snapped. "Think. Think of *him* for once. Even if you walk tomorrow, Ransom's death will be news for months. Whatever else you and I may have done, we've at least kept Carlo's life to himself. But 'The Return of Chris and Mary' will be the stuff of TV movies. You're not just asking me to do something for you. You're asking me to risk changing Carlo's world forever."

Mary looked up again, her gaze level. "How do you know," she finally said, "that I'm *not* thinking about Carlo?"

"Because you couldn't be."

"You are so very good at believing the worst of me."

"It's hardly a natural gift, Mary. I came by these feelings the old-fashioned way—you taught me."

Her face closed against him, as if she were withdrawing all feeling.

Then she shrugged. "Have it your way, then. I am, as usual, a cold-blooded bitch. I'm forcing you to put our son through publicity hell to spare me the minor inconvenience of a trial—or, at most, life imprisonment. Because I know how hard you'll work to spare *Carlo* the further trauma of having a murderess for a mother."

Paget watched her face. "Why?" he asked softly. "Why force me to do this? Just tell me that much."

"Because I know you'll do whatever it takes to win whatever you decide to win." Her voice was quiet, bitter. "Isn't that what every client wants?"

Paget found himself looking at the scratches on her neck, then at the table. "No," he finally said, "there's something else. I need to know what's really happening here."

For a moment, Mary was silent. Paget could not tell whether she was considering what he had said. Then she sat straighter, looked him in the face.

"What's really happening here," she answered crisply, "is that Mark Ransom was a pervert and a swine, who at the moment that I shot him was especially deserving. Or, as I put it more neutrally to the police, at the moment that the gun went off."

Paget stared at her. "The police," he repeated. "Why did you stop answering Monk's questions?"

"Because I was *tired,* half in shock. Because, however good my reasons, I'd *killed* someone. You can't know how that feels—you don't believe it, and yet you're scared to death nothing will ever be the same." She paused. "For the first time in my life, I stopped coping, that's all. I think I have a decent excuse."

"That's a reason not to talk to them at all, not tonight anyhow. But once you've started . . ."

"I wanted to persuade them, don't you see. Wanted all this over with—to get out of this building without ever needing you or anyone." She paused, exhaling, head bent forward. "The questions became confusing. I couldn't recall things clearly, couldn't follow him anymore. I was afraid of making a mistake."

"How can the truth," Paget asked quietly, "be a mistake?"

"I don't know." Mary shook her head, as if to clear it. "You feel like someone in a Kafka novel. Like they're going to misunderstand something you said, or did or didn't do, or something you didn't remember quite right. That tape . . ." She paused, touching her face with the fingers of one hand. "I was dislocated. I just had to stop talking, that's all."

Paget folded his hands. "Do you have the wherewithal to talk to me? Monk told me only a little, on the elevator up."

Mary gazed at him. "You'll do it, then?"

She seemed unsure again; it was as if she were too vulnerable to be sure that she had won.

"What I'm agreeing to do," Paget said, "is find out what the D.A.'s thinking. For that I'll need to know precisely what it is you told them."

Mary nodded. "All right," she said.

She seemed to reach within herself. When she spoke again, it was in a monotone—repeating her litany of a dead actress; a squalid weekend in Palm Springs; the dark side of a famous senator; a celebrated but perverted writer; a brutal attempted rape; the gun firing; a spreading bloodstain—as if she were dictating a recorded message. When it ended, an hour had passed, and Paget felt exhausted.

He was quiet for a time, organizing his thoughts. It was odd, he realized; one of the things that slowed him was a recurring image of the day James Colt had died. Paget had told the story to Carlo more than once. He had gone to cash a check and heard the news from a bank teller; tears had begun running down her face as she tried to count out money. He pushed the memory aside.

"Do I know," he finally asked, "everything the police know?"

Mary gave him a look of quiet understanding; he had not asked her about the events themselves. "What you know," she answered, "is everything I told them."

He watched her. "Would you like to finish up with Monk—once you're rested?"

"No." Her voice was clear and cool. "I used to be a lawyer, you may recall. Any tape I give is evidence at trial, mistakes and all. I want you to talk for me. Persuade them there should be no trial."

Paget's eyes met hers. Let her know, he thought, that I'm studying her face. "What about a lie detector test? Those aren't admissible, and they'll likely want one, if only to cover themselves if they drop the case."

"I don't believe in them." Mary's gaze remained steady. "I don't believe they can measure guilt."

"We can do it in my office. If we don't like the results, the D.A. never sees it."

"No," she repeated. "He abused me, and I killed him. I told them that. The only question they're facing is the degree of guilt. I want you to persuade them that they already have the answer."

Paget watched her. A minute, perhaps more, waiting for his silence to work on her. She said nothing.

"Tell me about the medical examiner," he finally said. "Everything she did."

Mary did that, eyes narrow with concentration. When she finished, he asked, "Were there powder marks?"

"Where?"

"On Ransom's shirt."

She leaned back in her chair. "Is that important?"

"I'm not sure yet."

She studied him. "They'll tell you, right?"

Paget let that hang a moment, unanswered. "I expect so," he said finally. "I suppose I'd better go see them."

"They'll be in now?"

"For this—yes. The D.A. himself will be in." Paget stood. "They hate cases like this, you know. Ninety-nine percent of what they get in, nobody gives a damn about. But there are too many ways that something like this, with well-known people, can go bad on them."

"What does that mean for me?"

"Politics, for openers. You have a dead Pulitzer Prize winner, accused of attempted rape by the celebrity who shot him. There isn't a voter with a pulse who won't have some reaction to this, no matter what the facts are or what the D.A. does. It means they're going to be very careful, and that nothing will happen very fast."

It seemed to deaden her; he could watch her imagine days, or even weeks, without an answer. In any other context, Paget would have felt too much compassion to press his advantage. "Which," he told her, "brings us once again to Carlo."

She looked up at him. "Forget," he said coldly, "that you're going to have to tolerate publicity that would make Liz Taylor vomit, or that Court TV will fight to televise your testimony in all its intimate details. You're going to have to *want* that. Because it's not just about who you are, or who Ransom was, or even the terrible stuff about

Laura Chase and our late and sainted senator. Your defense lays out as a feminist cause—a fight for justice for all the powerless victims of date rape. No competent defense lawyer would try to win this case at trial without first trying to win it in the media. Including me.

"There's only one difference. Any other lawyer would love that. I'll hate you for it. Because of the son I'll be living with every day. You should think very hard about having *that* kind of lawyer defend *this* kind of case."

When he finished, Mary was gripping the table.

"You were always good," she finally said, "on television."

Paget simply stared at her. In a softer voice, she added, "I'll try to make things right with Carlo."

Paget did not answer her. Instead he opened the door, said briskly to the matron, "We're through here," and let them take Mary to her cell without saying anything more.

The district attorney occupied the corner office of a bleak green maze that housed two lawyers in cubicles that a rabbit would resent. Paget's guide, a wiry woman in her mid thirties who had introduced herself as Marnie Sharpe but said little else, steered him through the door. Her air of humorless containment suggested to Paget that she was a lawyer, not the D.A.'s secretary, and that she was already feeling the weight of some responsibility for Ransom.

The D.A. had claimed one of the few decent spaces in the building. There was nothing one could do about the three small windows— neo-Stalinist architecture, Paget thought—but McKinley Brooks had twice as much room and no roommates. There was an Afghan rug, a leather chair, one potted palm, and a wall big enough to house the usual photo collection of a public man: Brooks with several judges, two mayors and, of all people, Luciano Pavarotti. His leather briefcase sat unopened on his desk, as if Brooks had returned hastily from home.

Brooks rose from his chair with a professionally amiable smile and the fluid grace of an ex-athlete still in his early forties and only now running to fat. The carefully trimmed gray Afro, slight double chin, and liquid eyes made him look, at first glance, like the slicker black version of a pleasant Rotarian.

"Christopher," he said in a gravelly voice that managed to make every word sound like a performance as Othello. "What are *you* doing here, nice uptown lawyer that you are?"

"Visiting a sick friend," Paget said easily. "Anyone seen Mark Ransom lately?"

From the corner of his eye, Paget saw Marnie Sharpe's mouth tighten.

"The medical examiner," Brooks answered. "Even as we speak. And you've met Marnie, I assume."

Paget nodded. "Just now."

"Please sit down, both of you. Marnie will be handling this for the office." Brooks looked over at Sharpe, adding, "Chris and I are old friends."

What that was intended to convey, Paget suspected, was that he should be accorded the respect due someone who had given money to Brooks's campaign. The good-humored civility was routine: even in a city as liberal as this one, it had taken a black man as smart and supple as Brooks to win election to a law-and-order post. What was not routine was Marnie Sharpe. Paget knew enough to know that Sharpe was not on the D.A.'s homicide team; it had taken Brooks a few short hours to think through the politics of dealing with Mary Carelli and to decide that it played best with a woman prosecutor.

As if reading Paget's mind, Brooks said, "Marnie's from our rape unit. She's ideally situated to be attuned to all the aspects of this matter."

That, Paget thought, was a particularly neat touch: a prosecutor who could reasonably claim to identify with Mary as possible victim, or could deflect charges of callousness if they decided to prosecute. Paget said evenly, "I appreciate your sensitivity."

Brooks smiled a moment, as if acknowledging the subtlety of the compliment. Something in the smile reminded Paget that, beneath his geniality, Brooks was as sentimental as a Venus's-flytrap. Paget, Mary, and even the pressures on Marnie Sharpe would get as much or as little consideration as Brooks's circumstances required.

Brooks's smile faded. "What *are* you doing here?"

Paget shrugged. "Miss Carelli is a friend of mine."

"The Lasko case." Brooks nodded. "Of course."

Paget felt Sharpe watching from the side, her wary, suspicious look seeming somehow to include both men. "I don't suppose," Paget said, "that either of you doubts this is traumatic for her. Even without all the publicity, stretching it out will make things that much worse."

"It's just a mess," Brooks agreed. "I'm sure you've already told her how little we enjoy things like this."

"Of course. But she's a little beyond the standard consolations. She's been beaten, forced to kill a man to keep from being raped, and thrown in a jail because she wanted to see me. The first two things you can't do anything about. The last one, you can."

Brooks held up a hand. "Please understand. We're not going to shove her in some cell with a bunch of drunks. She'll be as comfortable as we can make her here."

"That's the key word: 'here.'" Paget appraised him. "Right now she's under arrest. Within forty-eight hours, you've got to file a complaint charging her with something, or let her go. You can rearrest and charge her anytime you want. But nothing that happens in the next forty-eight hours is going to turn this into a case. And making someone like Mary Carelli wait two days for you to spring her is bad practice and worse politics."

Brooks spread both hands. "We have to be *cautious*, Chris. We've got a corpse on the first floor who was America's most famous living writer when he checked into the Flood this morning."

Paget turned to take in Sharpe. "How much of Ransom's work have either of you read?"

Sharpe stared at him in silence. "A few of his books," Brooks answered.

Paget kept looking at Sharpe. "Then is either of you really surprised that Ransom tried to rape someone? Because a lot of literate women in this country won't be."

Sharpe seemed to tense; there was, Paget thought, something brittle about her. It would make her harder to deal with, and the only place it might ever work for him was if they went to trial. "We have to go on the evidence," she said. "Not on what he may have written. Or was planning to write."

"Which brings us," Brooks said quietly, "to this nasty tape about Laura Chase and Senator Colt." He paused. "Millions of people still love the man. Including me."

Paget nodded. "You met him, as I recall."

"I *campaigned* for him." Brooks shook his head. "When his plane crashed, two friends and I drove three thousand miles across the country in a state of shock to see them bury him. It was like we couldn't let go." He gazed at Paget. "The country," he added softly, "has never quite let go."

That was right, Paget thought. Perhaps it was that Colt's plane crash at night in the California desert, three months after Laura Chase had died, had seemed so arbitrary and irrational. With his blond hair and grace of movement, his smile and quick wit, James Colt had seemed at forty impossibly young to be President; yet there had been something bracing in the thought, as if only a country whose best moments lay ahead would choose him. One had not thought of James Colt and thought of death; perhaps that was why the shock of it remained imprinted on the mind like the images of his memorial service: his ash-blond widow, painfully stoic; the unformed face of his teenage son, transformed by the wishes of those watching into an eerie replica of the father.

"Is it true," Paget finally asked, "that James Colt junior plans to run for governor?"

Brooks nodded. "So I understand."

Paget appraised him. "You certainly *do* have your troubles," he said finally. "Which you might do well to leave behind."

"If only we could, Christopher. If only we could."

Paget considered him. "All right," he finally said. "So the M.E. doesn't like the powder marks."

Brooks's eyes widened in mock surprise. "Very perceptive," he answered. "There *were* no powder marks. No gunshot residue of *any* kind. Nothing."

"And so?"

"So it's a problem. The M.E. can't always tell us what *did* happen, but she can pretty much always tell us what *didn't* happen. And what didn't happen here is that Miss Carelli shot Mark Ransom from two, three inches. Not even close."

"That's surprising," Paget said. "Mary's usually so precise. I guess she forgot her ruler."

Brooks's smile was a narrowing of the eyes, quickly passing. "Nice jury argument. But with Ransom eight hours dead, we can't ignore that. And it's going to keep us thinking for a while."

"Come off it, Mac. Ransom was *attacking* her at the moment the gun went off. Mary could have been wrong. Ransom could have been shrinking back from the gun. Consider the possibilities."

"And I'm sure you'll suggest all that to her. Just as possibilities, of course."

Paget shrugged. "When she thinks about it, I doubt she'll be able to swear to a distance."

"But then," Brooks went on, "there's cutting off Monk's questions. It just doesn't sit right with some of the people you're asking to believe her. And she *did* ask for a lawyer."

"Law school graduates are funny like that. And she didn't ask for a lawyer—she asked for me. It was more like calling a friend, or a priest."

"A priest?"

"Someone who would feel sympathy," Paget said coolly, "as she has every right to expect."

"She will certainly get sympathy. But just like you're not a priest, I'm not an ostrich. One possible construction of pulling the plug on Monk is that she saw she was in trouble."

For the first time, Paget felt a moment of fear. "A far more humane construction," he retorted, "is that she was a bit under the weather." He turned back to Sharpe. "How many rape victims ever report what happened? Maybe fifteen percent, even people like Mary Carelli. They feel ashamed, they feel guilty, they feel alone, and if they report it, then they get to explain it all to some man they've never met, while they're still semitraumatized. Mary Carelli got to explain herself within three or four hours of killing the man who tried to do it, sitting with Monk in an environment where she was utterly lost. So she felt disoriented, attacked, ashamed, and, yes, probably as 'guilty' as any normal person would feel who has just shot someone to death. Even though she's innocent under the law."

Sharpe's face was taut; Paget realized that it was herself, not Mary, whom she saw as under attack. "We know about rape," she answered. "*I* prosecute any case that's righteous. Even if I think we'll lose."

"I'm well aware of that." Paget looked back to Brooks. "You have a fine record on sex crimes, Mac. The people who care know that. Don't throw it away by coming out on the wrong side of a bad case."

Brooks's gaze was cool. "Give me a reason to spring her, Chris. One I can explain to people."

Paget had a bleak, wasted feeling. "I have a reason," he finally said. "But not one I'd like explained to anyone."

Brooks looked curious. "What is that?"

How little, Paget thought, he wanted to say this, with or without Sharpe in the room. "My son, Carlo. He's fifteen now and lives with me." Paget exhaled. "He's also Mary's son."

Brooks stared at him. "Sweet Jesus Christ," he murmured. "So *that's* why you're here."

"That's why I'm here."

Paget felt shamed; he had expunged Brooks's debt to him by cashing in his personal life, and that of his son, in the hope of a favor. "There are aspects of Carlo's life which have been ... difficult. But those things have been private. This won't be. He'll get to work through whatever his mother has done with the help of the media. It would help if he didn't wake up tomorrow to find her still in jail."

Sharpe seemed to have removed herself. Brooks gazed at his hands. "What is it," he asked, "that you want us to do?"

"Just listen. Give me every chance to show you this isn't a case before you decide to bring it. And in the meanwhile, let her go."

Brooks looked up. "Will she take a lie detector test?"

"No. On my advice."

Brooks raised an eyebrow. "Of course," he finally said, "she could finish up with Monk."

"She could. But for the moment, I'd like to handle this."

"Because nothing *you* say to us can be used at trial."

"Because that's the way *any* competent defense lawyer deals with your office."

"But you're asking—"

"And because," Paget finished evenly, "the prosecution has the burden of proof. I don't think you have a case. If I'm right, then I'm doing *you* a favor, simply by pointing out why. Plus you get some notion of what I'm thinking."

Brooks looked to Sharpe, then to Paget again. "Okay," he said. "Full disclosure. We decide to bring a case, we'd have to lift our skirts anyhow."

"Better find another metaphor, Mac. At least for press conferences."

Brooks gave Paget a wintry smile. "I wish this case weren't so unpleasant, Christopher. You and I would have such fun. . . ." Abruptly, he picked up the telephone, dialed a number he already knew. "Are you about through with him?" he asked into the telephone, and then said, "We're with Ms. Carelli's lawyer—please come on up," and put down the phone.

"The M.E.," he explained. "She's finished making nice with Ransom."

A moment later, a slim blond woman came through the door and extended a cool hand. "I'm Elizabeth Shelton," she said. "The medical examiner."

"It seems," Paget said, "that you've been quite busy."

She gave him a quizzical smile. "It's been a very long day," she responded, and she pulled up a chair between Paget and Sharpe.

"We've been having a candid chat among friends." Brooks waved a hand at Paget. "Chris understands your problem with the gunshot wound. Maybe you can tell us what else you found."

"Very little. Almost nothing, in fact."

"What do you mean?" Paget asked.

She looked quickly at Brooks and, when he nodded, back to Paget. "One thing I mean is that there's an absence of the physical evidence I'd like to have. Bullet angle, for one thing. If the bullet goes through, we can trace the path from the body to where the bullet lodges and tell you not only the angle but where he got shot within a couple of feet. But here, the bullet lodged in his spine."

She spoke with a cool precision, clinical but not unpleasant.

"What else?" Paget asked.

Shelton considered him. "The other thing," she said finally, "is there is almost nothing about Ransom's body that confirms what Miss Carelli told us."

"Well," Paget said mildly, "he *did* have his pants down. That's not standard dress for interviews."

"No." Her eyes and voice were cautious. "So I swabbed his penis and tested for traces of seminal fluid. You'd expect fluid on a man who'd recently had an erection, even without ejaculation. Nothing."

"Is that test one hundred percent reliable?"

"Almost no test is. But I'd expect results." Her look grew more intent. "As it happens, I'm no fan of Mark Ransom. But I can't tell you he's a rapist, or even an attempted rapist."

"All right. What else did you find?"

"Miss Carelli said that Ransom reached for the gun before it fired. But there aren't any powder marks on his hands. Again, it depends on how it happened, but powder marks would tend to confirm what she told us." She hesitated. "And of course, there's the fact that she didn't fire from two or three inches or, in my opinion, anywhere within two or three feet.

"In short, Mr. Paget, there's very little about Ransom's body to tell me that Miss Carelli didn't shoot him while they were strolling in the park."

"There were," Paget said evenly, "a few things about Miss Carelli."

Shelton nodded. "Scratches, for example. I took samples from both of their fingernails. There was skin under Miss Carelli's nails, but none under Ransom's."

"What's the reliability there?"

"Low," she concluded. "And we can't even tell *whose* skin it is—in fact, we usually can't. But one of the things we try to do is rule out possibilities. Here, I can't rule out the possibility that Miss Carelli scratched herself and broke a nail in the process."

Shelton's calm was unnerving; she knew her field, conceded what she had to, and seemed utterly dispassionate. In the right case, she would make a devastating witness.

"You also looked," Paget prodded, "at that rather nasty bruise."

For a moment, Shelton looked puzzled. "Yes." She nodded. "Miss Carelli's left cheek."

"Then did she pistol-whip herself? Or is she just allergic to champagne?"

To the side, Brooks gave the perfunctory smile of a lawyer who appreciates a problem. "No," Shelton conceded. "It looks like a slap."

"With an open hand?" Paget asked.

"Yes."

"Relatively recent?"

"Yes."

"And Ransom, I assume, was right-handed. So that he could have struck Miss Carelli on the left cheek."

"Yes."

"A couple of blows like that," Paget said to Brooks, "and I'd have shot Ransom myself. And if Ransom slapped her, it makes everything she told Monk a lot more plausible and renders the notion that she later decided to scratch herself impossible to explain. Add the tape of Laura Chase and James Colt, which gives Ransom's own sexual problems the awful ring of truth, and you've got no reason to doubt her.

"Which gets me to the last thing—motive. *Our* motive is simple: the man was trying to rape her, and she shot him. The bruise on her face supports that. But if he *wasn't* trying to rape her, why on earth does someone like Mary Carelli shoot a man she only knows through books?"

Brooks nodded. "No motive."

"None at all," Paget responded crisply. "No motive, no witness, no case. Leaving the only possible disposition a decision by the D.A. that Mary acted in self-defense." Paget finished more slowly, his gaze covering Sharpe and Shelton. "There are a lot of people out there, a lot of them women, who will know intuitively that's what happened once they see Mary Carelli on television. Gunshot residue won't mean a damn to them. Because they'll *know.* And because after Clarence Thomas and Willie Smith, they *also* know how easy it is for a man to walk away."

Sharpe frowned; Shelton stared at the rug. "The women's movement," Sharpe finally said, "is too important to too many women for any of us not to do our job."

Beneath her didactic tone, Paget sensed as much pride as principle. "I understand," he said mildly. "But my point was that part of your job—and Mac's—is not to waste moral or political capital on a case that you can't win. Forgive me if I made the point inartfully."

Sharpe stared at him, unbending and unmollified. "Artfully enough," Brooks said finally. "Can we agree, for the moment, to leave Laura Chase and James Colt out of this? At least as far as the press is concerned?"

Paget nodded. "I imagine so."

"All right." Brooks seemed to expel a short breath. "If you care to wait upstairs for a while, you can take Mary Carelli home."

Paget felt more tension easing from him than he had known was there. "Thank you," he said.

"Just part of my job, Christopher, as you point out. But there are other parts. I assume that what might be called the Paget family will forgive us if we finish the job before signing off on self-defense."

"Of course."

Shelton stood up. "I'll walk you up there," she said. "Perhaps it will move things along."

"I'd appreciate that." Paget shook hands with Sharpe and then Brooks. "I'll be back in touch. Perhaps in a couple of days."

"Do that," Brooks said, and then Shelton whisked him out the door.

In the hallway, she said, "Better me than Marnie Sharpe, I thought."

Paget smiled. "Is that 'M-a-r-n-i-e,' as in the Hitchcock film?"

"Yes. And it's perfect for her. Marnie has two obsessions—her job, and movies." She pushed the elevator button. "You know, I really did look for things to support Mary Carelli's story. I just want an answer."

Paget nodded, and then recalled something Mary had said. "Didn't you examine scratches on Ransom? On his buttocks?"

Shelton paused. "I'm still working on that."

Her voice had a faint troubled undertone. As he waited for Mary, it was that, rather than Sharpe's antipathy, that stayed with him.

FIVE

THE GUARD BROUGHT Mary to a small open space at the front of a row of cells housing spaced-out hookers, chattering druggies.

"Bye-bye, Rosebud," someone jeered, "pretty boyfriend," and then the elevator door closed behind them, and they were alone.

She slumped against the wall. "How," she asked wearily, "did you get me out?"

Paget pushed the button. "Just reminded them of what they didn't have. They'd have gotten there without me."

She was silent. The elevator creaked downward. Both of them, Paget thought, would be content to stay sealed in this space, as long as no one bothered them.

The elevator opened.

Through the glass doors of the entrance, a crowd of reporters was waiting, cordoned by police. Their muffled voices echoed in the lobby.

Mary recoiled. Paget stopped walking; for all that he had said, he was not prepared for this so soon.

"What do we do?" she asked.

Paget saw a cameraman spot them through the glass and then jostle for position. His movement spread through the crowd. Paget felt a flash of anger, at the media and at Mary.

"I'll make a brief statement," he said finally. "Then we'll go. Just be the dazed but dignified victim." He turned to her, heard the bitterness in his voice. "This is the first time anyone will have seen you since Ransom was shot. Your face will be the lead for every news flash. All that people will remember—what Carlo will remember—is how you looked."

She nodded slowly, as if only his words mattered, not his tone. Then she took his arm.

Paget looked down at her hand. "This is the first time anyone will have seen *us*," she said quietly, "since Washington. What they'll remember is how *we* looked."

Her voice and gaze were level now. Paget had the sudden weary certainty that the separation of their lives since then had been an illusion; decisions once made, he thought, can never be unmade, and debts to the past can never be discharged.

The night before they had testified in the Senate, Mary had called him.

"I have to see you," she had said.

It was almost one o'clock, and Paget had been unable to sleep. Two months before, they had shared the bed he lay on, but now that was impossible.

"Why don't we just talk," he said.

"I need to see you, Chris. In person."

"Exactly what is it you want?" he asked. "It's all been said."

"This isn't about Lasko." Her tone was cool, determined. "It's personal."

He looked out at the darkened room, at nothing. "Where?" he finally asked. "Here?"

"I don't want people to see us together—the two key witnesses, right before we testify. Someone might think we were deciding what to say." Her voice held a trace of irony. "Meet me at the Jefferson Memorial. You told me once you liked it there."

The night was chill with autumn. Framed by a half circle of cherry trees, the outer shell of the dome was dark; in the pale light within, Jefferson was a solitary stone figure, gazing outward as if waiting for visitors who might never come. Paget turned, walking toward the cement plaza that faced the Tidal Basin. The water was inky black; beyond, centered within a grass rectangle perhaps a mile long, the Washington Monument was a darkened obelisk, tip disappearing into the night. At the far end of the rectangle the Lincoln Memorial was so distant that it looked like a tourist's replica. Paget was alone.

"Hello, Chris."

He turned. Mary wore dark wool slacks, a silk blouse, a tailored jacket over her shoulders, silver earrings. In the moonlight, her face looked tan and her hair glossy, as if newly washed. She could have been going on a date.

"From what I read," she said, "you've had a busy two months. Since last we spoke."

"As have you, I hear." He paused, examining her face. "What's curious is that it seems to have agreed with you."

"Oh, I'm all aglow."

Paget almost smiled in spite of himself, and then he took a second look at her.

"I'm pregnant, Chris."

He paused, stunned. "You're sure of that?"

"Very."

He turned, staring at the darkened pool. Then he looked back into her eyes. "Whose is it?" he asked.

She stiffened, almost imperceptibly, and then gave a thin smile. "That's hardly flattering."

Paget shrugged. "The last two months," he answered, "have beaten the romantic clean out of me."

Mary looked away. "So much so that our last weekend slipped your mind?"

He was silent. "You know better," he said finally.

She moved closer to him. "The sad truth is, Chris, that a lot of things slipped our minds that weekend."

He folded his arms. "Why are you telling me this tonight? *Especially* tonight."

"Because sooner or later, I'd have had to tell you." She paused. "I thought later you might appreciate having known it now."

"And why, I'm forced to wonder, is that?"

She squared her shoulders. "Because I'm keeping it."

Paget stared at her. "You must be joking."

"No." Her voice had a determined edge. "I'm Catholic, you'll remember."

In his confusion and astonishment, Paget almost laughed. "All I heard from you was how much you wanted to escape the 'trap'— parents, church, your troglodyte ex-husband who wanted you to have children and 'use your education in the home.' If you were driven by profound religious feelings, it certainly escaped me. Or did you experience an epiphany while we were making love that Sunday morning, and wish you were at Mass?"

Mary frowned. "You were always very clever. But I *am* a Catholic, happy or not. You never know what something means until you're there. There are a thousand things I wouldn't expect you to understand."

Paget found himself gazing past her. "Mary Carelli," he murmured. "The Bride of Christ." When he turned back, her face held nothing but watchfulness. "Forgive me if I suspect some other agenda."

In the darkness, her body seemed to slump. Paget wanted to ask how she felt, and then she straightened again.

"At this point," she said coolly, "it hardly matters what you think."

The words made it sound final, irretrievable, pushed him into another realm: this woman, of all women, might have his child. In their silence, he found himself looking for changes in her body that could not yet have occurred.

"Do you get tired?" he finally asked.

She looked down. "A little. But not sick."

He nodded. "Maybe you should sit."

They sat on a bench overlooking the pond, several feet apart. The night seemed colder yet.

"What is it you want from me?"

In profile, she smiled at the murky water. "Marriage, of course. A ranch house in Potomac."

He waited, silent, until the smile faded.

"Nothing," she said. "Just for you to know. Whatever you do in the future, you do."

Paget watched her. " 'In the future'?" he repeated. "If I follow your logic, timing is everything."

"If you think it is." She stared fixedly at the pool. "I suppose it depends on what value things have for you, one over another. The only thing I'm sure of is that I'm going to have a baby."

Paget felt his eyes narrow. "And," he said, "that you're testifying before the Senate tomorrow."

"Yes." Still she did not look at him. "I don't think that particular men's club gives exemptions to unwed mothers."

Paget realized that he was facing in the direction of the White House, shrouded by night and leafless trees. "We'd better go, then."

Mary turned, searching his face.

"Yes," she finally answered. "We'd better go."

Her Volkswagen was parked in the darkness beneath the half circle of trees. Paget walked her there, hands in his pockets, waited as she unlocked the door.

Sliding into the seat, she looked up at him again. "It's going to be a long night yet. At least for me."

He watched her taillights until they disappeared.

The next morning, entering the hearing room, she looked as if nothing had happened.

She broke away from her lawyer, came toward him at the back of the room. Her carriage bespoke poise and serenity; Paget was certain that he alone noticed the trace of sleeplessness beneath her eyes. The reporters and photographers taking their positions, the senators and staffers gathering at the raised wooden bench, ignored them both.

"Will you be watching?" she murmured.

Paget nodded, glancing around them. "You realize," he said quietly, "what all of this could mean."

Mary drew closer, looking up at him. "My life has changed already," she answered with equal quiet. "And not because of Lasko."

She turned and walked toward the witness table.

He found Carlo in the library, watching them on television.

The room was dark; the colored images of Paget and Mary came through the glass doors of the Hall of Justice as if emerging from a cave. Gazing at his parents on film, Carlo did not turn or speak.

Paget touched his shoulder. "I'm so sorry. There wasn't time to tell you."

Carlo raised his hand, asking for quiet.

On the screen, Paget and Mary were surrounded by reporters, cameras, police. The lens zoomed in for head shots; as if by instinct, Mary leaned against his shoulder, gazing back at the camera. Her face held pain and vulnerability and a kind of wounded strength.

It was perfect, Paget saw. But, at least in this way, Mary no longer surprised him.

Fifteen years ago, he had learned that her face was made for the camera.

The picture changed, recapturing that moment as he remembered it.

A dark-haired woman in her late twenties, leaning forward to speak into a microphone, gaze calmly raised to the row of senators looking down at her. Waiting in the witness room, Paget had seen her on television as if for the first time: wide-set dark eyes; high cheekbones;

full, even mouth; a faintly cleft chin whose clean lines finished a kind of sculpture. A face even more vivid on-screen.

The newsman's voice-over echoed in Paget's library. "It was as a young lawyer," the narrator was saying, "that Mary Carelli first came to national attention. In televised hearings of the Senate Commerce Committee's investigation into the William Lasko scandal, Ms. Carelli confirmed charges by Christopher Paget—now her attorney—of corruption against the chairman of the Economic Crimes Commission."

On the screen, the voice-over was replaced by the bourbon drawl of Senator Talmadge of Georgia. "Miss Carelli," Talmadge said deliberately, "I would ask you to describe for this committee, as precisely as you can, how you first became aware of the possibility that Chairman John Woods was leaking Mr. Paget's investigation to William Lasko in order to save the President from embarrassment—or worse. In addressing this pivotal question, I must caution you that as far as we can determine, you alone know whether Mr. Paget is telling the truth about Chairman Woods's involvement."

Paget felt Carlo's shoulders tense; it was as if, Paget thought, even the outcome of events before his birth was once again in doubt.

"I wish I could tell you, Senator," Mary was saying on the screen, "that I would be happy to. But the night of August twenty-seventh contained the most frightening and disillusioning events of my life, and my strongest desire is to leave them behind."

Mary paused. In the silence, the camera panned the hearing room. Suddenly she was a small figure in an oak paneled cavern with ornate chandeliers, confronted by a panel of thirteen senators, staffers at their sides, reporters and photographers jammed into the seats behind her.

As the camera returned to her, Mary seemed to square her shoulders, as she had the night before. "Nonetheless," she finished quietly, "I will do my best."

For the next hour, Mary had held the country transfixed.

Alone in the witness room, Paget had been utterly still, watching television with millions of others. Not knowing what she would say, knowing only that when she was done, it would be his turn to testify.

The events she described were dramatic enough: the death of a witness; the attempt to kill Paget; the night that Mary and Paget had found Jack Woods, the chairman of their agency, about to destroy the evidence Paget had hidden in his desk. But what Paget found so riveting was Mary herself: not simply the tension of what she would say, but the wonder of how she said it. Her voice and expression ranged through sadness and humor, idealism and failed ambition, to fear and resolve and, finally, fatalism. She had lost much and learned much, she seemed to say, and now had come to speak the truth.

Watching her, he at first felt mere surprise, then felt a kind of wonder. It was as if, Paget thought, he had never truly known her.

When at last it was over and she rose from the witness table, Paget heard the door open behind him.

It was Talmadge's aide, a bespectacled man hardly older than Paget. "You're on next," the aide had said.

Paget felt an odd surprise. He followed the aide into the hearing room, still lost in what he had seen and heard.

Mary was walking toward him, followed by reporters hoping for a quick quote. Reaching Paget, she stopped.

Surrounded by reporters, their faces were perhaps two inches apart.

"Did you see me?" she asked.

"Yes," Paget had said simply. "I saw you."

Now, on television, their son saw the moment.

Captured at a distance, her lips moved silently, then his. Faces close, a portrait of intimacy.

"Before the death of Mark Ransom," the narrator was saying, "the names of Christopher Paget and Mary Carelli had not been associated for over fifteen years."

Abruptly they were in close-up again, standing outside the Hall of Justice. Paget could still feel the chill, see faces shouting from the semidarkness as if in a kind of nightmare.

A mustached reporter thrust a microphone at them; instinctively, Mary leaned back. Her hair touched Paget's face.

"Are you representing Miss Carelli?" the reporter asked.

"I'm *helping* Miss Carelli. She doesn't need a lawyer."

"Then you and Miss Carelli have a personal relationship."

Watching, Paget saw Carlo stiffen, felt the life he had constructed for them slipping away. On the screen, he answered evenly, "Yes— we're friends," and, facing the crowd, held up one hand.

"I have a brief statement. All that Miss Carelli asks is that you listen and then let her begin what you surely understand must be a long process of healing."

Paget had gathered his thoughts, searching for a sound bite. Now, with his son, he watched himself.

"At approximately twelve o'clock this afternoon," he began, "in a suite at the Hotel Flood, Mark Ransom attempted to rape Miss Carelli."

There was an eruption of sound, flashbulbs popping, shouted questions. Paget ignored them.

"It was under the pretense of business," he continued, "as these things often are. It was unexpected, as these things often are. And it was undeserved, as these things *always* are."

Paget paused. They were quiet now, waiting for more.

"There was a struggle. A gun fired. What resulted is that rarest of tragedies—an attempted rape where the result is tragic for both the rapist and the victim."

Mary looked down, as if stricken, and then silently back into the camera.

"Mark Ransom's death *was* tragic. Mary Carelli no more wished this talented but tormented man to die than she wished him to assault her. And that is *her* tragedy—that she must forever live with the memory of his assault and the memory of his death.

"That there will be no charges I am certain. But what I deeply hope is that those who know Miss Carelli only as a public figure will now extend to her the same compassion as those of us who truly know her."

On the screen, Mary was in close-up. Paget saw with astonishment that there were tears in her eyes.

As the police had hurried them to the limousine, Mary had taken his hand. She did not let it go until the door had closed.

They were alone then, behind the darkened windows of the one-way glass, separated from the driver by a glass shield.

"That," Mary had said, "was close to perfect."

Paget looked past her. Reporters and cameras pressed blindly against the windows, unable to see. "Yes," he answered. "Just like always."

She drew back. "I suppose we've had enough togetherness. At least for now."

"Yes. I suppose we have."

They said nothing more. The limousine circled the block twice, losing the reporters, and then dropped him at his car.

Carlo pushed the Mute button. In the glow of the television, he looked older than he had that morning. Behind him, pictures flashed without sound, mouths moved but spoke no words.

"Why isn't she *here*, Dad? Why didn't you bring her home?"

"ABC sent a limousine and got her to a hotel, with guards to protect her privacy." Paget hesitated. "She's better than you might expect— it's just that she's so tired."

Carlo shook his head. "But she's alone."

"I know. But I also know *her*. It's what she needs."

Carlo paused and then sat straighter, as if tensed against a blow. "Tell me what happened," he said. "Everything."

Paget sat next to him. Then, as clearly and simply as he could, Paget repeated what Mary had told Monk.

Carlo's eyes seemed never to move. For Paget, their fixity was worse than tears. "Do they believe her?"

"They don't know." Paget gazed at the silent television. "From their perspective, no one knows the truth but Mary."

Carlo seemed to search his face. "Do *you* believe her?"

Pausing, Paget replayed his son's tone of voice; the question was not about Mary but about Paget himself.

"Yes," he answered. "Essentially."

Carlo was quiet. "Since I've lived here," he asked, "have you ever done a murder case?"

"No."

"Then you should tell her you can't do it."

Paget felt weary. "It's more complicated than that."

"But you can't represent her, Dad, if you don't even believe her."

"You misunderstand me, Carlo. I appreciate we're talking about your mother. But we're also talking about a human being, charged with murder and scared to death. When you're facing *that*, you forget things. Or your story isn't coherent. Or you don't say something because it will make you look less attractive, even if it doesn't mean you're guilty." Paget tried to speak more gently. "Being your mother is a real argument for canonization, but even saints aren't perfect."

Carlo seemed to search his words for meaning. Finally, he asked, "You did love her once?"

Paget looked at him. How to talk about this, he wondered, when every word might carry an unspoken subtext: Carlo's life was an accident.

"I thought she was beautiful, Carlo, and even more than that, I thought she was an extraordinary woman." Paget paused. "Did I love her? Did she love me? I honestly don't know."

"Why not?"

"Circumstances came between us before we had a chance to know. We were two very willful people, who didn't really trust each other. We disagreed violently about politics, and then we were thrust into a situation that was very public and very painful—congressional testimony that destroyed Jack Woods, a man she worked for and deeply admired, and ruined the President they both supported. Our relationship simply became impossible."

Carlo cocked his head. "Did you even try?"

Paget heard the question that Carlo had not spoken: Didn't I make it worth trying? "I know it's hard to understand," he said at length. "You would have been the reason, but we didn't *know* you then. I'm sure that sounds strange now, but you were just an abstraction—you weren't *you* then." Paget hesitated. "We had no plans to marry, no real basis for believing that it would work, and a lot of reasons to think that it wouldn't. That kind of marriage is no favor to a child."

Carlo's voice turned stubborn. "Then why didn't she have an abortion?"

"I'm not sure. She could have done it, and I'd never have known." Paget paused again, searching for an answer that Carlo could accept. "But the ultimate answer is that—even if we didn't know you—we both loved you too much already to miss out on who you would turn out to be." Paget touched his shoulder. "We wanted you. We just didn't want to be married and didn't particularly think you'd want us to if you'd had an informed vote."

"Did you ever talk about it?"

"Not really. Most affairs like ours end with little to show for it. We've been lucky—we've got you, which is much more than either of us could ever have expected." Paget tried to smile. "As for you, you got a whole life out of the deal, and me for a father at that."

Carlo did not smile. Paget heard his son's next question before he even asked it.

"Why did she give me up?"

Perhaps a hundred times, Paget thought, he had prepared for this moment, discarding a hundred different answers. "She didn't really want to," he said finally. "Basically, I forced the issue."

"Why?"

"You were with your grandparents more than Mary—she was traveling a lot. Your grandparents were loving people, but they were *old* people. She knew that." Paget looked at him intently. "Perhaps I was selfish. But I was pretty adamant on the subject, enough to go to court over it. She knew that too."

"What did *she* say about it?"

"In the end, she agreed that it was best you be with me. But it was very hard for her to let you go, and harder still to stay away."

"Why did she?"

Paget paused. "To let me be your family," he finally said. "To not be the fantasy perfect mother, flitting in and out—to let you and me work things out when things got tough. However complicated my feelings about her may be, I know that Mary Carelli has character, and you should admire her for that."

For a long time, Carlo just gazed back at him, doubt struggling with the desire for resolution. "It's pretty confusing—if you're me."

"I know."

"Then she comes back, and now this. . . ."

Carlo's voice trailed off. As if reciting a catechism, Paget murmured, "It's okay, son. It's going to be all right." Said that, and then heard himself saying these same words to a frightened seven-year-old boy, eight years before.

But Carlo, of course, did not remember.

"I'm pretty tired," he finally said.

Paget knew the conversation was over, at least for a time. "Sure. But if you want to talk, wake me up."

Carlo nodded, and stood to leave.

Paget hesitated. "How was your game?" he asked.

For a moment, Carlo looked blank. "Oh," he answered. "Fine."

Briefly, Paget considered asking who had won and how Carlo had done, wanting to know but afraid his son would see this as indifference to his mother. The moment passed. Silent, Paget watched Carlo climb the stairs.

He felt more tired than he could remember. But then lying had always done that to him, especially to Carlo, and long before this.

PART TWO

THE INVESTIGATION

JANUARY 14 – JANUARY 22

ONE

"THE WAY TO shut this down," Paget told Teresa Peralta, "is to show Brooks that Mark Ransom was who Mary Carelli says he was."

For Terri, the moment possessed an eerie normality. They were sitting in Paget's office the next morning. The ten lawyers and staff could talk of little else. Reporters prowled the lobby, and the receptionist fended off requests for interviews. But Paget was having his calls held, and his office was quiet.

Seemingly well rested, Paget had reprised Mary Carelli's statement to Monk with the professional detachment of a lawyer who had been handed the defense of a total stranger. The only apparent difference was the newspaper folded on his desk: the headline read: MARK RANSOM SLAIN; the subheading added: "TV Interviewer Claims Rape Attempt"; and the photograph was of Mary Carelli in close-up, swelling beneath her left eye, head resting against Christopher Paget's face.

He followed Terri's gaze to the newspaper. "This is difficult, obviously. All the more reason to start thinking like a lawyer."

The remark was a concession to feelings that preempted any discussion of them. What he needed, Terri saw, was to deal with Mary Carelli as if she were not part of his life.

"It's pretty simple," Terri answered. "We need some prior acts of abuse. Something we can get before a jury."

Paget nodded. "If we can show that Ransom raped someone before, McKinley Brooks would toss this case quicker than a dead mouse on his kitchen floor. Assuming that the judge would let us prove that."

"There *is* the bruise." Terri paused, surprised at her own anger. "I mean, aren't blows to the face good enough? Or does some creep unilaterally deciding you want him inside you qualify that as foreplay?"

Paget shook his head. "Hardly. But we have to look at this from Brooks's perspective. He's got a case that could ruin his career, not a clue what really happened, and the only witness, Mary, saying what any woman would say who didn't want to go to jail."

"But what if we don't find anyone? What if Mary's the first?"

"Then it's a problem."

"I feel sorry for *any* woman who's some guy's first victim. Who's going to believe *her*? Maybe, after a while, she doesn't want to believe it herself. Maybe, day after day, she has to see this guy again." Terri stopped herself. "Even if there *is* someone, I think we'd have a tough time getting her to talk about it."

Paget considered her. "You were a rape counselor, I recall from your résumé."

Terri looked away, surprised. "Just for a semester," she said, "and more in helping with the legal than the emotional side of things. I don't think I was very good at it—I was busy, and it seemed to take a lot out of me."

Paget gazed at the photograph of Mary. "It just struck me," he ventured, "that a woman with a bad experience might talk more easily to you. And that in the remote event this thing ever goes to trial, it might be better if you did the questioning as well."

"I haven't got that much trial experience. A few misdemeanors with the public defender, and that's it."

Paget nodded. "That would bother me," he said, "if you were someone else."

The tacit compliment surprised her. Mary Carelli was Carlo's mother; at a time when Paget must surely feel great anxiety, however he might hide it, he had enough confidence to trust Terri and enough perception to treat her with some tact.

"Do you really believe that?" she asked, and then felt more embarrassed. The Richie effect, she thought; she was no longer used to compliments.

"Not a word of it," Paget said. "I'm just shopping for a feminist lawyer that everyone on the jury will want to adopt. Someone to offset Marnie Sharpe's warmth and humor."

Smiling, Terri wondered if Paget was helping her cover her own awkwardness. "Then I want to help," she said. "I'm sorry if I sounded funny about it."

Paget seemed to appraise her. "No matter," he said finally. "Rape's a subject that anyone normal feels funny about."

Especially, Terri thought, when it happens to someone you know. She searched for a change of subject.

"What," she asked, "did you think of Marnie?"

Paget leaned back in his chair. "Distrustful, I suppose. And brittle."

"Try steely. I've seen Marnie quite a bit, in court and because she's on the board of the Women Trial Lawyers." Terri paused. "Can I give you some advice?"

"By all means."

"First, don't make her angry. Somewhere inside Marnie Sharpe is a little girl who knows the boys don't like her and wants to hurt them back for it. And she can't make McKinley Brooks the enemy, even though he's kind of set her up. Which leaves you.

"Speaking as one professional to another, you're the kind of man—attractive, polished, seemingly secure—that Marnie despises most. It will be easy for her to feel that beating you would make her whole somehow. And like a lot of unhappy people who can function in the real world, she'll find a socially acceptable way to rationalize her own needs. Not just to Brooks but to herself."

Paget nodded. "I've often thought that a lot of lawyers would be tower snipers if they'd failed the bar exam."

Terri shook her head, wanting to make sure he understood. "Don't make her into a caricature. And *never* underestimate her, 'cause Marnie Sharpe was *always* first in her class. This may sound like pop therapy, but sometimes it helps me to see people as not too much older than Elena, my five-year-old. To me, Marnie is the kid who always did better than everyone else, even though she wasn't the smartest, because working by herself gave her the only sense of mastery she ever had." Pausing, Terri realized that Paget was close to smiling. "Sometimes I take this stuff a little far. It's just that I can imagine you thinking that maybe Brooks made a mistake if Marnie ever had to take this case to trial, and I'm not so sure he did."

"I was just thinking that you read my mind. How do *you* suppose Sharpe will be in court, then?"

"Tough. Hard cases don't scare her. Rape prosecutions *are* hard; she's used to trying cases like this one, where there aren't any witnesses and the evidence is circumstantial. So she's won some cases she should have lost.

"There's something very admirable about her, really. She's made rape her issue—not just prosecution but better counseling and support—and she's earned a lot of gratitude from the women she's helped. And she'll have thought of absolutely everything, down to the sixth permutation, because that'll be all she ever thinks about. To a jury, that comes off as trustworthy and professional. They may not love her, but they'll absolutely believe her."

Paget walked to the window, to stare down at the bay. The water was slate beneath gray skies; there were a couple of sailboats, a luxury liner, and a Honda freighter bringing cars in from Japan. "I liked my version of Marnie better," he said.

For the first time, Terri heard a note of worry. "Of course," she observed, "this time Marnie's going after Mary Carelli."

"I wonder," Paget said quietly, "how that cuts."

Terri tried to read his mood, gave up. "From my perspective," she began, "Mary Carelli is the whole case. So it's a good thing she's a defense lawyer's dream."

"How so?" Paget turned to her again. "I mean, from *your* perspective."

Terri nodded. "When I was at the P.D.'s office," she began, "we represented a lot of people who could hardly speak their names: drugs, alcohol, mental illness, simple illiteracy—you name it. Most of them couldn't even lie well. I tried to keep myself from getting too excited when I found out some client had told me the truth—I might begin to expect it. That was when I started wondering what practicing law did to the psyche.

"But Mary Carelli is more than just credible. She's successful, well educated, articulate. She's a role model for women. She has a very sympathetic story to tell, and there are a lot of people who are ready to support her. She understands the legal process. She's even TV trained, and she was a natural before that—I mean, her testimony before the committee was sensational."

"Yes." Paget looked out the window again. "I saw they ran that again last night."

"She was great," Terri finished. "And of course, she's absolutely beautiful."

Paget did not answer. Terri paused, wondering how he felt about this woman, whether part of him still loved her. "Is Mary all right?" she finally asked.

"More or less." Paget seemed to hear her first, unspoken question. "Forgive me if I sound cold. I'm just trying to see Mary as I would any other client. To me, precisely because of all the things you mention, Mary's someone a judge or jury might turn on if Sharpe could give them a good enough reason. And if I understand Sharpe at all, she'll be deeply offended if she thinks that Mary's using *her* issue as an alibi."

Terri considered him. "How bothered are you with the gaps in Mary's story? The bullet, for example."

Paget shrugged. "I'm less concerned with whether *her* story is completely right than with what Brooks and Sharpe can prove. Or what they can't prove, such as that Mary had any other motive than rape."

Terri hesitated. "I can see you have to detach yourself a little."

Paget nodded. "There is one area," he said finally, "where detachment fails me. Carlo. He knows who his mother is, but almost no one else does. We never wanted to bring any publicity down on him."

"I understand." Terri paused again. "Isn't that going to be kind of hard now?"

"It is." Paget stared down at the newspaper. "I wasn't expecting to represent her."

Nor, Terri was suddenly sure, did Paget want to. And if that was true, it made no sense that he *was* representing her.

"Before," she said quietly, "I didn't think you were being cold."

"I appreciate that." For the first time, Paget sounded tired. "I just want to bury this thing. Quickly."

Confused, Terri searched for something to say next. "How do we do that?"

"First, we hire a detective named Johnny Moore." Paget sat, crisp again. "When Johnny was an FBI agent in the sixties, he spent three years with the Weather Underground as a double agent, so he's used to looking strangeness in the eye. The white-collar stuff I do bores him to tears, so it'll be a relief to Johnny when I ask him to turn Ransom's sex life upside down.

"Beyond that, we should at least consider speaking to Dr. Steinhardt's daughter. Find out if she had any idea that Ransom was using Laura Chase's psychoanalysis as an aphrodisiac."

Terri looked across at the picture of Mary, imagining what had happened. Her stomach felt tight. "Does the media know about that part yet?"

"No."

"That tape gives me the creeps. With or without James Colt." Terri folded her arms. "Mark Ransom's little version of 'virtual reality.' "

"That's why it may be useful, from our point of view." Paget considered her. "For now, that seems like a place to look."

Terri nodded. "What do you want *me* to do?"

"Didn't I tell you?"

"Not specifically."

"Talk to Mark Ransom's one and only ex-wife. They were divorced five years ago, with an astounding lack of publicity." Paget gave a fleeting smile. "You might ask if it was just his books she didn't like."

Within two hours, Johnny Moore had called Terri with a Manhattan telephone number for Ransom's ex-wife.

"Melissa Rappaport," Moore said. "Took back her name. She's a free-lance editor, works at home."

"How'd you find her?"

"She was hiding out in the white pages, just like a real person. Maybe she figured divorcing Ransom would buy her a normal life."

Moore's voice was less sardonic than matter-of-fact—mild, pleasant, and faintly Irish. Terri trusted him instinctively.

"How do you think I should approach her?"

"Oh, I wouldn't wear a mustache or anything like that. The best way is what you'd probably do on your own—call her up, tell her who you are and that you want to talk with her. Just be ready for an answering machine: she's probably been called by everyone from *The New York Times* to *Women's Wear Daily,* asking how she feels about the great man dying with his pants off. Keep your message short, clear, and professional."

"I keep thinking Chris should do this."

"No, he's right. Chris is hotter than Warren Beatty after being on those TV clips, and if she's already press shy, a call from him would make things worse. Besides, you'll be an island of feminine calm in a sea of media maggots whose idea of a story is screwing and death—preferably in that order, although for some publications it's not a requirement."

Terri found herself laughing. "I'm sorry," she said, "this really isn't funny."

"Of course not. That's why I make jokes about it."

Terri thanked him and hung up.

She found herself staring at Melissa Rappaport's number, and then at what little else there was to stare at. Her office began to annoy her—it was half the size of Paget's, and she'd put nothing in it but a pre-school picture of Elena. Time to stop living like a transient, at work as well as with Richie; maybe she was doing okay here. A couple of posters, something like Picasso or Kandinsky, might make things feel permanent.

Just call the woman, Peralta. Quit stalling. You were always good at talking to people, and at least they'd listen to you.

Anyone but Richie.

Best not to think about that. Richie loved Elena, in his way, and Terri's job now was to make sure that they raised Elena to be as secure as she was smart. If Terri tried hard enough, she and Richie could make it so.

What would Christopher Paget think, Terri suddenly wondered, if she couldn't get Mark Ransom's ex-wife to even return a phone call?

It would help, Terri decided, to have an image of the woman she was calling. But it was hard to picture Mark Ransom's wife. All she could come up with was that Melissa Rappaport would feel far too shocked to carefully weigh the messages of strangers, distinguishing one from another. And all that she could do, Terri decided, was to say what she herself might respond to.

She composed a speech for the answering machine, committed the basics to memory, and dialed the number Moore had given her.

The telephone began ringing. One ring. Two. Three. Four. Terri was not sure what would happen if a real person answered.

"Hello," the cool voice said. "You have reached 501-7216. You may leave a message at the tone."

Melissa Rappaport, Terri thought, wasn't one for insincerity, such as that she was glad to hear from whoever called, or for false promises, like that she'd call back soon or ever. The voice had the crisp economy of someone who got to the point: Terri suddenly envisioned a thin woman, restlessly pacing her apartment, and began mentally editing her message.

The beep sounded.

"This is Teresa Peralta," Terri began. "I'm an attorney in San Francisco. Our office represents Mary Carelli."

Terri imagined the woman stopping to listen, surprised at who was calling, poised on the edge of hostility.

"It feels foolish to tell you how much I hate bothering you about something this painful, and then to ask you to call back anyhow. I'm asking because this is so painful for Mary Carelli. I need to help her make sense of this, emotionally as well as legally.

"You may think that you can't help, or just that you don't want to. All I ask is that you not decide until I've told you all I can about what Mary says Mark Ransom did."

In her mind, Terri saw the woman standing over the machine, caught between the wish to know and the desire to be left alone.

"You can listen," she continued, "and then not tell me anything. Anything you do choose to tell me will be confidential unless you say otherwise. I'm not the press, and I don't think people's lives are entertainment—yours, Mary's, or Mark Ransom's.

"I can be reached at work, (415) 939-2707, or home, (415) 232-5455.

"Thank you for considering this."

Slowly, Terri put down the telephone.

She checked her watch, saw that it was eleven-forty-five, and decided not to go to lunch for fear of missing the telephone. She wasn't hungry anyhow.

No one called. At two-thirty, her stomach felt concave, her blood sugar seemed to have gone into deficit, and she had begun debating whether it was all right to ask her secretary to get her a sandwich.

In Manhattan, Terri realized, night had fallen.

When the telephone rang, Terri was certain it was Richie.

"Terri Peralta."

"Hello." It was the cool voice of the tape. "This is Melissa Rappaport."

Terri sat upright. "I'm so glad you called me," she said. "Really, thank you."

"Really," the voice answered, "I'm not sure why I did."

The voice was cultivated and very cautious. Keep this going, Terri thought, engage her. "I promised to tell you what happened," she tried.

There was silence.

"Would it be better," Terri asked, "if I came to New York?"

"Just to satisfy my curiosity?" The voice paused again. "What *is* it you want?"

Terri gazed out at the bay, unseeing. She imagined Melissa Rappaport in the darkened bedroom of her apartment, weary from a day's worth of calls she had not answered, connected to Terri by a thread she could break simply by hanging up.

"I guess part of what I'm asking," Terri responded, "is whether the Mark Ransom that Mary describes is anyone you recognize."

"And if it were?"

"Then I could at least tell Mary Carelli she's not alone—that she's not the only one who can imagine what your ex-husband did to her." Terri's voice grew softer. "It's awfully lonely to accuse someone of trying to rape you."

There was silence. "In other words," Melissa Rappaport finally said, "did Mark ever use force."

"I was going to ask that, yes."

"No." The voice was toneless. "He never used force."

Terri tried to replay the words; heard something careful, literal. "Was there something else?"

"Yes." The word had a certain edge. "You said that you would tell me what happened. Or, more precisely, what Ms. Carelli says happened."

Terri felt deflated. "Where would you like me to start?"

"Perhaps," Melissa Rappaport answered, "with how Ms. Carelli happened to find herself in Mark's suite."

Terri stood, striving to remember all that Paget had told her. "He said he wanted to talk to her. About an interview."

"She knew him, I assume."

"No."

"Then why did Mark contact her?"

There was a moment's pause. Terri hesitated, trying to track the careful cross-examination. "What he first told Mary," she answered, "is that he liked watching her on television."

This time, the silence was much longer, the voice a little flatter. "Watching her on television."

"Yes."

"Really. I'd have thought her a bit dark for Mark's tastes. But then I hadn't seen him in several years."

"What were his tastes? That is, when you knew him."

More silence; Terri froze, fearful that she had gone too far. "I'm sorry," Melissa Rappaport said. "That last was a pointless remark. It may take me a couple of days of living with Mark's death to get the emotional range just right."

Terri had begun to feel the long-distance voice as if connected to her nerve ends. For the first time, she was certain that the rigid self-control sealed off some well of feeling.

"I'm sorry," Terri answered quietly.

"No matter. The etiquette for this conversation has yet to be written." There was another pause. "Tell me, how is it that Mark is supposed to have—to put it politely—introduced the subject of sex?"

"He suggested that she sleep with him in exchange for an interview."

"For an interview?" Over long distance, Melissa Rappaport's mirthless laughter was close to eerie. "We are *not* discussing Garbo or Howard Hughes. Mark Ransom was hardly a rare commodity. If the price of far too many words from Mark was sleeping with him, then he's screwed every talk show host but Regis Philbin."

Terri felt humiliated. "What he said, to put it *less* politely, is that he liked to fuck women he'd seen on film."

She heard the edge in her own voice a moment after she spoke. Perhaps, Terri thought, that had caused Melissa Rappaport's latest silence; she was about to hang up.

Tonelessly, Melissa Rappaport said, "What a very charming story."

"Our client didn't think so."

"No. I suppose she wouldn't have." There was another pause. "But what makes it so implausible is the idea of Mark offering his face on television as if that gave him sexual leverage."

Terri hesitated. "Not just his face. He was going to talk about a new book."

"Less plausible yet. We in what the more precious among us might call the 'literary community' may find it rather melancholy, but the publication of a novel is rarely the stuff of prime time television. Even a novel by Mark."

Again, Terri heard some buried emotion, a faint rueful edge. "I think," she answered with studied calm, "that *this* book might have been different."

"Different? I must confess that I don't even know what *this* one was about. I suppose I'm feeling a little left out." Rappaport hesitated, and then spoke more quietly. "You see, on top of everything, I used to edit his novels."

Terri thought she heard the last vestige of widowed intimacy. "It wasn't a novel," she said. "It was a biography."

"Biography?" Rappaport sounded surprised. "Not autobiography? That *is* a departure. Who was it that Mark found so uniquely worthy?"

"Laura Chase."

There was silence. Terri waited, heard nothing. Decided to speak again, go for broke. "He had a tape. Of Laura Chase talking to her psychiatrist. He asked Mary there to hear it."

"I see." Rappaport's voice seemed oddly detached. "What is on the tape?"

Terri hesitated. Paget had instructed her not to discuss the tape unless it was a strict necessity: knowledge of the tape would cause a scandal, outraging James Colt's family and those who loved him still. "This part isn't public," she said. "I don't think anyone wants it to be."

Terri's own words came back to her as tentative, untrusting. "What makes you suppose," Rappaport said in a cold voice, "that *I* do."

Terri felt the tension run from Rappaport to her, the thread between them close to breaking. "It's about Laura Chase and Senator Colt," she finally said. "A weekend in Palm Springs just before she died, where she drank too much and took too many pills." Terri paused. "Colt brought two friends with him. On the tape, Laura Chase describes what they did to her."

There was more silence. Then Rappaport asked quietly, "Did Mark actually have her listen?"

"Yes." Terri heard the tightness in her own voice, paused once more. "That excited him, Mary says. He tried to rape her while the tape was still playing."

The silence lengthened. It was more than seconds, perhaps close to a minute, before Melissa Rappaport spoke again.

"I think perhaps I should talk with you," she said. "In person."

* * *

Paget picked up the telephone. Without preface, she asked, "Is Carlo all right?"

For a moment, Paget did not respond. Dark had fallen, and the lights of the city were bright and clear; it reminded him of the moments, only an evening ago, before her telephone call had changed everything.

"Terrific," he answered coldly. "Not only are both his parents famous once more, but this morning there were reporters outside when he went off to school. He'll never be lonely again." Paget paused. "Of course, his friends don't know where to call, given that we've had to change our telephone number. But I'm sure the press will ferret it out."

Mary ignored his tone. "Do they know about me?" she asked.

"Not yet. But think what a career-maker that'll be for our son. I rather like imagining Carlo's face on the cover of *People,* superimposed on his birth certificate."

There was quiet. "Do you have to be like this?"

"Oh, I certainly think so." Paget stared out the window. "Someone once told me that sarcasm is the safe alternative to expressing anger. And I'm far too civil to be angry at such a difficult moment in your life. To invert what I said to our TV friends last night, those who truly know you should try to extend the same compassion as those who know you only through the media."

Paget sensed, rather than heard, a sharp intake of breath. "You know, Chris, you really are a bastard."

It was curious, Paget thought, that any words from her could still carry the memory of hurt. "You already told me that, Mary. On a particular disenchanted evening, fifteen years ago."

Mary was silent for a moment. "All right," she said dismissively. "Then let me be redundant on a subject I care much more about. How *is* Carlo?"

Paget found himself gazing at Carlo's picture. "How Carlo is," he answered, "is worried and confused. Not just about you but about us, in the past as well as the present. This has opened up a lot for him that you and I both know would be far better buried."

There was another silence; it came to Paget as the sound of something Mary had decided not to say. "You may not believe this," she said at last, "but if there were anything I could have done to stop Mark Ransom from doing this to all of us, including jump from the twenty-third story of the Hotel Flood, I would have done it."

Paget leaned back in his chair. "Well," he said at length, "it hasn't been a dead loss. You certainly have Carlo's sympathy, even if you find my response a little wanting. In fact, *Carlo* seems to find my response a little wanting."

"What does he say?"

"Very little. Sometimes, with Carlo, you have to read between the lines. But he seems to want me to exhibit more compassion, and us to act more like his parents than two strangers." Paget realized that his gaze had not moved from the picture; Carlo, a year younger, smiled back from a time of seeming innocence. "I suppose there are certain archetypes that arise from something deep in all of us, like it or not. Such as those involving mothers and fathers."

"Yes." Mary's voice was drained of feeling. "Mothers and fathers. Which brings us back to what I, or we, can do for Carlo now."

"It's quite simple. Get me off this case."

There was more silence. "Other than that," she answered quietly.

It was a moment before Paget felt his own anger. "Then why," he said, "did you ever ask the question? Had you read somewhere that caring was good form?"

She did not answer. Paget sensed her framing some retort, then repressing it with effort. "I have my reasons. And they *are* mine."

Paget felt his eyes narrow. "When, Mary, were your reasons ever anyone else's?"

Paget heard her exhale, the sound of impatience. "This gets us nowhere. I asked about Carlo, not you."

Paget stood, angry, then found his self-control. "All right," he said. "Short term, the only thing I can think of is for you to give him some reassurance that you're okay and, as you put it during your unexpected visit, that you care a little."

Mary was silent. "You asked me for dinner," she said coolly. "Maybe I should accept. That way you and I can pretend for Carlo that we're not the Addams Family."

Paget hesitated; the image of Mary inside his home felt more invasive than the cameramen outside it, the pretense it would require far more wearing. But he had already lost control of things, and the sole remaining question was how Carlo would respond.

"Let's do it on Friday," he said at length. "By that time I'll have revisited Brooks. If we can get some time alone, we can talk about whatever's happened without your coming to the office."

"Fine," she answered briskly. "I certainly wouldn't care to invade each and every one of your private spaces. Incidentally, what *has* happened?"

With surprise, Paget absorbed the fact that she had killed a man yesterday and yet had talked mainly of their son. "My associate's going back east to see Ransom's ex-wife. Terri thinks there's something there but has no idea whether it's helpful stuff or just emotional confusion."

"And you're sending some associate—this Terri—rather than go yourself. How old is she?"

"Twenty-nine." Paget paused, then added softly, "The exact age you were when the Lasko case went down."

With equal quiet, Mary answered, "That means nothing."

Paget began pacing. "You wanted me to represent you, and you won. Now you'll have to start trusting me, just like any lawyer you were desperate to have."

"Do you trust me, Chris?"

"No." Paget gazed out the window. "But then I wouldn't anyhow. I only trust my clients when long experience has taught me that I can."

Mary did not answer. Something in her silence made Paget feel less than human and then wish for a way out.

"Has the press bothered you much?" he asked.

She seemed to consider whether to even respond. "Not much. The guards have kept them away. And room service has exceeded my expectations."

How was it, Paget wondered, to be a prisoner in a strange hotel room? "A few days," he said, "and we should be able to get you out of town. In the meanwhile, don't talk to the press until we've both worked out a script."

"Then we should do that." Her tone was businesslike again. "I may be going on *60 Minutes* this Sunday."

"You've *already* talked to them about it? The day after Ransom dies?"

"Not me," she said coldly. "My agent. As you said, this is now a problem in public relations. And that's who deals with public relations when I'm too devastated to speak for myself."

The uneasy mix of irony and truth made Paget feel a kind of shame. "How *are* you?" he asked.

"Fine. Wouldn't you be?"

"No."

"Then you have one more reason to admire me," she said, and hung up.

"Why New York?" Richie asked. "I thought there was no travel in this job."

Bringing Elena home from day care, she had found him intently focused on the computer in the bedroom of their apartment, creating a complex graph that represented his imagined new enterprise. The computer, Terri realized, symbolized the differences between them: Richie looked at the screen and envisioned his ideas turning into money; Terri remembered what the screen had cost them. Forty-five hundred dollars, sitting on their charge card.

They had argued for two days, until Richie had worn her down, and then spent another three days while a newly energized Richie had dragged Elena, Terri, and her MasterCard through a half-dozen computer outlets, excitedly querying salespeople about the latest options. At the end, Terri was exhausted from watching Elena, and Richie had a laser printer and the best new color graphics.

"I said not *much* travel," she told him now. "Almost any law job has *some* travel."

"But why you?" he queried. "It's *his* girlfriend."

Once more, Terri was glad that she had not told Richie about Paget's son; her own confidences to Richie had a funny way of coming back with a little twist at times when she felt most vulnerable.

"Not girlfriend, old friend. And I feel good that Chris trusts me to do this."

"So it's 'Chris' now." Richie gave an exaggerated shrug. "Absolutely, then . . . whatever 'Chris' wants."

"Don't be an ass, Richie. Do you want me to call him 'Mr. Paget,' like Mary Tyler Moore used to call her boss 'Mr. Grant'?"

She felt Richie watch her, saw him choose a lower key. "What it is," he said, "is I've got plans, dinners with people who might invest in Lawsearch. I can't be baby-sitting Elena."

" 'Baby-sitting'?" Terri repeated. "You mean the thing teenagers do with kids who aren't theirs?"

"You know what I mean," Richie snapped. "Tied up."

"Maybe you can talk to them during the business day."

"Can't. They've all got jobs."

Terri searched his face for conscious irony, saw none. "Yes," she said. "A surprising number of people do."

Richie flushed. "That's abusive, Ter. How can I share my plans with someone who uses them to hurt me?"

For a moment, Terri found herself just observing him. Thin, wiry, with curly brown hair and intense black eyes, which had always made him seem consumed by some compelling inner vision. When she first met Ricardo Arias, he was only twenty-two. But he had struck her as different from anyone she'd ever met—full of ideas, yet always in motion, driven to make his best dreams real. Between Richie then and now were a law degree, the MBA she had helped him pay for, and three jobs he had not kept, and the endless motion seemed less that of an achiever than of a wind-up toy Terri had placed before Elena in the living room, to distract her while they talked.

"I'm sorry," she said. Partly for the thoughts. Partly to deflect him.

"It's okay." Richie kept his voice deliberately flat. "Maybe you don't always hear the way you talk to me."

The words were meaningless. Did she imagine, Terri wondered, the triumph in his eyes whenever she backed down, or had he taken so much out of her that she, like him, had begun to believe that every hurt was meant to help steal from the other some essential self. "I guess I worry about the dinners," she said finally. "Our credit's at the limit."

"It can't be helped. I can't get their attention during the day. Besides, dinners are a better place for them to get a feel for me."

Terri said nothing. In Richie's mind, a fancy restaurant, and not their bare apartment, spoke to who he was. Only Terri seemed to see Richie at the dining-room table they had never owned, the down-payment money lost on his last deal, the new dresses she too seldom bought Elena. The night before their latest move, when the last place had gone condominium, she had found herself staring into a packing box and thinking that the fruits of their marriage were their old college yearbooks and two honeymoon albums, complete with funny captions that seemed to have been written by some other woman.

"Mommy," Elena asked, "can we have macaroni and cheese tonight?"

She was standing in the doorway, holding her wind-up duck. A beautiful five-year-old with Richie's eyes. The real fruit of their marriage.

"Sure, Lainie." Richie scooped Elena up in his arms. "Mommy'll make that. Daddy likes it too."

Terri went to the kitchen, Elena and Richie chattering behind her.

That night, she did not sleep. The next morning, she left money for a baby-sitter, drove Elena to day care, and caught an eight-thirty flight to New York.

TWO

MELISSA RAPPAPORT WAITED in the doorway of her apartment.

Terri had not expected this. And something about Rappaport herself put Terri on edge; a too-slim woman in her forties with a thin face and marmoset eyes that shone with a bright intelligence. She wore little makeup, and what might have been unruly black hair was tamed by a hairstyle short enough to be severe. Her clothes enhanced the impression of someone too serious to care about frills—gray slacks, turtleneck sweater, flat black pumps, no jewelry at all. Even Terri's wool suit and white blouse felt inappropriate and overdone.

Rappaport's hand, extended to Terri, felt fragile. "You've come so far," she said. "Mark would have been flattered."

"I appreciate your seeing me."

"Yes?" The word held a note of denial, as if Rappaport wished to forget her own suggestion that Terri come. "Well, please step in."

They walked through an alcove, past a library with bookshelves from floor to ceiling, and entered the living room.

The room was spacious, furnished with spare iron sculpture and abstract prints. The hardwood floors were a bleached white, and the furnishings were white Italian leather; the absence of color lent the sensation of someone who had bled the emotion from her life.

"May I bring you some coffee?" Rappaport asked.

Terri sensed that she would rather busy herself than talk; she projected the neutral and slightly distracted air of someone who had been snatched from thought by a visitor of no great interest.

"Black coffee would be nice," she said, and Rappaport left the room.

The front wall was virtually consumed by a rectangle of glass. Through the window, Central Park in winter looked like a moonscape—grass shrouded in snow, empty paths, a pond frozen to an icy mirror. Clouds darkened the distant towers of the East Side, casting shadows across bare trees; their naked branches reminded Terri of the sculpture in the room itself. Staring into the park, Terri wondered how a free-lance editor could afford the view.

As if to answer, Melissa Rappaport spoke from behind her. "This apartment was Mark's originally. Of course, the furnishings are quite different now."

Terri nodded; there was little here that matched her sense of Ransom. "The view is lovely," she said.

"Thank you." Rappaport handed Terri a china cup and saucer, gesturing toward the couch. "Please sit down. You won't mind if I stand— I sit all day."

"Of course."

Rappaport stood with her hands in her pockets. Her posture lent a certain mutability to the moment, as if a change of mood would send her to the door. Terri decided to say nothing.

"Your telephone call," Rappaport said at length. "I suppose it shook me." Her tone was neutral, as if she were speculating about the emotions of someone else.

"I'm sorry," Terri said.

"We were married for almost six years, you know. I sometimes hear people say divorce is easier without children. . . ." The woman shrugged, cutting herself off.

"How did you meet?" Terri asked.

Rappaport's lips formed something halfway between smile and grimace. "I was Mark's editor. At Doubleday."

"That must have been quite interesting."

"Challenging. Mark had such talent—he was like a volcano, spewing words in wonderful bursts and torrents. There was life on every page. It was just that he loved each phrase too much, could never slaughter his babies." Rappaport's voice had a staccato intensity Terri had not heard before. "I suppose I gave him the structure he needed, a sense of where passion became excess."

"That's important," Terri said. "For me, sometimes it's the difference between finishing a book and picking up something else."

Rappaport looked at Terri more closely. "Have you read anything Mark wrote?"

"The novels, mostly." Including, Terri did not add, the one she had reread on the flight east, to refresh her memory.

"What did you think?"

Terri sipped coffee, considering her answer. "I liked the lush way he used language—for another writer it would have been too much, but Mark Ransom could immerse me in a world where I didn't want to turn the pages too fast. Also he seemed to feel his male characters from the inside, even the worst ones, so that I could believe that they were particular human beings and not types."

There was life in Rappaport's eyes now, a hint of challenge. "And?"

Terri met her gaze. "And," she said slowly, "the way he wrote about women made me uncomfortable."

The strange semismile reappeared, as if this were familiar ground. "Why, exactly?"

"Because he never wrote from a woman's point of view. They were always seen from the outside, either as bitch goddesses or as something for two men to compete for. The sex was conquest. . . ." Terri paused. "I didn't get the feeling Mark Ransom liked women, that's all."

"When I met him, that's not quite how it seemed to me." Rappaport's tone held the trace of ancient argument, with someone else than Terri. "Writers need understanding; fear impairs it. Mark had great understanding of everything but women because we frightened him so much."

"But why?"

Rappaport shrugged. "I think it happened to Mark the way it happened to other men I've known—their mothers. I never met Siobhan Ransom, but my sense is that she made Mark live his boyhood under a sort of military occupation of the mind and heart—no privacy, much guilt, few male activities, and tremendous pressure to succeed or lose her love. And his father was a cipher." Rappaport turned to the window. "Mark was sterile, you know. He couldn't have children."

"No. I didn't know."

"No one was supposed to. It hurt him very badly." Rappaport became pensive. "I used to think Mark believed that somehow his mother had stolen his manhood. And that beneath Mark's sexuality was an anger born of fear."

Terri nodded. "They ran an old tape of him on television last night, denouncing the pro-choice movement. He tried to be ironic, but he seemed to feel such anger. Not just at abortion but at the women who spoke up for abortion rights."

"Oh, I think Mark took all that personally somehow." Rappaport clasped her hands; Terri had begun noting the small aimless gestures of a woman trying not to reach for a cigarette. "I tried not to feel any anger of my own but to understand why Mark had become the way he was."

Terri looked at her curiously. "Was that hard?" she asked.

"Yes." Rappaport turned to her. "But *I* cared. For Mark's sake, and for the sake of what Mark wrote."

"Did you feel that his writing became better. I mean, in *that* way?"

"In *that* way, I did nothing for him, in his writing or in his life." Rappaport's voice was quiet, bitter. "But then Mark's writing didn't kill him, did it? Your client did. That's why you're here."

Terri was silent, unnerved by the shift in mood. Then she asked, "Did Mark ever watch Mary Carelli? Or talk about her?"

"No. Of course not."

"Why 'of course not'?"

"Because she's neither interesting nor appealing." Rappaport frowned. "I understand that she's quite beautiful and that people watch her interviews, but to me she's all surface and calculation."

But what did *he* think? Terri wondered. "Plus she wasn't Mark's type, you said."

"It was a cheap remark—or wounded, perhaps." Rappaport snatched a black purse from the coffee table in front of Terri and reached inside for a cigarette. "Really, I'm a bit sorry I troubled you to come. You called me at a moment of disequilibrium."

Her tone was dismissive. Terri felt something akin to panic; Rappaport seemed to be slipping away, as if she had taxed her own patience. Instinctively, Terri said, "I felt you reacting to Laura Chase."

The cigarette paused in front of Rappaport's lips. "Was that what it was?"

The question sounded rhetorical. "Yes," Terri repeated quietly. "I think it was Laura Chase."

Carefully, Melissa Rappaport picked up a silver lighter, snapped forth a flame, and took one deep drag of her cigarette. She smoked hungrily, Terri thought, like a man.

Terri broke the silence. "Did Mark ever talk about Laura Chase?"

Rappaport sat at the other end of the couch and placed an ashtray in her lap. She looked not at Terri but at a Kafkaesque print, distorted rectangles and broken lines. "Mark," she said finally, "was obsessed with her."

"Obsessed?"

"I chose that word with care. Mark read everything there was about her, had a scrapbook of publicity pictures, knew all about her marriages and the hundreds of men she'd slept with, all the apocrypha about Laura and why she died—a preoccupation so morbid that, in my mind, it became a sort of mental necrophilia. And he'd heard the rumors about James Colt, of course. I think he even *imagined* himself as Colt: to him, it made sense that one of the most powerful men in America would take a woman who, Mark once wrote, 'was the primal image at the heart of every male, half goddess and half slave.' " She gave a mirthless laugh. "Mark even made me watch her movies, over and over, until I knew every line as well as he did."

"Made you?"

Terri saw Rappaport nod slightly. "Not literally. I *wanted* to, you see, so that I could understand what went on inside him." Rappaport took another drag. "I was in my early thirties when I met him, but I hadn't that much experience with men."

"What did you expect to learn?"

"How to be a woman, of course. I was less than certain of myself that way—sexually." Her tone was still ironic, but her mouth was set in a line. "I was trying to learn what so appealed to Mark about Laura Chase, and he was going to learn to love that part of me that wasn't her at all. Or so I thought."

Terri shifted in her chair. She had begun to feel Rappaport resonate with the echoes of a long-ago psychic explosion, from which the current woman had been reconstructed with great care. "Laura Chase," she said, "was not much like you or me or anyone else I know."

"Do you mean bleached blond and voluptuous, with a mock-sexy voice and an air of undereducated precocity? Or do you mean alcoholic, nymphomaniac, and wholly lacking in self-esteem?" Rappaport paused, as if listening to herself. "In the end," she continued more softly, "all I shared with Laura Chase was a lack of self-esteem. And that, it now seems clear, was exactly what I'd started with."

Terri's coffee cup was half full; she had not touched it in some moments. Finally, she asked, "Was that because of how he treated you?"

Rappaport shook her head. "He treated me that way because that was who I was. Toward the end, when he lost interest in me, I grew more desperate."

"Lost interest?"

"Physically—he wouldn't react to me. It made me *try* harder, as it were. I'd always believed that I was smart but not that I could make someone love me. During the day, I'd slash words, scenes, whole chapters, imposing enough discipline on his talent so that people would want him." She paused, staring fixedly at the print. "At night, I would do anything Mark asked."

Terri's voice felt tight. "But he didn't mistreat you."

"No. He simply pretended to."

It was a moment before Terri understood. "He invented scenes of some kind?"

"Of a particular kind." Terri saw that the cigarette had burned close to Rappaport's fingers. "He would pretend to rape me."

Silent, Terri reached over and took the cigarette from Rappaport's hand. The woman seemed not to notice. Placing it in the ashtray, Terri saw that her own hand was shaking.

"How did he 'pretend'?" Terri asked.

"With my cooperation, of course." Rappaport's words, measured and toneless, had the inevitability of catharsis. "Every night I would call him from work, to tell him that I was leaving. Then I would ride home on the subway, wondering whether it would happen. It was part of our game.

"You see, what made it work for Mark was that he would never tell me. I would open the door and find a darkened apartment, not knowing whether he had gone out or was inside, waiting.

"I never knew until I felt Mark smother my mouth.

"I never knew how, or which room. All I knew was how worthless it made me feel." Rappaport's profile was still and white, and her gaze seemed directed at something outside the room. "Sometimes he left without saying anything at all. Like a stranger who had raped me."

Terri was conscious of her own body, small, taut, leaning forward. "Did you ever tell anyone?"

"No. It was just a game we played." Rappaport's eyes shut. "But he's dead now, isn't he."

Terri's throat was dry. "When we spoke," she said finally, "something connected all this with Mary Carelli. I thought then it was the tape."

"The tape?" Rappaport touched her eyes. "Of course, you had no idea what you were dredging up."

Terri watched her. "Can you talk about it?"

Rappaport nodded, silent.

Terri waited. When Rappaport spoke again, her eyes had opened, and her voice was dry and precise.

"The apartment was dark, as if it might happen. But he had been going out more, playing our 'game' less and less. I didn't expect him to be there.

"When I saw a faint glow from the bedroom, and then a shadow crossing it, I was almost grateful.

"I was alone in the hallway, bracing myself, when he came through the door.

"All I saw was a flash of red hair."

Abruptly, Rappaport stood, as if at a sound that only she heard. "He threw me over his shoulder, too hard. I remember my head snapping back, being dazed. Before I knew what was happening, he had thrown me facedown on the bed, pulled up my dress, torn my underwear and stockings from behind.

"Mark took me that way.

"I still didn't understand. Then he grabbed the hair at the nape of my neck and wrenched my head up. To show me.

"The light was from the television screen. He had a stag film on the VCR.

"It was Laura Chase.

"She was very young, before she became a movie star. There were two men with her. It looked like she was crying.

"Mark's face was next to mine, watching the two men take her as he had me, from behind. I didn't know that I was watching too, until I began to cry."

Rappaport paused, tears in her eyes. "When the film was over, I knew that I would never be with Mark again. But I didn't know why Laura Chase had killed herself until I spoke to you."

Terri looked away. "I'm so sorry."

Melissa Rappaport turned to her. "Don't be. It was the last time I was ever with a man." Her smile seemed more painful than her tears. "You see, *that* was what I learned from Mark."

"That," Paget's voice said, "sounds like what we needed."

From a telephone booth, Terri watched the baggage carousel spin.

Drained by a long flight spent thinking of little but Melissa Rappaport, she still held the scrap of paper with Paget's new telephone number. "If she's willing to testify," she answered. "And if the judge will let it in."

For a moment, Paget did not answer; the sound of someone paging a John McDermott echoed in the cavern of an airport at night. "Would you mind dropping by here?" Paget asked. "I hate to keep you, but I'm seeing Brooks and Sharpe tomorrow morning, and it would help to know exactly what she told you."

Terri hesitated. It was seven-thirty and the sitter had said that Elena was asleep. Paget sounded anxious, and something about Rappaport had made her feel more alone.

"Give me directions," she said.

A half hour later, Terri found a three-story white Edwardian with bay windows, a slanted roof, and a spotlit palm tree that seemed to have migrated from Los Angeles. She stopped to examine the tree, struck by its incongruity.

"I keep hoping it'll die," Paget's voice said. "But the thing's obnoxiously healthy."

As Terri looked up, he rose from a lawn chair on the front porch and came down the stairs, dressed in jeans and a white Irish fisherman's sweater.

"I like it," she told him.

"You and Carlo." He gave the tree a look of mild bemusement. "That foolish palm is why I bought this place."

"Because of a tree?" She turned to look again. "This must be the world's most expensive palm."

"Tell that to Carlo." Paget stood next to her, contemplating the tree. "After he came to live with me, we went out one day to look at houses. Nothing interested him until we saw this place, and then I could hardly get him to leave. He told me we had to live here because the tree looked like home."

Terri glanced at him, surprised. "Where had he been living?"

"Boston, of course. The date palm capital of Massachusetts."

Terri smiled. "Kids' minds are really funny. Elena once asked me why Richie and I hadn't taken her on the honeymoon."

Paget cocked his head. "That's one question that Carlo's never asked."

Terri was quiet. "So," she finally ventured, "whose idea was the spotlight?"

"Mine. Or so Carlo informed me." Paget turned to her. "Ever notice how literal little kids can be?"

This was not, Terri thought, a conversation she had ever imagined. "Sure. I try to be pretty careful about what I say to Elena."

Paget nodded. "We drove away from here, Carlo still chattering about the palm tree. The whole thing was so bizarre I could hardly keep from laughing—I was about to spend a million dollars to buy a tree I couldn't stand. So I turned to Carlo and said with utter seriousness, 'Don't worry, son, not only will your doting father buy this house, but I'll get the lighting on the tree just right.' It was one of those remarks you make to a kid which is really for the amusement of another adult—or, in my case, because I was laughing at the idea of myself as a father." Gazing up at the spotlight, Paget shook his head. "It was also a mistake. Carlo remembered every word."

Terri smiled at him. Silent, Paget kept his eyes on the tree; she had the sense that he needed to talk about his son but seldom did, so that now he felt embarrassed.

"We'd better go in," he said. "I'm keeping you."

"It's all right. Richie's out, and I wanted to tell you about Rappaport."

Opening a beveled double door with a brass knob and door kick, Paget led her inside.

The interior made Terri's preconceptions seem foolish. She had vaguely imagined the movie-set trappings of inherited wealth—the oak paneling, brown leather, and oil paintings of dead ancestors more appropriate to some private men's club. The actual decor was light: white walls and blond hardwood floors, with track lighting and bright splashes of color everywhere—a deep-red Persian rug, vases and silk flowers in various hues, an eclectic assortment of vivid prints and oils, which somehow enhanced each other rather than clashed. Passing the library, Terri saw a long marble fireplace and then a shelf full of games, which, like geologic periods, seemed to trace Carlo's passage from seven to fifteen. Terri felt a moment's envy, for Elena's sake more than for her own: Christopher Paget's house felt as if the same people had lived here for a while, adding pieces of themselves over time, secure in the knowledge that this was their home.

"That's a lovely fireplace," Terri said.

Paget nodded. "Carlo always liked me to build a fire for him, read stories in front of it. When he was younger, the library was his favorite room."

"Your whole home is beautiful, really. Did you do all this yourself?"

Paget nodded. "That's what explains all the primary colors," he said. "Carlo and I have a complete lack of subtlety no decorator could match."

Smiling, Terri felt the seemingly light remark bring Paget into focus: he was clinging to a life that might now change irreparably, and for the wrong reasons. It lent an unsettling note of worry to this lightness about Carlo.

"Where is he?" she asked. "I've never met him."

"Studying, I hope." Paget glanced up the staircase. "If you don't mind, perhaps we can chat in the kitchen. I was just cleaning up."

Paget looked slightly uncomfortable, as if concerned that his manners had lapsed. Terri realized that he preferred that his son not walk into the middle of the kind of conversation this was likely to be; thinking about Mark Ransom and his mother, she was sure, had already been hard enough.

"That's fine," she said. "I like any kitchen that I don't have to cook in."

The kitchen was what she now expected: high-tech, track-lit, spacious, light. On the other side of a bleached wooden counter were two white leather-covered barstools, where, she guessed, Paget and his son ate breakfast. Terri declined a glass of wine and sat with her hands folded in front of her. Paget leaned casually against the counter, as if to help her relax.

"Just tell me about Rappaport as it happened," he said. "From beginning to end."

For forty minutes, Terri did that.

At odd intervals Paget would interject a question, as often about how Rappaport looked or acted as about what she said. Terri sensed him piecing together this woman from whatever Terri gave him, adjusting the picture here or there, with the dispassion of an archaeologist reimaging a long-dead creature from a few scraps of bone. His face showed nothing save a slight narrowing of the eyes; Terri could not tell whether this reflected a reaction to what Rappaport had told her or to Terri herself.

When she had finished, Paget walked to the refrigerator without a word, poured a glass of white wine, and held it out to her. "If you don't want this," he said, "I'll drink it."

Terri realized that she wanted it. When she had sipped awhile, Paget said, "A few more questions."

"Sure."

He leaned back on the counter, regarding her. "Did she say Ransom had other women?"

"I assumed that." It sounded foolish, Terri felt, and was. "She didn't say so."

Paget nodded. "When she said Ransom had lost interest, did she mean that literally, or was she talking about some failure of performance?"

Terri hesitated. The question had not occurred to her. "I'm not sure."

"Did she know anything about Ransom's sex life outside her own experience—from Ransom himself, or anyone else?"

"I didn't ask her that." Terri stared at her wine. "I should have."

Paget smiled faintly, shaking his head. "Perhaps at a deposition. Not when you're watching a self-possessed woman unravel because she's telling you things you want to know but wish had never happened to her, until you're no longer sure you even want her to keep talking."

Terri felt surprise, and then something like relief. "I felt ashamed," she said. "Like I was taking something from her."

"I think not, in the end: it's what Ransom did to her that's awful, not the facing up to it. What strikes me is how much she seems to have taken out of you." He paused for a moment. "Do you always fool yourself when something's bad?"

Terri hesitated. "This shouldn't be."

Paget shook his head. "What she told you is quite extraordinary, and it connected you to what she felt. That's how you know you're not a sociopath, or dead."

Terri kept gazing at the glass. "It was unbelievable," she finally said.

"I really don't know how you got her to say all that." Paget poured himself some wine. "But by doing it, you've given Mary far more credibility than she could ever have on her own."

"Do you think they'll drop this now?"

"Quite possibly. One problem with Mary's story is that Ransom's connection to her is so arbitrary—it's like deciding to rape Barbara Walters because you saw her on *20/20*. I can understand Brooks and Sharpe thinking that there must be something more." He paused, as if trying to imagine himself as Sharpe. "What the D.A. has to accept," he finished, "is that, like Melissa Rappaport, but for reasons only Mark Ransom could ever have explained, Mary Carelli became the object of his Laura Chase fetish."

Terri finished her wine. "There *is* one difference. Which got Mary where she is."

"Which is?"

"She wouldn't play the game."

Paget considered her. "Mary Carelli," he said, "has never played anyone's game but her own."

His voice had a faint sardonic edge. Terri was still trying to decipher that when she discovered with surprise how very much Mary Carelli resembled their son.

"Am I interrupting?" Carlo asked them.

How long, Paget wondered, had Carlo been standing there, and what had he heard?

Carlo looked from his father, to the wineglasses, to Terri. With perfect composure, Terri slid off the barstool, extended her hand to Carlo, and said, "I'm Terri Peralta, your father's associate. So all you're interrupting is your father attempting to make sense of things, and me attempting to listen with my usual respect. Unfortunately, I'm doing better than he is."

Carlo's air of uncertainty eased a bit; through intuition or sheer luck, Paget saw, Terri knew that the surest way to disarm Carlo was to poke fun at his father.

"That explains the wine," Carlo answered. As he turned to Paget, his expression was more equable. "You guys were talking about my mother."

Paget nodded. "Terri's trying to help me prove that Mark Ransom was what your mother says he was."

Carlo looked at Terri again. "Do you think you can?"

Paget watched Terri appraise Carlo's face, react to the confusion she saw there. "Speaking strictly for myself," Terri said, "I think Mark Ransom did stuff like this long before he made the mistake of picking on your mother. If I'm right, then there are other women out there who didn't have the wherewithal to protect themselves the way your mom did. We've been trying to figure out how to find them, and what made your mother more able to take care of herself."

Terri, Paget realized, had neatly covered their conversation, putting a benign spin on the ambiguous comment Carlo might have overheard. The boy began fidgeting, as if not wishing to talk more but afraid of missing what else might be said.

"I assume," Paget ventured, "that your original purpose was not to meet Ms. Peralta, but to raid the refrigerator. Ice cream, or milk?"

"Both, actually."

Terri glanced at her watch. "I should be going."

The comment sounded perfunctory, Paget thought; Terri had the relaxed posture of someone with nowhere to go. "Why don't you have some ice cream," he suggested.

Carlo nodded. "I can spare a little."

"What? And create another chubbette?"

Paget looked at Terri's small frame, slim wrists. "In which life?"

"This life. I'm absolutely convinced that somewhere in Latin America, there's another Hispanic woman named Teresa Peralta who's wearing all the doughnuts I ate in high school." Terri turned to Carlo. "Because of me, she weighs at least three hundred pounds, and no one asked her to the winter prom."

"It's okay," said Carlo. "Our winter prom was awful. No one danced."

"So have some ice cream," Paget said.

Terri gave a theatrical sigh. "When I'm this tired," she said, "I've got no social conscience."

Carlo sat next to Terri, while Paget dished out two bowls of ice cream. "What about you?" Terri asked Paget.

"Never touch the stuff. Especially now."

"Why not now?"

"So I can recognize myself when they run old clips of the Lasko hearings. . . ."

"The truth," Carlo interjected, "is that my father runs five miles every morning and weighs himself six times a day. He wants to make the cover of *Seventeen*."

"*American Bride*, Carlo. And every parent needs a hobby to help compensate for disrespectful children. I've selected vanity, and I'll thank you to respect that."

Terri laughed. "Do you two always carry on like this?"

"Only when Carlo gets gratuitous reinforcement." Paget looked from his son to Terri. "Unfortunately for me, he seems to have found his natural audience."

Terri grinned at Carlo. "I guess he's right," she said, and then turned to Paget. "I don't want to hurt your feelings or anything, but during the Lasko hearings I was an eighth-grade cheerleader."

Paget looked at her in mock horror. "Tell me," he said, "do you even remember Paul McCartney's group before Wings?"

Carlo pointed to Paget. "Do you even remember *him?*" Carlo asked.

"Vaguely," Terri said. "But your mother has aged quite well."

Carlo burst out laughing. "Your move, Dad."

"I was just thinking, Carlo. Before I yank the barstool out from under her, you might want to ask Terri all the questions I'm too old to answer—stuff about dating, acne, things like that. You might even ask her why a superficially presentable fifteen-year-old, despite living in these modern times of which I am so dimly aware, can't get a couple of mere parents to let their daughter go out with him. Although, on reflection, Terri may only be able to help you with the daughter."

"What is this?" Terri asked Carlo.

Carlo put down his spoon. "I've got this girlfriend, Jennifer, only she's more like my girlfriend at school. Her parents won't let her go out on weekends." He frowned. "It can't be *me*—they don't even know me."

"Then maybe that's the problem."

Carlo turned to her. "What do you mean?"

Terri finished her ice cream and put aside the bowl. "I had the world's greatest mother, all right? She wasn't the way these people sound—I could talk to her about anything, and she trusted me a lot." Terri propped her chin on her hand. "But it was an unwritten rule that nobody took me out until they spent a little time around the house."

Carlo looked curious. "Did she ever say why?"

"I think mostly so my mom would get some handle on who they were." Terri paused, reflecting. "Also," she went on, "I think she wanted the boys who took me out to remember I had a family, someone who cared. Like Jennifer's parents, she had a lot invested in me."

Terri, Paget thought, had a gift for talking to Carlo on equal ground.

"True," Carlo said. "It's just that being around *those* people doesn't sound like a lot of fun."

Terri nodded. "Probably not. But what my mom said it told her was whether a boy thought I was worth the trouble." Terri's expression turned questioning. "Do you think Jennifer's worth the trouble?"

Her tone held neither challenge nor reproof, as if the right answer was whatever Carlo felt. Watching Carlo reflect, Paget began to believe in Terri's mother.

"Yes," Carlo said. "I really think she is."

Terri smiled. "What's she like?"

"Really nice. Good sense of humor." Carlo paused. "She's just really nice to be with."

"Carlo," Paget observed mildly, "can make Venus de Milo sound generic. Jennifer probably has an IQ around one fifty and looks something like Winona Ryder."

"No," Carlo answered. "She's just nice."

" 'Nice,' " Terri said lightly, "is a hard concept for your dad to grasp."

"I get 'nice,' " Paget protested. "That's like Santa Claus, isn't it? Or Harvey the Rabbit?"

Terri and Carlo smiled at each other. When she was truly amused, Paget saw, Terri's grin cracked white and sharp. Carlo's smile in return was more genuine than Paget had seen it lately; with foolish surprise, he realized that his fifteen-year-old son not only liked this woman but thought she was attractive.

"Hopeless," Carlo said.

Turning, they both looked amiably at Paget. "Hopeless," Terri agreed.

Paget smiled. "That's what shock treatments are for." He turned to Carlo. "At the risk of introducing a grim note of realism, how is your English paper going?"

Carlo gave a comic wince. "It's going. And so am I." He turned to Terri, hesitated, and then said seriously, "Thanks for helping with my mother."

"I'm happy to. But it's really your father." She touched Carlo's shoulder. "All kidding aside, she can't do any better."

Carlo seemed to consider that. "He certainly works hard enough," Carlo answered. Saying goodbye to Terri, he went back upstairs.

Paget turned for a moment, as if listening to his footsteps, and then looked back at Terri.

"I appreciate that," he said. "Things have been a little tough around here lately."

"I'm sure." Her face was thoughtful again, and then she gave a small smile. "This much is true—ten years ago, *I* was a teenager."

Paget smiled back. "Now I *do* feel old. Perhaps I should be consulting your mother." He leaned back on the counter. "Do you still talk to her a lot?"

"A fair amount." Terri hesitated. "There are a few things we find it hard to talk about."

"I guess that happens. You get married and develop a zone of privacy."

Terri looked away. "I suppose that's it," she said, and glanced at her watch. "God, it's nearly ten. I really should go."

"Sure." Paget felt embarrassed. "I'm sorry to have kept you."

"You didn't. This last was nice, after Melissa." Terri gazed at her wineglass. "Part of me," she added finally, "wishes I only knew about Mark Ransom through books."

Paget nodded. They walked together to the door.

The night air was cool and crisp. "This may not be the time to mention it," Paget said, "but there's Dr. Steinhardt's daughter. Specifically, whether she had any sense of how Ransom was using the tapes."

Terri looked up at him. "You'd like me to go see her?"

"I'd like you to go see her." Paget paused. "Hard or not, you did well today."

Terri smiled faintly. "All right."

Turning, she stepped onto the porch, gazing down at the tree-lined street. At night, the three-story homes were covered by darkness. In the streetlights some distance away, a woman with a large dog moved from light to shadow, shadow to light, reappearing and then vanishing again. Terri folded her arms, as if against the cold.

"Where are you parked?" Paget asked.

She did not turn. "Just a little way. Maybe a block and a half."

Paget watched her. "Would you like me to walk you to your car?"

Terri was silent, and then said simply, "Please."

THREE

SHARPE AND SHELTON were waiting with Brooks in his office. Feeble morning light came through two windows with a view of several parking lots and a highway overpass. The room, Paget thought, had looked better at night.

"I understand," Brooks said briskly, "that you have a little something to share with us."

Paget nodded. "My associate saw Mark Ransom's ex-wife. It turns out that Ransom had some peculiarities that should sound quite familiar."

Brooks raised an eyebrow. "Then we're all anxious to hear about them."

Their anxiety, Paget thought, registered in distinctly different ways: Brooks's expression was one of calm neutrality; Shelton looked interested but somewhat uncomfortable; and Marnie Sharpe folded her arms and sat straighter, as if extending a courtesy for which she had little patience and little time to someone she had little inclination to trust.

"The short is this: Ransom had rape fantasies and a sexual obsession with Laura Chase." Paget paused. "Mary Carelli got to see them converge."

Brooks's gaze came as close to a stare as he ever permitted. "The wife says all that?"

"More or less."

"You'd better lay it out for us."

Paget kept it succinct, letting the story speak for itself. No one interrupted. At the end, Brooks whistled softly. "That, Christopher, is truly disturbing."

Shelton, Paget saw, was examining her hands. Sharpe's unwelcoming look had become one of intense concentration. *"I* thought so," Paget said. "And it explains what Ransom did to Mary better than she ever could."

Sharpe gave a short shake of the head. "Not to my satisfaction," she said slowly. "Even assuming that Ms. Rappaport wants to come forward, which you haven't said, I doubt it's admissible."

"Admissible?" Paget turned to Sharpe. "We're not at trial yet. What we're discussing is an issue of fairness."

Sharpe's face closed against him, and her tone became didactic. "The issue *I'm* raising is relevance, which also happens to govern admissibility. You're suggesting that her story involves a prior similar act. But Melissa Rappaport *consented* to this particular practice. That is *not* a rape and therefore does not suggest that what your client says happened was part of a pattern of nonconsensual sex. The reason a judge wouldn't let it in later is the reason it doesn't satisfy us now."

The "us," Paget thought, was an assertion of authority. He paused to ensure that he responded with sufficient tact. "That's far too literal, Marnie. There is such a thing as psychological truth. Two different women, five years apart, confronted something in Ransom that is *very* particular. The reason to believe Mary Carelli is the same reason I get this into evidence at trial—because it makes what Mary told you *feel* right. Which is exactly what you'd argue if this were a rape prosecution."

Sharpe gave him a thoughtful look. As Brooks watched her, silent, Paget realized that Sharpe had started to invest in the case and that Brooks had moved from prosecutor to referee, carefully weighing his own interests.

"Will she testify?" Brooks asked.

Paget turned. "I don't know, Mac. I hope never to ask. It would be fairly uncomfortable, and not just for Rappaport."

Brooks considered him. "If you mean would we *enjoy* that," he said finally, "of course not."

Brooks, Paget saw, had followed him perfectly; his pretense of opacity was meant to force Paget to speak their understanding aloud.

"Actually, I was thinking of James Colt."

Brooks's mirthless smile came and went. "The one who's dead," he asked, "or the one who's running for governor?"

"Both," Paget answered, "and all the people who admired the father and support his son. Including the widow Colt and her very wealthy family. None of whom, as you've already conceded, will be eager to watch you add Laura Chase's less than glowing memories to the family annals."

"That tape," Sharpe cut in, "will be in the public domain as soon as Ransom's publisher gets someone to finish the book. Whatever your client's motives, she has virtually guaranteed that the Laura Chase biography will sell a million copies. The damage to the Colt family will already be done, and it won't be the fault of this office."

That was right, Paget knew. And if Mary was indicted, her story could merge with Laura Chase's, creating a media event that would lead them straight to Carlo. Once again, he felt the trap in which Mary had placed him: his best chance to protect Carlo was to prevent an indictment.

Slowly, Paget turned to Brooks. "You *have* listened to the tape, I assume."

Brooks nodded. "I have."

"Then speaking strictly as a human being," Paget continued, "how did you feel hearing Laura Chase's voice when she describes James Colt watching as his two friends had her?"

Brooks was quiet for a moment. Shelton turned toward a window with no view; Paget guessed that she, too, had listened to the tape.

"Speaking strictly as a human being," Brooks answered slowly, "what I was—God help me—was fascinated and repelled."

"And do you think simply *reading* about it would be quite the same experience as *listening* to it?"

Brooks's eyes narrowed. "No. I don't."

"Nor do I. And while we're about the business of calculating audience shares in the millions, how many million people watched the Willie Smith trial?"

"On Court TV," Brooks said flatly.

Paget nodded. "On Court TV. Because I would absolutely do that, Mac. If this case goes to trial, I'd insist that the judge let them show it nationwide. Then, like any defense lawyer in his right mind, I'd ask to play that tape. I don't know about your standing in the polls, but your Nielsen ratings will go right through the roof."

Brooks folded his hands in his lap. "And James Colt's family?"

"I've never been interested in politics." Paget paused, then finished softly. "That family means nothing to me. As I mentioned the last time, I have my own."

Paget heard Sharpe's curt intake of breath. Brooks looked from Paget to Sharpe and back again.

"There are problems, Chris. New ones."

Brooks's reluctant tone troubled Paget more than bluster. "Such as?"

Brooks looked to Sharpe. "More discrepancies," she said. "At least one seems quite serious."

Don't seem anxious, Paget thought. Turning to her, he assumed an expression of polite inquiry. Her lips tightened, as if she was nettled.

"To begin with," she said finally, "Mary Carelli told Inspector Monk that the blinds were drawn when she came to Ransom's room. Monk thought that sounded peculiar. So he asked the waiter who brought the champagne from room service. The blinds were open—he's quite sure of that."

Paget tried looking puzzled. "From which you extract what, exactly?"

"We're not sure, obviously. But it raises the possibility that Ms. Carelli closed the blinds for reasons of her own."

"Can you suggest a reason that makes her indictable?"

Sharpe looked at him closely. "We don't indict people," she said in cold tones, "for closing their blinds. But people sometimes close blinds so other people can't see what they're doing."

"Which," Paget answered, "raises the possibility that Ransom closed the blinds because he was planning to rape Mary Carelli and that she didn't notice or didn't recall. Assuming, that is, that the waiter remembers the precise status of each individual window shade in each of the many rooms he no doubt visited that day—a question you might care to ask him before making too much of this."

Behind Sharpe, Elizabeth Shelton smiled faintly. "I did," Sharpe retorted. "He distinctly remembers Ms. Carelli. He thought Mr. Ransom was a lucky man."

"He certainly *tried,*" Paget said. "But then, as Somerset Maugham once observed, 'luck is a talent.' "

Sharpe flushed; Shelton's smile was replaced by a closer scrutiny of Sharpe. In quick succession, Paget had two impressions: that Shelton did not care for Sharpe, and that something was troubling Shelton that Paget did not know.

"Forgive the levity," he said to Sharpe. "I'll ask Mary about the blinds, of course. Is there something else?"

"Yes." Sharpe looked distinctly unmollified. "Ms. Carelli says that she never left the suite. But another guest believes that he saw her enter the suite as he got off the elevator. I should say *reenter;* the guest was returning from lunch at about one o'clock, well after Ms. Carelli says she arrived."

For the first time, Shelton spoke. "One o'clock," she said carefully, "is the approximate time of death."

Paget turned back to Sharpe. "Is this guest certain it was Mary?"

"He only saw her from behind. But it was a dark-haired woman, around five feet eight or so, who carried herself like Mary Carelli."

Paget considered her. "Assuming that it was Mary, I expect what he saw was Mary arriving, perhaps earlier than he thinks."

A brief triumphant expression crossed Sharpe's face. "She wasn't arriving," she answered. "No one came to the door. The woman let herself in."

Sharpe had gained confidence, Paget realized. It was as if she knew that the same calculation which had caused Brooks to stick her with Mary Carelli gave her much more leeway than usual. He decided to speak for Brooks's benefit.

"But what does it mean?" he asked. "Ransom's rape fantasies and the Laura Chase tape *mean* something."

Without responding, Sharpe turned to Shelton. Her look was a curious admixture of deference and command; Paget perceived that Shelton had been summoned to speak on cue.

"There's one more thing," Shelton said slowly.

"What is it?"

Shelton turned from Sharpe, speaking to Paget as if they were alone. "Do you remember that night, on the elevator, when you asked me about the scratches on Ransom's buttocks?"

"Yes."

"I've gone back over them, thought about it quite a bit more." She paused, then added quickly, "I don't think they were made until after Ransom died."

Paget stared at her. "After?"

"Yes. Not seconds after, or even a couple of minutes. Appreciably after."

Paget tried to organize his thoughts, found none. "On what do you base that?"

"The scratches themselves." Shelton's gaze held his. "The normal scratch, such as those you saw on Mary, are like a red welt. The red color comes from bleeding under the skin, broken capillaries. But Ransom's scratches are white."

Paget noticed that Brooks had gotten up and was standing behind Shelton. Reluctantly, Paget asked, "What does that tell you?"

"Ransom's skin was damaged, just as Mary Carelli's was. But there was no bleeding, no burst capillaries. Because, in my opinion, his heart had stopped pumping blood." Shelton leaned forward, hands clasped in her lap. "It's really just a matter of gravity. A dead person's blood ends up in the lowest extremity, like a garden hose after you turn off the spigot. By the time the buttocks were scratched, most of Mark Ransom's blood had gone to his chest."

Paget touched the bridge of his nose. "Are you certain of that?"

"Not certain. No."

"But it *is* your opinion," Sharpe interjected.

Shelton gave a reticent nod. "What I would testify, if asked, is that what I have just told you is more probable than not."

"Which means," Sharpe said to Paget, "that Ms. Carelli waited at least thirty minutes to call 911. Before which she left several scratches on the buttocks of a corpse, quite possibly to make Ransom's death look different than it really was."

Paget gave her an incredulous look. "That's bizarre. This is San Francisco, not Transylvania."

"That may be." Brooks stepped between them, as if he had heard enough. "And it may be too little to indict on. But it's too much to ignore. For now, we're going on with this."

FOUR

Teresa Peralta opened the door of Mark Ransom's suite.

She hesitated; for a moment, Terri felt that if she did not enter, nothing would happen to Mary, and Ransom would still be alive. Then she stepped inside and saw the bloodstain on the carpet.

She was still staring at it when Paget and Johnny Moore came in behind her.

It was a moment before she turned. "Could you see me from the elevator?" she asked.

Paget nodded. "Clearly enough."

It was a little after eleven-thirty in the morning, roughly the time that Mary had arrived, four days prior. The door bore a sign that read: CRIME SCENE—CITY AND COUNTY OF SAN FRANCISCO. KEEP OUT. A policeman had broken the tape sealing the door; he waited for them by the elevator.

Terri looked around the room. The furniture was unremarkable— two end tables, a bookshelf, a small desk. The two windows of the sitting room faced east, across the city and toward Berkeley; there was enough morning sun left to make the room somewhat bright.

"You couldn't have seen my face, though," Terri said.

"No, the angle's wrong, and there's also the distance. Johnny and I paced it off at about sixty feet. But even three or four seconds would be enough to describe height, weight, and hair color." Paget looked down at the bloodstain. "Put it this way," he finished slowly. "I could tell the difference between you and Mary Carelli."

A sudden shadow fell across the bloodstain.

Terri and Paget looked up. Johnny Moore had pulled down a blind and was walking toward the second window. "Makes a difference," he said, and yanked down the other blind.

It was like instant dusk: a bright room, suddenly dark enough to sleep in. Johnny Moore's ruddy face and white beard had turned gray.

"It's depressing," Terri said to him.

"Unless you're Edgar Allan Poe." Moore walked to the end table by the far side of the couch and switched on a lamp. The effect was dim and unnatural, like a lamp in one corner of a windowless cell. "Maybe it was Ransom's idea of romance."

"Ransom's idea of romance," Paget answered, "was 'Mutant Cheerleaders in Bondage.'"

Terri shook her head. "There's no way," she said slowly, "that I'd have felt comfortable in this room."

Paget gazed at the stain and then at Terri. His look was curious, reflective. "Of course," he observed, "you know what happened here."

"That's not it." She looked around the room. "This just doesn't feel right. If it had been me, and Ransom had pulled down the blinds . . ."

She stopped there. "You'd have left?" Paget asked.

She folded her arms. "I don't know."

Paget regarded her another moment. "In any event, it seems that it would have made an impression on Mary."

Moore walked to the middle of the room. "Probably so, before she shot him. *After,* telling it to the cops, what happened might have gotten pretty confused. Like reading *Ulysses* for the first time."

Paget smiled faintly. "You like the Irish writers, don't you?"

"The Irish who *stayed.*" As he glanced down at the stain, Moore's Irish lilt became slightly more pronounced. "Personally, I always thought Mark Ransom's work would gag a vulture."

Paget ceased to smile. "Not unlike Marnie Sharpe's theory of this case."

Moore considered him and then nodded toward the couch. "Why don't we three rest awhile," he said, "on the Mark Ransom memorial love seat. You can explain why Miss Carelli defaced the poor man's arse *after* she shot him."

"Oh, that," Paget said. "Because then he couldn't complain, of course."

Terri realized that she was hugging her shoulders. "Would you two mind," she asked quietly, "if I pulled up the blinds?"

"I'll do it," Moore said. He opened the blinds and looked back to Terri. "It was becoming a bit like a séance, wasn't it?"

Paget stood to the side, watching her face. "Johnny's spent far too much time among the dead," he said finally, "and I spent too much time with Ms. Sharpe this morning. I'm a little off my feed."

Staring at the coffee table, Terri imagined the tape of Laura Chase. After a moment, she asked, "What's Sharpe thinking?"

The two men sat on each side of Terri. Paget was quiet, ordering his thoughts. Resting his feet on the coffee table, Moore gazed slowly around the room.

"It's pretty simple," Paget said. "Sharpe's been arranging and re-arranging the facts—or the absence of facts—until Mary comes out a liar.

"First, Mary says Ransom tried to rape her. To which Sharpe, or Shelton, says that there is no sign of seminal fluid and hence no evidence of sexual arousal. And as we know, there was no penetration."

Terri felt cold. "Mary kept making mistakes. She should have let Ransom deposit the evidence."

"You're beginning to sound like me," Moore told her. "That is, of course, the irony of Sharpe's scenario."

"Granted," Paget said. "But fact two, according to Shelton, is that Mary's statement that she shot Ransom from two or three inches isn't even close."

Moore nodded. "I ran that one past my forensics guy at Berkeley. Take a Walther .380, and the absence of gunshot residue, and he says Shelton has to be right. Liz Shelton's a professional; to get someone to testify against her on *this* point, you'll have to find a whore."

Paget shook his head. "If I put on some hired gun, Shelton would kill him. I'll have to find another way around it."

"In other words," Moore said carefully, "things happened much too fast for Mary to be sure."

"Of course." Paget paused. "But there's also the lack of gunshot residue on Ransom's hands. Mary says they struggled and the gun went off. Residue would help confirm that. There wasn't any."

"And needn't be," Moore answered. "Depends on how it happened."

Paget shrugged. "The next thing is the blinds. Mary says they were drawn when she got here. But the room service waiter, who has no ax to grind, says they were open. It's hard to miss the difference. From which Sharpe no doubt posits that Mary drew the blinds, presumably after she shot him, and presumably because she didn't want to be seen."

Moore got up from the couch without responding, looked through one window, then another. Arriving, Terri had seen that the Flood was not a perfect rectangle but a courtyard surrounded by two wings that faced each other. Ransom's suite was near the center of the top floor; through the window, the city and the bay were framed by wings on either side.

Moore pointed to the right. "I'll have to check it out," he said. "But from here it looks like the last couple of windows on that wing could see into this room. At least it's something you'd think about if you were standing here, wanting privacy."

Paget considered that. "It works best," he said, "if this waiter isn't sure. That way, the blinds are drawn when she gets here, which makes better sense for us than Mary *or* Ransom pulling them down."

Moore sat again. "I'll find the waiter."

Watching them, Terri was struck by their total absence of sentiment. Moore did not ask if Mary was telling the truth; Paget's focus was on what the prosecutor could prove. Neither showed passion or outrage. Which, Terri thought, was more to be expected in Johnny than in Paget: Mary Carelli was the mother of his son.

"That gets us," Paget continued, "to Mary's fingernails as compared to Ransom's. There are scratches on both Mary and Ransom, but Shelton was only able to find traces of skin under *Mary's* fingernails, not Ransom's. To Sharpe, the least that means is that Ransom didn't scratch her."

Moore leaned back on the couch. "Interesting," he said, "but not very compelling. It's kind of like listening to someone's theory about life on other planets. Maybe, you think, but you can argue it a thousand different ways, and who knows?"

"Until we get to Sharpe's little surprise. The scratches on Ransom's backside." Paget's face was so expressionless that, to Terri, it reflected some deliberate effort. "Shelton's theory is that the scratches weren't made until a half hour or so after Ransom died. If you believe that, it gives them two things: the passage of time, and the calculated alteration of a crime scene in the most cold-blooded way—the disfigurement of a corpse. And that pulls it all together for them."

Terri felt reality slip from her grasp. The day before, listening to

Melissa Rappaport, she was certain that she had found the truth. But in the suite where Ransom died, truth had become a kaleidoscope: the pattern kept shifting, as did her sense of Paget himself. That, and the strangeness of the room, put her off balance.

"The case Sharpe is making," Paget said, "is that Ransom died in another way than Mary described, for some other reason than rape." Paget gazed at the bloodstain. "Then Mary pulled down the blinds and for over a half hour worked on Ransom's body, and her own. She pulled down his pants, scratched him, scratched herself. And when she'd done all she could, she called 911 and kept on lying until she got too lost. After which," he finished softly, "she called me."

The last words seemed to have taken him somewhere else. As if to reclaim him, Terri said, "Ransom *hit* her."

"Oh, something happened in this room. Just something quite different from what Mary described. That is, if you're Sharpe."

Moore considered him. "How sure is Liz Shelton about *this* one?"

"Sharpe's pushing her some, although I expect there's only so far she gets pushed." Paget shrugged. "I think I could get her to say she's not sure."

The last phrase jarred Terri again; it was the pragmatic calculation of a defense lawyer, not the musing of a friend or lover.

They fell silent. "Give me a *reason*," Moore said at last.

"Sharpe has none," Paget answered. "She can make up a how, but she can't figure out a why."

He stared out the window, chin propped in his hand. After a time, he asked Moore, "Have you seen what you needed to see?"

"Pretty much." Moore stared, spent another minute checking the drawers of the end table and desk, and then said, "Let's go."

Outside the room, they stopped for a moment, looking around the corridor. There was little there: more doors; a smoke alarm; a mail slot across from Ransom's suite. No telephone, Terri thought, nothing of interest to anyone who was thinking clearly.

She paused, making sure that the policeman who waited could not hear.

"What's Sharpe's point," she asked Paget, "about Mary being in the hallway before she called 911?"

"No idea—just a discrepancy. But I'm sure Sharpe's working on it." Paget nodded toward the mail slot. "Probably figures Mary found herself with a half hour to kill, scribbled a few postcards on Ransom's rear end, and then mailed them to all her friends."

Moore gave Paget a quizzical look; all at once, Terri felt how shaken Paget was.

"By the way," Paget asked her, "will Steinhardt's daughter talk to us?"

Terri nodded. "For a fee."

"A fee? What on earth for?"

"A research fee, she says. She keeps her father's papers."

Paget shook his head in disgust. "I suppose she needs money," he said, "now that Mary's spoiled the sequel," and then turned to Moore.

Moore shrugged.

"Pay her," Paget said.

FIVE

CARLO CARELLI PAGET gazed at his parents, two profiles in the candlelight.

They sat in the dining room, poised between salad and dessert, at the end of the long mahogany dining table where he and his father always sat. The chandelier was dim; two white candles in brass holders created a pool of light that made the Persian rug seem richer, the crystal brighter, the room closer and more intimate. At his father's suggestion, Carlo sat at the head of the table, one parent to each side.

He watched them, trying to pretend that he was not doing so. The talk between them had been strained. His father, dressed in a white silk shirt and black wool slacks, was even more self-contained than usual. His mother seemed subdued, less electric than the woman he had seen on Sunday. She still looked beautiful, Carlo thought, but a little sad.

"Do you always eat like this?" Mary asked him. "By candlelight, I mean."

Carlo nodded. "When it's dark. I guess it's kind of a tradition."

"How did that start?"

"Dad?" Carlo turned to Paget, wanting to bring him closer to the moment. "You remember these things."

"That's because you were seven." Paget smiled. "Parents spend all this time building memories, and then they're devastated to find out that what their children remember about being little is when they backed up the car without looking and ran over the cat."

"Did you run over the cat?" Mary asked.

As his father turned to her, Carlo thought he seemed almost reluctant, as if forced from the familiar refuge of teasing him. "No, someone else did," Paget said. "But it was an awful day—the car was going quite fast, and Fluffy was, shall we say, unsuitable for viewing. I had to take care of it before Carlo got home, and then explain that Fluffy had gone straight to heaven without passing go. I felt like a murderer."

Carlo flinched inwardly. Mary stared at his father; Carlo saw the careless phrase come back to him in a narrowing of the eyes. A moment's signal seemed to pass between the two adults, a rearranging of their gazes in which his father apologized, Mary accepted. It put Carlo even more on edge; his father, whom he thought of as so graceful, did not seem himself.

"What did Carlo say?" Mary asked politely.

"He asked me to describe heaven, and then a few days later we got Fluffy the second."

Mary smiled. "That must have been hard for you."

"The part about heaven, or the cat?"

"Heaven." Mary tilted her head. "Not anything you used to spend a lot of time on."

"That's not fair. Believing as I do in the perfectibility of man, I simply assume that heaven can be realized here on earth, through the achievement of a balanced budget and a comprehensive program of national health insurance."

Carlo was silent. To him, they seemed like two actors, speaking lines they neither felt nor cared about, but expert enough not to be awful. He wished that he could imagine them without this veneer: younger, maybe the age of his dad's associate Terri, and in love with each other. But he could not understand them, or even explain to himself why it was so hard to think of Mary as his mother.

Lightly, she asked him, "What do *you* believe?"

She had no idea, of course—she couldn't have. That was part of why this seemed so difficult; his parents must have talked so little about him that she had to learn about his life as if he were the son of a business acquaintance.

"Nothing," Carlo said flatly. "I don't believe in any of that stuff. I could never get how Jesus' mother comes home, pregnant, tells this guy that God did it, and he buys that."

Something flickered in his mother's eyes. Now it was *his* turn, Carlo thought; he hadn't even sounded right to *himself*. But he couldn't tell what had hurt her, or how to get out of it. All at once he wanted dinner to be over.

"Well," his dad put in, "Joseph did get a son out of it all, if only on loan." His father turned to Mary, smiling a little. "My failures as a parent are worse than you imagine. Religion is one thing, but what's truly disturbing is that Carlo doesn't want to be a lawyer."

"Too many lawyer jokes?" Mary asked him.

Carlo felt a touch of gratitude; even a return to banter was better than where he had just been. "My dad *is* a lawyer joke," he said. "Always working, and always on the phone. I call it 'Lifestyles of the Rich and Compulsive.' "

"Well," his father answered mildly, "your mother gave it up, so I suppose there's precedent. And I expect she likes what she's doing now far better."

"Do you?" Carlo asked her.

She smiled. "Oh, yes."

"What is it you like? Being on television?"

Mary considered him. "It depends," she said finally, "on how you mean that. I've gotten to live lots of places—New York, Los Angeles, even Rome for a time. But what television really does is take you far beyond your own life. It's like plugging into this enormous current: suddenly you can meet almost anyone you want, ask them almost any question you want, and they *want* you to, because they want to be part of the current. Television gives me a license to be part of things. And instead of just watching other people help me know what to think, *I* help other people do that."

Mary's voice was animated. Carlo saw his father looking at her; for once, the look was without facade or wariness, as if she had spoken some deep truth about herself.

"Who did you like meeting most?" Carlo asked.

Mary smiled. "Well, lots of them are at least *interesting;* I've known the last three Presidents, and interviewed people like Gorbachev and Mitterrand and Margaret Thatcher—whom I absolutely admired, by the way; she had her own program, and people reacted to *her,* not the other way around." She paused, remembering. "But the best was An-war Sadat, and his death was a tragedy."

"Why him?"

"Because he was an unquestionably great man—everyone who met him knew that, almost at once." She leaned forward, as if trying to help Carlo feel what she had felt. "He was so *himself:* visionary, but plainspoken and completely honest. He seemed to transcend time or place, which was why he was able to envision peace with Israel while everyone else stayed trapped in their own history. I could feel that even in how he treated *me*. A lot of Arab men have trouble talking to women, but Sadat talked to *me* directly, like an equal, as if I were the most important person in the room. He was like that with everyone."

There was life in Mary's face now. Carlo felt a kind of closeness; she did not know how to act like a mother, but she could talk to him as herself.

"It's hard to imagine," Carlo said. "Being you, having everybody know you."

"They don't really *know* me. They have an *image* of me, or maybe they like my work—it's nice when people come up and tell you that. Although," she added with a sardonic smile, "the last few days, I could have done without people knowing me at all. So it depends, I suppose."

Carlo hesitated; she seemed objective enough that it might be safe to talk about it. "Aren't people going to sympathize more," he asked, "because they like you?"

"Some do. ABC's getting lots of wires from people giving me support, and various women's groups want me to speak out—less about *me*, really, than the whole issue." She paused. "Maybe it'll help me get through this thing."

Carlo felt his father retreat within his own thoughts. He wanted to reach out to her.

"Are you doing okay?" he asked her. "I really kept wishing I could see you."

Her smile seemed genuine, even grateful. "I'm all right now," she said. "For the most part anyhow—I spend a lot of time thinking about it." Her voice became quieter. "It's odd, Carlo. I've been so used to controlling things, and this thing just happened. It still doesn't seem like a part of me. But it is, for the rest of my life."

Carlo had the sudden sense of a lonely woman, speaking to him alone.

"I'll help you," he said. "Any way I can."

From the corner of his eye, Carlo saw his father's gaze, abstracted and unfathomable, directed at the candles. But his mother's returning look was intent. "The best way you can help me," she said, "is to keep living your life. It's how *I've* always been, and it'll make me feel better if you can be that way now." She reached out, touching his wrist. "Your father and I are two very capable people."

Her fingers felt warm, light. It was good, Carlo thought, to have his mother touch him.

"Okay," he said finally. "But I'll bug him about it."

Her hand tightened around his wrist, as if feeling something she could not ask in words. "That much," she said softly, "would be nice."

Watching them together was so strange, Paget thought. As strange as the moment he had first seen them: a woman he knew but did not know, her two-day-old son.

Mary lay in the hospital bed, pale and drained of energy. The baby, this stranger with matted black hair and an old man's face, wrinkled its features and yawned without sound. The baby's wristband read "Carelli."

"Does he ever make noise?" Paget asked.

She nodded. "Short squalls, mostly. He doesn't seem to be a complainer."

"Just as well, considering." Paget hesitated. "Does he have a name?"

Mary nodded. "Carlo. At least that's what's on the birth certificate."

"Carlo Carelli?" Paget looked at the baby. "A bit ethnic, don't you think?"

"It's my grandfather's name." Her voice was quiet. "The man I most remember loving."

Paget gazed at her. "Whose name," he finally asked, "is on the birth certificate?"

Her answering gaze was cool and level. "Yours."

Paget turned to the window. The room was cold and spare; it felt like prison. "I suppose," he said finally, "I should be grateful that you didn't name him Frank. After your ex-husband."

Mary did not smile. "No chance of that," she said. "Any more than there'll be more husbands."

Paget found his eyes drawn to the baby, stretching, hands making random fists. Funny, he thought; they don't really do anything, and still you watch them. "Who will take care of him?" he asked.

"My parents. At least for a while."

"Your *parents*." Paget shook his head in wonderment. "You can't stand them—with good reason, you once tried to persuade me."

"It's only for now." Her voice turned bitter. "I may be a disgrace, but I'm one of theirs."

"That hardly seems best."

"Neither does day care. And he *is* my son."

Paget's voice was soft. "And mine, I'm given to understand."

Mary stared at him. "Had it been up to you, Chris, Carlo wouldn't have lived past gestation."

Silent, Paget gazed at the baby, resting against Mary's shoulder. Finally, he asked, "What will you do?"

"I don't know yet. Just not practice law."

Paget put his hands in his pockets. "I'd like to help."

She gave him a long look of appraisal. "I'm grateful for what you've done. Really. But I don't need you anymore." She looked down at the baby's head. "From time to time, we can talk."

"I'd like to *see* him, Mary."

She gazed back up. "How often?"

He hesitated. "I'm in California now. But whenever I can."

She watched his face a moment and then nodded. "All right."

Paget could find nothing else to say. Wordless, he looked at the baby and then at Mary again.

Slowly, she held Carlo out to him.

Paget took him from her. Carlo's hair was soft against his face; the baby's skin smelled fresh and new. Paget had not known how this would feel.

"Time to go back," a brisk voice interrupted.

It was a red-haired nurse behind him. She took Carlo from his arms. "You the dad?" she asked.

"Yes," Paget said. "I'm the dad."

Walking alone to the car, Paget realized that there were tears in his eyes. He did not know for whom.

"Well," Mary said, "I think it went pretty well tonight. At least at the end."

Paget turned from her, closing the glass doors to the library so that Carlo could not hear them.

"Sit down," he said.

They sat facing each other, Mary on the couch, Paget in an armchair to the side, the spotlit palm tree filling the window behind them. Mary felt tense; the polite tone he had assumed for Carlo's sake was gone.

"What is it?" she asked.

Paget did not answer. His expression was so devoid of sentiment that she recalled again that Christopher Paget was the man who had most frightened her since she had left her father's home.

"This is *me*," she said coldly. "Save the ice-blue stare for witnesses and unruly spaniels, where it works."

His expression changed but slightly. "Are you going on *60 Minutes*?" he asked.

The indirectness of the question unsettled her. "Yes," she finally said. "We should seize the moral high ground."

"Ah, yes," Paget said. "The moral high ground, our accustomed territory. Just be careful to remember when you're lying."

The insult was so casual that it was as though he had slapped her in slow motion; it took Mary a moment to realize that she was taut with anger and apprehension.

"Spit it out, Chris, whatever it is. Or do you still enjoy pulling the wings off flies?"

He raised his eyebrows. "Was I too subtle? All right, then: you're still a liar, but you've lost your touch. Your story's getting threadbare."

"Damnit, tell me what's wrong."

Paget shook his head. "I'm going to ask you a few questions. If you can't bring yourself to tell me the truth, at least don't insult me by lying."

Mary paused, then she saw she had no choice. Folding her arms, she said, "Have it your way."

Paget leaned back in his chair, appraising her. Finally, he asked, "How long did it take you to call 911?"

"I don't know. Really."

"Less than a half hour, or more?"

She hesitated. "Perhaps more."

Paget's eyes narrowed. "What about Ransom?"

Mary gazed at the rug. Quietly, she answered, "He was dead."

"How did you know that?"

"Because he never moved." She infused her tone with the slightest edge: "I guess you had to be there."

"You're not a doctor," Paget shot back, "and that answer won't do. Why didn't you call for help?"

"I suppose I was in shock."

Paget watched her. "Were you? Or are you trying shock on for size?"

Mary looked back up at him. "We're all different," she said coldly. "That night in Washington, when you nearly killed Jack Woods, your first reaction was to call the Washington *Post*. But I don't recall you phoning 911."

Paget looked at her. "You had it right about one thing," he said in clipped tones. "I didn't give a damn whether your good friend Jack was dead or simply had a dental problem. Any more than he, among other people, ever cared about whether I lived or died."

Mary stiffened. "That's not fair."

"I am so sorry. Tell me, was there some reason you preferred *Ransom* dead, as opposed to merely disheartened?"

"No." Her voice rose. "Of course not."

"Then let's return to the question you so neatly avoided by turning the spotlight on me: why so much time passed before you called 911."

Mary stood, eyes averted, gazing out at the palm. "This may not sound attractive," she finally said, "but I was frightened for myself."

"Why, exactly?"

"Because I felt as if it were my fault. That I could have avoided it." Mary paused, remembering her own fear, then finished quietly, "And that people wouldn't believe me."

"What did you do?"

She shook her head. "My brain felt sluggish—it was like trying to run when you're waist deep in water. I couldn't think—you can't believe it's real. It takes time to accept—"

"What did you do?" Paget repeated.

Mary closed her eyes. "I really don't remember."

She heard Paget get up, walk close behind her until she felt him through her nerve ends in the back of her neck.

Softly, he said, "Someone saw you outside the room."

It startled her. "Is he sure?" she asked.

"Yes. The only question is why."

Mary realized that her eyes were still shut, her arms folded again. "I can't answer that," she said.

"Can't, or won't?"

Make him stop, she told herself. Turning, she looked straight at him. "I was confused. You're going to have to accept that, and make the district attorney accept that."

Paget's face was inches from hers. "Four days ago," he said quietly, "you didn't tell Inspector Monk that you left the room."

"That was four *hours*," she retorted, "after Mark Ransom's death. I was a mess. I mean, can you think of any rational reason for me to be out in the hall?"

"Not unless you knocked on doors, trying to get help."

"I didn't." Mary paused. "As I said, I was confused."

"Were you also confused about the blinds?"

Mary stepped away from him, sat down. After a moment, she repeated, "The blinds."

"They were open when you got there—despite what you told Monk." Paget still stood, looking down at her. "Who closed them, Mary, and why?"

"Why?" She hesitated, feeling helpless, unable to explain. Finally, she said, "Because I felt ashamed."

Paget sat beside her. "Ashamed?"

"Yes." She turned to him. "I didn't want anyone to see."

"To see what? Ransom?"

"Everything." She turned to him. "After I shot him, I thought about running, hoping no one had seen me—crazy things. I couldn't say that to Monk."

"So you lied about the blinds."

Mary leaned back from him. "The term is 'confused,'" she said coolly. "I was confused."

"Too confused," Paget asked, "to kill Ransom from a safe distance, pull his pants down, leave scratch marks on his buttocks, scratch your own neck and thigh, and then dream up a rape attempt detailed enough to fly?"

Mary felt numb, and then the terrible knowledge of how alone she was came over her. "They can't believe that."

"Why? Because you're so eager to help them out?"

"No," she said dully. "Maybe some of what I said was a mistake. But they can't believe I'm a murderer."

"They believe that you defaced a corpse a good half hour after his death. That makes murder a bit less of a stretch."

As if by reflex, Mary touched the bruise beneath her eye, now blue-green. "Do they think he was dead," she asked, "when he did this?"

Paget did not answer. "Tell me," he finally said. "Did you already know Mark Ransom?"

She stared at him. "God, no . . ."

"Because Sharpe's next step will be to look for some connection between Ransom and you. If there is one, tell me now, or I really will leave you to twist in the wind."

Mary felt her anger turn to fear. "Before he called," she said, "I'd never met him. I swear it."

"That had better be right. It's quite enough that Monk has on tape several answers that are either implausible or, as you now admit, inaccurate. Not to mention that you and Shelton's autopsy are essentially at odds." Paget's voice grew quiet. "I can't say you've done very well this time around."

Mary's face grew cold. "It's hard to choose what's more offensive—Mark Ransom or you, afterwards, grading my performance."

"So hire Melvin Belli, Mary, and restore your faith in men."

All at once, Mary felt drained. "You don't believe me at all, do you?"

"Not true. I believe about every other word. Assuming, of course, that you throw in the commas."

Mary stood again. "You know, I've had about enough of this."

Paget shrugged. "You should count your blessings, Mary. Your fifteen-year-old son believes in you. As for me, *I* believe in sparing Carlo needless pain, which is all the motivation I require."

"Fine." Mary reached for her purse. "Are we through here now?"

"For the moment. But take my advice: no specific comments on TV—just heartfelt generalities about your ordeal and that of victims everywhere. I don't want yet another 'mistake' I have to clean up later."

Silent, Mary watched him. "I'll say good night to Carlo," she said.

The limousine was outside when she returned. Paget walked her to the door. Outside, she turned back to him, uncertain of what she was looking for.

His face was without expression. "Enjoy *60 Minutes*," he said. Then he softly shut the door, and Mary was alone.

"It was a nightmare," Mary said softly. "I've heard women say that, but I never really knew."

In the library, Carlo and Paget watched her, their only light the glow from the television. The camera panned her hotel suite, framing Mary and her interviewer, then moved in until Mary's face filled the screen. Her expression was troubled, inward, as if too caught in painful memory to remember the lens.

The interviewer became only a voice. "Can you describe your feelings?" he asked.

Paget glanced at Carlo, tense and still, the Sunday paper on the couch beside him. The headline read: RANSOM DEATH UNRESOLVED.

Sharpe, Paget knew, had preempted Mary's interview.

The article was plainly Sharpe's idea. The reporter quoted her as being "concerned with discrepancies between Ms. Carelli's statement and the physical evidence"; "puzzled by Ms. Carelli's cessation of her interview"; "resolved that the concern with rape which has defined my own career not foreclose a neutral inquiry"; and "hopeful that the public will not forget that a gifted man died in this city." The sole photograph was of a younger, much more appealing, Mark Ransom.

Paget had managed to insert a quote. "Puzzling over tests and slides," he said, "should not distract us from a central truth—Mary Carelli was forced into a tragic act for which there is no reason but attempted rape." But it could not change the pressure Sharpe had shrewdly put on Mary: to respond in detail and on television, or look evasive.

On the screen, Mary gazed down. She seemed mute, battered. "It still seems unreal," she finally answered. "One minute, it's as if it must have happened to someone else. Then I feel my own terror as a physical thing—his breath on my face, body pressing down on me, hands tearing at my clothes." She paused, touching her cheek, and then finished softly, "The shock when he hit me."

"Did he say anything?"

"Yes. I can't repeat it. Not yet." She stopped, then murmured, "I'm sorry. I can't even call him by his name."

"Would you like to stop?"

"No." Slowly, she shook her head, seemingly less for emphasis than in confusion. "Perhaps I'm doing this too soon. But no." She looked up, eyes imploring. "It's like that, you see. You're all right, and then . . ."

"Perhaps this isn't timely," the interviewer said, "but I thought perhaps you might care to comment on certain questions that seem to puzzle the district attorney's office."

Mary's face froze for a moment, and then she looked bewildered. "I'm not sure I even know what they are. Or why they have them. He tried to rape me. . . ."

Once more, her voice trailed off.

"Perhaps," the interviewer prodded, "this will be an opportunity to put some of those things to rest."

Mary nodded.

Carlo leaned forward. "What are they doing?" he demanded.

Paget felt his own tension. "I'm not sure yet."

"For example," the voice went on, "the district attorney suggests that the bullet which killed Mark Ransom traveled from at least three feet, in contrast to your claim that the gun went off while he was on top of you."

For a moment, Mary looked surprised. To Carlo, Paget murmured, "The D.A.'s fed him questions."

On the screen, Mary had composed herself. "What they don't seem to understand is how quickly things happen and how stunned you are." Her voice was calm again. "It was over in seconds. He had just slapped me. I was hurt, frightened for my life. At the instant the gun went off, he must have been falling back—from one split second to another, a bullet could have traveled a few inches, or more than that. Some nights, that's all I think about—the moment he died—but it's so hard to see it in terms of distance. It's more—I don't know—impressionistic than that, and far too shocking for clarity." She paused. "I don't wish to offend anyone, but for someone to blame me for imprecision is really quite callous."

"Damn," Carlo said. "That's good."

Paget did not answer; he could imagine too clearly Sharpe's reaction as she watched.

"The D.A. also suggests that you did not call 911 for at least thirty minutes."

Mary shook her head. "I really have no sense of time about that day. As I told a friend, shock makes your brain sluggish, as if you're trying to find your way through a darkened house that isn't yours. The one thing I knew clearly was that this man was dead." Mary looked back at the camera. "If that weren't true, I could never forgive myself, no matter what he'd done to me."

"Do you recall what happened during that time?"

"No, only fragments." Her voice was soft, puzzled, as if explaining to herself. "I really think what happened is that I came out of shock and called 911."

Watching, Paget felt relief. "I think she's gotten through that," he said.

Carlo turned to him. "You sound as if she's guilty."

Paget mentally cursed himself. "Not guilty," he said. "On trial. The D.A.'s put her there, and she's doing well."

"Our sources indicate," the reporter was saying, "that you've refused to take a lie detector test."

Paget stood. "That bitch . . ."

Carlo turned. "Who?"

"Sharpe." Paget looked at him. "Sorry. Let's just watch, okay?"

Turning back to the screen, Paget saw Mary's look of tired resolve. "As you know," she said, "I began my career as a lawyer. Lie detector tests are so notoriously inaccurate that no court, anywhere, will allow them to be used as evidence. Every district attorney in this country knows that, and every D.A. *should* know that anything which can't be used in court shouldn't be used to damage someone's reputation." She paused. "You know, it's hard to believe what's happening here."

"I don't mean to suggest that you did something wrong."

"Good," she said firmly, "because I'm not the one who's done something wrong. I don't blame you for asking questions. But I *do* suggest that you have to evaluate your sources, and their motives." Her voice turned cold. "Whoever they are."

"We always try to do that," the interviewer said. "One way is to get your response, as I'm doing now."

Mary nodded. "I understand. I'm just very disappointed in the use of selective truths, by anonymous sources, to create a false impression of something that was so simple and traumatic." She paused, as if belatedly astonished. "My God, does anyone think I *wanted* this to happen? Does anyone think I *wanted* this man to die? Does every woman who is raped have to endure snickers for being victimized and insinuations for fighting back?"

"Don't go too far," Paget murmured.

"That certainly is not our intention," the interviewer responded. "By asking these questions so close to Mark Ransom's death, we run the risk of offending you and countless others. But however uncomfortable this may be, for us as well as you, it's unethical to sit on questions when they're brought to our attention."

Mary frowned. "I'm a journalist, as you are. But I've also become the victim of an attempted rape. And I know, and you know, that our society is still unfair to women who are victims of rape."

"I agree." The interviewer paused. "May I ask you one more question—as a journalist."

Watching, Paget recognized her expression: to anyone else it might seem thoughtful, but Paget knew it as deep wariness. "Of course," she answered.

"What we have been told," the interviewer said, "is that another guest at the hotel, looking through his window, saw you pulling down the blinds in Mark Ransom's suite."

Paget felt Mary's surprise like a contagion, knew that Sharpe had concealed this fact from him for just this moment. Duck this, Paget instructed Mary mentally, any way you can.

"Let me ask *you* a question," Mary retorted. "Has the district attorney told you *why* I went to see Mark Ransom?"

"Why do you ask?"

Mary nodded. "No. I didn't think so. And *I* won't tell you, although it would explain a great deal. Because it involves the reputation, and the feelings, of people other than myself." She paused, looking directly to the camera. "What you should demand of your sources is full disclosure: that they tell you exactly what was found in that room. And once *they* refuse to tell you, the one thing you will know is that *you* have been very badly used."

Despite himself, Paget laughed aloud: Sharpe had warned Mary, and now Mary was warning Sharpe.

"What's she talking about?" Carlo asked.

"The tape," Paget said. "As a good Democrat, McKinley Brooks does *not* want to answer to James Colt's family. Your mother just took that tape and stuck it in Marnie Sharpe's ear." In two days, Paget thought but did not add, no one will remember that Mary used it to avoid a question.

"I have *more* questions," Mary went on, "that people should ask themselves." Her gaze was steady, her voice crisp and clear. "Why is it," she asked, "that in the case of a sex crime, so many people remember the sex and not the crime?

"Why are the victims of rape, already so devastated in their own hearts and minds, cheapened in the eyes of society?

"Why does the justice system treat them as if they have committed a crime?

"Why are these women so often made to feel like they asked for what no sane person would want?

"Why, tonight, is this happening to me?"

Her voice had thickened. Carlo leaned forward, as if to help her finish.

"I'm not sure," she said to the interviewer, "that you can ever know how that feels. But hundreds of thousands of women know, and now *I* know."

On the screen, her picture froze in close-up. Her eyes shone with tears.

SIX

FOR TERESA PERALTA, Beverly Hills was a mirage.

It seemed far too lush for winter: the manicured sweep of lawns, the tropical mix of vegetation, the surprising bursts of pink and white, were like false spring. The sun was bright, the sky blue and crisp, the palm trees lining Santa Monica Boulevard seemed to float and vanish in the shimmering subtropic light. It made calling on Steinhardt's daughter seem even more unreal.

At the end of a winding driveway on Canyon Drive, tucked behind shrubbery and green trees, Steinhardt's white stucco home was a collection of rectangles and jutting squares; almost as high as it was wide, it looked as if it had been constructed by an imaginative child with a sense of light. There were many windows and skylights; the trees had been pruned to admit sun from every angle. When a Hispanic maid led her to the living room, Terri found herself beneath twenty-foot ceilings, surrounded by shafts of light.

In Spanish, Terri said, "This is a beautiful room."

The maid seemed surprised. Then she answered in the same tongue: "It is just as Dr. Steinhardt left it," and went to find his daughter.

Terri looked around her. Something in the decor was too calculated, she decided: the prints were too carefully selected, the vases too perfectly placed, and the sculpture—African here, Asian there—seemed chosen to reflect their place of origin rather than a passion for the things themselves. It was more like visiting an art museum than a place where someone lived.

"It always struck me as a room full of specimens," a husky voice behind her said. "Rather like a butterfly collection, but even less alive."

Turning, Terri saw a sharp-featured woman in her thirties, tall and slender in a coppery silk jumpsuit, with tinted ash-blond hair and long red fingernails. Her eyes were a vivid green; beneath this chic veneer, her carriage had the tensile alertness of a greyhound. Terri's first impression was of a woman who trusted no one.

"I'm Jeanne-Marc Steinhardt," the woman said, adding dryly, "My mother was French."

There was something bloodless in the reference, as if she were speaking of a vase and not a person. Terri extended her hand.

"Teresa Peralta." Smiling, she added, "My mother was Guatemalan. Still is, actually."

"How nice for you." Jeanne Steinhardt looked past her at the room. "Mine slashed her wrists when I was five. For years, I thought it was the art."

What, Terri wondered, should she say to *that?* "Then I'd change the decor," she finally answered.

Steinhardt turned to face her. "Oh? And what would your mother favor? Although I'm afraid an oil of the Madonna and Christ child would be incongruent with my background."

Terri felt herself tense; the sole ambiguity in Steinhardt's remark was whether its bias arose from class or race. "Many of us," she said evenly, "used to favor a framed portrait of James Colt. Preferably one that glowed in the dark."

Jeanne Steinhardt looked surprised and then moved her lips in an expression of chill amusement. "I take it," she said at last, "that you know what's on that tape."

Terri nodded. "I've stopped lighting candles for James Colt, if that's what you mean. And so did Mary Carelli, after Mark Ransom played it for her."

Jeanne Steinhardt stared at her openly, as if appraising and reappraising. "Yes," she said. "I saw her on *60 Minutes* last night. Impressive. Please sit down."

Silent, she led Terri to a long couch in the middle of the room, a white cotton fabric with an Aztec design. Terri sat at one end, Steinhardt at the other, hands folded, legs carefully crossed.

It was time, Terri thought, to soften her tone. "Your mother," she ventured. "That must have been hard."

"I barely remember her." Steinhardt gave an elegant shrug. "It's less a loss than an absence."

Terri tried to imagine her life had Rosa Peralta been "absent." It was, Terri found, like imagining that she herself did not exist. In that moment, she saw the emptiness she sensed at Jeanne Steinhardt's core as the absence of love.

"As you say," Terri answered, "I've been fortunate."

Steinhardt made a dismissive gesture. "You came about my father, and his tape."

Terri nodded. "About the tape, and about Mark Ransom."

Steinhardt gave her a curious look. "What is it that you care to know? Seeing that your client has already killed him."

Terri was silent for a moment, gazing out the window. There was a pool outside, a long oval that contrasted with the lines and angles of the house itself. A Hispanic poolman stretched over it with a long wire net, reaching for a tropical leaf that marred the blue surface of the water.

"How was it," Terri asked, "that Mark Ransom acquired that tape?"

"That part's quite simple." Steinhardt gave a thin smile. "I called him."

That, Terri thought, was no surprise. "For what reason?" she asked politely.

The question was perfunctory; Terri was quite certain that she already knew the answer: money. Steinhardt was silent for a moment. "Because," she answered coolly, "I found listening to it so educational."

Terri hesitated. "Wasn't it confidential?"

"That was certainly my father's intention. He left instructions that all tapes were to be destroyed by his executor." Steinhardt permitted herself another cold smile. *"I'm* his executor."

Terri tried to choose a neutral voice. "Don't you have problems with the psychiatrist-patient privilege?"

"Oh, I think not. Laura Chase moved beyond my father's ministrations, as it were, when she put the gun in her mouth and pulled the trigger." The husky voice seemed to drop a register. "Perhaps Laura felt she'd graduated."

Terri paused again, off balance. Beneath this woman's icy air of intelligence and self-interest, Terri felt another emotion which she could not identify. "Still," she said carefully, "people might argue that Laura would have wanted to protect her privacy."

Steinhardt shrugged. *"They* might. But I don't expect to hear from *her* about it. Which left me quite free, my lawyer confirms, to contact Mark Ransom."

Steinhardt seemed to be speaking by rote, Terri thought: there was a certain relentless quality to her indifference, as if she wished to ensure that it was noticed.

"What did you tell Ransom?" Terri asked her.

"Just enough." The clipped words had a faint derisive edge. "That I admired his work. That I'd read an article he'd written about Laura Chase—'Flesh Become Myth,' I believe he called it. That I shared his interest in Laura's death. And that, were he interested, I might let him listen to my father's tapes." She smiled at the coffee table. "At a price to be negotiated, of course."

"What did he say?"

"That he wanted to meet me." The strange smile reappeared. "So we did. Sitting in my father's office, with the door locked, surrounded by his tapes."

The image of their meeting, Terri found, unsettled her. "Where is his office?" she asked.

Steinhardt gave her a look of surprise. "Here, of course, in my father's home. So very private, so very *him*."

Terri hesitated. "May I see it?"

"If you like."

Steinhardt led her through a hallway hung with Flemish tapestries and opened a white door. She stood in the doorway, arms crossed.

Terri entered the room. It was sparely furnished, almost entirely in white—including the couch for patients to lie on and Steinhardt's leather chair at its head. The empty couch and chair were haunting, Terri thought; they reminded her that Steinhardt could not help Laura Chase.

"As sterile as an operating room," Jeanne Steinhardt said from the door. "But then someone once called my father 'The Surgeon of the Mind.' "

Terri turned. "Where are the tapes?" she asked.

Steinhardt pointed. "Through here."

In the wall, between the couch and the chair, was a door Terri had not seen. Steinhardt walked quickly past her and unlocked it.

The second room was dark.

Steinhardt switched on a black desk lamp. Terri saw shelves, books on psychiatry, a single desk, two black chairs, no prints or vases anywhere. The room was wholly impersonal.

"The inner sanctum," Steinhardt said in a mocking stage whisper. "My father's cerebral cortex. Or, perhaps, his essence."

Terri walked toward the bookshelf on the far wall. It was honeycombed with slots, as if for tapes of someone's favorite music. But these tapes, in white plastic cases, were coded with Roman numerals, numbers, years, dates. Removing one, Terri felt unclean.

"It could be anyone," Steinhardt said behind her. "How does it feel to hold someone's life in your hands?"

Staring at the tape, Terri replayed Steinhardt's words, her tone of voice, sensed some feeling she still could not grasp.

"How did you know which tapes were of Laura Chase?"

"My father had an index." Once more, the voice turned sardonic. "I showed it to Mark Ransom when we met. Rather like a shopping list."

It was difficult, Terri found, to look at Steinhardt. She edged along the shelf, her gaze sweeping hundreds of tapes. Then found a gap; one shelf, then half of another, were empty.

"That space represents Laura Chase," Steinhardt told her. "Her cure took quite some time."

Terri was silent for a moment.

"Ransom took them?" she finally asked.

"Yes. That was part of our negotiation." Steinhardt sounded almost amused. "He wanted to work at home."

Terri stared at the last shelf of tapes, less to inspect them than for something to do.

There was, she saw, another gap. It was small, two empty slots where tapes would fit. She placed her fingers there. "And this?" she asked. "Also Laura Chase?"

"I don't know." Steinhardt paused. "If so, they would have been out of order."

Terri looked at the tapes on either side. If she understood Dr. Steinhardt's code at all, they belonged to two separate patients; the numbers and numerals were different, and the dates overlapped.

"*Was* there anything in this space?"

For a moment, Steinhardt looked puzzled. "I'm not sure. I noticed that the other day. But I couldn't remember."

"If there *were* tapes, could Mark Ransom have taken them?"

Steinhardt shrugged. "It's possible, I suppose—once or twice I let him listen in here, alone. You know, when he couldn't wait." Steinhardt's voice turned dry. "He seemed to like communing with Laura in the room where she had most exposed herself—figuratively speaking, of course. How he must have wanted to *be* my father."

Terri felt a kind of chill. "Would the index show if tapes were missing?"

There was a moment's silence. "It would have. Yes."

Terri began to turn, then was stopped by a black and white photograph, the ascetic face of a man in his sixties.

It hung on the wall by itself. The man's face was thin, his skin like parchment; his eyes, pale and translucent, betrayed no feeling.

"Your father?" Terri asked.

Steinhardt nodded. "I hung it myself, just before Mr. Ransom's visit. It seemed somehow appropriate."

Terri was quiet for a moment. Turning, she asked, "Can you tell me about that?"

"Of course." Steinhardt took one chair, Terri the other. "It was really quite amusing, in its way."

The dimness of the room, Terri realized, was oppressive. "In *what* way?" she asked.

"The way he changed. When he arrived, Mark Ransom projected this restless energy—a prisoner in his own skin, a red-haired Irishman wrestling with his devils. It was something you could feel if he'd never said a word." Steinhardt gazed around her, profile almost leonine. "But once he got here, in *this* room, it was like he'd entered a cathedral. When I showed him the tapes, all he could do was stare.

" 'Play one for me,' he asked." Steinhardt's voice became almost teasing, as if replaying the moment. "So I did. Just one."

"The one he played for Mary Carelli?"

"Oh, no. Like Laura herself, I wanted to save the best for last." Steinhardt flicked back her hair. "For him, the sound of her voice was enough—Laura Chase, returned from the dead."

"What did he do?"

"He just sat there, hunched forward, listening. He hardly moved." Steinhardt smiled. "And when it was over, he offered me a hundred thousand dollars.

"I told him, more in sorrow than in anger, that his offer was deficient. And then I told him about Laura's last tape." The strange smile returned. "The one with James Colt."

It had been a game between them, Terri realized. Quietly, she asked, "What did Ransom say?"

"Oh, it was more how he looked that confirmed my sense of value. His face was—how should I say it—so *avid*." Steinhardt's voice took on the jaded tone of a woman mocking a discarded lover. "It felt as if I had offered him Laura Chase herself."

Terri imagined the moment with something close to horror. In return for money, Jeanne Steinhardt had set far more in motion than she could ever have imagined.

"What happened?"

"We reached an agreement, sitting here in this room. Two hundred and fifty thousand dollars, plus thirty percent of any royalties." Steinhardt gazed up, as if addressing her father's picture. "The last ten percent," she said in a mordant tone, "was for letting Mark take Laura home with him."

Terri watched her face. "Did he say how he would use the tape?"

"No. But I assumed that he would use it to promote the book. The tape goes far toward explaining her suicide, don't you think?" Pausing, Steinhardt still gazed at her father's photograph. "Laura's, that is."

For a moment, Terri found she had lost her train of thought. Then she asked, "Did he ever talk about playing the tape for Mary Carelli?"

"No." Steinhardt turned back to Terri, her voice edged with contempt. "But then he also failed to tell me that he saw the tape as foreplay. With my limited imagination, I merely saw it as the basis for a number-one best-seller regarding Laura's suicide. You know, the book that finally tells the world 'Who Killed Laura Chase.' "

Terri paused. "In connection with Laura Chase," she asked, "did he mention *any* other women?"

Steinhardt paused. "I do recall him mentioning Lindsay Caldwell," she finally said. "Although the connection wasn't clear to me."

Terri hesitated, surprised at this mention of the distinguished actress, still beautiful at forty, and as well known for her social causes as for the Oscars she had won. As an undergraduate at Berkeley, Terri had heard Lindsay Caldwell speak on women's issues. Drawing on her own painful evolution from "Barbie Doll to Superwoman," as Caldwell dryly put it, the talk had been surprising for its candor and universality. She was, Terri thought, the polar opposite of Laura Chase—the kind of woman whose politics and persona Mark Ransom would most resent.

"What did he say about her?" Terri asked.

"The first reference I don't exactly recall. I do remember Mark asking if I knew her. Which I don't."

"Did he ask whether she had some connection to Laura Chase?"

Steinhardt shook her head. "He didn't, and I don't know. But unless I'm wrong, Laura died when Lindsay Caldwell was barely out of her teens."

Terri's gaze moved across the shelves to the space where two tapes might have been. "Did Lindsay Caldwell ever see your father? Professionally, that is?"

"I didn't memorize the index, if that's what you're asking." Steinhardt hesitated. "When I listened to the tapes, I confined myself to Laura Chase. The last tape, really."

"Why was that?"

Steinhardt's expression turned cool, her voice cooler. "The circumstances of her death intrigued me."

Terri paused again, decided not to pursue it. "A moment ago," she said, "you mentioned Ransom's 'first reference' to Lindsay Caldwell. Was there another?"

"Yes. He called me from New York. I had asked to read what he had written, to be sure he truly understood the implications of Laura's tape. He was going to be here, he explained, to see Lindsay Caldwell. He sounded quite pleased with himself." Steinhardt gave a faint smile. "I never saw his draft, and he never met with Caldwell. He was scheduled to meet with her one day after Mary Carelli."

Terri paused. Quietly, she asked, "May I see the index?"

"No." Steinhardt's voice was level. "I'm afraid you can't."

The woman's gaze was watchful, impenetrable—rather, Terri thought, like the cold face in the photograph.

"Perhaps," Terri said, "you can look at it yourself. All I want to know is whether Lindsay Caldwell was a patient of your father's."

Steinhardt's look turned curious. "To what end?"

"I'm not sure, quite. Perhaps she knows something about the tape."

"Well, you'll have to ask Miss Caldwell about any relationship to my father." Turning, Steinhardt gazed at the rows of tapes. "After Mark Ransom and I made our arrangement, I burned the index."

Once again, Terri was surprised. "Why?" she finally asked.

Steinhardt's eyes moved to her father's picture. "For the same reason," she answered coldly, "that I now intend to destroy these tapes. Because I had done what I set out to do."

All at once, and for the first time, Terri understood what Steinhardt had done. And then she saw, as Steinhardt still did not, how pointless all of it had been. Softly, she said, "This was never about money, was it?"

"Oh, it was." Steinhardt's smile was bleak. "If I made Mark Ransom pay dearly for that tape, I thought he would have no choice but to use it. And I dearly wanted him to use it."

Terri nodded. "Because of your father."

"Yes." Steinhardt's eyes became fierce. "Have you ever listened to that tape?"

"No."

"It was a revelation to me. For almost fifty minutes, Laura Chase talks about how worthless James Colt had made her feel. By the end, she was sobbing convulsively. My father spoke only to ask for more detail about what they did to her. And then he told Laura that her time was up." Steinhardt's voice became so raw that it sounded painful. "By the time the tape was over, I knew that my father was a collector and we were his specimens. Every one of us."

But no one else, Terri thought, would hear what Steinhardt heard. Quietly, she asked, "When did your mother kill herself?"

"Thirty years ago. She died quite anonymously. No one remembers her, including me." Steinhardt's face had turned to stone. "But now, because of me, no one will ever forget who murdered Laura Chase."

"I find it refreshing," Johnny Moore told Terri, "that this case offers us at least one celebrity who's still alive."

Terri sat on the balcony of a suite at the Beverly Hills Hotel, courtesy of Christopher Paget, speaking into the first cordless telephone of her experience. Moore would make her smile, Terri thought, if she weren't so depressed.

"Do you have a number for her?" she asked.

"Just her answering service. I took the liberty of leaving a message on your behalf: 'Call Teresa Peralta, attorney for Mary Carelli, regarding Mark Ransom.'" Moore laughed softly. "An adequate attention getter, I would think, even in la-la-land. Otherwise, I'd have left a message from Ransom himself."

Terri gazed across a courtyard filled with flowers, watching the sun fall into an ocean she could not see. "I wonder if she'll call me."

"That may depend," Moore answered, "on why Ransom wanted to see her. Or she *him*—although I find that harder to understand."

His voice was sardonic. "Jealous?" Terri asked.

"You've caught me out, Ms. Peralta—what a man we have lost in Mark. Of course, I'm quite put out with *her* too. All that feminist propaganda decimated my happy home."

"Really."

"Oh, yes. Surely it had nothing to do with my rotten hours, sporadic drinking, mysterious absences, and dubious friends. After all, Harriet Nelson would have understood."

"Those were the good old days," Terri gibed, "before they started giving women jobs."

"Now, that," Moore answered lightly, "is what's ruined the American family. Millions of women can actually leave their odious husbands and not starve to death. It's a poor society that pins its hopes on marriage counseling."

Terri smiled. "My only question is whether Richie can afford to leave *me*."

"The family meal ticket, are you? Then go make partner, and you'll inspire the love that lasts forever. In the interim, just be sure he's on your health plan."

Terri felt a touch of shame; even joking about Richie was like a betrayal of their secret. "It's not that bad," she said. "I'd never let it be."

Strange, Terri thought, asking Johnny to believe what she could not believe herself.

"Oh, Terri," he said gently, "is there no romance left?"

It was as if Moore understood her and wished to make her smile again. But his feelings would not be hurt, she thought, if he could not see her.

"Thanks for everything," she answered, and said goodbye.

She was watching the sunset when the phone rang again.

Tense, she answered, "Teresa Peralta."

"Hi, Ter. What's this message about your not coming home?"

She slumped in the chair. "I've got more business than I thought. Another witness—at least maybe."

Richie sounded put out. "Yeah, well, we really need you here."

No questions about her day, Terri thought—not that she'd feel comfortable telling Richie other people's secrets. "I'll be home tomorrow night," she said. "Unless this person can't fit me in until later."

"So tell him to see you tonight."

"I'll try." Suddenly Terri felt tired. "Can I talk to Elena?"

"She's not here. When I got your message, I asked Janie to keep her for the night."

"Why?"

"I've got another investor dinner. Janie said it was fine, that Lainie and Tess do well together."

For a moment, Terri wondered whether sending Elena to a neighbor's was some obscure form of punishment, not for Elena but for her. "I thought I told you that Elena doesn't like Tess all that much."

"Really? I guess I forgot."

"You were at your computer." Terri stood, watching the falling sun become a ribbon of orange. "Maybe you didn't hear."

"I guess not. Anyhow, getting out makes kids more independent." Before Terri could retort, he shifted subjects. "Listen, Ter, there's something I was wanting to talk to you about."

Why, Terri wondered, did she feel a knot forming in her stomach. "What is it?"

"It's about capital. We're still a few thousand short of seed money."

"Maybe we can sell my body."

"I'm *serious*."

Terri rubbed her temple. "So am I. We don't have money—just a new computer I can't seem to pay off. Maybe you can sell that."

"I need it for my business. Besides, it's all deductible—you've got to factor in the tax benefits."

"We don't have any more money," she said slowly. "It's that simple."

There was a long silence. "That's what I wanted to talk with you about."

The headache, Terri realized, started in the cords of her neck and ended at her eyes.

"What, exactly?"

"Your pension plan." Richie paused. "We can borrow against it."

Terri touched her eyes. "I'm not sure we can."

"We can, though. I checked with your accountant, at the firm."

"You *called* her?"

"You weren't *here*, all right? Lighten up, Ter. I didn't take the money or anything. Nothing can happen until you sign the papers."

Until, Terri thought. Finally, she said. "I haven't been here that long. It's probably only about five hundred dollars."

"Nearly thirteen hundred." Richie began speaking faster. "You can borrow up to *half* of that, at a cost of less than eighty dollars a month. No monthly payments, even—they just take it off the top of your check."

"You mean, like having your wages garnisheed?"

"Listen to yourself." Richie's voice rose. "This is what I mean about complete nonsupport. Except it's even worse—you try to humiliate me to control me."

Terri sat down. "I'm sorry," she said. "I don't want to humiliate you. I just want us to get a grip on our life. I can't *predict* anything, Richie—there's always something else." She paused, struggling to explain. "You begin to talk, and I feel paralyzed. My stomach gets like this fist."

Richie's tone softened. "I'm sorry, babe. I forgot how rules-oriented your mom was. All those limits."

Why was it, Terri wondered, that so often with Richie she did not know how she felt. She might be angry, somewhere, but all she felt was numb. "It's not my mother, Richie. It's me."

Richie gave a knowing laugh. "Okay, *you*. Then ask yourself whether a few hundred bucks is worth all this time on the phone. You're eating into our profits, Ter."

It was dark, Terri suddenly realized; she had not seen night fall. "I'll think about it," she finally said. "Okay?"

"Great." Richie was upbeat again. "We can talk about it as soon as you get back."

Terri paused. "Listen, if for any reason I'm home late tomorrow night, please keep Elena home, all right?"

"Sure. I'll take her out for dinner at some place she really likes, then maybe for an ice cream float." He paused, as if struck by a new thought. "Listen, why don't the three of us go to Tilden Park this weekend—take a picnic, ride the train. Great family day."

Something in his energy, Terri thought, made her wearier yet. Then she remembered how much Elena liked the train. "That sounds fine," she told him, and said goodbye.

For a while, she simply sat in the darkness. Terri thought about room service, wondered about Lindsay Caldwell, about Richie and herself; did nothing. She felt unreal—adrift in a tropic night, away from her daughter, waiting for a call from someone she had seen only at a distance or on film.

The telephone rang, snapping Terri to alertness.

"Hello," she said.

"Hello. Is this Teresa Peralta?"

The voice was clear, unadorned; Terri had always thought of it as stylish midwestern. "Yes," Terri answered. "Thank you for calling."

"You're welcome," Lindsay Caldwell said. "But then you knew I would, didn't you?"

SEVEN

"Is this about Mark Ransom," Lindsay Caldwell asked Terri, "or Laura Chase?"

They sat on the deck of Caldwell's glass-and-redwood beach house at Malibu Colony, watching the morning sun dance on the ocean. Wearing blue jeans and a white sweater, Lindsay Caldwell seemed smaller than the woman Terri remembered seeing; with her tawny hair, clear blue eyes, and look of watchful intelligence, she appeared less like a film star than like a casually affluent suburban mother who did graduate work on the side. The sole difference was the businesslike authority, neither flaunted nor concealed, of a woman who produced her own films and thought her own thoughts; at whatever cost, Lindsay Caldwell had found out who she was.

"I'm not sure," Terri answered. "On the telephone, you said that I must know that you would see me. I don't even know why Mark Ransom wanted to see *you*."

Caldwell's expression mixed appraisal and surprise. "You don't," she said flatly.

Terri shook her head. "What I thought," she ventured, "is that you might have been a patient of Dr. Steinhardt's."

"It's a decent guess." Pausing, Caldwell turned toward the water. "There was a time when I ran through therapists like some women run through lovers, although what *I* was shopping for was a father. But no, I never tried that particular Freudian." Caldwell's tone became quiet, reflective. "Although I've told myself often enough that no one could have saved her, or helped Laura save herself."

The last caught Terri by surprise. "You *knew* her?" she asked.

This time, Terri thought, Caldwell's look had a certain furtive quality, as if her answers were themselves a form of probe. Slowly, she nodded. "I was quite young then. Nineteen, in fact."

Terri paused a moment. It was difficult to accept that Lindsay Caldwell would give her time, harder still to ask her about a legendary actress without knowing what the point was or why Caldwell would care to answer. Terri felt less lawyer than star-struck voyeur.

"Was that what Mark Ransom wanted to see you about?" she asked.

Caldwell raised an eyebrow. " 'That' being . . . ?"

"Laura Chase?"

Caldwell nodded. "Yes. That was why Mark wanted to see me."

Caldwell's tone was neither helpful nor hostile; Terri had felt more warmth from the woman who had spoken on the Berkeley campus than from the one sitting next to her. She decided to pursue a different tack.

"I heard you speak at Berkeley once," she said. "What was so effective was that you used what had happened to you, like sexual harassment or trying to get artistic control, to bring you closer to things that bothered me and all the other women I knew. But it's hard for me to relate to Laura Chase at all."

Caldwell's look became interested, more personal. "It's because you don't *want* to—none of us does. Laura was an exaggeration of everything women most fear in ourselves: a needy victim, full of short-sighted guile, who played into male fantasies and traded a sense of herself for any form of 'love' that would keep her from feeling alone." Caldwell paused. "If you've never, ever, had those thoughts about yourself, then you're either delusional or have such remarkable strength of character that you need to tell me how you've done it."

There was no edge in Caldwell's words, simply an unsparing self-knowledge that embraced them both. "I'm more delusional," Terri said simply. "Some days it works better than others."

For the first time, Caldwell smiled. "It's like trying to be a feminist—some days it works better than others. But, at least in my experience, it beats the known alternative."

Terri nodded. "Unless you're Mark Ransom."

"Iron Mark." Caldwell's tone was flat. "A man truly in touch with his primal self."

Terri hesitated. "Did you know him—I mean, before he called?"

"Oh, yes. We met at a symposium at Yale on 'Women in Film.' Someone thought it would be entertaining to invite him." Turning, Caldwell gazed out at the water. "We had a disagreement, it's fair to say, regarding Laura's place in the pantheon of role models. It was hard to gauge Mark's strongest emotion—his passion for Laura Chase or his instinctive dislike for me. I was less confused: I remember calling him 'the poet laureate of the centerfold.' " Caldwell frowned, shaking her head. "What a complete waste of time. It's so much more effective to speak for your own beliefs than to ridicule someone else's."

The breeze picked up, rippling Caldwell's hair. She looked clear-eyed, a little younger than she was, yet etched with the self-knowledge that time brings. Terri felt momentarily at peace; she watched the ocean, the line of white where waves struck the sand and, farther out, long strands of kelp undulating with the ebb and flow. A lone runner grew small in the distance, vanished. The air was heavy and smelled of salt.

Finally, Terri asked, "Why did you decide to see him?"

Caldwell kept watching the water, as if she found it soothing. "He discovered I'd known Laura."

"What did he say?"

"That he wanted to talk to me about it. Personally."

Caldwell's answers were becoming terse again, a little distant. Perhaps, Terri thought, another direction would help things flow.

"Laura Chase was much older," she ventured, "and even then, you couldn't have been much alike."

Caldwell shook her head. "More alike than you think. I'd been locked up in boarding schools for years, rebelling against my father through the usual well-considered means—drinking and boys." Caldwell paused. "There got to be a lot of boys. The angrier my father was, the less it mattered who I did it with, even boys I hated. Back then, they called it promiscuity. I forget what Radcliffe called it when they threw me out."

Terri had not known this. But Caldwell spoke the words with a tired familiarity, as if she had traveled this road many times before, in search of understanding.

"How did you meet Laura Chase?" Terri asked.

"That part was easy. As you may or may not know, my father ran Paramount then, so they stuck me in the family business." Caldwell's voice became dry. "Eventually, I developed a perverse desire to be more important than he was. But my first job was a minor role as Laura Chase's kid sister, for which my major qualification was to be more or less flat-chested."

"I've never seen that one, I guess."

"It never got made." Caldwell's voice grew softer. "Laura killed herself just before our biggest scene."

For a moment, Terri was silent. Then she asked, "What was she like?"

Caldwell's eyes narrowed. "In retrospect, I suppose the most obvious thing about her was a kind of ruined sensitivity—she wanted to love and be loved but was far too needy to find that in any way that wasn't self-destructive. One day, she would sleep with an extra for the most fleeting sense of security. The next day, she'd stay in her trailer until the director begged her to work. But she could never find enough within herself to figure out how to get things right." Caldwell's tone turned rueful. "What she did have was an uncanny sense of what was wounded in other people. Especially when the wounds were like her own."

It was best, Terri decided, to see where this might go. "It's funny— I've read a lot about your parents or your politics or how you got to make your own films. But I don't remember you saying anything about Laura Chase."

"I've never talked about her." Caldwell gazed toward the water. "Not in public, at least."

Terri paused. "Why was it," she asked, "that you were willing to talk with Mark Ransom?"

"He said that he had tapes. Of Laura, talking to her psychiatrist." Caldwell paused. "It came as a surprise to me."

"Is that how he became aware that you knew Laura Chase— something on the tapes?"

Caldwell turned to her. "Can I ask why you care?"

The question was edgy, guarded. "Ransom had a tape," Terri answered, "from a few days before she died. It's about a weekend in Palm Springs—Laura Chase meeting James Colt and two of his friends. What happened to her was bad enough that it may explain her suicide."

"And she mentions me?"

Terri was startled. "Were you there?"

"In Palm Springs?" Caldwell turned away. "God, no."

Her voice held a hint of pain. "As far as I know," Terri answered, "Laura didn't talk about you on that tape. Ransom must have had another one."

Caldwell looked at her again. "He told me he had all of them."

Terri nodded. "What he tried to do with Mary Carelli was trade the tape for sex." She paused, and then added, "That particular tape seemed to excite him."

Caldwell stood and walked to the railing of the deck. She leaned there, palms flat on the top rail, staring out at the ocean. "What you're trying to establish," she finally said, "is that when Mark met Mary Carelli, he had some sort of premeditated sexual agenda and that the tapes were a part of it."

"Yes."

Caldwell shook her head. From the back, the gesture suggested not denial but weariness. When she turned, she seemed a different woman, vulnerable and self-doubting. "You simply don't know what you're asking. But then Mark Ransom did know. And if I understand what I saw on *60 Minutes*, Mary Carelli could use a friend." She hesitated, looking intently at Terri. "If I tell you what happened, I decide whether and how it gets used."

It was a statement, not a question. Terri nodded. "All right."

Caldwell searched her face. Finally, she asked, "What is it that you want to know?"

Terri reflected. "Maybe where to start is what Ransom said was on the tape."

Caldwell looked at her for another moment. "Just enough to convince me to see a man I loathed."

"What were you afraid of?"

"Several things." Caldwell's voice and gaze were steady now. "Beginning with the week I spent in Laura's guesthouse."

Terri said nothing. She was learning to know when words were needed and when silence was better than speech. Lindsay Caldwell seemed in control of herself; if she had decided to talk, it was for her own reasons, and all that Terri needed to do was listen.

"I was a mess," Caldwell began. "Drinking every day, screwing more or less at random. Some days I'd wake up pretty close to a blackout drunk, uncertain whether the fragments of memory were real or some twisted dream. A couple of times men called me and I couldn't remember who they were or what I'd done with them." Caldwell paused. "Even when they told me.

"That was how I was when I met Laura—drunken, careless, and lost. Like Laura herself."

The words came easily, as if Caldwell had said them to herself a thousand times. But speaking them aloud produced a rough edge in her voice Terri had not heard before, on-screen or in person. "Laura knew that," Caldwell continued. "She had radar for the wounded. Before the first scene we did together, she seemed remote and hardly real, as if she were another species of woman. But she was the one who realized that my hands weren't shaking out of fear but because of what I'd done the night before.

"It was an adaptation of a William Inge play—she was a glamorous woman from Chicago, returning to her tiny hometown, and I was the bookish sister, too scared to leave. The first scene was supposed to be in my bedroom, both of us putting on makeup for a dance while we talked about her life." Caldwell shook her head. "I knew my lines well enough, but eyeliner was beyond me. My hands shook too much.

"So Laura improvised. She took the eyeliner from my hand, said, 'Here, let me show you,' and applied my makeup while we finished the scene. It was instinctively perfect, just right for the relationship between the two sisters, and the lines flowed from there. The director loved it.

"Afterwards, I thanked her. She gave me that funny smile she had—like she knew your worst secrets and didn't care—and said, 'If you're going to drink like that, wait until they need you enough to clean up after you.' And then she went off to her dressing room.

"That night, when I was walking to the parking lot, I felt a hand on my arm. It was Laura. 'Are you at least taking the night off?' she asked. I wasn't, of course—I'd been semi fixed up with a bit actor who I knew in my heart wanted to tell his friends he'd fucked Leon Caldwell's daughter. Which was exactly why I was going to let him do it." Caldwell shook her head. "I don't know why, but I couldn't tell Laura that—it was like she knew me too well. After a moment, she said, 'You'd better come home with me.'

"I didn't think about arguing. I just went."

To Terri, the words sounded like a fissure between one part of Lindsay Caldwell's life and another. Caldwell turned to her. "Laura took care of me," she said simply.

Terri hesitated. "In what way?"

"Every way." Caldwell looked past her. "She had a beautiful house in the West Hollywood Hills, with so much luxury it was almost a spoof—a deliberate one, I think, like Laura's film persona. But Laura herself became a different woman. Off came the dress and cosmetics, up went the hair, and Laura suddenly looked something like a home-maker. It was as if, for Laura, coming home, and having company who wasn't a man, was a relief.

" 'I always wanted a sister,' she told me, 'and now I've got one. Thanks to William Inge and Twentieth Century–Fox.'

"Before I knew it, she'd fixed up the guesthouse, found me some clothes to wear, and we were sitting at a table by the pool, nibbling Caesar salad and watching the sun go down, while Laura told me all about her childhood. No drinks in sight, either—just iced tea."

Caldwell paused. "It was funny," she went on. "I felt taken *over*, like I was a blank screen on which Laura was projecting her need of the moment. But I also felt taken *care of*, without being judged, which my father had never made me feel. At some point in the evening, I just gave in to it.

"I told Laura things I had never said to anyone."

Even at twenty years' distance, Terri thought, the words sounded lonely.

"And then," Caldwell said in a flat voice, "Laura lit the candles on the table and told me about her father raping her, repeatedly, until she blacked out."

Terri froze, staring up at her. "It was plain to me," Caldwell said. "Even then. What had happened with her father was more shock than any adolescent could handle, and it changed the way she felt forever. She was worthless, men were a frightening mystery, and the only thing she took from it was an instinct for pain. Which she would experience, again and again, without ever comprehending why.

"When she finished, I was crying." Caldwell hesitated. "It should have been for Laura," she said softly. "It wasn't, really. For the first time, I had begun to understand myself.

"When I looked across the table, I realized she thought it was for her. She stood up, came closer." Caldwell paused. "When she kissed me, I felt too selfish to object.

"We went to the guesthouse then, Laura carrying the candles." Caldwell began walking in random circles. "She was very tender, not like the boys I'd known. I suppose she'd pleased so many men, wished for so much she'd never gotten, that she knew just how to be with me.

"I let her undress me, kiss my nipples, do everything she wanted. That first time, it was all her, and she took care of me." Caldwell stopped, turned to Terri with a look of pain. "Just like she wanted someone to take care of her.

"Afterwards, she told me she had never been with a woman before. That it was like inventing her own language instead of speaking someone else's. And now we could invent it together." Slowly, Caldwell shook her head. "For a time, I just lay with my head in her lap, listening to her talk. Until turning my face didn't seem very far to go.

"It was like that for a week."

Caldwell looked away again, her gaze following a lone gull that had swooped down on the beach. "We would go to the studio together, come home and cook dinner, drink nothing but milk. Every night, we would swim together, in the nude. Afterwards, she would towel me off and help me practice my lines. Almost as if I were a child.

"She asked for very little. Just to take care of me, as she wanted to be taken care of, and to get affection in return." Caldwell paused. "For that one week, I gave that to her."

Terri was silent. How many lives, she thought, have their painful private moments, too intimate to be shared with strangers, too powerful to forget. Finally, she asked, "Is that what Ransom knew?"

Caldwell watched the gull. "Part," she said. "Perhaps not all."

Terri hesitated. "What did he want from you?"

Caldwell's eyes grew cold. "A private interview. In his hotel suite."

"What did you think that meant?"

"Some private indignity. Something far less tender than occurred with Laura." Caldwell's voice was quiet. "If I had any doubts about that, they ended with Mary Carelli."

"Were you going to go?"

"I was going to *listen* and then deal with him somehow." Caldwell's tone grew crisp. "I have two children now, a husband whom I very much love and don't care to hurt. I'm sure they'd try to understand, but still . . . And what about the others, who see me as a symbol of the women's movement, pro and con? Did you catch the furor when the president of NOW admitted being bisexual?"

Terri nodded. "Yes. I did."

Caldwell paused. "Twenty years ago, I learned that at any given time, some people can be one thing or another. But that's harder for a lot of other people to understand than equal pay for equal work, and I don't want to help some yahoo like Jesse Helms confuse the two—as cowardly as it may be to skip this chance to educate the public."

Terri was silent, sensing something left unsaid. "What else," she asked quietly, "did Ransom know?"

Caldwell's searching gaze became a stare. "What makes you ask?"

"Because you wanted Ransom to tell you something that you didn't know." Terri watched her. "Just as you've hoped that *I* can."

Caldwell's face seemed to pass through a series of changes, from surprise to resignation to a deeper level of anguish. Then she looked at Terri again, even more closely than before. "You have a kind of gift," she said. "A silence, almost a stillness, while someone talks to you. You've drawn them out before they learn how much you see."

Terri felt her own surprise; what Caldwell said sounded true, and yet she had not quite known it. "It's not meant to harm," Terri answered.

Caldwell studied her in silence. Finally, she said, "Let's walk, all right? I feel like a prisoner."

Terri kicked off her heels. They followed the redwood steps down to the beach and began walking on the sand, Caldwell looking like a woman on vacation, Terri like a yuppie on a lunch break. They would have been an amusing pair, Terri thought, except for the look on Caldwell's face.

"It was during that week," Caldwell began, "that Laura told me about James Colt."

Terri glanced over at her, surprised.

"How long was that before she shot herself?"

Caldwell knelt, rolling up the bottom of her jeans. Quietly, she answered, "Ten days or so."

From her tone, Terri knew that she need ask no further questions. They resumed walking, both silent.

After a time, Caldwell spoke again. "I had heard the rumors, of course. About how she and Colt would meet in secret, even how she fantasized about becoming First Lady—which was impossible, of course. But it was still strange to hear Laura talk about making love to 'the future leader of the free world,' as she mockingly called him, the blond handsome man we saw on television talking about courage and sacrifice and social justice." Caldwell looked over at Terri. "Somehow, knowing made me feel lousy. James Colt was a hero to me—I wanted him to be a little better than the last six guys I'd slept with. Too good to be taking advantage of Laura's weaknesses like some sleazy producer banging her on the couch and then going home to his wife and son.

"But what was worse, I realize now, was how Laura talked about him.

"He was this mysterious force she didn't understand. Laura wanted to believe in him, but she felt a deep resentment too—she referred to him as 'God almighty' as often as she used his name. The one thing that was clear to me was that Laura was at his beck and call. Even her jokes about him were the wisecracks of a slave." Caldwell paused, shoulders hunched forward. "It made me think about my life."

Terri looked over at her. "Then Laura taught you something."

"More than you can imagine." Caldwell looked away. "I was there the night James Colt asked her to meet him in Palm Springs."

Surprised, Terri said nothing. Simply watched her.

Caldwell turned toward the water, standing where the waves, dying at their farthest ebb, met the sand. The wind rippled her honey hair, glistening in the sun. The ocean lapped at Terri's feet.

"We were in the guesthouse," Caldwell said in the same quiet tone, "in a pink bedroom with mirrors on the ceiling one of her husbands had installed. I was lying with my head on her shoulder, watching my own reflection as Laura stroked my hair."

For a moment, Caldwell's voice had a dreamlike quality. "I was neither happy nor sad. I felt peaceful and at the same time sort of lost. Like this wasn't really me, just sort of a space I was occupying until something changed in me and I started on a different life than the one I'd brought to this house.

"Then Laura began to talk."

The rhythm of Caldwell's speech changed again, quickening. "What was so good between us, Laura said, was that it was so gentle. There wasn't any taking, only giving to each other, because all we wanted was to love and be loved. I had given her something that she'd never had before." Caldwell's voice grew lower. "In the mirror, I saw that Laura's eyes had filled with tears.

"I turned to her then, confused and somehow frightened." Caldwell paused. "She thought I was turning out of love. So she smiled, even with the tears, and then kissed me.

"When the telephone rang, she was saying, 'I love you too.' "

For a moment, Caldwell's voice had caught. Terri tried to imagine the moment: Lindsay Caldwell lost at nineteen, Laura Chase reaching out to her. To her surprise, what she felt most clearly was how overwhelmed Caldwell must have been.

"It was Senator Colt," Caldwell said. "Laura held the phone out so I could hear his voice.

"It was so strange. I was lying naked in bed with another woman, perhaps the most famous actress in the world, listening while someone who might become the next President asked her to spend the weekend in Palm Springs."

Caldwell looked down. "He talked for a while—I couldn't hear him clearly. In the mirror above me, Laura's face got very clouded, and then I felt her draw up her knees.

" 'Who are they?' she asked."

Caldwell shook her head. "She didn't have to say anything more— I could see her eyes reflected back at me. No matter how he'd put it, Laura knew what he had in mind for her, and *I* knew she knew.

"Suddenly my skin felt cold, and then Laura reached for my hand.

" 'I'm not sure,' she told him. 'I'll have to think about it.'

"He started talking again. As she listened, her fingers clasped mine tighter. Just before she hung up, Laura said, 'Suppose I'm not available. Just suppose, Senator Colt, that *I've* found someone else.' "

Caldwell knelt to scoop up a sand dollar, inspected it in silence. "It was a moment before I realized," she said at length, "that Laura was talking about *me*."

Terri glanced at her again. As the path of her story moved toward its end, Caldwell's voice seemed to be losing resonance. Even her steps had slowed. "When Laura hung up," Caldwell said, "I felt as if I'd made a commitment.

"I should have been glad for her—that she hadn't said yes right away. But what I felt was this kind of suffocating pressure. That Laura might reject James Colt for me. That if she stayed away from men, or drinking, it would be for me. That it all depended on *me*.

"I'd given myself over to Laura, and now, suddenly, I wanted to be away from Laura." Caldwell paused. "And while I was lying there, thinking that, Laura laid my head between her breasts.

"That night I almost ran away."

Caldwell shook her head. "I couldn't," she added softly. "When Laura fell asleep, her arms were still around me."

Terri gazed ahead, walking in tandem with Caldwell at the edge of the water. The sun was in midflight now, the sky winter blue, the light-streaked water aqua gray as it reached the whiteness of the sand. But Caldwell's story of Laura Chase made it all seem surreal, a dream.

"How did you leave?" Terri asked.

Caldwell gave her a sidelong glance. "In the only way possible," she said at last. "I told her the truth."

Terri said nothing. After a time, Caldwell continued as if she had not stopped. "Sitting at breakfast, with Laura holding my hands. Not because I was honest. Because I was selfish, and scared, and couldn't think of any other way.

" 'Why?' she kept asking, with tears running down her face, sobbing, until I told her everything." Caldwell's speech quickened, as she was drawn back into the moment. "That I was confused. That she frightened me. That I was too much like her. That being secret lovers was no life. That I had to find my own life." Caldwell paused, drew in one sharp breath, and then finished quietly: "That I could never love her as she wanted to be loved."

There was silence, and then Terri realized that she was walking alone. Caldwell had stopped behind her, touching her forehead. "It was like if I told her everything," she murmured, "Laura would let me go."

Terri waited a moment. "What did she do?"

"I got my wish." Caldwell looked up, face ravaged with pain. "It was as if I'd shot her.

"She dropped my hands. Just looked at me. Mouth half open, no sound at all. Only her eyes moved." Caldwell paused, voice slowing for emphasis. "I've experienced a lot before and since, including things my father said or did that were crueler than people can imagine. But I have never seen a face that wounded.

"I don't know how long we were sitting there, a few inches apart, saying nothing. And then she whispered, 'I'll have to go with him now.' "

" 'No,' I said. 'It's not about *me*. I don't *want* it to be about me. Don't go for *you*. Because you don't want *anyone* to treat you like that.' "

Caldwell gave a humorless smile. "Great advice, right from the self-help library—I was ahead of my time. But I was the only one who heard it. For Laura, I could have been speaking Swahili." Caldwell's voice became bitter. "And, of course, I knew that."

"But it's true," Terri said. "You can't supply some other adult with something they don't have. Any more than you can sustain a relationship by offering up your sense of yourself as a kind of bribe. In the end, everyone loses."

Caldwell gave her a complex look of irony and understanding. "Are you talking to me, Teresa, or to yourself?"

Terri hesitated. "To you, at least."

"I see." Caldwell paused, searching Terri's face. "Well, then, if you're talking to me, then there's a little more to the story, and the ending is a little more dramatic.

"The night Laura died, she called my apartment."

Caldwell turned toward the water. "It was an hour or so before she shot herself. I hadn't needed to be on the set, hadn't seen Laura at all, had tried not to imagine her weekend in Palm Springs. I was thinking about going out and picking someone up." Caldwell paused. "To prove to myself that I was straight.

"Somehow, I knew it was her.

"She was drunk, and alone." Caldwell folded her arms. "As people will when they're drunk, she kept repeating herself. And what she said, over and over again, was, 'I need you tonight.' "

A tremor seemed to move through Caldwell's body. "She scared me. Her voice was like a child's. It made her sound so insatiable.

" 'Please,' Laura said. 'I went with him.'

"The way she sounded—I just didn't want to hear. I didn't know who I was more frightened of: Laura or myself.

"All I knew was that I had to stop her from saying 'I need you.' " Caldwell's eyes shut. "I told her I had a date."

Inwardly, Terri winced.

"After I said that," Caldwell went on quietly, "Laura began sobbing. Hurt, almost animal sounds. It was like I could feel her shiver through the telephone.

"There was only one thing I could think to do. I told her goodbye and hung up." Caldwell had begun pacing in half circles, as if confined by the apartment she was remembering. "Then I turned out the lights. As if I were afraid that Laura might find me."

Caldwell stared down at the sand. "The telephone rang, again and again. I sat there in the dark perhaps an hour or so, afraid to answer. Just listening to it ring.

"Then it stopped."

Caldwell turned to Terri. "I'd never known that silence could be so profound. Perhaps it was the darkness. For I'm not sure how long, I couldn't move. Then, without realizing why, I got up and drove to Laura's.

"There were no lights. When I rang the doorbell, no one answered— no Laura, no maid. The door was locked.

"I was relieved." Caldwell shifted slightly, turning away from Terri. "I thought Laura had gone out. Then I remembered the guesthouse.

"There was a moon. I found the path around the house, through the flowers and shrubbery, which came out by the pool.

"The pool was dark. I stared into it for a moment, looking for something, hoping not to find anything. Then I noticed that the lights were on in the guesthouse.

"When I reached the door, it was ajar.

"I stood there, suddenly afraid. And then I knew why I had come."

Caldwell paused, gazing down. In Terri's imagination, her posture mimed that of a nineteen-year-old girl, twenty years before, deciding whether to step through a half-open door. And then Caldwell said, "I went in.

"The bedroom door was open.

"Inside, the light was pale yellow. The first thing I saw was the telephone by the bed. It was off the hook, dangling by the cord, which stretched to the floor until it disappeared in shadows. The receiver made a throbbing sound that seemed to echo in the room.

"Laura was on the bed.

"She was naked, her hair was wet, she was lying on a bath towel. For a second, I thought she'd just passed out after going for a swim. Then I saw the revolver in her hand, blood and hair scattered across the pillow. The back of her head was gone."

Terri flinched. "I turned away," Caldwell said softly. "After that, I never looked at Laura again. Except on film."

Terri wanted to reach out to her, then felt that this would be pointless. "What did you do?" she asked.

"I was in a trance. I stood there, my back to Laura, as if I'd been anesthetized. What penetrated, finally, was the relentless screeching of the telephone." Caldwell's voice had steadied. Each word was precise and clear, as if she were describing a picture she had memorized years before. "It kept beeping until I couldn't stand it anymore. All I could think of was to stop the sound. When I hung it up, and the sound stopped, it was like my brain reconnected to some sort of reality.

"Someone had to know." Caldwell paused. "It was foolish and empty, but I couldn't leave her alone like that.

"I picked up the telephone. When the Emergency operator came on, I said, 'Laura Chase has killed herself.'

"There was this long silence—I'm sure she thought I was some sort of crank. Finally, she asked who I was. I realized that I didn't want to say. So I answered, 'Just a friend.'" Caldwell shook her head. "It sounded so miserable.

"She kept asking who I was. Somehow, it made me angry. 'Damn you,' I snapped. 'She's put a fucking bullet through her brain,' and slammed down the telephone.

"After that, I just walked out.

"I didn't look back and didn't run. It was like turning away from Laura had taken all the energy I had. I walked to the car like a robot, switched on the ignition, and started down the driveway.

"When I got to the end, I had to stop for a moment, to remember where I was going, which way to turn. Then I started home." Caldwell paused. "I'd gone perhaps a quarter mile when I saw the ambulance, lights flashing, coming toward me in the other lane."

Caldwell looked at Terri. "That's when I knew for sure that the whole thing had been real.

"I just kept driving.

"That night, I couldn't sleep. The next day, when I could finally stand to open my door, Laura looked up at me from the morning paper."

Remembering, Caldwell's eyes seemed uncomprehending. "I kept waiting for them to come. They never did. No one had taped my call. They didn't have my fingerprints. No one knew about me and Laura." Caldwell looked away. "No one knew I was even there."

Terri said nothing. There was a long silence, and then Caldwell raised her head. She looked determined, almost defiant. "For years," she said, "I've read articles about the mysterious caller, about 'Who Killed Laura Chase.' But I'm the only one who ever knew the answer." Turning back to Terri, she finished in a steady voice. "*I* killed Laura Chase."

"No," Terri answered. "You didn't."

Caldwell looked at her. "Oh, I know all the right answers. I've had years of therapy to master them. Laura killed Laura. Or society, or Hollywood, or her father or Senator Colt or a thousand men in between. Even swine like Ransom, who built their fantasies on an idea of Laura which has damaged countless other women almost as badly as it damaged her. I *know* all that. But there's still one question for which those answers don't work at all.

"I keep asking myself, What would have happened to Laura if she'd just gotten through that night? For *that* there is no answer."

Terri shook her head. "But that was twenty years ago. You have a whole life to look at now. Not just the senseless thing that Laura did when you were nineteen and even your own life made no sense."

"My own life," Caldwell echoed. "I'm still sorting out how much of *that* I owe to Laura. After that night, I hardly drank again. I didn't go out for almost a year, and when I did, the sport fucking was over. Laura's death was like a fault line. Did she make me a feminist? Or a mother? Or a filmmaker? Or a wife? Or some or all of them? I'll never know that, either."

Terri waited, then asked quietly, "What is it that you thought Mark Ransom might tell you?"

"Part of it was what he might tell my husband, or my children. But there was more." Caldwell frowned, as if struggling to articulate something too enormous to be captured in a few words. "All this time, I've talked to Laura in my head, asking why she did it, what I meant to her. But when she answers, it's in my voice." She paused. "I wanted to hear *her* again, talking *about* me but not *to* me. I thought I might learn the truth."

"Do you think Laura really knew the truth, whatever it is?"

"Perhaps not." Caldwell turned to Terri, as if in search of understanding. "But how could I know the tape existed and run away from it?"

Terri studied her face. "So Ransom promised to bring a tape. Where Laura talks about you."

Caldwell nodded. "I suppose the police must have it now."

"No." Terri hesitated. "When he died, Ransom only had one tape. The one he played for Mary, about James Colt. The second tape he described to you, he didn't have."

Caldwell looked surprised, and then her eyes went cold.

"That bastard," she said.

EIGHT

"SO FAR," MOORE said to Christopher Paget, "it would appear that Ransom was either celibate or had taken up the 'solitary sin,' as my old priest used to call it. At least for the last two years."

They sat on a bench at the foot of California Street. To their right, the cable car line swept up California to the top of Nob Hill, where Ransom had died; ahead and to their left, Market Street ended at an open plaza, behind which stood the Ferry Building, its venerable clock tower showing a little past 2:30. Behind them were the four adjacent towers of Embarcadero Center, each housing about thirty floors of offices; the crowd around them seemed equal parts tourists and professionals, with a scattering of street people and three or four strutting pigeons, looking for food. On a nearby bench, a harmless lunatic, dressed in the jeans and seaman's jacket he had worn every day for years, shouted his usual mix-and-match fragments about conspiracies: today's special seemed to feature the CIA, Mary Lou Retton, and the New York Museum of Modern Art. Moore, who could not stand to lunch indoors, consumed the last bit of his salami sandwich.

Paget looked at him. "Nothing?"

"Nothing. And I don't just mean a laudable absence of attempted rapes. I mean the virtual absence of attempted dates." Moore made a short, choppy gesture of emphasis. "Nothing in the columns. No trips with women. Not a single female person, so far, who will admit to screwing Ransom anytime this decade. Either the act was so dreadful they've repressed it, so forgettable they thought dear Mark was merely sneezing, or sex just wasn't on his agenda for the nineties."

"That simply can't be. Not after his call to Lindsay Caldwell."

"I know, I know." Moore's eyes narrowed. "Poor woman. I always liked her."

"I still do."

Moore nodded. After a time, he said, *"Our* little girl's done well."

"Terri, I assume you mean. My only question about Terri is whether she knows how good she is."

Moore became quiet for a moment. "There's something sad about her, don't you think?"

"I *think*, yes. But I honestly don't know what, or why—it's more a sense, like quicksilver, which comes and goes in an instant. Terri's very private, and she holds on tight."

"Unlike you," Moore said sardonically. "The Mr. Rogers of white-collar law, so warm and fuzzy. It goes without saying that you've not met the husband."

"No." Paget found himself squinting at the sunlight. "Why do you ask?"

"Just a sense of my own. Something she said in passing."

Paget examined him. "Ah, Johnny," he said lightly, "you're not falling in love, are you? Not with my twenty-nine-year-old married associate."

Moore shook his head. "Too old," he said. "There's just too much sadness in the world, that's all, and it's far too late for either of *us*."

Paget smiled. "Personally, I've pinned my hopes on Carlo. It keeps me from becoming maudlin when I start performing mental tricks like doubling my age or adding up how many years I've already lived past Mozart. When I turned forty-five, the results of either calculation were rather melancholy."

"Still," Moore said, "you at least owe Ms. Peralta a pat on the back when she returns. This Lindsay Caldwell thing—"

"This Lindsay Caldwell thing," Paget put in, "reeks of sexual black-mail. It's a weird variant of what Mary says happened to her: trading tapes for sex, except that Ransom had tremendous leverage on Cald-well and none at all on Mary. Which, one assumes, is why he resorted to rape. And why Mary felt free—however inadvertently—to spare Lindsay Caldwell a private meeting with someone who no doubt had given considerable thought to her debasement."

"Except," Moore retorted, "that there *was* no second tape, and Mark Ransom has been living the life of Saint Augustine."

"Oh, there was a tape about Caldwell, all right—Ransom must have listened to it before he called her. Which leaves the question of where it is."

"I've no idea." Moore turned to him again. "If it comes to a trial, Chris, can you get Caldwell's story into evidence?"

Paget shook his head. "In justice, I should. But I probably have even less chance than with Melissa Rappaport. Nothing happened: Ransom scheduled an interview and then died first. The only consequence to Lindsay Caldwell is that somewhere, perhaps in one of Ransom's homes, exists a very nasty tape that will give Marnie Sharpe hours of listening pleasure."

Moore considered that. "Jeanne-Marc Steinhardt," he finally said, "paid her dear old mum a real tribute. So meaningful to the dead, so helpful to the living."

Paget was silent for a moment. "No price," he answered softly, "is too great for the truth."

Moore looked at him. "If there's any dirt on Ransom, Chris, I'll find it."

At seven-fifty, Paget found Terri in her office, looking drawn in the fluorescent light.

"Why aren't you home?" he asked.

Terri brushed back her hair. "By the time I got in from Los Angeles, Richie had taken Elena out to dinner." She smiled faintly. "Father-daughter night, he called it. So I decided to take a little more time to process things."

There was a hesitancy in her voice; except to see Elena, Paget guessed, some part of her was not eager to go home. "In the past six days," Paget said, "you've interviewed Melissa Rappaport, Jeanne Steinhardt, and Lindsay Caldwell. Processing *that* should take some time."

Terri watched him. "I suppose, for me, it will."

"For you?" Paget smiled. "As opposed to whom—the truly insensitive in general, or Johnny and me in particular? Or have your glaring personal inadequacies prevented you from noting that you've gotten three strangers to tell you things they've never told anyone else and perhaps never would have."

"That's part of what bothers me." Terri's shoulders drew in. "Knowing this stuff—it makes me feel responsible for them."

"You made them promises, Terri. I promise you I'll keep them." Paget watched her face. "Somewhere along the line, I've started trying to notice the damage I'll do before I do it. I do have a couple of questions, though."

Some of the strain seemed to vanish from Terri's face. "Sure."

"Are you hungry? Because I am. And have you ever eaten at Piano Zinc?"

Terri looked surprised. "What about Carlo?"

"He had a game. So I fed him on the way back, to save homework time, and then watched him shuffle up the stairs toward his English paper like a prisoner on death row. Which is close to how I'm feeling about being here now."

Terri smiled. "Then the answers are 'yes,' 'no,' and 'I'd like to.' "

Le Piano Zinc was a crowded art deco café with mirrors on two sides, light-pink walls, framed Parisian posters. The slender, mustached maître d' and Paget spoke briefly and amiably in French, and then Paget introduced Terri in English. The maître d' smiled, shook her hand, and led them to a table in a quiet corner. The minute or two spent doing this reminded Terri of how little she knew about Paget's life.

"I didn't know you spoke French," she said.

"College French, and poor at that. I practice on Robert, who indulges me. It's the last vestige of my first ambition."

"Which was?"

"To live in Paris and be Hemingway. Problem was, there'd already *been* a Hemingway."

"Why didn't you try someone else?"

Paget smiled. "That was the ultimate problem—I couldn't 'find my own voice,' as it were. When I didn't sound like Hemingway without the machismo, I sounded like Faulkner without the genius. And too few people read the Faulkner who *was* a genius."

Terri appraised him. "You know, sometimes I can't tell when you're serious."

"Believe me, it's completely intentional." Paget smiled again. "Some of the things I'm serious about embarrass me."

Somewhere in the flippant remark, Terri thought, was an element of truth. "You're serious about Carlo," she said.

Paget nodded. "About Carlo I'm absolutely serious." He paused, then added lightly, "Poor kid."

The throwaway line hung there for a moment. What was it about

Christopher Paget, Terri wondered, that so often made her feel as though they were having a two-track conversation: the first level what Paget said, the second and much more obscure level what Paget might communicate if she ever got close enough.

"How has it been," she asked, "raising him alone?"

Paget's eyes narrowed; Terri could not tell whether this was in contemplation of the question itself, or of why she had asked it.

"In a way," he said finally, "that's like asking what it's like to be me: it's all I know, so I've got no perspective on it. I suppose raising Carlo makes me acutely aware of all my deficiencies; I'm sure that makes me much more anxious than I'd be if I were married, and much more a burden to Carlo." He paused. "Although, in my own childhood, I learned that a rotten marriage is also rotten for the kid, and in ways more subtle and insidious than Carlo's teenage resentments of me."

"Is that why you never married?"

Paget looked surprised and then laughed. "I *was* married. Just not to Mary Carelli."

"To whom?"

The waitress, Terri realized, was hovering near their table. Paget turned to her with a wry expression, as if in search of rescue.

"Will you be having wine this evening?" she asked.

Paget turned to Terri. "*I* will," he said, "if you insist on having this particular conversation."

Terri hesitated and then saw that, in some small way, Paget's remark was to signal his acceptance of her as something more than just a lawyer. "Sure," she said.

"Do you care what we're eating in terms of red or white?"

"No." She smiled. "Richie and I drink from jugs, not bottles, and according to what's already open."

Paget turned to the waitress, said, "The Meursault, please," and then faced Terri again.

"As I remember," she said, "I'd just asked who you were married to."

"Oh, that. Her name was Andrea Lo Bianco."

Terri cocked her head. "Why does she sound so familiar?"

"She was a principal dancer for the San Francisco Ballet." Paget smiled briefly. "After we divorced, she joined the ballet in Paris, funnily enough."

"Was it funny?"

"Not terribly. But divorce rarely is."

Terri hesitated. "Was that before Carlo came?"

Paget shook his head. "A year or so after. The two events were not unrelated."

The last remark, delivered matter-of-factly, had an undertone of regret. "She didn't want him?" Terri asked.

Paget gazed at the tables around them, almost idly. "It was far less personal than that, and more complex. Andrea had never wanted children, because of her career and temperament, and I didn't really care—I'd never thought that much of myself as a putative father. Her dancing was demanding, and when she was home, Andrea could pretty much count on having my attention." Paget paused. "She knew about Carlo, of course, but when he actually came to live with us, our marriage changed quite a lot. In fairness to her, Carlo required a good bit of attention then, although that was hardly his fault, either. And for my own part, I felt I had no choice at all."

Buried somewhere in the last two sentences, Terri thought, was a piece of the puzzle that was Paget's relationship to Mary Carelli. "Why was that?" she asked.

Paget looked off into the distance. "He had some emotional problems," he finally answered. "Today's shorthand, I suppose, would be that Carlo lacked self-esteem."

The remark carried a painful trace of understatement. In the time it took the waitress to pour their first glass of wine, Terri decided to bury two questions she badly wanted to ask: "What problems?" and "How did Carlo come to live with you?"—the second of which, she was somehow sure, would drive Paget back within himself.

Smiling, Paget raised his glass to her. "To a marvelous career," he said, "for a lawyer who's already better than most."

Terri felt pleased and embarrassed, all at once. "Hardly. But thanks."

Paget gave her a droll look. "Someday, Terri, you'll learn to accept a compliment. Perhaps your friend Johnny and I should take turns forcing them on you, until you acquire the knack. It'll be a lot easier for us than for you."

"I don't mean to be like that. It's just that when people say nice things about me, I feel as though I've fooled them."

Paget smiled in acknowledgment. "The impostor syndrome. I know it well. Inside every self-assured professional lives a frightened neurotic who prays that he can somehow succeed before his clients discover the fraud. It's the guilty secret that drives us all."

"You too?"

"Me too." Paget grinned. "Even though, viewed from the outside, I'm clearly an incredible talent."

"Not to mention," Terri added, "Marnie Sharpe's forbidden fantasy."

Somehow the image piqued Paget's sense of the absurd. He started laughing and couldn't stop. "God," he said, "the mental pictures . . . ," and began laughing again. There was a sudden carelessness about his smile that made Terri want to keep it there: for a moment, she could imagine the young man he had been, before time and circumstance had changed him. And in that same moment, she realized how attractive he still was. The perfect match, she thought foolishly, for a prima ballerina.

"Mary, Andrea . . . ," she said, smiling. "Do you ever fall in love with Wasps?"

"Never; it's the tragic flaw that keeps me apart from Marnie. Ever since I was young, I've had the deep-seated fear that I'd grow up to marry an eastern type named Muffy, and then she'd give birth to twin loaves of Wonder bread."

Terri shook her head. "You can relax," she said. "Carlo is not your white-bread kind of kid. More like an Italian film star."

"Takes after his mother," Paget said lightly. "Goes to show what careful planning can do."

Again, Terri sensed something unspoken. It changed her mood ever so slightly; perhaps he had made her think of Elena. She finished her first glass of wine. "What I can't understand," she said finally, "is why you didn't think you'd be a good father."

Paget poured them both more wine. "For the same reason that I didn't think that *I'd* had a particularly great childhood. Too often, people do with their children what their parents did with them. *My* parents had parents too—who was I to think I was any better?"

"You are, though."

Paget shrugged. "Sometimes people can rise above themselves. If the need's extreme enough."

"And Carlo's was?"

"Yes." Paget hesitated. "Carlo's was."

The reluctance had crept back in his voice. Terri realized that, for whatever reason, Paget had been more candid with her than was his custom; perhaps it was safe to give something in return.

"*My* parents fought," she said. "Or, more accurately, my father fought, and my mother tried to protect us."

"From what, exactly?"

"He drank. And when he drank, he got violent." Terri looked up at him. "It's something I've never really talked about."

Paget considered her. "Why not?"

"I'm not sure." Terri hesitated. "When you're young, you realize the family doesn't want people outside to know. It gets to be a habit." She touched her chest. "Intellectually, you understand all that. But it's what you feel here . . ."

Paget sipped his wine. "Your mother never left him?"

"No. She's Catholic and believes in the rules, no matter what." Terri stared at the table. "And there were five of us. I was the oldest—there are two still at home, and Mom's still watching out for them."

"How did she do that? Protect you, I mean."

"I don't know." Terri exhaled, began again. "I guess part was that she was so watchful, pretty much all the time. When my father drank, he heard insults where there weren't any. You never knew when it would hit. When I was little, I remember closing my eyes, covering my ears." Terri folded her hands. "Sometimes my mom had to stand up for us. But mostly she kept us out of the way, tried to calm things, kept up with our classes and activities. My father saw it as some sort of conspiracy, almost. But it was just my mom taking care of things the way she had to do."

Paget gave her a reflective look. "What did you learn from all that?"

"That there's nothing I can do for her."

"What I meant was: for yourself."

Terri touched her wineglass, tracing the circle at its rim. "To avoid fights," she finally answered. "And to take care of things myself."

"It stands to reason." Paget's tone changed, as if to signal a change of subject. "Tell me about Elena."

Terri felt a knot in her stomach she had not known was there. "Do you mean: what has Elena learned from me?"

Paget shook his head. "That's your question, Terri. It wasn't mine. I've got no right to strip-mine your personal life."

She looked up at him, surprised. His gaze was even, almost gentle. The tears in her own eyes startled her. "I'm sorry . . ."

Christopher Paget, Terri realized, had reached across and briefly touched her arm.

"For what?" he said. "You're my friend, okay? I've decided that arbitrarily, because Carlo likes you. It's an awesome responsibility, but since there are two of us, we can probably handle it."

All at once, Terri felt relief course through her, warm and sudden. Lightly, Paget resumed the conversation. "Sometimes, as Freud once said, a cigar is only a cigar. I really did want to know about Elena."

Terri smiled. "Oh, Elena's wonderful. She's very imaginative, poetic almost, and she has this incredible fantasy life. She's much more like Richie that way—I'm so literal, and about as poetic as a pair of Birkenstocks." Talking about Elena, Terri realized, made her feel more like herself. "This is probably a mother speaking, but I'm sure that Elena will be someone out of the ordinary—a sculptress or a terrorist or something."

"Maybe she'll content herself with vandalism." Paget thought for a moment. "What are you going to do about her schooling?"

Terri frowned. "I'm not sure. I'd like to pick somewhere permanent to live, with good schools. But we really can't afford a house."

Paget looked surprised. "I can't swear to it, but the last time I looked, we paid our associates a living wage. In fact, although you were gracious enough not to say it, I had the distinct impression you left the P.D.'s office less for my charisma than to double your salary."

Terri smiled. "It *was* the money. And I'm not complaining. It's just that Richie works at home right now."

"What does he do?"

"He's trying to start his own company." Terri paused. "He's very bright, really, very inventive. Like Elena, Richie sees things that I really don't. It's just that sometimes, I think, someone like that finds it difficult to work for other people."

"Are you ready to order?" the waitress asked.

As Paget finished ordering, Terri looked around them. The tables were filled with couples and foursomes, some smiling, some serious and intent, their profiles reflected in the mirrors. These days, Terri and Richie seldom ate out alone; when they did, Terri enjoyed looking at the other faces and imagining their lives. Sometimes she would pick a man and woman, trying to figure out which date this was or why they were together. It caused her to wonder now what she would think were she someone else, watching herself with Christopher Paget.

"A penny for your thoughts," Paget said. "Or would you like a raise?"

Terri smiled. "I was just thinking that I liked this place."

Paget nodded. "I like rooms with a little animation. This way I don't feel like I'm communing with my ancestors." He seemed to hesitate. "On the subject of raises, we review our compensation every year. You're doing well with us, and it might make the joys of ownership look a bit more doable."

Terri looked at the table. "Thank you. It's nice of you to take an and interest. But there's daycare, too, and I can see some other expenses coming up."

Paget looked quizzical. "Does Richie watch her in the afternoon?"

"No." Terri paused. "He's busy at home."

The quizzical look vanished, replaced by the blank expression that, Terri had come to realize, concealed thoughts Paget did not wish to show.

"Perhaps you can work it out," he finally said. "Elena sounds like a special kid. I know when Carlo came to me, I decided that education and stability were what he needed most. It was worth the pain of paying for it."

Terri hesitated. But there was no point in discussing her fights with Richie, his insistence that children were flexible and could be happy anywhere. "When it comes to money," Terri joked, " 'pain' is a relative concept. I mean, don't you own a railroad or something?"

Paget laughed. "The *government* owns America's railroads, including Great-Great-Grandfather Kenyon's. As for the money I inherited, I never touch the stuff."

Terri looked at him a moment, trying to decide whether he was serious. "You're kidding."

"Of course not." Paget smiled. "Are you familiar with the theory of devolution? That's what happens when your great-great-grandfather passes down a ton of money, creating three of the most useless generations that ever walked the planet. It's like a curse. Shortly after college, I decided that my only hope was to make my own money. Which I have."

"So when Carlo talks about how hard you work . . ."

Paget nodded. "Sad but true. That didn't help with Andrea, either."

For a moment, Terri felt dull-witted, trying to process how this changed her idea of him. The thing that came to her was that, more than most people, Christopher Paget had his own idea of himself and had never wished to tamper with it. Finally, she asked, "What do you do with all the money?"

"Except for the occasional gift to worthy causes, it's in trust for Carlo and my theoretical other children, who grow more theoretical by the day." Paget smiled again. "The dirty trick I've played on Carlo is that, for purposes both legal and philosophical, the money actually goes to *his* children—which is as far into the future as I can postpone the curse. Carlo gets a more than comfortable life income, but only after I die. By which time, I trust, he will have developed what used to be called character."

Terri laughed. "That's appalling. Does Carlo know?"

"Oh, I've told him. Just last year, once he was secure in the more spiritual aspects of my paternal devotion."

"What did he say?"

"As I recall them, his precise words were, 'Then there's no point in putting rat poison in your cabernet.' I nearly choked up with real tears." Paget smiled again. " 'Don't worry, son,' I said. 'You've still got me.' To which Carlo responded, deadpan, 'Then you're just going to have to work a little harder.' "

"He really said that?"

"Absolutely. But the truly frightening thing was that his grades shot up next quarter."

Terri smiled. "I liked watching the two of you—the joking back and forth."

"It's my way of showing affection, and I fear I've passed it on." Paget's tone was dry. "But then I had to give the boy *something*. As matters stand, Carlo's the last of the Pagets."

"You never wanted more?"

"I just never had the right situation, and now I'm pretty much out of time." Paget glanced at her. "Are you and Richie planning on another one?"

Terri sipped her wine. "I don't know yet." She paused a moment. "We didn't plan Elena, really."

Paget nodded. "Birth control is tough these days, given that IUDs and the pill can kill you. If I were Johnny Moore, I'd say something like: 'The marvels of medical science—condoms to condoms in a single generation.' And once you're pregnant, the options aren't so hot."

"I really couldn't have done anything else." Terri stared at her wineglass. "It was time, I guess. Richie wanted a commitment—we'd have gotten married anyhow, he said, and he really wanted children. And I'd always had this strong sense of wanting to build a real family, one that's intact and free from conflict. That still means a lot to me."

Paget appraised her for a while. "This may be presumptuous," he said, "but have you ever wondered if you're still trying to fix your family of origin?"

Terri looked up at him. "No," she said quietly. "But sometimes I've wondered if I'm too much like my mother."

Paget paused, as if sensing that he had gone too far. "Perhaps *I'm* too much like someone who's divorced and has spent far too much time thinking about why." His voice was dismissive. "Probably the biggest gulf between my generation and our parents is that self-examination frightened them to death, whereas we're attuned to every quiver of the id and ego. It's tiresome, I'm sure."

It was uncanny, Terri thought: Paget seemed to know what questions to ask, when to talk, when to listen, and when to retreat under cover of self-deprecation. Either he was more sensitive than he cared to show, or he was getting a better fix on her than she herself had or wanted anyone else to have. It was unexpected, and somewhat unnerving.

"Not tiresome," she said lightly. "It's just that I'm too tired for all this stimulation."

Paget laughed. "Tell that to Carlo. The other night, when I was philosophizing about something or another, I heard him murmur, 'Get the hook.'"

"Like in vaudeville?"

"Uh-huh. The kid's ruthless. But it may be a line worth remembering."

Paget, Terri realized, was telling her that she controlled the depth and rhythm of their conversation, was free to pick and choose. All at once, she felt relaxed again: grateful for the evening and for everything that he had said.

"This was nice of you," she said.

He smiled. "I thought you and Carlo said I didn't get 'nice.'"

Terri raised her glass. "No," she said. "You get it."

Almost in spite of himself, Terri thought, Paget looked pleased. Lightly, he said, "I'll put that one in the bank, Terri," and changed the subject to work.

Dinner arrived; ahi tuna for Terri; cassoulet for Paget. The food was wonderful, Terri thought; they shared a little, and went over Steinhardt and Caldwell again, all the way through crème brûlée and a glass of port.

"Do you have any idea," Paget asked as they finished, "who the other two tapes belonged to? The ones Steinhardt couldn't identify?"

She shook her head. "No way to tell that they even existed, except to find them: the index is gone, and for all we know, it's just a gap. Does it matter?"

"Probably not. I'm just curious, that's all." Paget thought for a moment. "If they do exist and Ransom had them, Sharpe will find them soon enough. She's probably at home right now, baking cookies and listening to Troy Donahue tell Dr. Steinhardt about his mother."

" 'Ids on Tape,' " Terri said. "Poor Lindsay Caldwell."

Paget nodded. He finished his coffee, asked Robert to call a cab for Terri, and paid the bill.

It was drizzling outside, a cool wetness that felt good on Terri's face, a pleasant complement to the glow of wine and port. Standing next to Paget, it occurred to her, suddenly and by surprise, that she had liked the last few hours of her life.

From the row of headlights cruising up Market Street, a battered yellow cab peeled off, heading down the side street where they waited.

"Your limousine," Paget said, "has arrived."

She turned to him. "Thanks for dinner."

"The least I could do." He smiled. "Short of a raise, which is coming."

There was mist in his hair, she saw. Suddenly, impulsively, Terri stretched to kiss him on the cheek, and then stepped back again. She felt like a kid.

Paget was giving her a quizzical smile. "What did I do," he asked, "to deserve that?"

Terri felt herself grin. "It was the wine," she answered, and got into the cab.

* * *

The next morning, while Paget was still at home, McKinley Brooks called.

It caught Paget by surprise. " 'Lo, Mac," Paget said. "What's up?"

"Any number of things." Brooks paused. "You'll want to see me, I think."

His voice was somber, almost hesitant. "Can you give me a preview?" Paget asked.

"Yup. We found another tape."

For a moment, Paget thought of Lindsay Caldwell. "What's on it?"

"She starts out talking about you taking Carlo. But then she changes the subject, it seems. To the Lasko case."

Paget stiffened. "What in hell are you talking about?"

"You really don't know?" There was another, longer silence. "Mary Carelli was a patient of Dr. Steinhardt."

NINE

MARY HAD STARTED, Brooks said, with Paget taking Carlo.

It made what had happened sound almost brutal, as if Paget had coldly planned to deprive Mary of her son. But on the warm spring afternoon that Paget had come to the Carellis', he had intended to stay for an hour or so and then resume his life.

Mary's parents lived in the North End of Boston, just off Hanover Street, in a brick walk-up distinguished from its neighbors by green shutters that needed paint. John Carelli had run a corner grocery store, while his wife, Francesca, raised seven children, of whom Mary was the last. They were both in their seventies, the store had long since been sold, and, at least to Paget, any life in the house had decamped with their last daughter, so different from the others.

Now Carlo lived in the home that his mother could not wait to leave, while Mary traveled incessantly. In two or three more years, she had told Paget, her new career as a journalist would be stable enough to let her stay in one city, pay for a live-in person to help her raise Carlo. Meanwhile, she said, her parents were at least better than her older brothers and sisters. Paget knew only that two of Mary's brothers drank too much; that an older sister had refused to raise Carlo; and that the distance Mary had traveled made relations with her siblings as bad as with her parents. Some of that, Paget guessed, was the result of her relentless drive. But it was as hard for Paget to imagine Mary bounded by this world of parochial schools, male dominance, and rigid structure as it was for him to realize that her oldest sister still referred to Carlo as "Mary's bastard."

When John Carelli opened the door, he stared at Paget as if he were a derelict. He was a short man with a face like a walnut, all knots and crevices, a stooped body, and sharp, suspicious eyes. Nothing about him suggested warmth or laughter; Paget sensed a soul in life's harness, living so fiercely by the rules of his church and culture that it had killed something inside him. Whoever remained, Paget guessed, had just enough life to despise Paget for being like his daughter.

They stood in a cramped alcove. Behind John Carelli, a dark hallway stretched past a series of doors; like a ghost, Francesca Carelli appeared in the hallway, opened one of the doors, and closed it behind her. In three prior visits, Paget had not met her; he could only sense that once she might have looked like Mary.

John Carelli ignored his outstretched hand. "She said you were coming."

Paget nodded. "To see Carlo."

Carelli did not move; everything in his posture said that were he younger, he would throw Paget out. Finally, he grunted, "He's in here," and led Paget to the living room.

Its only adornments were heavy drapes that were completely drawn, a crucified Jesus, a still life of a pear and apples, and family pictures from which Mary was missing. The dark room smelled stale, as if no one had opened the windows for some time. There was nothing of Mary, save for the slim, dark-haired boy in front of the television, eyes vacant, watching reruns of a cop show. In profile, the boy had long eyelashes, delicate features.

"Carlo?" Paget called.

The boy did not look up. Paget knelt beside him. "I'm Christopher," he said. "I've come to see you."

Hesitant, the boy turned to him; as before, Paget was startled by the clear blue eyes. But they held neither recognition nor interest: two years was a long time in the life of a seven-year-old, and the boy did not remember him.

"Would you like to go outside and play?" Paget asked.

The boy did not answer. Paget touched his shoulder. "Maybe we can go to a park."

Quickly, the boy shook his head. "I want to watch this."

Paget looked up at John Carelli. "Do you have a baseball or anything?"

Carelli scowled. "This is what he likes to do."

Paget glanced at the boy, still intent on the television, and then back to Mary's father. "I'll just be here, then. Don't let me keep you from whatever you were doing."

John Carelli was silent for a moment, and then he left the room. Paget sat next to Carlo.

The show was about the California highway patrol. "Who are the good guys?" Paget asked.

The boy pointed at the television. "Him, and him."

"What are their names?"

"John and Ponch. They're on TV every day."

"Do you watch them every day?"

The boy nodded, eyes not moving from the television.

"Why do you do that?" Paget asked.

"Because John is my best friend." The boy hesitated. "Sometimes Ponch is too."

"Do you ever play with other friends, outside?"

Slowly, the boy shook his head.

"Why not?"

The boy looked vaguely frightened. Finally, he said, "I'd miss John and Ponch."

The answer had a bewildered sound, as if the idea of doing something else was overwhelming. Paget had the sudden desire to rip down the blinds, throw the windows open. Instead he watched television in the gloomy room, saying little, sitting beside Carlo Carelli.

On the television, the two highway patrolmen helped a mother and father look for a small boy named Timmy, who had gotten lost in a mountainous state forest. At least, Paget thought to himself, they had let Timmy play outdoors.

He forced himself to settle back, miming the boy's attentiveness.

After a time, he felt Carlo's shoulder touching his. He glanced over. The boy's gaze at the television was more intent than ever, as if he was afraid to acknowledge what he had done.

Paget said nothing. Then, without speaking or looking over, Paget lightly put his arm around him. The boy was very still. As they watched John and Ponch look for Timmy, Paget felt the boy lean into him, ever so slightly.

On the screen, Timmy had encountered a bear.

"Maybe," Paget said gently, "you'd better sit in my lap."

The boy seemed to hesitate. Without saying anything more, Christopher Paget picked him up.

When the bear went away, Carlo remained in Paget's lap. He was still there at the end, as Timmy and his parents hugged each other.

"My daddy's dead," Carlo said.

Paget rested his face against the top of Carlo's head. "Who told you that?"

"Papa."

"Who's that?"

Silent, Carlo pointed down the hall.

"What does your mommy say?"

The boy shrugged. The small gesture, like the boy himself, felt fragile.

Looking up, Paget saw John Carelli standing in the entryway. The hard look in his face said that Paget's time was up.

"Is there a park around?" Paget asked. "I was going to ask Carlo to play with me."

"He doesn't have time," John Carelli said. "We eat at five-thirty."

How, Paget wondered, had Mary ever escaped this, and how could she stand to think about Carlo here? "That's nice of you," he answered pleasantly, "but I wouldn't want Mrs. Carelli to go to the trouble of feeding me. Thank her for me, though." Paget paused, allowing himself a moment's petty enjoyment at the old man's look of anger, and then added, "I'll just feed Carlo after we've played. Is seven-thirty all right, or did you have something special planned?"

John Carelli stepped forward, blocking his path. "We didn't know you were staying."

For the dead, Paget thought but did not say, time is a never a problem. Then he felt the boy stiffen in his arms, as if aware of his grandfather's disapproval. He stood, scooping Carlo up in one arm, so that the boy could not see the warning look he gave John Carelli as he walked toward him.

"Well, I am," he said in a cheery voice meant for Carlo. "It's not every day that I have a boy to play with."

Carelli did not move. As they reached him, Paget politely said, "Pardon me," as if stepping into a crowded elevator, and firmly pushed the old man back with his free hand. Slung against Paget, the boy saw nothing. "I'll let myself out," Paget said over his shoulder. "Do enjoy your dinner, and thank Mrs. Carelli for her hospitality."

"Well," he said to Carlo when they got to the car, "where do we go from here?"

The boy shook his head; Paget realized that he had not seen him smile.

"What *I* figured," Paget said, "is that we'd go to a playground and then to dinner. What do you like to eat?"

The boy hesitated. "Pizza?" he ventured.

"Pizza it is. All we need now is a playground. It's been years, Carlo, since I've been on the slide."

The boy pointed to his suit. "You can't go like that."

"Oh, that just makes it more fun." Paget eyed him. "Do you ever do things you're not supposed to do?"

Again, the boy shook his head. "Papa won't let me."

Paget nodded. "Papa just wants to take care of you. But I'm thirty-seven years old, so I get to slide dressed any way I want to."

Carlo looked at him. "You're as old as my mommy, I think. She's thirty years older than me."

Paget smiled. "That's really not very old. At least your mommy doesn't seem old."

"Do you *know* her?"

Paget nodded. "Your mommy and I are friends."

The boy hesitated. Finally, he asked, "Did you know my daddy?"

Paget looked at him, and then he smiled again. "Why don't *I* be that, just for today, and you can help me find a park."

The boy's eyes changed, as if trying to remember how the subject had shifted. "What's your name?"

"Christopher." Paget turned the ignition. "And I'm ready to play."

The playground was small, cramped, but filled with mothers and children and a few old men on benches. Paget took a red rubber ball from the car. "Ever play catch?" he asked.

Carlo shook his head. "Only at school. They don't let me much— I'm not very good."

"I'll bet you're better than you think." He pointed to a swath of grass. "Here, I'll help you practice."

Haltingly, Carlo backed out onto the grass. Paget tossed the ball underhand. The boy flinched; when he clutched at the ball, it had already hit his chest.

"We'll start over," Paget said. "From closer."

He knelt a few inches away and tossed the ball more softly. Carlo dropped it again.

"That's okay," Paget said. "When I was a kid, I had to practice a lot."

"Were you good?"

"Not at first. But in the end, I got good."

On the fourth try, Carlo caught the ball.

He moved like his mother, Paget saw; he would be a tall boy, and even now the length of his arms and legs caused a little awkwardness. But his hands were quick enough; his problem was not reflexes but confidence and opportunity.

Carlo caught the ball again.

"You see," Paget said. "You're good."

Once more, Carlo shook his head. "I'm not good. You're just letting me be good."

Paget smiled. "It's you who's catching the ball. Not me."

"They'll never let me play." Carlo's voice was flat. "I could ask them for a million years, and they'd always tell me I'm not any good."

In these few words, Paget saw Carlo's life. He knelt beside him on the grass. "What's wrong?" he asked.

For the first time, Carlo spoke in a flippant voice. "I hate myself," he said. "I want to kill myself, that's all."

The boy's expression was so curious, Paget thought; half teasing, half searching. All at once, he felt despairing, at sea. By a kind of instinct, Paget said lightly, "If you killed yourself, Carlo Carelli, I'd have to eat the pizza alone."

The boy watched him for a moment. Then, for the first time, Carlo almost smiled. "Then I won't until later," he said.

"You would appear to have a problem," Larry Colvin said to Paget. "Or more accurately, Carlo does. At least on the basis of two visits."

When, Paget wondered, had his college friend Larry become so soft-spoken, his words so measured. And then it occurred to him that he had almost never known a mental health specialist who, at least in a professional mode, did not seem gentle to the point of sedation. Even his office—an upstairs room in his brick town house near Beacon Street—was subdued.

"I'm no child psychologist," Paget answered, "but I did take 'I hate myself, I want to kill myself' to be some sort of clue."

Colvin nodded, his fine, sensitive face reflecting sadness and a little curiosity. "To speak in shorthand, he's emotionally deprived—too little warmth, too few stimuli, not many reasons to feel good about who he is. The biggest problem with the conditions in which he lives is that he's internalized them all. Because he doesn't get much love, Carlo believes he's not worth loving."

Paget shook his head. "Short term, I really don't see that changing."

"Can you talk to the grandparents?"

Paget felt a moment's anger. "For God sakes, Larry, these people live in some other world. Mrs. Carelli won't speak a word—for all I know, she's been autistic for the last seventy-five years. As for the odds of meaningful dialogue between the father and me, one of us would have to die and be reincarnated." Paget paused. "When I came back to the house and asked if Carlo had report cards from school, Mary's father wouldn't answer. I had to threaten him with a court order even to get Carlo here."

Colvin nodded. "Do you think *I* could talk to them?"

"You can try. But you'd be talking in Morse code across a cultural Grand Canyon—you're young, highly educated, and, even worse, believe in insight-oriented therapy. These people are in their mid seventies, pickled in the Catholicism of the late Pope Pius, and members of a generation where even the well-educated believe that asking themselves any questions will destroy the foundation of their lives. It would be like Mozart meeting Genghis Khan for drinks."

Colvin got up, walked to a shuttered window, and threw it open. Outside, the cobblestoned street looked fresh-minted in the sun of a spring afternoon; the leafy branch of an oak tree, stretching toward the window, rippled with a fitful breeze. Colvin stared out the window.

"This city," Colvin murmured, "was a great place to grow up. I still love it, especially on days like this."

"But it's no good for Carlo. Not the way he's living."

Colvin nodded. "The thing is, he's really quite a bright boy. And, somewhere inside there, quite a sensitive one. For someone with so little stimuli at home, he follows things, even has something of a capacity for humor."

"I can feel that. Even in the little time we've had together, I've noticed that irony is something he gets and that it's safe for him. But the Carellis don't bring any of that out."

"How is he with you?"

Paget hesitated. "He doesn't show a lot of emotion—I'm sure that's true generally. Each time I visit, Carlo seems a little gladder to see me. But he doesn't like being touched, and I can't hug him at all. It's sort of sad."

"Everything you say, Chris, is pretty much what I'd expect." Colvin paused for a moment. "How about the mother?"

"I finally tracked her down in Rome—you may have seen her on the evening news when the Red Brigades killed Aldo Moro. It's going well, she says: two more years, and she'll be back in New York and able to rescue Carlo from her parents."

Colvin turned to him. "That takes him to nine years old, at least."

"I know." Paget hesitated. "I can see the pattern in the report cards I got from school. He's going downhill."

"It's not just school, Chris. It's pretty much everything. Self-esteem, ability to relate, even comfort with his own body. The next two years are critical." Colvin permitted himself a final note of irritation. "Does the mother know what she's getting into with this boy? I mean, does she have some sort of plan?"

Paget shrugged. "To have an au pair, I assume. Preferably someone with a working knowledge of English."

Colvin sat down again, expression curious and intent.

"Forgive me, Chris, but I think I'm permitted liberties with a friend that I would never take with a patient. How is it that two bright, obviously sophisticated people like you and the woman I watched during the Lasko hearings ended up with an unwanted child?"

The phrase "unwanted child" pierced Paget's heart and mind: the image it left was Carlo in front of the television, alone. "I can see why you don't usually take those liberties," he answered. "People in your business aren't supposed to make their clients feel guilty."

"Guilty? You look miserable." Colvin's voice softened. "Which is part of why I ask."

"*I* was a lonely kid—I never wanted to create one." Paget paused. "Although I've been reminding myself for the past four days that I survived."

Colvin leaned forward. "Are you happy with that answer? I mean, for yourself."

Paget shrugged. "Spare me, Larry. Next you'll have me drawing pictures to see whether I include arms and legs and have smoke coming out the chimney."

"Spare *me* the deflective wit, all right? You can even skip Carlo for the moment. What I'm saying, pal, is that this is important to *you*."

Paget smiled faintly. "My God, you're sounding like a human being again. I should have 'unwanted children' more often."

Colvin gave an impatient shake of the head. "Cut the shit, Chris."

"All right," Paget said. "The cold truth is that had it been my decision, Carlo would never have been born. I feel terrible about that, and even worse about how he's living." He paused, adding quietly, "As for Mary, she wanted him for reasons of her own. In that way, Carlo may already have served his purpose."

Colvin looked puzzled. "What do you mean?"

Paget paused. "It's a personal thing. Really."

Colvin searched his face. "All right," he finally said. "We'll stick to current events. Have you told your wife—Andrea, is it?"

"Not much about the last few days—she's touring Europe right now." Paget hesitated. "As a general matter, Andrea treats the fact of Carlo like something that happened in another world, perhaps because she finds it painful. Denial, I think they call it."

Colvin seemed poised to ask a question, then did not. At last, he asked, "Do you think Mary has a clear impression of how Carlo's living now?"

How, Paget wondered, to explain Mary as fairly as he could, yet leave out those things that Colvin did not need to know. "Mary has a clear impression," he answered. "She just doesn't *feel* it the way you and I might feel it."

Colvin leaned forward. "I thought, from what you said, that she despised her parents and pretty much hated her whole childhood."

Paget nodded. "All true. After seeing Chez Carelli at first hand, I'm amazed that she accomplished all she did. But becoming who she is took pretty much all she *had*. Mary's very tough now, in a cut-and-dried sort of way. She doesn't process bad experiences; she just leaves them behind. Just like rules. She learned that her parents' rules were a trap, so she invented her own and still does her damnedest not to care about anyone else's. If you have a problem, Mary would say, fix it however you need to. Don't feel sorry for yourself, and don't whine to *me* about it.

"Mary's so completely practical that it's become a form of ruthlessness. And like a lot of self-invented people, the distance she's come, and her success in getting there, has made her judgmental in a social Darwinist sort of way." Paget paused. "Although I would guess that it's part of Mary's creed never to pass moral judgment on herself."

Listening, Colvin watched Paget's face. "You seem to know her well," he finally said, "for so short a time spent together."

Paget found himself staring out the window. "Mary Carelli," he answered, "is someone to whom I've given a great amount of thought."

"Does she ever ask you for anything?"

"It's worse than that: she won't *take* anything. I don't know why."

Colvin seemed to reflect. "Okay," he said. "So why doesn't she feel Carlo's situation?"

"It's simply this: some part of Mary must think that Carlo can survive all this. Because she did."

Colvin paused for a moment. "Do you think that?"

Paget stood, walked to the window. "No," he answered. "Carlo's not a clone of Mary. There are other things inside him."

Colvin was quiet. After a time, he joined Paget, and the two friends gazed out the window together.

"You're right," Paget said. "This *is* a great city. I've liked it since you first showed me around, in college."

Colvin turned to him. "What are you going to do?"

Paget shook his head. "I have absolutely no idea."

Standing in front of the door, John Carelli shook his head. "You can't see him," he said.

"Why not?"

"Because this is my home." His voice was rough. "I'm sick of you hanging around."

"Next time, I'll see him elsewhere. Is Carlo here?"

John Carelli folded his arms. "You make my daughter pregnant, you think that gives you rights? *Anybody* can make a girl pregnant if she lets him. That doesn't make him a father, *or* a man."

Paget stared at him. Quietly, he said, "How true."

Carelli flushed. "You're a rich, spoiled boy. Carlo's never going to be like you—or Mary."

There was only judgment in this house, Paget thought. Carlo would see himself only in the Carellis' eyes, the son of a flawed woman, another person not worth cherishing.

"Have you given any thought," Paget asked, "to what *Carlo* will be like when he grows up? Or is it more rewarding to hate a daughter than to love a grandson? Because I've looked at you, Mr. Carelli, and there's no love in you." Paget paused. "If there *were*, you'd see that Mary's real sin was not sleeping with *me* but leaving her son with *you*."

John Carelli raised his hand to slap him. Paget grabbed his wrist; suddenly he felt exhausted. "I'm sorry," he said softly. "I had no right to say that. Please, I've just come to say goodbye."

Slowly, John Carelli reclaimed his hand. "Leave him be," he said. "You've done too much harm already, stirred Carlo up for nothing. Now leave him be."

"Papa?"

It was Carlo, standing behind his grandfather in the alcove. He had left his television program; from the living room, Paget heard the disembodied voices of John and Ponch. The boy looked up at him, eyes the shape of his mother's, their color as blue as Paget's own. "Northern Italian recessive," Mary had called them, as if dismissing any father at all.

"Hi, Carlo," Paget said, and then looked to John Carelli.

"Five minutes," the old man said. "Then I call the police."

Silent, Paget nodded, and then Carelli moved aside.

Paget knelt by Carlo. "Will you watch with me?" the boy asked.

Paget shook his head. "I'd like to. But I can't."

Even to his own ears, the words sounded empty.

"Are you going away?" Carlo asked.

Paget nodded. "I have to go now."

"Why?"

"Because I have to go to my house." Paget hesitated, trying to explain. "I live in California, where John and Ponch live."

Carlo looked down. "That's far away, isn't it?"

"Yes."

The boy nodded. "My mommy goes away."

"I know. But she'll be back. Mommies always come back."

"Will you come back?"

"Uh-huh. Someday."

Carlo went to the living room. When he returned, he was holding the rubber ball that Paget had given him. He put it in Paget's hand. "When you come back," he said, "bring this."

"But I wanted you to keep it."

Carlo shook his head. "We can play with it. If you come back."

Paget felt Carlo press the ball into his palm. When Paget closed his hand, Carlo did not let go of the ball; Paget's fingers curled around the boy's.

There were tears in Carlo's eyes. "What's your name?" he asked Paget. "I forget."

"Christopher." Paget paused, gazing at the boy, and then spoke before giving himself time to reflect. "I'm your father."

Carlo looked blank for a moment; Paget thought he saw a faint spark of hope, and then the boy glanced over his shoulder, as if afraid.

Paget picked up the boy and held him close. Carlo was stiff, uncomprehending. Then, slowly, his arms went around Paget's neck.

"I'm your father," Paget murmured again, "and it's going to be all right."

Paris was as beautiful as Paget had remembered.

It was a fresh spring afternoon, two days after he had left Carlo. Paget sat alone at Les Deux Magots, the outdoor café on the Boulevard St. Germain that he had haunted during his college year in Paris. He had liked it then for the boulevard's walking street show, and the corner café still offered a glimpse of every variety of Parisian—street jugglers, elegant women, would-be artists, older people who walked their dog and would stop for a glass of wine at this café or next door at the Café Flore. Near the entrance were the sculptures of two Chinese merchants from which Les Deux Magots derived its name; across the street was the forbidding stone mass of the twelfth-century cathedral of St. Germain-des-Prés, its small garden surrounded by an iron fence and graced by Picasso's bust of the poet Apollinaire. Paget watched a tall, dark-haired woman cross the street with the self-conscious grace of a runway model; it reminded him again that he had missed Andrea by one day and that she would dance tonight in Prague, six hundred miles away.

Idly, reflexively, Paget touched the briefcase full of papers.

"Basking in nostalgia?" the familiar voice asked. "Or imagining an evening with that slightly overdone brunette I saw you watching?"

Paget turned. "Nostalgia," he answered. "I was counting the years since last we met."

"Five," Mary said. "Would you like to talk here? I wouldn't mind a glass of red wine. I'll buy, of course, given that you've come all this way."

Paget nodded. "In that case, I'll have one too."

It wasn't until Mary had slipped off her coat and sat across from him that he started to absorb the changes in her. She was a woman in her thirties now, whose assertiveness had become self-possession. Her clothes and makeup were perfect as well: not too much of anything, but enough to suggest taste and an eye for detail. Even her speech, now well modulated for television, was clearer and more polished. Paget didn't know whether the better analogy was to a fine wine or a chameleon: there was nothing about this woman that suggested she and John Carelli belonged to the same race, let alone the same family. Even to Paget, she felt like a stranger.

"Why did you pick this place?" she asked.

"When you said you'd be in Paris, I thought of it." Paget glanced toward the street. "Not only is it good for people-watching, but this corner has a rather rich history—street battles of various kinds, even a few beheadings."

Mary smiled faintly. "And naturally, you thought of me. For my taste, though, that cathedral is a bit grim. I can't imagine spending any time there."

"Be respectful. In the thirteenth century, clerics died there, defending it from attack by students from the Latin Quarter. Not to mention the Huguenots who had their tongues yanked out for heresy."

A short, bustling waiter, officious and classically French, interrupted and took their order. When he left, they were silent for a time.

"You came about Carlo," she said at length.

"Yes." Paget paused. "I want him to come live with me."

Mary raised an eyebrow. "Just like that."

"No, *not* just like that. As I said on the phone, I've visited him several times lately, taken him to a child psychologist, gotten enough sense of your parents that I don't require any more. Carlo needs a father—or, more accurately, needs a parent. I told you how unhappy he is, how he reached out to me."

She made a brief dismissive gesture. "Chris, you can't possibly know what you're doing."

"In what sense?"

"In every sense." Her tone was impatient. "You can't just declare yourself a father and start making decisions."

Paget leaned forward. "I didn't declare myself a father, *you* did—the night before we testified. So here I am."

Mary shook her head. "I've asked you for nothing. Or haven't you noticed?"

"That's not true, Mary. You asked me for a great deal. Just not since Carlo was born."

Her eyes widened. "Is that what this is about? Making yourself feel better? Because what's done is done, and you'll just have to live with that. It's far too late for regrets."

"I know that very well," Paget said coldly. "But it's not too late for Carlo. In two years, it will be."

The waiter brought two glasses of red wine. The wine sat before them, untouched.

"Since when," Mary asked at length, "did you become such an expert in child development? I already know there are problems, because I know my parents. Believe it or not, it bothers me to leave him there for a couple more years, until my career gets straight. But I'll be able to change that. What suddenly makes *you* the one right answer?"

Paget decided to change tactics. "Look," he said quietly. "I'm not. And this isn't some sort of contest between the two of us. It can't be, for Carlo's sake."

"He's *my* son, Chris. I can't give him up. It really is that simple."

"It isn't, though. Because Carlo's not an inanimate object. Although if he keeps living in your parents' home, he may well become one." Paget's voice rose. "Damn it, the night I called, I *told* you how things are—as if you should even *need* that."

"I *am* coming back." She gave him a look of disbelief. "Really, this is grotesque. You never wanted to be a father, never wanted Carlo, and, until this moment, paid him less attention than one of your precious paintings. This conversation must be happening in a dream."

Paget stared at her. "Make up your mind, Mary. Am I the bad

parent who never wanted Carlo, or the man you effectively disowned as a father the moment Carlo was born? Because 'whatever suits my need of the moment' cuts no ice with me. Not, at least, on the question of this boy."

There was a subtle change in Mary's expression, as if she had deliberately forced patience on herself. "How much thought," she finally asked, "have you actually given this?"

"As much as I could, in the time allowed. Not as much as I will." Paget stared at his wineglass. "It's obvious that Carlo needs special tutoring, physical activity, and, most of all, consistent love and attention." He looked up at Mary. "Someone, every day of his or her life, has to make Carlo believe that he's the most important thing in it."

She smiled slightly. "You make it sound like a form of atonement, or a crusade. Of course, you used to be good at crusades."

"Not a crusade. Just a lot of time spent, and a certain sensitivity." Paget paused again. "In other words, the things neither of us got from our own parents."

"Which you alone have to give." Mary leaned forward. "Tell me, is Ms. Pavlova aware of your new ambitions?"

Paget hesitated. "If you mean Andrea—no, not in detail. But I'm sure we'll work it out."

"Oh, I'm sure." Mary gave him a sardonic smile. "I can so easily imagine it. 'Back from six straight days in Pittsburgh, my love, dancing *Giselle?* Carlo and I are going out to his Little League game, but you can meet us later at McDonald's.' Assuming, of course, that they have Little League in San Francisco. Do they?"

"They must."

Mary shook her head. "Honestly, it doesn't sound like you have much of a clue. You had an emotional reaction to my parents and caught a plane to Paris, *both* of which I completely understand. But that is *not* much basis for changing Carlo's life."

Suddenly Paget had the feeling that Mary was testing him, or perhaps just tormenting him—he could not tell which. It created feelings of hope and desperation.

"I'm *good* with him," he said. "I don't know why, but I am. The rest will come."

She gazed at him. "Are you so desperate," she asked, "to be good with someone? If so, maybe you should start closer to home. How *is* your marriage, I'm forced to wonder. Given that you propose to sandwich my son in the middle of it."

It's fine, Paget wanted to say. And then, because she was Carlo's mother, he told Mary something closer to the truth. "Andrea," he said slowly, "has more emotional requirements than some. It's all right as long as I'm available."

"Don't you think you should talk to her a little more before bothering *me* with all this?"

"I have." Paget paused. "The best way to describe her reaction is 'distant.' "

Mary frowned. "Then I suggest you withdraw your application and resume your former life."

Paget shook his head. "I've seen too much of Carlo," he said. "It may sound cold, but this is *not* a decision Andrea can make for me. Because if she did, and Carlo suffered for that, it would end our marriage. And *that* is what I've told her."

Mary watched his face. Around them, as the afternoon moved toward evening, men and women in business suits had changed the mix of the crowd, and the waiter seemed to wish that Mary and he would drink their wine or leave. Paget ignored him.

"No," Mary said finally.

Paget tensed. "Why not?"

"Because if Carlo does come, you'll have as good as ended your marriage. Which would make you a busy single father with a young son bearing the weight of a divorce. Carlo would feel guilty, and you might well resent him." Mary's gaze hardened. "What makes that a better life than the one I'll give him in two years?"

"Honestly?"

"Of course."

"Because he's in deep trouble, for all the reasons I described to you on the phone, which I know you understand too well." Paget's voice slowed. "And because I'm the right parent for that boy. If I didn't know that, I wouldn't be here."

Mary shook her head. "Go home, Chris. Save your marriage. In two years, I'll rescue Carlo from my parents. As I told you when Carlo was born, you've already done enough."

Paget looked into her eyes, as coolly and directly as he could. "Which gets us," he said, "to the bottom line of this discussion."

Silent, Mary watched his face. "What, precisely, are you referring to?"

"To the papers I've had prepared, awarding me legal and physical custody. And, of course, to the reason that you'll sign them. For the sake of politeness, we'll call it 'career considerations.' "

Her eyes widened, almost imperceptibly. "You're joking."

"No. Like many women, you've come to value your work. After an honest self-appraisal, you've seen the tension between career and motherhood, and recognized the expanded role a father can play. In this case, me."

She smiled coldly. "You seem to forget, Chris, that the same 'career considerations' affect us both."

"They don't, though. Because we're nothing alike. For one thing, as you once were fond of pointing out to me, I'm rich." Paget leaned forward. "Seven years ago, I just stopped caring. I don't give a damn what happens to me now. So I'm content to sit here until you tell me that same thing—that *you* don't care what happens to *you*." He finished quietly: "Perhaps, while I wait, we can have a bottle of wine."

It was odd, Paget thought, that her smile lingered, becoming a smile of appraisal. Even as she said, "You really *are* a bastard."

Paget felt tired. "I'm not, though," he said slowly. "I hate doing this. Just as I hate you for making me do it."

Mary shook her head. "That you hate *me*—that's no surprise to me. That you hate doing this the *way* you're doing it *would* be a surprise, if I believed it." She stared at her wineglass. "No, the real surprise is that you *are* doing it. Never, seven years ago, did I see this day coming. Never did I imagine you wanting to raise him."

She was pale, Paget saw.

"I'm sorry," he said. "I truly am. But if you don't do this, we'll be in court, with me waving Carlo's birth certificate and asserting my paternal rights by any means I can. Any at all. And that will do you no good at all. Nor Carlo, either."

For an instant, her eyes shut. "No doubt."

"No doubt," he softly echoed her. "And don't ever doubt I'll do it."

"Oh, I believe you." Her voice was thin, remote. "You have the papers with you, I imagine."

Nodding, Paget reached into the briefcase, placed the papers on the table. Mary read them carefully, like the lawyer she once had been.

"What do you intend to call him?" she asked. "I don't think 'Carlo' should change."

" 'Carlo Paget,' I thought."

She looked at him. "Carlo *Carelli* Paget."

Paget nodded. "All right."

Quickly, almost carelessly, she scrawled her name wherever it was needed.

"Did you know," she asked, "that Carlo likes blueberry waffles?"

Paget shook his head; it was surprising, he thought, how painful this felt, and how enormous.

"Well," she said, "I'm sure he'll tell you."

Abruptly, Mary stood. Paget saw a change come over her face, a shocked, wounded look—pain, anger, disbelief at what he had done. She seized her untouched wineglass, staring down at him; for an instant, Paget was sure that she would throw the wine in his face.

Turning, she drank until the glass was empty, and placed it down before him.

"Congratulations," she said. "You're Carlo's father now."

She turned, never looking back, and walked quickly away.

TEN

WHEN PAGET APPEARED in Brooks's office, there was a tape recorder on the desk, and Marnie Sharpe was with him. No one shook hands.

"You'll want to hear this," Brooks said.

The drizzle streaking the windows seemed to pervade the room. The D.A. did not smile; there were none of the usual graces. To Paget, Sharpe had the gaunt, angry look of a bitter saint.

"Where did you find it?" Paget asked.

Sharpe leaned forward. "At Ransom's home in Key West," she snapped. "Just how stupid do you think we are?"

"Not stupid, Marnie. Paranoid, perhaps."

Her mouth compressed. "It's hard to believe that you didn't know about this. And once they hear what's on the tape, no judge will believe it, either."

Paget tried to control his temper, and his nerves. "Why on earth would I conceal something so easy for you to find?"

"That's simple. You knew Carelli was Steinhardt's patient. You just weren't sure that Ransom had the tape. So you tried to shut us down, quick, before we figured things out." Sharpe paused. "The only other possibility is that your client lied to *you*. As to that, I *do* believe that Mary Carelli is a congenital liar. But it now appears that you're the perfect couple."

Paget stared at her. "Grow up," he snapped. "No one asked if Mary was a patient, so no one lied about it. This isn't kindergarten—the job of a defense lawyer isn't to tattle to the principal. Nor is this case a personal thing between you and me."

Brooks raised his hand for silence. Quietly, he said, "We should play the tape."

Paget nodded. "I thought that was why you asked me here. Because if your purpose was to permit your staff to instruct me on my character, or that of Mary Carelli, you should know that the only person I answer to is me."

"Consider us instructed." Brooks placed his finger on a button. "I've fast-forwarded over the preliminaries, like who she is and what she does, so you can get right to the meat."

Brooks pressed the button.

There was a moment's silence, and then Paget heard the voice of a man, emotionless and disembodied in the gloomy room.

"Was there something in particular," he asked, "that made you come here?"

More silence.

"Yes," she answered. "Three years later, I still can't leave it behind. I keep having this dream." There was a pause. "It's as if I shut it off by day, but at night I lose control."

Paget could identify the speaker—not the woman he had first known, but the more polished woman he had met in Paris. But without her face and gestures, there was something naked, almost haunting, in her voice. Some part of him, much deeper than the lawyer, did not wish to hear more.

"Can you describe the dream?" Steinhardt asked.

"Of course." Mary's voice sounded parched. "It's the same every time."

Paget became aware of Sharpe's stare, angry and intent.

"Tell me about it," Steinhardt prodded.

"I'm in Paris," she said, "at the church of St. Germain-des-Prés. In life, I've never seen it, except from across the street. But in my imagination, the inside is as gloomy as I remember the outside being on the one day I was there—dark and vast, so that the inner walls as they rise above me disappear in shadows. Behind the altar is a sculpture of Jesus, crucified and suffering, like the one my parents had." The voice became sardonic. "Except, of course, much larger."

"In the dream, why are you there?"

Paget became aware of Sharpe and Brooks, gazing fixedly at the tape. As it turned, Paget could imagine Mary in the white room Terri Peralta had described to him, staring at a blank ceiling, with Steinhardt sitting behind her, an unseen voice.

Mary answered softly. "To ask forgiveness for my sins."

"Are you alone?"

"I've left my son, Carlo, across the street, sitting at an outdoor café. Even in the dream, I feel guilty about leaving Carlo by himself. But this is something I must do, and I never want Carlo to know my sins."

"Are they forgiven?"

Mary's voice became muted, subdued. "At first, I have no sign. There is no one else there. I hear nothing, feel nothing. For a moment, it's as if the dream is telling me what I always told myself when I was young: that the Church is as empty as the Latin Mass became when I first heard it in English. That God either has left it or was never there." Her voice grew lower. "Then I go outside and receive His answer.

"Carlo is gone."

Voice thickening, Mary paused. Paget folded his arms, staring at the floor. He no longer knew, or cared, whether Brooks or Sharpe was watching.

"In his place are two empty glasses." She paused. "One for me, and one for Chris. And then I know."

"What do you know?"

"That Chris has taken Carlo, and that I must let him." Her voice became ashen. "That my sins are past redemption."

There was silence. "Who is Chris?" Steinhardt asked. "And what are your sins—in the dream, that is?"

More silence. "Do you know Christopher Paget?"

"I know *of* him. The young man who testified at the Lasko hearings."

"Yes." Mary paused. "Chris has Carlo now."

Paget could imagine Steinhardt making choices, deciding whether to pursue reality or dream. His hands clenched.

"And your sins?" Steinhardt asked.

"In the dream, or in real life?" Her voice became cooler, almost defiant. "Because in real life, sin has little meaning to me."

"The dream, then."

"You can't understand them," she said, "without some background. Did you actually watch the hearings?"

Paget realized that his posture was as it had been in the witness room, as he watched Mary fifteen years before: taut, leaning forward, living from word to word.

"Yes," Steinhardt said. "Like millions of others, I was fascinated."

Mary's voice was bloodless now, that of a lawyer describing someone else's case. "And did you watch my testimony?"

"With great interest."

"Then we need to start with one essential fact."

"What is it?"

Mary paused. Then, in a cold, flat voice, she said, "I lied."

There was a long silence. Brooks stared fixedly at the tape; Sharpe
at Paget. "Concerning what?" Steinhardt asked.

"Several things." Mary paused again; Paget could only wait. "I'm
sorry," Mary said, "but that tape makes me nervous."

Abruptly, Paget, reoriented, became aware that Brooks and Sharpe
were watching him.

"Why is that?" Steinhardt asked.

"Isn't it obvious?" Mary sounded impatient. "If it got out, what
I'm telling you could ruin me. Really, I don't know if I should be here
at all."

Paget touched the bridge of his nose; somehow, the reflexive gesture
helped him shut out everything but Mary's voice.

"But you felt you needed to come," Steinhardt said.

"Yes."

"Why, precisely?"

"The dream." Mary's voice was flat. "As I said, I don't like losing
control."

"Then let me reassure you. The tapes are for my use only, and only
to assist me in your therapy. By state law, they are subject to the
doctor-patient privilege, which I would ardently insist on even were
there no such law. So whatever you tell me is as confidential as if there
were no tapes."

There was a quiet vehemence to Steinhardt's words that Paget found
disturbing. Perhaps, he thought, what troubled him was Jeanne Steinhardt's comment about "specimens"; more likely, it was listening to
Steinhardt's assurances to Mary, five years later, in the office of the
district attorney. He looked first at Brooks, then at Sharpe, making
the point without words.

"All right," Mary told Steinhardt.

There was more silence, and then Steinhardt spoke again. "You
mentioned lying to the committee, as you put it. Perhaps you could
tell me what you meant."

Paget leaned forward. Then Mary said quietly, "Some of what I told

Senator Talmadge was true—the parts about Jack Woods. The chairman. My boss." She paused, and then her voice became clipped and systematic, as if reciting a litany.

"It was true that Jack spied on Chris for the President.

"It was true that Lasko had Chris's witness killed because Jack told Lasko that Chris was meeting him in Boston.

"It was true that Jack helped cover up the reason for the murder.

"It was true that Jack tried to stop Chris before he found out that Lasko had funneled money to the President.

"And it was also true that, because of Jack, Chris was nearly killed.

"All in all, I told the truth a good deal of the time." Mary paused. "What I didn't tell Talmadge is that *I* had helped Jack do every one of those things."

Paget felt the silence on the tape merge with the silent stares of Brooks and Sharpe, directed at him. He tried to focus on the tape recorder.

"You wanted to protect yourself?" Steinhardt ventured.

Mary sounded almost amused. "I wanted to stay out of prison. Even without that, the life I had worked so hard for would have ended if I had told the truth." She paused, voice softer. "And of course, I was pregnant."

Sharpe, Paget realized, was wearing a strange smile.

"Did Chris know about you?" Steinhardt asked.

"Know what?" Mary answered, and then the tape clicked off.

Sharpe leaned forward. *"My* question exactly." Her voice mimicked Steinhardt's: " 'Did Chris know about you?' For example, when *you* testified before the Senate."

Paget looked at her coldly. "I take it there's a second tape. Why don't you just listen and find out?"

"Don't bullshit me. You *know* there's a second tape, and you know that *we* don't have it."

Paget paused, feeling a moment's respite from his sense of vertigo, of things spinning out of control. "I don't have a second tape," he said. "And if I did, the only person I'd give it to is Mary Carelli. Who's the only person entitled to it." Paget looked from Sharpe to Brooks. "As for *this* tape, it will never become public—at least in a court of law—and both of you damn well know it."

Sharpe shook her head. "Only if Mary Carelli doesn't screw up on the stand, and only if her lawyer makes absolutely no mistakes. And, you surely agree, that lawyer can't be you."

Paget looked quizzical. "So that's what you're after—me out of the case."

Sharpe frowned. "Don't flatter yourself. We're not talking about my personal preference in defense lawyers; we're talking ethics. This case isn't about Mary Carelli—it's about *you* and Mary Carelli, and perhaps even your son, as I think you knew all along. I can't even begin to count your ethical problems."

Paget turned to Brooks. "Mary's conduct is at issue here, not mine. I'm not charged with anything, nor am I a witness to anything. Whether I continue to represent her is *my* decision, not yours."

Brooks shook his head. "You're walking a *very* fine line here. For two weeks now, you've told us that Mary Carelli had no motive for killing Ransom but self-defense. Now we've got a motive: Ransom had a tape that could ruin her for the rest of time, as she herself admits." He nodded to Sharpe. "And *I've* got the M.E. and the head of my rape team telling me this case has zip to do with rape, except the one your client tried to fabricate as cover. Which, if proven, may help us get to murder one."

"As far as the jury goes," Paget retorted, "you've still got no motive. That tape is subject to doctor-patient privilege. No judge in his or her right mind can listen to Steinhardt promise Mary that the tape is confidential and then let you put it before the jury."

"We've considered that," Sharpe put in. "Now you consider *our* case. There's no question Carelli killed him—the only question is why. So first we put on the tape recording of her interrogation by Monk. Then we bring on Liz Shelton to show how Ransom couldn't have died the way she said and how the physical evidence suggests a cover-up that includes defacing a very dead body. The room service waiter and the guest who saw her give us a couple more lies. And just as Carelli really begins to smell, we rest." Sharpe paused for emphasis. "Without ever saying a word about Steinhardt."

"Also without," Paget answered, "ever making it past reasonable doubt. I file a motion, the judge throws your case out, and we all go home."

Sharpe shook her head. "You file the motion, and you lose. We also keep out Rappaport, because she *consented* to whatever Ransom wanted. That leaves you with only two alternatives.

"The first is to argue reasonable doubt, keep Carelli off the stand,

and let the jury wonder why your feminist heroine has chosen to hide behind her lawyer. You will no doubt conclude, as I would, that choice one involves a very big risk.

"The second, of course, is to have Mary testify in her own defense and let me cross-examine her.

"Maybe, although I doubt it, she can survive all the inconsistencies arising from the Monk interview, Liz Shelton's analyses, and the two witnesses. But there is nothing in the doctor-patient privilege that prevents me from asking *whether* she saw Steinhardt as a patient, *why* she didn't tell Monk that, and *if* Ransom had a tape that would end her career.

"If she says 'yes' to that last question, she's merely hurting. If she says 'no,' she's history. Because the judge already knows she's lying and, I'm pretty damn sure, would let me find a way to get the tape in."

It was strange, Paget thought, how this relentless woman could make him think of the pain of Mary's dream and not the coldness of her lies. "Assuming," he said quietly, "that the tape hasn't already found its way into the morning papers."

Sharpe shrugged. "I'm not responsible for what they print."

"Why not?" Paget snapped. "You were the last time." His voice grew cold. "And if you play games with this tape, any games at all, it won't be Mary who's history. Because first I'll get a mistrial, and then I'll nail you to the wall."

Sharpe flushed. "I can certainly understand," she said, "why *you* want those tapes concealed."

"Do you? Then you should have no trouble believing me." Paget turned back to Brooks. "Are you enjoying this?"

"No." For the first time, Brooks looked uncomfortable, as if he wished he were somewhere else. "Under the circumstances, no."

Paget paused. "Under *what* circumstances?"

"We're charging her with murder." Brooks shook his head, as if hearing bad news for the first time. "We've got no choice."

Beside him, Sharpe looked triumphant. Paget felt stunned. "That's a real mistake," he said.

"The only mistake," Sharpe put in, "would be turning down our deal."

"Deal?"

Sharpe nodded. "Your client pleads to voluntary manslaughter, and we recommend the minimum sentence. A few years' prison, and this tape never comes out."

Brooks leaned forward. "Think about it, Chris. It protects Ms. Carelli from far worse."

Keep your head, Paget told himself. "And, with all respect, protects you from the political consequences of a backlash in Mary's favor. Not to mention the considerable distress of the Colt family."

Brooks summoned an equable expression. "I prefer to think the ends of justice will have been satisfied. And on a less ethereal note, I'm not as worried about 'backlash' as I used to be. Such an ugly word anyhow, I think we would all agree. As for the ire of James Colt's family, I would argue strenuously that the Laura Chase tape isn't relevant anymore and should never see the light of day." He spread his arms. "Besides, I can't imagine that a trial could be good for anyone—for Ms. Carelli, for you, or for your son. So talk to her, Chris, and get back to me. We won't indict until I hear from you, and if she signs on, we'll handle this with all the civility we can manage."

The D.A. was massaging him, Paget thought, as he would any defense lawyer with a guilty client in a mildly troublesome case. He stood, numb with disbelief. "This isn't a month's stay in a Best Western," he said. "It's the end of Mary's life, and she'll surely understand that."

"A conviction for murder one," Sharpe answered, "is the end of Mary's life. Compared to that, this is a sabbatical. Tell her that."

Paget turned to her. "Could you write that down for me? I don't want to miss a word."

Silent, Sharpe got up and opened the door for him. It was, Paget thought, the ultimate gesture of dismissal.

"Good luck," he said to Brooks, and walked through the door.

When Sharpe and Paget were on the other side, she shut the door behind them, as if to say something she wished Brooks not to hear. "When you first came here," she said in a flat voice, "I had some sympathy for you, believe it or not. Now I know you're just another user. So I want *you* to know that you're using the wrong issue, for the wrong woman, in the wrong case. That's what I'm going to prove."

She turned and stalked back to her office, the brisk click of her heels sounding on the tile floor.

ELEVEN

"DID CHRIS KNOW?" Steinhardt had asked.

Alone in his office, Paget imagined the second tape.

He was certain that it began with the night in Washington, fifteen years before, when Mary helped him evade Lasko's men at the airport. The night they had found Jack Woods rifling Paget's desk, clutching the memo that would destroy William Lasko and the President. The memo of a dead man. The witness Lasko had ordered killed, Alec Lehman.

For an instant, Paget remembered, Woods's face had frozen in surprise. Then it had settled into closed-off pride, looking from Paget to Mary and back again. His broken nose lent a hint of violence.

"What the hell are you doing?" Paget had demanded.

Woods had remained silent, giving the room a searching glance. Only the desk was between them. The overhead light cast a sickly yellow tint on the bare walls.

The desk touched the wall to Paget's right. But between the desk and the left wall was a four-foot space. Woods gauged it, then turned back to Paget.

Paget felt a sudden wave of anger. "Give me the memo."

Woods shook his head. Paget's anger began turning to disbelief. "It was you all along," Paget said.

Woods stared at Paget with contempt. "Nothing justifies the fuck-up you've made. You're a fool, with no sense of proportion."

"And you're a low-rent John Dean, Woods, with the ethics of a war criminal."

Woods answered in a smooth, indifferent voice. "Lehman's dead. I didn't want that, but there it is. There's only you to say this memo ever existed. And there's no one over me for you to say it to."

They were both to the side of the desk now, three feet between them. Woods was framed by the darkened window, Capitol Hill spot-lit behind him. The two men watched each other.

"If you want to walk out of here," Paget answered, "you'll have to kill me yourself. I know it all now. Most important, I know where the money was going."

"I'll bite," Woods said negligently. "Where?"

"The President."

For five minutes, still tensed and watchful, Paget had spelled it out: a one-and-one-half-million-dollar "contribution" to kill an antitrust case, the one witness who could prove that, Alec Lehman, whose memo Woods now held—whose death Woods had caused.

Woods's response was unnaturally calm. "You've lost," he said simply. Without this memo, no one will believe you."

The words covered Woods's careful slide toward the door. Paget slid back his right foot, to brace himself.

Woods suddenly dipped his shoulder and shot forward, knocking Paget against the desk. Paget bounced off and punched up from the rib cage. Woods's teeth clicked.

Pain ripped through Paget's forearm. Woods rocked, then caught himself against the wall.

Paget lunged for the memo. But Woods was too quick and too strong. He sidestepped as Paget stumbled past, off balance. A fist cracked into Paget's cheekbone. He staggered, then sprawled facedown on his desk, seeing a sudden purple haze. The haze cleared. In front of him was an onyx bookend, a squat hunk of rock. He grabbed it left-handed and spun.

What Paget hit was teeth.

Woods's hands jerked up to clamp his mouth, as if to hold it to-gether. Paget cocked the bookend, then hacked at Woods's forehead.

Paget heard Mary scream.

As Woods tottered on his heels, Paget hit him again.

Woods staggered, eyes glazed. Then he slid slowly down the wall. Paget gaped at him, breathing hard.

Mary stood in the doorway, staring. Woods was sprawled gracelessly on the floor, like the victim of a sudden stroke. His mouth was oozing blood.

Mary looked up from Woods, and then saw Paget's face.

She froze, irresolute, turned to run. Paget caught her and threw her against the wall. She made a little sound, like a hurt cat. Her fingers covered her mouth.

Paget moved toward her.

She shook her head like a mechanical doll. "No. No, Chris. You can't believe . . ."

Paget shook her hard.

"Lehman," he demanded. "It was you and Woods."

Mary stared at Paget.

"Tell me, damn you, before I mash your fucking face into the wall."

Her words escaped in twos and threes. "That night . . . the first time we went out . . . you said you were going to Boston. To meet a key witness." She caught her breath. "I called Jack, after I got in. Jack called Lasko."

Paget clamped her shoulders. "Goddamn you."

Her voice jumped. "No one knew Lasko would kill Lehman. I could hardly sleep."

Paget shook her. "I was there, remember?"

The personal thing was close to the surface, passing unspoken from Mary's eyes to his. "Please, Chris," she pleaded, "let me talk."

Paget slowly eased his grip. Her mouth worked soundlessly, then started. "I never talked to Lasko or anyone at the White House. I never wanted you hurt. I didn't know, really. I didn't know what I was into. I just tried to help Jack control the case. I couldn't expose him after the Lehman thing. He said we were both in trouble, because I'd known what he was doing. That's the only reason I kept helping him."

"Including tonight, when you called him from the airport? That *is* what happened, isn't it?"

"Yes, damn it. Now let me go."

"Did you call anyone but Woods?"

She shook her head. If that was true, Paget thought, perhaps he had some time before Lasko's people, evaded at the airport, figured out where he was. He let his hands drop.

Mary straightened and smoothed her hair, seemed to retrieve some of her poise. Something in Paget had admired that, even then.

Her eyes softened. She spoke quickly, looking at him. "Chris, you think I was with you because of the case. Maybe I used that a little.

But I didn't have to come to you this weekend. And I didn't have to stay. I did that because I wanted to."

Two days before, Paget remembered, they had made love. It seemed much longer. "I've had the privilege of listening to your speeches about politics, remember? You were just another weapon they could use. To pry the memo out of me, and give it to Woods."

She nodded her concession. "All right. But if I'd kept you away from Lasko, or gotten this memo, you'd be safe. I cared for you. You were good at things, gentle underneath—and so free. Money does make you free, you know."

"No, I don't know."

"Chris, please let's not lose this too."

It was no good, Paget realized. Slowly, he shook his head. "What I very much don't want to lose," he answered, "is my life."

A touch of panic crossed her face. "Give me the memo, Chris, and I can protect you. There isn't anywhere you can go with this. Not Woods, the White House, or anywhere else."

She was right, Paget knew. He looked over at Woods. He was still unconscious, but Paget's time was running out. He turned to Mary and pointed to the chair behind his desk. "Sit over there."

Paget reached for his telephone. In quick succession, he made two phone calls. When he had finished, a police lieutenant in Boston knew about everything except Mary, and a reporter from the Washington *Post* was hurrying from home to meet him outside.

"Why didn't you tell them about me?" Mary asked.

"I have my reasons."

Woods moaned but didn't move. Mary glanced at him dispassionately. "You know, he was right. You don't have enough proof to do to him what you've done to Lasko."

Paget shrugged. Her eyes were imploring now. "Chris," she said urgently, "there has to be some way to make this better."

Paget did not answer. His watch showed 9:43; in a minute or so, the reporter would be parked in front of the building.

Paget picked up the telephone and placed his last call.

An operator answered. "Police Emergency."

"Yes. I'd like to report an incident. The address is the ECC Building on D Street, Northwest, room 327. I've just caught a man trying to burglarize my desk. I knocked him unconscious, possible concussion. I'll need a couple of officers and maybe an ambulance."

Mary bolted upright. The operator repeated the address. "We'll have someone there within three minutes," she said.

"Thank you."

As Paget put down the phone, Mary lunged for the door, half tripping over Woods.

Paget caught her by the wrist.

She struggled, then stopped. Paget pulled her back. "The cops will be here in about two minutes. I have to leave. I'm giving you a choice—stay or go."

Mary stared at him furiously. "I want to leave."

Paget forced himself to be very calm. "Choice one is to stay and tell the truth. That Woods said he called Lasko about Lehman, that you called Woods tonight, and that after that he broke into my desk—"

"I didn't know he was going to do that," she interjected.

"And along with that, you can do your Miss Innocence routine and try to wriggle out. If you can pull that off, I won't stop you."

Her eyes were black pools. "And if I leave?"

"Then I give your name to the *Post*."

She clutched Paget's shirt. "Do you know what that would do?"

"I figure disbarment at the very least. You've got about a minute to decide."

She dropped her hands. "I'll stay, damn you."

"Good. Tell the police I'll be by in the morning."

Woods was moaning, the blood caked on his mouth. The memo still lay by his hand.

Paget picked it up and started to leave.

"You're a bastard, Chris." She said it in a clear, quiet voice.

Paget turned back. She was watching him, with an odd, expectant look. "My reporter friend will be calling the police," he said, "at exactly midnight. To check your statement on Woods, for his article. If you change your story or tell the cops where I am, you'll be reading about yourself tomorrow morning."

Mary's mouth parted. It was strange, Paget thought; he had never seen her more beautiful.

He turned and walked out.

He glanced back, once, as he rounded the corner. Mary was staring down at Woods. The yellow light was surrounded by darkness. The room looked like a cell.

"Did Chris know about you?" Steinhardt had asked Mary.

Chris knew everything.

There was a knock on the door, and Terri Peralta came in. "What's wrong?" she asked.

"Did you find Mary?"

"Yes. She'll be here in about an hour."

Paget nodded. "Close the door," he said. "There are a few things I have to tell you."

It was somehow touching, Paget thought, to watch Terri's attempt to listen like a lawyer, devoid of judgment or emotion. It made his own feelings a bit more bearable.

When he had finished, Terri simply sat there for a moment. "Why did Mary tell you she was pregnant?" she finally asked. "At least when she did."

"Insurance, I would guess. That night in my office, neither of us could know what we were getting into—a Senate investigation, national television. We were both improvising, with Jack Woods lying there on the floor. I was trying to save my life and, as Mary saw it, she was trying to save *her* life." Paget paused. "By the time we got to the hearing, I guess Mary wasn't sure I'd still protect her."

"Would you have?"

"I had hoped that no one would ever ask about her." Paget leaned back, remembering. "When Talmadge did ask, there were so many things going through my mind.

"The hearing room was quite imposing: leather chairs and a long wooden bench, raised so that you had to look up from the witness table; thirteen senators staring down; cameras everywhere.

"Millions of people were watching me. I had come so far with this since I'd seen Alec Lehman run down on a Boston street, since William Lasko had tried to do that to *me*. In the last two hours of testimony, I had settled my accounts with Lasko, with a President I didn't even know, and, most personal of all, with Jack Woods—who represented everything in government that I despised.

"I had to decide whether to go all the way, or to end it with a lie.

"In a way, it was Woods who put me there.

"Mary had finished him, of course—I couldn't have nailed Woods without a second witness. Skipping the question of morality, her testimony that morning was a thing of beauty. With complete self-confidence, she had told the truth about Woods by claiming that he had 'confessed' what Mary in fact already knew. Then she covered for herself, absolutely certain that Woods could never implicate her in any convincing way without implicating himself."

Paget watched his words register in Terri's eyes: their client was a liar and worse, and Paget had always known it. "Which brings us," he said slowly, "back to me.

"Talmadge asked a question with a lengthy preamble, as senators seem prone to do on television. But when he finally got to the question, it was, 'Did Miss Carelli have any involvement in the death of Alec Lehman, the obstruction of your inquiry, the leaks to William Lasko, or the alleged cover-up of illegal contributions to the President himself.'

"I remember looking up at him, composing my answer. Thinking about Woods, and Mary, and the baby she would have.

"Just as I began to answer, a camera flashed."

Paget gazed at Terri. "I lied, of course. *Time* magazine captured the moment in mid-sentence and put it on their cover."

Terri met his gaze, impassive. "Is that why you've never talked about it?"

Paget nodded. "I don't know," he said softly, "whether it was that so many people thought I was a hero, or the lie itself. Whatever, the Lasko case had done something to me, and I was through with it."

"Does anyone else know?"

"Only Mary." Paget hesitated. "And now you."

"Not Carlo?"

"Definitely not Carlo. Not, at least, until someone finds the second tape."

All at once, Terri's shoulders slumped. "Oh, Chris," she said quietly. "I'm so sorry."

"Don't be," he said. "Mary and I both made our choices. We're the perfect couple, and Carlo is a lucky boy."

Terri shook her head, almost angrily. "He *is* lucky. What you did was out of love—it's something a parent does for a child." She finished more gently: "It's something my mother would have done for me."

"That's the most attractive view. But I didn't do it just for Carlo." Paget turned, watching the rain spatter his windows. "Perhaps, to some degree, I did it for Mary herself. But I don't think it was just that, either. Maybe it comes down to this: I needed Mary to tell the truth about Jack Woods, so I helped her lie about herself."

Terri's gaze was steady again. "That doesn't explain raising Carlo."

"If you believe Mary, I was searching for atonement." Paget looked away. "I know this much: the day in Paris, when I threatened her with the truth unless she gave up Carlo, was one day Mary thought would never come. And today, listening to her confess on tape, was a day *I* thought would never come. For any of us."

Terri was silent. Finally, she said, "If that tape gets into evidence, Mary doesn't have a prayer, does she?"

Paget shook his head. "Not only does the tape give her a motive, but the motive is to conceal that she's already committed perjury. After *that*, no jury will believe her about anything."

Once more, Terri hesitated. "Do *you* think Mary planned to murder Ransom?"

"I have no idea."

Terri looked pensive. "What I don't understand is why she wanted you to represent her. Of all people, you're the one least likely to believe her."

"Oh, Mary's reason's clear enough to me." Paget turned to her. "I'm the only person alive that Mary absolutely believes to be as ruthless as she is—at least if I want something badly enough. She's seen that twice: that night in Washington, when I wanted to finish Woods, and that afternoon in Paris, when I felt I was saving Carlo." Paget paused. "Because of Carlo, I have something to lose now. It was Mary's turn to play the perjury card. To force me to represent her."

"With what's on the tapes, though, why would she want you?"

Paget gave a bleak smile. "They're the best motivator of all. The first tape damages me by implication, the second no doubt finishes the job. If I don't manage to suppress either or both—not so coincidentally giving Mary her only hope of beating this—Carlo will get a rude surprise regarding *both* his parents."

Terri touched her eyes. "What are you going to do?"

"I don't know that, either." Paget hesitated. "I may not have a conflict in the literal sense—I'm no longer chargeable with perjury, and I have no personal knowledge regarding Ransom's death. But in the deepest way, my own interests are very much at stake."

"Or Carlo's interests."

Paget shrugged. "In a family, it's hard to keep them separate: what the parent does, or doesn't do, invariably affects the child. That's why Mary was right to give up Carlo. For whatever reason."

"Have you thought of telling him?"

"A thousand times. And the answer I keep coming up with is 'not unless I have to.'"

Terri hesitated. "He's not a frightened seven-year-old anymore. He's a different boy."

Paget considered that. "How different, I wonder. Most kids, when they learn some hard truth about a parent, make their peace with it in private. That's a bit easier than learning in the full glare of publicity that your mother—who's already charged with murder—obstructed justice fifteen years before, was morally implicated in the killing of a government witness, and went hand in hand with your father to lie about it to the United States Senate." Paget shook his head. "What would your mother do with *that* one?"

Terri gazed at the floor. "I don't know, Chris. I really don't."

She sounded tired, distant. "I'm sorry," Paget said quietly. "I know how disappointed you must be."

"In what?"

"In me." Paget found it painful to say more. "Look, I'll take you off the case, help you find another job—"

"*No.*" Terri stood. "You just don't get it, do you?"

Paget stared at her. "Get what?"

"You said I was your friend. All right, I get to *care* about you as a friend." Her eyes were alive again. "You're a much better person than you allow yourself to believe, so this hurts me that much more. But that's all you're seeing, damn it. *I'm* not fifteen."

Paget watched her face, unsure of what to do. "You owe me nothing, Terri. I chose *you* as a friend. You didn't choose me."

The smallest smile appeared at the corner of her mouth. "Sometimes," she said, "you really *are* hopeless."

When the telephone rang, Paget was still looking at her.

"Mary Carelli," the receptionist said, "to see you."

For a moment longer, Paget gazed at Terri. "Send her in," he answered.

* * *

When Mary entered, turning to Terri with open curiosity, Paget realized that the two had never met.

It was strange to see them facing each other: Mary nearly a half foot taller, with her air of sophistication and command; Terri, still young, with that look of level intelligence, of seeing things clearly. They seemed very different.

Terri extended her hand. "I'm Terri Peralta," she said. She did not smile; it was no doubt difficult, Paget thought, to first encounter a client within moments of learning that she was amoral, a gifted liar, and, quite possibly, some form of murderer. Add that Mary was Paget's ex-lover and the less than stellar mother of a teenage boy whom Terri seemed to like, and Terri's poker face was an achievement.

"Yes, of course." Smiling slightly, Mary gave Terri a quick once-over, which Paget thought less than polite. "Chris, as is so often the case, seems to have forgotten his manners. Including any explanation of why it was so urgent to see me."

"Now that you're here," Terri answered, "I'm sure that Chris will make it up to you."

Terri's tone, cool and undeferential, transformed her from Paget's associate into a woman with thoughts of her own. It seemed to bring Mary up short.

She turned to Paget, as if to dismiss Terri from the room. "Are the two of you through?" she asked him. "If not, I can wait outside."

Beneath the polite inquiry, Mary's message was clear: Whatever Paget had in mind, she did not wish to discuss it in front of Terri. "Oh, no," Paget said casually. "We're ready to meet with you now."

For an instant, Mary looked off balance. "Perhaps," she said, "it would be better if we talked alone."

Paget took his time. "I have no secrets from Terri," he answered. "And neither do you."

Mary stared at him. "What do you mean, precisely?"

"That as long as she works on this case, and whatever it turns out to involve, Terri will know everything."

Something new crossed Mary's face, doubt and a trace of humiliation. How much does she know? the expression asked. Turning to Terri, she said, "Chris must have great confidence in you."

Terri nodded. "*He* can, so *you* can. But I have things I can be doing." She turned to Paget. "Think you can handle this alone?"

Paget felt himself smile. "I think so." He paused, then added, "Thanks for your help."

Mary looked from Paget to Terri and back again.

"Sure," Terri said easily. She went to the door, gave Paget a final glance, and left.

Mary watched the door close. Then, as if to dispel her own tension, she said lightly, "There's something a little proprietary in how she looks at you, don't you think?"

"Something a little human. I'm trying to get used to that."

Mary continued, as if impervious to his tone. "I'd guess she has a crush on you, actually. But then I'm sure that even the mailroom boy pines for you hopelessly—"

"Is this your idea of diversionary patter?" Paget interrupted. "Because if you're auditioning for *Private Lives*, I wouldn't expect a long-term contract."

She stopped abruptly, sat down. "All right," she said quietly. "What's wrong?"

"Why don't *you* tell *me*? For once."

Mary turned to the window. Waves of rain hit the glass, a drumbeat of sound. Her tone was subdued. "Do I get a clue?"

"Just one. Think of something a client with any intelligence would tell her lawyer." Paget's voice grew softer yet. "Or something a mother with any decency would tell a father."

Mary could not seem to turn from the window. "They found a tape."

"Yes."

She leaned back in the chair. "Where?"

"At Ransom's apartment."

Mary's eyes shut. "What, exactly, is on it?"

"It's *your* tape, Mary."

She shook her head. "It's been five years. I was in somewhat of a state."

"So was I, listening to it."

"Please, Chris."

"All right. It begins with your dream, in the cathedral of St. Germain-des-Prés." Paget paused. "It ends with your perjury before the Senate."

She expelled a short breath, eyes still closed. "I never meant you to hear that."

"Why? Did you think I'd forgotten?"

She shook her head. "The dream."

"It enhanced your image. Really, I was pleased to discover that your subconscious believes in sin."

Mary swallowed. In a trembling voice, she said, "And your associate knows all this."

"You have an odd sense of priorities. The *district attorney* knows all this." Paget's voice went cold. "They're issuing an arrest warrant."

Slowly, Mary nodded. Her eyes remained shut.

Paget leaned forward. "If I retained any sense of humor about this, I'd say we were having a crisis of confidence."

"I'm sorry." Her voice was soft. "I truly am."

"So am I. Particularly because there seems to be a second tape out there, one that is no doubt worse for me."

"Yes," she answered dully. "Far worse."

"Would you mind looking at me while you admit to screwing me and, potentially, our son? After all, they say that the eyes are the windows of the soul."

Mary turned and opened her eyes. It was a look more naked than he had seen that night in Washington. The night when he had found out who and what she really was.

"What would you like from me?" she asked.

"Some approximation of the truth. Because if *you* lie now, *I* walk— no matter what."

She stared at him, silent.

"Tell me about Steinhardt," he demanded.

"I saw him once. Five years ago, for two hours. I never went back."

"Why not?"

"Perhaps it was like confession: tell it once, and it's over." She gave a small shrug. "There was something haunting about it—him, the room, the tape. Talking about it at all." She paused. "You know how Indians used to believe that a photograph would steal your soul? When I left, that's how I felt about those two hours."

"Did you stop having the dream?"

Mary's face hardened. "That," she said, "is none of your concern."

Paget watched her. "Why are there *two* tapes?"

"Because I was there so long. As I recall, he had to change tapes."

"What's on the second tape?"

Mary shook her head. "Some of what I said is *my* property, as *all* of it was meant to be until Mark Ransom started pawing it. I don't feel the need to discuss it with you, and I won't."

"There is, I assume, more about the Lasko case."

"Nothing that should make *my* situation any worse—I'd already confessed to perjury. To the extent that it concerns you, the missing tape tells what you knew." She paused, adding quietly, "It also concerns the circumstances of Carlo's adoption, as it were."

Paget appraised her. "Where's the second tape?"

"I don't know." She turned away. "For your sake, and for Carlo's, I hope they never find it."

"Ransom didn't say?"

Mary hesitated, as if deep in thought. "No. He didn't say."

Paget waited until she looked at him. Quietly, he asked, "Did you murder him?"

Mary turned back to him, composed. "He tried to abuse me," she said coolly. "I executed him."

Paget could think of nothing to say. At length, he asked, "Why did Ransom call you? The truth, this time."

She nodded. "To tell me he had the tape."

"Your tape, or the tape of Laura Chase?"

"Both." She paused. "He made it clear that his interests were both professional and personal."

"How so?"

"Professionally, he wanted to use the Laura Chase tape to promote his book." She looked down. "Personally, he felt we should have a 'private interview' about my past."

"Was he more explicit?"

"He didn't have to be." Her eyes raised. "His tone of voice was worse than anything he could have said."

Paget paused. "What did he say about the tape itself? Your tape, that is."

"He described what was on it—in detail. To leave me in no doubt he had it."

"Did you ask him to bring the tape to San Francisco?"

Her eyes filled with anger. "Yes."

"But he didn't?"

She stared at him. "It seems to me," she said coldly, "that you and your friends at the D.A.'s office just finished listening to a tape. I suppose my good friend Mark just forgot to bring it out."

"But he did remember to bring the Laura Chase tape."

"Of course." Her voice was edged with contempt. "As I told Inspector Monk, it seemed to excite him."

Paget watched her face. "Why San Francisco?" he asked.

"He told me that he had a private interview with another famous woman." Contempt turned to bitterness. "That he wanted us 'back-to-back.' That he wanted to 'compare notes.' "

That, Paget realized, had the ring of truth—but only if one knew about Lindsay Caldwell. "Did he mention any names?"

"No. He was going to be 'discreet,' he said." She paused. "Even on the telephone, I could feel his hands on me. That was why I bought the gun."

"So you lied to Monk about receiving threatening calls."

"Of course." Mary looked pensive. "If I had told him the truth—that Ransom was blackmailing me—then I'd have a motive for murder, wouldn't I?"

"Not to mention that purchasing the weapon begins to sound more than a bit like premeditation."

Mary shrugged. "Anyhow, they can't prove I got no calls. I'm better off with that than I am with the truth."

Paget smiled faintly. "Getting by with one lie out of six or so leaves something to be desired. Whatever made you think you could go one-on-one with someone like Charles Monk and come out ahead?"

"I didn't want to look guilty." She gave him a sardonic returning smile. "I suppose my past success had made me overconfident."

"That's unfortunate. The average homicide cop is smarter than the average senator, and much more attentive to detail." He paused. "Just for fun, why don't you tell me exactly what *did* happen in that room."

Mary searched his face. "Does it matter?"

"What do you mean?"

"The tape of Monk questioning me is admissible, isn't it?"

"Yes."

"Then that's the story I'm stuck with."

"True," Paget said. "And that's unfortunate as well. You didn't tell Monk about Steinhardt. You didn't admit to blackmail. You forgot about closing the blinds. You got the gunshot distance all wrong. You denied leaving the room after Ransom died, which you clearly did. And as far as Liz Shelton is concerned, you have no respect for the rear end of a corpse. Compared to all that, making up nonexistent phone calls is a stroke of genius."

Mary's gaze was level. "Too bad. Because the essence of what I told them was true."

"Define 'essence.' " Paget's voice went cold. "I can hardly wait."

Mary breathed in again. "Ransom abused me," she said slowly. "And I killed him." She touched her cheek. "If that weren't true, *this* wouldn't have happened. Please, trust me this far."

"What *did* happen?" Paget asked again.

"What I *said* happened. Insert the tape of *me* with that of Laura Chase, add the blackmail that came with it, and what I told Monk is pretty much the truth." Mary paused. "With allowances for shock and a few omissions."

"Like the blinds?"

"Yes. *I* pulled them down."

"Why?"

"Because Ransom asked me to." She looked down. "Things hadn't come to a head."

"And leaving the room?"

Mary folded her hands. "I thought about getting help. Then I figured I hadn't thought quite hard enough."

"About what?"

"About what to say and what to leave out."

"Is that why you delayed in calling—because you were refining your story?"

"It was hard for me to think, that's all. Looking back at it, I really *was* in shock." Her voice lowered. "A lot had been done to me, emotionally and physically, and then I'd killed the man who'd done it."

Paget waited for a moment. "You should know," he said at last, "that they'll take a plea of voluntary manslaughter."

She faced the window again. The clouds had thickened, blocking the view; the rain spattering the window seemed to come from a wall of gray. "And if I don't agree?"

"Then you go on trial. For murder one."

For a long time, Mary was quiet. "What are my chances?" she asked.

Paget hesitated. "It's a tough case," he finally said. "For both sides."

"Why tough for them?"

"They can't get the Steinhardt tape in. Unless, possibly, you take the stand."

"And for us?"

"If you *don't* take the stand, they play the tape of what you said to Monk and then show all the problems with your story. After that, the jury will wonder why they should believe in a woman who's lied to the police and then declined to testify." Paget paused. "Frankly, to the extent that I believe you at all, it's only because Melissa Rappaport and Lindsay Caldwell lend you some credibility. Granted, the jury doesn't have the advantage of knowing you as well as I do, but they probably won't have the advantage of seeing Rappaport or Caldwell, either. I doubt the judge will let the jury hear them."

Mary turned to him. "Which means I have to testify."

"I think so." Paget gazed at her. "More specifically, you have to explain your misstatements to Monk, admit the blackmail you forgot to mention, and then persuade the jury to believe you anyway."

She smiled slightly. "That's all?"

"Not quite. You will also have to admit the Steinhardt tape was damaging, while avoiding any mistakes that would strip you of the psychiatrist-patient privilege and allow Sharpe to play it for a jury. Because if they get to hear you admit lying to the Senate, it's over. And Marnie Sharpe will be looking for any way she can, including tricks as dirty as she can get away with, to make sure that happens."

"Why?"

"Because she's ambitious. As ambitious as you were."

Mary's face turned grim. "Ambitious, perhaps. But she doesn't have nearly enough to lose."

Paget shook his head. "In the middle of the night, when she's alone with her private thoughts, I think Marnie Sharpe has as much to lose as anyone."

"And you, Chris?"

"If that tape comes in, I may have a lot to lose. And so may Carlo." Paget paused. "Which is why McKinley Brooks suggests that I sell you this deal."

Mary considered him. "I plead guilty, and the tape stays buried. Is that the deal?"

"Yes."

"How neat."

"Whatever," Paget said softly, "made you think they wouldn't find it?"

Mary's eyes narrowed. "Because *I* didn't know where it was. And if I didn't tell them about it, the police wouldn't know to look."

"Bad judgment, Mary. As I said, you're losing your touch."

Mary sighed. "All right," she said finally. "What would you do?"

"I won't say. Brooks and Sharpe want me to make a choice for you, and their choice at that. I refuse."

"Despite what you and Carlo have at risk?"

"Despite that. *You* put me here, because you thought I'd play to win. That's the 'essence' of *you*—manipulative and completely without conscience—and I despise you for it. But I won't let the D.A. turn your trick around on me and make me play to lose." Paget shrugged. "Your killing, Mary. Your choice."

She was quiet for a time. "If I go to trial, will you defend me?"

"What about Carlo? After all, he *is* our son."

Mary looked down. "The way I see it," she said slowly, "is that Carlo's mother is either an admitted murderer or a potential perjurer with a chance to be innocent of murder. Which I am." She looked up again. "So the only question is: Will you represent me?"

Paget got up, walked to the window. Again weighed Melissa Rappaport, Lindsay Caldwell, the odds that whatever Mary had done was not premeditated murder. And, finally, thought of Carlo.

He went to the telephone. "I'll call Brooks," he said.

Mary looked relieved. But all she said was, "I'm sure you'll think of something."

Brooks's secretary answered on the second ring. Paget told her who he was, and waited.

"Hello, Christopher," Brooks said. "Long time no speak."

"No deal, either."

Beneath the opening banter, Brooks had sounded tense; now Paget could measure by his silence how little more he relished this trial than Paget himself. "You needn't be precipitous," Brooks said. "Really, I didn't expect you back so soon. If you want more time to think, take it."

"Don't need it. I'm bringing her in for photographs and prints. All I want is a few courtesies."

He could hear Brooks exhale. "All right. Anything else?"

"One suggestion. Keep Ms. Savonarola under control. For both our sakes."

"I read you," Brooks said, and hung up.

Paget turned to Mary.

She looked hopeful, watchful, scared. The look reminded him of the moment before she had testified in the Senate, first pregnant with Carlo, when she had gazed into his face.

He did not need to tell her what was coming: the reporters shouting questions, the flashbulbs popping, the cameras. Nor did he need to hear the voice-over that night, as he and Carlo watched alone:

"This afternoon in San Francisco, television journalist Mary Carelli was charged with the murder of America's most celebrated writer, Mark Ransom."

PART THREE

THE WITNESS

JANUARY 27 – FEBRUARY 10

ONE

FIVE DAYS LATER, Mary Carelli was in court.

Terri and Paget stood next to her, facing Municipal Court Judge Caroline Masters, Terri's former boss at the public defender's office. The occasion, the arraignment of the accused, was the most humdrum grist of the criminal mill. Paget would plead Mary innocent, and Judge Masters would set another meaningless date: the preliminary hearing in municipal court, where all that Marnie Sharpe had to establish was that there was "probable cause" to believe that Mary Carelli had committed a crime, an event as routine as singing the national anthem before a football game.

The arraignment, Terri knew, was likely to be Caroline Masters's first and last appearance in the case; another municipal court judge would likely preside over the preliminary hearing. After the prosecution showed probable cause, the muni court and its judges would have finished their work, and the case would be dispatched to the relative grandeur of the superior court, the forum of higher jurisdiction, to be tried by a superior court judge.

The sole reason Judge Masters had borrowed such an impressive courtroom was that this time the mill was grinding on Mary Carelli, and space was needed for all the media people who wished to watch it happen. The sterile courtroom where Caroline Masters usually processed the minions of muni court—traffic violators, parking scofflaws, and petty disturbers of the urban peace—could barely accommodate the defendants and their sport-coated lawyers; the more spacious courtroom specially assigned for *People v. Carelli* could absorb a greater crowd, and its oak bench, high ceiling, and wood-paneled walls would show well on television. Watching Caroline Masters and knowing her aspirations, Terri was certain that she enjoyed this respite, however fleeting, from processing the dregs of the justice system in a room that looked like public housing.

"How do you plead?" Judge Masters asked.

Paget paused. "Not guilty," he answered calmly.

Judge Masters gazed at the participants, stretching out the moment. At one long table, both dressed in gray, were Marnie Sharpe and a young male assistant D.A., who Terri guessed had been selected for his ability and inexperience, so that Sharpe would have competent help without being challenged by a seasoned homicide prosecutor with ideas of his own; McKinley Brooks was nowhere in sight, for what Terri was certain were reasons of political prudence. At the other table were Paget, Terri, and Mary Carelli, Mary in a simple black dress, Paget dressed with a bit less dash than usual. Even Caroline Masters seemed to have given her appearance some thought: her black robe looked freshly pressed and her straight black hair newly cut, and her gold-and-onyx earrings and red-orange lipstick nicely complemented a deep tan acquired at her time-share in Puerto Vallarta. But as with other things about Caroline, Terri had no idea whom she might have vacationed with or what she might have done; in two years of work, Terri had learned little more about Caroline Masters than that she was quite ambitious and very smart.

It was not, Terri thought now, that Caroline had not been pleasant to her—in her incisive way, she had quickly concluded that Terri had enough talent to make her worth Caroline's time. But the advice she had given had been strictly professional; Caroline, Terri learned, drew a wall around herself. What, if anything, she was protecting, Terri did not know; Caroline acknowledged her passion for privacy only by making it seem impersonal. "The way for a woman to survive," she once told Terri, "is to make men see you as a lawyer. If they see you as a *woman*—someone with fears or a troubled marriage or a lover who's broken your heart—they'll start seeing weakness that they'd never see in a man. It's sad but true." To Terri, the comment seemed too stark, the flip side of some hurt that Terri could not see. Since she had been appointed to the court, Caroline had not changed; Terri would see her come alone to bar functions, nursing one drink carefully, determined to be nothing but a judge. By consensus, Caroline Masters was a good one.

"The defendant," Judge Masters repeated for the record, "has entered a plea of not guilty to the charge of murder." She stopped a moment, allowing the court stenographer to catch up, and then turned again to Paget. "Has the defendant arranged for bond?"

"Yes, Your Honor," Paget answered. "Five hundred thousand, by agreement with the district attorney."

Judge Masters nodded. "In that case, Mr. Paget, we are required by statute to set the preliminary hearing within thirty days. Do you wish to waive the ten-day period?"

It was, Terri knew, the standard inquiry. In practice, the preliminary hearing was worthless to the defense; by waiving the right to a hearing within ten court days, the defense lawyer typically lost nothing of value, and in exchange gained time to prepare by putting off the setting of a trial itself. From her expression and tone of voice, that was what Caroline Masters expected of Christopher Paget.

"The defendant," Paget answered pleasantly, "chooses not to waive time."

For the first time, Judge Masters registered surprise, her raised eyebrows making her thin face seem longer, her expression more intent. At the prosecution table, Marnie Sharpe had turned to look at Paget.

"Might I inquire," Judge Masters said to Paget, "as to why you want the prelim so promptly? As you may know, our docket is stacked up like planes at the airport. If you're going to discommode the court, it ought at least to serve your client's interests. It's not apparent to me, Mr. Paget, that this does."

Already on edge, Terri began to lose hope. The question was vintage Masters; it was Caroline's habit to decide what lawyers should do, and lawyers who did otherwise affronted her sense of strategy. But that she was so direct in saying so told Terri that Paget was not among those defense counsel who, by virtue of their experience in murder prosecutions, might get some slack from Caroline Masters. Sharpe, who had shown a moment's surprise and annoyance, now looked pleased.

Tense, Terri watched Paget frame his answer. But Paget seemed unaffected; perhaps only Terri could tell how uncertain he was that he could draw Judge Masters into a plan that had little precedent.

"There are several reasons," Paget responded. "But one, I think, should suffice. My client is a television journalist. She does *not* make her living in the state, but in New York and around the world. Yet at the insistence of the district attorney's office, in the person of Ms. Sharpe, Ms. Carelli is not allowed to leave the state until the case is over." He paused. "Apparently, Ms. Sharpe is concerned that Ms. Carelli is going to escape justice. In truth, all Ms. Carelli wants to do is escape Ms. Sharpe's misguided charges. But if what Ms. Sharpe requires for Ms. Carelli to resume her life is to get this trial over with, that's what Ms. Carelli wants—just as quickly as these charges warrant." Turning to Sharpe, Paget inquired amiably, "I assume, Ms. Sharpe, that you're prepared to show probable cause within the statutory period."

Caroline Masters did not appear sympathetic; she did not yet see, Terri realized, what Paget was about to do. As for Sharpe, she was openly annoyed.

"Of course," she told Paget with asperity, and then turned to the judge. "If it would make Mr. Paget happy, the People could show probable cause by the close of business today."

Judge Masters gave her a curious look. "That won't be necessary," she said. "Just as I wonder if it's necessary to keep Ms. Carelli on quite so short a tether."

"*We* think so." Quickly, Sharpe sought the cover of her office, making her judgment institutional. "Mary Carelli has considerable resources, and the charges pending, in our view, make her a serious flight risk." Sharpe turned to Paget and Mary, speaking with a certain bite. "The court will remember, as will Ms. Carelli and Mr. Paget, the case of William Lasko. After Mr. Lasko's conviction, with his appeal pending, he fled to Costa Rica. It took several years for the United States government—with all its legal and diplomatic resources—to secure Mr. Lasko's return. Where the district attorney has not insisted on prohibitive bail, the least we can do is not facilitate that kind of risk." She turned again to the judge. "We therefore join Mr. Paget in requesting the promptest prelim possible."

Terri knew that the gratuitous reference to the Lasko case, and therefore to the tapes, was meant to put Paget on edge. But his face showed nothing. "We appreciate Ms. Sharpe's endorsement," he responded pleasantly, "if not her analogy to William Lasko. And for the record, Ms. Carelli prefers Bolivia."

Sharpe stared at him; for the first time, there was laughter from the press. Caroline Masters raised her gavel with a look of annoyance, signaling her intent to run a tight courtroom, and the noise subsided.

"All right," she said crisply. "We'll need an estimate on time. How long, Ms. Sharpe, will you require to show probable cause?"

The usual prelim, Terri knew, consisted of a couple of witnesses and lasted one to two hours. For an important homicide case, it might run on for the morning; for someone as careful as Marnie Sharpe, it might extend to midafternoon.

"One day," Sharpe responded. "Max."

"All right." Judge Masters turned to her courtroom deputy, Charlie McWhorter, a paunchy factotum who seemed to predate the courtroom and, perhaps, the court itself. "Charlie, find out from Department 20 when they can hear this."

"Pardon me, Your Honor." Paget stepped forward. "Might I be heard on the question of time?"

This time, Masters showed genuine surprise. As she paused before answering, Terri watched the judge begin to wonder where Paget might be heading. "The prelim is the D.A.'s show," she said flatly. "Were you intending to cross-examine?"

"What we're intending," Paget answered, "is to challenge the D.A.'s entire case."

Sharpe spun to look at him; Terri heard another, deeper murmur from the press. There was no laughter at all.

The judge's aquiline features had rearranged themselves into a stare of incredulity. "You intend to challenge probable cause?"

Paget nodded. "Specifically, we intend to *refute* probable cause and to ask this court to dismiss all charges against Mary Carelli."

In the silence, a reporter murmured, "Jesus Christ!" There was a babel of sound. Paget glanced at Terri, as if to say: It's all right, and then Judge Masters's gavel cracked like a whip.

"How long," she asked in hostile tones, "do you expect that process to take?"

"Two weeks," Paget responded blandly. "Give or take a day."

"*Your Honor,*" Sharpe cut in angrily, and then Judge Masters waved her silent; to Terri, the gesture said: I'll take care of this myself. Terri wished she did not have to watch.

"This is unheard of," the judge snapped at Paget. "And two weeks' cross-examination is absurd."

With whatever effort, Paget looked unruffled. "Not just cross-examination, Your Honor. We intend to challenge the admissibility of certain prosecution evidence; to put Ms. Carelli on the stand; to put on other witnesses and evidence; and to proffer the testimony of at least two further witnesses in closed sessions in the chambers of the court itself." Paget turned to Sharpe. "And now that Ms. Sharpe knows our plans, I expect she'll want a bit more than one day. Our two-week estimate includes several days for the prosecution."

For the first time, Masters's look of irritation betrayed a certain interest. "As I said, Mr. Paget, I've never seen this done. The role of a preliminary hearing is *not* to replace a trial—even if the prosecution loses for lack of probable cause, they can refile if they find more evidence. Nor does the defense have an automatic right to put on its case in advance of trial."

Paget nodded. "That's correct, Your Honor, as a general matter. But my understanding of the law is that at a preliminary hearing, the defense *is* entitled to establish an affirmative defense. Self-defense is an affirmative defense to murder, and preventing rape is a form of self-defense."

Caroline Masters examined him for a while, suspended between annoyance and intellectual fascination, and then permitted herself a thin smile. "That's also *my* understanding of the law. Which may or may not be terribly fortunate for you. Seeing that you propose to give Ms. Sharpe a preview of the entire case."

Paget smiled back. "If I'm right, Your Honor, a preview is all that Ms. Sharpe will ever get."

Masters looked dubious. "There's a big difference between 'probable cause' and 'reasonable doubt.' In my experience, the D.A. *never* blows 'probable cause.' It's hardly a daunting standard."

"Daunting enough," Paget answered, "if the D.A. doesn't have it."

"I would like to be heard," Sharpe demanded. When Terri turned, she saw that Sharpe had grasped the table with both hands. "Mr. Paget's ten-day ploy has now become transparent. He means to rush the prosecution into a minitrial before the case is ready."

"And you bit, Counselor, didn't you?" Masters's tone was dry. "Do you still think Ms. Carelli's such a flight risk, or are you willing to loosen her bonds?"

Sharpe shook her head. "The People will not change their position on flight. We *will* be ready within the ten-day period, and simply ask that the prelim be set at the end of that period."

"Very well." Turning back to Paget, Masters used her most ironic tone. "Is there anything else, Counselor?"

"Just one more thing, Your Honor. The matter of Court TV." Paget paused. "I've had several discussions with their representatives, the short of which is that they very much want to televise all public sessions of the prelim. On behalf of Ms. Carelli, I request that they be allowed to do so." Glancing over at Sharpe, Paget added, "The prosecution purports to bring these charges on behalf of 'the People.' We believe that 'the People' should be allowed to watch."

Masters was silent for a moment, examining Paget with an opaque expression, and then looked to Sharpe. "Ms. Sharpe," she asked, "have you some thoughts on this?"

"Yes," Sharpe answered succinctly. "This trick is worse than the last. Having invented an unnecessary hearing on the question of probable cause, Mr. Paget now proposes to use it to generate so much prejudicial publicity that it will be impossible to ever select a jury once we *do* prove probable cause. The People are opposed."

"Mr. Paget?"

"My reaction is that having invented an unnecessary charge of murder, Ms. Sharpe now proposes to hide it." Paget paused. "The primary concern regarding pretrial publicity is the *defendant's* right to a fair trial. Ms. Carelli believes that fairness is best served by full disclosure." Once more, Paget looked at Sharpe. "Indeed, listening to Ms. Sharpe, I'm reminded of Justice Cardozo's dictum that 'sunlight is the best disinfectant.' "

When Sharpe began to retort, the judge cut her off. "Enough, both of you. I think I understand the argument. I will say to Ms. Sharpe, without prejudging what should be done here, that a defense request on this issue is entitled to great weight." Masters turned again to her deputy. "Now I really would like to see the calendar."

McWhorter brought a bound logbook to the bench. Masters motioned him closer. Bending over the logbook, they murmured to each other. Then Masters turned to McWhorter, said a few final words; he nodded and then retreated to his desk at the side of the courtroom, looking bemused.

Caroline Masters surveyed the courtroom. To Terri, she seemed to sit straighter, look even more like a judge. "All right," she announced. "The preliminary hearing will begin on February 10 and will continue five days a week until concluded." She paused, looking from Paget to Sharpe. "Generally, this would go to Department 20. But it's my current intention to delegate my normal caseload to a judge pro tem and to handle the prelim myself."

With that, Terri knew, Paget had achieved what he wanted. "Thank you, Your Honor," he said.

Masters nodded to each side. "Mr. Paget, Ms. Sharpe. See you in two weeks. And thank *you* for this morning's entertainment."

"All rise," the deputy called out. As the courtroom stood, Caroline Masters walked from the bench.

In the eruption of sound, Terri felt the release of tension. Mary uttered her first words in an hour. "Congratulations," she murmured to Paget. "For a single father, you're remarkably well prepared."

"Congratulate Terri," he answered coolly. "The reason I'm so well prepared is that after two straight nights of research, she knows more about preliminary hearings than God *or* Marnie Sharpe."

Mary turned to her. After a moment, she said, "Thank you."

Terri nodded. "You're welcome," she said. But Mary had already turned away; Terri stood there, wondering what it was about her that Mary so disliked.

Marnie Sharpe broke into her thoughts.

She had walked briskly up to Paget, reaching him before the press did. "Never," she said, "have I seen someone cut their own throat with such aplomb. At least not since Peter Sellers stopped playing Inspector Clouseau."

"Peter Sellers is dead." Paget smiled. "That's the wrong joke, Marnie, from the wrong woman, about the wrong movie. The film I had in mind was called *Les Misérables*. You know, the one where a maniacal policeman pursues the innocent for twenty years." He paused, adding lightly, *"This* film, at least, promises to be shorter."

When Sharpe turned and walked away, Terri knew that Paget's nonchalance had only fed her anger. Which was, against Terri's better judgment, precisely what Christopher Paget had set out to do.

Christopher Paget's sailboat knifed the water.

Terri watched him. She knew nothing about sailing or the boat itself, a trim twenty-footer. But Paget knew what he was doing; slim and alert, he gazed intently at the water ahead, weight shifting easily with the waves. Johnny Moore, who had clearly done this before, helped with the sails. Terri leaned back against the inside of the boat; it sliced the bay at a forty-five-degree angle, tilting her forward. She looked out at Angel Island and the Golden Gate, breeze cool on her face.

It was the morning after Mary's arraignment, and unseasonably warm. The three of them needed to talk. Johnny Moore, who hated meetings and liked the outdoors, had told Paget that in this weather he preferred to meet in the middle of San Francisco Bay; when Paget had called to ask her about it, Terri volunteered to pack sandwiches. "That clinches it," Paget said, and asked what she wanted to drink. The only person who did not like Johnny's plan was Richie.

"What kind of job is this?" he had demanded as she pulled out blue jeans and a sweater.

"The kind that supports us," Terri had answered. Then she had dressed Elena and driven her to day care, Richie's nameless irritation trailing after her.

After an hour or so, they docked at Angel Island. Wooded and green in winter, the hilly island rose above them and curled around the waterfront. The only sound was the wind and the cries of gulls; behind them, more gulls walked stiffly down the dock, searching for scraps of food. They sat hunched inside the sailboat, looking out at the terraced hillsides of Sausalito and, beyond that and to their left, the distant skyline of the city, white and sparkling. Paget and Terri drank mineral water; Johnny sipped at a long-necked bottle of Beck's beer, looking contented in the sun.

"This is better," he said. "I feel mummified in offices. Especially yours."

Paget shrugged. "My view is nice."

"I suppose. The problem is that the building works me over. I step inside, start breathing air that's been filtered by God knows how many machines, and then surrender to an elevator that's run by remote control instead of by a person. By the time I've risen twenty floors, I've given up all control over my destiny, and the only reminder of normal life is when I look about a quarter mile down through your window, and I can't even open that. I feel like a fish in an aquarium."

Paget turned to Terri. "Remind me," he told her, "to look for space in a trailer park. Something human scale, for Johnny's sake."

There was an unwonted edge in Paget's voice; Terri decided the moment needed some lightness. "I like it this way," she answered. "You provide a decent office, and Johnny takes me sailing. Between the two of you, you're almost satisfactory."

Moore smiled at her fondly. "That's my most fervent endorsement," he said, "since my ex-wife passed up our anniversary dinner for an evening of group therapy. And to think that all I needed to make her happy was to bring Chris along."

They stopped talking for a moment, gazing out at the city, each with their own thoughts.

"Would someone please tell me," Moore inquired at last, "why you two are challenging probable cause? That's like standing in front of a bullet and asking it to stop."

As Paget leaned back, squinting slightly, Terri could read how uncertain he still was. He looked not at Moore but at the city.

"This case," he said, "is going south. I want to try and end it before it crosses the border. The prelim is our best chance."

Moore regarded him. "You don't want them to find the second tape."

"That's very much part of it," Paget answered. "Do you have any idea where it could be?"

"No. But even the police have had no luck—it's like dear Mark mislaid it." Moore paused. "Am I correct in understanding that this tape is worse for you than her?"

Paget shrugged. "Aside from whatever it says about me, and whatever it might do to Carlo, I have the strange feeling that it would do Mary no good at all. In spite of what she says."

Terri watched Moore hesitate, take in how difficult Paget must find this conversation. "I wouldn't think worse of you, Chris, if you *were* just looking out for yourself and Carlo. She's put you in a terrible place, and long ago."

Paget's eyes narrowed further. "But *I'd* feel worse. As I did then, lying to serve my own interests, as well as Mary's. It surely has come back to haunt us all."

It's haunted *you*, Terri thought, all along. A single lie, for better reasons than you can believe of yourself, changed the course of your life.

"Ah, well," Paget said. "The problem now is to deal with it. Whatever I have at stake, our client is Mary Carelli."

Moore appraised him. Finally, he asked, "You still don't believe her, do you?"

"No. She's hiding something from me. But I don't know what, or why, and there's no point in even asking. I just don't want Sharpe to find whatever it is."

"But do you really think there's any chance to beat Sharpe at the prelim?"

"After the arraignment, yes. *Some* kind of chance."

Moore pulled on his beer, plainly skeptical. "Because you sucked Sharpe into an early prelim?"

Paget nodded. "That, and Caroline Masters. I counted on her being intrigued enough, and ambitious enough, to handle the prelim herself. It was obvious that she'd prefer doing this to cases of sidewalk spitting. What was less obvious—but I think very much on her mind—was that two weeks on television could shoot her up the judicial ladder." Paget paused. "Which, although I was far too circumspect to even hint at it, was precisely what I offered her."

"But why would you *want* her?" Moore asked. "In my observation, the woman's a real piece of work. Piss her off, and what she'll offer *you* is two weeks in the eighth circle of hell, and on television at that. I can see the promos now—'Watch Christopher Paget, turning on a spit.'"

Inwardly, Terri winced; perhaps better than Moore, she could feel the pressure of a televised hearing bearing down on Paget. But Moore was too honest and professional to withhold his doubts for the sake of tact. Paget turned to Moore with an expression of weary patience. "Why did I want her? Because Terri told me I should. Does that make you feel better?"

"That makes me feel a *little* better." Moore looked over at Terri. "Please, reassure me."

Terri hesitated; inadvertently, Moore and Paget had reminded her how much was riding on her judgment of Caroline Masters, and how much Paget had begun to trust her. "I used to work for her," Terri said at length. "The first thing you notice about Caroline is that she has immense self-confidence, and an overwhelming—and generally justified—belief in her own intelligence. She's smart enough to see where Chris is going, and one of the few judges with guts enough to throw this out. Assuming that she *buys* where Chris is going. Which she's more likely to than most."

Moore looked curious. "Why is that?"

The wind shifted, rippling Terri's hair. She leaned back, gazing at a sailboat that cut across her line of vision. "Because like any judge," she answered, "Caroline is a real person, with real opinions. Her personal life is an enigma, but her personal *beliefs* aren't: if you'd taken off her robe and introduced her to Mark Ransom, she'd have told him to go fuck himself. And she used to be a defense lawyer. You can make yourself a judge—and Caroline's a good one—but you can't make yourself a whole different person."

Moore nodded. "But you can," he ventured, "make yourself a *Superior* Court judge."

"Or, even better, an *appellate* judge." Terri paused. "Everyone at the P.D.'s office knew *that* was Caroline's goal. At some point, the politics of letting Mary off are going to cross her mind. Depending, of course, on how Mary looks on the stand. And, Chris tells me, on the publicity Mary intends to generate."

Moore frowned again. "Before we leave Judge Masters's more human qualities, there's something else about her." Moore glanced over at Terri. "Perhaps it's just that she's so determined to be in charge, and therefore a sexist reaction on my part, but I've the funny sense that Judge Masters may not like men much. Of which variety our friend Christopher is indubitably one."

"And so was Mark Ransom." Terri paused, intent on showing Johnny that at least they had thought this through. "Chris and I parsed this until, as he put it, we felt like a couple of soothsayers reading the entrails of a goat. Because she's a woman who's new on the bench, Caroline is very sensitive on the issue of bias, both other people's and her own. She strives not only to *be* fair but to *look* fair. What I can't tell you is how that cuts. Will she bend over backward not to show favoritism to the female defendant, or to the female prosecutor? It's probably a wash.

"Anyhow, I'm not sure that Chris and Caroline won't have better chemistry than Caroline and Marnie Sharpe. Caroline likes to be on the cutting edge of the law, and she admires creativity almost as much as she does intellect." Terri smiled over at Paget. "For sheer creativity, what Chris did yesterday is hard to beat. In her own way, Caroline seemed almost grateful."

Moore pondered that. "You seem to have put Judge Masters through everything but a Rorschach test."

"It's the trial lawyer's favorite game," Paget observed. "Psychoanalyzing the judge. I've been wrong so many times that I figured it was Terri's turn."

Moore studied him. "Now that you have Caroline Masters, you must also have a plan to impress her."

Annoyance crossed Paget's face; it was a sign, Terri knew, of how worried he was. "Eat your sandwich," Paget answered, "while I try to figure out some way to keep your excitement under control."

For a while, they fell quiet. Terri sat between Paget and Johnny, eating her lunch, content. The water lapped at the boat. In the distance, the city looked like a dream.

"It would be a lovely world," Moore observed at length, "if life were as gentle as this."

Paget nodded, silent. For an instant, Terri imagined she read his thoughts: I hope Carlo's will be. Idly, he tore the crust of his sandwich into bread crumbs, lobbed a couple to the sea gulls. Finally, he said, "At least let's try to make the world safe for Mary Carelli, shall we?"

Moore turned to Paget, face troubled again. "Let's hear it, then."

"To start, our defense is an evidentiary nightmare." Paget leaned back again. "We all know what rings true about Mary's story—something between Mark Ransom and women was very badly wrong. That's what this whole obsession with Laura Chase suggests and what, in their different ways, Melissa Rappaport and Lindsay Caldwell made clear to Terri. To me, they help make Mary's version of Ransom credible. The problem is that—as the law now stands—Judge Masters isn't likely to let them testify before the jury." Paget paused. "If that's true, then what happened to Rappaport and Caldwell will be like the proverbial tree falling in the woods: in the jury room, Rappaport and Caldwell won't exist."

Moore thought for a moment. "But they'll exist for Caroline Masters."

"One hopes." Paget tossed another bread crumb, watched a gull scoop down to skim it off the water. "If Terri can persuade them, we ask Rappaport and Caldwell to tell their stories. Sharpe will insist that the judge hear them first in chambers, so that she can argue that their testimony should be excluded. Should Judge Masters decide against us, neither woman will have to face the ordeal of public testimony. But while the judge may erase them from the hearing, there's no way that she can erase them from her mind. And it's Masters who decides whether this case goes to trial."

Moore examined him. "You're going to need more than that."

"I know, I know, but it's at least a start." Paget paused again. "Even the smartest of judges likes to appear evenhanded. If Masters turns us down on Rappaport and Caldwell, we'll ask her to split the baby. Specifically, to rule that Mary's tape is inadmissible, and to order that any misuse of the information therein will result in the dismissal of the case. And if *that* doesn't work, there's the tape of Laura Chase. I don't want to reveal it now, if for no other reason than because it would look so gratuitous. But in chambers I'll insist that the Laura Chase tape is at least as relevant as Mary's tape—given that it's part of Mark Ransom's sexual pathology—and ask that it be played in open court. The Colt family notwithstanding."

Moore gave a low whistle. "All that," he said, "would make Sharpe *very* angry."

"Yes. I'm counting on her."

A gull swooped, capturing a bread crumb without breaking the speed of its flight. Moore watched it rise again, as if toward the sun, and then turned to Terri. "I thought the idea was not to engage Sharpe's pride."

"This is *my* call," Paget cut in. "Not Terri's. For whatever reason, Marnie Sharpe disliked me on sight. Perhaps for my own sake, perhaps because she thinks I'm helping Mary rip off the rape issue for her own self-preservation. That means that charming her is hopeless, but it also means that she's carrying around some psychic baggage. My guess is that if I'm careful about how I do it, I can goad her into a mistake." Paget turned to Moore. "The only advantage I have over Marnie is that, smart as she is, I'm some sort of symbol to her. Whereas to me, she's simply a technical problem. Like quantum mechanics."

Moore hesitated. "If goading Sharpe is a positive benefit," he said finally, "then you're off to a flying start. Or so it appeared from the peanut gallery."

Paget seemed to contemplate the whiteness of the city; in the distance, the afternoon sun made its buildings shimmer with light. "I understand that it's risky," he answered. "But we don't have many cards. At the least, we'll find out before trial just how good Sharpe really is. And in a hearing like this, without a jury, my lack of recent practice in trying homicide cases should hurt a little less."

Moore gazed out to the city. "What happens," he asked finally, "if

Judge Masters goes along with you? Suppose she rules 'no probable cause.' Can't the D.A. just dig up more evidence, satisfy probable cause, and take Mary to trial then?"

"It depends. If the prosecutor fails for lack of evidence, they can refile if they come up with new facts. The tape, for example." Paget sipped his mineral water. "But until and unless they do that, Mary walks. Forever."

"You're taking a pretty serious chance, it seems." Moore looked from Paget to Terri and back again. "If this strategy is so inspired, why don't real defense lawyers use it?"

Paget smiled faintly. "Because they know better."

"You make it *sound* good enough."

Paget turned to him. "What it is, Johnny, is a terrible risk; Caroline Masters saw right away how desperate we are, no matter what face I put on it. Masters hit the nail—probable cause is far too easy to make out, and if I lose, we'll have previewed our case so thoroughly that Sharpe will crucify us when it comes to jury time. And on the evidence that now exists, I lose."

Moore seemed to squint. "Am I correct in assuming that the purpose of this little outing is to make me feel the heat?"

"Of course."

"In other words," Moore said slowly, "you need a real live act of rape. Within the next two weeks, no facsimiles accepted."

Paget nodded. "Sometime, somewhere, Ransom has to have crossed the line. The problem is that women don't report these things."

Moore turned to Terri. "Do you agree with that?"

Terri gazed at her feet. "Yes. I do."

"Then all I can do," Moore said, "is try."

For another moment, they were silent. "I'm sorry to be so bald about it," Paget offered in half apology, "but I need to give Judge Masters something to hang her psychic hat on when she's thinking about Rappaport and Caldwell, whose testimony she may never acknowledge and whom the press may never see. If I can, maybe we win. If not, Mary loses."

And you, Terri thought. And, more important to you, Carlo. Once more, she admired Paget's stoicism and felt his fear.

Moore was looking at her. After a time, he asked, "Would you consider going on television?"

Interrupted from thought, Terri felt confused. "To do what?"

"To ask for witnesses." Moore hesitated. "Try as men may, I suppose something like this strikes a chord in women that we simply can't replicate. *You* obviously feel it."

"I still don't follow."

Moore shrugged. "Perhaps it's a bad idea. I just wondered if some appeal for information about Mark Ransom, perhaps on CNN, might scare up a witness. A request for help from women, by a woman lawyer, on behalf of a woman defendant." He glanced over at Paget. "Is that insane?"

Paget, Terri realized, had been looking at her for some moments. "I hadn't thought of it," he said. "It's hard enough to ask something so intimate of someone sitting right in front of you—which Terri's done so well—let alone of an audience of women you can't even see. We'd likely learn nothing, and look desperate in the bargain."

For a moment, both men were silent. Neither looked at Terri.

"If you want me to," Terri finally told them, "I'll do it. God knows we need a break."

TWO

"THAT'S A TRICKY ONE," Elena Arias announced to Carlo Paget.

They sat hunched over a black onyx coffee table in Paget's library, arranging small odd-shaped blocks in a precarious high-rise. The purpose of the game was alternately to place the blocks one upon the other, without causing the edifice to fall. Dressed in jeans and a T-shirt, Carlo sprawled with his long legs stretched on the rug; Elena, pretty in a pink dress, with her hair freshly combed, was on her knees; the pile of blocks they had constructed—a rickety multicolored tower with angles jutting everywhere—violated every rule of aesthetics and, as far as Terri could see, of gravity. Elena, who had just placed a round peg on top of the block beneath it, was delighted with herself. Carlo looked bemused.

"I never lose to five-year-olds," he said in mock frustration. Carlo glanced up at Terri, who sat on the couch sipping wine. "Do you see any way out for me?"

"You're on your own," Terri answered. "I thought you were the house champion."

"For eight years running." Carlo smiled. "But that's against my father, who has the spatial-reasoning capacity of a primitive fern. He didn't prepare me for Elena."

But he had, of course, Terri knew; the pile of blocks was a tribute to Carlo's deftness at selecting moves that would keep Elena in the game, as all the while he acted as if she had forced him to the wall. The tower Carlo and Elena were creating was like a minihistory of Paget's relationship to Carlo; the younger player gaining confidence while the older, groaning and protesting, lost at great length and with great ingenuity. Elena, who played with more daring than sense, had stretched Carlo's gifts to the limit.

"Your mother won't help me," he told Elena.

"She can't help *you*." Elena jabbed her chest. " 'Cause *I'm* her kid."

Carlo raised his hand for silence, signaling his awareness of all that was at risk. With utter gravity, he trained his eyes on the rickety tower. The windows of Paget's library cut the late-afternoon sun into squares of light on the black onyx table and inside the marble fireplace; across one of the squares fell a shadow of a frond from Carlo's palm tree. Carlo's wrist caught the light as he suspended his block over the tower, moving downward with excruciating slowness, block pinched between his thumb and index finger. Terri held her breath.

Slowly, carefully, he placed the block on Elena's peg. The peg leaned one way, the block beneath it another. The tower began to teeter.

With the terrible inevitability of a chain reaction, the blocks crashed in a heap.

Carlo stared at the rubble as if galvanized. "Total devastation," he said to Elena. "I can't believe it."

"But you *tried*." With sudden concern, Elena touched his hand. "I bet you can still beat your daddy. That means you're the *second* champion. Next to me."

Carlo laughed out loud. "Five years old," he told Terri, "and she's already learned condescension."

Terri smiled. "It's not condescension, it's codependency. Elena's taking care of you."

Carlo gave her a look of exaggerated concern. "Are you codependent," he asked, "if you go to a movie that your girlfriend wants to see?"

"Only if the movie's terrible." Terri appraised him. "Does this mean you got Jennifer out of the house?"

"Yeah." Carlo grinned. "Like you said—I went over there a couple of times and sat around and talked with them."

"Was that okay?"

"It was fine." Carlo's face clouded. "Except half the time they wanted to talk about my dad's case. At least that's what they called it—'your dad's case.' "

Terri's eyes flickered to Elena, who was beginning a new tower with a child's unselfconscious concentration. "Jennifer's parents don't know who your mom is?"

Carlo shook his head. "No."

He looked down, silent for a moment. Terri decided to say nothing, just to wait. She sipped her wine.

"The whole thing," Carlo said at last, "makes me feel weird. Like I'm hiding her. Like I'm hiding *out*."

Terri glanced at her daughter. "Elena," she asked, "could you help Chris with the hamburgers? He's all alone on the deck."

Elena considered this. "How do I help him?"

Carlo smiled at her. "Tell him not to cook the hamburgers on high, because it makes them dry inside." He turned to Terri. "It drives me nuts."

Terri looked at Elena. "It sounds like Chris needs help."

"Definitely," Carlo affirmed to the little girl. "Just tell him 'no dry hamburgers.' "

Elena stood straighter, as if affirming the importance of her mission. " 'No dry hamburgers,' " she repeated, and scampered down the hallway.

Carlo grinned after her, clearly pleased at the notion of his father being instructed by an officious five-year-old, aware that Carlo was the source of her message. Terri smiled as well, and then realized with sudden guilt how glad she was that Richie had not come.

It had been awkward at first; Paget's invitation had been for all of them, and what it had finally come down to was that Richie had asked Terri to refuse. Richie didn't feel like it, he said; he'd be bored. Terri could only guess the deeper reasons: that Richie resented her friendship with Paget; that Richie was too proud to spend time with someone he could not impress; that Richie did not care for social settings that he could not control.

In this case, Terri at first had acceded to his wishes, and then their pointlessness had made her angry. The upshot was that Terri had pleaded business reasons to Richie; offered Paget a lame excuse for Richie's absence; and come because she wanted to. Alone, she did not have to fear that Richie would try to solicit Paget as an "investor," or dread the exaggerated politeness on Paget's face as he mentally took Richie's measure and filed him away. But to be ashamed of Richie made her feel guilty; what made her feel better was the chance to talk with Carlo about something that mattered.

"Don't your friends," she asked him, "know who your mother is?"

He shook his head. "Not really. I'm in a new school this year, and she's never around for people to know about." A pained expression crossed his face. "I mean, what do I say? Butt into the middle of some conversation and say, 'Have I told you that Mary Carelli's my mother?' Especially with all this stuff on television, and then the way some people at school talk about her . . . *I'm* not afraid, but I'd only make *them* feel bad."

For a moment, Terri tried to imagine not telling people that Rosa Peralta was *her* mother, and then she saw that what divided her from Carlo was what he could not bring himself to say: that Mary as a mother did not seem real to him, so that claiming her would feel like pretense.

"What *do* your friends say?"

Carlo reflected. "Some people don't say a lot," he answered with irony, "because it's my *dad's* case. Other people feel sorry for her." He paused. "I guess a few think she did it."

"You 'guess'?"

Carlo's handsome features hardened. "One guy on the team said she was probably sucking him off and then Ransom just got out of hand." His eyes narrowed. "You know—like she was going to let him beat her up too, only it got too real for her to like it."

Terri watched his face. "Do you believe that?"

"No." He hesitated. "I don't know her, really. But she just doesn't seem like that to me."

Terri put down her wine. "Like what?" she asked.

Carlo looked away, as if struggling for words. "Like someone who wants to be pushed around, or would even *pretend* to want that." He turned to her. "Look, I know there's stuff I don't know . . ."

What, Terri thought, do I say to that? For a moment all she wanted was to pass the buck to Paget, whose buck it rightfully was, and not make some snap judgment that might hurt both father and son. But that, she concluded, was the coward's way out, and Carlo deserved better—even from her.

"*I* don't know," she answered evenly, "what you know or don't know. But yes, I imagine there are things your mother and father haven't told you."

Carlo's eyes turned stubborn. "I'm not some kid. I'm old enough."

Terri nodded. "I understand, and so does your dad. But what makes you think that he's protecting *you?*"

"Because he always does. Too much, sometimes. It's like he *worries* about me so much."

Terri could imagine too well how a seven-year-old who spoke of killing himself would tear Paget apart; the painstaking years of care when Paget battled the boy's self-hatred; the constant habit of watchfulness, too ingrained for Paget to dispel. Could see perhaps better than Paget that, whatever his lingering wounds, Carlo no longer was that fragile boy and had no conscious memory that he ever had been. And that without this understanding—which Paget would never wish to give him—Carlo might feel weakened by a primal sense of his father's fears for him.

"Do *you*," she asked Carlo, "tell your *dad* everything you do? Or think, or feel?"

Carlo shook his head emphatically. "No."

"Why not?"

Absently, he began putting blocks back in their box; his fingers seemed to know from memory where each piece fit. "Because," he answered, "there's some stuff you don't want anyone to know—especially a parent. I don't know how to explain why something feels private—it just does. Not even 'cause you feel ashamed always, or even embarrassed. It's just *yours*, that's all, and it's important not to talk about it unless it's even more important that someone know."

"But what's the test for when that is?" Terri spoke more quietly. "That's the problem *I've* always had."

Carlo looked up from the blocks. "I don't know. I guess when talking will help you more than hurt you—that is, if you really need to talk. And when the other person is a person who needs to *know* and won't be too hurt by what you say."

Terri gazed at the shadows from the palm tree, falling across the room. "What makes you think," she finally said, "that your father's any different? Suppose he hasn't told you everything he knows, or everything he's afraid of. That doesn't mean that he lacks confidence in you or doesn't think that you're adult. All that may mean is that he's protecting your mother, or even himself. Sometimes, adults need privacy even more than teenagers—they've had a lot more time to do things they're embarrassed about or ashamed of. And as far as your mother goes, it's not your dad's place to talk about her life. Or mine. *She* makes those calls, and we all have to respect that."

Carlo stood, turning to the window, hands in his pockets as he stared out at the palm. The stance was so much like Paget's that Terri wondered, not for the first time, about the line between genetics and simple emulation. Once again, she tried to imagine the seven-year-old boy as Christopher Paget had found him.

Carlo turned to her. To Terri, his face looked suddenly older. "I want to go to the hearing," Carlo said at last. "To be with them. But I've been afraid to ask."

Surprised, Terri felt she had exceeded her limits, searched for the temporizing question. "What about school?"

"They're my father and mother, and she's on trial for murder. That's a little more important than school." His voice became intent, persuasive. "I wouldn't find out any more by being there than anyone else who's there, and isn't even in this family. But it would mean I'm there for her, instead of hiding out in school. What either of them tells me about their lives is up to them."

Terri watched him, suddenly sure that—at this moment—Christopher Paget would be proud of his son. And, Terri hoped, could also manage to be somewhat proud of himself.

"All you can do," she said simply, "is ask him. Silence isn't fair to either one of you."

Carlo considered that. "He's just so sure he's right, sometimes."

Beneath Carlo's plaint, Terri felt the tension in Paget that was making him seem peremptory, even to her. But she could not tell Carlo about Paget's fears that Sharpe would find the second tape; or the days in which Johnny Moore had not found a single witness; or the nights Paget spent trying to find a way to cross-examine Monk and Shelton; or the mock courtroom session in which Paget had torn Mary's testimony apart until her eyes blazed with anger; or the endless pressure of trying to give interviews that would do more good than harm.

"That's just how it looks," she finally answered. "You know the strain he's under. In a week, we're going to court."

"I know." Carlo shifted from one foot to another. "But this case seems to be changing him."

"How so?"

"He's got a really short fuse with me." Carlo hesitated. "I think part of it is my mother. He never really says anything. But somehow I don't think he's very fair to her. Really, I don't know why he ever wanted to defend her."

How, Terri wondered, to be fair to Christopher Paget and still conceal the facts? It made her appreciate the painful intersection of Paget's lawyering for Mary with his parenting of Carlo, in which the truth could not be spoken. "It's easy to misread your dad—especially when he spends more time looking out for other people than caring how he looks to them." Terri paused. "But there are two things that I'm sure of. The first is that he desperately wants to win this case. The second is that he loves you very much."

"I love him too, and I respect him a lot." Carlo paused, as if to say more, and then chose to end with a throwaway line. "I just don't want it to go to his head."

Terri watched him, realizing that Carlo had said all he cared to say. She decided to join his attempt at levity. "It won't go to his head. Not with Elena deflating him. I can imagine her out on the deck, saying 'No dry hamburgers' like a talking parrot. Your poor father."

Carlo smiled back. "You'd better go save him. I'll clean up the blocks to preserve his sense of order."

When Terri came to the deck, she was surprised to find Elena sitting on Paget's lap, alternately monitoring the hamburgers and gazing out at the bay, blue-gray with failing light.

Standing behind them, Terri decided that the backs of their heads made a nice picture: Elena's straight brown hair next to the copper waves at the edge of Paget's collar. They did not see or hear her.

"What do you do at home?" Paget was asking.

Elena thought. "Play," she announced. "With toys. Sometimes Daddy's there and Mommy's not. On vacation days from school."

"You go to school?"

"Course. Mommy takes me to Explorer Preschool. It's good except for Janie."

Paget turned to her. "What's Janie's problem?"

"She pulls my hair." Elena's voice turned indignant. "The teacher made her take two time-outs the other day. *Two.*"

Paget smiled. "Bad day for Janie."

"Bad day for the *teacher,* you mean. She said she had a headache." Elena paused. "Sometimes Mommy gets headaches. Daddy says she worries too much."

The two of them looked out at the bay. It was past five, and the sun had begun setting behind the Golden Gate; the bay was silver, the sailboats were flecks of white. "What *I* think," Paget said, "is that your mommy works very, very hard. Sometimes people who work hard get headaches."

Elena considered that. "My mommy's not home, always. But Daddy's home."

Paget seemed to reflect. "That's because your mommy works with *me*," he answered, "so she can make money for food and clothes *and* your house. Sometimes that happens in families—one person takes care of everyone else."

Elena looked at the hamburgers. "Mommy cooks dinner too."

"Then maybe sometime you and your dad can cook it for your mom." Paget smiled. "Because your mom is very nice, and both of you are lucky to have her."

"It's true," Terri interrupted, smiling. "I *am* wonderful, and the whole wide world is lucky I was born."

Paget turned, surprised. "I was going to cover that," he said. "But the hamburgers would have turned to carbon."

"Hi, Mommy," Elena said. "Chris says you're nice."

"But I only say that behind her back," Paget told Elena. "It's easier that way."

Although Elena did not understand, she knew that Paget had made a joke and that she was included in the spirit of it. Elena smiled up at her mother, as if she were a third adult. "That's right," she told Terri. "You're nice. It's easier that way."

Terri laughed. "You know what'll be nice, Elena? Dinner. But only if you go to the bathroom first. Better go ask Carlo where it is."

Elena ran back down the hallway, happy to have a question to ask Carlo.

"Thank you," Terri said to Paget.

"For what?"

"For telling Elena that her absentee mom is not so bad."

Paget gazed at her. "Someone else," he said, "should be doing that job."

Terri gazed past him, at the bay.

"What I meant," Paget amended quietly, "is that sometimes it's hard to speak for yourself. Especially in families."

Terri turned to him. "Actually, there was something I wanted to talk to you about. If you have time after dinner, can Carlo watch Elena for a minute?"

"Sure." Paget hesitated. "If it's about going on TV, you don't have to do that. Let Johnny keep digging for a witness. After all, it's *his* job."

Terri paused a moment; the hearing was so much on Paget's mind that, much more than usual, he had begun projecting his thoughts onto others. "TV's okay, really. But this isn't about that."

"Can I ask what it *is* about?"

Terri gave a small, embarrassed shrug. "Carlo," she said.

THREE

"WHEN YOU ANSWER a question," Mary Carelli murmured, "never look at the person who asks it. Gaze directly at the camera." She paused, adding dryly, "That's how the audience knows you're sincere."

Terri nodded. "All right."

Mary raised an eyebrow. "You sound a little dubious."

"It seems artificial, that's all. Now that I'm here, it's difficult for me to imagine talking some other woman out of her home, long distance, and into a courtroom to describe herself being raped. Assuming that Mark Ransom ever did that."

Mary shrugged. "That's why *I'm* here. When it comes to television, or Mark Ransom, I can imagine almost anything."

They sat on an empty soundstage that CNN had borrowed from ABC's San Francisco affiliate, waiting for the interview. In nine days, Johnny Moore had found nothing that would tie Mark Ransom to a sexual assault—no reported incidents or even rumors. The preliminary hearing was five days away.

It was that which had pushed Christopher Paget into letting Terri go on television. Even then he had seemed reluctant; only when she insisted was the interview set.

Involving Mary had been Paget's idea. "You're the lawyer," he said, "but Mary's the supposed victim. Besides, she's famous and does this all the time. For Mary, a touching plea for help will be just another star turn." His voice turned cynical and a little weary. "Just keep her off the 'facts,' for lack of a better name."

"But aren't we assuming," Terri asked, "that her story is basically right? Isn't that the point of looking for another victim?"

Paget had shrugged. "All that *I'm* assuming is that Ransom was a pig. The only question is whether he was this particular kind of pig."

"And whether," Terri answered, "anyone will say so."

Now, sitting next to Mary Carelli, Terri wondered who might watch. She envisioned a lonely woman who had hidden an assault from friends and family, perhaps buried it so deep that it seemed a vague memory she no longer quite believed in, real only in the fear she felt when she walked alone at night, or when she experienced that first unwanted glance from someone she'd misjudged. The woman that Terri imagined would not talk to anyone.

"You look pensive," Mary told her.

Once more, Terri had the sense that Mary was examining her, and with little liking. It put Terri even more on edge. "I was just imagining our audience," she answered. "I mean, would you come forward?"

Mary smiled. "I *did* come forward."

Terri turned to her. "You had no choice," she said simply. "Ransom was dead. If he'd lived, and simply raped you, *then* you'd have had a choice."

Mary glanced around the soundstage—its blank partitions behind them, three chairs, two cameras pointing at them like armed guards. "You don't believe me," she said.

Terri examined her. "I don't *understand* you," she said at last. "So I don't know whether I believe or disbelieve you." She paused, adding softly, "All I know is that it doesn't really matter."

Mary gave a sardonic smile. "Because you're a lawyer? Or because of Chris?"

"Because I'm a lawyer. That's part of who I am." Terri paused, adding pointedly, "Just like being a wife and mother is part of who I am."

"You make it sound like you've signed on for life."

"I signed on for life," Terri answered, "the day I had Elena. In that way, I'm a pretty simple person."

Mary's smile turned skeptical. "How many people have underestimated you, I wonder."

"It depends on the person." Discussing herself, Terri felt an odd detachment. "For some, there was nothing to understand. They had me pegged just right."

Mary looked at her curiously. "If I've touched some nerve," she finally said, "I'm sorry."

"You didn't touch anything. I just want to get this over with."

"You seem as tight as a spring." Mary smiled. "Look at it this way—

it's like going to court, but the questions aren't as intelligent. It should be no problem at all for anyone as smart as Chris thinks *you* are."

Chris again, Terri thought, and then wondered if this cool, detached woman had so distanced herself from her own emotions that she no longer knew what they were. Any sense of Mary Carelli seemed to slip from her grasp; beneath the self-preserved veneer, Terri saw only glimpses—pride, solitude, and, most elusive of all, a hint of wounded puzzlement, as if Mary could not understand why no one understood her. As for Mary's true feelings for Christopher Paget, or for their son, they were hidden from view; Terri felt them only in the sense that they were connected to Mary's resentment of her.

"Did you know," Terri asked, "that Carlo wants to go with you to court?"

Mary's face changed utterly. "Surely Chris won't let him."

"I think he may, and hope he does. Carlo very much wants to. Particularly for your sake."

"He *can't*." Mary's voice turned hard. "He simply can't. Really, I don't want him to hear this."

Terri paused again. "What would be worse for him," she answered, "is for his mother and father to treat him like a child."

"That's not for you to decide." Mary's voice was tight with urgency and anger. "You have no idea what this is all about. You have no idea what *Carlo* is all about. None at all."

Terri stared, startled at the visceral intensity she saw on Mary's face. And then, like a cold finger on her spine, she felt for an instant that Mary Carelli was capable of murder if something pierced to the core of her. But what that core was, Terri could not know.

"At this point," Terri answered softly, "it's really for Chris to decide, isn't it? Whatever you won't or can't say to me, perhaps you should say to him. Assuming, of course, that there's something *else* Chris doesn't know."

Mary hesitated, as if surprised, and then gave Terri a long glance of appraisal. "You're a very perceptive woman, Terri, and a bright lawyer. But this isn't a lawyer's problem, and *I'm* the only woman who owns it. Don't tamper with this, please. I'm asking you not to."

Tamper with *what?* Terri wondered, and then the interviewer came onstage.

A brisk, slender man in his forties, Greg Cook looked like someone who burned calories just by standing around. In quick succession, he reacquainted himself with Mary, was introduced to Terri, and had ushered them back into their chairs, with microphones clipped to their blouses. Terri drifted through it all like an automaton, still suspended in her conversation with Mary.

"We're running this on the nightly news," Cook explained. "You can watch yourselves at seven this evening."

The filming started. After a few preliminaries—introductions, Terri's office telephone number—Cook demanded of Mary, "Why are you here?"

Mary leaned forward, focused on the camera. "Because we believe that what Mark Ransom tried to do to me, he may have done to someone else. If so, I ask them to come forward now, to testify on my behalf."

"How would that help you?"

Mary looked grave. "Because it's a sad fact of life that any woman claiming to be the victim of a sexual assault faces a high threshold of disbelief." She paused, her expression open, candid. "That's all the more true when the woman is charged with murder, and attempted rape is her sole defense."

Cook nodded. "But this, you would agree, is an extraordinary step."

"I would. But what is truly extraordinary is that four out of every five rapes go unreported." Mary's voice quickened, became more urgent. "We believe that hidden behind these statistics—this collective fear that society has too long fostered in *all* women—at least *one* woman may be watching whose life Mark Ransom changed."

To Terri, she seemed too crisp, more political than personal. Behind tortoiseshell glasses, Cook raised his eyebrows. "But—and I speak as a matter of psychology, not morality—why should a woman who is too traumatized to help herself relive that trauma by helping you?"

Exactly, Terri thought. She turned to Mary, as if she were the nameless woman in the audience, fearful and waiting for an answer.

"Because," Mary said calmly, "the issue transcends what happened to me. True, my life and freedom are at stake, as is the public reputation I am fighting to maintain: I'm either a victim and exonerated, or guilty of some degree of murder." Mary paused, as if daunted by her personal abyss. "But the ultimate issue is whether victims everywhere will speak out against rape and thus diminish the number of victims to come. True, I ask for help, and I need it. But it is also true that anyone who helps me offers hope to countless others."

"All surface and calculation," Melissa Rappaport had said of Mary. Perhaps this cut too deep for objectivity, but to Terri, Mary's answers were the slogans of a movement, not simple words of pain.

On impulse, Terri asked, "May I say something?"

Cook and Mary turned, as did the cameras. Cook looked curious, Mary perplexed. Then Cook said, "Surely, Ms. Peralta."

Terri found she could not speak; her few seconds of confusion seemed infinite. "For someone who's been raped," she began at last, "rape is not a cause." Terri paused, searching for words; suddenly it was not hard to look into the camera. "It's deeply personal, and it can make a woman feel cheap, and damaged. We're not talking to 'women' about 'protecting' other women. We're asking a lone woman to remember something she never reported to anyone, something she has tried very hard to stuff somewhere and never think about." Terri paused again, then spoke, her voice softer. "Because after it happened, that was the only way she could think of to protect herself."

At the corner of Terri's vision, Mary's face was cold. Cook seemed surprised. "You seem to be arguing against the purpose of this interview."

Terri gazed down, feeling chastened and exposed. When she looked up again, it was at the camera. "I'm not arguing with anyone," she answered quietly. "I'm not even talking to anyone here. I'm talking to someone I don't know, who may be watching by herself, or with a husband, or with children, or her friend. But no matter whom she's with, she's completely alone. Because *she's* the only one who knows."

"Are you saying that she should *not* come forward?"

"No." Terri inhaled, forcing herself to speak slowly and clearly. "I'm saying that if she *does* come forward, it should be to help herself. Because, as if she were partners with the man who raped her, she's hidden the rape inside her until she's become a different person."

Cook nodded. "You obviously have some empathy with the people you're seeking out."

Turning from the camera, Terri felt cut off from the woman she had imagined. "I was a rape counselor," she told him. "In law school."

Cook gazed at her a moment. Then he said, "Teresa Peralta, Mary Carelli, thank you for appearing on CNN nightly news," and the interview was over.

Mary looked startled, and then composed herself. "Thank you," she said. Terri said nothing.

In the elevator down, Mary finally spoke. "No wonder you were nervous. You have no idea of television, or how to help me."

Terri turned to her. Very softly, she said, "But it didn't happen to you, did it?"

Mary stared at her, as if to respond. Then she said only, "I have a rally at two o'clock. I should change. Please drive me to the hotel."

Now, six hours later, Terri sat with Richie on the couch, watching the news. Elena played nearby with the blocks, which Carlo had given her.

There was a clip of Mary Carelli, addressing a crowd on the steps of the Hall of Justice. Dressed in a simple blouse and skirt, she looked less militant and more a victim; with each applause line, Terri could feel the pressure on McKinley Brooks.

"You are here," Mary said, "because you have chosen to believe in me. For that I feel deep gratitude and great humility. But in the larger sense, you have rallied for every woman who has ever felt the shame and tragedy of rape."

"That's pretty good," Richie remarked. "Universalize it. Make it bigger than she is."

Terri nodded. "It's fine for this. I just don't think it works for soliciting witnesses."

"Earlier today," the voice-over said, "Ms. Carelli and one of her lawyers, Teresa Peralta, made a last-ditch appeal for any woman to come forward who has suffered alleged abuse at the hands of Mark Ransom."

Making her appeal, Mary looked and sounded rational. Her expression was wounded, yet composed. "She's good here too," Richie said.

When the camera shifted to Terri, her own face startled her; she looked tentative, disconcerted, more like a victim than the victim's lawyer. She felt herself flush. Then heard herself say, in a voice less firm than she remembered it, "as if she were partners with the man who raped her, she's hidden the rape inside her until she's become a different person."

When it was over, Terri sat on the couch with her hands folded, half listening to the sound of Elena's play.

"I don't know, Terri," Richie said at last. "I'm not sure that came off like you wanted it to."

He said this in a tone of concern, as if to help her do better next time. Except that Richie knew, as she knew, that next time would never come.

"I did the best I could."

"I know, Ter. I think it's just the wrong pitch, that's all. The woman you imagine sitting there with her husband and kid is going to look around her and decide not to reach for the phone." Richie gave a fatalistic shrug. "You can't really blame her. I think a lot of women get themselves in situations they know they should have avoided. I mean, put yourself in their place."

Terri did not answer. Finally, she said, "I think I'll just play with Elena for a while, check my messages on voice mail. Maybe someone will call."

"Sure." He paused. "What about dinner?"

"I'm kind of tired. Think you could fix macaroni and cheese? Elena would probably help."

"How about ordering pizza? I've got some work to do on the computer."

Terri looked at him. "Just no pepperoni, okay? Elena peels it off."

When the pizza arrived, only Richie's half was pepperoni. There had been no calls on voice mail. "Too bad," Richie said in sympathy. "But I think it really is like I said."

Four hours later, when Terri checked for the seventh time, there had been no messages at all, and Richie was asleep.

Silently, Terri undressed, put on a long T-shirt. She lay next to Richie in their bed, watching the red numbers of the alarm clock mark the minutes she could not sleep.

At one forty-five, she was still awake.

The telephone rang.

Terri started, and then tried to reach over the alarm clock to stop the ringing before Richie awoke.

"Hello."

Terri heard a faint hum, but no voice. Beside her, Richie was stirring. "What the hell . . ."

Terri placed one hand on his shoulder. "Hello," she tried again.

For a moment more, Terri heard the hum, and then a woman asked, "Is this Teresa Peralta?"

Terri felt herself tense. "Yes. It is."

"I thought I recognized your voice." There was a moment's pause. "I'm sorry to call like this. But I couldn't sleep."

"How did you get my home number?"

"I started calling information everywhere in the Bay area." The woman gave a shaky laugh. "If I hadn't gotten Berkeley on my third try, I might have stopped."

"That's all right." Terri hesitated. "Can you tell me who you are?"

"Yes." Another pause. "My name's Marcy Linton."

Terri thought for a moment. "The writer?"

"You've read me?"

"Yes." Terri felt delayed surprise. "In *The New Yorker.*"

"That's very nice." There was a genuine politeness in the voice, as if, in the middle of the night, Marcy Linton was glad that a stranger had read her stories. "And, of course, I watched you on television. It touched me."

"Yes?"

"Yes." A final pause. "You were talking to me."

FOUR

THREE MORNINGS BEFORE the preliminary hearing, Teresa Peralta found herself in a rented Ford Escort with snow tires, steering through a valley in the Rocky Mountains—jagged peaks of black and white, wooded hillsides so steep they seemed to tumble toward the dirt road. To her left, a sheer embankment dropped to a glistening stream, whose gray and silver eddies were broken by logs or branches that had run aground in shallow water and dammed more clumps of driftwood behind them, white with new-fallen snow. The road ahead was covered with ice; in the morning sun, the white terrain was close to blinding.

Terri downshifted. She had not thought to bring sunglasses; she squinted at the road, steering gingerly, tense with the effort of driving for the first time on an ice-slick surface. A frightened deer skittered from the roadside at the sound of tires crunching, the hum of an engine. There was no one in sight.

As she drove, the mountains at the valley's end became higher and closer; it enhanced her sense of smallness and inadequacy. Her sole consolation was that she was learning to recognize those feelings and to fight her way through them. Marcy Linton, Terri was sure, must be even more apprehensive than Terri herself.

Linton was writing a novel, she had explained, in a cabin ten miles west of Aspen owned by her uncles. It was where she had brought Mark Ransom, she said, four years before. On the telephone, she had left it at that.

Twenty minutes farther, with the valley's end looming in her windshield, Terri found the gravel drive.

It wound to the left, down a hill, over a narrow bridge of railroad ties that crossed the stream, and then through more pine trees, until it ended in a circle looping past a wooden shed that housed a new Jeep

Cherokee. By the shed were more trappings of rural life in winter—a mini snowplow, a stack of cordwood covered by a tarpaulin. To the side of the circle, a freshly shoveled stone walkway climbed a gradual hill, to the cabin.

It was two stories of wood and glass, with a stone chimney and an atelier, where, Terri assumed, Marcy Linton wrote. Through the glass front door, a slender woman peered out at Terri.

The woman was dressed for the outdoors—boots, jeans, green sweater—and her long strawberry-blond hair was pulled back. But the heavy clothes made her look too slight; there was something about her that seemed more suited to the city. As the woman stepped outside, Terri saw more clearly her pale skin, probing hazel eyes, and delicate face, pensive and lightly freckled. She was startlingly young.

"I'm Marcy Linton," she said. "I'm glad you could find me."

Her voice was clear but almost whispery. When she extended her hand, it felt fragile, as if Terri were cupping a bird in her palm. "Thank you," Terri answered. "I'm glad you could *call* me."

Linton gazed at her boots, as if checking them for snow. "Have you ever written?" she asked, and then glanced up at Terri. "I know that sounds foolish, and a little vain, but I think most writers survive partly by imagining how others must feel. The way you described my feelings was so perfect that it was like calling someone who already knew."

Terri shook her head. "I've never written—I wouldn't know how to start." She gave Linton a curious look. "I didn't expect you to be so young and to have written so much."

"I'm twenty-eight." Linton tilted her head. "And you?"

"Twenty-nine."

Linton looked off into the distance. After a time, she said, "Whenever I imagined talking about this, it was to a white policeman with the blank, somewhat cruel expression of an Aztec carving." She paused. "I suppose I made him look like Ransom."

Terri appraised her. Linton could put feelings into words, and Terri liked her instinctively. But they were still standing outside, as if lingering on the threshold of Linton's story, more painful than she made it sound.

"Do you have coffee?" Terri asked. "I'm pretty cold."

"Oh, sure." Linton sounded chastened. "Come on in."

The inside was more elaborate than Terri had imagined: a stone floor of odd-shaped pieces; a marble fireplace; high ceilings; an expanse of glass window, which framed the mountains. There were animal skins on the floor, and above the fireplace, the head of an elk stared into space.

Linton followed Terri's eyes. "My uncles kill things," she said. "I can't work in this room."

Terri nodded. "I've never been able to imagine hunting. Or even owning a gun."

Linton gazed at the elk. "Oh, I own a gun now. But not for that."

Terri paused a moment, wondering what next to say. "Do you ski at all?" she asked.

"Not really." Linton did not turn. "I used to come here for the quiet."

To Terri, Linton's voice carried a trace of sadness, perhaps loss. Then Linton shrugged, as if to herself. "Do you like anything in your coffee?"

For an instant, Terri thought of Melissa Rappaport, making coffee as she avoided mention of Mark Ransom. Even here, where Ransom had come but once, Terri felt him as an unnamed presence who had broken the quiet, the reason Marcy Linton had a gun.

"Just black," Terri answered. "Thanks."

Linton disappeared.

Terri sat on a couch behind a heavy oak coffee table. On its lower shelf were two volumes of poetry, a thick book on impressionist painting, and a collection of Stieglitz photographs of Georgia O'Keeffe, which included several nudes. The volumes lent an urban sensibility, the slightest hint of female sensuality, as if to subvert the oppressive maleness of the room itself.

"He liked this room, he told me."

Reentering, Linton spoke in matter-of-fact tones. Her voice had none of Rappaport's pained ironic intellect; it was as if she were relating puzzling scraps at the margins of her memory, looking for clues to what had happened. She held a mug of coffee out to Terri, then sat on a heavy chair across from her.

"So," she asked, "will I have to testify?"

"Only if you want to." Terri hesitated. "We won't make you."

Linton considered that. Finally, she said, "But the only way to help is to be a witness." Her voice was measured and subdued.

"Yes," Terri answered. "I'm afraid so."

Linton nodded, almost to herself; it was as if the silent gesture helped her absorb the truth. "Will it be public?"

"If Judge Masters thinks it's relevant to whether Ransom tried to rape Mary Carelli." Terri hesitated. "And if she's even thinking about throwing out the case, she'll want it public—for her own sake. To keep from getting pilloried as a biased woman judge."

Linton sipped her coffee. "That's a lot of pressure," she said. "On the judge, I mean."

There was something tired in the phrase, as if the thought of too much pressure on anyone made Linton feel enervated. Terri had first encountered Linton's short stories while riffling through *New Yorker*s in the waiting room of her obstetrician: lately, Linton's characters seemed to spend more time deciding whether to open their apartment door than they did on the other side of it. Terri, who admired Linton's sensitivity, found the increasing tentativeness of her people distressing, as if they bled strength from Terri herself. Yet, looking at Linton, Terri felt that whatever inner balance Linton had achieved belonged to *her*, and that Terri had no right to challenge it.

"There's a lot of pressure on everyone involved," Terri said at last. "If you do this, it's got to be for yourself. Because everyone else in that courtroom will have their own agenda, and they're going to play for keeps. Even Chris, my boss." Terri hesitated. "Perhaps Chris most of all."

Linton stared at the floor. "It's hard to know what to do with this."

In these few stark words, Terri felt a deep loneliness. "Do you think," she ventured, "that we can just talk it through?"

Linton looked up at her. "And afterwards, if I don't want to testify?"

"Then it never leaves here." Terri paused. "I just stick it where I stick my own stuff. The things *I* never talk about."

Linton seemed to search Terri's face. Then she said simply, "Let me tell you about it."

Why, Terri wondered, was she herself so much on edge. She took one deep breath, nodded, and continued to sip her coffee, watching Linton over the rim.

"I was twenty-four," Linton began, "and three years out of Barnard. I'd come here to write the novel I'm hoping to write now."

The clipped last sentence, Terri thought, had an undertone of damage. "What is it about?" Terri asked. "Or is that a dumb question?"

"Not dumb, just difficult." Linton looked at her shoes again. "Perhaps I'm a short story writer, not a novelist. Some people just can't do both." Linton glanced up at Terri. "Mark Ransom could, of course."

Terri hesitated. Part of Linton seemed disjointed, shaken beneath the calm. "Did you admire him?" she asked.

"As a novelist, yes. Our sensibilities were totally different, and his politics weren't mine. But page to page, he was a master of narrative and character. His characters weren't slight, at least not his men—he could make them struggle, breathe, quiver with surprise and change for twelve, thirteen hundred pages." Linton shook her head. "We were nothing alike, and I thought there was nothing like him."

"How did you meet?"

"Here, that one time. At a writers' conference." Linton's voice grew quiet. "I timed my arrival in Aspen to coincide with two events—the beginning of my novel and meeting Mark Ransom."

Terri felt puzzled. "Did you expect to spend any time with him?" When Linton looked somehow hurt, Terri added quickly, "What I mean is that someone like Ransom must have had friends here, people competing for his attention, dinner plans in advance."

A quiet pride crossed Linton's face. "I'd already been published in *The New Yorker*. People knew my work." Then, as if to herself, she added softly, "Young writers have no sense of proportion. If they *did*, they'd never write."

Terri tried to imagine Mark Ransom caring about Marcy Linton's delicate fiction; it was like van Gogh being intrigued by Japanese watercolors. Finally, she asked, "Did Mark Ransom know your work?"

"He knew *of* my work." Linton's voice grew softer yet. "Before the conference, John Whitley, my editor at the magazine, called Mark himself. To tell him to 'take care of me.'" Linton looked away. "John is a very nice person. When he later asked if Mark had caught up with me, and I said yes, he looked quite pleased."

Again, Terri thought, a few oblique sentences conveyed much more: the small literary world to which Linton aspired; the naïveté of Linton's benefactor; her desire for approval; her fear of shattered friendships and notoriety had she denounced Mark Ransom as a rapist.

Except for the exotica of Linton's chosen milieu, Linton had limned in a moment the dilemma of any woman raped by a respected man in a small town or university, or after an office party. It made Terri feel small.

"What is it?" Linton asked.

Terry shrugged off her depression. "Sympathy pains, I guess. I had a vision of this benign, white-haired editor, so pleased that Mark had honored his request, and how lonely that must have made you."

"John has black hair and is far too thin to look benign. But yes, I did feel lonely.

"The morning I saw John, my mouth felt swollen, and I still hurt inside." Linton paused, staring down at her lap. "When Ransom did it, I wasn't wet."

Terri realized that she had crossed her arms. Quietly, she asked, "How did it happen?"

Linton nodded slightly; the small gesture seemed irrelevant to Terri's question, as if Linton were reviewing some thought of her own. "I was so vain," she said softly, "to have published at twenty-three. I thought what I did with words was so extraordinary that even Mark Ransom would want to read them."

Like her characters, Terri thought, Marcy Linton was having trouble opening the door. Terri waited, wondering how much of this reticence was the woman herself, how much she owed to Ransom. When Linton said nothing more, Terri asked, "When did you first meet him?"

Linton seemed to be summoning a specific memory. "It was the last night of the conference," she answered. "At the bar of a glitzy hotel called Little Nell, jammed with writers and snow bunnies and slick men in ski clothes. But I found him right away, from the mellow voice and all that red hair. When I introduced myself to Mark, his smile of recognition thrilled me. '*Marcy Linton*,' he said, 'the most famous twenty-three-year-old writer since Sylvia Plath. John Whitley says you'll have even me reading short stories again.' He grinned down at me. '*Short stories*, of all things.' "

Linton looked pensive, as if ashamed at some secret foolishness. "Except when I'm on some sort of literary high, I'm not very confident at social things—I'm more of the quiet observer type, I think. But the instant Mark clasped my hand, it was as if I felt connected to the confidence he gave off: bolder, almost brash.

"Suddenly it seemed right that America's most famous writer was interested in me.

" 'Maybe you don't *have* to read short stories,' I told him. 'I've just started my first novel.' "

" '*Good,*' he answered. 'Short stories are to novels what raisins are to wine—you can either shrivel your characters or let them breathe.' He laughed. 'I don't know what kind of metaphor that is, but it's how I *feel.*'

" 'Well, I'm going to let them breathe,' I answered. 'I just hope they don't get vertigo.' " Linton paused; her persona shifted from an excited twenty-four-year-old to the cautious woman Terri sat with now. "Listening to myself," she said with quiet irony, "I know why I never talked about this. My own bravado is far too painful to remember."

Terri waited, then asked simply, "What happened next?"

Linton touched her wrist, as if tracing a scar. When she spoke again, her voice seemed chastened by some hidden censor. "Mark looked at me for a moment. 'If you've just started,' he told me, 'I suppose I'll have to wait.' He sipped his drink and then, as if a new thought had just struck him, asked, 'Did you bring any pages?'

"God, I thought, he wants to *read* them. I was scared and excited, but more excited than scared. 'I didn't have to bring them,' I said. 'They're here, because *I'm* here. Living in a cabin, off by myself, until I finish.' " Pensive, Linton added softly, "I thought it made me seem more serious about the novel I'd just started. But what it must have told Mark Ransom was that I was available—away from the hotel, with no roommates and no boundaries, eager for him to think well of me."

Beneath the bulk of her sweater, Linton's frame appeared to settle, becoming smaller. "For a moment, as I remember it now, his eyes seemed to glitter. At the time, I thought that this was a moment when one writer recognizes another—older to younger, but members of the same species. Then, very politely, he said, 'I'd be flattered if you'd let me read them.'

"I remember imagining: What if Mark Ransom found a woman writer he admired enough to say so." Linton shook her head. "In the narcissistic way of young people who've been told they have talent but have yet to learn the limits of it, I began to imagine the bright dinner parties, the influential articles in the *Times* and *New York Review,* the great literary friendships that would start with this meeting.

My own celebrity." Her voice, soft and clear, held a trace of self-contempt. "What a fool I was—how romantic, how unlike the people I've come to write about. It humiliates me just to think of it."

"Why?" Terri asked. "Were you supposed to be immune to dreams?"

"Not immune. But clear-eyed. Enough not to invest someone else with the power of my own fantasies."

Terri shook her head. "It's normal to look up to someone older, to want to be like them, or be close to them. It's just that for women, that can present a special problem. Because, in his mind, the man you've started to invest in may already have his fingers on the top button of your blouse."

Linton gazed at Terri. "We're supposed to know that," she said finally. "*You* must have always known that. But somehow I forgot."

"The penalty for forgetting," Terri answered quietly, "shouldn't be rape."

Slowly, Linton shook her head; once more, the gesture seemed to take her inward. "I offered to meet him the next morning, for breakfast. 'Don't worry,' he told me. 'I'd like to explore this country. If you'll be in tomorrow, why don't you let me find you?' He made it sound like an adventure. A game, almost.

"The next day, I was so excited that I could hardly write. I laid out all the bottles of wine my uncles had so that Mark could make his choice, then presliced some cheese and wrapped it in cellophane to keep from running around the kitchen when he got here, acting nervous like I do. About every half hour I would get up from my desk and look out the window for a car. It got so hard waiting that I almost called him.

"Around four-thirty, when I'd finally settled into my writing, there was a knock at the door.

"It was Mark Ransom.

"He had fresh sushi from town, and an expensive bottle of wine. 'First things first,' he told me. 'Put these in the refrigerator, and show me a quiet place to read.' "

Reflectively, Linton glanced upstairs. "I took him," she said quietly, "to the atelier. The place where I wrote.

"I had fifty pages waiting for him. Fresh and clean, worked and re-worked. The absolute best that I could do."

Her tone became flat, as if from the effort of memory. "He settled into my chair, leaning both arms on my desk, waving me away. He seemed totally intent on what I had written." Linton's voice fell. "I remember thinking that he wanted to know my work. To know *me*."

It was strange, Terri thought, to listen to Linton after reading her stories. In her speech, as on the page, Linton was a minimalist: she conveyed her pain by indirection, in a few understated words. "You felt that he cared," Terri ventured.

Linton watched her. "What I felt," she said with equal quiet, "was that I had opened myself to him."

She turned to the fireplace. "I came down here, made myself busy. Opened the wine he had brought, to let it breathe. Started a fire. All the time wondering what he thought of my pages." She shook her head. "Writers have this great protection: unlike singers or actors, we don't have the terror and ecstasy of confronting our audience. But now I would, and it was Mark Ransom." Her voice lowered. "I felt so vulnerable.

"By the time he finished, an hour had passed, and it was dark." Once more, Linton shook her head. "When I heard his footsteps coming down the stairs, I wanted to run.

"He walked into the living room." Linton paused. "He just stood there, saying nothing. Giving me this enigmatic, knowing look. I couldn't stand the silence.

" 'So,' I said, 'should I throw it out?' When he didn't answer right away, I cursed myself: instead of sounding clever and self-confident, I was a supplicant, and the smile I pasted on to cover that felt like a rictus." Linton folded her hands. "I already felt naked, and he hadn't even touched me."

Terri gazed around the room. In the present, it was perhaps noon; through the windows, Terri saw that sunlight made the boughs of snow-covered pines glint with crystals, saw more sun streaking the jagged peaks on the far side of the valley. But what Terri imagined was a window blank with darkness, a room made close by firelight, dancing on the stone slabs and the skins of animals. A man with glittering eyes and a slender young woman, facing each other in silence, a few feet apart.

"What did he say?" Terri asked.

Linton stared at the fireplace. " 'Oh, I wouldn't throw it out,' he said, and gave this little smile. The smile gave the words an almost casual cruelty; what it said to me was that his answer was less about the merit of what I'd written than the pitiable way I'd asked the question." Linton turned to Terri, fresh pain in her eyes. "At night, when I still think about it, I wonder whether he'd intended all along to strip away my confidence."

Somehow, Terri felt the fragility of her own body. "And did he?"

Silent, Linton nodded. "In school," she finally said, "before I found writing, I was a pleaser. As a young girl, I stayed out of trouble, watched everyone else to know what to do and not do, killed myself to get the best grades I could. All to *please* other people." She paused. "When Ransom said that, it was as if he'd taken away my writing and I was a little girl again.

"All I could say was, 'Can we talk about it?'" Linton's voice returned to the present. "It sounded *so* pitiful.

"Mark just laughed. As if that, and *I*, were trivial.

"'Of course,' he said. 'A little wine will warm me to the subject.'"

The first sliver of anger pierced Linton's voice. "It was so completely patronizing. As if he had to drink to work up any interest. But I was helpless to say, or even feel, anything like that." Her tone became bitter. "I poured the wine, like a waitress trying to please a customer. Like the pleaser I used to be.

"'Go ahead,' he told me, 'have some wine, and sit. It's really not so bad.'" When Linton shook her head yet again, Terri saw it as a self-directed reflex of puzzlement and wonder. In a flat voice, Linton said, "That finished me."

"How do you mean?"

Linton seemed to swallow. "I've never liked to drink that much—it usually makes me queasy, not myself. But what he said made me feel like such a joke. I didn't *want* to feel like myself." She continued with painful slowness. "I sat next to him on that couch, put two glasses on the coffee table. When I filled my glass to the top, Mark Ransom smiled down at it."

Terri felt cold. There was a moment's silence, and then Linton spoke again. "He waited to start in on my pages until I'd finished a glass of wine and begun another." Linton hunched forward. "And then he told me what he thought."

"What did he say?"

"It wasn't just what he said, but the cold, analytical way he said it. He made my pages sound like a slide under a microscope—something with scientific interest but no life. Which, I've come to believe, has become the central problem with so many of my characters." Linton turned back to Terri. "When a good editor works with young writers, he or she will let them build some confidence—get some pages under them, speak only to what is most important. But Mark Ransom was more brilliant and incisive than any editor I'd known, and he was completely without mercy, scene after scene." Linton stared at the coffee table. "Every so often, between comments, he would pour us both more wine. And of course, I was grateful to drink it."

Linton, Terri realized, had turned pale. "By the time he got to his last comment," she said softly, "I felt paralyzed—with wine and with humiliation."

There was something missing, Terri realized, from what Linton had just said. "What," Terri asked, "was his 'last comment'?"

Linton touched her face. "What ruined the pages, Ransom told me, was the bloodless way I write about sex.

"I felt myself go numb. When I could finally speak, my tongue felt thick." Remembering, Linton bowed her head. "The scenes were about David, my boyfriend, and me."

Terri could think of nothing to say, and Linton spoke again. " 'I *liked* that part,' I told him. 'It's *real*. They're both intellectuals, and so young, so inexperienced. They're still scared of feeling, and smart enough that they can hide it.' I felt desperate, almost pleading. 'Later in the book,' I said, 'they'll *know*. This is just the start.'

"It seemed almost to make him angry. 'It's like they're negotiating a contract,' he told me. 'Sex isn't an insurance policy, you know.' He stopped, taking one long look at me. 'What sex *is*,' he almost whispered, 'is spontaneity, and danger.' "

Linton was staring, as if transfixed by memory. "That one comment," she said quietly, "and I felt the whole thing turn on me. Everything he'd done was not just about my book, but about *me*.

"When he put his arm around me, the room started to spin."

Linton had begun to speak without expression. It was as if Ransom were about to touch her again; Linton had not stopped him in life and so could only remove herself in memory. She became close to inaudible. "I went stiff, felt too sick to struggle. And then, as if I belonged to him, he reached inside my blouse and put two fingers on my nipple."

Terri looked away; she found it easier to listen than to watch Linton's face. But when Linton spoke again, it was in tones not of hurt but of mild astonishment. "Do you know what he did then? With my nipple between his fingers, he took my face in his other hand and asked, 'Do you ever watch Laura Chase?' "

Terri felt herself freeze, did not know for how long. When Linton spoke again, she had been silently staring at the floor. "Are you all right?" Linton asked.

It reminded Terri that Mary Carelli had asked much the same question; when, Terri wondered, had she started losing her detachment? It made her feel as fragile as Linton sounded.

"No," she answered quietly. "This gets to me, and then I feel selfish. It's your pain, not mine. I'm just asking you to open it up to the world."

Linton shook her head. "Don't feel selfish. You just *feel*, that's all. It's why I'm opening up to *you*."

You give me too much credit, Terri thought. She told herself to be a lawyer, get Linton talking again. "He asked you about Laura Chase," she said.

Linton looked at her another moment, and then her gaze grew distant. She nodded again, her body making a rocking movement, and briefly shut her eyes. "When he said that," Linton answered softly, "a shiver ran through me. It was like realizing that you'd missed the clues—that someone you've thought of as merely singular is, in fact, insane."

Linton's eyes opened. "Perhaps it was the fire, the stone floor, the elk head on the wall. Suddenly I felt like I was under the spell of something primitive. It was like being in a nightmare, yet being lucid, all at once. I saw his madness clearly, knew that it was becoming my reality. And then his thumb and forefinger tightened on my nipple."

Linton turned toward the empty fireplace. "That," she said slowly, "was when I pulled away.

"His eyes got big. He simply stared at me, and then he smiled." Linton nodded, rocking herself. "It was what he'd wanted me to do.

"I was still caught up in his eyes when he slapped me.

"My neck snapped back, and then I fell against the arm of the couch. I saw yellow flashes, tasted blood inside my mouth.

"He got up on his knees, waiting for my eyes to open. And then he ripped open my blouse." Her voice dropped. "It was like it wasn't enough for me to feel him. He needed me to watch him."

Linton closed her eyes. " 'Shall I hit you again?' he asked softly.

"I couldn't talk, couldn't move. I just shook my head.

" 'Then show me your breasts,' he said. 'And keep your eyes open.'

"My bra unhooked in the front." Linton's eyes opened. "Even then, unhooking it was hard. My fingers couldn't move right."

Terri wanted a drink of water, she found. But she couldn't speak. As if in a trance, Linton kept on talking. "When I was uncovered," she said, "he just looked at me. I had this crazy hope—if he liked my breasts, perhaps it would end there. I was so pathetic that I tried to smile at him. But my mouth was swollen, and I couldn't make it."

" 'That's good,' he said. 'Eyes open now.' His voice was soothing but impersonal, like a doctor's. And then I felt his fingers on the clasp of my jeans.

"When I began to wriggle, he slapped me again.

"I started to cry. *Eyes open*,' he said angrily." Linton looked pale again. "He made me unzip my jeans, pull them off. Even to myself, I looked so thin.

"At first, he let me keep my panties on." Once more, Linton nodded to herself. "He opened my legs, forced his knees between them. I had to watch while he undid himself."

Linton's eyes were dry. Terri, watching, struggled for control. "When he was finished," Linton said quietly, "he told me to hold his penis while he pulled my panties down. To keep him hard.

"I did that.

"When he had me naked, he pushed me back. I felt his wool sweater, his face against my neck. And then I felt *him*." Linton looked away. "He didn't care whether he hurt me."

Linton's voice became tired, as if with shock. "It hurt. But I was too afraid to close my eyes. I tried finding something to look at." She paused. "So I lay there, staring up at the elk head, while he had me.

"Afterwards, he made me cook him dinner. Without any clothes, while he watched me.

"I did that, still in shock, like a little robot homemaker. Then I cleaned up." Linton shook her head. "The more I moved, the more it hurt. And he just watched me.

"I was cleaning up the living room, wiping beneath the wineglasses, when I saw the stain on the sofa." She looked at Terri. "It was right where you're sitting now."

Terri could only stare at her. "I turned the cushion over," Linton said softly, "so my uncles wouldn't see the stain. For all I know, it's still there."

Terri got up, walked to the window. Her legs felt weak; perhaps, Terri told herself, she had been sitting too long.

"Would you like to go for a walk?" Linton asked.

Terri turned to her. "Is that all right?"

Linton nodded. "I need to stop this. At least for a while." She paused, touching her chest. "It's almost a physical thing. To talk about it hurts in here."

God, Terri thought, there can't be any more. She followed Linton to the hall closet, borrowed a ski parka and some boots, went outside.

It was crisp and still; the cold felt good on Terri's face. Silent, they began walking toward the road. There was no sound except the crunch of their boots on crusted snow.

It was midafternoon, Terri realized. Daylong sun had warmed the pine boughs; once or twice the branches bent and their burden of snow fell to the ground, needles stirring with the fall. Terri and Linton walked side by side. For perhaps a quarter mile, neither spoke.

"When did he leave?" Terri asked.

Linton paused, staring out. "The next morning."

Terri let it go for a time. They reached the bridge of railroad ties; Linton stopped and leaned against the railing. Next to her, Terri watched the icy flow of the stream, listened to the water rush beneath them.

Terri turned to her. "Why did he stay?"

Linton shrugged. "Because he wanted to."

Terri kept watching her. Linton leaned forward, arms resting on the railing, cradling her chin. "It was as if," she said quietly, "he wanted things normal. To believe that I'd felt something more than pain."

"And you?"

Linton shook her head. "I was a shell."

Terri was silent.

"Have you heard of the 'Stockholm syndrome'?" Linton asked.

Terri nodded. "I think so. Isn't that where victims begin to identify with the kidnapper, because they're so afraid?"

"It was something like that. I was in shock, torn loose from my moorings. I wanted to pretend that nothing had happened. And at the same time, I was afraid of what he'd do if I asserted myself at all." Linton turned to Terri, hazel eyes full of confusion and self-doubt. "Can you understand any of this?"

Terri was quiet for a moment. "Yes," she said finally. "I can."

Linton turned to the stream. "That night, he slept with me. I couldn't sleep at all."

Terri tried to imagine lying in bed with the man who had raped her. It was like recoiling from a flame; the thought left a residue of shock.

"In the middle of the night," Linton said softly, "I felt him reach between my legs.

"It was semidark. The only light was from the bathroom; I'd gone to wash inside me, and left the light on and the door ajar. Like a child afraid of the night." Linton paused. "It hurt to be touched there.

"Suddenly he stopped. For a moment, I thought I was safe. Then he got up, pulled aside the sheets to uncover me. As he turned, his profile caught the light from the bathroom, and I saw that he had an erection.

"I lay there, stiff. But when he opened my legs, I reached out to him. So that he wouldn't hit me again.

"He pushed against me, trying to get in. I was wondering if it was dark enough to close my eyes." Staring at the stream, Linton shook her head. "Then I realized that his penis wasn't hard."

Linton turned to Terri. "He flung my arms away, got back up on his knees, still between my legs. Just staring down at himself. He became so still that it frightened me. I didn't move, could hardly breathe.

"For a crazy moment, I thought he'd kill me. Because, somehow, I'd failed him." Linton was shivering in the cold. "And then, without a word, he gathered his clothes and went downstairs.

"I lay there for hours, a prisoner in my uncles' house, listening for sounds from below. The sun came up; there were streaks of light across the bed. Every once in a while I heard him pacing the stone floor. All

I could do was pray that he would leave without wanting me again."
Linton paused. "Then I heard him coming upstairs."

In her imagination, Terri heard Ransom's footsteps on the stairs.
Felt herself waiting, as Linton had.

"I covered my shoulders," Linton said. "When I looked up again,
he was standing at the foot of the bed.

"The look in his eyes was so peculiar: confusion, anger, fear. He
stared at me as if I had tried to destroy him.

"Once more, I was sure that he would kill me.

"He came closer. Then he sat on the bed, placed one hand on my
lips, and said in a whisper, 'You can never tell anyone.'

"I stared at him, and then I nodded. He looked into my eyes, as if
deciding whether to believe me. Then he whispered, 'Good. Because
that never happened to me before.'

"I didn't know what he was talking about. And then it came to
me." Slowly, Linton shook her head. "He wasn't asking me to hide
his rape," she said with quiet bitterness. "He was asking me to
hide his failure."

Terri was silent. When Linton spoke again, her voice held a kind of
amazement. "Even then, his only feeling was for himself. He left without saying another word."

Terri turned to her. "After that, what did you do?"

"I got dressed and sat down to write, as if it were a normal day. An
hour later, I was staring at a blank page." Linton stared at the floor.
"The scene I was writing was between a man and a woman, about to
make love.

"For weeks, the book wouldn't come. I left here, took time off,
tried writing different scenes. What I was really trying to do was lose
myself in a story. Nothing worked. Mark Ransom had killed something in me—in life, and in fiction."

"You never told anyone?"

"I just couldn't do it." Her voice went flat. "It would make such a
mess. Part of me felt, somehow, that I'd let him do it. Then, when I
got away from here, it was almost as if it hadn't happened." Again,
she shook her head. "As you said, I just stuffed it somewhere. Sometimes the only way I knew that it had happened was how careful I
was to avoid Mark Ransom. So *I* wouldn't feel dirty and ashamed."

"And David?"

"We broke up. Before, I thought maybe I could let him get close—emotionally, that is." Linton paused. "I just never did."

Terri hesitated. Finally, she asked, "Did you ever think of telling him?"

"Sometimes. But I never could really imagine it. David was a law-yer—shy about his feelings but very aggressive and literal about every-one else's rights. If I'd told him, he wouldn't have stopped there. And he would have taken what happened with Mark Ransom personally." Linton sounded weary, defeated. "Sometimes I think men and women see these things so differently."

Terri searched her face. "The book," she asked. "What was it about?"

The bitterness left Linton's face; its residue was another look, more distant yet profoundly sad. "It was to be about David and me. Only a better, wiser version of us both." Linton's tone grew softer. "Like many writers, I used fiction to bring order to the world, make life and people as I wished them to be. Including me."

"And you're trying to write it again?"

"Yes. But it's not going well." The bitter smile returned. "I seem to have lost the feeling for it. Perhaps, as Mark Ransom suggested, I'm a writer of short fiction—'little people, little feelings, little stories.' "

Terri was quiet. Finally, she asked, "What do you call the novel?"

"Now? Nothing." She shook her head. "When I gave it to Mark Ransom, I called it 'The Pursuit of Happiness.' " She turned to Terri again, her eyes glistening. "I can't seem to be happy, if I ever was."

Terri did not know what to do or say, except to touch Linton's shoulder. "Marcy," she said gently, "you don't have to testify. No one will ever know."

For a time, Linton regarded her, and then spoke with equal quiet. "No," she said. "Maybe I'll never finish 'The Pursuit of Happiness.' But if I testify, perhaps someone else will understand why I'm so damned glad Mark Ransom's dead."

FIVE

"THAT'S A TERRIBLE STORY," Paget said.

They sat at a restaurant in the mountains above Aspen, one night later. Paget had flown out to help make Marcy Linton comfortable with him and to prepare her for what was to come. He had been candid and factual; although more reserved with Paget than with Terri, Linton was determined to testify. But watching Linton become the centerpiece of Mary Carelli's defense, Terri found herself resenting Christopher Paget for the relief he felt.

She looked around, pretending to enjoy the room. On another day, she would have. The restaurant Paget had managed to find was a long drive into the mountains and set off by itself; a rustic cabin that offered excellent food and, in the kennel just below, dog sleds for hire. Inside were candlelit tables, rough walls, and, through the windows, a view of snow filtering through the pines and aspens that covered the mountainside. They sat in a corner; the other tables were filled with twosomes and foursomes in jeans and boots and sweaters who had come for the food rather than to be seen. Beyond the murmur of the room, close and convivial, Terri could hear dogs yipping below, their cries echoing in the mountains.

"I'm sorry," she said. "I guess I'm not very good company."

"Oh, you've been surprisingly lifelike." Paget seemed to wince at his own words. "Forgive me. Sometimes I don't know what to say, when a simple 'What's the matter' would do nicely. What *is* the matter? Marcy Linton?"

For once, Terri thought, his intuition had failed him; she was better prepared for banter than for serious talk. She searched for something that would seem like enough to explain her mood and, at the same time, invite a change of subject. Finally, she said, "It's just how Richie sounded last night, I guess."

Paget tilted his head in inquiry. "How was that?"

"He's not happy about my being here." She smiled faintly. "I'm never sure anymore how attractive Richie really thinks I am, but he's absolutely certain that *other* men find me compelling."

Paget looked mildly surprised. "Me, for example?"

Terri nodded. "Uh-huh."

Paget seemed to consider that a moment. "You *are* compelling, of course. But that misses the point of our relationship. As professionals, or as friends."

"I know that. But Richie never will."

Paget stared out the window. His gaze was distant, directed at the mountainside. "Sometimes," he said quietly, "people just need a safe place to go."

The waiter cleared their plates and wineglasses, took coffee orders. For once, Terri did not want dessert. She felt Paget watching her again.

"Linton's our one chance to win," he said finally. "And getting this out may well help her."

"That's much too easy." Terri stared at her coffee. "What gives us the right to play with other people's lives, for reasons of our own? What gives *me* the right to open them up like that?" Suddenly Terri needed to deflect the conversation. "Sometimes, I wonder if I was really made to be a lawyer."

Paget's smile was unimpressed but not unkind. "Is that what we were talking about—your fitness as a lawyer?"

She looked up at him, and then his smile disappeared. Softly, he asked, "What happened to you, Terri?"

She felt startled, confused. When she spoke, her voice sounded thin. "I became a lawyer. That's all."

Paget shook his head. "Something happened to you," he said. "If you're paying attention, as I've been, it's not even that hard to spot."

All at once, Terri felt exposed, angry at the tears she had to fight. "Can we go now?" she said. "I'm tired."

"Of course."

Quickly, Paget signaled the waiter, paid the bill. His manner was smooth and pleasant; the only change was that he let Terri keep to herself. On the way to the car, and for some time after, he said nothing at all.

The night was cold and dark. Through the windshield Terri could see a crescent moon; a black expanse of sky above the mountains; more stars than she could see in San Francisco, undimmed by fog or city lights. The only sound was the engine running.

They drove, two stiff and silent profiles, staring through the window at the dark. Terri felt herself hold on tight.

"I'm sorry," Paget said quietly.

Perhaps, Terri thought, it was the way he said it. She had curled up in the seat, tears running down her face, before she was aware that he had stopped the car.

They were at an observation point above the valley, a thousand feet of darkness.

"Are you all right?" he asked.

"No." Terri felt her emotions plummet in a free-fall with no end in sight. "I'm not all right. I haven't been all right for a long time."

Despite the tears, her voice was cold and clear.

"What is it, Terri?"

They sat there, Paget turned toward her, Terri staring out the window. It was easier that way.

"Five years ago," she said at last, "someone raped me."

He was quiet for a time. "And you've never told anyone."

Just look at the stars, Terri told herself. "It was stupid," she said.

Once more, Paget fell silent. Terri felt herself swallow, began again. "The man was a law professor in his forties—married, with two kids, and Hispanic like me. He'd done criminal defense in East L.A., worked with Cesar Chavez. Some of us saw him as a kind of role model." Terri paused. "Especially me.

"In my third year, a few months after Elena was born, he asked me to be his research assistant on a paper he was writing. I was flattered that he'd asked. But I did it because Richie had decided to add an MBA to his law degree, and we needed the money." She paused again. "From the start, Richie was jealous. The man was appealing in his way—black mustache, dark intense eyes—and Richie was sure that he was interested in me. But not so sure that he didn't want me taking his money."

Terri stopped, replaying the note of bitterness in her voice. So funny, she thought: her eyes were wet, but her throat felt dry.

"What," Paget inquired gently, "was this man's name?"

Terri hesitated; somehow naming him made it real again. "Urbina," she said at last. "Steve Urbina."

In the darkness of the car, Terri closed her eyes.

"If this is too much," she heard him say, "we don't need to talk about it."

There was a knot in her chest; she could not seem to get it loose. Talk about it, she told herself, as if it were a case. As if it were someone else.

"It was late Sunday afternoon," she finally said. "Richie and I had taken Elena on her first outing to Tilden Park. It was warm outside. We put Elena under a tree in one of those portable car seats while Richie and I ate our picnic. I was wearing a sundress, Richie his hiking shorts and a sweatshirt, and Elena had on a pink T-shirt that said 'Baby Power' or something foolish like that. I remember thinking that we were a family, and how glad I was that I'd decided to have Elena.

"We spent all afternoon there, remembering things about college and looking at Elena, who didn't do much but sleep and squall." Terri felt herself holding on to the memory. "But then babies don't *have* to do very much, do they?"

"I've never really had one," Paget said. "I envy you that."

"It was such a good day. We decided to go home, barbecue something on the roof of our apartment building, while Elena slept." Terri hesitated. "And then, after we put Elena in her bassinet for the night, we were going to make love."

For a moment, Terri tried to recall her marriage to Richie before it began carrying the weight of her successes, his jealousies and fits and starts. It was more painful than she had allowed herself to know. She stayed there, lost in what she felt as Christopher Paget's infinite patience.

"When we got home," she said at last, "there was a message from Steve Urbina.

"I'd forgotten to give him some research notes; could I drop them at his house?" She shook her head. "The thing I remember was that Richie was so pissed.

"I called Urbina and told him I'd be right over—it wasn't far. I didn't worry about him—I mean, he was a little flirty, but nothing serious, and home was where his wife and kids were. Actually, at the time I didn't even think about those things." Terri opened her eyes, looked out at the stars. "And besides," she said in a flat voice, "forgetting the notes was my fault.

"I went out the door, with Richie still angry.

"Steve Urbina's house was this stucco sort of Spanish place in Albany, with an apple tree in front. I got there in about fifteen minutes and hurried to the door.

"I was in such a rush to get back home that I tripped on one of his kids' tricycles.

"I was sitting on the walk with the notes scattered next to me and my sundress pulled up around my thighs, looking at my knee, when I realized he was watching through the screen door.

"It was strange for a second: he startled me, and I couldn't tell how long he'd been standing there. But all he said was, 'Let me take a look at that.'

"The scrape was pretty bad, with some surface bleeding. When he knelt beside me, I pulled my sundress down so that only one knee showed. 'We keep Band-Aids and Mercurochrome for the kids,' he said. 'That may need hydrogen peroxide too.'

"When I picked up my notes and followed him inside the house, I didn't hear anyone else.

" 'Mattie and the kids are visiting their grandmother,' he said. ' 'Fraid I'm the only nurse around.'

" 'It doesn't matter,' I told him. 'Just show me where the bathroom is, and I'll take care of this myself. It'll be practice for Elena.'

" 'Oh, come on in,' he answered, and steered me into his bedroom. 'Just sit on the edge of the bed, and I'll get the stuff from the master bath. I can't have you suing me for maintaining a dangerous condition on my own front walk.' "

Terri paused. "I was dumb," she said dully, "but he was so paternal, as some men can be, that I thought it made him feel better. I just sat on the edge of the bed.

"In a minute, he was back. He had cotton balls, hydrogen peroxide, and a large Band-Aid patch. Very carefully—respectfully, almost—he waited for me to pull my dress up and then dabbed peroxide on the scrape.

"It stung—I flinched a little. He looked up at me, concerned, and asked if it hurt. When I told him 'A little,' his touch got even softer."

Terri looked down. "It wasn't sexual to me, but I remember thinking for a moment that his gentleness was nice, kind of warming." She paused, adding softly, "Richie was never that gentle."

She fell quiet for a time, suspended on the edge of what had happened to her. "When he put on the Band-Aid," she said finally, "he pressed down on each edge very carefully, to make sure it stayed on. And then he reached up beneath my dress and pulled my panties down."

There was something in Paget's perfect stillness that made Terri falter, as if the effort of his self-control tore something loose inside her. "It happened so fast," she told him softly. "Really, it was over before I could believe it."

Paget said nothing. She touched her eyes. "Maybe the worst part," she said at last, "is that I didn't do anything. I don't have any excuse—not like Marcy Linton. I just froze."

" 'No,' I told him. And then he pushed me down on the bed and leaned his elbow against my throat. He was already standing between my legs. I was so easy for him." She shook her head. "He was coming inside me before I even started to cry."

Gazing out at the stars, Terri stopped herself from crying. "Afterwards, he stood between my legs, staring down at me as he zipped up his pants. When he said that no one would believe me, I knew that he had done things like this before." She shook her head. "He was far too confident, and he'd chosen his victim far too well."

Terri swallowed again. "Once I promised, he handed me back my panties. He just watched me while I put them on. He'd felt me respond to him, he said—that was why he'd done it. And then he told me it was time to leave."

Terri leaned her face against the cold window of the car. "I drove home in a daze, I don't even remember how. When I got there, Richie wanted to know what took me so long. He kept badgering me about why I needed to waste family time on Steve Urbina." Terri paused. "I was so unresponsive that, in one of his lightning changes of mood, Richie suddenly became cheerful. He wanted to take a picture of me in my sundress. I remember trying to smile for him." Terri's voice became wondering. "It's his favorite, he says. He still keeps it over his computer."

Terri turned to Paget. "That night, Richie fucked me twice. One for himself, I remember thinking, and one because I'd been at Steve Urbina's.

"I never told anyone. I couldn't explain, couldn't face Urbina." Her voice was parched. "I couldn't bring myself to even mention him. I wrote a one-page letter resigning my job, didn't go to graduation. I don't know whether I was more afraid of seeing Steve Urbina or I thought, somehow, Richie would know." Terri shook her head in wonder. "I felt it was my fault. That was why I became a rape counselor—to try to understand. What I learned was how many women this happened to, far more than most men seem to realize. But I could never talk about it. To anyone."

Pausing, Terri looked down. "Not only was I a coward, but I never seriously considered *not* being one. How did I ever ask Marcy Linton to do this?"

Paget watched her. "How can you have blamed yourself?"

"Because I let it happen." Terri paused. "Because I protected everyone but me."

Turning to the window, Paget gazed out at the night. "I hate that," he said softly. "I hate it for *you.*"

Almost to herself, Terri shrugged.

"Why," Paget asked finally, "did you never talk to your mother? You surely didn't think that *she* would blame you."

His tone was not judgmental; it was as if he wanted to understand her, and this was a piece that mattered.

"No," Terri answered, "I didn't think that. Looking back, I just didn't want to admit that I'd started doing what she'd always done—keeping things from Richie, keeping the peace. For both our sakes, I couldn't tell her that."

Paget turned to her. "Then who do you talk to?"

She thought for a moment. "You," she answered quietly. "I guess I talk to you."

SIX

TERESA PERALTA STEPPED from the shower.

Richie turned to look at her. It was strange, she thought; she had been naked with him countless times before, and yet tonight it made her edgy.

He put down the toothbrush, taking her in. "Coming to bed soon?" he asked.

She wrapped a towel around herself. "In a while. I have to dry my hair, take off my eyeliner. Unwind a little. It was a long flight and a longer two days."

Richie gave her the thwarted look she had come to know too well. "It's not like I've seen you much lately." His voice rose in complaint. *"I'm* the one who's your husband. Not Chris Paget."

Terri tried to understand why she felt guilty. "I know who you are," she said tiredly. "And I know you're my husband. In nearly six years of marriage, I've never *not* known that."

Richie was silent for a moment. Terri turned to the mirror, dabbing at her eyes with makeup remover. "Why didn't you call last night?" he asked.

Terri's guilt became defensiveness. "It was late, and I had a lot to think about." Terri paused. "If you were so concerned, you could have called *me.* I gave you the number."

"Was *he* with you?"

Terri stopped to look at him. "No," she answered quietly. "I just didn't want to call."

Richie put both hands on his hips. "I can't believe this."

"Then believe *this,* Richie. I've never been unfaithful to you, and I never will." Terri paused. "There's nothing you can do to change that, one way or the other. It's just the way I am."

Richie stood there watching her. In a lower voice, he said, "I don't want you working with him."

Terri felt a moment's anger, then felt tired. "You have an exclusive on my body, Richie. But you can't set the conditions under which I'm going to support you."

He flushed. "You know, that's a really telling remark, Ter. It's what you do—emotional abuse and economic castration."

It felt so unfair that Terri did not stop before she spoke. "When it comes to economic castration," she retorted, "you're a self-made man."

Richie stiffened; then, curiously, Terri thought she saw a fleeting triumph in his eyes, as if he had gotten what he wanted. Very softly, he said, "I don't know whether I'll ever forget what you just said."

"All that I meant to say," Terri answered wearily, "is that you should quit worrying about Chris and start worrying about Elena. *And* me."

"I thought our interests were synonymous." He stood straighter. "In a real family, Terri, that's how it's supposed to be."

Married all this time, Terri thought, and she was still not sure when Richie meant to be manipulative and when he was merely obtuse to any feelings but his own. She supposed it did not matter. "Let's stop fighting," she said. "Please. I just got home, and tomorrow the hearing begins."

He lowered his voice still further. "Your job. That's all you seem to think of now."

Terri picked up her hair dryer. "Tonight," she answered, "that's pretty much true."

She switched on the dryer, using its sound as a buffer. Richie lingered in the doorway of the bathroom, watching with an expression of stubbornness. Then he shrugged and turned away. Something in the gesture told Terri that their quarrel had not ended.

Terri stood in her transient zone of peace: the light of the bathroom, the drone of her hair dryer. Looked at herself in the mirror: the serious eyes, the first lines at their corners. Thought of Elena, sleeping in her bedroom, face lineless and untroubled, so much like Richie's that Terri still found it startling. And then her mind wandered again to Marcy Linton. To the way Mark Ransom had broken her down, used her fears and vulnerabilities until Linton felt a kind of paralysis. To whether Terri had any right to make her face a trial.

Tomorrow it would begin.

She finished. With more deliberation than normal, Terri put things away, hung the towel up. And then she breathed in, once, and walked into the bedroom.

Richie was waiting.

He lay propped up on one elbow, torso showing, half covered by the bed sheet. Even before he pulled the sheet down to make room for her, Terri knew that he was naked.

"Come here, Ter," he said. "It's no good for married people to end the night like this." He gave his most ingratiating smile. "Afterwards, I'll rub your back."

In the dim light from the lamp on Richie's side, Terri walked naked to the bed. "I'm really tired," she parried. "Think we can take a rain check?"

He shook his head, smiling as if to say that his insistence was well intended, that he knew what was best for them. "It's early yet," he answered lightly. "And I have to reclaim my territory."

"Really, I don't think that I could even come."

Persisting, his smile seemed to become an act of aggression. "Then we'll do the short version, rather than the deluxe."

What, Terri wondered, was the difference?

She turned out the light, slid inside the bed on her stomach. Passive resistance, she thought; maybe he'll give up. She felt his hand lightly stroke her thighs; his touch was idle, aimless, as if he had nothing on his mind. Then it came to rest between her legs.

"Come on, Ter," he murmured. "Just for a little while."

His hand began to move again, small strokes where it had rested. Mentally, Terri shuddered.

As he touched her, Terri moved on her stomach, calculating the value of sleep. If she resisted, a quarrel would ensue. Richie could be relentless in his anger; the fulcrum of their marriage, Terri realized, was his uncanny sense of when her resistance would become fatigue. She could not afford to be tired; she owed Christopher Paget and Carlo, owed *herself*, the best she could offer as a lawyer.

How many times, Terri wondered, had Richie been inside her? How much would this time matter?

How long had she been dead this way?

Silent, Terri rolled over on her back. Richie's murmur of satisfaction seemed to come from some great distance. He would enter her without words, she knew; like many things, the act of sex was something that took Richie deep within himself, until Terri felt a bystander. She no longer thought of what they did as making love.

Sliding across her, Richie put his hands beneath her bottom, to move her as he wanted. She felt him push inside her. As he went as deep as he could, moaning his pleasure, she draped her arms across his back and wished that he were someone else.

The next morning, Teresa Peralta found herself with Christopher Paget on the fourth floor of the Hall of Justice, Mary Carelli between them, pushing through a lobby jammed with reporters.

Three broad-shouldered police ahead of them parted the crowd— reporters with microphones or notepads; photographers with flash- bulbs; cameramen with minicams mounted on their shoulders, backpedaling to film the progress toward the courtroom. Terri glanced sideways. Mary Carelli looked composed and determined; Paget's ex- pression was abstracted, removed from his surroundings, as if focused on the hearing ahead. In the last days, Paget's face or Mary's had been on the cover of four weekly magazines and on every network news- cast; inside the courtroom waited the cameras of Court TV. Terri had hardly slept last night; she wondered if Paget had slept at all.

At the end of the green hallway she saw the double doors of the courtroom. From the side, reporters shouted questions, flashbulbs hissed, footsteps echoed off bare walls. In another minute or so, they would be inside, and it would begin.

Instinctively, she looked at the boy walking next to her: Carlo Car- elli Paget, awkward but handsome in a coat and tie, looking so much like his mother that Terri thought some reporter would surely notice. Carlo turned to her, flashed the crooked, uncertain smile she had come to recognize; once again, Terri hoped that her advice to Christopher Paget would not damage a boy she had come to care about.

A flashbulb exploded in their faces.

She touched Carlo's arm, too quickly for anyone to see. Then she forced herself to look straight ahead, the dots of light from the flash still blurring her line of vision.

Thirty feet from the doors of the courtroom, Terri saw Paget turn at the sound of a question.

The noise had grown louder; the media people were backed against the doorways as if they had hit a wall. It was a red-haired woman reporter whose question had pierced the din: she slid behind the police and stood looking from Mary to Carlo.

"Who *are* you?" she asked Carlo again.

Carlo gazed down at her with a pained expression, as if trapped in an awkward social situation by a drunken and rude adult. "I'm Carlo Paget," he murmured.

Turning, Terri saw that Mary Carelli was stiff with alarm; Paget began pushing in front of her to get to the reporter. "He's my son," he snapped in a preemptive tone.

Carlo looked at him, as if startled. Then a slight smile of amusement crossed his face, relieving his look of tension. "I can't deny it," he said to the reporter.

The crowd kept moving toward the door. "What are you doing here?" the reporter asked. "Learning about the law?"

"No," Carlo answered calmly. "I'm thinking about medical school. In case I don't make the NBA."

Paget had stopped to watch him; it was as if, Terri thought, he was seeing who Carlo Paget had become.

"You don't want to be a lawyer?" the reporter asked.

From the side, a minicam moved in on Carlo. He glanced over, taking that in, and then looked back at the reporter. "Not at all," he told her. "I just want to be a son." He turned to face Paget and Mary. "Christopher Paget is my father, and Mary Carelli is my mother. And all I really have to say to anyone is that I'm very proud of them both."

The reporter was momentarily speechless. Touching Terri's arm, Carlo gave Mary a slight smile, shot a grin at Paget, and turned back toward the doors. Then they opened, and Carlo Paget walked through.

PART FOUR

THE PROSECUTION

FEBRUARY 10 – FEBRUARY 12

ONE

"ALL RISE," the courtroom deputy called out. "The Municipal Court for the City and County of San Francisco, the Honorable Judge Caroline Clark Masters, is now in session."

A handsome woman on the worst of days, Caroline Masters looked close to regal as she surveyed a courtroom filled by media representatives from around the world, with a small section reserved for members of the public who had lined up outside for the privilege of attending in hour-long shifts. More reporters watched in adjacent rooms fed by closed-circuit television; two cameras in each corner of the courtroom broadcast the hearing nationwide. On the steps of the courthouse, a coalition of women's groups carried signs and placards asking justice for Mary Carelli.

Mary herself stood beside Paget; the awe of finding herself in the cockpit of a crowded courtroom, charged with premeditated murder, showed in the way she grasped the table reserved for the defense. On his other side, Terri looked tired and troubled. Carlo sat behind them in the first row; Johnny Moore had joined him and sat primed to feed Paget scraps of information for use in cross-examination.

Turning, Paget glanced at Marnie Sharpe. She looked pale. But her alertness of expression said that she was ready. Paget was certain that she, like him, had committed every pertinent fact to memory; had designed and redesigned lines of questioning; and had prepared herself against surprise. The one edge he carried to the courtroom was how much he had at stake.

From the bench, Caroline Masters appraised them both. The judicial frown she wore seemed the residue of pleasure and anticipation.

"Ms. Sharpe," she began, "Mr. Paget. A few ground rules. I suggest you listen carefully.

"First, the presence of television is a responsibility, not a chance to entertain. There will be only one 'personality' in this courtroom—and you're listening to her."

The judge paused, her voice becoming crisp and surgical. "Second," she continued, "we will be ruling on contested points of evidence— whether certain witnesses are relevant or other evidence should be made public—by holding private sessions in chambers. The transcript of those proceedings will be sealed, so as to avoid prejudice to all participants. If anyone alludes to the subject matter of those proceedings without my prior permission, this court will personally bring them before the disciplinary committee of the California State Bar."

This, Paget knew, was a warning not to mention the Laura Chase tapes; James Colt; Steinhardt's recording of Mary; or the proposed testimony of any witnesses to Mark Ransom's sexual character until Masters ruled on them in private. The pressure of those issues, Paget thought, made even Masters seem apprehensive.

"Third," the judge went on, "I reserve the right to pull the plug on all or part of these proceedings. If either the People or the defense makes an argument, or even asks a question, which I believe is designed more to create bias than to advance their legitimate interests, they will be severely penalized.

"Do I make myself clear?"

"Yes, Your Honor," Sharpe said.

Paget nodded. "Quite clear, Your Honor."

"Good." Masters looked down at Paget. "Not to single you out, Mr. Paget, but you singled yourself out by asking for this. I expect exemplary behavior."

"The court has every right to that," Paget answered mildly. "From everyone."

Masters raised her eyebrow. "I'm sure *everyone,*" she said with the slightest edge, "is as aware of that as you are." She turned to Sharpe. "I've suggested opening statements. Do you have one?"

"We do," responded Sharpe. She stepped to the podium, looking up at Caroline Masters, and the hearing began.

"This," Sharpe opened, "is a simple act of murder."

Her voice quavered slightly, Paget thought, as if her larynx had been squeezed. But it was a good first sentence, and he was certain that the words themselves were crafted to get better.

"Mary Carelli admits shooting Mark Ransom to death. The one thing standing between the People and 'probable cause' is Ms. Carelli's story about *why* she killed him." Abruptly, Sharpe's voice was etched with scorn. "Or, I should say, her *stories.*

"Because if Ms. Carelli presumes to testify before this court, she must tell the court a far *different* story than she told Inspector Charles Monk."

This was clever, Paget saw: make Mary's credibility the focus of her argument; suggest that Mary will insult the court by lying; and then, in chambers, finish the job by asking to introduce a tape in which Mary admits perjury before the United States Senate. Next to him, Mary watched the prosecutor intently, as if preparing for cross-examination. Paget dared not look at Carlo.

"Let us start with the only things about which Ms. Carelli appears to have told the truth to anyone.

"Mark Ransom *did* contact her.

"Thereafter, Ms. Carelli *did* purchase a gun.

"She *did* come to San Francisco, at her own expense, without telling ABC or anyone else.

"She *did* go to Mark Ransom's suite with the Walther .380 hidden in her purse.

"And then, at about noon, Mary Carelli shot Mark Ransom to death.

"Right there, we have a probable cause for first degree murder." Sharpe paused for effect, and then her voice dropped. "And from there on," she added, "things get much worse for Ms. Carelli."

Caroline Masters leaned forward, betraying her interest. Terri was utterly still. The courtroom was far too quiet for Paget's liking.

"Mary Carelli claims to have purchased the handgun because of anonymous phone calls, to her *unlisted* number, which she failed to report to anyone.

"She says that Mr. Ransom lured her to the hotel room with information regarding Laura Chase." Sharpe paused. "On that point," she said dryly, "I will say nothing for the moment. I simply ask the court to keep that claim in mind.

"She says, even more fundamentally, that Mr. Ransom tried to rape her." The contempt returned to her voice. "That while maintaining an erection, Mark Ransom scratched her throat and leg and threw her to the ground. And then, in the ensuing struggle, that she shot him from a distance of two to three inches."

Sharpe paused and then began speaking in staccato sound bites, perfect for television. "Here is what we will show.

"There is *no* evidence of sexual arousal.

"The only skin beneath anyone's fingernails was found under *Ms. Carelli's.*

"There is no extraneous sign of a struggle.

"And as the medical examiner will tell us, Ms. Carelli's tale of shooting from two or three inches is off by at least two or three feet, rendering her entire story of the shooting implausible at best."

Sharpe stood upright, as if galvanized by sudden anger. "What Ms. Carelli appears to have done," she said with scorn, "is to fashion a fashionable defense from an issue which is far too real to far too many women to be so cheaply used." She turned to gaze at Mary. "Indeed, it seems that the only reason Ms. Carelli did not accuse Mark Ransom of child abuse is that she has reached the age of majority. For there is about as much evidence of child abuse as there is of rape." As she paused, the two women stared at each other. "Of course," Sharpe added quietly, "once one shoots someone else to death, one can speak without fear of contradiction. About the *dead,* one can say just about *anything.* The only boundaries are *this* one woman's sense of honor, and of truth."

Caroline Masters had begun to look impatient; her expression said that she did not require rhetoric. But Paget could imagine all too clearly the first few moments of the evening news.

"Unfortunately for Ms. Carelli, there is more.

"At first blush, these discrepancies seem merely a grab bag of anomalies.

"For example, Ms. Carelli told Inspector Monk that when she arrived at Mr. Ransom's suite, the shades were drawn.

"We will produce three witnesses. One saw Ms. Carelli and Mr. Ransom sitting in a sunlit room with the shades up. The second witness saw Ms. Carelli draw the blinds herself." Sharpe's voice rose, became relentless. "And the third saw Ms. Carelli outside the room. *After* Mr. Ransom died.

"Ms. Carelli told Inspector Monk that she called 911 as soon as possible.

"The medical examiner, Dr. Elizabeth Shelton, estimates that Mr. Ransom had been dead for the better part of an hour when Ms. Carelli placed that call."

Suddenly Sharpe's voice grew quiet. "*Ms. Carelli* claims to have scratched Mr. Ransom's naked buttocks in the struggle to defend herself."

She paused again, speaking each word slowly. "But Dr. Shelton believes that when Mark Ransom received the scratches, he was well beyond struggling. Specifically," she finished softly, "Dr. Shelton believes that Mr. Ransom had been dead for a good half hour when Ms. Carelli chose to scratch the buttocks of a corpse."

The audience emitted different sounds: shocked exclamations; murmured questions; the rustle of people turning to each other. Masters raised the gavel. The audience fell silent, waiting.

"Dead for a half hour," Sharpe repeated. "The half hour, we will suggest, that Ms. Carelli was casting about for a story to tell."

Sharpe focused her gaze on Masters. "And what will all this tell *us?* That Ms. Carelli lied to the police, to cover her crime. Just as she must lie to the court."

Masters's face was grim; Paget could not tell whether it was intended to foreclose the thought that Sharpe could prejudice her, or to express her determination that Mary Carelli could not lie with impunity.

"And what of motive?" Sharpe inquired mildly. "As a matter of law, we need not show one. Motive is not an element of the crime, and as to the elements themselves, we have more than enough for probable cause." Sharpe's voice rose again. "But we *do* have motive. We will present that evidence to the court, in chambers, and ask the court to rule that it is admissible."

Paget began to rise. Sharpe was skirting Masters's instructions, touting evidence the judge might not permit her to present in public. When he hesitated, fearful of drawing too much attention, Masters cut in. "On Mr. Paget's behalf," she snapped, "you've crossed the line. When I asked you not to talk about proceedings in chambers *after* the fact, I assumed that you would refrain from describing them *before* the fact. Or is there some distinction that eludes me?"

Sharpe had frozen. "No, Your Honor," she said in chastened tones. "I apologize for any error."

Masters frowned. "If that's what it was, Counselor. Move on."

But Sharpe had lost the force of her argument. She paused and then chose to wind up.

"Your Honor," she started again, "only one more thing need be said.

"Rape is a deep and serious societal problem. It should *not* be the issue *de jour* for a media-wise defendant, desperate to avoid the consequences of murder, eager to tell whatever story she thinks will work." Sharpe had recovered her confidence. "What Mary Carelli *says* is unworthy of belief. What Mary Carelli *did* is commit premeditated murder, and that is what the evidence will show." Sharpe stood straighter yet. "With respect, Your Honor, this court *must* find probable cause to hold Mary Carelli for the murder of Mark Ransom."

For a moment, she stood silent at the podium, gazing up at Caroline Masters. When she turned and walked back to her table, taking the room's energy with her, Paget felt respect and apprehension. Mary Carelli looked away.

"Listening to Ms. Sharpe," Paget began, "my first thought was that speeches are *not* evidence, and sound bites are not facts."

There was silence in the courtroom; Paget knew he already had the attention of the media. But Masters's narrow face registered displeasure, as if anticipating a personal attack on Sharpe.

"My second thought," Paget continued evenly, "was that rape is far too serious a matter to be treated as casually as the People have treated it this morning." He turned to Sharpe. "As serious a matter as the beating of a woman—the kind that leaves her bruised and in shock. And that is far too serious a *fact* to slip the prosecution's mind.

"Yet, somehow, it did."

Paget paused. "Listening to the prosecution's pastiche of circumstantial evidence, I was reminded of a somewhat troubling evening I spent a year or so ago.

"It occurred, of all places, at the movies."

Masters's shoulders moved, a small gesture of impatience. "I was with my son," Paget went on, and then turned to Carlo and Mary. "Ms. Carelli's son."

Mary gave him a slight smile of appreciation; behind him, Carlo nodded. Then Paget turned again, fearful of losing Judge Masters altogether. "The film concerned the assassination of a President, and it was Carlo's first exposure to the subject. And, like Ms. Sharpe's opening statement, it was gripping entertainment."

Masters seemed to sit back to see him more clearly, torn between curiosity and concern about Paget's choice of subject. Paget saw Sharpe half rise, searching for an objection she could put into words.

"The film's director," Paget continued, "managed to slice and dice every stray fact regarding the assassination until he came up with a compelling case that a conspiracy of Cubans, gay men from New Orleans, right-wing fanatics, CIA operatives, missile manufacturers, *and* the Vice President of the United States had murdered the President and then covered it up for thirty years, all with the assistance of countless members of Congress and the Chief Justice of the Supreme Court." Paget paused. "It was absolutely riveting entertainment. And like Ms. Sharpe's opening statement, its origin is circumstantial evidence." His voice slowed. "Circumstantial evidence," he repeated. "A dangerous thing, when it is left to brew too long in the fever swamp of a prosecutor's imaginings."

Paget gazed at Sharpe until her face was stiff with anger. "Movie theaters," he said coolly, "are the proper venue for fantasy and myth. *Not* courtrooms." He turned back to Masters. "Nor is any courtroom the proper place for the tissue of speculation Ms. Sharpe has just presented.

"I will not try the court's patience with a story of my own. Nor will I offer previews for all those watching of the evidence *we* will offer the court in chambers. I will merely offer the court one statement of fact, and make of the court one simple request.

"The statement is that Mark Ransom abused Mary Carelli. That is why she shot him, and that is what we will show." Paget turned to Sharpe again. "The request is that the court count how many times Ms. Sharpe's version of the facts turns gauzy under cross-examination." Paget paused, looking back at Masters. "And then," he finished softly, "I will ask the court to consider just whose credibility really stands at issue.

"Thank you, Your Honor."

There was silence; Masters looked surprised that he was finished. Walking to his chair, Paget found that what he felt was not relief but depression.

It was the spare approach: poke holes in the prosecutor's story; offer no story of your own; promise only to stick to the facts as they unfold. Viewed charitably, it could be read as prickly integrity. It was also, Paget knew, the only thing that was safe to offer Caroline Masters; Mary had no story that Christopher Paget could believe.

Taking the witness stand, Charles Monk sat with his head raised stiffly, turning to look about the courtroom. His face was devoid of all expression; to Mary, he had the unperturbed look of a snapping turtle that had stuck its head out and did not see anything of concern. According to Johnny Moore, he had testified in thirty-seven homicide prosecutions; thirty-six had ended in conviction. On the table next to him was the tape of Mary's interview, edited to delete the identities of Laura Chase and James Colt.

Quickly, Sharpe established that the tape was what Monk said it was; that it had been in their custody; that Mary had been advised of her rights—in short, that it was admissible. Stiffly, Mary watched the methodical grinding of a first-class prosecution team at work; when Monk began playing the tape, she felt helpless.

Sharpe had two purposes, Mary knew. To prove that she shot Mark Ransom, for there were no eyewitnesses to the crime itself. And, more devastating, to show that Mary had tried to mislead Charles Monk.

Snippet by snippet, Sharpe began to accomplish both. Mary listened to her own voice proving how foolish she had been.

Relentlessly, Mary's words began to support Sharpe's case. She had purchased the Walther after Ransom called. She had told no one of her trip to San Francisco. She claimed that Ransom had attacked her after becoming aroused. She believed she had scratched his buttocks. The scratches on her body were Ransom's. She had shot him at very close range, with his hands on her wrists. She had noticed that the blinds were already drawn. She had called 911 as soon as possible. Her words came to her as sometimes cool, sometimes weary or confused, even angry once or twice. But always she sounded lucid. Her voice did not suggest a woman in shock; Mary, listening to herself as if to a stranger, was afraid to look at Carlo.

The courtroom was still.

When the tape ended, Mary felt heads beginning to turn, as if to reexamine her. Judge Masters eyed her with a new wariness.

They had *not*, Mary realized, played the 911 tape.

But then Sharpe and Monk were on to other things. Crime scene procedures; the presence of her fingerprints in several spots in the living room—an end table, a desk filled with stationery—as if she had been moving around the room at will. Only to her, Mary thought, would the woman Sharpe described sound trapped and desperate.

"In short," Sharpe's relentless voice was asking, "Ms. Carelli's fingerprints seemed to be all over the living room, on numerous pieces of furniture?"

"That's right."

"Was any of this furniture toppled?"

"No."

"Or damaged?"

"No."

"Or seemingly displaced?"

Monk shook his head. "No," he said slowly. His gold-rimmed glasses glistened in the light.

"Was the champagne bottle tipped over?"

"No."

"Or the glass?"

"No."

"Or the tape recorder?"

"No."

She placed her hands on her hips. "Put another way, was there anything in the room itself which suggested a struggle between Ms. Carelli and Mark Ransom?"

For a moment, Mary felt bewildered; she had not realized how the absence of evidence could be made to look.

"No," Monk answered calmly.

"Or anything which suggested other than that, prior to the shooting, Ms. Carelli and Mr. Ransom had simply been talking?"

"Objection!" Paget stood. "Calls for speculation. Lack of foundation."

"Overruled."

"No." Monk's deep voice sounded resonant, satisfied. "Nothing whatsoever."

Paget gazed at Monk with an air of puzzlement.

Watching, Terri felt as bemused as Paget looked; Monk was an experienced witness, whose testimony had consisted of Mary's own words and a series of simple facts. She did not know how Paget could attack him.

"Before you questioned Ms. Carelli," he asked, "did you send her to the hospital?"

For a split second, Monk seemed to hesitate; Terri guessed that the first question had surprised him. Very calmly, Monk answered, "No."

It was, Terri knew, the terse answer of an experienced witness; Monk did not wish to look defensive, or to temporize before he knew where Paget was going.

"As I understood your testimony," Paget said, "you saw no sign of a struggle, is that correct?"

Monk paused again. "Not in the room itself," he said. "No."

Turning, Paget glanced at Johnny Moore, now standing at the side of the courtroom. In less than a minute, Moore moved an easel to the center of the courtroom; suddenly the easel held a three-by-five foot photograph of Mary Carelli. There was stirring in the courtroom; the dark swelling on her cheek lent her eyes an air of shock. Judge Masters looked from Mary to the photograph as if at a double image; the well-groomed woman in the courtroom staring at herself as a battered victim. The contrast was striking.

"Do you recognize this photograph?" Paget asked.

"Yes." Monk spoke in measured tones. "It's a police photograph, from the crime scene. Blown up, of course."

"And is that how Ms. Carelli appeared when you first saw her?"

"Yes."

"That *is* a bruise on her cheek, is it not?"

"Yes."

"And her eye was swollen?"

Monk nodded. "Yes."

Paget raised an eyebrow. "Yet according to your testimony, there was no sign of a struggle."

"In the room itself," Monk responded. "That was what I said."

Pausing, Paget gave him an incredulous look. "In the room itself," he repeated. "If the coffee table had been chipped, would Ms. Carelli be on trial here? Or would you have charged her with vandalism as well as murder?"

Terri tensed. "Objection," Sharpe snapped. "The only purpose of *that* question was harassment."

"Sustained." Masters turned to Paget. "Don't even try to rationalize that one, Counselor. And don't insult the witness *or* this court by doing it again."

"Forgive me, Your Honor. I'll try to make the point in a less polemic fashion." Paget again faced Monk. "Could you please look at the photograph, Inspector."

As Monk turned to Mary's bruised image, Paget backed away from it until he stood next to the witness stand. Together, he and Monk gazed at the picture like two visitors to a gallery. "Would you say," Paget asked conversationally, "that Ms. Carelli's face showed 'signs of a struggle'?"

Monk nodded. "With a bruise like that, physical violence is one possibility."

"As a result of your investigation, are you aware of any *other* possibility?"

"No," Monk answered carefully. "Not that we are *aware* of."

"And in fact, Ms. Carelli told *you* that Mark Ransom had struck her as she tried to defend herself."

"Yes. She did."

"But you didn't take her to the hospital."

Monk blinked; Terri saw that the change of subject had come so quickly that it seemed to undermine his confidence.

"No." Monk paused. "She said she didn't want to go."

Still gazing at the picture, Paget tilted his head. "Do you think that was a judgment that *this* woman should have made?"

Monk turned to him. "I thought she *could* make it, yes."

"Are you a doctor?"

Monk looked annoyed. "No."

"Do you know, for example, whether Ms. Carelli had a concussion?"

"No." For the first time, Monk showed some desire to explain. "When we got there, Ms. Carelli was calm, well-spoken, and sensible.

The bruise on her face was not near as ugly as that blowup makes it appear. If *she* didn't want to go to the hospital, *we* didn't want to force her."

"But you didn't want to release her, either."

"Of course not." Monk frowned. "She'd not only killed Mark Ransom; she was the only person who *knew* what went on in that room."

"So forced with a choice between questioning Ms. Carelli or taking her to the hospital first, you questioned her. Is that correct?"

Monk hesitated. "Yes."

"How soon after arriving at the Flood did you begin to question her?"

Monk stared at the ceiling. "Roughly three hours."

"And where did the questioning occur?"

"The police station."

"What did you do with Ms. Carelli in the meantime?"

Monk hesitated. "For forty minutes or so, we kept her there. Mostly for the medical examiner."

Paget gave him a sideways look. "To take various tests?"

"Partly."

"Like fingernail scrapings?"

"Yes."

"And reexamining the scratches on the body?"

"Yes."

"So you had time to poke and prod Ms. Carelli for your own purposes, but no time to take Ms. Carelli to the hospital for the purpose of ensuring her well-being."

"Objection." Sharpe stood. "Misstates the prior testimony. Inspector Monk has already testified that Ms. Carelli didn't *want* to go to the hospital."

"Sustained." Once more, Masters frowned at Paget. "Stick to the facts, Mr. Paget."

"Of course, Your Honor." Almost immediately, Paget asked Monk, "So there were roughly two hours that Ms. Carelli spent waiting for you to question her?"

"Yes."

"And these were spent at the homicide bureau?"

"Yes."

"Alone?"

"Yes." Monk paused. "We tried to be sensitive to her rights, Mr. Paget. I'm sure we'd have heard from you if I'd detailed another homicide inspector to chat with her without Miranda warnings."

Paget stared at him. "Speaking of sensitivity, Inspector, did you bring in a rape counselor?"

"No."

"Or a doctor?"

"No."

"Or bring her any food?"

"I don't know." Monk paused. "I know we gave her some coffee."

"With cream and sugar, I hope." Quickly, Paget looked up at Caroline Masters. "My apologies, Your Honor."

Masters, Terri saw, wore a faint smile of amusement. "Respect, Mr. Paget, is never having to say you're sorry. Move on."

"Thank you." He turned back to Monk. "At this point," Paget asked, "did you know how long Ms. Carelli had been without sleep?"

"No."

"Or food?"

"No."

"You never asked?"

Monk hesitated. "Not directly, no."

"But you did know she'd been beaten?"

"She said she'd been hit. If that's what you mean."

"I appreciate the fine distinction, Inspector. Let me put it another way." Pausing, Paget pointed at the picture. "You *did* see that bruise?"

"Yes."

"And Ms. Carelli had already told you that Mark Ransom had tried to rape her."

"Yes."

"And you knew that she had shot him."

"Yes."

"It also appeared from the room that she and Mr. Ransom had been drinking champagne."

"Yes."

Paget looked from Mary to Judge Masters, then back to Charles Monk. "So at the time that you questioned her, at least as far as you knew, in the last eight or so hours, Ms. Carelli's only nutrients were champagne and coffee."

"I suppose so."

"And during those eight hours, you had reason to believe, Ms. Carelli had been struck, sexually assaulted, and forced to shoot someone."

Monk stared at him. "She *wanted* to answer questions."

"Wouldn't *you*, Inspector? Wouldn't any normal person who shot someone in self-defense want at least to say that?"

"Objection," Sharpe cut in. "That question is argumentative."

"Sustained," Masters said. But her face and voice told Terri that Paget's point was made.

Paget still faced Monk. "Are you familiar with the medical definition of shock, Inspector?"

"No." Monk was clearly nettled now. "But I have a layman's experience of shock, gained in twenty years of dealing with violent crime. And in my experience, Ms. Carelli had none of the loss of focus that *I* associate with shock."

Paget stared at him. "I guess we'll have to take your word for it—seeing that there was no doctor on the scene. But are you really comfortable trying to nail Ms. Carelli for discrepancies in what she told you, after eight hours of the trauma you've just acknowledged, without offering her so much as a Big Mac and fries?"

"*Objection,*" Sharpe called out. "This is a court of law, not a high school debate. Rhetorical questions have no place here."

"Mr. Paget," Masters said, "please show the rules of evidence some respect. And for that matter, give the court at least modest credit for intelligence. I got the message five questions ago."

Paget smiled. "Then I'll be happy to sit down," he said.

Sharpe stood. "A few brief questions," she said.

Masters nodded. "Go ahead."

Sharpe faced Monk. "Who terminated your interrogation?" she asked.

"Ms. Carelli."

It was a good opening question, Terri realized. Unable to attack the tape itself, Paget had undercut the basis for it—that Mary was equipped to talk at all. Now Sharpe would try to show that Mary was in full control.

Sharpe went on. "So Ms. Carelli felt free to decide not to answer any more questions."

"Of course."

"When she refused to continue, did Ms. Carelli seem disoriented?"

"Objection," Paget said. "We've already established the witness's lack of medical expertise."

"I'm not asking for a medical opinion," Sharpe retorted. "I'm asking the kind of questions any layperson is entitled to answer: 'Did Ms. Carelli seem confused?' "

"Overruled," Masters said. "The witness may answer."

"No." Monk paused. "I remember thinking that Ms. Carelli was unusually poised and very smart—remarkably so for a woman who'd just shot someone to death." Monk paused again. "The thing that really struck me is that she turned off the tape herself."

Listening, Paget did not change his expression. But Terri knew how much these questions had to hurt; the woman Monk described more closely resembled the cool voice on the tape than the battered face on the easel.

Sharpe moved closer. "Did Ms. Carelli ever ask for food?"

"No. As the tape indicated, she asked for water."

"Did she ever ask for a doctor?"

"No."

"Or for time to rest?"

"No."

Sharpe nodded. "After the end of the tape," she said softly, "did she ask for anything at all?"

"Yes." Monk looked from Mary to Paget. "Yes," he repeated. "She asked for a lawyer."

"This," Marnie Sharpe said on the television, "is a simple act of murder."

Terri and Paget sat in the library, reviewing Terri's notes to help prepare for Elizabeth Shelton. Reporters were clustered outside. They had shouted questions as Paget had driven Terri and Carlo into the garage: the questions were as much about Carlo's acknowledgment of Mary as they were about the trial.

Paget looked up at the screen; in dispassionate tones, he said of Sharpe, "She did well today."

Terri paused, sensing how the loneliness of the hearing must bear down on Paget when he had so much at risk. They had done little but work, avoided all personal subjects; now she wished that there was something she could do for him besides be a lawyer. "You did well too," she told him.

He shrugged. "You're kind to say so. But all I did was nibble at the edge. It's not nearly enough."

He sounded tired, Terri thought, and it was only the first day. "A lot of it's up to Mary," she answered. "You can't kill this case on cross-examination. No one could."

"Let us start," Sharpe was saying in the background, "with the only things about which Ms. Carelli appears to have told the truth to anyone."

Terri watched her for a moment. Quietly, she said, "What *is* the truth, I wonder."

Paget leaned back on the couch, staring into the empty fireplace. Except for the lamps and the spotlit palm in the window, the room was dark; in profile, Terri could not read Paget's face. Finally, he answered, "I try never to ask myself that."

"Because you don't want to know?"

"Partly that." He turned to her. "It feels almost like superstition— that there's some reason that I *shouldn't* know."

"And the other part?"

"The other part is that knowing is impractical." He smiled faintly. "The truth might inhibit my imagination in constructing a defense."

"About the *dead*," Sharpe was noting quietly, "one can say just about *anything*."

"It's a funny game we play," Terri said at length. "It's not about the truth. It's about burdens of proof and rules of evidence—what the prosecution knows, whether they can prove it, whether we can keep things out or cast doubt on what comes in."

Paget nodded. "That may be morally unsatisfying, on a human level. It's what I think civilians find so disenchanting—the feeling that a trial is Kabuki theater and *not* a search for truth." He shrugged. "Of course, they forget that the system is freighted with other values, one of which is that a civilized society is *not* about retribution at any cost. If it were, we'd just skip trials and start tearing Mary's fingernails out until she told 'the truth.' Whatever *that* is."

"Specifically," Sharpe was saying, "Dr. Shelton believes that Mr. Ransom had been dead for a good half hour when Ms. Carelli chose to scratch the buttocks of a corpse."

Paget looked up at the screen. "If I can't do something with *that,*" he said softly, "Mary's close to finished."

In Terri's mind, she heard Monk testifying again, tracing Mary's fingerprints as she drifted about the room at will, touching lamps, tables, drawers in a stranger's hotel suite. Doing what? Terri wondered. And was Ransom still alive, or dead on the floor?

"Do you think she's still lying?" Terri asked Paget.

Paget stared at her. "Yes," he said in a reluctant voice. "At least in part. But I don't know *which* part. Nor do I want to."

Terri considered him. "I'm sorry," she answered softly. "But I think I'd like to know."

"Then do me a favor, Terri. Just don't tell me." He hesitated, then added softly, "I think it's enough to know the truth about our own lives."

Terri fell quiet for a time. "I keep wondering," she ventured, "what happened to the second tape. And, for that matter, to the Lindsay Caldwell tape."

For a moment, Paget looked upstairs, as if afraid that Carlo might hear them. "I have no idea," he finally said. "But seeing as how you've asked, I don't think the tape got lost by accident."

Terri stared at him. "Mary?" she asked.

Paget nodded. "I think so. But I really don't know how. And if that's so, I don't care to know. For my own sake."

On the television, Sharpe's opening statement drew to a close.

"What *I* care to know," Terri said finally, "is what happened in that room between Mary Carelli and Mark Ransom. Perhaps for *my* own sake."

Paget considered her. "But we never *will* know," he answered. "I just hope we never learn what's on that tape."

On the screen, Carlo's face appeared. Paget looked up.

Carlo gazed into the camera. "Christopher Paget is my father," he said simply, "and Mary Carelli is my mother. And all I really have to say to anyone is that I'm very proud of them both."

Paget shook his head. "God," he murmured. "I never wanted this."

The newsman's face returned. "The only comment from Mr. Paget or Ms. Carelli was a press release from Mr. Paget's office, which said only: 'Carlo Carelli Paget is our son. And all we really have to say to anyone is that both of us are proud of him.' "

"The phone was ringing off the hook," Paget said. "Mary and I decided quickly: no interviews on the subject of Carlo, or with Carlo. It's the first thing we've agreed upon in years."

Terri reflected. "I think she really loves him, in her way. It's just not a way I recognize."

Paget became pensive. "You know what I did when she first told me she was pregnant? I asked whose kid he was."

Terri looked at him. "That was a long time ago, Chris. Whatever you said doesn't matter now."

After a time, Paget turned to her. "I really am sorry to be keeping you from Elena."

"I miss her. But this will be over, without Elena thinking much about it." Terri paused for a moment, realized again that she was no longer quite sure where Elena's life was going. But there was nothing she could say to Paget, except to add, "It's Carlo I'm most worried about."

He gazed at her, as if to ask her something. Then he said simply, "I'm afraid of this hearing. For Mary, for me, but most of all for him. I've taken such a chance, it seems."

That was right, Terri knew; the Court TV legal experts were already second-guessing him, and there was more risk than they knew.

"Let's keep going," Terri said. "I've got some thoughts about Shelton."

TWO

Watching Elizabeth Shelton on the stand, Paget recalled that he had liked her instinctively.

Some of it, he decided, was her look of clear-eyed intelligence; she gave the impression of an inner balance in which no hidden angers or ambitions prevented her from being fair. The other part was the subtle sense that—as good a professional as she was—Shelton found her role in life the source of a certain amusement: her tailored suit and bright orange scarf signaled her awareness that she did not have to play medical examiner for a jury, and thus could reach into the closet for something she liked. It made Paget sorry that he did not know her in some other context and that *his* role was to try to discredit her.

But for now, he could only watch her help Marnie Sharpe build the bricks and mortar of a prosecution case.

In a few questions, Sharpe qualified Shelton as an expert in forensic medicine and criminology, with an extensive background in both, and then got to the heart of things.

"Did you examine the medical evidence," Sharpe asked, "with an eye toward corroborating Mary Carelli's initial story?"

Shelton folded her hands. "Yes. I did."

"And was there such corroborating evidence?"

From the bench, Caroline Masters watched intently. "With the exception of the bruise on her face," Shelton responded, "I found none."

"*None,*" Sharpe repeated for emphasis.

Briefly, Shelton nodded; the reluctance of the gesture signaled her dislike for bombast. "That's correct," she answered.

"In a moment," Sharpe said, "I'll ask you to elaborate on that. But Mr. Paget's questions of Inspector Monk bring something else to mind. When you performed your various tests, Dr. Shelton, Ms. Carelli was present, was she not?"

Shelton nodded again. "For a time," she answered. "When I first arrived at Mr. Ransom's room, some of my work involved inspecting Ms. Carelli for signs of violence and other physical evidence."

"And that was when?"

"Perhaps one-fifty. A short time after Ms. Carelli first called 911."

"And did you speak with Ms. Carelli?"

"Yes."

"Could you describe that conversation?"

Shelton paused, looking gravely at Mary Carelli. "Among other things," she said quietly, "I asked her whether Mr. Ransom had penetrated her and whether she wished to receive medical attention."

"And what did she answer?"

"No. To both."

Sharpe nodded. "Could you describe her manner?"

Shelton seemed to reflect. "I would say that she seemed in some distress—still frightened a little. But quite sensible."

"In your opinion, did she exhibit signs of shock?"

"No." Shelton looked at Mary again. "We had a conversation, and the conversation tracked. She seemed appropriately concerned for her own situation."

Sharpe tilted her head. "Did she mention Mr. Ransom's situation?"

Shelton seemed to hesitate. "Her only mention of Mr. Ransom," she said, "was with regard to certain marks on her body—scratches, the bruise. Ms. Carelli attributed them to him."

"And do *you* attribute those to him?"

"I'm unable to. With the sole exception of the bruise on her face, the medical evidence simply does *not* support Ms. Carelli's version of events."

Sharpe nodded her satisfaction. "Could you describe the procedures on which you base that conclusion?"

"Certainly." As Shelton half turned to Caroline Masters, Sharpe moved to stand only a few feet from her. The result seemed an intimate conference among the three of them, two credible professionals advising the finder of fact. It made Paget acutely aware of his gender, and of Mary's isolation.

"We start," Dr. Shelton went on, "with what I would call Ms. Carelli's basic account. That is, her explanation of the physical evidence—which, as I understand it, has remained constant throughout."

It was a shrewd introduction, Paget thought, and obviously rehearsed, for it carried the suggestion that Mary was a liar. Mary's narrowed eyes, watching Shelton, hinted at a sense of betrayal. As he turned briefly to Carlo, he saw that his son looked pale.

"She's good," Terri whispered.

"That basic account," Shelton continued, "is relatively simple: that Mr. Ransom assaulted Ms. Carelli; that in the process he slapped her and scratched her thigh and neck; that during a pause in this same struggle, she was able to produce a Walther .380 from her purse; and that, as they wrestled for it, the gun fired into Mr. Ransom's chest from a distance of two or three inches."

Shelton paused, briefly scanning the courtroom as if to ensure the attention of her audience. She had it, Paget knew; the room was still. "As to Mr. Ransom himself," she went on, "he was found lying on his stomach, with his pants down to his knees. According to Ms. Carelli, this was the result of his attempt to rape her, during which he achieved and maintained an erection." Turning to face Judge Masters directly, Shelton spoke softly but clearly. "There were also scratches on his buttocks. Again according to Ms. Carelli, she inflicted those scratches while fighting off the attempted rape.

"With *that* understanding of Ms. Carelli's account, I employed certain procedures myself, and worked with the crime lab in employing others."

Sharpe turned to Paget. "Will you stipulate, Mr. Paget, to Dr. Shelton's qualification to address work done by the crime lab? Or do we need another expert?"

Paget hesitated. But a second expert might only make things worse; better to take a chance that Shelton would at least be fair. "So stipulated," he answered.

Nodding, Sharpe paused a moment, further drawing in the courtroom and, more important, the judge. Unusual for her, Judge Masters had not spoken in some moments. Her expression was unselfconscious and utterly rapt.

"Could you describe for us," Sharpe asked at length, "each of these procedures."

Shelton nodded. "Certainly," she answered crisply, and turned directly to the judge.

"First, there are the scratches on Ms. Carelli's neck and thigh. Ms.

Carelli says that Mr. Ransom made them. So we examined Mr. Ransom's fingernails for traces of skin."

"And what was the result?"

"We found none."

Sharpe's voice became more pointed. "And if Mr. Ransom *had* scratched Ms. Carelli, would you expect to find skin traces in his fingernails?"

"It's not a foolproof test. But yes, generally."

"Did you also perform that test on Ms. Carelli's nails?"

"Yes."

"And did the test work *then?*"

"Yes." Shelton spoke quietly, to Caroline Masters. "There were traces of skin beneath Ms. Carelli's fingernails."

Leaning forward, Masters asked her first question of the hearing. "Were you able to determine *whose* skin?"

Shelton shook her head. "No. Unless there's enough skin, we usually can't."

"Thank you. Go on, Ms. Sharpe."

Sharpe looked at Shelton with a faint, curious smile. "Did you find anything *else* under Ms. Carelli's nails?"

"Yes."

"And what did you find?"

Shelton paused. "Microscopic fibers of nylon."

Paget stiffened. Sharpe had never told him this; her smile had anticipated his own surprise. "In your opinion," she asked, "what is the origin of the nylon fibers."

Shelton turned toward Mary. Softly, she said, "There's no way to be certain. But they're consistent with Ms. Carelli's panty hose."

"And were there any traces of nylon under Mr. Ransom's fingernails?"

"None."

From behind him, Paget heard a low, tense buzz; the media people understood the wound that Shelton had just dealt Mary Carelli and now were poised for more.

"As you understood Ms. Carelli," Sharpe went on, "Mr. Ransom was sexually aroused during the alleged attack. Is that correct?"

"Yes."

"Did you attempt to corroborate that?"

"Yes." Shelton turned to Masters. "Prior to orgasm, and even intercourse, it's usual for the erect penis to emit a small amount of semen, sometimes enough to cause pregnancy without ejaculation. To determine whether that has happened, we swab the penis for any residue of semen."

"And did you do that," Sharpe asked, "with Mr. Ransom's penis?"

"Yes."

"And what was the result?"

"There was none." Shelton kept her eyes on Masters. "We found no secretion."

"Indeed, did you find any evidence, of any kind, that Mr. Ransom was sexually aroused?"

"No. None."

Sharpe stood straighter, moving back a couple of steps; both her tone and her posture bespoke a new command. "Let us move to the fatal gunshot wound. Originally, Ms. Carelli told Inspector Monk that she and Mr. Ransom had struggled with the gun and that it had fired into Mr. Ransom's chest from two to three inches. Was the crime lab able to form an opinion as to that?"

"Yes. It's not consistent with the evidence."

"When you say 'it' . . ."

"I mean that the gun was not fired from two to three inches or, in their opinion, from anywhere closer than at least two to three *feet.*" Pausing, Shelton turned to the judge again. "As you know from your own experience at the P.D.'s office, near gunshot wounds leave distinct residue."

"I *do* know," Masters said dryly. "From my own experience in cross-examining *you,* I learned great respect for gunshot residue. As I did for your skills as a witness."

The remark, pleasant yet somewhat Delphic, caused Shelton to smile but made Sharpe freeze for a split second, appraising Caroline Masters. When Sharpe began again, Paget sensed a shade less confidence. "Could you tell us what the powder marks in *this* case showed?"

"Yes. The weapon was a Walther .380, and the bullet was a Winchester Silver Tip—high-tech equipment, by the way. From two to three inches, *that* gun and *that* bullet would have left a distinct charcoal-gray circle of gunpowder on Mr. Ransom's chest, several inches in diameter." Shelton paused. "Here, there was no residue of powder. None."

"And what do you conclude from this?"

"Start with this fact: the nearest that gun could have fired and left no gunshot residue is at least two feet and probably closer to three." Shelton turned to face Mary. "From which we conclude that Ms. Carelli shot Mr. Ransom not from two or three inches but from two or more feet."

Mary's eyes met Shelton's. Between them, Sharpe nodded slowly, as if silenced by the gravity of what she had just heard. Then she asked softly, "And what about Ms. Carelli's story of a struggle for the gun?"

Shelton still gazed at Mary. "No sign of it," she answered with equal quiet. "No fingerprints. No powder marks on Mr. Ransom's hands. As you might expect had there been a struggle."

The courtroom was quite still. Paget knew why: the cumulative effect of Shelton's crisp testimony and calm demeanor was devastating to Mary Carelli. It was hard for Paget to sit there as if nothing were amiss.

"On the tape," Sharpe asked, "Ms. Carelli said that she called 911 as soon as possible. Do you recall that?"

"Yes."

"And how long after that call did you arrive at the Flood?"

"Not long. Perhaps fifteen minutes."

Sharpe paused. "And how long, in your opinion, had Mr. Ransom been dead at the time you arrived."

"It's hard to be precise. But some little time—close to an hour, at least."

"On what do you base that?"

"His blood had begun collecting in his chest cavity. When the heart stops pumping, the blood flows to the lowest point in the body and stops there. It's really just a matter of gravity. But it doesn't happen all at once." Shelton paused. "In my opinion, the pallor of Mr. Ransom's skin suggested that the process had well begun."

"From which you conclude. . . ?"

"That Mr. Ransom had been dead at least one-half hour when Ms. Carelli called 911. Perhaps more."

"Do you know what Ms. Carelli *did* between the time that she shot Mark Ransom and the time that she called 911?"

Shelton still looked at Mary. Softly, she said, "I can only surmise."

"Indeed." Sharpe paused. "Which brings us to the scratches on Mr. Ransom's buttocks. Did you form a medical opinion as to those?"

Shelton's eyes flicked toward the judge, then looked away. As Masters stared down at her, Shelton's eyes fixed on some middle distance. "Yes," she answered slowly. "I did. After a great deal of thought."

"And what," Sharpe prodded, "was that opinion?"

Shelton turned to her. "That the scratches were inflicted *after* Mr. Ransom's death."

The courtroom murmur rose again and stayed suspended between crescendo and diminuendo, sustained by new voices and questions.

The gavel cracked. "This is a courtroom," Masters snapped, "not an audience participation show. If some of you don't get that, you can watch these proceedings on television, with everybody else." She turned to Sharpe, frowning as if the prosecution were at fault. "Proceed."

Sharpe nodded. "On what," she asked Shelton, "do you base your opinion?"

Shelton turned to Mary again; this time her gaze was reticent, almost an apology. "On the scratches themselves. Unlike the usual scratch, such as those on Ms. Carelli, there were no burst capillaries or other signs of bleeding." Pausing, Shelton seemed to exhale. "From which I conclude that the blood in Mr. Ransom's buttocks had already departed. Because his heart had stopped beating."

The courtroom was silent again. For the first time, Caroline Masters gazed not at Elizabeth Shelton but at Mary Carelli. Whose eyes had shut.

"Let us step back," Sharpe was saying, "and take *another* look at the medical evidence. A look which follows the evidence itself, *not* Mary Carelli's story."

Paget rose. "Is there a question in there somewhere," he inquired, "or is Ms. Sharpe about to announce her candidacy for higher office?"

Masters gazed at him. "Is there an objection in there somewhere?"

"Yes, Your Honor, to the form of the question. I can't find it." Paget stepped forward. "I've let Ms. Sharpe go on for over an hour, without objection. But when she begins to sound like Charles Laughton in *Witness for the Prosecution,* it's time for someone to remind her that *she* is not the witness and that speeches are not facts."

"You've let Ms. Sharpe go," Masters rejoined, "because her questions aren't objectionable. But speeches are." She turned to Sharpe. "No preambles, Counsel."

"Very well, Your Honor." Sharpe faced Shelton again. "Based on the medical evidence, Ms. Carelli shot Mr. Ransom from several feet, is that correct?"

"Yes."

"So that, in your view, it is also possible that the blow to Ms. Carelli's face was *not* inflicted in a hand-to-hand struggle but in some other way."

"Objection," Paget snapped. "Calls for speculation."

"I agree," Judge Masters said. "But for what it is worth, I'll take Dr. Shelton's speculation."

"Yes," Shelton said to her. "It's possible. In my opinion, Ms. Carelli's bruise *was* caused by a slap to the face. But there is nothing to say *how* that slap was inflicted, or under what circumstances." She paused. "Or even, necessarily, that it was Mr. Ransom who slapped her."

"And in your view, there is nothing to show that Mr. Ransom was sexually aroused?"

"Objection," Paget said again. "These questions have been asked and answered. Only this time they're leading."

Masters nodded. "True enough, Mr. Paget. But I'll allow Ms. Sharpe some leeway to summarize the evidence."

"No," Shelton said to Sharpe. "There's no evidence of sexual arousal."

Sharpe paused. "Nor," she said, "do Mr. Ransom's fingernails suggest that it was *he* who scratched Ms. Carelli."

"That's correct."

"Because the only fingernails with skin beneath them were Ms. Carelli's."

"Correct."

"And it was under *Ms. Carelli's* nails, not Mr. Ransom's, that you found traces of nylon fiber."

"Yes."

"Consistent with Ms. Carelli's panty hose."

"Yes."

Sharpe leaned back. "Based on the medical evidence, how would you characterize Ms. Carelli's story?"

Shelton gave her a considered look. "What I would say is that certain *parts* of Ms. Carelli's story—the gunshot distance in particular—

are not consistent with the medical evidence. Everything else but the slap is unsupported."

Sharpe nodded. "Then let me pose you an alternative, based on the same medical evidence." She paused, voice rising in a rhythmic cadence. "Is it possible that Ms. Carelli murdered Mr. Ransom and did not call 911 until roughly forty minutes later, during which time she pulled his pants down, scratched his buttocks, scraped her own thigh and neck and tore her own panty hose, all the while concocting a phony defense of rape?"

"*Objection!*" Paget stood, walking forward amid the shocked murmur of those watching. "The question partakes of the fantasy I described in Ms. Sharpe's opening statement. It's hypothetical, calls for speculation and, because it misstates, distorts, and selectively ignores the evidence, lacks any reasonable foundation. Put another way, it's moonshine."

Judge Masters smiled thinly. "And I suppose you don't like it, either. Most of what you say is valid, Mr. Paget—technically speaking. But we don't have a jury to protect from prejudice here, and I'm capable of according Dr. Shelton's response whatever weight I think it's worth." She paused. "And for the record, I do think it's worth hearing."

Turning, Paget saw Mary's face, suddenly fixed and white. Terri looked down; behind them, Carlo had a wounded, helpless expression. In the silent courtroom, Paget's walk back to counsel's table seemed to take too long.

He sat, arranging his face into a look of bored resignation.

"In my opinion," Shelton told Masters, "the medical evidence is more consistent with Ms. Sharpe's hypothetical description than it is with Ms. Carelli's version of events."

Sharpe nodded. With evident satisfaction, she said to Caroline Masters, "That's all I have, Your Honor. At least for *this* witness."

"Very well." Judge Masters looked at Paget. "Does the defense have questions of this witness?"

"Yes, Your Honor. Quite a few, actually."

The judge glanced at her watch. "We'll take lunch break, then. Back at one-thirty."

Without ceremony, Caroline Masters rose and walked off the bench. The courtroom erupted. Paget stood there a moment, lost in thought. When he turned, Carlo had come to Mary and stood gazing down at her, trying to smile as she tried to smile back. They looked so much alike that it hurt Paget to see.

"Come on," he said to Teresa Peralta. "We've got work to do."

Paget rose from the defense table, walked forward a few feet, stopped to face Elizabeth Shelton. The spot that he had chosen was on the other side of Caroline Masters; as Shelton turned to face him, the judge watched them both. Until Paget spoke, there was no sound at all.

Quietly, he asked, "You don't know *what* happened between Mary Carelli and Mark Ransom, do you?"

Shelton appraised him for a moment. "No," she answered. "I wasn't there. I can only assess the medical evidence."

"So that you can't testify to whether or not there was a struggle."

"No."

Paget paused. "Or, for that matter," he asked softly, "to whether Mr. Ransom attempted to rape Ms. Carelli."

"No." Shelton paused. "All that I can determine is whether the evidence tends to support Ms. Carelli's claim that an assault occurred."

Paget gave her a sideways glance. "Among that evidence is the swelling and bruise on Ms. Carelli's face, correct?"

"Yes."

"And at the time you examined her, you determined that this bruise had been forcibly inflicted."

Shelton paused; her intelligent face held a trace of puzzlement that she did not try to conceal. "Yes."

"And to your knowledge, the prosecution does not claim that Ms. Carelli *arrived* at Mark Ransom's suite in that condition, does it?"

"To my knowledge, no."

Paget nodded. "In your opinion, was the damage to Ms. Carelli's face inflicted by an open hand?"

"So I understand."

"By someone using his right hand?"

"Yes."

"And was Mr. Ransom right-handed?"

"So I understand."

Paget glanced up at Judge Masters. She was watching Shelton with an air of dispassionate interest; Paget imagined her remembering, perhaps without fondness, cases where Elizabeth Shelton had doomed Masters's clients to a verdict of guilty. He turned back to Shelton.

"Do you have a view," he asked, "as to whether the person who struck Ms. Carelli was right-handed?"

Shelton paused. It was a moment, Paget knew, where she could choose to hurt or help him: only Shelton knew whether or not she had an opinion, and unless she volunteered it, there was nothing Paget could do. His tension rose with each second of her silence.

"Yes," she said quietly.

"And what is that opinion?"

Shelton seemed to draw a breath. "That it is much more probable than not that the blow to Ms. Carelli was inflicted by a right-handed person."

Paget nodded. "And what are your reasons for that?"

"There are two, really. As a matter of habit, a right-handed person would strike such a blow with his right hand. The fact that it also involves violence, which in turn suggests spontaneity, reinforces the likelihood that the assailant was acting on instinct." Shelton paused. "The instinctive reflex of a right-handed person is obvious."

Paget watched her face. "There was a second reason, you said."

Quickly, Shelton glanced at Sharpe. "A more marginal one," she answered. "The blow was struck with considerable force. A right-handed person will have more power in his, or her, right hand and arm."

Paget tilted his head. "Incidentally, is Mary Carelli right- or left-handed?"

Shelton turned to Mary. In a cool, clear voice, she answered, "Left-handed, I believe."

Paget nodded. "In your opinion, could Mary Carelli have inflicted this kind of damage by slapping herself?"

Shelton kept looking at Mary. "That's *conceivable,*" she finally said. "But no, it's not very likely. It's never been my hypothesis that Ms. Carelli did this to herself."

On the bench, Caroline Masters looked from Shelton to Mary. "How many such blows," she asked, "would it take to inflict more serious damage?"

Shelton turned, her face pensive. Paget sensed that, like Marnie

Sharpe, Shelton was troubled by the thought that Mary was using the issue of rape to cover an act of murder but that, more than Sharpe, Shelton was also troubled by doubts she could not name. "It's hard to say," she told Judge Masters. "With repeated blows, the possibilities range from a fractured cheekbone, broken teeth, nose, or jaw, and, of course, a concussion." Shelton looked back to Mary. "If the victim loses consciousness and falls, other injuries could result. Perhaps more serious."

"What effect on the victim's consciousness and perceptions might such a blow cause?"

The judge was engaged now, Paget thought; Caroline Masters had not wholly lost the defense lawyer's habit of mind, and the question was a good one.

"Again," Shelton answered slowly, "it's hard to say."

"Would the possibilities include shock and an impairment of vision?"

Shelton considered her. "Shock is a medical term, Your Honor, involving a cluster of symptoms I did not observe in Ms. Carelli. But some degree of disorientation is clearly possible."

"So that the victim's perception of events, or memory of them, might be less precise?"

"That could happen, yes."

"Thank you, Dr. Shelton." The judge turned back to Paget. "Excuse me, Mr. Paget. The court was curious as to those points."

"As were we." Paget wondered whether the judge's intervention was on Mary's behalf, out of concern for a possible victim, or whether Masters was settling some intellectual score with Shelton from another case. He moved closer to the witness stand, stopping when he had found his next line of inquiry. "Following up on the court's questions, you take issue with Ms. Carelli's memory that the gun fired two or three inches from Mr. Ransom's chest, correct?"

"Yes."

"But you concede that it *could* have fired from two or three feet?"

Shelton's voice turned colder. "That would be the minimum distance, yes."

Paget nodded. "It is also true, is it not, that you cannot determine the angle from which the bullet was fired."

"Not in this case, no."

"Nor can you tell whether, at the moment of impact, Mr. Ransom was recoiling."

"No."

"Or leaning back for any reason."

"No."

Paget paused. At the margin of his vision he saw Mary hunch forward, as if to help him. "So there is nothing in the medical evidence," he said, "which precludes the possibility that in their struggle, the gun became pointed at Mr. Ransom and that he recoiled, shrinking away from it at the moment of discharge."

Shelton gave him a calm, level gaze. "I can't *preclude* it," she answered, "but there are things which argue against that. Ms. Carelli claims that Mr. Ransom was wrestling her for the gun, and yet the only fingerprints we found on it were Ms. Carelli's." She paused, frowning. "Also, were he falling back with his hands in front of him, a shot from two or three feet would likely leave a residue of powder on his palms and fingers. We found none."

Paget hesitated. Shelton had just hurt him; lulled by her air of candor, he had forgotten how good she was. He struggled to find another question before he looked too rattled. "But you don't know," he managed, "whether Mr. Ransom was grasping the gun itself or Ms. Carelli's wrists."

"No."

"Nor do you know the position of his hands at the instant that the gun went off."

"No."

It was, Paget thought, the best he could do. "Let us move," he continued, "to other points of your direct testimony. You testified, did you not, that Ms. Carelli seemed lucid at the time that you first spoke to her."

"Yes."

"But you weren't present when Mr. Ransom died."

"No. Of course not."

"Then you have *no* understanding as to whether, from the moment of death until she called 911, Ms. Carelli was in shock. Or at least, as you put it, disoriented."

"No."

"So that, in contrast to Ms. Sharpe's hypothetical scenario, in which

Ms. Carelli spent that time in a state of hyperactivity, creating evidence and mutilating corpses, it is entirely possible that Ms. Carelli was seized by torpor and confusion."

"Objection," Sharpe cut in. "Mischaracterizes the prior testimony."

Masters gave her a quizzical look. "Does it? If so, not by much. Overruled."

"That is *possible*, yes." Shelton's voice became firm. "My answer to Ms. Sharpe's question was based on anomalies in the physical evidence. Anomalies which did not support Ms. Carelli's account of events between the time of Mr. Ransom's death and the call to 911."

"Speaking of which," Paget said, "have you ever heard the 911 tape of Ms. Carelli's call?"

Slowly, Shelton shook her head. "No. I have not."

Paget turned to Masters. "Your Honor, the prosecution has already stipulated to the admissibility of that tape. I would ask leave of the court to play it for Dr. Shelton."

"For what purpose?" Sharpe interjected. "Everyone acknowledges that Ms. Carelli placed the call and, moreover, that the call was *not* to Dr. Shelton. I don't know what you could possibly ask her about."

"It's simple," Paget responded. "Dr. Shelton has testified to Ms. Carelli's lucidity at the time of her arrival, based partly on her tone of voice and the content of her speech. I'd like her to compare her impressions of Ms. Carelli *then* to Ms. Carelli's earlier call to 911."

"I object," Sharpe answered. "We have not attempted to qualify Dr. Shelton as a voice interpreter. Or, for that matter, as a mentalist. Her earlier testimony was based on a doctor's physical impression of a woman sitting right in front of her."

"That's true," Masters answered, "but you also attempted to use Dr. Shelton's impressions, at least by implication, to cover Ms. Carelli's mental state for a good half day. I'm going to allow the tape to be played."

When Paget turned, Terri already had the tape recorder on the table in front of him. She smiled with her eyes: this line of questioning had been her suggestion. Beside her, Mary stared at the tape machine with a somewhat haunted look; Paget could not tell if this was because she did not wish to relive the moment of her call or was thinking of another tape, which she hoped never to see.

Terri switched on the tape recorder. As it spun, Paget suddenly saw Carlo, listening intently for the sound of his mother's voice.

The courtroom was silent.

"San Francisco Emergency," the male voice called out.

No one answered. The voice snapped again, "San Francisco Emergency."

There was yet more silence. Then, quite softly, Mary said, "There's been an accident."

In the courtroom, her tone was thin, uncertain. It was as if she were repeating a dream she vaguely remembered, to someone she did not know.

"What happened?" the man asked.

"There's been an accident," she repeated. Her voice was weary; its tone said that her explanation was perfectly adequate and that he should listen more closely.

Listening, Caroline Masters narrowed her eyes, as if at some subtle alteration in her perception. The expression on Shelton's face was one of deep concentration.

On the tape, the man became more patient. "What kind of accident?" he asked.

There was a long pause. In a tone of disbelief, Mary said, "A gun went off."

Paget turned to Mary. Staring down at the table, she slowly shook her head. To Paget, the gesture bespoke a tragic wonderment, the helpless desire to reach back in time, change what had happened.

"Someone's been shot?"

"Yes." The voice quavered. "I think he's dead."

"Where are you?" he demanded.

"The Hotel Flood." There was a long pause. Then, in a tone of mystified apology, Mary said, "I can't remember the room."

"Who is this?"

"Wait," Mary interjected. "It's registered to Mark Ransom. A suite."

The last words held an odd note of relief, as if Mary had been frightened by a loss of memory.

"Who is this?" the voice demanded.

"Just come," Mary answered shrilly, and hung up.

When Paget gazed at Mary again, she had turned to Shelton with tears in her eyes. Shelton had lost color.

The audience was silent. A few shifted in their seats, some looked away. Paget was reminded of the eerie feeling he had once had, listening to the taped words of a flight crew in the moments before their airplane crashed.

Softly, he asked Shelton, "Does that sound like the woman you remember?"

Shelton gazed up. There was no good answer to the question; Mary's voice on the tape sounded shaky enough that to answer "yes" would make Shelton seem unfeeling. "No," Shelton said at last. "In person, she sounded somewhat different."

"How so?"

"When I saw her, she seemed to think slowly but to be in control." She paused. "The voice on the tape sounds more *distant*, I suppose. More overwhelmed."

"And the woman on the tape," Paget said, "was also much closer to the events the prosecution faults her for not remembering quite as well as it would like."

"Objection," Sharpe called out. "This time *I* don't hear a question."

"There was none," Caroline Masters said. "Do find a question, Mr. Paget. A proper one."

"Surely." Paget turned to Shelton again. "So you would concede," he pursued, "that her tone of voice in speaking to you does not mean that trauma didn't affect her behavior that evening—either alone with Mr. Ransom's body or answering questions from Inspector Monk?"

"I would concede that, for what it is worth." She gave Mary a cool, quiet gaze. "As Ms. Sharpe pointed out, I'm not a mentalist."

"Then we'll return to the physical evidence—which, I believe you testified, contained 'anomalies.' "

"Yes."

"And one of these anomalies was that, unlike Ms. Carelli, your test turned up no skin samples under Mr. Ransom's fingernails?"

"Yes."

Paget looked puzzled. "Did Mr. Ransom have long fingernails?"

Shelton paused. "No. Not at all."

"But Ms. Carelli did."

"Yes. In fact, she'd broken one."

Paget paused. "Isn't it easier to retrieve skin samples from someone with long fingernails?"

Shelton nodded. "Easier, yes. But it's common to do so with fingernails of ordinary length, from a man."

"Were Mr. Ransom's nails of 'ordinary length'?"

Shelton hesitated. "They were a bit shorter, I think. It appeared that he'd just clipped them."

"Might that affect the test?"

"It might, Mr. Paget. But if you take this line too far, one is left to wonder *how* Mr. Ransom managed to scratch Ms. Carelli."

There was a murmur in the courtroom; with one thrust, Shelton had stopped Paget's momentum and refocused attention on the prosecution's case. Stunned, Paget tried to summon a weary look, as if he had expected this. "It is nonetheless true," he said, "that your test doesn't always work."

"Yes. That's true."

"So that Mark Ransom could have scratched Mary Carelli and yet not collected enough skin beneath his nails to show up on his test."

"That's possible, yes." Shelton paused for emphasis. "But in the majority of cases, that test works. At least for scratches as deep as Ms. Carelli's."

Shelton had begun to fight him, Paget realized: partly out of professional pride and partly, he suspected, because whatever Shelton's doubt about the evidence, her experience told her that too much was wrong with Mary's story. He tried to search for a lower key. "One of the areas I found most troublesome," he said, "was that regarding Ms. Carelli's panty hose. I'd like to ask a few questions and see whether there might not be some other way to look at it."

Shelton gave a small shrug. "All right."

"You testified that you found nylon fibers, of the kind appearing in Ms. Carelli's panty hose, under *her* nails but not under Mr. Ransom's, is that correct?"

"Yes."

"And in part, it was based on that conclusion that you agreed with Ms. Sharpe that Ms. Carelli might have fabricated evidence."

"In part, yes."

Paget paused. "I don't know precisely how to broach this, Dr. Shelton, but putting on panty hose involves considerable effort, does it not?"

Shelton gave him a long, speculative gaze, which culminated in a slight change in her eyes. "It can," she said.

Paget nodded. "And in the course of that effort, it's a common thing for panty hose to rip."

Paget felt Masters's expression hover between interest and amusement, and then decide on interest. Shelton's eyes narrowed slightly. "Yes," she said with an expert's gravity, "panty hose commonly rip." She paused. "At least in my observation."

"So that in the normal act of putting on panty hose, as Ms. Carelli did that morning, it would be possible to rip them."

"Yes. Of course."

"And it would also be possible, in the normal course of putting on panty hose, for Ms. Carelli to get fibers of nylon under her fingernails."

Shelton watched him. "Yes."

"Common, even?"

She hesitated. "I suppose not uncommon."

Turning, Paget nodded to Terri, whose questions these were. Then he looked out at the media people, crowding the benches between the cameras and behind the dock of the court. Perhaps half, as he already knew, were women; most wore skirts or dresses. "I wonder, Dr. Shelton, if you could cast an eye with me on the representatives of the media."

"Objection." Sharpe stood. "I don't know what diversion Mr. Paget intends, but we've moved far afield from the evidence surrounding Ms. Carelli's shooting of Mark Ransom."

"You really don't know what Mr. Paget intends, Ms. Sharpe?" Masters paused, eyes sweeping the press. "*I* know, and I'm curious about the answer. If only because this is yet another indignity to which women are subjected."

Sharpe flushed. "I don't find much amusement here, Your Honor."

"Nor do I, Counsel. And as I understand Mr. Paget's underlying point, it's very serious indeed."

"Thank you, Your Honor." Paget turned back to Shelton. "Taking a rough count of the press, I'd guess that around fifty or so are women. Would you agree?"

"I haven't counted. Sitting here, I see a number."

Paget nodded. "And what percentage of those women reporters," he asked softly, "would have nylon fibers under their nails if you subjected them to the same test that you administered to Ms. Carelli?"

Paget watched the faces in front of him focus on Elizabeth Shelton; beneath the particulars of the question, Paget sensed the press absorbing its subliminal impact—the instinctive fear of being falsely accused. "I have no idea what percentage," Shelton answered.

"But certainly some."

"In all probability. At least a few."

"None of whom, we can assume, murdered anyone on the way to the courthouse."

Shelton looked out at the faces as if searching for suspects. Without smiling, she answered, "I assume not."

"Thank you. Having eliminated the media as suspects, I'd like to return to Ms. Carelli. You've already agreed that she could have gotten nylon fibers under her nails simply by putting on her panty hose." His voice softened. "But it is also possible, is it not, that Ms. Carelli could have grasped the panty hose in an effort to stop Mark Ransom from pulling them off."

For a long time, Shelton simply stared at him. "Yes," she said finally. "That's also possible."

"And these various possibilities tend to undercut Ms. Sharpe's hypothesis that Ms. Carelli manufactured evidence."

Shelton looked pensive. "They *cast doubt,*" she corrected, "on one element of that hypothesis. But in addition to the absence of skin under Mr. Ransom's nails, we also have the absence of semen and the apparent infliction of postmortem scratches on Mr. Ransom's buttocks."

Paget nodded. "Let's take the semen first. That test is hardly foolproof, is it?"

"No test is. But in the vast majority of cases, erections cause secretions well before ejaculation."

"But not in all cases."

"No."

"And even in cases where there *may* have been secretions, your test is not one hundred percent?"

"No." Shelton sat straighter, a note of professional challenge entering her voice. "But you may have noticed, Mr. Paget, that your questions presume an unusual confluence of test failures. I believe that our tests are better than that and, for that matter, that *we* are."

Paget paused. He was coming to the most delicate part of his examination; he could not afford to antagonize Dr. Shelton. "I was not suggesting," he said easily, "that you and your office are not highly professional. Merely that your office handles the cases you are given and that this particular prosecution case is highly circumstantial."

Sharpe rose again. "Mr. Paget complained about speeches. I'd like to register my own complaint. Particularly when Mr. Paget's only purpose is to attack the prosecution."

Paget turned to Sharpe. "My only purpose," he said, "was to clarify any misunderstanding. In the course of which I thought it appropriate to distinguish between *Dr. Shelton's* professional competence and *your* case."

Masters leaned forward. "That's quite enough, Mr. Paget. Press on."

"Thank you, Your Honor." Paget turned back to Shelton. "Am I correct in understanding, Dr. Shelton, that a significant part of the prosecution hypothesis regarding fabricated evidence are the scratches on Mark Ransom's buttocks?"

Shelton considered him. "It's a part, yes. I wouldn't care to characterize its significance."

"But you concede, do you not, that you could be mistaken—that the scratches could have occurred *before* Mark Ransom died."

"Again, it's possible. But based on the lack of bleeding, the absence of damaged capillaries, I believe that the scratches occurred *after* Mr. Ransom died."

Paget looked at her. "Are you familiar, Dr. Shelton, with the procedures employed by paramedics in answering a call to 911?"

"Yes, I am."

"And is there a uniform procedure in San Francisco County when they first attend the victim?"

"Yes. Unless the condition of the body makes it obvious that the person is dead, the paramedics *must* try to revive him or her. That means attempt to get a heartbeat, putting on pads."

"And did they do that to Mark Ransom?"

"I understand that they did." Shelton paused. "Mark Ransom had a single wound; under the guidelines, they could *not* conclude that he was dead."

"And that would involve checking Mark Ransom's heartbeat?"

"Among other things, yes."

Paget summoned a puzzled expression. "But at the time you examined Mr. Ransom, wasn't he lying facedown on the carpet?"

"Yes." Shelton hesitated. "My understanding is that they rolled him over. But once they determined that Mr. Ransom was dead, they restored his body to the position in which they found it."

Paget nodded. "In other words, they found him on his stomach, flipped him on his back, and flipped him on his stomach again. Is that correct?"

"That is my understanding, yes. Less elegantly put."

"And in doing so, they had to handle Mr. Ransom's body."

Shelton's eyes narrowed. "Yes."

"The body of a man who, according to your report, weighed roughly two hundred and twenty-five pounds."

"That was his weight, yes."

"And they do all this quite rapidly, correct?"

"They *should*. On the assumption that the victim may still be alive."

Paget paused for a moment, looking from Caroline Masters, intent and quite still, back to Elizabeth Shelton. "Isn't it possible," he asked softly, "that the *paramedics* inflicted those scratches on Mr. Ransom's buttocks?"

Shelton stared at him a moment. There was silence; then, at length, she nodded. It seemed less an answer to Paget's question than a gesture of admiration. "Yes," she answered finally. "I don't know how likely it is, but that's possible."

"And, it is fair to say, the existence of that possibility undermines the hypothesis Ms. Sharpe posed to you?"

"To a point." When Shelton spoke again, her words were softer, directed at Paget alone. "But if Mark Ransom scratched Mary Carelli, and the paramedics scratched Mark Ransom, whose skin was under Mary Carelli's nails?"

The thrust was so perfect, its delivery so sincere, that Paget felt the entire painstaking cross-examination slide slowly out from under him. He did not need the courtroom murmur to know how badly she had wounded him. Was grateful, even, that it gave him time to think.

Masters's gavel landed. "Mr. Paget," she inquired. "Do you have anything more?"

"Just a couple of questions," he said casually. "You've named two possibilities for the origin of the skin beneath Ms. Carelli's nails. The first is that she scratched Mr. Ransom, which, although you posit it happened after his death, could have happened before. Is that correct?"

"Yes."

"You also posit that Ms. Carelli may have scratched herself in an effort to manufacture evidence."

"Yes."

"Isn't there a third possibility?"

Shelton gave him a guarded look. "Such as?"

Paget moved forward. "That in the struggle to keep her panty hose on—in her struggle to prevent this man from raping her—Ms. Carelli scratched her own thigh."

Shelton frowned a moment, staring at her lap; Paget felt her reviewing the evidence, less for this specific question than to ask herself what was fair. Then she looked up at him again.

"Yes," she answered softly. "That's possible."

Paget felt his own relief. "Thank you, Dr. Shelton," he said. "That's all I have."

She nodded, giving him a faint smile, and then Paget sat down.

Sharpe was quickly on her feet. "I was struck, Dr. Shelton, by something you said. I believe it was—and I paraphrase—that Mr. Paget's questions presume an unusual confluence of test failures. What did you mean by that?"

Shelton thought for a moment. "What I meant to say was that for Ms. Carelli's account to be right would involve a sequence of botched tests and skewed judgments involving this office, as well as a high degree of coincidence."

Sharpe nodded. "Specifically, it would require the tests to have missed skin under Mr. Ransom's fingernails."

"Yes." Shelton corrected herself. "Although it's not uncommon that there is no skin to find."

Sharpe frowned. "But it would also," she prodded, "assume that the tests missed evidence of sexual arousal."

"Yes."

"And for Mr. Ransom to have no gunshot residue on his hands, despite Ms. Carelli's account of their struggle."

"Yes."

"And for him to be rearing back when she shot him."

Shelton nodded. "Yes."

"And for Ms. Carelli to have ripped her own panty hose."

"That's all true."

"And unless Mr. Ransom's scratches were caused by paramedics, it would also require for you to be wrong about *when* they were inflicted."

"Again, yes."

Sharpe looked incredulous. "Have you *ever* been that wrong?"

Shelton tilted her head. "I certainly hope not."

"And in your opinion, what does all that render Ms. Carelli's story?"

For a long moment, Shelton looked across at Mary. "Medically implausible," she said quietly. "To my regret, I simply don't believe her."

THREE

MARY CARELLI SEARCHED Carlo's face.

They sat at a corner table in the Café Majestic, an elegant Victorian room with ceiling fans and a pianist playing quietly in the background. As she had expected, the other diners shot them glances of recognition. But she had asked Carlo to dinner despite the possibility of this; the one thing that had disturbed her more than Elizabeth Shelton's last words was the way that Carlo had tried to cheer her.

Mary wished he had not come to court. But she did not want him to feel that his presence was a burden; Chris had made the decision, and it was done. "I haven't told you," she said finally, "how much it means to have you with me. The problem is that I'm not used to depending on anyone, so I end up feeling guilty." Smiling faintly, she finished: "Assuming that's a phrase I should be using."

She watched him attempt a smile of his own. As best he could, Carlo was trying to love someone he no longer knew; in the face of what Marnie Sharpe had placed before him, Mary found this both touching and painful. "You'll be all right," Carlo said finally. "Dad forced her to back off a lot."

The comment carried wistful undertones, as if Carlo hoped that his father's determination meant that *he* believed in Mary. But all that Mary could do was to tell Carlo that she believed in Christopher Paget. "He's doing a wonderful job," she answered. "He has a hard case, you know."

Carlo gave her a querying glance. "How do you mean?"

Mary steeled herself. Her job was to make him believe that she was unburdening herself, rather than trying to spare him something. "There are things I didn't tell the police," she said softly. "For reasons of my own. Chris's problem with me is that he's guessed that."

It hurt to see him struggling to be stoic and adult; once more, Mary questioned the delicate judgment involved in having Paget represent her. In a flat voice, Carlo asked, "Is it too late to tell him?"

"For some things, far too late." Mary paused. "Whatever my reasons *then,* Carlo, I have very good ones *now.* Please just accept that."

Carlo nodded slowly. "Okay."

Mary watched him wonder. She had not known how hard it would be to forfeit her son's trust, how deeply he had captured her. But she must leave Carlo with at least one parent to be proud of.

"There is one thing," she said, "that I do need *you* to know about."

It seemed to reach him. "You're my mother," he answered. "Whatever you need to say to me, it's all right."

By instinct, Mary shrank from thinking of herself in terms of need. But it was better for Carlo to think she needed him than to understand that it was his needs that were driving her. She put her hand on his. "There's a tape," she said, "of me talking to a psychiatrist. Mark Ransom had it."

Carlo had not yet learned Paget's pose that surprise was beyond his emotional range; alarm and confusion crossed his face before he found composure. "Does the D.A. know?" he asked.

"Yes. They think that's why I killed him." She paused. "There'll be a recess tomorrow or the next day. For a conference in chambers, while your father tries to keep the tape out of evidence."

"So Dad already knew?"

"*Now* he knows. But only because they found it." Mary kept her voice level; don't show him how hard this is, she told herself, or how scared you are of what Marnie Sharpe could do. "It concerns my time as a lawyer," she finished. "Things I'm deeply ashamed of."

"But to *kill* over it? That's what they think?"

"The tape would ruin my career." Mary gave a thin smile. "I seem to have given some people the impression that would be enough."

Carlo shook his head; Mary could not tell whether it was in disbelief that anyone would think that or at what she had just told him.

"That *isn't* enough," she said softly. "Not to murder someone."

Carlo was silent for a time. "And the things Dad *doesn't* know. . . ?"

"Belong to me."

Carlo was staring at her hand, still on his. Then he turned it, so that her hand rested in his palm, and closed his fingers around hers.

His silent simple gesture brought Mary close to tears. "While Chris is trying to defend me," she said quietly, "there are certain things he doesn't ask and things he doesn't need to know. What I wanted *you* to know is that his problems as a lawyer are far worse than you can see. Worse, even, than he may know." Her voice grew softer yet. "For that you can blame me."

Mary saw his perceptions shift again, a kind of relief running through him. Realized, with sadness and satisfaction, how much this boy's sense of himself had come from Christopher Paget.

"He's been a good father," she said. "Hasn't he?"

"Yes. He has."

To Mary, he seemed glad of the change of subject, and to know that he could speak well of Paget without offending her. As for her, she felt exhausted—anything was a better subject than the things she could not tell anyone, Carlo most of all.

"Does Chris have any kind of social life?" she asked. "I really have no idea."

Carlo's look mingled surprise with a certain amusement. "Do you mean a woman? Or just going to cocktail parties and stuff like that?"

"Women, I suppose." Mary paused. "I just wonder what he's been doing with himself all these years."

"He doesn't tell *me* much. But there are always one or two women around, usually good-looking and smart and with great jobs. He just never seems to get attached to them." Carlo shrugged. "Maybe some of it is that he's a parent, and a lot of the people he's gone out with don't have kids. But there's a part of him I think they never really get to see."

"Like me, I'm told." Mary smiled. "If you asked either of us to get in touch with our feelings, we'd probably need a map."

Carlo gave her a mischievous look. "Then for all either of you knows, you're still in love."

Mary laughed. "He's not *that* out of touch," she said in a facetious tone. "And the part of me *I* know about can't stand him." She paused again, voice softer. "It's funny, though. When I first knew Chris, I thought he was the most arrogant man I'd ever met, as strong-willed as I was, and certain of his own rightness. He seems so much more human now, more aware of his own flaws—even when he's being an absolute bastard." She smiled a little, shaking her head. "The strange thing is, instead of liking that, it makes me a little sad. Like we've both gotten older."

Carlo reflected for a moment. "It's hard to think of him as older. To me, he's always looked the same. Ever since I first came here."

His last phrase, outwardly careless, seemed to ask Mary why she had let him go. She searched for something else to say. "What was Andrea like—his wife?"

"I don't remember much, except that I thought she looked kind of like you." He considered a moment and then shrugged; it seemed a teenage gesture of incuriosity, dismissing things that had nothing to do with him. "I think they just kind of drifted apart."

Mary nodded. Carlo had been young enough, and Paget sensitive enough, that the boy had never blamed himself. "Perhaps he'll find someone else."

"I don't know." Carlo seemed to reflect. "The one I think he really likes is Terri, and she only works for him. Besides," he added, as if this closed the subject, "she's got a husband and a five-year-old kid."

Mary smiled. It was surely not her place to say what instinct told her: that Teresa Peralta was falling in love with Christopher Paget, husband or no, and whether or not Terri would ever permit herself to face that. "Chris and Terri can still be friends, you know. It doesn't have to be passion."

He gave her a wry look. "Now you sound like Dad. Listen to him sometimes, and sex doesn't matter at all. Especially for me."

Mary laughed. "That's not how *I* remember Chris." The thought stopped her, and then other images ran through her mind—a night in Washington, an afternoon in Paris—much more bitter and more lasting. She stifled them, recaptured her smile. "We were a disaster as a couple," she said. "But when it came to picking a father for you, I did pretty well."

Carlo raised his water glass. "Then here's to all of us." He paused, then added, "I know you're going to win, Mom."

What she could not tell him, Mary thought, was that winning and losing had many faces. That when she had awakened the night before, sweating yet cold in a room that at first she did not recognize, her nightmare had been not of prison or disgrace but of Carlo Carelli Paget, listening to the tape they must never find.

Mary touched her glass to Carlo's. "To all of us," she said. "And, most of all, to you."

FOUR

THE ROOM SERVICE waiter was a dapper Hispanic in his mid thirties, Paul Aguilar, with a black mustache, slicked-back hair, and a confident smile. The act of testifying before the world seemed not to bother him at all.

"Can you identify," Sharpe asked, "the woman you saw with Mr. Ransom?"

Her manner was relaxed; Paget guessed that she had worked with Aguilar extensively, and that he made a good witness.

"The defendant, Miss Carelli." Aguilar straightened in his chair, pointing at Mary. "Even without seeing her on television, Miss Carelli would be hard to forget."

"How gallant," Mary murmured to Paget. On the other side of him, Terri watched Aguilar intently; Paget sensed that he already concerned her.

"Once Mr. Ransom let you in, what happened next?"

"The usual thing. I asked him where to place the champagne bucket, and he said the coffee table. So I put it there in front of Miss Carelli."

"At that time, did Ms. Carelli say anything to you?"

"Nothing, except to thank me." He smiled, as if in pleasure at this brush with the famous. "She seemed very nice."

"Was there anything unusual in her manner?"

"No. She was just like I'd expect her to be."

"And how was that?"

"Classy." Aguilar seemed to wrinkle his nose at the word. "That's not exactly what I mean. Very poised, very relaxed, like someone who always knows what to do."

Sharpe, Paget realized, was asking Aguilar to paint a word picture of a woman at ease, self-possessed and unconcerned. He made the snap judgment not to object.

"Did she seem worried about anything?"

Aguilar's shrug said that the thought had never occurred to him. "Not that I saw."

"Or unfriendly to Mr. Ransom?"

"No." He gave a smile of bemusement, as if still deciphering Ransom's death. "She didn't look hostile at all. I thought they were friends, spending a few hours alone." He smiled again. "In my business, you see that a lot."

On the bench, Masters frowned. "He's making this seem like a date," Mary whispered to Paget.

Paget turned to her slightly, still watching Masters. "I'd make it look worse by complaining," he whispered back. "Let's hope that this guy hangs himself."

"Did Mr. Ransom say anything?" Sharpe was asking.

Aguilar nodded vigorously. "I said something to *him* about how much I liked his books. So he told me that compliments like that were what kept him writing. He made me feel good I'd spoken up." He gave a sheepish smile. "I'm a room service waiter, you know. It's not my place to push myself on people."

With one innocuous question, Paget thought, Sharpe had made both Ransom and Aguilar seem more human. He felt Mary tense beside him.

Sharpe paused for a moment, as if preparing some ultimate thrust. "During this time," she asked, "did you happen to notice whether the sitting room blinds were closed or open?"

"Open. Definitely."

"And how are you so sure?"

Aguilar smiled. "Because I remember Mr. Ransom had a nice view of Berkeley, across the bay. So I looked out, imagining I could see my cousin's old house." He turned, explaining to Masters, "I used to spend a lot of time with him. My cousin, I mean."

Caroline Masters nodded. To Paget, her expression said that Aguilar's charm was lost on her; quickly, Paget adjusted his impression of how far he could go on cross.

"Before you left," Sharpe continued, "did Mr. Ransom do anything else?"

"He signed the check, of course." Aguilar smiled again. "Then he gave me a nice tip, clapped me on the back, and winked."

"He winked?"

"Yes. Like to tell me he was lucky." He spread his arms, as if to affirm the pleasure of life itself, the understanding of one man for another. "You know, that he's alone with this beautiful woman and feeling good."

Masters's frown had deepened. She turned to Aguilar. "Are you sure he didn't have something in his eye?"

Aguilar looked puzzled, as if Judge Masters did not appreciate this moment of shared humanity. "No," he said. "It was a wink."

"I see," Masters said in her flattest voice. "Go ahead, Ms. Sharpe."

Sharpe gazed at her for a moment. When Terri turned to him, Paget whispered, "I don't think Caroline will be checking into the Flood very soon. At least not without bringing her own champagne."

But Sharpe was moving closer to the witness, with an air of expectancy Paget did not like. "Before you left," she asked quietly, "did either Mr. Ransom or Ms. Carelli say anything else?"

Aguilar nodded. "Yes. Miss Carelli did."

"And what did she say?"

Aguilar turned to Mary, as if Sharpe had trained him to do so. Softly, he said, "To hang out the privacy sign."

Sharpe paused, letting the moment sink in. There was a first faint murmur in the courtroom, and then Sharpe asked, "Did Ms. Carelli say why?"

"No." A rueful shake of the head. "If a woman wants to be alone with a man, I don't ask why."

Sharpe nodded, as if he had said something profound. Then she turned to Masters. "No further questions."

Masters was gazing at Mary. As Masters looked away, Paget whispered to Mary, "Is that true?"

Mary still watched Masters. "Yes," she murmured. "It is."

Paget turned from the witness, listening as Johnny Moore bent forward from the first row, whispered his advice. Nodding, Paget stood and then walked toward Aguilar. "Good morning," he said pleasantly.

Aguilar nodded; the impression was of a relaxed and friendly man in a service business, meeting another member of the public. "Good morning, sir."

"*Was* it morning," Paget asked abruptly, "or afternoon when you went to Ransom's suite?"

Aguilar blinked. "Morning, I think. Late morning."

"And you worked from seven to five that day, correct?"

"That's my usual shift."

"That covers breakfast, lunch, and early dinner, correct?"

"Yes."

Paget gave him a curious look. "Have you any idea how many rooms you visited that day?"

"No."

"A lot?"

Aguilar furrowed his brow. "A fair number."

"If I told you that my investigator had checked the room service slips with your name on them and counted forty-three, would that seem out of line?"

"No. I keep busy—it could have been that many."

"Other than Mr. Ransom's suite, can you describe the occupants of any other rooms you served that day?"

"No." Aguilar paused. "It was fresher then. You know, the first time I talked to the police."

"But you also talked to my investigator, Johnny Moore, two days later. Is that correct?"

"I remember Mr. Moore. Yes."

"And do you also remember Mr. Moore asking the same question I just did: whether you recalled anyone else you served that day?"

"I guess so."

"And your answer was the same, wasn't it—you didn't remember anyone else, did you?"

Aguilar folded his arms. "I guess I didn't. These people were celebrities."

Paget moved close, ignoring the last sentence. "Nor," he asked softly, "did you remember whether anyone else had the shades up or down, did you?"

Aguilar began to look unhappy. "No," he said. "Mr. Ransom's room was the one I remember."

Paget nodded. In a tone of sudden understanding, he said, "Because you recalled looking out at Berkeley."

Aguilar leaned forward, as if eager to seize on the reason Paget had given him. "That's right."

"Do you make it a habit to look out at Berkeley? That is, when you get the chance?"

"When I think about it." Aguilar smiled. "The views in the Mission District, where *I* live, aren't so hot."

Paget smiled back. "Do you happen to recall," he asked pleasantly, "how many rooms you visited that day that had views of Berkeley from the tenth floor or above?"

Aguilar stared at him. "No."

"Twelve rooms," Paget said in the flat voice of authority. "And three suites. All with views of Berkeley. Does that sound right to you?"

Aguilar paused, giving him a trapped, wary look. "Could be."

"Must have been quite a nostalgic day for you," Paget observed.

"Your Honor," Sharpe called out. "That wasn't a proper question, and this has gone too far."

"It wasn't," Masters agreed, "and this has. Move it along, Mr. Paget."

The judge did not, Paget saw, look particularly annoyed. "Are you still quite sure," he asked Aguilar, "that *Mr. Ransom's* shades were open?"

"Yes."

"Because it is one of fifteen rooms you saw that day with a scenic view of Berkeley?"

"No." Aguilar's voice was emphatic. "Because of Miss Carelli."

"Miss Carelli." Paget stretched out the name. "Yes, she does seem to have captured your imagination."

Paget lent the last three words a faint sardonic edge. Caroline Masters caught it, he saw; a fleeting smile came and went. But Aguilar did not seem to follow him.

"Yes," he agreed, "I remembered her."

"How long were you in that room, Mr. Aguilar?"

Aguilar shook his head. "No way I can recall."

"You're trained, are you not, to get in and out of a room quickly?"

"Yes. People like their privacy."

"And all you had to do in this case was set down an ice bucket and two glasses, is that right?"

"And have Mr. Ransom sign the check."

"A simple job, right?"

"I would say so."

"So that if you told Mr. Moore that you had been in Mr. Ransom's suite for about a minute and a half, would that still sound right?"

Aguilar paused. "I guess so," he finally said.

"So that your testimony for Ms. Sharpe this morning is based on roughly ninety seconds in one of forty-three hotel rooms you visited that day. Is that correct?"

Aguilar's mouth set in a stubborn line. "I remember what I saw."

"And what you saw, you believe, was that Ms. Carelli seemed 're-laxed'?"

"Yes." Aguilar nodded. "She seemed comfortable with Mr. Ransom."

Paget stared at him. "Did they actually say anything to each other?"

Aguilar looked from Paget to Johnny Moore, sitting next to Carlo in the front row. "Not that I remember."

"Or say anything to you *about* each other?"

"No. Not that."

"Or touch each other?"

Aguilar stared at him. "No."

"Or even smile at each other?"

"No."

"In other words, each of them *talked* only to you, and *smiled* only at you, and yet you concluded they were 'relaxed' with each other."

"Mr. Ransom did order champagne, sir." Aguilar paused. "And then he winked at me."

Paget smiled. "Are you sure, Mr. Aguilar, that Mr. Ransom wasn't simply attracted to *you?*"

There was a ripple of laughter. Aguilar looked indignant. "Of course not."

"Really? But he *touched* you too, correct?"

"He clapped me on the back."

Paget shook his head. "I wasn't there, Mr. Aguilar, but it sounds pretty suggestive to me. Seems like a good thing you got in and out of there in ninety seconds."

The courtroom erupted in laughter. Sharpe was quickly on her feet. "Objection, Your Honor. Mr. Paget is badgering this witness."

"Really?" Masters asked her. "According to the testimony *you* just elicited, within a couple of minutes Mr. Aguilar served some champagne, sized up Ms. Carelli, observed the state of the windows, relived a few childhood memories, offered his views on literature, and did a little male bonding with Mr. Ransom. I'd love to know what happened in the other forty-two rooms."

Paget found himself laughing with everyone else. Sharpe waited for the sound to die. "With respect, Your Honor, that summary is unfair to this witness. And it misses two central points: that the blinds were open when Ms. Carelli *arrived* and that, when Mr. Aguilar *left,* she asked him to ensure her privacy."

Masters nodded. "In my fascination with Mr. Aguilar's interpretive powers, I forgot to mention that I was sustaining your objection." She turned to Paget. "I understand your point, Mr. Paget: this witness's views regarding Mr. Ransom and Ms. Carelli are merely conjecture. Do you have anything else?"

Paget hesitated, disappointed; Masters's intervention, as favorable as it seemed, had saved the witness from potential devastation. Now he had to deal with the most difficult point of all. "It was your testimony, as I recall, that Ms. Carelli asked you to hang the privacy sign."

A vigorous nod. "That's right."

"After all this, are you sure it isn't possible that *Mark Ransom* asked you?"

"Positive."

Paget did not like the sound of that. "How can you be sure?"

"Because it stuck with me—Mr. Ransom winking, and then Miss Carelli *asking.* Like he *knew* it was going to happen, and she wanted that too."

Paget felt himself losing ground, asking questions he was not sure of in an effort to recoup. "Knew *what* was going to happen?"

"You know." Aguilar looked awkward. "Sexual intercourse. I mean, you couldn't read it any other way."

Paget tried to sound indignant. "Do you assume, Mr. Aguilar, that every time a man and a woman want to talk in private, it involves sex?"

"No," Aguilar protested. "I don't think that at all. But you see a man and a woman in a hotel suite at noon, the man ordering champagne and the woman asking to be alone, and you've got to figure the odds have just gone up. That's how *I* saw it, and *I've* got to figure that's how *Mr. Ransom* saw it. Which is why it stuck in my mind that Miss Carelli was the one that wanted privacy."

Paget felt like a fool. "You've got the edge on me there," he snapped, "by ninety seconds. But there are certain things you don't know, do you? Like whether Ms. Carelli simply wanted privacy to talk."

Aguilar eyed him. "No, I don't know," he finally said. "One way or the other."

"A judicious answer," Paget said coldly. He turned to Masters. "I'm through with this witness, Your Honor."

She nodded, giving Aguilar a speculative gaze. "Redirect, Ms. Sharpe."

"No, thank you, Your Honor." Sharpe smiled faintly. "Since my last objection, I've been content with the job Mr. Paget has done on our behalf."

"Which is it?" Terri murmured. "Ransom never got it up, or Mary the seductress?"

"Both," Paget whispered back. "Marnie's idea must be that Mary lulled Ransom into being all alone, then shot him."

Terri nodded. Together, they watched John Hassler take the stand.

He was a pleasant, open-faced man in his late forties, an insurance executive from Chicago with a twenty-year marriage and two teenage daughters. Sharpe added to this estimable life the fact that Hassler was a guest at the Flood on the day that Mark Ransom died, and then asked, "In fact, Mr. Hassler, weren't you on the same floor as Mr. Ransom?"

"That's right. I met him in the elevator, coming up from breakfast when he was checking in."

"You recognized him?"

"With that face and all the red hair? Couldn't miss him. So I said hello." Hassler shook his head sadly. "He was a nice man—friendly. Polished but very engaging."

"How long did you speak to him?"

"For five minutes or so. We were walking in the same direction, so he invited me into his room. I was curious about the suites, so we sort of checked it out together." He paused. "As I said, a nice man."

"What did you talk about?"

Hassler's expression mixed pleasure with regret, as if reflecting that this was one of the last encounters Mark Ransom had with anyone. "He showed me the suite—which was quite spacious—and talked about some writers from Chicago whom he knew. He was very complimentary of them, and of the city. Then he looked at his watch and gave sort of an embarrassed smile. He said he wished that we could chat more but that he had to take a shower." Hassler shot a glance at Mary. "He told me that a woman was coming to his suite in an hour or so, and he didn't want to smell like an airplane breakfast."

"Did he tell you why she was coming?"

"No." Hassler paused. "But the way he looked and sounded, it wasn't business. At least he didn't give me any reason to believe it was."

"Did he say whom he was seeing?"

Hassler shook his head. "No. Just that I'd know her if I saw her. He sounded pretty pleased with himself—I must admit I was curious."

Paget glanced at Mary; through the stoic mask, her eyes flashed anger and contempt. On the bench, Masters wore a slight frown, directed at no one.

"What happened then?" Sharpe asked Hassler.

"Nothing. We just shook hands, and I went around the corner to my room."

"How long were you there?"

"I had a business lunch at one, so it was maybe a couple of hours. I read some memos and worked the phones a little."

"Did you ever see Mr. Ransom again?"

Hassler looked down. "No. Later that night, after I heard, it was like someone walking over my grave."

"Did you ever see the woman who came to his room?"

Hassler hesitated. "Yes. I *think* so."

"Could you explain?"

Slowly, Hassler nodded. "It was about noon, and I'd gotten bored with the stuff I was reading. So I got up, yawning and stretching a little, staring out my window without anything much in mind.

"It wasn't a very good view. The Flood is shaped kind of like a block **U**, with two wings facing each other and surrounding an inner courtyard. I was on the end of one wing, so all I could see was the opposite wing and a few rooms on the right side of the **U**, where Mark Ransom was staying." Hassler paused. "I guess at some point it occurred to me to wonder which windows belonged to his suite. Seeing as how I'd been there."

"Did you do that?"

"Uh-huh. I began sort of counting windows, trying to remember how far along the back of the U his suite was." He paused. "That was when I saw her."

"Her?"

"Yes." Hassler glanced at Mary. "A woman, with long black hair. Standing in a window."

"What did she do?"

"She seemed to look out for a minute, as if she was staring at the bay. Then she pulled down the blinds, and I couldn't see her anymore." He averted his gaze from Mary. "But I figured it was the woman who'd come to see Mark Ransom."

"And why was that?"

"The position of the windows, for one thing. It seemed right."

Sharpe paused for a moment. "Was there anything else?"

"Uh-huh."

"And what was that?"

Hassler looked down. In a quiet voice, he said, "She was undressed."

There were whispers in the courtroom; quickly, Masters gaveled for silence, face grim. Paget's mind seemed to have gone blank. The one thing he could think of was Carlo.

Pausing, Sharpe showed no emotion. "I want to be clear on this," she said. "You saw her through a full-length window, am I correct?"

"Yes." Hassler glanced at Mary. "The woman I saw wasn't wearing anything. Nothing at all."

"How did you know that?"

Hassler looked away again. "There was a patch of black between her legs."

"Pubic hair," Sharpe said flatly.

Hassler sighed. His voice sounded feeble. "It was a long way off, but yes. Pubic hair."

Beneath the table, Paget realized, Mary's fingers grabbed his suit jacket. Her face was flushed.

"This window," Sharpe asked. "How many windows was it from the end?"

"Three, I believe."

Sharpe nodded. "And did we later show you Mark Ransom's suite, and three suites on either side?"

"Yes."

"And did you count the windows?"

"Yes."

"And what did you discover?"

Now Hassler looked quite miserable. "What I discovered," he answered, "was that Mark Ransom's sitting room contained the third window from the right."

Paget rose. Quickly, he said, "The window you looked at was at least one hundred fifty feet from your own, was it not?"

Hassler nodded; the look he gave Paget was half ashamed, half apologetic. "I would think that's fair."

"So you couldn't see her face, correct?"

"Not at all." He explained, "I *could* see height and coloring."

"Anything else?"

"Only that the woman was slender."

"Let me show you something."

Quickly, Johnny Moore had the easel out again; another picture appeared, this time the distant color image of a dark-haired woman, gazing out a window at the Flood. "Your Honor," Paget said, "we're prepared to establish that Mr. Moore took this photograph through the window of Mr. Hassler's hotel room and that the woman in the picture was standing in Mark Ransom's suite."

Judge Masters turned to Marnie Sharpe. "Any objection?"

"Yes. I don't know what this is."

"True, at the moment. But I'm going to allow it, subject to proof. And unless you doubt Mr. Paget's word, you may wish to reach some sort of stipulation."

Sharpe frowned. "Very well, Your Honor."

Paget stepped forward. "Mr. Hassler, let me direct your attention to this photograph and then to the defense table."

Hassler looked from one to the other. "I have, sir. To both."

"All right. You'll note that *this* woman, although clothed, is standing in the full-length window, looking out as you described her. Does this approximate the view you had that day?"

"Yes. As I recall it."

"And can you identify the person in the picture?"

"No." Hassler looked embarrassed. "But like the woman I saw that day, her height and coloring resemble Ms. Carelli's."

Paget nodded. "So in your view, the woman in this picture bears the same resemblance to Ms. Carelli as the woman you saw?"

"Yes. It's hard to say, of course. But it could be the same woman."

"It could be, yes." For the first time, Paget smiled. "But actually it's Ms. Carelli's virtual twin. My associate, Ms. Peralta."

Masters gave a thin smile of her own. Paget turned to the defense table. "Would both of you mind standing?"

They did, Mary looking grim, Terri expressionless. "As you can see," Paget said to Masters, "the principal differences are Ms. Carelli's considerable height advantage, Ms. Peralta's lighter hair, and, as Ms. Carelli would be frank to admit, some fifteen years in age."

Judge Masters looked from the picture to Terri. "I've seen better likenesses, Teresa. But I suppose that's Mr. Paget's point. It's nice to have you in my courtroom, incidentally. Even in a nonspeaking part."

"Ms. Peralta will be speaking," Paget said, "when the defense puts on witnesses."

"Good, Mr. Paget. Not to denigrate your skills, of course." Masters paused. "I assume that you have more."

"Just a little." Paget turned back to Hassler. "Take another look at the picture, if you will. Given the distance between your window and those at the back of the U, can you even be certain that you're looking at a window on the precise same floor?"

Hassler cocked his head. "Not from looking at this. No."

"Or from looking through your window on the day in question? We are, after all, talking about a view from at least half the distance of a football field."

Hassler considered that. "No," he said finally. "I can't be sure that I wasn't looking at someone on a floor above, or a floor below."

"And in fact, didn't you assume that the woman you saw was in Mr. Ransom's suite because of what he *led* you to assume about his activities?"

Hassler looked confused. "I'm not sure I know what you mean."

"Let me put it another way. Would you have associated this woman with Mr. Ransom's suite if he hadn't implied to you he had some sort of date?"

Hassler's eyes narrowed. "Maybe not," he said finally.

"Indeed, sitting here today, are you certain that the window you saw was the third window from the right?"

"I don't know." Hassler shook his head. "After he was dead, these kinds of details become more important."

"In truth, isn't what got your attention not the sequence of the windows, or whose window it was, but the unexpected sight of a woman without clothes?"

Hassler looked chastened. "It startled me, I'm sure."

Paget paused. "And attracted you?"

Hassler raised his head. "I suppose so, Mr. Paget. Whoever it was, she was attractive. I'll admit to you that I didn't turn away."

"Nor, after seeing her, did you count windows."

"No."

"So that you're not at all certain that the woman you saw was standing in Mark Ransom's suite."

Hassler looked from Sharpe to Paget. "No," he said in a hollow voice. "I can't be sure."

"Or even confident?"

"No." Hassler looked away. "Not even that. What I saw was a naked woman. It could have been Mark Ransom's suite."

"Or not."

Hassler nodded. "Or not."

"It is also true, is it not, that you saw no one else through the window. *Not* Mark Ransom, or any other man."

"That's true."

"So that the faceless woman you saw could have been fresh from the shower, and quite alone."

Hassler reflected. "Yes, you're right. The woman I saw could have been alone."

Paget paused for a moment. "Given all of these uncertainties," he asked, "and the potential prejudice to Ms. Carelli, why did you come forward?"

"I didn't *want* to." Hassler gave a helpless shrug. "But I met the man, and now he's dead. What could I do but tell the district attorney what I saw, and let them decide what to do with it?"

With a trace of weariness, as if his worst expectations had been confirmed, Paget slowly looked at Marnie Sharpe. Then he turned to the witness again. "Oh, you fulfilled *your* responsibilities," he said. "Thank you, Mr. Hassler. I have no further questions."

* * *

Sharpe was quickly up, an edge in her voice. "Did anyone, from either the police or the district attorney, coach you as to what you saw through the window of your hotel room?"

"Objection," Paget called out. "The scope of redirect is confined to matters addressed in cross-examination. Never once did my questions suggest that Ms. Sharpe suborned perjury."

Sharpe looked indignant. "Mr. Paget is deliberately misunderstanding, and overstating, the thrust of my question."

"Your Honor," Paget said to Masters, "let me make the thrust of *my* last question clear to Ms. Sharpe. My question implied—and I am now saying flat out—that it was shoddy for the People to prejudice Ms. Carelli's hearing by offering testimony which is at once so inflammatory and so flimsy. Period."

"All right, both of you." Masters turned to Sharpe. "I appreciate Mr. Paget's feelings, if not his every turn of phrase. We will likely never know *who* Mr. Hassler saw in that window, but we will surely *all* remember her mode of dress—as you no doubt intended."

Sharpe bristled; she had trouble, Paget realized, dealing with rebukes. "Our only intention," she said, "was to present evidence of what happened in that suite. I hope that the court will accept that."

"The court accepts that," Masters responded in a milder tone, "if not the probative value of this particular testimony. I'll allow the question, but I suggest that you wrap this up quickly."

"Very well, Your Honor." Sharpe turned to the court stenographer, a middle-aged black man who sat to the right of Masters. "Mr. Sanders, could you read back the question?"

He picked up the tape of paper from the machine, squinting at its shorthand symbols, and then read: "Ms. Sharpe: 'Did anyone, from either the police or the district attorney, coach you as to what you saw through the window of your hotel room?' "

Hassler shook his head. "No. Not at all."

Sharpe continued. "And what you described here is what you told our office on your own initiative?"

"Very definitely." Hassler paused. "I saw what I saw."

"And do you, despite the questions asked by Mr. Paget, continue to believe that it is more likely than not that the woman you saw was in Mark Ransom's suite?"

Hassler furrowed his brow. "More likely than not?" he asked Sharpe.

"That's my question, yes."

Hassler paused. "I'd have to say 'yes' to that," he finally answered.

Sharpe paused; Paget watched her decide that this was the most she could do. "No further questions," she said, and then Hassler left the stand, leaving Paget to wonder if the unclothed woman was Mary Carelli.

Edward Tench was a hawk-faced investment banker with dark-rimmed glasses, a crisply tailored suit, and an incisive air to match, as if he were accustomed to persuading conference rooms full of people to do what he wanted. He smoothed back his dark hair, straightened his red tie, and awaited Sharpe's next question.

"So that at about one o'clock," Sharpe asked, "you returned to your room at the Flood?"

"Yes," Tench answered. "I'd just finished an early business lunch and wished to call my office."

"And your suite was on the twenty-third floor. Mr. Ransom's floor."

"Yes."

"When you got off the elevator," Sharpe asked, "did you see anything?"

"Yes." Tench leaned forward, as if impatient with the structure of the questioning. "But perhaps I should explain its elevators. The elevator *I* took was at the far end of a long hallway, containing suites or rooms that face toward Berkeley. I was, I believe, two suites past Mark Ransom. So that I turned in the direction of his suite."

"Thank you," Sharpe said dryly. "And what did you see?"

"A woman, standing in front of the door to one of the suites."

"And what did this woman look like?"

Tench looked over at Mary. "From where I was standing, I couldn't see her face. But she was quite tall, about five feet eight, with long black hair."

"Do you recall what she was wearing?"

"I really don't, although I have the odd impression that she wasn't wearing shoes. What I do recall clearly is the shine of her hair, the way she carried herself—quite straight, like a model. There aren't many women who look like that from any angle."

A self-confident professional, Paget thought, determined to get the most out of what he knew, and then some. Without much material for cross, Tench would not be an easy witness—particularly, Paget added to himself, because the woman he saw was more than likely Mary Carelli.

"What did she do?" Sharpe asked.

"She stood there for a moment, staring at the door. Then, very abruptly, she stepped inside. It was as if she'd heard the elevator open and didn't want to be seen outside the room."

"Did someone let her in?"

"No," Tench said. "She let *herself* in."

For an instant, Paget imagined Mary Carelli standing in the hallway. But he could not imagine why she had been there.

"From her movements," Sharpe was asking, "did this woman appear to be injured in any way?"

"No, again. She moved very quickly." Tench paused. "I had the fleeting image of a dancer, perhaps a tennis player. A woman with confidence in her body."

"I'm going to enter a belated objection," Paget said. "I wonder if the witness could refrain from sharing with us his rich cultural experience and points of reference, and just stick to facts. Truly, I don't know whether this woman was a model, a dancer, an athlete or, for that matter, had recently had a steel rod implanted in her spine. And neither does this witness."

Masters smiled briefly and then turned to the witness. "In light of Mr. Paget's request, Mr. Tench, I wonder if you could confine yourself to what you actually saw."

"Of course, Your Honor." Tench looked vaguely thwarted. "I was only trying to be helpful. It's been my understanding that in the law, as with investment banking, one's experiences shape one's observations."

"Oh, they do," Masters agreed. "By the way, how long did you observe *this* woman?"

Tench seemed to reflect. "It couldn't have been long."

"Because from what you describe," Masters continued, "it sounds like ten seconds at the outside."

Tench looked nettled for a moment. "It was probably that."

"Oh, well," Masters rejoined. "One's experience can enhance the most fleeting observation. Press on, Ms. Sharpe."

Now Sharpe looked annoyed. It was a very good day for Caroline

Masters, Paget thought, regardless of how the lawyers were doing; the first newspaper pieces about the judge were already starting to appear, and clips of her courtroom style would surely be featured on the nightly news. But how that might affect her, Paget could not guess.

"Your Honor," Sharpe finally said, "I wonder if I could ask Ms. Carelli to stand and turn her back to the witness."

"Mr. Paget?"

There was nothing he could do. "Certainly, Your Honor. Ms. Carelli would be pleased to turn her back to this witness."

Judge Masters smiled at one corner of her mouth. "Ms. Carelli," she said.

Mary rose, gazing at the witness. Then, slowly, she turned from him.

She could not help it, Paget realized; the image of a dancer or a model leapt easily to mind. For a strange moment, he remembered her standing naked in front of the Vasarely in his apartment, quite graceful and quite straight.

Now, in what seemed to be a lifetime later, Mary Carelli gazed out at the courtroom full of media people, come to watch her on trial for murder. She held her head high, kept her eyes still. Paget watched her face.

"That looks like the same woman," Tench said. "Or put another way, the woman I saw looked as Ms. Carelli does now."

Mary's face showed nothing. The courtroom was still.

"May Ms. Carelli sit?" Paget inquired.

"Of course," Masters said. "Thank you, Ms. Carelli. Any more questions, Ms. Sharpe?"

"None, Your Honor."

As Mary sat, she shot a querying look at Paget. How much does this hurt, the look asked, and what can you do with him?

Very little, Paget thought. He did not even rise from the table. In his most languid voice, he asked, "Tell me, Mr. Tench, was this nameless, faceless mannequin you saw for less than ten seconds in a dim hallway at least wearing clothes?"

There was a ripple of laughter. Masters raised her gavel and then thought better of it, looking over at Tench. His mouth formed a grimace in what, Paget thought, was meant to convey perfunctory amusement and a sense of his superiority.

Sharpe stood again. "Really, Your Honor, this isn't comedy."

"Far from it," Paget answered. "But this witness's powers of observation are so extraordinary that when he could not recall the woman's clothes, I feared the worst."

Masters's shrug suggested that her amusement was running low. "For the record, Mr. Tench."

Tench turned to Paget. "Yes," he said in a tone of weary condescension. "The woman was dressed."

"That's a relief," Paget answered. He turned to Masters. "Given that Ms. Sharpe wishes to avoid comedy, I have no further questions."

"Ms. Sharpe?"

"No." She looked at Paget with asperity. "There's nothing to ask."

"You may step down, Mr. Tench." He did so, looking irritated at his abrupt dismissal.

Masters, too, had begun to look annoyed. "Tempers seem to be fraying here," she said. "I'd like a half-hour recess, and then we'll meet in chambers. The topic will be certain evidence proposed by the prosecution to conclude their direct case."

The tape, Paget knew. But as Masters slammed the gavel, finishing public proceedings for the day, Paget found himself still wondering why Mary had left the suite. And then he turned to see his son, staring at his mother with new questions in his eyes.

No matter what doubts he had tried to plant today, Paget realized, the look on Carlo's face told him how much Marnie Sharpe had managed to achieve.

FIVE

LIKE HER COURTROOM, the chambers that Caroline Masters used were borrowed: the tomes on evidence, treatises on trial practice, and bound jury instructions belonged to another judge, and the heavy furniture and green leather chair were unrelieved by any touch that was Masters's own. It did not seem to matter; three days into the hearing, Caroline Masters looked at home.

She leaned back in the chair, fingers interwoven beneath her chin, gazing thoughtfully at the tape recorder Sharpe had placed in front of her. The only persons present were Terri, Paget, Sharpe, and her assistant.

"The media," Judge Masters said, "don't know what they're missing. Which is precisely how I intend to keep it."

"What are we authorized to say?" Sharpe asked.

"Nothing. You'll tell the press, as I have, that these private sessions are to rule on disputed points of evidence. Period. You will not describe what the points are or what is in dispute."

Sharpe leaned forward. "It seems to me," she ventured, "that Mr. Paget wants selective publicity—nationwide television for some aspects, and a lead-lined vault for anything that sheds some real light on Ms. Carelli."

"This isn't about what Mr. Paget wants. It's about *my* quaint notions of decency." Pausing, Masters looked at each lawyer in turn. "As I understand it, the parties intend to treat me to a tape of Ms. Carelli's psychoanalysis, another tape providing some distasteful insights into the relationship of a dead film star with a revered United States senator, and testimony from three women regarding Mark Ransom's sexual habits and/or his misuse of the tapes in question. If this stuff turns out to be admissible, I'll admit it. Until then, I'm more concerned with protecting the particular people involved than I am with the 'people's right to know'—or, for that matter, the *National Enquirer*'s right to supplement their usual fare about Peter Lawford's final days and sex between women and apes." She turned back to Sharpe. "Do I make myself clear?"

Sharpe hesitated, as if to protest the focus on her. Then she nodded.

"Good. Because if you feel like I'm picking on you, Marnie, you're right." Masters's voice grew quieter. "Like half of America, I watched Ms. Carelli on *60 Minutes*. But unlike most of them, I knew precisely where the interviewer's questions came from. And I was forced to ask myself: Does Marnie Sharpe only care about the privacy of women who've *actually* been raped? Now, this morning, you wonder aloud about keeping information private which could cause great hurt to any number of people, before the court even determines that it's fit to be evidence." Masters glanced at the tape recorder, then back at Sharpe. "I don't know what's on this tape. But if the press prints anything about it until and unless I decide that it's admissible, and I trace that story to your office, I will hold you personally responsible. Have I made *that* clear enough?"

"Yes," Sharpe said, with an edge in her voice. "You have."

Paget glanced at Terri, silently wondering whether these stringent procedures reflected the judge's reaction to the seriousness of the case, or something else. But Terri looked as surprised as he.

"During our private sessions," Judge Masters continued, "it will be necessary to bring in a stenographer and have a record of what's said. But I intend to make this as comfortable as possible for the women who've come forward. This experience will be bad enough for them, and for my part, I think the courts should make every effort to encourage women who've been victimized to say so. Which means, among other things, that *I* will be the primary questioner. If anyone then wishes to ask anything for the sake of preserving the record on appeal, of course they may. But if I conclude that the particular testimony offered will *not* be used in open court, then I'll have that transcript sealed from the press to protect the women involved. As for the tapes, I'll play them *without* a stenographer, given that they speak for themselves." Once more, Judge Masters glanced at each lawyer. "Is that agreeable? If not, tell me now."

There was silence. Usually, Paget knew, the judge would be more observer than participant. He watched Sharpe calculate Masters's response if she objected; his own guess was that the judge would tell her to go to the court of appeals. But the hearing was going too well for Sharpe to risk alienating the judge, and Masters's resolve to guard the privacy of Mary and certain witnesses did not affect Sharpe's case on the merits.

"We have no objection," Sharpe responded.

"Nor," Paget said, "does Ms. Carelli."

"I would think not," Judge Masters said dryly. "How do you wish to proceed, Ms. Sharpe?"

"By playing this tape, Your Honor, which *does* speak for itself." Sharpe glanced at Paget. "I will say only that it is a tape of Ms. Carelli's psychoanalytic session with a Dr. William Steinhardt; that we found it in Mark Ransom's home in Key West; and that we are prepared to authenticate should the court deem it admissible."

"And I," Paget responded, "will say only that the tape is so obviously privileged that the prosecution's sole purpose is to prejudice the court. Once the court has listened to it, that damage is done."

"I'm going to have to hear it, Mr. Paget. And then I'll hear your argument. You'll just have to trust my mental discipline."

"Thank you, Your Honor." Paget's response was formulaic; once Judge Masters heard the tape, her perception of Mary and her lawyer might be changed beyond repair, the contest for the judge's mind and sympathies lost.

As she switched on the tape, Sharpe seemed to wear a secret smile. At that moment, Christopher Paget hated her; what he felt was not the adversarial passion of a defense lawyer, Paget realized, but the visceral anger of the guilty at a prosecutor's pleasure. He sat back, trying to keep the shame and apprehension from his face.

"I keep having this dream," Mary said.

As before, her voice sounded naked, haunting; repetition did not lessen Paget's dislike of listening. "It's as if I shut it off by day, but at night I lose control."

Staring at the cassette, Judge Masters's face had none of its usual hauteur. It appeared that she did not wish to look at anyone.

"I'm in Paris," Mary went on, "at the church of St. Germain-des-Prés."

Her voice echoed in the room. With its dark wood paneling, the window admitting one square of light, the chambers seemed charged by Mary's words with the character of a confessional. The lawyers were quite still.

"Why are you there?" Steinhardt inquired.

Mary's voice was quiet. "To ask forgiveness for my sins."

The voices went on: Steinhardt querying, Mary responding; both speaking softly, as if afraid they might be overheard. Caroline Masters looked away.

"Are they forgiven?" Steinhardt was asking.

"At first, I have no sign." As she described the dream, Mary sounded tired. "Then I go outside," she finished, "and receive His answer.

"Carlo is gone.

"In his place are two empty glasses. One for me, and one for Chris. And then I know."

"What do you know?"

"That Chris has taken Carlo, and that I must let him." Her voice was defeated. "That my sins are past redemption."

In silent inquiry, Masters looked up at Paget. He met her gaze, nodding. She studied his face a moment; then, with a self-conscious fixity, resumed watching the tape as the voices went on. At the corner of his vision, Paget sensed Sharpe interpreting the silent exchange.

"Who is Chris?" Steinhardt asked now. "And what are your sins— in the dream, that is?"

A long silence. "Do you know Christopher Paget?"

"I know *of* him. The young man who testified at the Lasko hearings."

"Yes." Mary paused. "Chris has Carlo now."

For a moment, Paget imagined that Terri's eyes shone. Then he remembered that she had never heard the tape.

"And your sins?" Steinhardt was asking.

"In the dream, or in real life?" Mary's voice became as cool as Paget remembered it. "Because in real life, sin has little meaning to me."

Caroline Masters's face was stone. In those few words, Paget thought, Mary had defined herself.

"The dream, then," Steinhardt said.

"You can't understand," Mary answered, "without some background. Did you actually watch the hearings?"

"Yes," Steinhardt said. "Like millions of others, I was fascinated."

"And did you watch my testimony?"

"With great interest."

"Then we need to start with one essential fact."

"What is it?" There was yet more silence, and then Mary's flat voice echoed in Judge Masters's chambers.

"I lied."

Masters's eyes narrowed: to Paget, the effect was that of a contemplative woman putting the pieces together. But watching her face seemed better than living with his own thoughts. Helpless, he saw her listen to Steinhardt ask more questions, to Mary's answers.

"Then let me reassure you," Steinhardt was saying. "The tapes are for my use only, and only to assist me in your therapy. By state law, they are subject to the doctor-patient privilege, which I would ardently insist on even if there were no such law. So whatever you tell me is as confidential as if there *were* no tapes."

Masters raised her eyebrows at Sharpe. As though reminding the judge to listen, Sharpe angled her head toward the tape recorder.

As Masters turned, Mary confessed to perjury before the Senate.

To Paget, it seemed that Mary repeated the name of Jack Woods relentlessly, like a curse. Once more, Woods betrayed Paget's inquiry, sent a witness to his death. The memory of hating Woods returned to him, fresh and keen.

"All in all," Mary finished, "I told the truth a good deal of the time." She paused. "What I didn't tell Talmadge is that *I* had helped Jack do every one of those things."

Judge Masters's eyes showed nothing, looked at nothing but the tape recorder. Paget could not read her thoughts.

"You wanted to protect yourself?" Steinhardt asked.

As before, Mary sounded amused. "I wanted to stay out of prison. Even without that, the life I had worked so hard for would have ended if I had told the truth." She paused, voice softer. "And of course, I was pregnant."

Paget inhaled. He felt Terri stir next to him, moving closer.

"Did Chris know about you?" Steinhardt asked.

In the silence, Masters glanced at him. Paget saw that she instantly understood the implication: whether Paget knew about Mary's complicity and, more damaging, whether he, too, had lied to the Senate.

"Know what?" Mary answered.

The tape ended.

Without speaking, Masters went to the door and motioned in the stenographer. A round woman in her forties, she set up her machine in a far corner of the office, trying to be unobtrusive. As she did that, Masters settled back in her chair, still silent.

Sharpe broke the quiet. "This tape reveals Ms. Carelli's motives," she said. "And it suggests, regrettably, that Mr. Paget has a serious problem of ethics stemming from his own involvement in the Lasko matter and in the Senate hearings. Obviously, there is a second tape, which discloses much more regarding Ms. Carelli *and* Mr. Paget." She turned to Paget. "But *we* don't know where it is."

Paget said nothing. Masters waited until Sharpe looked back at her. "There's only one thing *I* want to know," she answered. "And that's what this tape is doing in a court of law."

Sharpe stared at her. "To listen to this tape," she rejoined, "is to know why Mary Carelli killed Mark Ransom. No one can say this tape isn't relevant to motive."

"Oh, it's relevant, all right. And if some court lets this into evidence, your chances of convicting Ms. Carelli go up about a thousand percent." Masters paused, stressing each syllable. "But there's just no way that *I* will. No way at all."

Sharpe sat straighter. "Without this tape, the court's proceedings are the shadow of truth. And determining truth is, or should be, our ultimate purpose. If courts become preoccupied with the *means* of justice, no one will believe that *any* court can serve the *ends* of justice."

Masters leaned forward. "Skip the pieties about 'justice,' Counselor. There's a psychiatrist-patient privilege in this state, and *this* tape falls as squarely within that as anything I can imagine." Her voice rose. "You've had me sit here listening to this woman's secrets, protected by law, without an argument worth making for getting this tape in. Your obvious and only purpose was to poison the court against Ms. Carelli and, it seems quite clear, against your opposing counsel. *That* is grossly unjust to both of them and contemptuous of me. Now do *you* fathom how *this* court feels about 'justice,' or should I spell it out for you?"

Sharpe looked pale. "No," she said quietly. "But I would just remind the court that, in a jury trial, I could ask a trial judge to rule without prejudicing the finder of fact."

"I understand." Masters's voice became more level. "But in my opinion, any judge who lets this in buys you two things: a guilty verdict at trial and a reversal on appeal. I suggest you try your case without it. As for me, I'll do my best to put this tape out of my mind."

There was momentary silence, the reticence of lawyers in the presence of an angry judge. The stenographer finished tapping her machine and sat staring into space. "Your Honor," Paget ventured, "I assume this concludes the prosecutor's evidence."

Masters looked to Sharpe. "Does it?"

Sharpe paused. "Subject to rebuttal witnesses."

"In that case," Paget said, "I intend to move for the dismissal of all charges against Ms. Carelli."

Masters's expression said that this trial balloon, floated to test the judge's early sentiments, would get very short shrift. "On what ground?"

"That the prosecutor's case, standing alone, does not support probable cause."

"You must be dreaming, Counselor. As *People v. Souza* put it so succinctly, probable cause means simply 'more evidence for than against.' Don't embarrass yourself by filing a motion."

How much of Masters's vehemence, Paget wondered, was the residue of the tape. "I'll certainly forgo the motion," he answered politely, "though I'm tantalized by the specter of victory."

For the first time, Masters seemed to consider smiling. "Don't let it keep you up," she said. "Anything else, anyone?"

"There is," Sharpe cut in. "I'd like to ask Mr. Paget if he intends to put Ms. Carelli on the stand."

Paget hesitated. With each day of trial, the risk of exposing Mary to cross-examination seemed to grow exponentially; the night before, he and Terri had debated for an hour the merits of keeping Mary silent. But now that the prosecution had carried its burden on direct, Mary's only hope was to build an affirmative defense, close to impossible without Mary herself. "My current intention," he said, "is to have Ms. Carelli testify."

"In that case," Sharpe rejoined, "there's some unfinished business with respect to this tape."

Masters looked curious. "Such as?"

"Such as whether we can ask Ms. Carelli if she visited Dr. Steinhardt; or if a tape existed; or if Mr. Ransom had it; or why she didn't tell the police about any of this. None of which topics, it seems to us, are privileged in the least."

"Perhaps not," Paget replied. "But Ms. Sharpe is attempting to evade the privilege by tricking Ms. Carelli into saying something about the tape—and thereby waiving the privilege against its disclosure—or by creating the aura of an undisclosed tape whose contents are unspeakably damaging."

"As the court has already suggested," Sharpe said mildly, "it's hard to imagine anything more damaging than the *actual* contents of Ms. Carelli's tape—unless it's her *missing* tape. And the law is clear: only the communications themselves are confidential, not the *fact* of the communications *or* the existence of the tape."

Once more, Paget was forced to admire Sharpe's preparation: for every point where she lost ground, Sharpe had a second and third approach, and now had added a softer tone to mute the judge's anger. If Judge Masters ruled in her favor now, Mary's cross-examination would be even more brutal and dangerous, with the disclosure of the tape itself at risk with every answer.

"You can explore those areas," Masters replied. "But questions like, 'Did you perjure yourself before the United States Senate,' or *any* question derived from the *contents* of the tape, simply will not do." She paused, looking from Sharpe to Paget. "If this tape gets into evidence, it will be because Ms. Carelli waived the privilege by blundering on the witness stand. Understand?"

"In other words," Sharpe pursued, "if Ms. Carelli testifies regarding the contents of the tape, or misrepresents them in any way, the People can play her tape in open court." She shot a glance at Paget. "Or the *next* tape—if we find it."

Paget's voice was clipped. "I'm sick of Ms. Sharpe's insinuations. As for her suggestion, it's impossible to make a ruling in advance. Whether there's a waiver depends wholly on what's said."

"That's correct," Masters responded. "But if *I* think any statement by Ms. Carelli fits the formula that Ms. Sharpe has just proposed, there's a waiver. Because—and I must stress this before Ms. Carelli takes the stand—the law protects privileged communications, not the fact of perjury."

"Forgive me, Your Honor," Paget said. "But it seems that Ms.

Sharpe has accomplished precisely what she set out to do: to plant the tape in this court's mind and to put Ms. Carelli at maximum risk."

Masters shrugged. "I've already reprimanded the prosecutor. But you *did* ask for this hearing, Mr. Paget." She turned to Sharpe. "What I *will* do is take this tape into the custody of the court. For everyone's sake."

"That's virtually unprecedented," Sharpe protested. "Our office can take precautions to protect this tape."

"So can I. Anything else?"

Sharpe hesitated. "No, Your Honor."

"Mr. Paget?"

"No, Your Honor. Thank you."

"Then we'll adjourn until tomorrow." Masters paused. "I don't know about all of you, but I've had quite enough."

The stenographer left. Masters stood, and then, as if in an afterthought, turned to Paget. "There is one thing I should say to you, Mr. Paget. It's this: You're as welcome in this courtroom now as you were before Ms. Sharpe played that tape. I don't care what you did or didn't know fifteen years ago, and I'm sorry Ms. Sharpe does." She glanced at Sharpe, and then faced Paget again. "Personal lives are a complex matter, and it will be a pity if what's private between you and Ms. Carelli doesn't get to stay there. I know your son's here watching, and appreciate the pressure you're under."

For a moment, Paget was speechless. He had been prepared for anything from Caroline Masters but compassion.

"*I* appreciate that, Your Honor. Truly."

Masters considered him. "There is, perhaps, one other thing I should say. In simple fairness, so that you can assess your alternatives." She paused again, then finished softly. "You've done a very nice job. And you're losing this case."

Paget stared into the martini glass. Straight up, no ice. His first in weeks.

" 'You're losing this case,' " he said to Terri, "does *not* require extensive analysis."

They sat at the Top of the Mark Hopkins, looking at the city as dusk fell. "Semantically speaking, no," Terri answered. "But it can mean either 'Your witnesses better be damned good' or 'Better cut a deal with Marnie while you've got the chance.' Or maybe 'Don't put Mary on the stand—you'll lose anyhow, and you'll just screw yourself up for trial.'"

Paget nodded. "I think it's one of the latter two. Maybe both."

"So do I. Unfortunately."

He smiled faintly. "It's one of the many things I like about you, Terri. You're honest."

She put down her wineglass, seeming to assess its contents. He could look at her then; the delicate face, crescent green eyes, the ridged nose that, Paget was sure, only she disliked. The woman he saw was smart and self-reliant, clear-sighted about everyone but herself.

"One problem," he told her, "is that Mary still won't take that deal. Even if they offered it."

Terri still gazed at her wine. "You kept the tape out," she said softly. "There was nothing more you could do."

"*Caroline* kept the tape out. At least for now."

She gave him a veiled look of worry; Paget watched her choose between sympathy and encouragement. "Tomorrow's our turn. We didn't expect to win now, remember? And Caroline did treat you well."

"She did, to my surprise." He paused, reflecting. "I find Caroline Masters completely inscrutable. I have the sense that something drives her besides sheer intellect, but I've no idea what it is. Or, really, who *she* is. It makes her impossible to predict."

"Then don't try, Chris. I don't think Caroline's your problem here, and you've got far too much to think about."

"I know." Terri's concern for him reminded Paget that she had worries of her own. "So how are things at home? And how's Elena?"

"Elena's great." Terri paused. "As for home, it's okay. Richie doesn't really understand the demands of this hearing—he takes it sort of personally."

Was there anything, Paget began to wonder, that Richie *didn't* think was about Richie? "That can be hard," he said.

Terri shrugged. "I just try to shut it off. Two weeks, and we're back to normal."

Her voice was flat. As if she heard herself, Terri asked, "How's Carlo?"

"Too quiet. I'm sure it's the implications about his mother and Ransom." Paget stared out the window. "More and more, I dread the day she takes the stand. Every time I drill her with questions, I find a new hole. Not to mention that Sharpe keeps coming up with new facts. It worries me, for Carlo most of all."

Nodding, Terri sipped her wine, said nothing.

"Sorry," Paget said after a time. "But if I don't say this stuff to you, it seems I don't say it to anyone."

Terri looked at him. "That seems to be our arrangement, Chris. In addition to doing trials, of course."

"Lucky for me. Not only do you listen to me brood without visible boredom, but you come up with terrific lines of questioning." He smiled. "You may have struck a death blow to the panty hose industry."

He watched her smile back. It lightened his depression for a moment, and then he thought of the tape again, and Carlo.

Terri glanced at her watch. "Melissa Rappaport should have checked in by now. I keep wondering if Caroline will let her testify in open court."

"Probably not." Paget finished his drink. "I just hope that Caroline remembers her whenever she remembers Mary's voice on tape."

PART FIVE

THE DEFENSE

FEBRUARY 13 – FEBRUARY 19

ONE

"HE TOLD ME to undress for them," Laura murmured.

Her smoky voice sounded plaintive, more bewildered than angry. Caroline Masters looked from the tape to Terri.

"What is this?" she said quietly.

Terri paused, torn from her image of Laura Chase lying on a white couch in a white room, Steinhardt an unseen voice behind her. "Please listen, Your Honor. I think we can show relevance."

"And *did* you undress?" Steinhardt asked.

"Piece by piece." A long pause. "Jamie told me what to take off and how to move."

"How to move?"

"Yes." Her voice fell. "While they watched me, I danced for them."

"Danced?"

"Jamie told me how to move," she repeated. Laura did not seem to answer questions; it was more that she was talking to herself, or what was left of herself. Her voice sounded dead. "When to turn around for them. What parts of me to uncover."

Masters looked at Terri. "James Colt?" she asked.

"Yes."

Slowly, Masters shook her head.

"What did you think about," Steinhardt was asking, "while you were doing this for him?"

"That I wanted to keep drinking." Her voice stayed flat. "We were in the recreation room of his friend's house. There was a bar there. They had everything they needed."

"So you drank more."

"Gin. Every time I took off something new. It helped me float away." Her tone became distant. "When I slid my panties down, and turned around for them, I imagined that I was about to go swimming. With *her*."

Masters's gaze seemed to turn inward; the effect was of someone who had removed herself. Terri's palms were damp.

"Then," Laura whispered, "he asked me to touch myself."

Paget and Sharpe's assistant looked at the floor. Marnie Sharpe sat with her arms folded. No one spoke.

"Touch yourself?" Steinhardt asked Laura Chase.

"At first just my nipples. Then moving my hands, like I was discovering new parts." Another pause. "After a while, he asked me to slide to the floor, and lean back against the bar."

"For what?"

"I masturbated. While they watched me."

The tape was silent.

"While I did it," Laura murmured, "I closed my eyes. Under my breath, so they couldn't hear, I whispered her name to myself."

Caroline Masters's eyes shut.

"Then someone put his penis in my mouth." Laura's voice became wispy. "I kept my eyes closed. I didn't want to know who it was.

"When he was through, and I opened my eyes, Senator James Colt handed me another drink."

Her tone was suddenly angry. The future leader of the free world, Terri remembered; that was what Laura Chase had called him, talking to Lindsay Caldwell. Lindsay had said it was the humor of a slave. But it was more than that: the phrase had a bitter irony. Terri's revulsion turned to anger.

It was all right, James Colt was saying. It was all right for Mark Ransom to treat Marcy Linton as his friends had treated Laura Chase.

Christopher Paget glanced over at Terri.

Don't get sidetracked, she told herself. You've got an argument to make. You asked to argue this yourself, and Chris agreed.

Laura Chase kept speaking.

"The second one stretched me out on the rug, and opened my legs again." Her voice became distant. "It made me think of that movie I made. Letting two men fuck me so other men could watch. I try never to think about that."

"You bought up all the copies, didn't you?"

"I hope so." Pain deadened her voice again. "But now it doesn't really matter, does it?"

There was silence, and then Laura's tone went cold. "It stopped mattering a long time ago."

"Tell me," Steinhardt asked softly. "Did anything else happen?"

"The other one rolled me over." There was a long pause. "He was hard again."

"Rolled you over?"

"Yes." Laura's voice held a faint note of anger. "They wanted to have me every way."

Steinhardt's voice was quiet. "That must have hurt you."

"Not really. My father used to do that." Her voice became flat again. "While it was happening, I looked up. Jamie was sipping his martini, watching."

Caroline Masters seemed to inhale, and then she opened her eyes.

"I'm afraid," Steinhardt said, "that our time is up."

Slowly, Masters shook her head. From the tape recorder, Laura said in matter-of-fact tones, "I may not be here next week."

"That's all right, Laura. Just call my secretary, and we can reschedule. We'll certainly need to talk about this more."

There was the faint sound of movement: Laura rising from the couch. "You know what's so funny about it?" she asked. "I can never come. Except with her."

Her voice broke. There was one sob, then the convulsive sound of Laura Chase, breaking down.

The tape clicked off.

For a long time, no one spoke.

Caroline Masters touched her eyes. "Just what," she said to no one, "am I supposed to do with *that?*"

"Let us play it," Terri answered quietly, "in open court."

Masters thought for a moment. Then slowly, she got up from her chair and summoned the stenographer.

As before, the woman settled in an unobtrusive corner. "All right." Masters looked to Sharpe. "What do the People say?"

"That tape should be suppressed." Sharpe's voice had an undertone of disgust. "It may be appalling, but it's not relevant to anything."

Masters stared at the tape. "It's relevant to some things," she said. "Why Laura Chase killed herself. Who James Colt really was. How he felt about women. If I were a historian, I would strongly argue that Colt is due a hard second look. But I'm merely a municipal court judge." She paused. "And, at the moment, I wish I weren't even that."

"I may agree with you, as a matter of personal philosophy," Sharpe answered. "But that has nothing to do with any issue in this case—which, after all, is about the death of *Mark Ransom*." Sharpe glanced at Terri. "What the defense is trying to do is create a scandal which will deflect attention from Ms. Carelli's culpability. And, frankly, make this case expensive for the district attorney by alienating a family that still matters, a son who is running for governor, and all the people who believe that the country's finest moment was cut short by a plane crash."

"The tape goes to who *Mark Ransom* was," Terri shot back. "Our defense is that Mark Ransom was a tangle of sexual pathology, at the heart of which was a need for physical and mental dominance of women as symbolized by his obsession with Laura Chase. Any political damage to District Attorney Brooks *or* Ms. Sharpe is the incidental cost of a case *they* wanted to bring." Terri paused. "I don't know how they can argue that the tape Mark Ransom played for Ms. Carelli—one that sexually aroused him in the moments before he attacked her—isn't relevant."

"In other words," Sharpe said to Masters, "make the victim so distasteful that it doesn't matter if someone murdered him. It's the world's tiredest defense strategy, Your Honor, dressed up as a feminist cause."

Terri shook her head. "Our strategy is to show this isn't murder at all, Your Honor. We ask that you not rule on the tape until you've heard all of our witnesses. Including the three witnesses Ms. Sharpe wants you to hear in chambers."

Masters looked at her. "But the only purpose of *that* is for me to rule on whether their testimony is admissible. And, therefore, can be part of the hearing on which the court determines probable cause."

"That's why I suggest you wait to rule on *this*. We think that the testimony of our witnesses, *and* the Laura Chase tape, should be taken as a whole."

"Who are they?"

"The first is Melissa Rappaport, Mark Ransom's ex-wife. The second is Marcy Linton, the writer."

Masters nodded. "I've read her stories. And the third?"

Terri paused. "Lindsay Caldwell."

Masters raised an eyebrow. "What does Ms. Rappaport have to offer us?"

"A description of Mr. Ransom's obsession with Laura Chase, and with rape. Among other things."

"What about Ms. Linton?"

"Mark Ransom raped her," Terri said softly. "In Aspen, four years ago. He came to her cabin, under the pretense of a literary meeting, to commit rape."

"And she's willing to say so?"

"Yes."

Masters looked pensive. "And Lindsay Caldwell?"

Terri tried to read her face. "Lindsay Caldwell," she answered quietly, "was the 'her' Laura mentioned. On the tape that I just played."

From the side, Sharpe turned to stare at Terri. Masters's eyes flickered. With equal quiet, she asked, "Can you explain the relevance of that?"

"Yes. Ransom told Ms. Caldwell that he had another, more explicit tape regarding her relationship with Laura Chase. He used it to arrange a 'meeting.' " Terri paused. "It was scheduled for the day after he met Ms. Carelli."

For once, Sharpe looked openly surprised; Terri watched her try to calculate the impact of what she had just heard. From the corner of her eye, Terri saw Christopher Paget's faint smile of approval, to assure her that she was doing well.

"Ms. Caldwell's also willing to come forward?" Masters asked.

"Yes. If you decide to let her testify in court, she will. In the meanwhile, we ask that you take all steps possible to assure that any appearance in chambers remain private."

Masters nodded, somber. "Of course."

"I admire Lindsay Caldwell," Sharpe put in. "But blackmail still isn't rape. Assuming that blackmail is what Ms. Peralta's implying."

"*Attempted* blackmail," Terri said. "*And* attempted rape."

Masters was gazing at the tape again. To Terri, she seemed unusually subdued.

"Explain your theory, Teresa. Step by step."

Terri nodded, organizing her thoughts. She was not as facile with words as Paget; what worked best for her was to be plainspoken. "In brief," she began, "Ransom's call to Mary Carelli was to blackmail her into being alone with him. The Laura Chase tape was something that excited him; he meant to use *Ms. Carelli's* tape to force her to have sex." Terri paused, speaking more deliberately. "When she refused, Ransom was already aroused by the Laura Chase tape. So he tried to rape Ms. Carelli, and she shot him in self-defense."

Masters looked from Terri to Paget. "How do you intend to acknowledge sexual blackmail without dealing with the existence and contents of Ms. Carelli's tape?"

"We have some thoughts about that," Paget answered. "But for now, I'd prefer not to share them with Ms. Sharpe."

"I think we're entitled to know," Sharpe put in, "if Mr. Paget intends some end run around the tape."

"What you're entitled to," Paget rejoined, "is what Mary Carelli gives you on the stand. As Judge Masters has already ruled."

Masters nodded. "I'm not here to force Mr. Paget's hand, Ms. Sharpe. You and I will find out together whatever it is she has to say. Then I'll decide if you can use Ms. Carelli's tape."

"And *this* tape?" Terri asked.

"I'm going to reserve ruling, Ms. Peralta, as you suggest." Masters gave her a thin smile. "Welcome to a speaking role, incidentally."

"Thank you, Your Honor."

Masters's smile faded. "As to your witnesses, I agree with Ms. Sharpe that Rappaport and Caldwell should be heard in chambers first." She turned to Sharpe. "Not so Ms. Linton. I want her testimony in open court."

Sharpe looked surprised. "Really, Your Honor, I'd request Ms. Linton also be heard in private. We need to explore whether her alleged experience was sufficiently similar to Ms. Carelli's supposed rape to qualify as evidence of a pattern on behalf of Mr. Ransom." She paused. "If this were a rape prosecution, it seems certain that the testimony of Ms. Linton would be excluded as too prejudicial to Mr. Ransom. At the Willie Smith trial, you will recall, the prosecution had three women ready to testify. The court excluded all of them."

Masters nodded. "I recognize the irony," she responded. "If Mr. Ransom had succeeded in staying alive, and you were prosecuting him for Ms. Carelli's rape, I would probably be forced to exclude Ms. Linton altogether. As much as I disagree with the law as it now stands." Her voice grew quiet. "But I don't have that problem, do I? Because Mark Ransom's dead."

"That's correct," Terri put in. "Under the Evidence Code, a victim's prior acts of violence are relevant to the question of self-defense. Including rape."

"Truly," Masters said dryly, "the law is a wonderful thing." She turned back to Sharpe. "How many times, Marnie, have you asked a judge to help you prove rape by letting in testimony like Ms. Linton's?"

"Often," Sharpe answered crisply. "And I've never won."

"If you ever have one in front of me, you might try again." With another brief smile, Masters turned back to Terri. "I'll hear Ms. Linton after Ms. Carelli. And please bring on Ms. Rappaport."

Melissa Rappaport wore a gray suit and an expression of birdlike alertness, which, for Terri, did not conceal her humiliation.

She sat across from Caroline Masters, her back not touching the chair. Terri sat next to her, Sharpe a little farther away; at Paget's suggestion, he and Sharpe's assistant had stepped outside. The stenographer sat in her usual corner. Rappaport had yet to speak.

Caroline Masters had set aside her robe; suddenly her manner had none of the edge she reserved for lawyers. Her posture was relaxed, her tone businesslike but pleasant, her expression one of mild inquiry. She seemed less a judge than a caseworker unraveling a complex family problem. It was a side of Caroline that Terri had not seen.

"I appreciate your coming," she told Rappaport. "The subject matter is inherently painful—human relations, and the turns they can take. Not to mention that this involves the death of a man to whom you were close, however complex those feelings might be." She nodded toward the stenographer. "I'm forced to make a record of what's said here. But please be assured that unless I have you testify, that record will remain sealed."

Rappaport merely nodded; despite Terri's best efforts to reassure her, it was as if she did not trust herself to speak. Terri was accustomed to the diminishing effect of courts, where the layman's every gesture bespoke some loss of self, but the difference between this woman in her own apartment and in Caroline's chambers was pronounced; even the nervous quickness of her movements seemed repressed. Her thumb and forefingers twisted an imagined cigarette.

"Your Honor," Terri asked, "would you mind if Ms. Rappaport smoked?"

The judge gave her a brief, quizzical look; she had always hated cigarette smoke, and Terri knew it. "Would you care to?" she asked Rappaport.

"Yes. Thank you."

Caroline reached into the drawer and produced a standard glass ashtray. "It's Judge Brookings's," she explained. "When I borrowed these chambers, I found this filled with nonfilter Camels. You don't smoke *those,* do you?"

"No. Menthol cigarettes." Rappaport's voice took on a shade of irony. "The benevolent brand that sponsors women's tennis."

Caroline nodded. "Yes. I can just imagine Martina wheezing menthol as she jumps the net. But you may live longer—every time I hear Judge Brookings cough, I think of anthracite."

With a half smile, Rappaport watched the judge push the ashtray toward her. "It's an indefensible habit," she replied. "And, like so much of what we do, self-inflicted."

" 'Man is the complicating animal,' " Caroline said. "Do light up."

Rappaport put a cigarette in her mouth. Her fingers were stiff; it took several flicks of her lighter to summon a flame. Terri watched Caroline take this in, await Rappaport's first drag. Quietly, the judge said, "I'd like to hear about Mark Ransom."

Above the cigarette, Rappaport's eyes froze. Caroline went on: "Ms. Peralta can help out, of course. But this isn't a formal proceeding, so we can have a conversation without the artificiality of court. Essentially, I'd like to know what you'd say if you *were* in court, so that I can determine its relevance to Mr. Ransom's death. If there is any."

Rappaport hesitated. "I'm not sure what's even *potentially* relevant to Mark's death."

Caroline Masters appraised her. "According to the defense, his sexual profile. I understand generally from Ms. Peralta that he had an interest in 'male dominance,' to use her words."

Watching Rappaport, Terri felt as if she had betrayed this woman. "When we talked in New York," Terri said to her, "you suggested that, pretty much from the beginning, Mr. Ransom had some unusual desires. I don't think the judge is asking for every last detail—just a sense of what Mark Ransom's needs were, including his interest in Laura Chase, and how he acted them out."

Slowly, Rappaport nodded. The way Terri had phrased it put the focus on Mark Ransom, not her. It seemed to give her a way to talk.

"The first thing that I noticed," she told the judge in a toneless voice, "was Mark's obsession with Laura Chase."

She sounded like an anthropologist, describing the obscure rites of a tribe she had studied from a distance. But Terri could hear the resonance behind the words.

"You call it an obsession," Caroline said.

"Yes. He read everything that he could find." Rappaport paused. "But much of it was visual."

"Her movies?"

"Not just those. Magazines, fold-outs. Old calendars from when she was a starlet. Anything." Her voice became flat. "Nudes, of course, were especially valued."

Sharpe gave an impatient shake of the head. "Your Honor, this trip through the backwaters of a dead man's sexual thoughts is both ghoulish and irrelevant. The question is not whether Mark Ransom subscribed to *Hustler* but why Ms. Carelli killed him in that hotel suite. Surely it wasn't for looking at pictures."

It was a shrewd intervention, Terri thought, intended to embarrass Melissa Rappaport while disrupting any rapport between her and Caroline. Terri saw the same thought run through the judge's mind. In unruffled tones, Caroline said, "I find this very helpful. And I assume that Mr. Ransom's obsession with 'pictures' was focused on Laura Chase. Is that correct, Ms. Rappaport?"

Rappaport nodded. "Yes."

Caroline leaned forward. "Other than looking, did this interest in Laura Chase erotica take any particular form?"

Rappaport took another drag on her cigarette; exhaling, she studied the cloud of smoke as if it held some interest. "Sometimes, he would take out pictures and lock the bedroom door." She shrugged. "I knew what he was doing—I'd had brothers, after all. But it seemed a bit arrested."

She said it in disdainful tones, but then looked down; Terri imagined the humiliation of trying so hard to please Mark Ransom, at such loss of self, to be put aside for photos of another woman. As if she had the same thought, Caroline asked, "Did you ever discuss that with him?"

"What was to discuss? You can fulfill your needs with photographs, or make love to your wife. But you can't do both."

"How did you resolve that? Or did you?"

Rappaport gave a thin smile. "Bondage. Of course."

The startling answer hung there a moment; beneath its deceptive casualness Terri felt a lacerating self-contempt. She looked away, as did Sharpe. Only Caroline Masters seemed unfazed; ten years at the P.D.'s office, she had once told Terri, broadened one's sense of possibilities.

"Is there some way in which you associate that with Laura Chase?" Caroline asked.

Rappaport looked past her. "Mark did. He told me that bondage freed a woman to find what was sexual inside herself, as Laura had. That Laura would have liked it." Her tone became bitter. "I tried to do what Laura would have liked."

Terri winced at Rappaport's psychic dissonance—a woman of intellectual achievement, acting out her husband's fantasies of a movie star who inspired feelings in her of both contempt and inadequacy. But Caroline seemed to sense that compassion required her to be clinical. In an even voice, she asked, "Did what Mr. Ransom wanted follow any patterns?"

"Yes." Rappaport's voice was dry. "My subjugation, physically and emotionally. That was what excited him." She looked away. "Although afterwards he could hardly look at me."

"Do you know why?"

"No." Her voice dropped. "Once I even suggested something to try to please him, to help him not be ashamed. He just became upset. Because *I* was the initiator, I think."

"Did this go on throughout your marriage?"

"At some point, Mark lost interest. No matter what I did." Rappaport stubbed out her cigarette, grinding it to a nub. "So we went on to other things."

"The rape fantasy?" Terri asked.

"Yes." Rappaport looked directly at the judge. "I would come home, and Mark would pretend to rape me. I never knew when." She paused. "I think it was the surprise that he liked most."

"But this was consensual."

Rappaport's eyes shut. "Yes."

"Did he ever hit you?"

"No." Rappaport paused. "Not to hurt, and never without my consent."

Terri watched Caroline Masters take that in. "Mr. Ransom's preoccupation with rape," Caroline ventured. "Do you also relate *that* to Laura Chase?"

"Only at the end." Rappaport glanced at Terri. "But Ms. Peralta seemed to think this important."

"What is it?"

Rappaport paused, reached for her cigarettes. Terri remembered Rappaport's face when she had first described this encounter, her own feelings when she learned that it was Rappaport's last with any man. But Rappaport's response to Caroline suggested that it was something of marginal interest, thrown out to help Terri; only the tremor in her hand showed how much the memory still cost her.

"It was the last time Mark and I had sexual relations of any kind." As if steadying herself, Rappaport took a leisurely drag. "As before, it seemed that he'd been losing interest in me—that the rape motif had played itself out, as it were. This time, however, he'd added a little something. When he threw me on the bed, there was a film of Laura Chase on the VCR." She shrugged. "Visually, it was of very poor quality."

For an instant, Terri flashed on Steinhardt, talking to Laura Chase. Did you buy up all the copies? Steinhardt had asked. I hope so, Laura had answered.

"A stag film?" Caroline asked. "With two men?"

Rappaport stared at her for a moment. "What I remember most about it," she said quietly, "was Laura Chase crying as they did it. That stuck with me, for some odd reason." She paused. "That, and Mark's renewed sexual vigor."

Caroline was quiet for a moment. "You said that was 'the last time.' You and Mr. Ransom separated after that?"

"Yes."

"As a result of this incident?"

"That and another." Rappaport put down her cigarette. "After he did that, Mark went to a bar with some friends. They stayed out late. He told me, when he arrived home drunk, of having a 'theoretical discussion' of certain sexual practices." She paused. "And then he wondered aloud if two of them could fuck me. While he watched."

Terri turned to her, startled. Rappaport looked quite composed, except that she did not notice Terri at all; quite suddenly, Melissa Rappaport seemed to be in a room by herself.

"Whatever Laura Chase did," she murmured, "he wanted *me* to do. I was never *real* to him. And neither, in the deepest sense, was Laura herself. Dead or living, we were both about his needs and fears. We couldn't be ourselves."

Slowly, Caroline Masters nodded. But Rappaport did not seem to see her, and no one wished to speak.

Quietly, Terri said, "I think you can see the relevance, Your Honor. Except for the issue of consent, the use of the Laura Chase film in a fantasy rape bears striking similarity to the role of Laura's tape in Ransom's attempted rape of Ms. Carelli."

Caroline turned to her, as if grateful to be refocused on the law. "I understand the parallel, Teresa. As we agreed, I'm reserving judgment until you've called your other witness."

"Then I'll reserve my argument," Sharpe said. "But with the court's permission, I'd like to ask Ms. Rappaport one or two questions."

Masters looked at Rappaport; she sat with her hands folded, unusually still. Masters turned to Sharpe again. "All right."

Nodding, Sharpe faced Rappaport. "When you were discussing bondage, you mentioned that your husband 'lost interest.' Could you explain what you meant by that?"

Rappaport watched her. "What I meant by that," she said, "was that it—I—no longer excited him."

"By excited . . ."

Rappaport lit a cigarette. "By excited," she said coolly, "I mean to convey the opposite of flaccid."

Sharpe gazed at her. "In other words, he no longer achieved erections."

Surprised, Terri remembered with embarrassment that Paget had raised the question after Terri first saw Rappaport, and that she still did not know the answer.

"Yes," Rappaport said finally. "Once or twice."

"And it was after these failures that Mr. Ransom contrived the pretended rape."

Where, Terri wondered, was Marnie going with this.

"Yes," Rappaport answered. "It was."

"You also mentioned that after bondage, he could hardly look at you. Did you associate this with guilt?"

"I don't know. Perhaps it was just embarrassment at what he seemed to need." Rappaport looked away. "Or at what I was willing to do."

Caroline, Terri saw, was looking at Rappaport with an air of concern. But in comparison to the woman Terri had met in New York, Rappaport seemed less highly charged, as if by acknowledging what had happened, she had started drawing out the poison.

"After he simulated rape," Sharpe was asking, "did Mr. Ransom also have trouble looking at you?"

"Sometimes. Yes."

Sharpe paused reflectively. "You already indicated that the 'rape motif had played itself out.' Did that involve a similar loss of interest?"

Facing her, Rappaport seemed stronger. "It involved a decline in frequency, if that's what you mean."

"It's partly what I mean. But did it also involve impotence?"

It startled Terri. "Did Ms. Rappaport mention impotence? I certainly don't recall that."

"Mark *wasn't* impotent," Rappaport interjected. "The time before the Laura Chase incident, he couldn't achieve erection." Her voice became bitter. "But that was obviously due to the limits of *my* appeal. With Laura Chase to help us, Mark was every inch the man he wished to be."

Sharpe shrugged, as if wishing to spare Rappaport further embarrassment. "Thank you, Ms. Rappaport."

Terri turned on the night-light, kissed the top of Elena's head. "Good night, sweetheart. I love you."

"Forever?"

"Forever," Terri answered firmly. It was a formula they had started; newly frightened by the concept of time, Elena had extracted a promise from Terri never to get old or die. It would not do to tell Elena that, tonight, Terri felt as old as her own mother.

She walked to the living room. "Long day," she said to Richie. "And another one tomorrow."

He sat at the coffee table, with index cards spread in front of him, coding them in red pen for input into his computer. Terri did not ask what plans this might involve; she had an almost superstitious fear of knowing, and Lindsay Caldwell was too much on her mind.

"Did you have time to put through that loan?" he asked.

Terri considered lying, to give herself the peace she needed. But she could not bring herself to do it. "I haven't signed the note yet."

His head snapped up. "Why not?"

"I still don't feel quite right about it."

"Damn it, I need that money for Lawsearch. You *know* that."

Terri felt the familiar weariness that seized her every time Richie wanted something. "And borrowing will gut my pension plan and tighten our cash flow. We're already maxed out on our credit cards and paying consumer interest without any end in sight."

He stood. "Look, Ter, this deal will pull us out."

"Then you should be able to find one more investor. Besides me."

His long appraising look ended in a distrustful half smile. "You envy me, don't you? You have to work for someone, and I have my own life."

Terri wondered yet again at how Richie could always change the subject, find some hidden and petty motive for her objections to his plans. "I don't work for *someone*, Richie. I work for you."

Richie shook his head. "We work for *each other*. Right now we can get by on what you make, and invest in the future." He paused, adding pointedly, "Besides, having me home is good for Elena. Don't leave her out of the family equation."

"I never do. But during your 'workday,' Elena's in day care. Which is another cost in our financial equation."

"Not during the summer. I figured out the other day that between June and September I saved us nearly two thousand dollars by working at home. Besides, she goes to public school this fall."

Terri moved to the couch and sat. "I'd like to look for another place," she said. "Somewhere near where we can afford to buy someday, and which has a public school we like. That way, Elena won't have to change schools."

Richie stared down at her. "We've got better ways to spend our money than moving, and the schools here are fine." His voice became accusatory. "I'm not going to do something with *my* daughter just because Chris Paget found some special school for his son and then fills your head with how great it all is while the waiter pours expensive wine. I'll be damned glad when this trial is over and we can have a family life without his fingerprints all over it."

Terri did not trust herself to speak. Finally, she said, "Why do you believe that I need help to worry about Elena? And why do you think I disagree with you just to cut you down? Because it isn't true, and it hurts to have you think that."

The half smile returned. "You always think I'm trying to manipulate you, don't you? Wear you down. There's a name for that, Ter. Paranoia."

Terri rose from the sofa and went to Richie. She put both hands on his shoulders, gazing up at him. "Am I real to you?" she asked.

He gave her a defensive look. "Real? You're my wife, Terri. You're a big part of my life."

She shook her head. "But am I *real* to you? Do I exist *outside* you? Does Elena?"

"Why are you attacking me, Ter?" Quick as a stage actor, his shoulders slumped in her hands, voice conveying mystified hurt. "We're a couple. We dream together, make love together, raise Elena together. We've made a family. Don't you see that every time you attack me it threatens that?"

Terri felt the numb helpless feeling creep over her again. She could think of nothing to say.

Gently, Richie kissed her forehead. "Let's not quarrel like this, okay? It's no good for Elena."

It was a familiar moment, Terri knew; the point where she could not go on, where Richie promised her peace in return for giving in. Suddenly the words rushed out. "Don't you see what we do? We both use 'family'—you to get me to do what you want, me to hide what I'm doing from myself." Her voice became pleading. "I'm dead inside, Richie. I don't *feel* anything."

He stared at her. "You're tired. It's no good for you to talk when you're tired—you lose perspective. Get some sleep." He paused. "Even better, wait till this trial is over and things are where they used to be."

Terri found she could not go on. She turned and walked out the door.

What, Terri wondered, am I doing? She was halfway down the hall before she knew that she was headed for the fire escape, to get some air. Richie did not follow; he knew that he did not need to.

The night air was cold. Slowly, Terri climbed the catwalk to the fourth floor. She stopped there, looking across the street at the student housing where they once had lived. They had not come, Terri realized, very far at all. And then she felt the tears on her face.

Why, she wondered, do men never seem to cry? Even the best ones, and even at the worst of moments.

She stayed there long after her tears had stopped, listening to the crickets in the cool night air, remembering the five years that had brought them to where they were. Tried to imagine the next five years, and then Elena's life to come.

She knew why she was afraid to do this. It was easier to keep busy day to day, the future no farther than next Saturday's matinee with Richie and Elena, or a picnic to which they took Elena and a friend from day care. Snapshots of a family, with both parents' arms around Elena. Pictures that hid, rather than revealed, the truth about her marriage.

At what age, Terri wondered, would Elena start absorbing the subliminal message of things unsaid and unfelt? At what point in childhood would she start to become like Terri, without ever choosing for herself? For what, when she was older, would she hold Terri to account—the marriage that Terri had stayed in, or the marriage that she had left? And with what damage would Terri send her to a marriage of her own?

She could find no answers. Standing there, Terri realized that she was tired and cold.

She had a trial to worry about, she told herself, Lindsay Caldwell to shepherd. The process did not stop because some defense lawyer had started to face her life.

She went back inside. Richie was still in the living room; the stacks of cards seemed only to have changed their sizes, some smaller and some larger.

"I agree with you," she said slowly. "We shouldn't talk until the hearing's over. And then we should talk seriously."

He looked up, eyes newly alert. "About what?"

She gave an apologetic shrug. "Maybe we both should take a little time off. To think."

His eyes narrowed. "Time off from work?"

"Time off from us."

He stood, his tone suddenly aggressive. "That we should separate, you mean. Why don't you just say that?"

Terri felt suddenly confused. "Live apart," she temporized. "Just for a while."

" 'For a while.' " His voice rose. "You'd do this to Elena, without even listening to me or going to see a counselor. Just walk out."

Already Terri felt guilty. "This *is* about Elena. Even if we're apart, we can always see a counselor."

Richie watched her with an odd, superior smile. "You're not being practical, Ter. We can't afford to separate."

"What do you mean?"

"I'm not leaving this apartment. Not while I've got a business to get up and running." His voice became cool. "If you pull the rug out from under me, I figure a court awards me around two thousand a month in interim support." He paused. "More, if they give me Elena."

It startled her; the conversation had spun out of control, with Richie pushing it into realms she had not contemplated.

"They'd never do that," she managed.

"Because you're a woman? Before you go running off, Ter, wake up and smell the coffee." His tone turned harsh. "The women's movement has arrived. Courts look at who the real parent is, not just gender. In *this* family, your role has been to provide, and *mine* to care for Elena."

Terri could not shake the sense of unreality; she seemed to have entered a world she did not believe in, armed only with a lawyer's rote responses. "I never *asked* you not to work."

The smile reappeared. "But you agreed to it, and I relied on that. And that's all I'll need to tell the judge."

Terri felt herself trembling at Richie's rising air of confidence. With a sudden terrible clarity, she knew that he had been planning for this moment, perhaps for a long time.

"I'm very slow," she said softly. "But once I learn something, I remember it."

He nodded. "This is ugly, Ter. I don't like even imagining it. But if you're going to bring it up, we should talk about reality."

Terri looked at him: the slender frame, the curly hair, the face in which she once had seen such life and imagination. The face of her husband, her adversary.

"I've got another witness in the morning," she finally said. "I'd better get some sleep."

"Sure." His voice was gentle now. "When I come to bed, I'll try not to wake you."

Terry felt something shiver inside her. "Please," she said.

That night, with Richie asleep beside her, she wept again.

In the morning, Terri found him in the kitchen. The coffee was already made.

He handed her a cup. "French toast coming up," he said cheerfully. "Your favorite."

She took the coffee, sat at the kitchen table. "Want some milk for that?" he asked. "Or half-and-half?"

For a long time, Terri merely looked at him. With sudden pitiless comprehension, she saw the moment for what it was: the sweetness after the storm, calculated to help her pretend that nothing had happened. "I may not be real to you," she said quietly, "but what you understand about me, you understand very well."

He turned to her, expression hovering between relief and apprehension.

Terri stood. "I'd tell you not to threaten me with Elena, Richie. But it may be far too late."

"*I* didn't threaten *you*. It was *you* who wants to separate."

"Don't twist things." She shook her head. "You told me to face reality. The sad reality of our marriage is that you're always three moves ahead of me, and I still can't bring myself to believe that there even are moves to make."

He stared at her. "What exactly are you saying?"

"That you don't love me. And that I haven't loved you for a long time, and hid that from us both." Terri paused. "If you want to blame me for something, blame me for that."

He flushed with anger. "Don't bullshit me, Ter. It isn't our marriage. You had this alleged breakthrough when you started spending time with Christopher Paget."

Terri walked silently to the sink, tossed the coffee down the drain, turned to face him again. "Chris and you don't belong in the same conversation. First, you're nothing alike. Second, this has nothing to do with him. It's all about *you*."

"I can't believe that."

"Believe it. It's *you*, Richie. You, and the fact that you can never accept that it's you. And never will."

He was silent; for the first time, Terri saw the panic in his mental calculation. "It's about Elena, Terri. Our daughter, remember?"

She felt a surge of anger. "Didn't you hear me? Don't use Elena to cover for yourself or to blackmail *me*." She paused, lowering her voice. "I've got a case to try, and I'm going to do it right. For as long as I'm doing that, you've got me to support you. As long, that is, as you don't touch me."

Terri turned and went to wake Elena.

Watching Caroline Masters greet Lindsay Caldwell, Terri thought that
they seemed like members of the same species, who recognized each
other without ever having met. Caroline's manner bespoke a respectful
sense of how difficult Caldwell must find this; Caldwell's quiet command seemed tempered by the knowledge that she could not control
what Caroline did. Both spoke softly; neither smiled.

"Did they get you past the press?" Caroline asked.

Caldwell nodded. "They took me through the underground garage
and then up a private elevator. I felt like plutonium."

"Which you are, in a way." Caroline Masters paused. "Unless I
decide they have to, I don't want the press to ever know that you
were here."

Caldwell glanced at Sharpe. "I appreciate that," she said, and the
four women sat, Caroline behind her desk, Terri next to Caldwell,
Sharpe a few feet back.

They were a strange assortment, Terri thought. Sharpe's alertness
suggested some deeper tension, whereas the case appeared to have
drawn from Caroline an unforeseen reserve of empathy. As for Terri,
she still felt her inexperience. But at least all three were lawyers; here
in chambers, Caldwell, with her tawny hair and chiseled profile, familiar only as an image on film, seemed startling.

Caroline faced her. "Tell me about Mark Ransom," she asked.

Caldwell nodded briskly, as if she appreciated the judge's directness
and would be equally direct. In the corner, the stenographer sat poised
over her machine. "It's quite simple," Caldwell began, "and quite
painful. Twenty years ago, shortly before she died, I had an affair with
Laura Chase. Mark Ransom found out."

Caroline's face was expressionless. "Did he make clear how he intended to use what he knew?"

"It was clear to *me*," Caldwell answered coolly. "And he made it
very clear that he was in control."

Caroline seemed to appraise her. "When you say that what Ransom
knew was 'painful,'" she finally asked, "do you mean something about
the affair itself. Or do you mean the fact of it?"

For a moment, the two women looked at each other; to Terri, their
silence had a sudden unspoken intimacy. "Not the fact of it," Caldwell
answered. "It was confusing to me then, but I've come to terms with

that part. People's sexuality can cover a wide range, and my range, it seems, made being with Laura a possibility—at least for that time. No, what was painful was that the circumstances were so tied to Laura's death." Caldwell paused, as if still processing the memory, and then went on. "The affair began two weeks before Laura shot herself, with Laura looking out for me at a time I badly needed someone. One week later, I abandoned *her,* out of fear of Laura's needs and my own sexuality. Her suicide completed the chain of cause and effect. *That's* the pain Mark Ransom touched."

Caroline's gaze was still level, unfathomable. "I've listened to Laura's last psychiatric tape," she finally said. "A few days before she died, three men used her with a callousness that was equaled only by the psychiatrist who listened to her." Her voice grew quiet. "What I've just told you can never go beyond this room. But it's something you should know. Before you start apportioning blame."

Terri looked at her in surprise. For the moment, Caroline seemed to have set aside the murder of Mark Ransom; her exchange with Lindsay Caldwell had the unsparing directness of two women concerned with matters deeper and more intimate than a criminal proceeding. Caldwell shook her head. "I was with Laura when James Colt called her," she answered quietly. "Both Laura and I knew what he intended. I left anyway."

Caroline folded her hands. "We've been speaking of blackmail," she said. "For Laura to put her decision on you was a kind of emotional blackmail. You didn't force Laura to go with him. Or to kill herself."

Caldwell looked away. "Mark Ransom touched one other thing," she finally said. "Although he may not have known it."

"Which is?"

"An hour before she killed herself, Laura called me, drunk and desperate." Caldwell's voice fell. "I rejected her again."

Caroline watched her. Softly, she asked, "Did you think Ransom knew that?"

"I didn't know. He certainly knew enough." Caldwell still gazed down. "I thought perhaps she'd called Steinhardt that night, and that Ransom knew that. I still don't know whether that would have made me feel better, or worse."

"But you wanted to know."

"I've *always* wanted to know. As much as I feared exposure, *that* was why I would have seen Mark Ransom."

Caroline was quiet. "It may be beside the point," she said at last, "but I believe in personal responsibility for personal choices. You were what—nineteen? Laura let *herself* go." Her voice hardened. "But if we're adding links in some chain of cause and effect, add Steinhardt and James Colt—or Laura's father, for that matter. It's not germane to Ms. Carelli's culpability, but the suggestion that Mark Ransom found *that* tape exciting is almost as appalling as the suggestion he was using it for sexual blackmail."

"And they are *both* suggestions," Sharpe pointed out. "Not *facts.* Nor defenses to premeditated murder."

Caroline Masters turned to Sharpe. "I'm not here to bail out Ms. Carelli. But it's probably fortunate that the prosecution isn't required to show the human decency of the victim." Once more, Caroline faced Lindsay Caldwell. "As the issues of guilt which must occupy Ms. Sharpe are confined to Ms. Carelli, perhaps we should turn to the nuts and bolts of your conversation with Mark Ransom."

Caldwell leaned back, looking out the window. "I was surprised when he called," she finally said. "But the first thing I really remember was when he said that he'd been hearing so much about me.

" 'From whom?' I asked him.

"He hesitated, then he answered, 'Laura Chase.' "

Caldwell paused. "I was at my beach house in Malibu," she said slowly. "In the living room. My husband was sitting next to me.

"When Mark said that, I started—quite literally. I remember looking over my shoulder. Roger was reading a novel by Philip Roth, half smiling to himself.

"In the most normal tone I could manage, I said, 'Really.' And then Ransom began laughing." Caldwell's voice became low and angry. "The conversation had hardly begun, and I'd already told Mark Ransom that there was someone in the room with me and that I was scared of Laura.

" '*Really,*' he repeated. 'Specifically, what Laura told me is that you're the most beautiful and sensitive lover she had ever been with.' It chilled me. And then his voice took on the unctuous tone of someone giving an exaggerated compliment. 'Coming from Laura, that's quite extraordinary, don't you think? It certainly impressed *me.*' "

Terri turned to glance at Caroline. But the judge's gaze had moved to her hands.

"The odd thing," Caldwell went on, "is that beneath the syrupy surface he sounded angry. As if knowing about Laura and me had thrown him off balance.

" 'Of course,' Ransom went on, 'toward the end, Laura had very poor luck with men—or women, it seems.' " Caldwell shook her head. "And then he said, in a horrible joking tone, 'The confusion must have killed her.' "

Caroline Masters looked up. "What did *you* say?"

"Roger glanced over at me. I realized that I'd been talking for some time and that he was becoming curious. So I said in the driest voice I could master, 'That's very droll, Mark. Where are you getting your material, the *Reader's Digest?*'

"Ransom laughed again. 'My Most Unforgettable Lesbian'? No, my material comes direct from Laura. In her own voice.'

"Almost by reflex, I said, 'Then I hope she called collect.' " Pausing, Caldwell looked at the judge. "It was so strange: I was trading black jokes with Mark Ransom about my affair with Laura Chase, trying to keep Roger from noticing how intimidated I was by whoever was on the other end.

" 'No,' Ransom told me. His tone was suddenly serious. 'But I paid for it quite handsomely.'

"Roger was looking at me now. 'What rights did you buy?' I asked Ransom.

"Ransom's voice got very quiet. 'Literary rights,' he said. 'To the tapes of Laura and her psychiatrist.' "

Caldwell paused again, looking at Caroline Masters. "For a moment," Caldwell told her, "I forgot where I was. I don't even know what I said. But for the rest of my life, I'll never forget what *he* said next. " 'Laura seems to have loved you,' he told me. 'And you seem to have left her to her fate. Which, as it happens, is the subject of my book.'

"For a time, I could hardly speak. 'What,' I managed, 'is the book about?'

" 'Laura's suicide,' he told me. 'The days and hours before she pulled the trigger. I mean to answer the question "Who Killed Laura Chase?" '

" 'Who *did?*' I asked, and then I realized Roger was staring at me.

"More quietly yet, Mark answered, 'Whomever I choose, Lindsay. Whom would you suggest?' "

Terri watched Caroline Masters imagine what Terri could see clearly: Caldwell in the beach house Terri had visited, trying to conduct one side of the conversation for her husband's benefit while she listened to Mark Ransom exhume the guilt of twenty years. Caldwell's voice turned dull, as if at the memory of her helplessness.

" '*What* would *you* suggest?' I finally said to Mark.

" 'That you listen to my tape of Laura, talking about you.' His tone became intimate. 'Then you'll give me a very private interview. If you're sufficiently cooperative, I may even consider you an "editorial consultant." '

"Roger had gone back to reading Philip Roth. 'Is that necessary?' I asked Ransom.

"There was a long silence, and then he said, 'Only if you want the tape.' "

"I felt sick. 'Why?' I asked.

"He was quiet again. 'Remember that little quarrel we had about Laura,' he asked, 'at the Yale symposium on "Women in Film"? You called me "the poet laureate of the centerfold," I believe.' "

Caldwell crossed her arms, as if hugging herself. "Something in those two sentences," she said to Caroline, "was as frightening as knowing he had the tapes.

" 'Yes,' I told Ransom, 'I remember.'

" 'I found you terribly arrogant,' he went on. 'But I didn't know then just how well *you* knew your subject. So I thought it was time that we have a much more intimate chat about Laura. *And* about centerfolds.' "

Caldwell sounded tired. "If I'd had any doubt at all about what he wanted," she said, "that ended it."

" 'That's not my favorite subject,' I said.

" 'But it's *mine,* Lindsay. Because I've always wanted to interview someone who slept with Laura Chase. And hearing from Laura about how it was to sleep with *you* suggests that you have much more to offer me than I could ever have imagined.'

"I couldn't think of anything to say. When I turned to look at Roger, he was smiling at his book again. And then Mark Ransom said, 'I want you for an entire day. Alone. I promise, of course, to bring the tape.' "

Caldwell's voice became wearier. "I agreed to see him. At a hotel room in Los Angeles. It would have been the day after he met with Mary Carelli."

Caroline was quiet for a time. "And you never told your husband?"

"Only in the narrowest sense. After I hung up the phone, Roger asked who it was. I told him it was Mark Ransom and he wanted to sell rights to a book about Laura Chase." Caldwell shook her head. "It wouldn't come to anything, I told Roger—it wasn't my kind of material, and Ransom wasn't my kind of writer. But I was going to meet him anyway." Caldwell's voice fell. "After all, I said to Roger, we were only talking about one day out of my life."

Caroline leaned back. "Why," she finally asked, "are you willing to come forward now?"

Caldwell seemed to ponder the question. "My reason has changed. When I first spoke with Terri, I was certain that the police had found the tape, or soon would. That my secret was out." She paused. "And I desperately wanted to hear what Laura had said."

"And now?" Caroline asked. "The tape is missing. Unless and until it's found, you're the only one who knows what happened between you and Laura Chase."

Caldwell gave her a level look. "That's true," she said finally. "But I also know what happened between *Mark Ransom* and me. And knowing that, I know who Mark Ransom was."

"And that makes silence difficult."

Caldwell nodded. "Until Steinhardt's daughter sold Ransom those tapes, *I* was content to live with what had happened. Because the only living person it hurt was me. That's not true anymore. Now Mary Carelli's on trial for murder, and the tape may surface anyway." She paused again, looking at Caroline Masters with an air of fatalism. "If you decide that what I know is relevant, I'll tell Roger and my son and daughter. And then I'll testify for Ms. Carelli."

Caroline Masters bent forward, as if in private contemplation. Terri could almost read her thoughts: that the matter of Mark Ransom was far more complex than she had imagined; that she did not wish to harm Caldwell or Melissa Rappaport; that she no longer saw the trial in terms of her own role.

"May I pose a few questions?" Sharpe asked.

Almost unwillingly, Masters turned to her. "Of course."

Sharpe pulled her chair closer, facing Caldwell.

"Do you know where the tape is?" she asked.

Caldwell shook her head. "No. I don't."

"Do you have any idea what might have happened to it?"

"No." Pausing, Caldwell looked puzzled. "I wish I did."

Sharpe cocked her head, as if equally bemused. "Did Mr. Ransom ever demand sex for the tape?" she asked.

"No. Not in so many words."

"Did he propose any kind of sexual activity between you and him?"

Caldwell stared at her. "Did he say, 'I'll trade the tape for sex'? No. Did he have to? You wouldn't ask if you'd been on the other end of the telephone."

"I understand. But don't you agree that, in the literal sense of his words, Mark Ransom could have been asking you for information—albeit of a very intimate kind?" Sharpe paused. "Perhaps pushing you, as journalists sometimes will, but after nothing more than the most sensational book he could write?"

Caldwell flicked back her hair. "Only if you believe that when a man says to a woman, 'I'd like to stay the night,' the literal sense of his words is that he admires your living room couch." She paused, adding in sardonic tones, "Perhaps pushing you, as men sometimes will, but only for a good night's sleep."

The sudden stinging irony startled Terri and seemed to snap Caroline out of her private reverie. Sharpe flushed, and then assumed a tone of exaggerated patience. "The literal sense of words *does* matter if you're in a court of law. I've prosecuted any number of rape cases where the man claimed that 'no' meant 'yes.' If that kind of Orwellian twist were evidence of guilt or innocence, one of those men would no doubt be raping another woman even as we sit here."

"Don't *you* twist this," Caldwell snapped. "The only reason Mark Ransom didn't try to rape *me* is that Mary Carelli shot him first." Caldwell's voice turned calm but very cold. "The curious thing about his call was how clear it was to me, whatever words he used, that part of Ransom's very sick thrill was that I was a successful woman and a feminist. Like you, I assume." Caldwell paused. "I can't help but wonder how *you* would have felt, Ms. Sharpe, if Mark Ransom had placed that call to you."

Sharpe pulled back, staring at Caldwell with an odd, hurt expression. "That's completely unfair."

"Is it?"

Caroline leaned forward. "I understand your point, Marnie. *And* Ms. Caldwell's. Do you have anything more?"

It took a moment for Sharpe to turn from Caldwell. "Only an observation," she said quietly. "We have no explicit request for sex, no blackmail which can be proven. And certainly no rape. Quite literally, Mr. Ransom did not come within four hundred miles of Ms. Caldwell. So all we're left with is a long-distance call that *Ms. Caldwell* conducted in a deliberately obscure manner and that is evidence of nothing more than Ms. Caldwell's private pain. Which is how it should remain—private."

Terri leaned forward. "That goes to the weight of the evidence," she replied. "*Not* its admissibility. The court should allow Ms. Caldwell to testify fully and completely. Ms. Sharpe can cross-examine. After that, the *court* can decide how it sees Mr. Ransom's call to Ms. Caldwell—which, as she points out, bears as much resemblance to a request for information as rape does to a honeymoon."

"The problem," Caroline rejoined, "is that it doesn't resemble rape, either. Which is Ms. Carelli's defense."

Terri felt Caroline deciding against her, reached for a new argument. "Ms. Carelli's defense," she responded, "involves this man's sexual character, and his sexual agenda in contacting Ms. Carelli. Which, as Ms. Carelli can attest, involves the same supposedly 'ambiguous' approach Mark Ransom used with Ms. Caldwell."

"But we're looking for admissible evidence on which to decide whether Ms. Carelli acted in self-defense and therefore can defeat probable cause. You'll admit, Teresa, that we're nowhere near what could be considered a 'similar act' to rape."

"It depends on *which* act we're talking about." Terri shifted ground again. "Let me suggest this: that the court wait until the entire defense case is in before ruling on whether Ms. Rappaport, Ms. Caldwell, and the tape of Laura Chase can be part of the record on which the court decides the issue of probable cause. That ought to assure the broadest information and perspective when the court *does* rule."

Caroline gave a small smile. "Never face today," she said, "what you can put off till tomorrow. If you're losing, that is."

Terri smiled back. "Never rule today," she answered, "if your ruling may be better tomorrow."

Caroline's smile faded, and then she nodded slowly. "All right, Teresa. You've preserved your position for the moment. I'll rule after your remaining witnesses." She turned to Caldwell. "I apologize for keeping you in limbo, Ms. Caldwell. But from the court's perspective, Ms. Peralta's request makes enough sense to honor it."

Caldwell nodded. "I understand."

"I hope so." The judge turned to Sharpe. "In the meanwhile, Marnie, if any new tape involving Ms. Carelli, Laura Chase, *or* Ms. Caldwell comes into your possession, you are to notify me immediately." She paused for emphasis. "Immediately, and privately. Because if *any* of these tapes is made public, and it's the doing of the prosecution, I'll be inclined to see that as a deliberate denial of due process. The sanction will be to dismiss this case. And in dismissing it, I'd feel impelled to set forth why."

Sharpe looked startled. "Is it really necessary," she asked, "for the court to assume responsibility for safeguarding so much evidence in such an extraordinary way?"

"It's necessary for my own sense of decency. For which *I* take responsibility." Caroline turned back to Caldwell. "If I decide to rule for Ms. Peralta, I'll give you reasonable notice. So that you can tell whomever you need to tell."

"Thank you," Caldwell said. "At some point, I may tell my family, regardless of what happens here. But whether and when is something I need to work out for myself."

Caroline was quiet. "In the end," she answered, "I may force you to. That's a decision that weighs heavily on me. But it's part of being a judge. So perhaps you can indulge me while I give you the perspective of a judge."

"Of course."

"Sexuality *does* involve a wide spectrum. But you couldn't have known that at age nineteen. And as simple as it seems, many people find facing that difficult at *any* age." Caroline's voice slowed, as if to make sure Caldwell heard her. "For almost twenty years as a defense lawyer and now a judge, I've been mired in questions of guilt and innocence—moral as well as legal. Of all the people involved with Laura Chase's death, your wounds seem by far the worst to me, and you have by far the least to answer for. Forgive yourself."

Caldwell looked surprised. Abruptly Caroline stood, extending her hand. "Good luck, Ms. Caldwell."

Caldwell took Caroline's hand. "And you," she said softly. "Thank you."

Caroline called her deputy. Within a minute, Caldwell and Terri, accompanied by two bailiffs, were in a freight elevator, silently thinking their separate thoughts.

Finally, Caldwell turned to her. "You were good, Terri. She was going to rule against you, I think."

"I think so too."

They got to the underground garage. Caldwell's limousine, black with opaque windows, was parked by the elevator. The bailiffs stood back; Caldwell's chauffeur waited on the other side of the car. "It seems," Caldwell said to Terri, "that I'll leave as I came, anonymously. It's a luxury I don't often get."

Terri was quiet, then she said, "I don't know how to thank you."

"You needn't thank me, and you needn't feel responsible. Really, I had no choice."

Terri watched her face. "At least Caroline Masters tried to make it easier," she said at length. "Much more than before, I'm really coming to admire her."

"You *should* admire her—she's an admirable woman." Caldwell paused, and then added softly, "But I think there's something else—a particular sensitivity. Something personal, perhaps."

Before Terri could question her, Lindsay Caldwell touched her shoulder. "I wish you well," Caldwell said, "with everything."

Caldwell disappeared into the limousine. Terri watched it drive up the exit ramp, a black car with an unseen passenger, and vanish.

TWO

TELEVISION FLICKERING IN the background, Christopher Paget poured Mary Carelli a glass of red wine.

"You still like Chianti, I imagine."

"Since even before you knew me." Her voice was dry. "Of course, I've learned to like better Chianti since I lived in Rome."

To Paget, the remark had a rueful undertone, which mingled pride in what she had accomplished with fear that it would soon be gone: to remember Rome was to acknowledge that she might never see it again.

Paget raised his wineglass. "To Rome."

Half smiling, Mary touched her glass to his. "To Rome," she said. "And to getting through tomorrow."

They sat in Paget's library on Sunday evening, the end of four days spent rehearsing Mary's testimony, while Terri handled Rappaport and Caldwell and then prepared for Marcy Linton. For the first two days, they had crafted Mary's testimony, confessing error or doubt when necessary; carefully treading through her interview with Charles Monk; designing, editing, and discarding verbal formulas until they found the answers they wanted. And then Paget had devoted the weekend to tearing those answers apart.

Now it was dark outside, and they were finished.

"You've worked hard," he said. "All you have to do is stay alert but calm."

Mary's smile became ironic. " 'Alert but calm,' " she repeated. "So easy to achieve. And such a perfect approach for a premeditated murderer."

For Paget, the remark had a surreal quality: a mordant joke from a calculating woman from whom he could not demand the truth, and in whose truthfulness he could not believe. But the most eerie part was that he could hear the comment either as a veiled confession or as understated bitterness that Sharpe—and perhaps Paget—believed her capable of murder.

"I think Caroline's ready to listen now," he said finally. "Whether she lets them testify or not, Rappaport and Caldwell have made an impression. Which means that Judge Masters is thinking about who Ransom was, rather than just wondering who *you* are."

Of course, Paget thought, *I* wonder who you are. But he did not say that: while their preparation was shot through with the fact of Mary's lies, they had treated that as an intellectual problem, and each other with civility. After four days, the two things Paget knew for certain were how facile and self-disciplined Mary Carelli still was.

As if in counterpoint, her face now appeared on television: first as a young witness before the Senate, then as a woman charged with murder. "Tomorrow morning," the voice-over said, "Mary Carelli faces the most critical moment of the hearing and, perhaps, of her life. The moment when she takes the stand."

Mary gazed at the screen, and then at Paget. "Don't worry," she said. "I won't blow this. Whatever else you think, you should know me well enough to know that."

The remark was matter-of-fact, but there was steel beneath it. "Just don't underestimate Marnie Sharpe," Paget answered.

Mary stretched her legs. "I've been studying her, Chris. I know exactly how she'll be."

Paget nodded; he could too easily imagine Mary, removed from all emotion, dissecting Sharpe while she went about her business. That her business was to prove Mary a murderer would make Mary all the more determined.

"I'm sure," he remarked, "that Marnie's every quirk is coded on your brain."

"It is." Mary's voice went cold. "I won't let her nail me."

"I believe you."

Her ironic look returned. "Yes? About that I suppose you do."

Paget smiled. But all that he believed in was Mary's resolve; he was far too skeptical of her innocence not to worry. He wished that he could fast-forward his life to the end of her testimony, find their defense still viable, their secrets safe from Carlo.

The seamed face of a prominent defense lawyer had appeared on Court TV.

"It's such a mistake," he said, "to put her on the stand. But then this whole strategy is a mistake. If Christopher Paget loses *here*, he's got no surprises left for trial. To me, this defense looks like a play written by a gifted amateur—flashes of brilliance, but a plot that won't fly. I think he's far too close to the case to be objective."

Paget turned off the sound. "We've done all we can," he said quietly.

Mary turned from the television. "We have," she said. "I should leave in a while."

She looked suddenly tired, Paget realized, and a little sad. Like a woman with nowhere to go.

When she glanced at the television again, the picture had changed. A much younger woman, she stood in intimate profile with Christopher Paget, in the moments before he testified in the Senate. And then Carlo's face appeared.

"Did you see the cover of *People?*" she asked.

He nodded. "Carlo. But I didn't read the article."

"They don't have much yet." Mary paused. "It's just as well that my parents are dead."

Paget nodded, lost in thought.

"Do you ever wonder," Mary asked softly, "what would have happened to us without the Lasko case?"

Paget gazed at her. "Without Carlo? Or with?"

"With, I suppose." Mary looked down. "That was a good night, Chris. A good weekend."

"It was." Paget contemplated his wine. "But it's impossible to project from a single weekend. We're so very different, after all."

She raised her eyes. "But could my *life* have been different? Would *I* have been different?"

Paget thought for a time. "I don't want to sound like a moralist," he answered, "and certainly not tonight. But by the time we made love that weekend, you'd already committed yourself to helping Jack Woods. Once that was done, the whole thing had an inexorable quality." Pausing, he switched off the television. "The truth, I think, is that people keep on being who they are and what they want. I don't think the fact that two people encounter each other truly changes either one. It may change their *lives*, perhaps, but not their essential selves."

Mary fell quiet. "You and me, you mean."

He nodded. "You and I made each other's *lives* wholly different. But that was because we encountered each other head-on, and then proceeded to be precisely who we were. As Malraux observed, 'Character is fate.' "

She studied him. "Carlo didn't make just your *life* different, Chris. He made *you* different."

Was that true? Paget wondered. Had Carlo made him any better, any wiser and more loving, than the man Paget's parents had sent into the world? "Perhaps," he said finally. "But then *children* are different."

The thought led him again to Carlo: how this trial might change his view of his own parents and, more subtly, of himself. It took Paget far away from Mary.

"I'm sorry," she said at last. "For everything. More than you'll ever know."

He looked up at her again. At that moment, fifteen years fell away; he saw her as she had seemed to him in Washington, making love on the weekend before he had learned what she had done. "I know you are," he answered. "I *do* believe that."

She searched his face, as if measuring the truth of what he said, hoping for something to take away from all that had happened. And then, very simply, she said, "Thank you."

As they watched each other, something changed.

It would have been possible, Paget knew for an instant, to reach out to her. To put aside their past and suspend all disbelief. To make love for a night, escape from fear. People do these things for different reasons and then, in the morning, leave the moment and their needs behind. He knew that Mary and he could do that. Knew, as he looked into her eyes, that part of Mary wanted to.

He did not know what stopped them. History, perhaps. Perhaps, for him, there were other reasons.

"The one thing you have left to do," he told Mary, "is sleep."

For another moment, she simply looked at him. "I'll call a cab," she said.

*　*　*

The courtroom was dense with silence; the extra reporters Judge Masters had admitted to hear Mary Carelli stood at the back of the room. Carlo and Johnny Moore watched from the front row; intent, Terri took notes.

Outside, groups of women with a sprinkling of men among them chanted and held a banner that read: RAPE IS NOT A RIGHT. Facing them, separated by the width of the concrete walkway leading to the door of the courthouse, a group of counterpicketers carried signs reading: JUSTICE FOR MARK RANSOM; THE VICTIM IS NOT ON TRIAL; DON'T MURDER THE FIRST AMENDMENT. The doorway was guarded by police; more police lined the rear of the courtroom.

"And why did you agree to see Mark Ransom?" Paget asked Mary.

The question was critical—it would determine the course of Mary's testimony and the line of Sharpe's attack. Sharpe did not move; even Caroline Masters's gaze, intent and unblinking, underscored the moment. Only Mary looked calm.

"He had a tape," she answered. "Of a session I had with a psychiatrist in Beverly Hills. A Dr. Steinhardt."

At the corner of his vision, Paget saw Sharpe tense with surprise. "Why did you visit Dr. Steinhardt?" he asked.

"Because I was in deep emotional pain." Mary paused, but her gaze at Paget did not falter. "There were things I had done—hidden things—of which I was deeply ashamed. I had no peace of mind."

Paget heard whispers exchanged behind him, saw Sharpe half rise in her chair, looking from Mary to Masters. But Masters, staring openly at Mary, did not see Sharpe.

"And you described those things to Dr. Steinhardt?" Paget asked.

Mary's face was a mask of shame. "In as much detail as I could." Her voice fell. "I thought it was in confidence."

"And why was that important to you?"

She looked down. "Because what I told him was so deeply personal."

Sharpe's body, Paget saw, was taut with repressed energy—concern that Mary's fear of secrets might gain sympathy, eagerness to argue that Mary had opened up the tapes herself as evidence. "And how," Paget asked Mary, "did you feel when Mark Ransom described the contents of the tape?"

"I was devastated." The memory appeared to drain her. "After he hung up, I went to my bathroom and vomited."

Paget paused, as if letting her collect herself. "Did Ransom say what he thought would happen if he disclosed the tape?"

"Yes." Mary raised her head. "He said that it could ruin my reputation, and my career."

"Did you agree?"

Mary nodded. "That was why I saw him," she said quietly. "To ask him—beg him, if necessary—to leave my past life where it belonged. In the past."

"You felt that desperate?"

Mary's eyes shut. "The things he knew tortured me. That's why I went to Dr. Steinhardt."

Paget turned to Judge Masters. "Might we have a bench conference, Your Honor?"

Masters looked surprised, as if still caught in Mary's testimony. "Yes. Of course."

Quickly, Sharpe and Paget approached the bench. Glancing toward the crowded room, Masters leaned forward, to speak out of earshot of Mary, the reporters, the microphones of Court TV. Paget felt the cameras follow him to the bench.

"What is it, Mr. Paget?"

"Ms. Carelli has said all she intends to about the tape. She's acknowledged that it exists; that it would damage her reputation and career; and that it was the reason she agreed to see Ransom. Which, we strongly believe, is an adequate substitute for disclosure of the tape itself—both from the standpoint of its impact on Ms. Carelli's actions and from simple fidelity to the truth. And because she's said nothing about the specific contents of the tape, Ms. Carelli has *not* waived her right to protect her conversation with Dr. Steinhardt."

"If this is fidelity to the truth," Sharpe said in muted tones, "then we should replace the scales of justice with Pinocchio. Ms. Carelli has *finessed* the contents of the tape, omitting *why* it was so harmful—that she lied to the United States Senate—while gaining sympathy for Mr. Ransom's exploitation of this nameless secret. For all that appears on the record, Ms. Carelli was ashamed of cheating at Monopoly."

Paget turned on her. "Does *that* end careers, Marnie, and ruin reputations? If you got caught cheating at Monopoly, would *you* throw up?"

"Only if I were looking for sympathy," Sharpe retorted, turning to Masters. "She's opened up the tapes."

"Regrettably," Masters answered, *"you* opened *this* up—when you got my permission in chambers to ask essentially the same questions Mr. Paget just asked. He's simply preempted you. If you want to play those tapes, you'll have to induce Ms. Carelli to say more than she has."

"Thank you," Paget said quickly. He walked away, leaving Sharpe still staring up at Masters. As Sharpe shrugged, Paget gave Mary a silent nod; one corner of her mouth formed the briefest of smiles. Glancing at Carlo, Paget saw his face relax.

"Please continue," Masters said.

Paget nodded. "Let me ask you this, Ms. Carelli: why did you bring a gun to Mr. Ransom's suite?"

"To protect myself."

"But why did you feel the need?"

Mary folded her hands. "His telephone call to me was filled with sexual innuendo and sexual blackmail."

"Could you be specific?"

Mary's shrug lent the suggestion of a shudder. "It wasn't just the words he used," she said quietly. "It was his tone—sniggering and systematically degrading. He expected a 'private interview.' He was going to 'interview' another 'famous woman' in Los Angeles. He wanted us 'back-to-back,' so that he could 'compare notes.' We could even discuss 'freedom of choice' and a woman's 'right to privacy.' " She shook her head. "Each word made my skin crawl."

Paget glanced up at Masters, as if to underscore the connection to Lindsay Caldwell. Then he asked Mary, "And what did you conclude from this conversation?"

"What Ransom so clearly *wanted* me to conclude," Mary answered coolly. "That he would trade the tape for sex. And that he would hurt me if I didn't."

Sharpe was on her feet. "Move to strike that last answer, Your Honor. It's wholly speculative—the witness is claiming omniscience regarding what Mark Ransom never said."

"Sustained." Masters turned to Mary. "We want the facts, Ms. Carelli. Please leave the interpretations to me."

Slowly, Mary nodded.

Moving forward, Paget asked, "Did you *intend* to trade the tape for sex?"

"I didn't *want* to." Her voice fell. "I just wanted to talk him out of it. Beyond that, I didn't really know."

"And yet you brought a gun."

"Yes," Mary looked at Masters. "But *not* to kill him. Because he frightened me."

"Then why didn't you tell the police?"

Mary paused, touching her eyes. "Because I didn't want anyone knowing what was on the tape."

"Is that also why, after Mark Ransom died, you *still* didn't tell the police about the tape?"

"Yes. It is."

"Didn't you think that the police would find any tape that Mr. Ransom had?"

"That's logical, of course." Mary turned back to Caroline Masters. "But I was in shock."

Paget nodded, satisfied. By asking the questions a skeptical judge or cross-examiner might ask, he was depriving Sharpe of points while helping Mary restore her credibility. And though Masters understood all this, she was plainly prepared to listen: Terri had done her job, and now Mary was doing hers.

"Is it your understanding," Paget asked, "that there are actually two tapes of you and Dr. Steinhardt, and that the prosecution has only the first?"

"That's my understanding, yes."

"Do you know the whereabouts of the second tape?"

Mary looked at Sharpe. "No," she said emphatically. "I do not."

A slight edge in Mary's voice hinted anger at the question; if she knew what had happened to that tape, Paget thought, then Mary was a gifted liar. But, of course, she was.

"In fact," Paget said, "Ransom didn't bring *any* tape, did he?"

"No tape of *me*." Mary looked troubled. "He did bring a taped session between Dr. Steinhardt and Laura Chase. Her death was to be the subject of his next book."

There was a stirring in the courtroom; until this moment, the press had not known about the tape of Laura Chase.

Now Sharpe was on her feet. "Your Honor," she interjected. "The People request a bench conference."

The two lawyers met in front of Masters. "That tape has not yet been admitted," Sharpe said. "Mr. Paget phrased the question indirectly, so that Ms. Carelli could slip in Laura Chase before I saw it coming. I didn't know that we'd invited her."

"What *are* your intentions," Masters asked Paget, "now that Ms. Carelli has so neatly summoned Laura from the dead?"

"To describe the contents generally," Paget said, *"without* mentioning James Colt." His voice quickened. "Laura Chase is dead; it's Ms. Carelli who has a claim on our compassion. And as Your Honor knows, the Laura Chase obsession goes to the heart of Mr. Ransom's sexuality. It's a central part of what Ms. Carelli says happened here—"

"The sexual acts described are quite different, Mr. Paget."

"True. But the obsession is all of a piece. And that's what triggered Mr. Ransom's abuse of Ms. Carelli."

"According to Ms. Carelli," Sharpe put in, "that unimpeachable source of truth."

"Save it for cross," Paget retorted, "where Mary can answer you."

Masters raised her hand. *"Enough,"* she said. "I'll allow a very general description. As Mr. Paget points out, there's no privilege here. And Mr. Ransom's sexual proclivities are clearly relevant to the defense. Let's get back on the record."

"Thank you," Paget said. Briefly, he nodded to Terri, and then faced Mary again. "Ms. Carelli, could you generally describe the contents of the tape?"

"Yes." Mary's voice was soft. "It involves a weekend Laura Chase spent with three men in Palm Springs. The men involved her in a series of sexual activities—exhibitionism, at first." Mary paused. "And then two had sex with her while the third watched."

Watching Mary, Paget felt and heard the crowd reaction—bodies stirring, exclamations. The judge cracked her gavel, and there was silence again. "Why did Mr. Ransom bring *that* tape?" Paget asked.

"What he *said* was that he wanted to discuss his new book on Laura Chase. Of which that supposedly was an integral part." Again, Mary hesitated. "He intimated that if I interviewed him on *Deadline,* it might help him forget *my* tape."

"What did you say?"

"That he'd misled me. That he'd held back the tape to continue his blackmail." Her voice grew faint. "His answer was that we should listen to the Laura Chase tape and then talk about it."

"And did you listen to Laura's tape?"

"Yes." Mary looked away. "He made me."

Paget cocked his head. "Was that after Mr. Aguilar appeared with the champagne?"

"Yes."

"And did you ask Mr. Aguilar to hang the Do Not Disturb sign when he left the room?"

"I did. Yes."

"And why was that?"

Mary turned to Caroline Masters. "I was there against my will," she said softly. "Because Mark Ransom knew things I didn't want *anyone* to know. The fact that Mr. Aguilar saw us was upsetting enough; I didn't want to have a cleaning person come in and see us talking." She paused. "And when Mark Ransom described the Laura Chase tape and then told me I had to listen, I knew I didn't want anyone walking in on *that*. I was far too ashamed of what was happening."

"You didn't make that request of Mr. Aguilar just to be alone with Mark Ransom?"

"Not in the sense that *he* interpreted it." Mary's voice hardened. "I don't want to disappoint Mr. Aguilar, but I consider Mark Ransom to have been the most twisted and distasteful man I have ever known."

Paget was silent for a moment, letting Masters absorb that. "Could you tell us," he asked, "what this 'twisted and distasteful man' tried to do once Mr. Aguilar left?"

"He tried to rape me." As if to answer some unspoken doubt, Mary turned to Caroline Masters, repeating softly, "Mark Ransom tried to rape me."

"Could you explain what happened?" Paget asked.

Turning again, Mary stared into some middle distance. "It began when he played the tape." Her voice became quiet now, almost frightened. "It was awful. As Laura Chase danced for these men, and then started touching herself, Mark Ransom grew more excited. When the sex acts began, it pushed him over the edge."

"Could you describe that?"

Mary's look of fixity lingered: it was as if she were replaying a tape of her own, searching for precision. "He began to drink quickly," she finally answered. "Glass after glass. I had the odd feeling that I was watching a perverted *Alice in Wonderland*—that if Mark Ransom could step through a looking glass and find himself with Laura Chase and those three men, he would have given up his soul."

There was another murmur from the spectators. Sharpe stood again. "The same objection, Your Honor. If anything, Ms. Carelli is taking more liberties than before."

Masters turned to Mary. "I agree with Ms. Sharpe, and I'm striking the last sentence of your answer. Just tell us what happened."

Mary shifted, folding her arms so that she seemed to hug her own shoulders. "For a moment, it was as if I weren't there anymore. He sat there listening, an odd smile on his face, just sat looking at me. Like he was hearing music from very far away—something beautiful, which he might never hear clearly. And then he put his hand on my knee.

"I pushed his hand away, looked up at him in surprise." She paused. "When my eyes met his, his gaze moved to his lap. Slowly, to make sure that I followed him.

"There was a bulge in his pants.

"It was as if we'd *both* stepped through the looking glass." She turned to Masters, speaking in an embarrassed tone. "I'm sorry, Your Honor. But what he said then, very soft and very low, was, 'I like fucking women I've seen on television. It's like I've made them real.' "

Masters gazed down at her. "It was so hostile," Mary told her. "They say that for some men sex is an act of violence, not of love. What I felt then was that Mark Ransom wanted to commit an act of violence—against me, and against who and what I was: a successful woman whom other women might actually admire." Her voice grew harder. "Mark Ransom hated women unless they were subservient. That's why forcing me to listen to Laura Chase's degradation excited him. That was why he wanted to break my will."

Paget saw Sharpe begin to rise once more, then think better of it. "What did you say to him?" he asked Mary.

"*No.*" Mary still faced Caroline Masters. "I said *no.*"

"And Mr. Ransom's response?"

"That if I had intercourse with him, the tape was mine." She turned back to Paget, finishing softly. "But if I didn't, my secrets belonged to the world."

"And you still refused."

Mary paused. "Not at first. I was too scared."

"What did you say?"

She looked down. "That I'd help him promote the Laura Chase book."

"But he didn't accept that?"

Mary shook her head. "He told me that was the *other* thing I'd do for him." Mary's voice fell. "After I undressed for him, like Laura."

"And you refused?"

"Not really." Her voice became puzzled. "It was more like an instinct. I knew I couldn't let him make me be Laura Chase." She turned to Masters, her words coming in a rush. "It wasn't a rational thing. It was a felt thing. I remember thinking that it would never end—that if I gave in now, he could force me anytime he wanted me, until my life wasn't worth living. I thought of all I'd done to become who I am, to stand for something. And then for a split second I thought of all the women who've given in to men like Ransom—whether for a job, or for their children, or for money to get by on, or just because they were too frightened to resist." Her tone hardened. "Some deep instinct made me want to fight back, no matter what. It was as though if I gave in, I'd lose *myself*. Forever."

In that moment, Paget imagined the people watching on television, imagined McKinley Brooks calculating the political cost of prosecuting this woman as he felt her intensity, saw her impassioned profile gazing up at Masters.

"What did you do?" Paget asked.

"I grabbed my purse. I wanted to leave before I *thought* more than I *felt*. To leave while I was still *me*." Mary seemed to swallow. "And then Ransom spun me around."

Paget stepped forward. More quietly, he asked, "What happened then?"

Mary straightened her skirt, the reflex of a woman imposing order on her own emotions. To the side, Paget saw Carlo again, face tight and miserable. The courtroom was silent.

"I was still holding my purse." Mary's voice was quiet but clear. "Suddenly he was on top of me, pulling down my panty hose, as Laura Chase described two men having sex with her while the third one watched."

There was a nervous cough in the courtroom.

"It was almost unreal," Mary went on. "Some part of my senses registered Laura Chase's voice, Ransom's face, the champagne on his breath. I still remember those things clearly." She touched her forehead, as if searching for some lost detail. "Another part fought him by instinct. But it's as if *that* woman lost her memory to shock. All that I can retrieve are fragments."

Paget nodded. "Was your memory keener when you talked to Inspector Monk?"

Mary shook her head. "No. It's not a matter of memory, but of trauma. If anything, the trauma was more debilitating when I was with Inspector Monk."

Glancing up, Paget saw Masters's unblinking gaze at Mary, as if by sheer intensity she might divine the truth. The hearing seemed to weigh on her now; she seemed less inclined to arid wit, more troubled by judgments yet to be made.

"Do you recall," Paget asked Mary, "how you received the various injuries described by Dr. Shelton?"

"Some. Not all." As Mary turned to Sharpe, her voice became cold and precise. "The only thing that I can say with certainty is that I did not inflict them *after* Mark Ransom died. *Any* of them."

The last phrase rang with anger and conviction; so far, Paget thought, Mary's demeanor was close to perfect. "Is there any injury you recall more clearly than others?"

"Yes." Mary touched her cheekbone. "The first blow to my face. I recall that very clearly."

"And why is that?"

"Because it was slow, deliberate, and brutal." She paused. "And because Ransom seemed to take such pleasure in it."

Paget saw Caroline Masters lean forward. He could almost trace her line of thought; this was the injury Elizabeth Shelton could not explain, inflicted by a man with a taste for bondage and simulated rape.

"Could you describe the blow?" he asked Mary.

"Yes. I was on my back. He had one hand on my chest, pinning me to the floor, staring at me with a hatred so intense that, for a moment, I stopped struggling." Mary's tone grew quiet. "That moment—and the look he gave me—has stayed in my mind like a freeze-frame. And then he hit me." She stopped, as if at the shock of memory, and then, slowly and pointedly, added, "Just as I told Inspector Monk."

To his left, Paget saw Marnie Sharpe frown; Mary was doing well, he knew, and this was the one piece of evidence for which Sharpe had no ready answer.

"How did Mark Ransom's blow to the face affect you?"

Mary's voice became toneless. "My neck snapped back, my head hit the floor. A jolt of pain went through my skull and eyes. It got dark— I think perhaps he'd started choking me." She stopped as if puzzled. "It was like I'd blacked out. The next thing that I remember is my legs spread apart, and Ransom kneeling between them. His pants were down."

"What did he do?"

Mary gazed at the back of the room. "He'd stopped," she said quietly. "His head was cocked to one side. And then, in the background, I heard Laura Chase's voice again." Mary's own voice filled with wonderment. "He was *listening* to her. As if he were listening for a cue."

Masters gave Mary a pensive look; as Paget had intended, Mary's comment resonated with Rappaport's last encounter with Mark Ransom. And then Mary added, "As I *also* told Inspector Monk."

That was good, Paget thought; Mary's testimony had begun to highlight the points where her statements to the police were congruent with the physical evidence or the account of other witnesses. With each moment, the misstatements stressed by Sharpe began to seem more petty and unfair.

"Did he have an erection?" Paget asked.

"Yes." For a moment, Mary closed her eyes. "As he listened to Laura, he held it in his hand."

"Did he seem ready to penetrate you?"

Mary's eyes opened. "Yes."

Masters leaned forward. "Could you describe," Masters asked quietly, "how it happened that Mark Ransom was shot? In the most factual terms you can manage."

Mary turned to her, as if startled by her intervention. "Mark Ransom was shot," she finally answered, "because he stopped to listen to Laura Chase."

Masters's brow knit. "Could you explain that?"

Mary nodded. "As he listened, it was like a respite. I had a moment of clarity—heightened awareness, almost. I felt the strap of my purse in my hand. All at once, I remembered what was inside it." Pausing, Mary sounded bemused. "A gun. The gun I had bought."

She made it sound, Paget thought, like an object of wonder and horror. "How did you get it out?" Masters asked.

Paget was helpless now; he had not expected Masters to interrupt the flow of their questions, rehearsed until it seemed natural. "I heard Laura's voice," Mary answered. "She was saying something like, 'He wanted them to have me every way.' And then it came to me.

" 'You can take me,' I told him. 'I'll let you do it, any way you want.' " Mary's voice became bitter. "He looked so pleased—my consent to being degraded was what he'd wanted most. And then I said, 'But only if you use a rubber.' "

Masters's look suggested surprise, perhaps unease at Mary's presence of mind. "How did he respond?"

"By laughing." Mary paused. "And then I said there was one in my purse.

"It seemed to startle him. Before he could answer, I started to reach in my purse." Mary's voice became tired. "When he pushed me back again, the gun was in my hand." She stopped abruptly.

"What happened then?" Masters asked her.

Mary stared at her hands. "His hands were on my wrists, grabbing. I kneed him." Mary's lips parted, mute, and then she said softly, "The gun went off."

Masters watched her. In level tones, she asked, "How close were you?"

Mary shook her head. "I don't know anymore. I just don't know."

"But you told the police two to three inches."

Mary shrugged, as if helpless. "I did the best I could," she said wearily. "I was trying to answer what they asked. I didn't know how they could make a wrong answer look." Her shoulders drew in. "I'd kneed him. He could have been falling back when the gun went off. I accept that what I thought was wrong. I wish I could tell you why. But I can't."

Paget saw tears in Mary's eyes. But her gaze at Caroline Masters was unblinking. In a soft voice, Masters asked, "His hands were never on the gun?"

"Perhaps they were. But I never told the police that. Because what I remembered was his hands clamped on my wrists."

"Did you close the window shades?"

Mary seemed not to notice the abrupt change of subject. Her voice was leaden. "Yes."

"Before the gun went off, or after?"

"I think after." Mary paused. "After, everything that happened is so vague. My only association with the window was that I was ashamed of what had happened. I know that doesn't make any sense." She shook her head, as if at an afterthought. "I was wearing clothes, though. He never got my clothes off. So I don't know who that man saw."

"Mr. Hassler," Masters said. "Was it you that *Mr. Tench* saw? Outside the room?"

In Mary's silence, Paget felt the slow dismantling of their preparations. It was as if the judge had required a closer sense of Mary than Paget could supply. "I think so," Mary said at last. "I think for a moment I was going to get help. But then I went back to the room without doing anything." She sounded bewildered. "I seem to have an image of being outside the door, not believing what had happened. That if I went back inside, he would be fine and the nightmare would be over."

Caroline Masters remained silent, waiting for more. Mary, stripped of the careful framework she and Paget had constructed, seemed to have started free-associating. From the corner of his eye, he saw Marnie Sharpe, intently scribbling notes.

"I felt I was sleepwalking," Mary went on. "I remember drifting around the room, moving from thing to thing. Touching each piece of furniture as if to find out what was real. I did everything but look at him." She paused, gazing up at Masters. "You see, it was so horrible the way he died. Staring down at me with the life slipping out of him, as if I had hurt his feelings. When I wake up at night, that's what I remember. That, and pushing him off me, feeling from his weight that he must be dead."

"But if you had to push him off," Masters asked, "how was it you shot him from at least three feet away?"

Mary shook her head; the movement had a dazed quality. "Perhaps he fell forward. But I don't know. I just don't know."

"Were your panty hose already torn?"

"Yes." There was pain in Mary's voice. "God, yes. Maybe *I* ripped them in the struggle, but yes. Afterwards, I wasn't capable of anything. Even sensible things. When I called 911, it was like just enough fog had lifted to see the telephone."

"Did you scratch Mr. Ransom's buttocks?"

"I must have—we were struggling." Her voice rose in sudden anger. "But *not* when he was dead. That's ridiculous. It's sick. The prosecutor's whole case is sick." Sharpe looked up from her notes. "Sick," Mary repeated to Sharpe. "But then ambition is a sickness. *I* know."

As Sharpe stared at her, a murmur rose from the press. Paget sensed that Mary's sudden challenge would become a defining moment in their memory of the hearing.

"Ambition may be a sickness," Sharpe said to Masters. "But murder is a crime. I object to Ms. Carelli's efforts at distraction."

Masters turned to Mary. "Whatever your emotions, Ms. Carelli, I will ask that you confine your answers to the questions asked."

"I *do* have emotions, Your Honor. I *have* been charged with murder. It's hard to be dispassionate. Or to feel apologetic to Ms. Sharpe." She paused. "But I will try, at least, to be responsive."

"Responsiveness," Masters said dryly, "will suffice."

The judge's shift of mood, Paget realized, was meant to signal that she was finished. "Might I ask a few questions?" he inquired.

"Of course, Mr. Paget." Masters smiled faintly. "Ms. Carelli is *your* witness, and I appreciate that my intervention here has been out of the ordinary. But I wanted to keep Ms. Carelli on track, and Ms. Sharpe from having to object."

Mary seemed to gaze at them with the passivity of exhaustion. The effect was far different from that of the poised woman who, unknown to those watching, had lied to the Senate: *this* woman was more flawed, more human, and, somehow, much more real. It came to him that beneath her seeming discursiveness and pain, the core of Mary's responses to Caroline Masters had been as flawless as was possible—every inexplicable act explained as trauma, each inconsistency blurred by shock and confusion. Suddenly Paget saw where he should go next. "When the police came," he asked, "did they offer you a doctor?"

"Yes." Mary lowered her head. "But I didn't want anyone touching me. I told them that."

"Did they then suggest a rape counselor?"

Mary shook her head. "No."

Paget was quiet for a moment. "When had you last eaten?"

"The night before." She paused. "That morning, I was too upset to eat."

"Did the police ask you *that?*"

"No."

Paget nodded. "So at the time they questioned you, you hadn't eaten for almost twenty-four hours."

"Yes."

Paget tilted his head. "How does going without food affect you?"

"I feel weak. It makes me impatient." Mary looked at Sharpe. "To me, that's how I sound on the tape of the interrogation—hungry and exhausted. I become a one-note person."

"Is that *all* you felt—hunger and exhaustion?"

"No. I felt disoriented." Her voice fell. "I was answering questions to answer them. Even when I didn't *know* the answer. By the time I asked for a lawyer, it was the only thing I could do."

Paget turned to face the courtroom—the cameras, the reporters standing in the back, the sheriff's deputies guarding the door. Then he saw Carlo, sitting in the front row, expression soft and focused on Mary, as if to get her through this.

Paget faced her again. Quietly, he asked, "Did you murder Mark Ransom?"

Mary straightened on the witness stand, raising her chin. "No," she said. "I did not."

"What *did* you do?"

"Defend myself. Because he wanted to abuse me. Because I was so terribly frightened. Everything that was happening, everything about who Mark Ransom was and what he wanted from me, scared me to my soul." Mary's voice grew quiet. "I didn't want to lose myself. That was why he died."

Paget was silent for a moment, and then he nodded. "Thank you," he said. "That's all I have."

Sharpe walked toward Mary, her right hand clasping the barrel of Mary's gun.

"What's she doing?" Terri whispered to Paget.

"Psychological warfare, I think. She wants to make Mary hold the gun."

Sharpe held the gun out to Mary. "This *is* yours, isn't it?"

Mary stared at her. She did not take the gun. "It looks like mine."

"It's been identified as *yours*." Sharpe thrust the gun toward Mary. "Take a closer look."

Mary gazed at the gun as if it were a foreign object. "It wouldn't help," she said quietly. "I don't know guns. And I'd rather not touch this or any gun, ever again."

Sharpe paused. Abruptly, she asked, "You'd never owned a gun before, had you?"

"No."

"And you didn't buy this one until *after* Mark Ransom called you?"

"I think so."

"I *know* so." Sharpe walked back to the prosecution table, put down the gun, and then turned. "The reason you gave Inspector Monk for buying *this* gun is that you'd received threatening calls, correct?"

Paget tensed; Sharpe had immediately headed for one of Mary's lies. On this, and other points, he had coached Mary to give the minimum answer, so as not to lie further.

"Correct."

"How many calls were there?"

Mary hesitated. "Two, I think."

"You *think?* The calls disturbed you so much that you bought a gun, and you don't remember how many?"

Mary folded her hands. "If that's a question, my answer is the same: I think there were two calls."

"You do remember the sex of the caller, I assume."

Mary nodded. "It was a man."

Sharpe placed her hands on her hips. "Then please tell us, in as much detail as possible, what this man said in his threatening call or calls."

It was what Paget had feared: that Sharpe would ask an open-ended question, requiring Mary to embroider the fictions she had already told. Mary straightened on the witness stand. "I don't recall precisely. But he said something about watching my house. That was why I bought the gun."

Sharpe gave her a skeptical smile. "He didn't happen to mention Laura Chase, did he?"

Paget half stood, thinking to object to the sarcasm. And then Mary said coolly, "No, he didn't. So I'm almost sure that it wasn't Mark Ransom."

There was another murmur from the courtroom, a cough that sounded like stifled laughter. Sharpe stopped, staring at Mary. "Did you think it was *anyone* you knew?"

"No."

"If you had thought that, you would have reported them, correct?"

Mary hesitated. "I believe so, yes."

"But you didn't report the call at all, did you?"

"No."

Sharpe paused. "Wouldn't it have *had* to be someone you knew?"

Paget saw the apprehension register in Mary's eyes. "You mean," she said calmly, "because my telephone isn't listed?"

Sharpe looked surprised. Mary had preempted her question and the trap that lay behind it. "Yes," Sharpe answered. "Among other things."

Mary nodded. In a tone of sympathetic puzzlement, she said, "I can't explain that, either."

Paget almost smiled. What stopped him was the look on Masters's face; her eyes seemed to narrow, as if she had registered how clever Mary was.

Terri had seen the same thing. "This would be better if we had a jury," Terri whispered. "Mary should just take her lumps and go on."

Terri looked tired, Paget thought. "You're right," he murmured back.

"In fact," Sharpe was asking Mary, "you never told anyone about the calls, did you?"

"No."

"Not the police, or friends, or anyone at ABC."

"No. No one." Mary paused. "Not even the person who sold me the gun. I didn't want to sound paranoid."

"Was that it? Or was it hard to describe calls you never received?"

It's not that hard for Mary, Paget thought to himself. "The problem isn't describing them," Mary told Sharpe. "That's *not* the reason."

Sharpe gave her a cynical once-over. "Didn't you buy the gun for the specific purpose of confronting Mark Ransom?"

The answer, Paget knew, was yes. "No," Mary said firmly. "The reason is that the calls reminded me that I was a woman who lived alone. Just as I told Inspector Monk." Mary paused, tilting her head. "You prosecute rape cases, don't you? Don't a lot of your cases come from women who live alone?" A final pause. "Or," Mary finished in a soft voice, "from a woman who has been *trapped* alone?"

Sharpe turned to Caroline Masters with a weary expression. "Your

Honor, would you again explain to Ms. Carelli that her purpose is to answer *my* questions, not to give speeches or pose questions of her own—rhetorical or otherwise."

Masters turned to Mary. "There *are* rules here, Ms. Carelli. You should confine yourself to giving Ms. Sharpe *answers* she doesn't like. So that she can ask more questions that *you* don't like."

Mary smiled faintly. "All right."

"All right?" Sharpe repeated in sarcastic tones. "If it's all right with you, Ms. Carelli, let's discuss another matter you never reported to the police—that Mark Ransom had a tape or tapes that were damaging to you. You failed to mention that, correct?"

"Objection," Paget interjected. "I already asked that question, and Ms. Carelli already answered. Imitation may be the sincerest form of flattery, but repetition is harassment."

Sharpe turned from Paget to Masters. "I can well understand why Mr. Paget wants to sweep this under the rug. In fact, the first hour of his examination swept so many things under the rug that he needed a shovel. But he can't inoculate Ms. Carelli against cross-examination—particularly on a foundational question to establish the premise for questions Mr. Paget never asked."

"Speaking of speeches," Masters rejoined, "your last sentence was sufficient. Ms. Carelli can answer the question."

Sharpe turned to Mary. "Yes," Mary answered promptly. "I failed to tell the police."

"And in fact, you led them to believe that your sole purpose in seeing Mark Ransom was professional."

Mary paused. "By omission, yes."

"By omission? Didn't you tell Inspector Monk quite an elaborate story about the news value of the Laura Chase tape, and your interest in the ethics of buying and selling people's secrets?"

Mary straightened in her chair. "What I said was true," she answered quietly. "What I didn't tell Inspector Monk was that the secrets Mark Ransom proposed to buy and sell included my own. Because, as I said, I was deeply ashamed."

Once more, Sharpe seemed to slow, and then find another angle of attack. "Didn't you also invent fictional dialogue for Mr. Ransom? Such as him telling you that truth is more important than privacy or sentiment, for the dead and for the living?"

Mary looked at her calmly. "He *did* say that. Laura Chase was the dead. *I* was the living." She paused. "Mark Ransom was using Laura Chase's secret for money, and mine for sex."

Sharpe nodded curtly. "Which must be why you told Inspector Monk that you were surprised to find Mark Ransom alone. You *did* say that, didn't you?"

"Yes, I did." Mary paused. "As I said, I didn't want to admit to blackmail."

"Is that also why you told Inspector Monk that you expected Mark Ransom to bring a publicist?"

Mary paused. "Yes."

"*That* wasn't a mere omission, was it? It was a lie." Sharpe paused. "A lie, deliberately invented to cover your purpose in coming."

Masters turned to Mary, as if awaiting her answer. "I don't know *why* I said it," Mary answered, "except that I was frightened and confused."

"But you didn't expect a publicist, did you?"

"No, I did not." Mary paused. "Nor did I go there intending to shoot Mark Ransom."

Sharpe turned to Masters. "I move to strike the last sentence of that answer as unresponsive."

"Granted." Masters turned to Mary. "Again, Ms. Carelli, confine yourself to answering the question which is asked." She gave a thin smile. "After all, this is municipal court. We have higher standards for responsiveness than do presidential debates."

There was a ripple of laughter from the gallery. But Paget did not join it; the faintly slighting comment signaled Masters's resolve to let Sharpe take her shots at Mary unimpeded by verbal sparring. The first flicker of worry crossed Mary's face. "I apologize," she said to Masters. "Being charged with murder is quite emotional. I'll try to repress that."

"Please do try. For your own sake." Masters turned to Sharpe. "Go ahead, Counsel."

Perhaps, Paget thought, he alone felt a new chill in the courtroom. "Let's talk," Sharpe said quietly, "about Mark Ransom's erection. Or erections. How many did he have—one or two?"

"Penises?"

"No." Sharpe's voice held a lethal patience. "Erections."

"I don't understand."

"You told Inspector Monk that Mark Ransom got an erection while listening to the Laura Chase tape, correct?"

Mary nodded. "He wanted me to see the bulge in his pants."

"How long was that before he tried to rape you?"

Mary looked puzzled. "I don't know when he first got it. I only noticed when he touched my knee."

"And how long was *that* before he tried to rape you?"

"Perhaps five minutes."

"What's Marnie's thing about erections?" Paget whispered to Terri.

"You can forget penis envy," Terri whispered back. "With Rappaport, as I told you, she was hinting at impotence. She knows something—or thinks she does."

Paget nodded. "I don't like this at all."

Sharpe moved closer to Mary. "And when he dropped his pants, you testified, he also had an erection."

"Yes."

"And quite a memorable one, in that you recall him stroking it."

"I remember that, yes."

"In fact, you now remember more about that erection than you recalled for Inspector Monk—to whom you said something like, 'It was an erection. I didn't stop to notice how special it was.' "

Mary paused. "I was in shock," she answered. "Days after, some details became clearer."

Sharpe's voice was staccato. "Why not how your panty hose ripped? Or why you closed the window blinds? Or what you were doing in the hallway? Or your reasons for wandering around the suite? Why Mr. Ransom's erection?"

"I don't know." Pausing, Mary seemed to search her memory. "I suppose certain details etch themselves on your brain out of sheer horror, and when the shock wears off, they have this awful clarity." She turned to Masters. "Mark Ransom stroking his penis while listening to Laura Chase describe her violation was one of those. And it defines him to the core."

"Move to strike the answer as nonresponsive," Sharpe said.

For a moment, Masters was silent, appraising Mary. "Denied," she said in a casual tone. "At the risk of sounding like far too many men, you asked for an erection, and you got one."

Again, there was muffled laughter. But Masters did not smile, and.

Paget, watching her, did not care for what he saw; something in her words and manner suggested her awareness of Mary's powers of invention, and the damage that Steinhardt's tape had already done.

Sharpe pressed on. "Was that the same erection as the 'bulge' you described, or a different one? In other words, was Mr. Ransom continually aroused from the time that you were sitting on the couch?"

Once more, Mary hesitated. "I didn't watch that, obviously. But I think so, yes."

"And between the time you first noticed his erection and the time you shot him, how long was it?"

"I'm not sure. Ten minutes, at least."

"And during those 'at least ten minutes,' you say, Mark Ransom tried to talk you into sex."

"Yes."

"And pushed you to the floor."

"Yes."

"And struggled with you."

"Yes."

"And tugged at your panty hose."

"Yes."

"And pinned you under him."

"Yes."

"Then slapped you."

Mary's voice became tight. "Yes."

"Scratched your throat."

Mary nodded. *"Yes.* To all of that."

"And, after all that, stopped to listen to the voice of Laura Chase."

Mary touched her forehead. "Yes," she said softly.

Sharpe stared at her. "And during all that time, and all those strenuous and distracting activities, this fifty-six-year-old man achieved and maintained an erection."

Mary stared at her. "I didn't think of it that way. I really don't know how to answer that."

Turning from Mary, Masters gave Sharpe a puzzled look. "Maybe," Terri whispered, "Marnie just wants to discredit Mary's story."

Paget shook his head. "I don't think that's it. She *did* mention the possibility of a rebuttal witness, didn't she?"

A look of concern crossed Terri's face. "Yes. She did."

But Sharpe had begun a new line of attack.

"You acknowledge telling Inspector Monk that you shot Mark Ransom from two to three inches, don't you?"

Mary nodded. "Yes. I've tried to explain my state of mind at the time."

"And you also told the police that Mark Ransom's blinds were closed when you came to the suite, correct?"

With Sharpe's second question, Paget saw with alarm where this was going. Sharpe would force Mary to trace every change in her story to some police discovery.

"Objection," he called out. "Asked and answered. How many times must Ms. Carelli repeat her testimony on direct?"

As Sharpe started to speak, Masters held up her hand. "I'm going to let this go awhile, Mr. Paget. Ms. Sharpe can make her point."

"Yes," Mary answered promptly. "That was what I first recalled."

"But you heard Mr. Aguilar testify otherwise."

Mary stared at her. "I did."

"And now, this morning, you acknowledge closing the blinds."

"The day Mark Ransom died, I was in shock. My recollection comes back in bits and pieces."

Sharpe gave her a look of open disbelief.

"And shock, I believe, is the reason you give for the delay in calling 911 estimated by Dr. Shelton."

"As best I understand my own actions, yes."

The courtroom was dead silent now. Paget saw Masters's eyes sweeping back and forth with each question and answer, as if watching a tennis match.

"But when you spoke to Inspector Monk," Sharpe pursued, "you said you called as soon as possible."

Mary hesitated. "That's what I thought at the time."

"Isn't it true that your story changed *after* you heard Dr. Shelton's account?"

"As a matter of the sequence of events, yes. But that's not why I testified as I have." Mary paused, turning to Masters. "Again, it's a matter of piecing together what happened."

"But you already acknowledged omitting any mention of the tape."

Slowly, Mary faced Sharpe again. "As I explained, the contents of the tape were painful."

"So painful that you hid the tape's existence until we found it."

Mary leaned forward. "That's a way of putting it," she said coolly. "But I wasn't just hiding from you. I was hiding from everyone but Dr. Steinhardt, the man I chose to trust with my own guilt and shame. What I did with Inspector Monk, in my confusion and shock, was follow the habit of years."

"Lying, you mean."

Mary flushed, faltered for a moment; Paget could feel her trapped awareness that Caroline Masters knew of her perjury. Then, very softly, "That's not what I meant, Ms. Sharpe. And you know that."

Sharpe slowly shook her head. "What *I* meant," she said with equal quiet, "is that you adjust your story not because your memory revives but to accommodate the testimony of other witnesses. And *you* know that."

Caroline Masters turned to Mary; to Paget, her expression was an odd combination of skepticism and regret. "That's not true," Mary told Sharpe. "What I *do* know is never to expect compassion. Not from you."

Sharpe stared at her for a moment. Then she shrugged, as if anything Mary said to her now was too self-serving to require a response. Despite himself, Paget admired that: by some effort of will, Sharpe was mastering her own sensitivity to attack, making herself cooler and more controlled.

"Speaking of compassion," she said, "you claim to have been wandering in the hallway—at which point Mr. Tench saw you—in contemplation of seeking help for Mr. Ransom. But you didn't *get* help, did you?"

Mary lowered her gaze. "Not then, no. As I said, it hadn't become real to me."

"Hadn't it? Isn't the *real* reason you were in the hallway to determine whether anyone had heard a gunshot, so you wouldn't be caught falsifying evidence?"

"No." Mary half rose in the witness stand. "That's not true."

"Really. Isn't *that* also why you closed the blinds—so you wouldn't be caught fabricating evidence?"

Mary seemed to brace herself. "According to your witness Mr. Hassler, I must have been fabricating evidence in the nude. But that struck me as so senseless I've decided not to 'adjust my story' to accommodate nudity."

There was a murmur from those watching; a bark of laughter. Paget saw Sharpe stiffen with anger. "No," Sharpe retorted, "what happened is that you undressed to disarm Mr. Ransom, and then shot him. After *that*, you closed the blinds. That *is* what happened, isn't it?"

"It is not." Mary's face was ashen, but her voice was edged with contempt. "Except in your own fantasies. And, perhaps, Mark Ransom's."

"Mr. Ransom *has* no fantasies. Tell me, Ms. Carelli, did you begin to wander about the room, determining the 'reality' of certain pieces of furniture, *after* you closed the blinds?"

Mary stared at her. "I honestly don't remember."

"You don't recall when you touched both end tables, the bookshelf, and the desk."

"No."

"Or why your fingerprints appear on the handle of the desk drawer."

"No."

"What *was* she doing?" Terri whispered to Paget.

Tense, Paget kept his eyes on Mary. "I have no idea."

Sharpe paused. "Weren't you, in fact, looking for tapes of your session with Dr. Steinhardt?"

Mary's eyes widened in surprise. "I was *not*," she said finally, "looking for tapes."

"Didn't you find one tape? And then destroy it?"

"When?" Mary's voice was shot through with incredulity. "How? Flush it down the toilet? As you must know, I never even entered the bathroom." Mary seemed overcome with anger. "Mr. Paget's opening statement was right. The prosecution's case is like a satire of conspiracy theories, written by a lunatic. But then it requires so much more imagination to convict someone who is innocent. Unless, of course, *you're* fabricating evidence."

By instinct, Sharpe moved forward. The sound from those watching was muted; Paget could almost feel them squirm with tension. Masters's gavel cracked.

The two women froze, looking up at Masters. Her face was angry and closed. "That's enough," she snapped. "I appreciate, Ms. Carelli, that Ms. Sharpe's cross-examination is intense. But your comment is unacceptable. To *me*." Her voice grew quiet. "I'm out of patience. The next outburst will be followed by a contempt citation."

Mary turned to her. "Forgive me, Your Honor. But those accusations are very difficult for *me* to accept. It's very hard for me to summon the one-way deference Ms. Sharpe seems to require while she tries to destroy my life."

From the public section, someone clapped abruptly. Masters's tone was cool. "The deference *I* require is to the court, from and among *all* participants. As for whether you receive justice here, that's on my head, not Ms. Sharpe's. You may find it reassuring that mere charges—hers *or* yours—impress me not at all." Masters paused. "The sole question before this court is whether there is sufficient evidence of probable cause. And I will decide that question as wisely and fairly as I know how."

Mary's face softened. When she nodded, it seemed less an acceptance of Masters's power than of her desire to be fair. "I apologize," she said quietly.

The judge gazed at her a moment and then said, "Please continue, Ms. Sharpe."

Sharpe moved in again. "Let us return, Ms. Carelli, to the tapes. Did Mr. Ransom describe what was on them?"

"Yes. He did."

"Did he suggest to you, in words or substance, that the tapes reflected on your honesty and veracity?"

Mary looked from Paget to Sharpe. "He did not *suggest* that. No."

Sharpe moved closer. "*Do* the tapes reflect on your honesty and veracity?"

"Objection." Paget stood. "I'd like a bench conference, Your Honor. Immediately."

Masters nodded. "I would expect you do."

Sharpe and Paget walked briskly to the bench. They kept their voices low. "What's the next question?" Paget demanded of Sharpe. " 'Bigger than a bread basket,' or 'Does it start with a vowel or a consonant?' " He turned to Masters. "If Mary has to answer questions like those, there *is* no privilege. And if Ms. Sharpe throws out any more hints—like 'Did the tapes concern your service as a government lawyer?'—there'll be investigative reporters crawling all over Mary's life."

Sharpe shook her head. "That was *not* the question I asked, Your Honor. The question I asked was whether the embarrassment and pain to which Ms. Carelli already testified relates to a failure of veracity."

Masters leaned forward. "We three *know* what the tape relates to. But that tape, and its contents, are not properly part of the record. And those questions aren't proper, either. Unless Ms. Carelli raises the contents of the tape themselves, I'm instructing you not to ask about them. Or, more devious, what Ransom *said* about them. Understood?"

Sharpe nodded. "Yes, Your Honor."

The two lawyers left the bench. "What was *that?*" Paget murmured.

Sharpe gave him a fleeting sideways glance, and then shrugged. "Never up, never in," she said, and turned to face Mary Carelli.

In an even tone, Sharpe said, "Our next subject, Ms. Carelli, is the moment you shot Mr. Ransom."

"All right," Mary answered. "But for the record, I don't remember it as the 'moment I shot Mr. Ransom.' I remember it as the end of a struggle, when the gun went off." She turned back to Masters. "You see, I don't recall *shooting* him. And I didn't *plan* to shoot him. I just wanted him to stop."

Good, Paget thought; it was another step back from murder, and one they had worked on together.

"Semantics aside," Sharpe said, "he let you reach into the purse unimpeded. Is that your testimony?"

"I told him that I was reaching for a condom, Ms. Sharpe. I'm sure he wasn't expecting a gun."

"How did you ever reach the gun? Hadn't he pinned you to the floor?"

Mary hesitated. "That's true," she said in a patient tone. "But when I told him about the condom, he took his weight off me."

"How did he do that?"

"I don't know, really." Her voice became weary. "But the hand he'd slapped me with was free, obviously. Perhaps he leaned on *that.*"

Sharpe's brow furrowed. "But when you pulled the gun, he was essentially on top of you."

"Yes."

"Too close to extend your arms in front of you."

"Yes."

Sharpe walked back to the prosecution table. She returned holding Mary's gun.

Silently, she placed it on the front rail of the witness box. "Could you show me," she asked, "how you held the gun and how close it was to your body?"

For a moment, Mary simply stared at the gun. Then she squared her shoulders, took it in both hands, and pointed it at Sharpe with her wrists bent to her chest. "Like this," she said coolly. "As best I remember."

Sharpe eyed the gun. "He was still on top of you, correct?"

"Yes."

"But he permitted you to pull a gun from your purse, clamp it in both hands, and assume the rather awkward position you're demonstrating now."

Mary held the gun steady. "He didn't permit me to do anything," she answered. "As I said, he grabbed my wrists."

"While he was still on top of you?"

"Yes."

Sharpe cocked her head. "Could you describe your relative positions?"

Mary placed the gun on her lap. "It happened so fast," she said.

"Just your best memory."

Mary's eyes narrowed. "He was kneeling between my legs, leaning forward. Both hands were on my wrists." She gave a melancholy shrug. "That's what I remember."

"And as he grasped your wrists, the 'gun went off,' as you put it."

"Yes."

Sharpe looked puzzled. "Didn't we just skip a step?"

"Skip a step?" Mary asked carefully. "I don't know what you mean."

"I mean the step where Mark Ransom obligingly released your wrists and catapulted backward so that you could shoot him from at least three feet."

The question was delivered with subversive innocence, in a tone so bland that it underscored the absurdity Sharpe meant to suggest. The buzz from the spectators was like a delayed reaction.

"Jesus," Terri whispered.

Paget kept watching. "No. I think it's all right."

Mary stared at Sharpe, face quite composed, her perfect stillness commanding silence in the courtroom. "As I told you," she said calmly, "I don't remember everything. But Mr. Ransom was a very tall man, and I expect his *arms* were three feet long. And I think they were extended, pinning my wrists to my chest." She clasped the gun between her breasts, aiming at Sharpe again. "Like *this*. So you see, the bullet could have traveled close to three feet if he'd never even flinched."

There were muted exclamations. Sharpe looked stunned.

"She walked right into that one," Paget whispered. "Wonder why she believed that Mary and I wouldn't think of it?"

Terri turned to him. "I wonder if it's true."

Looking up, Paget saw Masters's faint smile at Mary. "All that matters," he said, "is that *Caroline* wonder."

But Sharpe had recovered. "He was leaning forward, you said. Not backward."

Mary put down the gun. "I don't know, Ms. Sharpe. Somehow the gun went off, and somehow the bullet traveled two to three feet. All that I know for certain is that I didn't mean for it to happen." She shook her head. "I only meant to scare him. To make him stop."

Sharpe placed her hands on her hips. "Isn't what happened that you bought this gun planning to shoot Mark Ransom, came to the Flood and killed him from a safe distance—after which you closed the blinds, scratched yourself, tore your own panty hose, and scratched Mark Ransom's buttocks, in an effort to claim rape? Isn't *that* what happened?"

"It's nearly over," Paget whispered to Terri.

"Pardon me," Mary said politely. "But didn't you skip a step? The part where I slap myself?"

Another, deeper sound. Terri murmured, "You know, I've never seen anyone quite like her."

Neither, it was clear, had Marnie Sharpe. "I didn't," Sharpe finally said. "Because when you pulled the gun, Mark Ransom swung at you by instinct. And then you shot him, just as you intended. *That's* what happened, isn't it?"

Once more, Caroline Masters turned to Mary. Pausing, Mary folded her hands. "No," she said calmly. "That is *not* what happened. Mark Ransom tried to rape me, and I defended myself." Mary's voice grew quiet. "A gun went off. But as tragic as that is, I'd defend myself again."

Slowly, Sharpe shook her head in silent disbelief. Then, in a tone of dismissal and contempt, she said, "No further questions, Your Honor."

"She survived," Terri murmured to Paget.

Paget nodded. "Yes. She did."

It took a moment for Masters to turn from Mary. "Redirect, Mr. Paget?"

Paget stood. "No questions," he answered. "None at all."

Masters nodded. "You may step down, Ms. Carelli."

Mary stood stiffly, seemingly unsure that it was over. She was still for a moment, as if preparing for the reporters outside, the cameras, the people who wished to cheer her, to revile her, or simply to collect her autograph. Then she walked across the courtroom, composed again, as she had been that day fifteen years before, leaving the Senate.

THREE

MARY FLASHED ON the screen, pointing the gun at Marnie Sharpe.

Paget and Carlo watched in the library. "In a tense confrontation," the narrative began, "Mary Carelli held her own with Prosecutor Marnie Sharpe. Refusing to wither under repeated attacks, Ms. Carelli fought back at the end of her testimony, dramatically affirming her innocence."

Carlo turned to Paget. "She *was* good," Carlo said.

He seemed to need reassurance, as if doubting the evidence of his own senses. "Very good," Paget answered.

He fell silent. He could not say to Carlo that Mary had *needed* to be good simply to survive; that drama was not innocence in the eyes of Caroline Masters; and that in the unsparing calculus of evidence—the relentless accretion of fact upon fact—Sharpe's attack had been telling. Nor could Paget say that the secrets Caroline Masters already knew, and that he hoped Carlo would never know, might have damaged Mary beyond repair.

"Do you think the judge believed her?" Carlo asked.

Carlo now seemed to have the caution of a lawyer, rather than the fierce loyalty of a son. It was painful to see. "Your mother gave her reason to," Paget answered. "Tomorrow morning, Terri puts on Marcy Linton. By this time tomorrow evening, Caroline Masters will know that Mark Ransom raped a defenseless young woman."

Carlo looked hopeful; it was as if he, too, would then be persuaded. "After that, the judge should *know* that my mother's telling the truth, don't you think?"

"Caroline's hard to read. But it will at least make Mary more credible, and much more sympathetic." Paget switched off the television. "This trial has been hard for you, hasn't it?"

Carlo shrugged. "In a way."

A glancing phrase, Paget thought, which held much more: children are meant to learn ambiguity and moral complexity in some other place than the trial of a parent, to never learn their parents' secrets, or even that they have them. "Like most of us," Paget said, "your mother has done things that she's ashamed of. But that doesn't mean that people shouldn't believe her. *All* the women who dealt with Mark Ransom seem to have suffered for it."

Carlo was quiet. "Do you think she'll ever tell me what was on the tape?"

Inwardly, Paget flinched; the conversation made him feel like a hypocrite, using Mary as a shield. "If she never did," he asked softly, "would you stop caring about her?"

The question seemed to give Carlo pause. He shook his head. "It doesn't have anything to do with me, really. Or her and me."

Perhaps, Paget thought, his son would never learn that the tape had everything to do with Mary and Paget, Mary and Carlo, and why Paget had raised him. "Then let it be. The hearing will be over soon." Paget paused. "Perhaps it will have taught you to be less like me—judgmental to a fault—and better able to separate the mistakes people make from their worth as people. As someone like Terri seems able to do."

Carlo gave him a curious look. "She talked you into letting me come, didn't she?"

"Terri?"

"Uh-huh. Because you've never done a one-hundred-eighty-degree turnaround on any 'no' I can remember."

Paget smiled. "I've always believed that consistency is a virtue. Of course it was Terri."

Carlo smiled back. "I know you, Dad. From *me* you've got no secrets."

Paget was quiet for a moment. "Just one or two," he said.

Teresa Peralta sat on the couch in Mark Ransom's suite, gazing at the bloodstained carpet.

It was six-thirty; at seven, she was meeting Marcy Linton at a nearby hotel, to prepare for the most important day in court she might ever have. But an hour before, on impulse, she had called Marnie Sharpe for permission to visit the suite again. Sounding tired from her cross-examination of Mary, Sharpe did not question her, leaving Terri to question herself.

Why was she here?

The truth, Christopher Paget had told her, was something he wished never to know. All that mattered was that Sharpe never find the second tape.

Where was it?

Terri sat back, reflecting.

Where, for that matter, was the Lindsay Caldwell tape? If Ransom had failed to bring that as well as Mary's second tape, despite his promise to both women, why had Sharpe not found the missing tapes in his home with Mary's *first* tape?

Terri stood, eyes moving across the furnishings.

Why, in the moments after Mark Ransom died, had Mary gone from the end tables to the bookshelves to the desk? Leaving fingerprints on each.

Because she was looking for the tape, Marnie Sharpe had suggested. That was wrong, Mary answered; she was in shock, wandering aimlessly. Not sure of where she was and what she was doing.

Terri opened the drawers of one end table, then another. A telephone directory. A Gideon Bible. Nothing else.

The bookshelf was no different. One drawer, empty. A few volumes of coffee table literature. Banal and impersonal, suited to a room where people came and went.

She found herself gazing at the bloodstain.

What had happened here between Mark Ransom and Mary Carelli, in the moments after Paul Aguilar had brought them champagne? Was Mary the naked woman standing in a distant window? What was Mary Carelli doing in the hallway when Edward Tench had seen her? While, inside the suite, Mark Ransom was lying dead.

Turning, Terri walked slowly to the desk.

On top were a pen, blank paper. She opened the drawer.

Empty, except for stationery and envelopes, imprinted with the address and logo of the Hotel Flood. A shield with a script *F*.

Closing the drawer, Terri gazed out at Berkeley, as Paul Aguilar claimed to have done.

Elena was there. Having dinner with her father while Terri worked again.

He was the care provider, Richie would tell the judge.

The unfairness of it seized Terri by the throat. *She* should raise Elena. At least she saw Elena as someone outside herself. As a person to be nurtured.

She turned away, standing over the stain Mark Ransom's death had left, lost in her own thoughts.

Finally, she looked at her watch.

Six-fifty. It was time to go; Mary's defense depended on Marcy Linton now, and there was much to do.

Terri picked up her purse and left the suite.

In the hallway, a uniformed policeman waited at the elevator Edward Tench had used. Terri turned toward it and then stopped, glancing at the mail slot.

She had stood here with Chris and Johnny Moore on the morning they first saw the suite.

What was Sharpe's point, Terri had asked, about Mary being in the hallway?

No idea, Chris had answered. And then he had made a bitter joke: "Probably figures Mary found herself with a half hour to kill, scribbled a few postcards on Ransom's rear end, and then mailed them to all her friends."

Terri turned and reentered the suite.

She walked to the desk. Opening the drawer, she took out an envelope, studied it, pensive. Then, without quite knowing why, she slid it in her purse.

She stood still for another moment. Then she hurried from the suite toward the elevator, to meet Marcy Linton.

"I can't find the tape," Johnny Moore said. "And neither can Marnie Sharpe."

He sat with Paget in the stern of Paget's sailboat. It was night, and the boat was docked; this time it was Paget who had felt too confined to meet inside. The lights of San Francisco climbed the hills behind them; more distant, the towers of the financial district glowed against the black. The night was quiet, still except for the muffled sounds of the city, the lapping of water against the hull. Moore and Paget drank beer.

"Mary had to have gotten rid of it," Paget answered. "Somehow."

Moore shrugged. "So Sharpe thinks, my sources tell me. And so *I* think. But the police combed every scrap of garbage at the Flood, and everywhere the garbage went. They even tore Ransom's toilet apart. Although, as Mary points out, there's not one bit of evidence that she even entered Ransom's bathroom."

"Yes," Paget murmured. "She was too busy touring the hallway."

Moore sipped his beer. "I've thought of the mails, of course. As has Sharpe. But with all its considerable advantages, the D.A.'s office hasn't found it. There's just no evidence that Mary sent it anywhere. Even assuming she could have."

"Not even care of ABC?"

"Not to ABC. Not to herself. Not to anyone." Moore paused. "Which leaves us with the notion that Ransom hid it somewhere and that Mary's telling the truth. As hard as that may be for you to believe."

"I haven't had much practice." Paget gazed out at the city. "They've checked Ransom's homes, of course."

"And his banks. And with any friend who claimed him." Moore paused. "Of course, unlike Mary, Ransom was at liberty. There's all sorts of places a clever man can hide something the size of a tape. Which, although I don't mean to press it on you, also enhances Mary's claim."

"You think it's destroyed?"

Moore shook his head. "No way that Mary could do it. And no way that Ransom wanted to. It's out there, somewhere."

Paget was silent.

"I'm sorry," Moore said softly. "I wish I could give you some peace of mind. At least while you're trying this case." He paused. "Better yet, I wish I could tell you I'd destroyed it."

"I'd never ask you to do that, Johnny."

"You wouldn't have to."

Paget was quiet for a time. "It's enough," he said finally, "that you've been looking after Carlo."

"No trouble. It's the nearest I'll ever come to having a son." Moore paused. "It's mostly rides to basketball, and he plays a good game."

"I'm sorry to be missing it."

Moore was silent. Finally, he asked, "Did he tell you about the other day?"

"I'm not sure."

"Someone from *US* ambushed him after the basketball game, with two TV reporters right behind him, cameras and all. Wanting to talk about his childhood."

"What did he do?"

"Just stared at them. I chased them off."

Paget felt a surge of anger, then of shame. "He never told me."

"He doesn't want to bother you. What with the hearing."

"Bother me? He's my son."

Moore gazed at him. "That's why he didn't say anything."

Paget fell quiet again.

"About Ransom and women," Moore said finally. "Still nothing. I begin to think there's nothing to find."

"What does *that* mean?"

"No idea, and such a loss to womankind." Moore tilted his glass to Paget. "Here's to Mark Ransom's undying potency. Now that he's dead, that is."

FOUR

SOFTLY, MARCY LINTON SAID, "Mark Ransom raped me."

The courtroom was still, tense, as crowded as for Mary herself; present for the first time, McKinley Brooks sat behind Marnie Sharpe. Moving closer to the witness stand, Teresa Peralta asked, "Could you tell the court how it happened?"

"Yes." Dressed in a simple skirt and a high-collared blouse, Linton was pale but composed. Her quiet voice had the edge of repressed emotion. "We were in the living room of my uncles' cabin. Drinking wine while Mark Ransom took apart my writing."

"He was critical?"

The word made Linton pause. "Brutal. His clear intention was to strip me of every scrap of self-respect."

Terri saw Sharpe rise to object to the answer, then hesitate. Quickly, Terri asked, "Did he succeed?"

Linton seemed to reflect, as if examining the extent of the damage. "He humiliated me. When he offered me wine, I wanted it." She gazed past Terri, as if explaining herself to the gallery. "I was twenty-four, and I'd been so proud. Had so looked forward to having Mark Ransom read my writing. And then he made me feel like nothing. Like I, and what I cared about, were contemptible to him."

Terri waited for a moment. "Who provided the wine," she asked, "you or Ransom?"

"Ransom. I didn't really like to drink."

"But you wanted to on this occasion?"

Linton nodded. "As he tore me apart, Ransom kept pouring, and I kept drinking."

"How did you feel?"

"Numb." Her voice grew quieter. "But that was better, really."

Terri nodded. She had prepared Linton carefully: despite an inability to sleep, and the burdens of carrying Mary Carelli's defense, Marcy Linton was facing her ordeal with composure. But that did not seem to diminish her ethereal quality; with her pale skin and slender frame, the sense of devastation Linton conveyed did not seem self-pitying but merely factual. Marnie Sharpe watched her without taking notes.

"Did any of Ransom's comments," Terri asked, "concern the subject of sex?"

"Yes," Linton answered. "At the end, after he had torn apart everything else, he ridiculed the 'bloodless' way I wrote about sex."

On the bench, Caroline Masters's gaze never moved from Marcy Linton. That was good, Terri thought. Her own role was merely to help Linton trace the parallels to what Mary Carelli had said: when Linton's testimony was finished, neither Caroline Masters nor anyone else should doubt who Mark Ransom was. If Terri did her job, by evening there would be no pickets seeking justice for Mark Ransom's memory, and Brooks and Sharpe would know how much this case could cost them.

"Did you answer him?" she asked Linton.

"I defended my writing, yes." Linton paused, distractedly touching her hair, more auburn than red in the fluorescent lights. "The scenes he mocked were about me and someone I loved. I told Ransom those scenes meant a lot to me."

The phrase had a valedictory note of sadness, Terri thought, that no lawyer could teach and even Mary Carelli could not replicate. "What," Terri asked, "did Ransom say after that?"

" 'It's like they're negotiating a contract,' he said. 'Sex isn't an insurance policy.' For a minute he seemed angry, and then he looked up and down my body. 'What sex *is*,' he almost whispered, 'is spontaneity, and danger.' " Linton paused. "Before I could answer, he put his arm around me."

Caroline Masters's posture was stiff, unnatural.

"What did you do?" Terri asked.

Linton stared past her. "I couldn't move, felt sick." She shook her head. "It was like being drugged. I knew what was about to happen, but I couldn't seem to stop it."

"In what way," Terri asked quietly, "did Ransom first touch you? Sexually, that is."

Linton looked down. "He reached inside my blouse," she said quietly, "and touched my nipple." Her eyes shut, as if to protect herself from those who watched and listened. "Then he took my face in his other hand and asked me, 'Do you ever watch Laura Chase?'"

There was a release of sound, a low collective gasp. Caroline Masters made no move to silence it. She looked stunned; even Terri, who was prepared for the answer, felt shaken by it.

"What did you do?" Terri asked.

"I shivered." There was a first tremor in Linton's voice. "It was as I told you—the fire, the darkness, the elk on the wall. When he said the name Laura Chase, it was as if I'd been trapped in some primitive ritual, by a man who was insane."

The courtroom was silent again. "What did you do?" Terri asked.

"I pulled away."

"And then?"

Pausing, Linton shook her head. "His eyes got so angry," she said softly. "But he smiled, as if I'd pleased him. Then he raised his hand, very slowly, and slapped me across the face." Linton began rocking. "My neck snapped back. As I fell back on the couch, I saw yellow flashes. There was blood in my mouth."

Slowly, Terri turned to Sharpe, and then to Caroline Masters. Sharpe's gaze seemed inward, reflective; Masters's mingled compassion and deep thought.

"What happened next?" Terri asked.

"He rose to his knees, waiting for my eyes to open. And then he ripped open my blouse." Linton's voice echoed with disbelief. "He told me to watch him do it.

"'Do you want me to hit you again?' he asked.

"I couldn't talk or move. So I shook my head." Linton's voice trembled now. "Then he told me to show him my breasts. And to keep my eyes open."

"Did you?"

Linton nodded, mute.

"I'm sorry," Terri said softly. "We need an audible answer for the record."

"I showed him my breasts," Linton said tonelessly. "And I kept my eyes open."

Terri ached with sympathy. She remembered that Linton had tried to smile at him, hoping that he would stop, but that her bruised mouth had hurt too much to move.

"What did he do then?" Terri asked.

"He made me unzip my jeans. Then take them off." Once more, Linton's eyes shut. "Then he told me to hold his penis while he pulled my panties down. So that I could keep him hard."

Terri felt drained. For the first time that day, she glanced at Christopher Paget. He watched her for a moment, and slowly nodded.

She turned back to Linton. "What happened then?" she asked.

"He hurt me." Opening her eyes, Linton seemed bewildered. "The way he did it was *meant* to hurt me. For days I hurt inside."

"Physically, you mean."

"Yes." Linton paused. "Emotionally, the hurt has never stopped."

Terri watched for a moment. "While he was raping you, Marcy, what did you do?"

"I lay there, staring up at the elk." She shook her head. "I was afraid that if I closed my eyes, he'd hit me again."

The whispers in the courtroom were quiet, deferential. Sharpe was scribbling on a legal pad; it might have been notes, Terri thought, except that the penstrokes seemed aimless. Then Terri caught Mary Carelli's split-second gaze, perhaps only imagined the smallest of smiles. If you get off, Terri thought coldly, you will owe a lot to Marcy Linton. And to me. She turned back to Linton.

"When it was over," she asked, "what did Mark Ransom do?"

Linton looked down. "He told me to cook for him. Without clothes."

"And did you?"

"I was afraid of him." Linton's voice became a monotone. "And he wanted to watch me."

The last sentence, with its silent weight of fear and humiliation, lingered there.

"Are you still afraid of him?" Terri asked.

Slowly, Linton nodded. "He didn't just rape me," she finally said. "He *changed* me. What he left behind was instinctive fear—of life, and of *him*. I know I can never stop him, no matter how many times he wants to do it." Her voice fell. "I don't believe he's dead. Really, I can't believe it. He's been inside me far too long."

Terri watched her. Softly, she asked, "Why didn't you defend yourself?"

Linton gave a helpless shrug. "I just didn't. I couldn't. He was too strong, and I had no way to defend myself."

"Do you wish you could have?"

"Oh, yes." Linton's voice became stronger. "Much more now, even, than when it happened. Because I know what scars he left behind." She paused again. "It's terrible to think about hurting someone else. But in the balance of a life, Mark Ransom lost his right to be safe from hurt when he decided to hurt *me*."

Terri nodded. "Since then," she asked, "have you taken steps to protect yourself?"

"Yes." Raising her head, Linton added quietly, "I bought a handgun."

The courtroom was still. Terri waited before asking her last question. "Why," she asked, "did you come forward now?"

Linton seemed to hesitate. But when she answered, her voice was clear and firm. "Because the only way left to defend myself from Mark Ransom is to tell the world *who* and *what* he was. Because women should do that for other women." Marcy Linton turned to Mary. "And because what Mary Carelli did, *I* should have done."

Rising to cross-examine Marcy Linton, Marnie Sharpe looked tentative. It was as if she were gazing at the specter of doubt.

"Good afternoon, Ms. Linton."

Linton nodded. "Good afternoon."

Watching in the silent courtroom, Terri thought how strange Sharpe must find this. Sharpe had a visceral hatred of rape; she had spent her professional life protecting its victims. Cross-examining a victim seemed to slow her; when she spoke, her voice was gentler and faintly sad.

"Let us agree," she said to Linton, "that Mark Ransom visited your home. And let us further agree that you and he had intercourse on the specific occasion that you just described. And that after that you cooked him dinner. All right?"

"All right."

"When did he leave?"

Paget turned to Terri. "How did she know to ask *that*?"

Terri shook her head, watching Linton. Softly, Linton answered, "The next morning."

"The next morning? How did *that* come about?"

Linton looked away. "He wanted to stay. I was afraid to argue."

"And where did he sleep?"

"With me." Linton hesitated. "At least some part of the night."

Sharpe nodded. "Was there some reason," she asked, "that Mr. Ransom did not spend the *entire* night in your bed?"

Linton flushed. "He went downstairs."

It was uncanny, Terri thought with apprehension; Sharpe seemed to know what to ask, question after question. "Was there a particular reason," Sharpe asked, "that Ransom went downstairs?"

Linton's shoulders drew in. "He tried to make love to me."

"Did you resist him?"

"No." Linton shook her head. "I was afraid."

Sharpe paused. "Fearful enough," she asked quietly, "to act like a lover?"

"Objection," Terri called out. "Ms. Sharpe is dragging the witness through needless pain, to no point. We've already established the act of rape and the fear that it caused. How long does the prosecution intend to spell out the forms that fear can take?"

Sharpe turned to Masters. "There *is* a point to this, Your Honor, which the People will make clear if necessary. Even on the record to date, the issue of consent justifies exploring whether Ms. Linton's subsequent actions are truly consistent with rape. But in fairness to this witness, I'll confine myself to a few more questions."

Masters nodded. "All right, Counsel."

Terri sat down, appraising Sharpe with concern. "There's nothing you could do," Paget whispered. "Caroline has to let her cross-examine."

Terri leaned toward him, still watching Sharpe. "Marnie knows what happened, and I don't know how. Marcy hasn't spoken to her. Or anyone, that I know about."

Sharpe had turned back to Linton. "Did you respond," she demanded, "as if you and Mark Ransom were lovers?"

Linton stared at her. "I didn't want him to hurt me."

"So you pretended?"

"Yes."

Sharpe folded her arms. "Then why," she asked, "did you and Mr. Ransom not have intercourse?"

Linton hesitated. "Because he couldn't."

"Couldn't what?"

Gazing at Sharpe, Linton seemed to regather strength. "Maintain an erection," Linton said quietly. "That was why he went downstairs."

Sharpe paused for a moment. "Was he embarrassed?"

"Oh, yes." Her voice rose. "But it wasn't just embarrassment. It was fear and anger."

"What did he say?"

"He made me promise not to tell anyone. Told me that he had never failed before." Linton's tone grew bitter. "It was as if I'd taken something from him. I suppose he considered his performance on the downstairs couch much more of a success."

It was, Terri thought, a nice retort. But Marnie Sharpe looked calm enough.

"Thank you," she said. "No further questions."

Paget glanced at Terri. "What was *that* about?" he asked.

Terri shook her head. "I'm going to try something," she said, and was back on her feet.

"Before Mr. Ransom raped you," she asked Linton, "you resisted him, correct?"

"Yes. I did."

"What was his reaction?"

As Linton gazed at her, Terri saw the comprehension in her eyes. "It seemed to excite him."

"And slapping you seemed to excite him also."

Linton nodded. "His eyes almost glittered. I think that was why he made me watch him and do things for him. He liked *forcing* women, dominating them."

Terri nodded. "And so the second time he wanted sex, you took the line of least resistance."

"Yes."

"You didn't struggle."

"No."

"He had no excuse to slap you."

"No. I didn't want to give him one."

Terri paused. "Instead you reached out for him, correct?"

"I was frightened." Linton's voice fell. "So I put my arms around him."

"And what happened?"

"He lost his erection." Linton shook her head. "It was so strange."

"Is it? Isn't the only difference between the two incidents that the rape—when he achieved penetration—involved violence and abuse? Whereas the time that he failed, you pretended to be his lover by consent?"

Linton was silent for a time. "Yes," she said. "That is the *only* difference. But then Mark Ransom hated women."

"But then Mark Ransom was a *rapist*," Terri answered. "It seems that when you reached for him, you saved yourself from more than just a beating."

Masters raised an eyebrow. "Was that a question, Ms. Peralta?"

Terri turned to her. "It was a *comment*, Your Honor. I *have* no further questions."

Masters looked from Paget to Terri. "Is Ms. Linton your final witness?" she asked.

Terri glanced at Paget. "Yes. Pending the court's decision on the admissibility of the testimony we tendered in chambers."

Caroline Masters nodded. "I'll hear argument on that at nine tomorrow morning." Turning, she faced Marcy Linton. "You're excused, Ms. Linton. And speaking for the court, your appearance here is very much appreciated."

Nodding, Linton stepped down. To Terri's hopeful eyes, she looked no worse—perhaps better—than when she had come. And then, as she had the night before, when Terri had told her of Steve Urbina, Marcy Linton put her arms around Teresa Peralta.

Terri parked her car in front of Mary Carelli's hotel.

It was dusk, the end of a silent drive from the courthouse. From the passenger seat, Mary looked out at the cluster of reporters, waiting for some final comment. "I wonder if I'll ever see them the same," she said. "Let alone be one of them."

Terri was exhausted, she realized: partly by Linton, partly by the tension of preparing to argue that Rappaport and Caldwell should be heard in open court. After a time, she said, "At least they should be friendly."

Mary nodded. "It was a good day—my best, probably. Thank you for that."

"You're welcome. But it wasn't me. It was Marcy Linton." Terri paused. "It's hard to feel elated. From Sharpe's questions, she's saving a surprise for us."

"Still, you *did* find Linton. Despite my considerable doubts." Mary turned to her. "You had something you wanted to ask me about?"

Terri waited for a moment. "The missing tapes," she said finally.

Mary's eyes narrowed. "What about them?"

Terri's stomach felt tight. "I'd like to know where they are."

Mary stared at her. "Why do you care?" she asked coolly.

"Because we need to find them before Sharpe does. And because I don't want Chris or Carlo hurt even more."

"Did Chris send you on this mission?"

Terri shook her head. "Chris has had to shut everything out, just to be able to defend you. This is for me."

Mary smiled faintly. "I thought as much. Do you have any ideas?"

Terri nodded. "Two, actually. One general and one specific. My general theory is that you got rid of them."

Mary's face turned hard. "And your specific theory?"

Terri felt herself take a deep breath. "That after Mark Ransom died, you put them in an envelope and dropped them down the mail slot."

For a moment, Mary was quiet. "You give me great credit for presence of mind."

"Yes. I do."

"Too much, and yet not enough." The mirthless smile returned. "What, for example, did I do for postage? Which, incidentally, pretty much rules out any foreign destination."

Terri looked at the reporters. A group of four hovered in the half-light a few feet from the car. "You had stamps in your purse," she said finally. "Or Ransom had some."

"Really? And after I picked Ransom's pockets for stamps, to whom did I address it? Myself?"

Terri shook her head. "The police would have found it."

"True, I'm not *that* foolish. But then where did it go? Surprisingly, I'd forgotten my address book. And any address I knew by heart probably would be somewhere Sharpe would think to look."

The conversation was becoming murky, unreal. Despite the sardonic edge in Mary's voice, her eyes were curious and quite intent; Terri could not tell whether this curiosity was about Terri herself, with whom she was playing some abstract game of mental chess, or about something else.

"That's what worries me," Terri answered. "Where you sent it."

Mary gave a short laugh. "Here's what would worry *me*. If I addressed an envelope in my handwriting, and then stuck the tapes inside, it would be like a signed confession. All Sharpe would have to do is find it."

"The tapes," Terri asked. "Plural?"

Mary shook her head. "It was *you* who said 'tapes.' I just repeated it. But it does point out another small problem with your theory: motive. The only tape that really hurts *me* was found at Mark Ransom's home." She paused, still watching Terri. "Is there anything else?"

Terri shook her head.

"No? Then thank you for the ride." Mary put her hand on the door handle, and then turned back. In a cold, quiet voice, she said, "Don't *ever* assume that I haven't thought of Carlo."

She snapped open the door and got out, closing it behind her with fearful gentleness. Then she walked toward the hotel, smiling at reporters as she answered their questions.

FIVE

THE LAWYERS SAT clustered in Caroline Masters's chambers, awaiting her decision on Rappaport and Caldwell.

Glancing around her, Terri saw dark circles under Marnie Sharpe's eyes. The media reaction to Marcy Linton's testimony had been to present Mark Ransom as a sexual predator: whether because of that, or private qualms, Sharpe looked as if she had not slept. Pensive, Terri turned back to Caroline Masters, the conversation with Mary Carelli still echoing in her mind.

Caroline nodded to the stenographer, then to Terri. "The witching hour has arrived, Ms. Peralta. Let's hear your argument."

Terri paused to compose herself. "This issue is critical to our defense," she began. "Because the relevance of both witnesses, *and* of the Laura Chase tape, is now very clear.

"First, Ms. Rappaport.

"Our defense is not simply that Mark Ransom attempted to rape Mary Carelli, but that he was impelled by a serious personality disorder: an obsession with Laura Chase, and a need to demean and dominate women which was so strong that it seems to have driven his sexuality.

"The man that Mary Carelli describes was sexually stimulated by a tape of Laura Chase engaged in sex with two men. The man that Melissa Rappaport describes was aroused by a *videotape* involving precisely the same thing."

Pausing, Terri saw that Caroline Masters listened with care, felt Sharpe intently watching. "Melissa Rappaport," she went on, "describes a man who required fantasies of bondage and rape to assure sexual performance. The man *Mary Carelli* describes was a rapist who beat her. And the bridge between these two women is Marcy Linton, whom Mark Ransom beat and raped and with whom, when she later feigned consent, Mark Ransom could not perform."

Terri's voice became quiet. "By the time he got to Mary Carelli, Mark Ransom knew what worked for him. But his 'journey of discovery,' as it were, began with Melissa Rappaport.

"Finally, Melissa Rappaport proves the relevance of the Steinhardt tape of Laura Chase to Mark Ransom's sexual *modus operandi*. The videotape had pictures, the Steinhardt tape words—Laura's own voice. But that was the only difference."

Sharpe, Terri saw, was scribbling furiously. She felt herself gaining confidence.

"Last," she said, "there is Lindsay Caldwell.

"Ms. Caldwell has shown great courage. Like Ms. Rappaport, she is willing to come forward, at whatever cost, because what she has to say is important."

Pausing, Terri saw Caroline's troubled look. Terri's voice became stronger, more emphatic. "Mary Carelli says Mark Ransom tried to blackmail her. So does Lindsay Caldwell.

"Mary Carelli says Mark Ransom wanted sex. So does Lindsay Caldwell.

"Mary Carelli says Mark Ransom hated women." Terri slowed her words, softened her tone. "And so does Lindsay Caldwell.

"Ms. Sharpe says that Mary Carelli is not credible. Can she say that about Melissa Rappaport? She cannot. Can she say that about Lindsay Caldwell? Again, she cannot. And then Mary Carelli *will* be credible, well beyond Ms. Sharpe's ability to argue otherwise."

Terri turned to Sharpe. "With respect, Ms. Sharpe's only hope is to bar their testimony—both here and, if necessary, at trial. Because if those two women testify, and become part of the record in *People v. Carelli*, the People will lose." Terri faced Masters again. "Except that, in reality, the *people* win only if Ms. Carelli wins. Because only the testimony of these two women can present a true account of who Mark Ransom was. And that is what the *people* deserve."

Pausing, Terri felt the passion in her voice. "The problem with proving rape, Your Honor, is that too often there are no witnesses. The victim faces the rapist alone, and then must face the trial alone. And so, too often, cannot carry the burden of proving what was done to her.

"That need not be. It is time for the law to acknowledge that every woman abused by a rapist can bring us closer to the truth." Terri paused again. "As can, so clearly, Melissa Rappaport and Lindsay Caldwell. The court should let them be heard.

"Thank you, Your Honor."

From the corner of her eye, Terri saw Paget smile; even more encouraging was Caroline Masters's seeming introspection. And then Caroline said to Sharpe, "I won't need argument," and Terri, stunned, knew that she had lost.

Caroline leaned forward. "That was ably presented, Teresa. I regret having to rule against you. But I must."

Stricken, Terri listened as Caroline went on. "Let us start with the Laura Chase tape. No privilege protects it, so that the only question is relevance. I've permitted Ms. Carelli to testify generally as to what is on those tapes." She paused, adding quietly, "Without naming names.

"Here, I should digress. I'm appalled by the contents of that tape. And I'm personally appalled that its protagonist, a man who sought the presidency, was so lacking in humanity as to disqualify him from an office which requires—or should require—empathy for the pain of others."

Caroline's face was hard, her voice incisive. "But the man is dead; his family survives. *Their* pain is worth considering. And I'm equally appalled by the use of Laura Chase's most painful and private moments, her confession to a psychiatrist, in the name of 'truth.' That not only hurts the living—Ms. Caldwell comes to mind—but even the dead deserve better." Caroline paused. "Laura Chase was used quite enough in life. No one asked her if she would also like to be used in death. Her entitlement to dignity did *not* die with her, and this court will not kill it."

Abruptly, Caroline stopped herself. Looking at Terri, she spoke more quietly, "I don't fault the defense for arguing relevance. If I agreed, none of what I just said would matter. And if the sexual acts described on the tape were similar to those Ms. Carelli attributes to Mr. Ransom, I *might* agree. But they aren't, so I don't.

"I feel much the same about Ms. Rappaport. To testify regarding her marriage to Mark Ransom would be to humiliate herself in public. *If* the acts Ms. Rappaport described were the same as those described by Ms. Carelli—rape, as in the case of Ms. Linton—I would agree with the defense that it might suggest that Mr. Ransom was prone to rape. But the heart of Ms. Rappaport's humiliation is that her actions were consensual. Which is the precise reason that her humiliation is irrelevant to Ms. Carelli's defense. At least as a matter of law."

Caroline stopped, folding her hands. "And then," she said slowly, "we have the matter of Ms. Caldwell. Each of us may have our private view on whether Ms. Caldwell did anything 'wrong.' Hopefully, our understanding of sexuality is broader and more humane than it was twenty years ago; certainly a nineteen-year-old can't be held accountable for the suicide of someone as complex and tormented as Laura Chase. But, absent extraordinary circumstances, that private matter should remain Ms. Caldwell's to live with, in private. Without becoming 'the woman who killed Laura Chase.'

"She is willing to forgo that right. I will not ask her to. I agree that her testimony suggests that Mr. Ransom's feelings about women were lamentable. But misogyny and blackmail do not prove rape." Pausing, she turned to Terri. "Indeed, they may even suggest a motive for murder."

That was right, Terri knew. She watched as Caroline Masters leaned back in her chair, as if to finish. "Finally," Caroline said, "there is fairness to the prosecution. It is hard to listen to Ms. Rappaport and Ms. Caldwell without developing a certain feeling about Mark Ransom. However, we are not in the business of deciding whether murder victims deserve to die, but simply whether murder was committed. I've tried to put their testimony out of my mind. It will not be part of the record on which I determine 'probable cause.'

"That's all. On the question of whether Ms. Carelli has proven her affirmative defense, I'll make my finding based solely on the testimony of Ms. Carelli and Ms. Linton."

Terri turned to Paget, the disappointment washing over her. He gave a small shrug: you've done your best, it seemed to say—we'll have to win without them. But, to Terri, the gesture did not quite cover the worry he felt.

Sharpe was leaning forward, as if to seize the moment. "Given that the defense has rested," she said in tones of confidence, "the People ask the court to enter a finding of probable cause without further proceedings. If the court needs argument, I can make it now."

"I *will* set a time for argument," Masters responded. "But you mentioned a possible rebuttal witness. You've decided not to call anyone?"

Pausing, Sharpe looked openly concerned. "Is that really necessary, Your Honor? I'm confident we've shown probable cause on the ample record which exists. Whether Ms. Carelli and Ms. Linton raise a reasonable doubt should be reserved for the jury at a subsequent trial."

Masters raised an eyebrow. "You *do* have a witness ready, correct?"

Sharpe hesitated. "Yes. One."

"But you'd prefer not to give Mr. Paget a preview of the utter devastation he or she will cause at trial. Is that it?"

Slowly, Sharpe nodded. "Not unless the court is in doubt on the issue of probable cause."

"I won't say *what,* if anything, the court is in doubt on. And I ask you not to read anything into my suggestion, other than my preference for a complete record on which to make whatever mistake I'm about to make. But that's up to you."

The dry remark reminded Terri that Caroline, too, faced political consequences, however she ruled; unlike traffic offenses or disorderly conduct, it was the kind of case that could cost her reelection. But it was the consequence to the district attorney that seemed to have struck Marnie Sharpe; her face was somber.

"Thank you, Your Honor." Sharpe hesitated, as if making a final decision. "We're prepared to call our witness now."

Masters glanced at her watch. "I'll hear him at ten o'clock. Meanwhile, we're on break."

Terri and Paget were in the hallway outside chambers before they could speak. "I'm sorry," she murmured. "I'd begun to believe we could win."

"Maybe you got through to her anyhow," Paget said quietly. "Hopefully, that's why she's making Marnie call Mr. or Ms. X."

"Whoever it is," Terri answered, "we're about to find out what it is that Marnie's always known."

Terri took an elevator to the first floor, avoiding reporters.

Here, the Hall of Justice broke into a maze of bleak green corridors. She followed one, then turned down another, until she found an empty telephone booth.

Glancing over her shoulder, she ducked inside.

There was a telephone directory, but the overhead light was broken. Terri squinted at the pages under "United States Government"; at length, she found the heading "Postal Service."

What did I do for postage? Mary had asked.

Beneath the heading was a page-long column of telephone numbers—area post offices, express mail, complaints, employment verification. The only one that looked promising was "Dead Letter Branch."

I'm not so foolish, Mary had said, *as to mail them to myself.*

This was foolish, Terri thought. But the conversation with Mary would not leave her; Mary's chilly exercise in logic was either a heartless game, played to no purpose, or designed to trace the rigor of Terri's thoughts.

They were not very rigorous, Terri knew. But she was certain that her opening premise was the same as Marnie Sharpe's: that Mark Ransom died in possession of the tapes.

Terri picked up the telephone and dialed.

"Dead Letter Branch," a woman's voice answered.

Hesitating, Terri formed a vision of her: black, substantial, and middle-aged, phlegmatic from years of inquiries.

"I have a question," Terri ventured.

"That's why we're here, ma'am."

"What I wanted to know is what happens if someone mails something but forgets to put the whole address on. Or any address at all."

"It depends." The woman coughed. "Sorry, but I can't seem to kick this cold. Anyhow, some things we just throw out. It depends on whether we think they have value."

"How do you determine that?"

"We open the parcel. If it's just a letter, and we can't tell where it should go from looking at it, we get rid of it. If it looks like something of value, we keep it for a while."

"How long?"

"Usually three months."

It was about five weeks, Terri thought, since Mary Carelli had shot Ransom. "What happens then?" she asked.

Terri heard the stifled sound of a repressed sneeze. "Then we sell it at auction," the woman answered. "If it doesn't sell, then we give it away or throw it out. Why, what did you lose?"

Terri paused, trying to envision the fate of Mary's tape at a public auction. "Cassette tapes," she said finally. "Like for a car stereo."

"Yeah, we might keep them."

The voice was becoming bored and taciturn. Once more, Terri hesitated. "If I described them, could you take a look?"

There was silence. "Didn't you already call about tapes?" the woman asked. "A few weeks back?"

Terri was stunned. "No," she said finally. "It wasn't me. I've never called before."

"Would there have been postage on them?"

"I don't know," Terri replied.

"Well, *this* isn't the lost and found, ma'am. If it had no postage and you want it, you got to go to the post office and look yourself. You know what zip code this got mailed from?"

"I know it was Nob Hill."

There was silence, then a sudden loud cough. "I think that's Station O," the woman wheezed. "Van Ness Avenue. You might go look there."

The witness was a round-faced man with thick glasses and a blond fringe of hair. His face was reflective but good-humored; his voice—deep, slow, and authoritative—had the trace of a southern accent. There was something quite gentle about him.

"Who," Terri whispered to Paget, "is Dr. George Bass?"

Wary, Paget watched him. "I don't know."

"And you're a psychiatrist," Sharpe was asking, "licensed in the state of Florida?"

Bass nodded. "That's correct."

Paget felt Mary touch his arm, suddenly tense. "What's *this* about?" she demanded.

"Just let me listen," he snapped. "If this guy's Ransom's psychiatrist, I'm about to object."

Sharpe moved forward. "And was Mark Ransom one of your patients?"

Bass nodded. "Whenever he visited Key West. He started about four years ago, and our last session was about three months back."

"When Mark Ransom first visited you, Doctor, what reason did he give?"

Bass looked faintly sad. "At first, it wasn't any reason he gave, so much as what he talked about."

"And what was that?"

"Women, and his feelings about them." Bass frowned. "It took me some time to get to what *he* saw as the root of the matter."

"And what was that?"

Bass paused. "Impotence," he said quietly. "Mark Ransom could no longer achieve intercourse with a woman."

There was a sudden startled buzz. Paget was on his feet abruptly. "Objection," he called out. "Is the witness speaking from personal knowledge? Because if not, his testimony is hearsay, and I request that he be excused."

"Your Honor," Sharpe responded, "Ms. Carelli is claiming an attempted rape by a man who, Dr. Bass now tells us, was impotent. Surely Mr. Paget is not claiming that Mr. Ransom lied to Dr. Bass about *that*."

"I have no basis for knowing," Paget responded. "Nor does Dr. Bass. The court should not hear his testimony."

Caroline Masters leaned forward. "It may seem archaic, Mr. Paget, but as a matter of evidence, Mr. Ransom's admissions on this subject are deemed so embarrassing as to be reliable. This witness may help shed light on Mr. Ransom's state of mind, and the question of sexual capacity is important. Overruled."

Sitting down, Paget could see the fear in Mary's eyes at Masters's ruling: Bass already looked like a good witness, and Mark Ransom's supposed impotence went to the heart of her defense. "No wonder," Terri murmured, "that Johnny couldn't find any women."

Silent, Paget wondered how long Sharpe had known this. Before Melissa Rappaport had appeared, he realized, and perhaps even before the indictment. It turned his understanding of the case upside down.

Sharpe was moving closer to the witness. "Was Mr. Ransom's impotence the result of some physical incapacity?"

Bass shook his head. "Mr. Ransom told me that he was capable of having an erection, but that he became flaccid whenever he attempted intercourse. Understandably, Ransom felt that he was not the same man."

"And this upset him?"

"To put it mildly. His chosen self-image was one of virility. It took a number of sessions before he could admit this, even to me."

Sharpe nodded. "And to what do you attribute Mr. Ransom's impotence?"

"According to Mr. Ransom, or my own analysis?"

"Your own analysis, Doctor."

Bass nodded. "The superficial answer is that Mr. Ransom disliked women. But the result of that hostility was guilt and ambivalence. About himself and his own sexuality." Pausing, Bass removed his glasses. "Mark Ransom wanted to subjugate, and even humiliate, women. But in his subconscious, he felt he had to inhibit himself. The ultimate result was impotence. You can view it as a kind of sexual policeman, dispatched by his conscience."

Terri leaned close to Paget. "Are we supposed to feel *sorry* for him?"

Slowly, Paget nodded. "At least see him as human," he murmured. "Marcy Linton hurt them—if not with Caroline, then with the public. Sharpe means to turn all that around on us."

"To what do you attribute Mr. Ransom's hostility toward women?" Sharpe was asking.

"In part to his feelings toward Siobhan Ransom, his late mother. She was a domineering woman and seems to have served as an archetype for any woman he perceived as strong and aggressive—those of independent accomplishment, or ardent feminists. Women who he believed might dominate him, or criticize him, or simply not think well of him. As I say, Mark Ransom was a frightened and vulnerable man."

To his left, Paget felt Mary's rising anger. The testimony regarding impotence was eating through her self-control; she stared at Bass with barely repressed rage. Once more, against his will, Paget wondered what had happened in Mark Ransom's suite.

Keep your concentration, he told himself. Look for a line of attack.

"How serious," Sharpe was asking, "did you consider Mr. Ransom's sexual problem to be?"

Bass looked grave. "Extremely serious, and very deeply rooted. At the time of our last visit, he had not been able to have intercourse for nearly four years."

Paget saw Caroline Masters's eyes widen. Sharpe waited a moment. "And did Mr. Ransom specify to you," she asked quietly, "the last time in which he achieved intercourse?"

"It was the same occasion that *he* blamed for his impotence." Pausing, he turned to Masters. "The rape of the young woman you saw yesterday—Marcy Linton. After that, Mark Ransom became impotent."

The courtroom was silent. Softly, Sharpe said, "No further questions."

Rising from the defense table, Paget saw Mary's sudden look of defeat. Behind her, Carlo stared at his shoes. Paget felt their reactions as his own; with her final question, to his utter disbelief, Sharpe had pointed Marcy Linton's testimony back at Mary Carelli.

Slowly, he walked toward Bass.

"You mentioned Siobhan Ransom as an archetype," Paget began. "Did Ransom develop a counterarchetype? That is, was there a particular woman who he imagined represented his *needs?*"

Bass watched him for a moment. "Yes. The actress Laura Chase."

Paget felt a spark of hope. "So he mentioned her in analysis?"

"Frequently."

"And what role did Ms. Chase play in Mr. Ransom's psychic landscape?"

Idly, Bass tapped his glasses. "In shorthand, she represented security and sexual fulfillment. The Laura Chase he invented in his mind would have done anything to please him. She not only would have catered to his sexual desires but, equally important, she would have *admired* him."

Paget gave him a curious look. "Did he specifically associate Laura Chase with sexual performance?"

"Yes." Bass sounded rueful. "He came to believe that with Laura Chase, he would have been the sexual man he wished to be. He saw her as someone mysterious, yet available; a woman who wanted to maintain a distinct and exotic role that was not in competition with him."

"Is it fair to call this preoccupation with Laura Chase a fetish?"

Bass nodded. "In a sense. It's not at all uncommon, Mr. Paget, for men with doubts about their sexuality to seek arousal through fetishes or rituals. I don't mean to sound insensitive, but the incident with Ms. Linton traumatized him. He was deeply afraid of failure."

Paget felt himself slow down. "Did Mr. Ransom also have a preoccupation with rape?" he asked.

"Yes. It was part of his desire to subjugate women."

"Is it fair to say that rape is a crime of violence rather than of passion? As evidenced by the blow to the face he inflicted on Ms. Linton?"

"I would agree, yes."

"And it's true that Mr. Ransom derived sexual stimulation from physically abusing women? Also as evidenced by Ms. Linton?"

"That is possible. At least it is consistent with his psychology."

Paget moved closer, glancing up at Caroline Masters. "It is even possible, is it not, that he might view slapping a woman's face as a way of achieving and/or maintaining an erection?"

"Yes. That also would be consistent."

"So that we have now identified two factors which helped Mr. Ransom achieve erection: striking a woman, and his fetish for Laura Chase. Is that correct?"

Bass gave him a thoughtful gaze. "Those could be factors."

It was time, Paget thought, to take a chance. "Did you ever become aware that Mr. Ransom had obtained tapes of Laura Chase's sessions with her psychiatrist, Dr. Steinhardt?"

"Yes." Bass looked defensive. "I don't approve, incidentally. I'm here because my patient was killed, and because Ms. Sharpe was quite insistent. In fact, I find it quite ironic to be here discussing Mr. Ransom's confidences."

"I understand," Paget said. "But fairness to Ms. Carelli requires that I pursue this. Specifically, did Mr. Ransom tell you that he had obtained the tape described by Ms. Carelli—one in which Laura Chase described having sex with two men?"

Bass nodded unhappily. "He did. Yes. He was quite excited about it."

"Did Mr. Ransom believe that this tape might restore him sexually?"

"Objection," Sharpe called out. "The question asks Dr. Bass to speculate."

Caroline Masters gave her a droll look. "People who live in glass houses, Ms. Sharpe, are likely to get glass in their eye. Carry on, Mr. Paget."

"That would be speculation." Bass paused. "But yes, I think so. I do know that once Mr. Ransom got that tape, he stopped seeing me."

All at once, Paget understood the doctor's rueful tone: Mark Ransom had chosen Laura Chase as a substitute for therapy, gone down what Bass believed to be a sad and fruitless path. "But after that, Doctor, he *did* see Ms. Carelli. So let's briefly reprise your testimony. Slapping women helped Mr. Ransom stay erect, true?"

"So it seems."

"The Laura Chase fetish also helped Mark Ransom stay erect?"

Bass nodded. "It was a primary source of stimulus, yes."

"So isn't it quite possible that stimulated by the Laura Chase tape and by slapping Ms. Carelli, Mark Ransom could have tried to rape her?"

"It's possible, yes. But after Ms. Linton, that would have put Mark Ransom at great risk of personal embarrassment." Pausing, Bass glanced at Mary. "It's difficult to envision him taking that risk with a woman like Ms. Carelli."

"But weren't women 'like Ms. Carelli'—independent women of achievement—the very type of women Mark Ransom despised and wished to subjugate?"

"True, on one level." Bass shifted on the witness stand. "But to me, the operative word is 'fear.' The man I saw was far too mired in fear to attempt penetration with an unwilling woman."

Paget's voice went cold. "That's called rape, Doctor. Which is the *third factor* we've identified as a sexual stimulus to Mr. Ransom."

"Indeed," Bass said. "But I saw the man for almost four years, and what you describe is hard for me to imagine."

It stopped Paget again. He stared at Bass, feigning incredulity, while he tried to think of a way to end on a better answer. "But isn't it possible," he finally asked, "that Mark Ransom could have achieved an erection under circumstances that would convince Ms. Carelli she was going to be raped, including the infliction of a blow to the face, whether or not he could actually do it?"

"That's possible, yes."

"Or whether or not, in the end, he intended to even *try* penetration?"

Bass looked at Sharpe, then turned again to Paget. Slowly, he answered, "I suppose that's also possible."

When Paget glanced up at Caroline Masters, her gaze was cool. But there was nothing more that he could do.

He turned back to Bass. "I have no further questions, Dr. Bass. Thank you for your patience."

Walking back to the defense table, Paget saw that Sharpe was already on her feet.

"During the four-year period of Mr. Ransom's treatment," she asked Bass, "did he ever discuss raping anyone?"

Bass shook his head. "No. As I said, the consequence of his attack on Ms. Linton tormented him. His fantasy concerning rape, when he acted it out, came at a great cost to *both* people involved."

"Did he indicate any predisposition to rape anyone again?"

Bass paused, looking at Mary Carelli. "No. None."

Sharpe nodded. "In fact, did Mr. Ransom talk of sexual contact with *anyone?*"

"No one."

Sharpe paused for a moment. "Did he ever mention Mary Carelli?"

Bass shook his head. "If he had a particular interest in Ms. Carelli, I was not aware of it."

"Thank you, Dr. Bass. No further questions."

As Caroline Masters excused her last witness, Sharpe walked to the prosecution table with an air of satisfaction. Watching, Paget felt disheartened.

From the bench, Masters faced the lawyers again. "I'd like to compliment both prosecution and defense on an admirable presentation of the evidence. I'll hear final argument at ten o'clock tomorrow morning."

Abruptly, she banged her gavel.

"All rise," the courtroom deputy called out, and Caroline Masters left the bench, the sudden tumult of the courtroom trailing after her, the legacy of Sharpe's final witness.

PART SIX

THE COURT

FEBRUARY 19 – FEBRUARY 22

ONE

TERESA PERALTA pulled up in front of the post office.

She sat in her car for a moment, watching the pedestrian traffic on Van Ness. It was one o'clock; men and women on lunch breaks filed in and out of restaurants and shops and the stereo outlet across the street, in no particular hurry. The desultory rhythm of normal life seemed alien to Terri; the day was unseasonably warm, and the brightness of the sun surprised her.

The cloistered world of a trial was unnatural, she realized; a forced obsession which so consumed its protagonists that they thought of little else. For two weeks, the hearing had been her life; the witnesses her chief concern; Christopher Paget and Caroline Masters and Marnie Sharpe and Mary Carelli her human reference points. She had watched them stumble, grow, confront the relentless pressure of the courtroom and of life in the third person—watching their every act replayed on television—until, finally, it was almost finished.

Chris was shut in his office, trying to adjust his thoughts to the testimony of Dr. Bass, refusing all calls from the press so that he could outline his final argument to Caroline Masters. Later, Terri would listen and offer advice. There was just one more thing she needed to do.

This would come to nothing, she believed. But if the tapes had not been destroyed—and while Mary had motive to destroy them, she lacked the means—Chris and Carlo were still at risk. If Terri could not find the tapes, at least she would know that.

Getting out of the car, Terri felt the breeze on her face, took in the vehicles that passed, the people in the crosswalk, the sounds of engines and car horns, the random buildings—some tall, some low, their irregular height like the rooftops of a toy city, built by a child. After she saw Chris, perhaps she would pick up Elena early from day care, drive her to the beach. They both needed that.

Terri walked into the post office.

It was dim, musty-smelling. Ten or twelve people waited with sullen detachment for three postal clerks to process their mail or retrieve a package. The bearded man in front of her hummed tunelessly, passing time to his own inner voice.

The beach was a good idea, Terri thought. Once the hearing was over, she would be free to spend time with Elena and deal with Richie.

She checked her watch. One-fifteen.

What was Caroline doing now? she wondered. Calmly nibbling on her usual salad, having made up her mind? No, Terri thought: Caroline might already have decided how to rule, but she would not be serene about it. The hearing, and the people it touched, seemed to weigh on her now. She would be thinking of those people as much as her career or even Mary; she could cause the machinery of justice to release them by freeing Mary Carelli or, with Mary, send them all to trial.

Terri would not, she decided, wish to be Caroline Masters.

She shuffled forward, imagining the moment when Caroline announced her decision. The thought led her to another: even less would she like to be Christopher Paget.

They had lost, Terri believed. Lost with the final witness.

"Next," a man's voice called.

Terri looked up in surprise. There was no one in front of her; a pleasant-faced Japanese postal clerk looked at her expectantly.

She walked up to the window. "Sorry," she said. "Absentminded."

"Sure." He was looking at Terri with an intelligent, curious expression; for the first time, it struck Terri that her face might be recognizable to strangers. Then he asked, "What can we do for you?"

Terri hesitated. "I'm looking for a lost package. Something with an incomplete address, or the address missing. It got mailed from Nob Hill, we think."

Perhaps, Terri thought, she only *imagined* that he looked curious. "You didn't mail it yourself?" he asked.

Terri shook her head. "No, a friend. We think she stuck it in the mail by accident." Feeling awkward, Terri joked, "She's absentminded too."

The man seemed to study her face. Then he smiled. "You'd be amazed," he said. "What was in there?"

What had she told the woman in Dead Letters? "Cassette tapes," she answered. "Like for a stereo."

He looked thoughtful. "I might have noticed that. We get some good stuff back there, and I play music all the time in my car. Offhand, I don't remember tapes."

Didn't you already call about tapes, the woman had asked, a few weeks back?

"Can I take a look?" Terri asked.

He hesitated. "There's no one back there now."

Terri smiled. "I promise not to take anything that's not mine. All I'm looking for are cassette tapes, really. Maybe in an envelope marked 'Hotel Flood.' "

He thought for another moment, and then shrugged. "We have a lot of things. I might have missed it." He motioned her around the counter. "Come on back—you've got an honest face."

Terri followed him down a hallway to an open room with metal shelves full of packages and a three-foot stepladder next to the door. "This is it," he said cheerfully. "If you find what you're looking for, come get me."

"Thanks," Terri said. Somehow, being in the room made her quest seem real. Her skin tingled; she did not dare look around her until the clerk had left.

She should have told Chris she was coming.

It was all right, she told herself. Chris was distracted enough. He did not want the tapes found by anyone else; if they were anywhere Sharpe or the media could get them, he would choose to have them first. And if Mary lost, and went to trial, it was all the more important that Terri find them.

Look systematically, she told herself. Don't become frenzied, glancing from shelf to shelf, and don't leave anything to chance. Then you can forget this.

There were shelves on three walls.

The first row of shelves took a half hour. She spent the time bending, stretching, using the stepladder, until her back hurt. She found a baseball glove, foreign currency, several watches, a box full of religious tracts, a cookbook with handwritten recipes stuffed in several pages. The scraps of lives, but no tape.

Once more she climbed the stepladder, peering over the top of a new shelf.

"Find anything?"

She turned atop the ladder. The clerk stood in the doorway.

"Not my stuff," she said. "But a couple of nice watches."

The clerk laughed. "You must really want those tapes. This room reminds me of the army. It's depressing."

Terri smiled. "If I start to need air, I'll let you know."

"Okay." He paused. "These tapes, they're not the Grateful Dead, are they?"

Terri shook her head. "No."

"Too bad. I really love the Dead." He went back to his customers.

She turned, resting on her arms, and glanced at the top of the next shelf over.

There was a ripped letter-size envelope, Terri saw, with a rubber band around the middle. Inside the envelope was the outline of a small rectangular object.

At least it was the right size, Terri thought. She paused, debating whether to break her discipline of a systematic search, and then climbed down the stepladder.

She slid the ladder sideways across the floor, then climbed it again, peering at each shelf as she went.

She got to the top, gazing down at the envelope. Finally, she picked it up.

It was light in her hand. When she turned it over, she saw the logo of the Hotel Flood with a line drawn through it.

Her hands began shaking. As she removed the rubber band, it fell to the floor.

She reached inside the envelope.

There was not one rectangle, her fingers told her, but two. She pulled them out.

Tapes.

Staring at them, Terri saw the Roman numerals. But it was a moment before she could accept what she was holding.

The first tape, she knew from Steinhardt's code, was of Laura Chase. Which meant that the second was Mary Carelli.

She stood there clutching the tapes, wishing that she had not come. Then she slowly climbed down the stepladder with the tapes and the envelope.

The rubber band was by the ladder. She picked it up, put the tapes in the envelope, and wound the rubber band tight around it.

The clerk was serving a customer. Terri walked behind him. "I found it," she said quietly.

He turned, smiling, and took the envelope from her hand. He glanced at it and looked up again. "Amazing," he said. "Goes to show what they say about perseverance."

He might not have noticed how strange she had sounded, Terri thought. She saw his customer watching them. "I guess so," she said. "Thanks for your help."

"Oh, you'll have to sign for it. We can't just let stuff go."

He left for a moment, returning with a sheet filled with descriptions of parcels, a column for signatures and addresses. His index finger rested on a line headed "Tapes, Flood." "Here," he said.

Carefully, Terri signed the index, the tapes held in her right hand. "Thanks," she repeated.

"Sure." He looked at her again. "Don't I recognize you from some-where?"

Terri managed a smile. "I have that kind of face," she answered, and left.

TWO

CHRISTOPHER PAGET found it hard to concentrate.

He walked to his window, gazing out at the panorama of the city—the green rise of Telegraph Hill, houses and apartments seeming to climb up its side; the sweep of piers with their luxury liners and tour boats; the blue expanse of bay. Since he was a child, Paget had loved this city, counted himself fortunate to live here; as an adult, he had taught Carlo to love it too, exploring its vistas and its nooks and crannies—a neighborhood Italian restaurant in North Beach, pocket parks with swings and slides, places to walk on Sunday morning for croissants or blueberry muffins.

On a normal day, these thoughts brought him contentment. Being part of a place that Carlo now wished to be part of made him feel that his life had added up to something, was not just about himself and how he had made his way. He no longer saw his decision to raise Carlo as something done for a lonely child: it had created a depth of happiness and pleasure that would have been beyond him on his own. Whatever else the accident of Mary Carelli had brought him, their careless weekend in Washington had brought him Carlo. Christopher Paget was lucky to be Carlo's father; looking at the city, defined by the days they had spent together, reminded him of that.

But today the view gave Paget little pleasure, and less peace.

From the beginning, he had believed Mary guilty of something, in some degree or another. Everything he knew about her, and every twist in her story, told him she was hiding something deeper and more obscure than what had happened on the day Mark Ransom died. But Paget had forced himself to focus simply on what the prosecution could prove. If he put Sharpe's case to an early test, he had reasoned, perhaps he could extract Mary from danger before the prosecutor learned what Paget himself did not know—by finding the tape or otherwise. And Marcy Linton had made a difference; there were times, despite himself, when Paget gave Mary's account some credence.

Now George Bass had shaken him to the core.

It wasn't merely the damage to Mary's defense—though Paget could see that in the faces of the media people as he had left the courthouse, hear it in the shouted questions he had ignored. Nor was it that Johnny Moore's failures now made sense, or even that Sharpe had transformed Marcy Linton—at least in some sense—into a prosecution witness. What was so painful was the realization that in spite of his best professional efforts and all that he knew about her, Paget had still wanted to believe in Mary Carelli.

Why blame Mary? he thought. She is who she is; only a fool invests in believing his client. Even when the client is the mother of your much-loved son.

Especially then.

Now there would be a trial, he believed, another ordeal for Carlo to bear. Searching for motive, Sharpe might find the tape: even if it was inadmissible, sooner or later someone from the media would ferret it out. There was no chance that the lucky reporter would conclude that hurt to Carlo Paget outweighed the boost to his or her career, piously cloaked in the public's right to know. And in the meanwhile, Carlo would be besieged by questions from all sides, and worst of all his own: whether his mother had killed Mark Ransom not because of rape but to save her own career, and then coolly lied about it until the lies entangled her.

There was a soft knock behind him.

As Paget turned, Teresa Peralta appeared in the doorway.

"Do you want to talk," she asked, "or should I come back?"

She looked as troubled as he was, Paget thought. "Stay," he answered. "I'm not functioning very well. Perhaps you can help."

Just her being there would help. But Paget could not tell her that. Too much of what he felt was no longer about Terri the lawyer, as good as she was, but about Terri the woman.

"Is it Bass?" she asked.

Paget nodded. "He seems to have set off a chain reaction. In the past hour, I've covered Mary, Carlo, the tapes, and my own monumental foolishness. I haven't come up with a line of argument."

She closed the door, stood leaning against it with her black purse clasped in front of her. "Tell me the worst part," she said.

Paget was silent for a moment. Then he asked, "Did you ever love someone so much it hurts?"

Terri nodded. "Elena."

"For me, it's Carlo. It's the only time I've let myself feel like that—perhaps I thought that loving a child was safe." He shrugged. "Loving someone is never safe. There's too much that can happen."

"And you're worried about what will happen to Carlo."

"To Carlo, yes. Perhaps, more selfishly, to Carlo and me." He paused. "I don't want this to go on for him. And I keep worrying about that tape. What on earth could have moved Mary Carelli, of all people, to bare her soul for a tape recorder?"

Terri watched him. "You're still afraid they'll find it, then."

"If they have a reason to keep looking. An ongoing prosecution will do nicely."

Terri's shoulders drew in. Softly, she said, "They won't ever find it, Chris."

Her tone was very subdued and very certain. "Because Mary destroyed it?" he asked.

"No. Because I have it."

Something in her voice kept Paget from saying anything. Slowly, Terri took an envelope from her purse.

She walked across the room and placed it in his hands. "There are two tapes inside," she told him. "One is Laura Chase, talking about Lindsay Caldwell. The second is Mary."

He stared down at the envelope. "How long have you had these?"

"For less than an hour." Her voice was still quiet. "I found them at the post office."

Paget looked up. "Mary told you?"

Terri shook her head. "I figured it out. After Mary shot Ransom, she put them in a blank envelope and slid them down the mail slot. That's what she was doing in the hallway."

"Then she lied about that too." Paget touched his eyes, slowly shaking his head. "If she was cool enough to do *that*, God knows what else she did. And lied about."

Terri walked away from him, sat in a chair, looking out. "I shouldn't have told you," she said. "Not today."

Paget shrugged. "You didn't want me worrying anymore—at least about the tapes. And you reasoned, correctly, that any decent defense lawyer wouldn't let this keep him from arguing the evidence before the court."

She looked up at him. "Do you want *me* to do the argument?"

"No. You've done far too much already." Paget's brain was sluggish, he realized; it was only as he spoke that it came to him that Terri was at risk. "You got these tapes yourself?" he asked.

"Yes. There's a storeroom for mail without postage."

Paget looked from Terri to the envelope and to Terri again. "They made you sign for them, I imagine."

"Yes."

"Then they can trace this to you."

"I suppose so." Her voice and eyes were steady. "Better me than you. Or Mary."

Paget sat next to her. Quietly, he asked, "Why did you do this?"

She was silent a moment. "Because I like Carlo," she answered. "And I like what you've done with him. He's been hurt already, and I didn't want him hurt anymore. Now, perhaps, he won't be."

"But you've got your own life, Terri, your own career. I didn't want you involved. Not like this."

Terri looked down. "I have trouble drawing lines sometimes. I know that. But if it were Elena, and me, wouldn't you have done the same thing?"

Paget gazed at her; the still, silent profile, the face he had learned to trust. "Then leave it at this," he said. "You gave me the tapes, and your responsibility ended. You didn't know what I'd do about them, and I never said. But you assumed I'd keep them safe."

Terri smiled faintly. "Did I?"

"Yes, you did. And that's what you'll say if you're ever asked. For my own peace of mind."

Her smile faded. "All right. If that's what you want."

"It's very much what I want."

They sat next to each other for a time, Terri staring out the window, Paget at the envelope. At length, she asked, "Can I help with your argument?"

"In a while." It was only when he spoke again that he was certain. "After I listen to this tape."

She looked over at him. "You want to do that? Now?"

"I can't *not* do it. Tomorrow, the next day—I'd have to listen to it, Mary's feelings aside." He paused. "I don't like this. But she's lied to me about too many things for far too long for me to worry about *her* feelings. And who's to say that Steinhardt was the only other person who knows what's on the tapes? If it concerns me, and what we did in Washington, I have to know."

"But why today?"

"Because until I hear it, I can't think about anything else."

Terri touched his shoulder. "I'll leave, then. Call me when you need me."

He gazed at her. Softly, Paget asked, "And what if that's now?"

Her eyes filled with confusion. As if sparring, she said, "You don't want me to know what you'll do with them."

"True." He looked away. "But you can know that I listened."

Terri's eyes did not move from him. In a quiet tone, she asked, "Why do you want me here?"

"As I said, I feel squeamish about Mary. But I just don't want to be alone with this." Suddenly Paget felt embarrassed. "All my life, I've never leaned on anyone. Tomorrow I'll go back to that. I suppose, for a day, I'm borrowing you."

She nodded, silent. After a time, she reached into the envelope, pulled out a tape. "It's this one."

Paget stood, walking to the credenza behind his desk, and produced a portable tape player. He put it in front of them. Inserting the tape, he briefly looked at Terri. Then he pushed the button.

As Paget sat next to Terri, Steinhardt asked, "Did Chris know about your involvement with this man Jack Woods?"

The tape crackled with static. Steinhardt's words had a ghostly quality; it reminded Paget of driving late at night through the Pennsylvania hills during a college trip he had made across the country, the distant voice of an evangelist the only sound that could come from his radio.

"What do you mean?" Mary asked quietly.

Steinhardt hesitated, as if confused. "Your involvement in obstructing the Lasko investigation."

"Yes." Mary's voice became a monotone. "He knew about that."

There was a long silence. "But as I recall his Senate testimony," Steinhardt said slowly, "he supported you."

"No," Mary corrected. "Chris *lied* for me."

Paget felt Terri glance at him, look away. Listening to Mary's taped voice, saying through the static what she never thought he would hear, was haunting. But at least, as Mary had described this tape, he had already heard the worst of it.

"Do you know why Chris lied?" Steinhardt asked.

More silence. "I know of one reason," Mary answered. "The night before we testified, I told him I was pregnant."

"With Carlo, his son?"

The silence became longer. "With Carlo. Yes."

"When you told him, how did he react?"

"We met by the Jefferson Memorial at night, so at first I couldn't really see his face. But his words were clear enough." Her voice turned briefly sad. "He thought Carlo wasn't his. He suggested I consider an abortion."

"And what did you say?"

Her tone sounded bitter. "That he must not think very well of me. And that I was keeping Carlo."

Paget's eyes shut. He felt Terri touch his arm. "It's all right," she murmured. "That was all so long ago. You couldn't know who Carlo would be."

"Then you didn't want an abortion?" Steinhardt asked Mary.

"That's what I told Chris." There was another pause, and then Mary's voice became muted. "But if he hadn't covered for me, what choice would I have had? Carlo would have had no father, and a mother in prison."

"Did you tell Chris that?"

"No." Another pause. "I knew I didn't need to."

"Why was that?"

"Because I felt him start to take in the reality of it—that I might be pregnant with his child. He began to look at me differently, to ask how I felt." Paget heard an ironic smile in Mary's voice. "He even said I should sit down. Like an inexperienced new father, not knowing what to do, amazed at the wonder of it all."

Listening, Paget felt the moment again: the darkness outside the memorial; the woman he did not trust but who might have life inside her; the sense that his own life was about to change. He still felt shaken by it.

"Did you love him?" Steinhardt asked.

Paget sensed Terri's gaze. "Yes." Mary's voice was cool. "As much as I can love anyone."

"You think you're not capable?"

"Not head over heels. Not to the point where I lose control, or lose sight of what I want. I can't let myself." Another pause. "I've never known whether that's a virtue or a fault. It just is."

"Did you think that Chris loved you?"

"I don't know. In a lot of ways, Chris was *like* me—he's very cool and controlled." Mary's voice fell again. "It surprised me when he wanted to raise Carlo."

Next to Paget, Terri slowly shook her head. "Mary never knew who you were," she murmured. "She still doesn't."

"Perhaps he did love you," Steinhardt was saying. "Perhaps *that's* why he helped."

"Oh, it was partly out of feeling for me, I think, *and* the baby I was carrying." Her tone changed again. "And partly because I could help him send Jack Woods to prison."

"Did you offer him that?"

"I didn't have to. He knew that if he covered for me, I would help him ruin Jack." Another pause. "And *I* knew how much he wanted that. Because I knew how much he hated Jack."

Paget turned to Terri. "She did understand me," he said softly. "Much better than you think."

"But you testified *before* Chris did," Steinhardt probed. "You didn't know what he would say."

"It was better that way." Mary's voice turned cold. "Watching me testify, Chris saw what I could do to Jack. And he also knew that if he turned me in, I would be forced to protect myself instead of repeating my story at Jack's trial." She paused again. "All Chris had to do was lie about me, and he would save a pregnant woman and destroy Jack Woods. I still don't know which one he wanted more."

Paget's surroundings—the airy office, the panorama of the bay—seemed to vanish. All that he could imagine was Mary in the sterile room Terri had described to him, telling their secrets to a tape recorder. "She told me the truth," he said to Terri. "This tape does no more harm to her. But it would have ruined me."

"And Carlo," Terri answered. "Imagine him listening to this."

"Jack Woods," Steinhardt was asking Mary. "What happened to him?"

"All the things that would have happened to me." Mary's voice turned grim. "He pleaded guilty rather than face a trial. Three years in prison were the least of it. His career was ruined. He couldn't even practice law."

"They took away his license?"

"Yes." Mary paused. "Much worse, they took away who he was. When he got out of prison, he was no one."

"Did you ever see him again?"

"Of course not." Mary's tone was ironic. "By then I was on my way. In one day, Chris Paget and I destroyed Jack and launched my career in the media."

"Do you feel guilt about that?"

"Not about *that*. Jack had blackmailed me into helping him because of what I already knew, until I was in far deeper than I ever wanted. I owed him nothing." Mary hesitated, voice softening again. "No, Doctor, I'm here for another reason. One we haven't even touched on."

Something in her tone made Paget tense. "Is it about Carlo?" Steinhardt asked.

"Partly." Her voice was hesitant. "But it's also about Chris. And me."

"That dream," Steinhardt said. "You're in the church in Paris, asking forgiveness for your sins. Is your sin giving Carlo to Chris?"

There was a long silence. "Yes," Mary answered softly.

"Has Chris been a good father?"

"I think so." Mary's voice sounded parched. "I've tried to stay out of the way. After years of trying to keep him away from Carlo."

"I don't understand, then. You believe Chris to be good with Carlo. And in the dream, you're asking forgiveness *before* you give Carlo to Chris. Not after."

There was a long silence. "You're an intelligent man, Doctor. But there's something I haven't told you. Or anyone."

"And what is that?" Steinhardt asked.

To Paget, Mary's silence was like the intake of breath. Then, very coolly, she answered, "Chris isn't Carlo's father."

The next moment was a blur. Terri's pale, stricken face. Feeling himself bend forward. Steinhardt's dry voice, asking the next question as if nothing had happened.

"Who *is* the father, then?"

Another silence, as if Mary could not bring herself to answer. Through his shock, Paget felt Terri's hand on his arm. "Jack Woods," Mary answered in a trembling voice. "Chris's enemy. The man we sent to prison."

"Oh, Chris." Terri's voice was anguished. Looking up, Paget saw the tears in her eyes.

It doesn't matter, he wanted to say. But he found he could not speak the words. Or any words at all.

"Why didn't you tell Chris?" Steinhardt asked.

Through the static, Mary's voice was faint. "At first, I wanted him to protect me. So I let him think the baby was his, to save myself."

"And later, when you gave up Carlo?"

"Chris flew to Paris, full of worry. He'd seen how Carlo was, living with my parents. I'd tried to put it out of my mind, tell myself it was temporary. Chris couldn't do that." Her voice was soft. "We sat at a café in the shadow of St. Germain-des-Prés, the cathedral in my dream, while he begged me to give him Carlo. And when that didn't work, he blackmailed me. For the son that was never his."

Paget covered his face. Some deeply irrational part of him wanted to turn back the clock and erase the tape from his mind. But when he felt Terri reach for it, he grasped her hand. "It's too late," he said softly. "For fifteen years, it's been too late."

The tears ran down her face. "I did this," she murmured. "I did this."

He shook his head. "*I* did. When you were younger than Carlo is now." He saw Terri swallow; the tape spun inexorably on—silence, then static, then silence again.

"Did you think about telling Chris then?" Steinhardt finally asked. "In Paris?"

"I couldn't bring myself to do it." Her voice fell. "I took the coward's way out. I tried every way I knew to discourage him. Just as I'd refused any help from him once Carlo was born. But this time, nothing worked." The irony returned, this time mixed with sadness. "He was Carlo's father, he told me. He was willing to sacrifice his marriage to save him—his own reputation, even. And mine."

"How did that make you feel?"

"That Chris would do anything he had to do." Her voice softened again. "And that in the end, I'd given Carlo the right father."

"The right father," Paget murmured, "for Jack Woods's son."

As Terri took his hand, Steinhardt spoke again. "Was that why you let him go, Mary?"

There was silence. "I let him go," she finally answered, "because Chris made me think. About who he really was, and who I wanted Carlo to be." Her voice became sad, yet certain. "You see, I realized that Chris wasn't really like me, after all."

In the quiet that followed, Paget shook his head. "Then what is your sin?" Steinhardt asked.

"That I could let my son go," she said softly. "And that I lied to Chris twice. The first to save myself, the second to save Carlo."

"Did you feel you were saving Carlo?"

"I thought of my own childhood. What Chris said about the damage to Carlo scared me." She paused. "But not enough to give up my career. Only enough to give up Carlo, and to use Christopher Paget one more time. And the only thing I can say to myself is that when I did it, I was thinking more of Carlo than of either Chris or me."

"Have you thought of telling Chris *now?*"

There was more silence. "I always do," she said, in muted tones. "But I tell myself that it would hurt them far too much." She paused again. "They love each other now. With every day I allow to pass, it would hurt them more."

"Then why are you so troubled?"

"Because I could lie about that. Because I could do what I did. Because I'm not troubled enough." Her voice fell. "Because there's something missing in me, and always will be."

Through his anger and anguish, something in Paget found the words both sad and frightening. On the tape, Steinhardt asked, "How does that make you feel?"

"Free," Mary answered softly. "Free, and very alone. Like no one can touch me." There was another pause; for a moment, Mary sounded close to tears. "What Chris could do for Carlo, I could never do. I could never feel enough. I only feel enough to stay away from them. To not face what I've done."

Perhaps, Paget thought, Mary was crying, but too quietly to be heard. Then Steinhardt asked, "Where are you going?"

"I'm leaving." Mary sounded weary, but composed again. "I came here wondering if I should tell Chris the truth. But I can't."

"That's not the only reason to seek help."

There was a final silence. "There's no help for who I am," Mary said quietly. "And never will be."

Terri let go of Paget's hand. A moment later, at the margin of his consciousness, he heard her switch off the tape.

Paget sat there alone.

The central act of his life, the raising of a son, had no more meaning than his lies to the Senate. They were the acts of a fool, mired in vanity and self-deception.

Did you ever love someone, he had asked Terri, so much that it hurts?

Elena, she had told him, and Paget had answered, For me, it's Carlo.

Jack Woods's son.

He did not realize that he was crying. Then Terri took him in her arms, pressing his head between her breasts, her face resting on the top of his head.

"I'm so sorry," she whispered.

When he looked up at her, she brushed the hair back from his forehead with her fingertips. "What can I do?" she asked.

"I need to be alone with this," he said. "It's a lot to sort out."

She nodded. "What will *you* do?"

"I have no idea." He paused. "About anything."

Terri let him go. For a moment, she stood next to him, hand resting on his shoulder. Then she started toward the door.

She stopped there, turning. "She's right, Chris. You're not like her. That's why it all happened."

He could think of nothing to say.

"I'll be in my office," she told him and left, closing the door gently behind her.

THREE

WITHOUT MAKEUP, Mary's eyes seemed hollow, her face drawn. She had the strung-out look of a woman too wired to sleep. Finding Paget at the door seemed to startle her, as if the hearing had eaten through her nerve ends.

"What do you want?" she asked.

Paget simply stared at her. Softly, he said, "You seem to have lost your tolerance for surprises."

Mary stared from the doorway, like a woman wrenched from her private space by someone who was threatening her. She made no move to ask him in. "Shouldn't you be preparing your argument?" she asked.

"I seem to be having trouble with it."

Her eyes narrowed. "And you've come here for my help."

"In a manner of speaking."

She paused, waiting for him to say more. He said nothing.

Finally, she stepped aside. The gesture was grudging, almost angry. When he walked to the middle of the suite and turned to her, she still held the door.

"You might want to close that," he said.

Slowly, she did. She stood, gazing at the doorknob, as if reluctant to face him. There was a new fragility to her movements, Paget thought.

Turning, she squared her shoulders. *"You're* behaving strangely," she said.

"Am I?"

"Yes." She paused. "I really don't appreciate this."

"What, precisely?"

"Your just showing up. What is it you want?"

Paget gazed around him, choosing a place to sit. The drapes were drawn; there was nothing of Mary in the antiseptic room. It was as if personal possessions were clues, to be hidden from intruders.

"The truth," he answered. "I'd prefer to hear it sitting down. But you can stand there if you like."

He walked to the couch and sat, gazing up at her with a look of mild interest. "You can start anytime," he said. "I've got till ten o'clock tomorrow."

Her mouth opened to speak, closed again. "What is it, damn you? Bass?"

Paget watched her. "I'm not here to discuss why I want the truth. I simply want it."

"Then you can leave. You already have the truth." She folded her arms. "Your cross on Bass was right. Whatever Ransom could or couldn't do, I was frightened."

"No," Paget said softly, "you were rational. And once I understood that, I knew the reason you delayed in calling 911."

"And what is that?"

"To cover up the murder you'd been planning." To Paget, his own voice seemed to come from a distance, very calm and very polite. "There *is* one point you can help me with. What were you doing in the hallway?"

"I was in shock, damn it." Mary stood rigid, clenching her fists, voice rising as she spoke. "Do you find some pleasure in tormenting me? Wasn't the trial enough for you?"

"No. It wasn't."

"Please, Chris, *leave*." Her voice sounded brittle. "Leave me alone. I don't want you here. The place I need you is in court."

"But I can't leave." Paget spoke with exaggerated patience, as if to a child. "You haven't answered my question."

"There *is* no answer."

"Oh, I'm sure there must be."

"Why? Because you've been talking to your diminutive friend, Ms. Peralta?"

Paget raised his eyebrows. "What does Terri have to do with this?"

"Will you *stop*." The first edge of Boston Italian appeared in her speech, as if her persona were unraveling. "I can't remember *what* I was doing."

"It may come back to you." Casually, Paget took the tape from his pocket and placed it on the coffee table, still looking up at her. "Why don't you think for a moment."

As if by reflex, Mary drew up her hands. Her face was white.

"Of course, you may not remember what's on *this*, either." Paget's voice became softer yet. "Five years is a long time in the life of a parent. And it's one third of the life of your son."

Mary turned to the window. In the silence, she was stiff and still, and then her shoulders began trembling.

Paget stood. "Look at me, damn you. You had the courage to kill a man. All that you did to *me* was change my life. It shouldn't be too difficult to look me in the face."

Silent, Mary shook her head. She did not turn. The tremors ran through her body.

"I lied for you," Paget continued. "I left Washington because of you, abandoned the career I'd wanted. I let my marriage founder and raised Carlo as my son, because of you. And now, because of you, I've found out what a joke it's all been."

Mary's head bent forward. Her body shook in spasms now, but still she made no sound.

"*Look* at me," Paget demanded. "You can use people, or kill them, or just warp their lives. People aren't real to you—*I'm* not real to you. You don't see anyone apart from what you want. For you, the only excuse I or anyone has for living is to serve as your pawn. So the least you can do is look at me."

Mary's back straightened.

Slowly, she turned to him. Tears ran down her face.

Paget struggled for self-control. It took all that he had; he felt no pity, but his voice was still soft. "Forgive me if I sound harsh," he said. "But I just found out that you arranged for me to raise Jack Woods's son as mine. And you know how *I* hate surprises."

Mary tried to speak, could not. Her hands touched her chest in a posture of grieving and shock.

"You're a remarkable woman," Paget said. "You helped me send Carlo's father to prison to save your own career, and used *his* son to make me help you. It's hard to put a name to that."

"Don't you *know*," Mary burst out, "why I went to Ransom's suite?"

"Of course. To kill him."

"*No.*" Through her tears, Mary's voice shook with pain and anger. "To do anything he wanted. So that you and Carlo would never hear that tape."

Paget was silent. "It's touching," he said finally, "to consider the sacrifices you've made on my behalf. The guilt may be too much for me to live with."

Mary seemed to blanch. She half turned from him, face wet with tears, arms crossed as if to hold herself in. Her shoulders quivered; she looked desolate and alone.

Paget did not move or speak. He simply watched her; his sole expression was one of distaste.

All at once, Mary sat down on the rug.

Her face bent to her hands; there was one convulsive sob, and then the sounds that followed were like keening. Whatever had happened with Ransom, the lies and torment that had come from it had pushed her to the edge. Now, at last, the second tape had shattered her: the Mary Carelli that Paget saw was the one woman he had never imagined.

Paget waited until the keening stopped. Walking across the room, he stood over her, holding the tape in his hand.

"Then tell me." The quiet in his voice was anger, barely controlled. "Everything. But not until you look me in the face."

For a long moment, Mary's face stayed in her hands. Then her face rose to meet his gaze. "It wasn't *me,*" she said, "who did those things with Ransom."

"The things you say Ransom wanted? Or killing him?"

Mary swallowed. "The things I did for him," she said at last. "Only killing him was me."

"Then tell me," he repeated.

Slowly, Mary nodded. "All right," she answered quietly. "But I can't talk about this with you standing over me."

Paget stifled a harsh response. He thought of pulling her up, then decided that he did not wish to touch her.

After a moment, he sat cross-legged on the floor, several feet from her. "You can start," he said, "with Ransom's first call."

Mary looked at her hands. "It was simple," she said at last. "Ransom described the tapes and said he'd give them to me." Her voice became muted. "One meeting at a time."

"Was he more specific?"

"He said that I had a choice. He could undress me in public or in private." Her tone turned bitter. "He wanted to be fair with me, he said. I should understand that in private, I would do anything he asked me to do. So I shouldn't assume that my 'private exposure' would be any less humiliating than 'public exposure.' "

"And you agreed?"

"No. I took his number and said that I'd call back. When I put down the telephone, my hand was shaking." Mary hesitated. "Then I went to the bathroom and threw up. Just as I said in court."

Mary paused for breath. When she began speaking again, her voice was weaker. "I couldn't imagine it: how this man could have *those* tapes; why he needed to do this to *me*. I couldn't sleep that night. I thought of everything—the Lasko case, Steinhardt, my career, Carlo. Even you. And then, after that, I imagined what Ransom must want." Her eyes shut. "In the morning, I called him back."

"What did you say?"

"That I would meet him." Mary's eyes remained closed. "If he gave me my choice of tapes."

For the first time, Paget hesitated. "You asked for the second?"

"Yes."

Paget fell silent. After a time, he asked, "Why did you buy the gun?"

Mary's eyes opened. "Because I was afraid," she answered simply. "Once we were alone, I didn't know what he would do."

Paget searched her face. "The night before, you came to see us. After eight years."

"I came to see Carlo." Her gaze was steadier now. "It was *me* who said that I'd meet Ransom in San Francisco. I was still torn about what to do. I thought, in a strange way, that seeing Carlo might help me."

"How?"

"Enable me to go through with it." Abruptly, she looked down. "If you and Carlo found out the truth, then no good would have come of letting you believe he was your son. I wanted to believe that good had come of it."

"And did you?"

"When I saw Carlo, I knew that he was happy. It made up my mind. Because I knew that good *had* come of it." Her voice fell. "Until now."

Paget looked past her, struggling for calm, felt his grip tighten on the tape. For this moment, he told himself, put your emotions aside. First you should know the truth.

"What happened," he asked, "when you got to the room?"

Mary still stared at the floor. "Ransom opened the door. He didn't say anything. Just looked at me, with a strange smile on his face. His expression was almost gloating, and yet I felt the tension beneath it. It was like walking into a nightmare.

"He still wouldn't talk. I put my purse on the coffee table, where I could reach the gun." Hesitant, she tried to look at Paget again. "Then I asked him to play the tape for me. *My* tape."

"And did he?"

Slowly, she nodded. "Listening to it—my voice, Steinhardt's questions—brought back how I'd felt. When I couldn't look at him anymore, he put his hand on my breast, like he did with Marcy Linton." Her gaze broke. "And when I didn't take it away, Ransom knew we had a deal. He'd never had to say a word."

Paget's stomach felt hollow; since Bass's testimony, he had not eaten. He found that he could not ask questions.

"The first thing he said," Mary told him softly, "was that we would share a bottle of Roederer Cristal. Because Laura Chase drank Cristal with her lovers. After she undressed for them." Mary touched her eyes. "Once the room service waiter left the suite, I knew that I would have to take off my clothes. That was why I asked him to hang the privacy sign."

Paget was silent. Mary had stopped crying; her shame seemed beyond tears. "Ransom put the tape between us," she murmured, "and watched me undress.

"When I was naked, he motioned me to the couch, to sit facing him. He positioned me in a certain way." The sudden anger in her voice was like the memory of hate. "He wanted to see each part of me, he said, without having to tell me what to show him. Because the tape I was about to hear demanded my total attention."

"Laura Chase," Paget said softly.

Mary nodded, still looking away. "I was to listen carefully, he said, while he inspected me. So that I could do for him what Laura had done for James Colt." Mary paused. "Then he made me drink a toast to Laura Chase."

Mary seemed to shiver again. Drained of defiance or calculation, she looked tired and too thin. But her narrative had taken on a relentless quality; Paget had wanted the truth, and now she would spare neither of them. "I sat there, listening to that tape: Laura Chase describing in a lost voice what she had done for those men, what they had *made* her do.

"With each act she described, Ransom would smile at me and then slowly move his eyes across my body." Mary paused again; for a moment, her voice was thick. "By the time the tape was over, the champagne was almost welcome.

"He still didn't speak. I sat there in his silence, watching him look at each part of me, taking his time. There was an almost casual cruelty in it, as if he were making sure that degrading me still held interest for him." Mary raised her head. "Then he smiled," she finished quietly, "and started to rewind the tape."

Mary's eyes stayed fixed on Paget. "He didn't need to say anything. When the tape finished rewinding, I would be standing in front of him, doing what Laura Chase had done.

"I asked him to close the blinds. 'Do it yourself,' he told me. 'That way I can see how you move.' "

Her voice had become flat; to Paget, it made what had happened seem inexorable. "I went to the window," she said. "Below me was the city, people going about their normal lives. I stood looking out, wishing I was one of them, not wanting to turn and face Mark Ransom. That was when John Hassler saw me."

The mood had shifted again; the flat words held an understated horror and, beneath that, irony—Mary had lied about what Hassler saw, but the scene as Hassler witnessed it was more illusion than truth. Softly, Mary said, "Then I heard Laura's voice again, and pulled down the blind.

"When I turned, Ransom stopped the tape.

" 'You're already naked,' he told me. 'So when I turn on the tape, I want you to start dancing. Please listen to Laura carefully.' Then he smiled again, and said, 'I want Laura Chase to be your teacher.' "

Mary swallowed again. "He tried to sound casual, in command. But I'd started to feel something desperate beneath it—as though if I got it wrong I would break some spell. Before, I was disbelieving, angry, ashamed. Now I felt frightened.

"When I began moving for him, he took his penis out.

"I felt like a courtesan. Dancing to make him hard, as Laura told me how." Color came to her face. "I did whatever Laura Chase did, desperate to be as Ransom imagined her, until I felt more like Laura than me. It was like losing my soul."

Paget shook his head. "Why did you do all that?"

Mary gave him a silent prideful look, the first semblance of her former self. "The tape he made me dance for would destroy Carlo," she said simply. "And the tape I didn't ask for would destroy *me*. I wanted them both."

"But to keep on ..."

"I was alone with him." Mary looked at Paget steadily. "As Mark Ransom watched me dancing, standing with his penis in his hand, I knew he was insane. I was afraid of what would happen to me if I couldn't make him hard.

"I kept listening to Laura. When Laura touched herself, I touched myself. And when it was time to slide down the wall and masturbate for Mark Ransom, I did that too." Her voice became callous, almost brutal. "It's not the first time a woman has pretended to come. Women my age were taught to be actresses for men, in all sorts of ways, first by our mothers. It was like a tribal skill, still there when I needed it. I was merely glad that Laura Chase had kept her eyes closed.

"When I felt his penis enter my mouth, I knew that it had worked." She paused. "I began to suck him. Just like Laura on the tape."

All at once, Mary stopped talking.

She pulled up her knees, hugging them close to her. Paget watched her force rhythmic breaths through her body, in and out and in again, until the quivering ceased. When she looked up, her face was naked once more: it was as if the long repression of her feelings had exhausted her. The wetness in her eyes was fresh.

"That was when it happened," she said quietly.

Her voice had changed again. It was sadder and softer, one human speaking to another; for once, appearing vulnerable seemed less like a choice she had made than all she could do. It made Paget feel a kind of dread.

"*What* happened?" he asked.

Her eyes opened wide, as though comprehending something for the first time. "As I sucked him," she said, "his penis started turning soft.

"He began cursing me in a strangled voice, telling me to suck harder. Nothing worked." Stopping, Mary took another deep breath. "I looked up at him. The back of my head was against the wall, his penis still in my mouth. He was staring down at himself. His eyes were angry and frightened all at once." She paused again, voice lower. "When his gaze met mine, his penis slipped from my mouth.

"He looked down again, watching himself shrivel.

"I was afraid to look away. I stayed very still, trapped between Ransom and the wall, watching with him. Every second he grew smaller scared me more.

"I was still watching when he slapped me.

"I looked up, stunned, eyes blurring with tears. He slapped again, looked down at himself, slapped me again, looked at himself. Like slapping me would make him hard.

"I spun away, the room turning black in front of me, began crawling toward the coffee table. In the background, Laura was still describing what they did to her. It made me crawl faster. When I looked back, he was still staring at himself." Her voice sounded shaken. "Tears were running down his face.

"It stopped me. I just knelt there by the coffee table, naked, watching him as he cried.

"Then he saw me."

Mary's gaze was fixed; she seemed to be looking not at Paget but at Mark Ransom. "The rage and humiliation came to his eyes. He stared at me like an animal, face red with anger, pants around his ankles. It was like he felt too much hatred to speak.

"He began walking toward me.

"His pants were still down, and his movements were jerky, almost bestial, as if his failure had swept away whatever made him human. Then he raised his hand again." Her voice took on a visceral intensity. "There was something primal about it—an absence of limits. Before, he wanted to punish me, to help make himself hard. Now he wanted to destroy me.

"Looking at each other, we both knew that.

"I grabbed my purse." She stopped again: in her silence, Paget felt the combustible moment when Mark Ransom's pathology triggered Mary's will to survive. "My fingers were numb. I could barely get the gun out.

"When I turned with it, still shaking, he was maybe six feet from me.

"His eyes widened." She paused at the memory. "For an instant, he just stood there. Then he started toward me again. He seemed so enraged that he could imagine nothing else but reaching me."

Mary's voice became staccato. "I was still on my knees. 'Stop,' I called out. He didn't.

"Now he was four feet away. I still couldn't shoot." Her eyes closed. "And then he called me a worthless cunt.

"All at once, I hated him enough to shoot.

"Maybe I could have stopped him—his pants kept him from moving fast. Maybe I could have shot him in the leg. It didn't matter anymore." Pausing, Mary shook her head. "All that abuse and then, with a single word, he made me the same person *he* was." She stopped again, and spoke her next words slowly and distinctly. "The only thing I cared about was killing Mark Ransom.

"My hands stopped shaking. He was four feet from me when I shot him in the heart."

The new calm in her voice gave Paget a chill. Her eyes opened again, staring past him. "He didn't so much fall as stop. His eyes were blind with shock. It was as if he were no longer in the room, and I was no longer there.

"He slumped a little. His face became sad, almost puzzled. Then he crumpled, sitting on the floor.

"Tears came to his eyes again. The last thing he did was mumble a single word." Mary's voice filled with wonder. " 'Laura.' He whispered the name 'Laura.'

"The blood drained from his face. I knew he was dead before he had fallen backward.

"Suddenly I was alone.

"I tried to take it in. A moment before, Mark Ransom might have killed me. Now he was a corpse with his pants around his ankles." The tone of wonder returned. "I was sitting next to him, naked in a strange hotel suite, with a tape filled with secrets sitting on the coffee table."

Paget tried to imagine it. But there were too many layers—shock, horror, shame, and disbelief—for him to understand how Mary could have coped. As if by reflex, he looked at the tape in his hand.

Her gaze followed his. "I had killed a man," she said slowly. "For a prosecutor, my tape would explain why. But without my tape, there was no explaining his naked genitals, exposed so I could please him. Or the tape of Laura Chase.

"On some level, even through my shock, I understood all that. It was like being under anesthesia but still conscious.

"I never really had a plan. It came to me in pieces—jumbled, out of order. The only thread was that I had come there to conceal the tape, and now I had to conceal why I'd come."

Her voice was thin, emotionless. It was as if she had been drugged and now was trying to reconstruct actions she dimly remembered and barely understood.

"It all seemed too hard," she said. "For a moment, I thought of giving up, just telling the truth. Then I thought of Carlo." She paused. "And, of course, myself."

There would be no more tears, Paget thought. She was too spent for emotion or, it seemed, dissembling. There was nothing left to hide.

"Finally," she went on, "I forced myself to look at Ransom. He was lying there, mouth open, sprawled on his back like someone who had died in the middle of dressing himself. And then the first thought came to me: there was no explaining *anything* with Ransom as he was." Her voice turned cold. "I couldn't explain why he was half naked, or why I was naked with him. Let alone why he deserved to die.

"I remember being angry. What he had done to me was not just a violation of my body, but of *me*. And yet I could tell no one.

"He *violated* me, I kept thinking. He deserved to die, I told myself—what he did was worse than rape." Her voice filled with discovery, as if replicating the moment. "Rape," she said simply. "The first cousin of sexual blackmail. The only explanation I could give them.

"But how had he gotten me there? I wondered. He could be a rapist, but not a blackmailer. And then I remembered: he was writing a book about Laura Chase.

"Of course, I thought—*that* was why you came. For a *story*. To hear him play that tape.

"I suppose it was like writing a play. It explained my presence, Laura's tape, the cassette player. And when I looked down at him, remembering his pathology, I realized that Laura's tape would help explain why he was naked."

Through his grief and anger, Paget felt a kind of fascination. "So you rolled him over," he said softly. "Because a rapist would have been on top of you."

Mary met his eyes and then slowly nodded. "He was heavy," she said softly. "I had to reach beneath his buttocks to flip him over. That was when I left the scratches, and broke my nail."

Paget touched his forehead. "I said it was the paramedics."

"*Sharpe* said I did it to fake a struggle. Not even *I'm* that cold. I hated touching him."

Paget felt his eyes close, heard a sliver of shame in her voice. "Once he was on his side, I gave him a push. He fell sprawling like a rag doll, more limber than in life, his buttocks in the air." She paused, and then added, in a tone of surprise, "As I looked at him, my story became real.

"I felt a surge of crazy energy. Don't *feel*, I told myself—just *do*. But I didn't know *what* to do." Her voice slowed, as if she were reliving the process of thought. "He hadn't penetrated me, of course. But I didn't know what that meant. So I thought of all the things a rapist might do before penetration, and did them."

Paget imagined her, standing naked over Ransom's body: half horrified, half rational, trying to think her way to freedom. His eyes opened. "You scratched yourself," he said.

"Yes." She paused. "And put a run in my panty hose. I didn't think about getting fibers beneath my nails."

Paget found himself trying to think with her, floundering and desperate, knowing little of police work. Quietly, he said, "There were still the tapes."

After a time, Mary nodded. "I knew that. But I couldn't think anymore. Not until I got dressed."

She looked bemused. "It was strange," she said quietly. "He'd taken so much from me. But with clothes on, I was more myself. Only Mark Ransom was naked.

"I walked to the coffee table and picked up the tape.

"I stood there, the tape clutched in my hand. Somewhere out of reach was another tape, which could ruin my life. But the tape I was holding would ruin Carlo's, and yours." She stopped for a moment, adding quietly, "Once I got rid of it, I could tell them I was only there because of Laura Chase, and hope they never found the other tape.

"One by one, I clicked off the possibilities.

"I couldn't throw my tape out the window. If I tried to flush it down the toilet, the cassette might get stuck there." She paused. "I'd started checking my watch, trying to fight the panic I was feeling. And then, for some reason, I remembered the mail slot in the hallway."

Mary began speaking faster. "In a kind of frenzy, I began looking for an envelope. I was too rushed to worry about fingerprints. Too panicky to look first where it was logical to look—the desk.

"I got to it last. When I opened the drawer, there were envelopes.

"Then I saw the other tape. I thought it might be *my* other tape, and that Ransom had been listening to it. But I didn't know; Steinhardt's numbering system meant nothing to me. I couldn't listen to it myself—I didn't have time, and I'd leave fingerprints on the cassette player.

"I just grabbed it.

"There was a pen in the drawer, but I couldn't use it—fingerprints again. All at once, I saw how stupid I was being. If I mailed it to myself, and they arrested me, the police would find it before I did." She paused, catching her breath. "And then something more basic came to me. I had no stamps.

"I started shaking.

"I couldn't stop myself. I took a pen from my purse and crossed out 'Hotel Flood' on the envelope. I stood there trembling while I tried to imagine the fate of an envelope with no postage and no return address, wending its way through the postal system."

Mary stopped, shaking her head. "I had no idea. The only image I could fix on was some bureaucrat sorting mail at the post office, uncaring and uncurious, throwing out the tapes because no one had sent them and no one could receive them." Mary gave a small, mirthless smile. "So I decided to put Carlo's fate in the hands of the government. The one thing that never occurred to me was that *his* fate was Lindsay Caldwell's."

Silent, Paget stared at the tape he held. She saw that and looked away.

"I put them in the mail slot," she said softly. "Just before that pompous investment banker got off the elevator.

"When I went inside the room and closed the door behind me, I knew I was out of time.

"I didn't really have a story. Only fragments." She paused again. "When I called 911, all I had were my own resources. As you've been so fond of pointing out, that was hardly enough."

For a moment, she was silent. Then she looked up at him again. "Of course," she said quietly, "I also had you."

His eyes met hers. "Why?" he asked. "Because you could manipulate me?"

"You underestimate yourself, Chris. You're the smartest lawyer I know. I also counted on your feeling for Carlo." Paget saw her hesitate, the shame in her eyes becoming a question. "I believed you'd protect the tapes better than anyone. And that, God forbid, if you ever heard them, you'd make sure that Carlo never did."

For a long time, Paget looked at her without speaking. "Fifteen years ago," he finally said, "I wasn't sure if Carlo was mine. But after he came to live with me, I stopped wondering. I didn't want to anymore." His voice grew softer. "My life may have disappointed me, partly on account of you. But at least I had a son."

The quiet words seemed to devastate her. Her shoulders slumped, and she looked away. "Withdraw as my lawyer, Chris. You don't have to go to court tomorrow."

"Do you think that will fix things, Mary? Knowing what I know? Holding this tape in my hand?" He paused, voice lower. "And it would be like telling the world you're guilty."

She gave a tired shrug. "I wonder if that's any worse than living with *this* has been. And I *am* guilty, I suppose. Because I'll never know whether I needed to kill him."

"Nor do I. If that matters."

She straightened, as if gathering strength. "I lied to you. You owe me nothing. I ask only that you never tell Carlo what you know." She looked into his face, a quiet plea in her voice. "I'll plead guilty, if you like. But destroy this tape, Chris. Please."

Paget watched her, not answering. Then he stood. "You've no right to ask for anything, Mary. But you're certainly free to hope."

He turned abruptly, and left.

FOUR

"How's it going, Dad?"

Carlo stood in the entrance to the library. He was trying to sound casual, Paget realized, but he had the abstracted gaze of someone who had spent the afternoon in thought, and his voice was too quiet. Paget did not want to look at him.

"I'm pretty tired." Paget stared at his drink. "I have a lot to think about."

His voice was not welcoming, nor did he wish it to be. He did not know what he would do about anything: reassuring Carlo was beyond him, and he did not have the resources to lie. All that he wanted from anyone was that they want nothing from him.

But Carlo could not know this. He walked inside, flicking on the illuminated chandelier. "This room is pretty weird without the lights."

Paget sipped his drink. "I'm capable of finding the switch."

Carlo paused, as if deciphering his mood. Quietly, he said, "You think she's guilty, don't you?"

Paget did not turn. "If you really care to know, Carlo, I'm sick of thinking about her at all."

"*Jesus.*" Carlo's voice rose with sudden strain: it still had the lightness of youth, but there was something new in it. "Why do you hate her so much? What did she ever do to you?"

The words had an angry timbre that Paget had never heard from Carlo and yet touched a chord of memory: it was like that of Jack Woods on the last night they had faced each other, with Mary Carelli—their lover—standing between them. The thought made Paget turn to Carlo.

The boy he saw now startled him. His face was older; it had the look of a man whom Paget had despised. The blue eyes were not Paget's at all.

How, Paget wondered, could he have failed to see it?

"It's as she's always said," Paget replied. "I'm an insensitive bastard."

Carlo stared at him, as if at a stranger. "You think she's guilty," he repeated.

Guilty of a thousand things, Paget thought. Guilty of this moment, as he faced the son who was no longer his and yet who felt the anger of a son. "You were the one who wanted to be there," Paget said. "What do you want from me now? To tell you that she's wonderful?"

Carlo reddened. "What are you angry at *me* for? *I* didn't ask for any of this. Or for either one of you."

Paget caught himself, expelled a long breath. "I know you didn't," he said tonelessly.

Carlo watched him. "You've been surprised in court before. You can't just fall apart on her."

"Who said I'm falling apart? I'm just sick of people leaning on me."

Carlo stiffened. "Like me?"

"Like your mother. It seems I've spent my life cleaning up her messes." Paget lowered his voice again. "It's complicated, and much too personal. You wouldn't understand."

"Try me."

Paget shook his head. "No," he said softly. "Thank you."

"You mean you'd rather take it out on me." Carlo's voice was raw. "Do you think you're alone? This hasn't been any day at the beach for *me*, you know. *She's* my mother, and I have to live with *you*."

"I'm sorry I've been such a burden." Paget answered politely. "Would you rather not live here?"

Carlo shoved his hands in his pockets. "Would you like me to go?"

The boy's words quivered with pain and anger. "I didn't want to have this conversation," Paget said. "I *don't* want to have this conversation."

Carlo turned from him. "All I wanted was to talk to you. It didn't have to be about *her*."

The stark request took Paget by surprise. For a moment, he saw not Jack Woods but a lonely seven-year-old boy.

"I'm sorry," Paget told him. "This case has taken a lot out of me. Too much, it seems."

Carlo looked down at him with Jack Woods's eyes. "Mark Ransom was a piece of shit."

Paget shook his head. "This isn't about Mark Ransom."

"Then what *is* it with you and her?"

"History."

"Fifteen years is too long to hold a grudge." Carlo paused. "She doesn't hate *you*."

"You don't know anything about us, Carlo. It was a mistake for me to do this. Perhaps it's best if Mary gets another lawyer."

Carlo stared at him. *"Now?"*

"Yes."

"But you can't do that. Not on the last day."

Paget faced him again. "She and I have already discussed it. She left it up to me."

Carlo paused, trying to absorb the implications. "What is it that I don't know?"

There was no use in lying. "Quite a lot."

Carlo sat down. Softly, he asked, "Did she admit killing him?"

The conversation was so pointless, Paget thought: the central issue between Paget and Carlo's mother was not Mark Ransom's murder, and had never been. "She *did* kill him," Paget answered. "The question was whether she killed him in self-defense."

" 'Was,' " Carlo quoted. "So now you don't think she's innocent."

The anxious questions annoyed Paget—he no longer cared whether Mark Ransom had deserved to die. But the only way to explain that to Carlo was to tell him the truth: Your mother lied to the Senate. She lied to this court. I covered for her fifteen years ago, and tomorrow, if I'm still her lawyer, I'll have to cover for her again. And by the way, you're not my son. I just found out she lied about that too.

"I don't think she planned to kill him," Paget said. "But I question my effectiveness. So does she."

"Because of that psychiatrist?"

"No. Because of *us*."

" 'Because of *us*,' " Carlo repeated. "What has *she* ever asked you for? You sit here telling me what a burden she is, and she's never even been around. And now that she is, and really needs you for once, you treat her like dirt."

Paget stood. "I *will* not talk about this, damn it."

"We're going to." Carlo rose to face him, voice trembling. *"You* drove her away, didn't you? She was never welcome here—"

"*Stop this,* Carlo. Right now."

Carlo shook his head. "*I* never had a mother because *you* never wanted me to have one. You wanted me to yourself. And now that I may lose her again, you won't lift a finger." Carlo paused, catching his breath, and then spoke more slowly. "I always looked up to you. But now I see how selfish you are. You say you're sick of my mother? Well, I'm sick of *you.*"

Paget clenched his fists, rigid with hurt and anger. "You have no right to be sick of me, Carlo. You don't know how little right you have."

Carlo's face was a mask of pain. "Don't talk down to me. I don't respect you enough to listen."

In one angry motion, Paget picked up his drink glass. Carlo's white face was three feet from him. Paget suddenly turned and flung the glass at the palm tree outside.

As the window shattered, Carlo flinched but did not move.

"Then you won't have to listen," Paget said softly, and left the house.

Teresa Peralta's headlights cut the darkness.

The beach was deserted. A full moon lent the ocean a touch of light, silver on obsidian, shimmering at low tide. But the sand itself was dull black, as if stained by an oil slick. At its edge, perhaps a hundred yards away, Terri saw the lone figure of a man, staring out at the water.

There were no other cars. She parked where the cement ended, got out. The man turned at the sound of her car door slamming.

Terri moved toward him, sand giving way beneath her feet. The night was still warm; she hardly felt the breeze in her face. The rolling tide was a deep susurrus of sound.

The man stood waiting, as if uncertain of who she was. His hands were shoved in his pockets; backlit by the moon, he looked slender and solitary. As she came nearer, she saw that he had not changed from court; his shirtsleeves were rolled up, and his tie and collar loosened. He looked much too young to have lived the life he had lived and to bear what it had brought him now. All that she wanted to do was hold him.

She stopped two feet away, looking up into his face.

"It's all a mess," Christopher Paget said.

Terri nodded. After hours of aimless driving, he had called her on his car phone, ostensibly to explain why he had not called her before; he had told her just enough for her to sense that beneath his emotionless words, Paget felt lost.

"The beach is where *I* come," she told him, "when it gets to be too much. But never at night."

Paget gazed at her. "Was there trouble with Richie?" he asked.

Terri hesitated. It was she, not Paget, who had suggested that they meet; it was not the night to explain her relationship to Richie, and there might never be such a night. Best to stick to the simple truth—that Richie had not objected much—and omit the reason: that Richie had commenced a relentless campaign to keep her, appealing to her sense of family while reading one self-help book after another, swearing that their marriage could be healed if only Terri tried as hard as he was trying. It made her weary, and guilty about her dead emotions. She felt as though by asserting herself she had changed him, so that now he—and Elena—deserved the second chance Terri was not sure she wanted to give. Letting her leave without complaint was part of the new Richie: if Christopher Paget would ever be one of Richie's weapons again, Terri sensed, it would be after she was bound to the marriage once more, perhaps by the second child Richie had begun to press for.

"Richie was fine about it," she told Paget. "He knows we still have work to do." She paused, looking into his face. "Do we?"

He gave a weary shrug. "I don't know."

"What happened, Chris?"

Paget did not answer. He turned from her, hands still in his pockets, and began walking along the edge of the water. Terri understood that she was to walk with him; they moved in silence, tide lapping near their feet, the Golden Gate Bridge to their back, scattered car lights moving slowly across it. To their left was a rocky hillside; above them, the sprawling stucco houses of Seacliff overlooked the water, much as Terri imagined an Italian hill town. Paget did not seem to notice; he was silent for a long time, and when he began to speak, he gazed at the sand in front of him.

He talked for perhaps an hour.

He told her everything. His voice was uninflected, yet unsparing of himself or anyone else. When he had finished, they had turned back toward the Golden Gate, and Terri was exhausted.

"What will you do?" she asked.

"I don't know." He paused. "It's like something's broken. I don't even know where to start."

Terri watched him for a moment. "It's so unfair, Chris. I feel that for you."

"Carlo?"

"Everything."

Paget gave a tired shrug. "Carlo doesn't know," he said. "If I'm looking for perfect justice, I suppose I'll have to look somewhere else. Mary seems to have that particular market cornered."

Terri moved closer. "She *is* his mother, Chris. When a parent isn't around, kids invent a person who makes them feel better about that. I think that's what Carlo must have done with Mary."

Paget's repeated shrug seemed the only way he had to slough off feeling. "That's how God made it big, I guess—by not being seen. So why not Mary?"

He was trying to sound fatalistic, Terri knew, but his voice had a weary undertone of bitterness. She waited him out.

"It's eight years of questions," he said finally. "We never really talked about his mother, or *why* he was living with me. Tonight was like a dam bursting." He paused, then, his voice lower, as if he was talking to himself: "Christ, what a fool I was."

Terri moved closer to him. "But there's nothing you can do about the past." Her own voice grew quieter. "Just as I wish I'd never found the tapes but know there's nothing I can do now. Just as there's nothing *you* can do to put off tomorrow."

Paget looked away. "God, I wish there were."

"But there isn't." She paused again. "You're going to have to deal with Carlo, and with Mary. But first you're going to have to keep on living with yourself. And whatever you do tomorrow will be part of that."

He turned away from her, toward the ocean. It was a gesture not of dismissal but of thought. Terri watched him stand there, framed by moonlight and black water. When she felt it was time, she moved beside him.

"You've been a lawyer for almost twenty years," she said. "Lawyers protect their clients."

Paget did not turn. "I wasn't her lawyer," he replied, "when I lied to the Senate."

"But you are now, Chris. Mary may not have told Caroline the truth, but it's at least as close to the truth as Marnie's version." She paused. "Whatever Mary did to Ransom, it wasn't murder. She was battered, degraded, and deeply frightened—close to breaking, it seems. What she did was somewhere between manslaughter and self-defense, and I doubt even Mary can know which one." Her voice gained intensity. "Think of her as just a client, if you can. How much does a woman have to take before killing a man is self-defense? Does she have to know to a moral certainty that he would *kill* her? For *me*, what he had already done, and what he was threatening to do, is more than enough."

"She *lied*, Terri. As always."

Terri waited. "Do you mean that she lied to Caroline," she asked, "or lied to you? Because if her sin for these purposes is that she lied to protect herself in court, you'd be the first to say that clients do that all the time. It's only *your* sin if you were part of it."

"You know I wasn't."

Terri nodded. "Then there's no problem of ethics here. You can argue the evidence. Or Sharpe's lack of evidence."

"And cover for Mary again."

"You can avoid that, Chris, by pulling out. You've got the right. But if you do, she won't just lose in *this* hearing. People will believe you're withdrawing because she's guilty of murder." Terri paused again, then finishied quietly: "And as much as I dislike her, I don't think she is."

"It's a little hard for me to care."

Terri hesitated. "She *did* try to protect you, in her way. At least with Ransom." She gazed at him intently. "I'd guess that most of the people you've defended are far more guilty than Mary. If you let this happen to her, that will become part of what you take from this. Do you want that?"

Silent, Paget bent to pick up a piece of driftwood. For a moment, he turned it in his hand. Then, as if gauging its capacity for flight, he slowly turned and flung it out to sea.

"It's not Mary I'm worried about," Terri told him softly. "It's you."

He turned to look at her. In the semidark, she could not read his face.

"It's Wednesday night," she said. "On Friday morning, you're going to wake up and start living with what you've learned. But you'll also have to live with what you've done. How would you rather face Mary and Carlo?"

"I don't know." His voice was equally quiet. "Really, I don't."

She moved closer to him, fingertips touching his shirt. "You may not be there for Carlo, or Carlo for you. How will you feel then, if you've abandoned Mary? And if you and Carlo still want to be together, dropping Mary will have made that harder. Impossible, perhaps."

"Ah, Terri . . ."

His voice, soft and despairing, trailed off to nothing. In the moonlight, his face seemed unspeakably sad.

"Carlo loves you," she said. "And he expects things from you. For better or worse, *you're* the person he's *learned* to expect things from." She paused, trying to find a way to reach him. "It may not be fair, Chris, but Carlo told you the truth as he understands it. The only thing worse than abandoning his mother is what you'd have to tell him to justify yourself."

Paget did not answer. Terri reached up, touching his face. "Finish this, Chris." Her voice was soft but clear. "Be yourself for one more day. Then you can choose who else to be."

FIVE

THE NEXT MORNING, Paget and Carlo rode in silence to the Hall of Justice.

Paget had not slept. The sun cut into his eyes; he had turned off the radio to banish the cheery morning voices. Carlo—it hurt Paget not to think of him as his son—preserved a taut and edgy quiet. Paget could not tell whether Carlo was upset about their rupture and his own part in it; afraid that speaking would increase Paget's withdrawal; or restrained by some reflex of manners. Carlo did not ask what Paget would do.

Paget could not have answered him. The ebb and flow of feeling had become an undertow; he was not sure enough of himself to reassure anyone else. He had never felt this lost.

As they approached the Hall of Justice, he glanced at the profile of the boy who sat next to him. Carlo's thin face had become handsome with age, but his eyes were bleak as they swept the warehouses and parking lots and treeless sidewalks, as if looking for something he could never find. His face seemed so familiar, Paget thought, and yet so strange.

It was like the death of a parent. When his mother had died, and then his father, Paget had felt a shift in the world that was beyond his ability to change or comprehend. They had given him little but money, one part of Paget knew, but nonetheless they were the touchstones of his life—the first people he had tried to love and, because he had tried to love them all their lives, the people who made him think most deeply about the nature of love, the limits of understanding, the curse of mortality.

Now there was Carlo. He had believed in Carlo and himself much more than he had ever believed in his parents, believed from the perspective of adulthood, as someone who had chosen to be a father, drawing on the lessons he had learned from being a son. He and Carlo had redeemed the shortfall of his family in a way that was mysterious to him: his fathering of Carlo was like a gift of understanding he had sent his parents, when it was far too late to do it any other way. But then he had believed that his parents, and Carlo, were kin.

It was too much to assimilate now, if he ever could, that the end of Paget's family had been Paget himself. Or that his attempts to redeem the past and his highest hopes for the future—his vanity, perhaps—had been focused on the son of Jack Woods and Mary Carelli.

And yet here Carlo was, still sitting next to Paget, as he had for the past eight years.

Carlo watched the street as if it were a war zone. Mary was arriving by herself; as they parked and got out, Paget sensed that the boy was looking for his mother. Whether they would drive her was the one question that Carlo had asked; when Paget said no, he had lapsed into silence again.

On the steps, Paget and Carlo edged through the media gauntlet. The reporters pressed too close; their open mouths and hectoring questions reminded Paget of a drunk in a bar, demanding his attention, oblivious to the fact that he wished to be alone. As with yesterday, their questions centered on Dr. Bass or on what Paget would next argue. As with yesterday, Paget did not answer. He had ceased to care about them.

The only thing he noticed, at the edge of his vision, was Carlo.

Silent, the boy glanced at him as they pushed through the crowd. This time, Carlo said nothing to the press in defense of his mother; Paget had become certain that Carlo feared pushing him over the edge. The thought unsettled him: Paget's last eight years had been devoted to helping Carlo to trust and to feel safe. To be a source of worry to Carlo violated some deep instinct; the residue was guilt, and then anger at Mary.

Why was he here?

The weeks since Ransom died had changed him. Waiting for the elevator reminded him of taking it with Mary on the night the police had brought her in, their encounter with the media just moments away. Now, alone with Carlo, he felt like a different man: as they walked down the corridor, the memory of his first appearance here, on the day he had demanded this hearing, was like a dream. Entering the courtroom, he wished that he had never entered it before.

Yet they were all here. Reporters, their faces now familiar. Terri sitting calmly, with her notepad in front of her, as if their conversation on the beach had never happened. If Terri wondered what Paget would do, she gave no sign. Last night, she had tried to help him by speaking to his heart, and now she would try to help by acting like a lawyer.

Next to her was Mary.

They had not spoken since he left her hotel room. Now she turned to watch him coming toward her. Her expression, a surface calm covering deep watchfulness, triggered yet another image: it was how she had looked when Paget entered the Senate hearing room and she had not known what he would say or do. Paget first saw the difference—a certain fatalism—when he drew within a few feet of her. She gave an almost imperceptible shrug, an indication that she was resigned to whatever happened, and did not much care.

He sat next to her without speaking. She turned away, as if she knew to leave him alone. But he felt something deeper from her: buried shame, and quiet apology.

In a moment, Caroline Masters would enter, and nothing else would matter.

Sharpe sat poised at the prosecution table. She had the tensile alertness of a lawyer ready to argue her biggest case; it was odd, Paget thought, how the past twenty-four hours had opened a gulf between them. He no longer felt like a lawyer, or even like himself.

Looking past her, Paget saw McKinley Brooks.

Unobtrusive, the district attorney sat on a bench behind Sharpe. Save for the day of Linton's testimony, Paget had not seen him since Mary had turned down the offer of a plea bargain and Brooks had filed murder charges. The reason Brooks was here now, Paget knew, was politics: he would get a feeling for the courtroom and for Judge Masters, to add to the soundings he no doubt had taken from his precinct leaders and in the neighborhoods. He sat with his hands folded on his stomach, inscrutable as Buddha; catching Paget's gaze, he gave a small smile, which did not reach his eyes. The stakes were too high, Paget thought, for Brooks to pretend otherwise.

"All rise," the courtroom deputy called out, and Judge Caroline Masters ascended the bench.

She, too, looked different. At the beginning of the trial, Masters would commence the day with an alert, expectant look that bespoke some inner pleasure; she was a woman at the height of her powers, and they were finally being stretched a little closer to capacity. But now there was something muted about her: her face was somber, her expression inward. Paget could no more read her thoughts than he could those of McKinley Brooks.

He had expected Judge Masters to give some preface, tracing her expectation for the argument with incisiveness and a certain dry wit. But Masters did not do so. Nodding to Sharpe and then Paget, she said simply, "This is a great responsibility. Please do your best to help me."

It was far better than a speech. When Sharpe approached the podium, her manner was respectful, and her opening words were soft.

"For the district attorney, as well, this case is a responsibility which has occasioned great thought. We have tried to address the issues responsibly and thoughtfully, and will try to do so now."

It was effective, Paget saw; she had caught the judge's mood and would not oversell her case. Caroline Masters, he realized, was not the only person who had grown.

"Mary Carelli," she said in the same quiet voice, "killed Mark Ransom. She admitted that long ago. And unless she can show self-defense, that killing is a murder."

It was strange, Paget realized: that was what he had said to Carlo at the beginning of their terrible—perhaps fatal—argument. Turning to Carlo, Paget saw pain etched in his face, as if he were hearing a chorus of voices arrayed against his mother.

"As the court knows," Sharpe went on, "proof of motive is *not* an element of murder. But as this court also knows, Ms. Carelli had a compelling motive." Here Sharpe paused. "A tape," she said succinctly, "which could ruin her life."

Alone among all who were there, Paget could hear the tape that no one but Terri had heard.

"All that stands between Ms. Carelli and probable cause," Sharpe said, "is whether she has proven self-defense."

The silence was complete. Sharpe had them now; she knew better than to raise her voice. "Ms. Carelli has *claimed* self-defense. But her attempt to prove that has proven only that she is unworthy of belief.

"The formal caption of this case is 'People versus Carelli.' In reality, it has been 'Ms. Carelli versus the evidence.' For the only thing that supports Ms. Carelli's *story* is Ms. Carelli's *word*.

"The court must consider, then, what Ms. Carelli has proven her word to be worth."

Better than Marnie Sharpe, Paget thought, *he* knew the answer. But in his own reaction, subjective as it was, Paget felt the shrewdness of Sharpe's argument. Short of proving Mary a murderer, Sharpe could prove her a liar. People—including judges—do not care for liars.

"Mary Carelli asks this court to believe her, just as she asked the district attorney to believe her before we brought this case. We therefore ask the court to learn from us, just as we learned from Ms. Carelli." Sharpe paused. "Learned, and kept learning, until we had no choice but to charge her with murder."

Caroline Masters leaned forward, frowning as she followed Sharpe's argument. She did not look at Mary Carelli, nor Mary at her.

"Part of what we learned," Sharpe said, "is that Mary Carelli cannot be believed.

"Ms. Carelli told *this court* that she visited Mark Ransom's suite because he had a tape—a tape so damaging that Ms. Carelli's lawyer insisted that it be suppressed. And yet, before we found that tape in Mark Ransom's home, Ms. Carelli had never mentioned it to us. Instead she invented an elaborate story about visiting Mark Ransom solely to hear a tape of Laura Chase." Sharpe lowered her voice. "Invented a story, coolly and plausibly, within an hour of shooting Mark Ransom dead."

There was a low murmur in the courtroom. Sharpe had given her argument a new and compelling thrust; rather than focus on the evidence, she would erode all sympathy for Mary, as a woman or as a victim. And perhaps, in the process, root out any sympathy Sharpe herself might feel.

"But the discovery of the tape," Sharpe went on, "answered all the mysteries of Ms. Carelli's story.

"We discovered that Mary Carelli had bought a gun after Mark Ransom first called her. Because, she said, she had received threatening phone calls.

"We thought it strange that these calls had driven her to that point of fear and yet that she had never revealed them to anyone. But when we found the tape, we also found the answer: Mary Carelli bought the gun to kill Mark Ransom. Because he had the tape.''

Sharpe paused again; her pauses, as well as her voice, had fallen into a rhythm. Paget felt it sweeping away Mary's fragile story.

"After she brought that gun to Mark Ransom's suite, and shot Mark Ransom to death, Mary Carelli told us that he had tried to rape her.

"We thought it strange that there were no secretions on his penis.''

There were no secretions, Paget suddenly realized, because—afraid for her life—Mary Carelli had sucked Mark Ransom's penis until he had gone soft.

The judge's frown had deepened. As if encouraged, Sharpe's tone became mordant.

"We thought it strange," she said with lethal clarity, "that Ms. Carelli had scratches on her neck and thigh and yet that *Ms. Carelli,* and Ms. Carelli alone, had skin beneath her fingernails.''

"We thought it strange that the scratches on *Mr. Ransom's* body seemed to have been made when he was dead.

"We thought it strange that Ms. Carelli claimed to have shot Mark Ransom from a mere three inches and yet left no gunshot residue.''

Sharpe paused again. "Perhaps, in fairness, I should amend my statement. Those of us without training as pathologists thought these things strange. But Dr. Elizabeth Shelton merely found it grisly. For she concluded, as *all* of us concluded in the end, that the medical evaluation best supports the thesis that Ms. Carelli had murdered Mr. Ransom, fabricated the evidence, and accused a dead man of rape.''

Sharpe raised her head, looking only at Masters. "A dead man," she repeated softly, "who, when he was alive, was impotent.''

The courtroom was still. Once more, Christopher Paget felt the truth that others did not know. Unwittingly and with reason, Marnie Sharpe had strung Mary's lies into a larger lie of her own invention: that Mary Carelli had gone to Ransom's suite intending to kill him. Mary had gone, Paget knew now, not to commit murder but to do as Ransom wished, to protect the son she had first sought to protect by lying to Paget himself. But Sharpe continued relentlessly, telling the truth as she understood it.

"The man who Mary Carelli swore had tried to rape her was incapable of raping anyone—"

"How do you explain Ms. Carelli's bruise, Ms. Sharpe?''

It was Caroline Masters; she had interrupted as if speaking Paget's thoughts.

"We don't know *how* she got it," Sharpe replied calmly. "What we *do* know to a moral certainty is that Ms. Carelli did *not* get it in the way she described to this court. And because we have been able to expose her other lies, Ms. Carelli's entire story rests on a bruise we cannot explain."

Masters raised her eyebrows. "That is *not* a mere anomaly, Ms. Sharpe. From the photographs, it appeared that Ms. Carelli had been beaten."

Beaten, Paget thought, in Mark Ransom's final frenzy. Because he failed to turn hard.

"What we *think*," Sharpe replied, "is that the truth is hidden in some part of the story Ms. Carelli cannot tell us, for fear of admitting guilt. My own theory is that Mr. Ransom struck her when she pulled out the gun. But the heart of the matter is this: Ms. Carelli cannot use one unexplained fact to avoid trial on a charge of murder."

Sharpe paused for a moment, peering at Judge Masters to see if she was satisfied. Masters looked back at her in silence; when Sharpe resumed again, the awkward interlude had leeched some certitude from her tone.

"With so little to say for *herself*," Sharpe told Masters, "Ms. Carelli has tried to portray Mark Ransom as a man too despicable to merit justice, or even our concern.

" 'Why bother with the evidence of murder,' her tacit message goes, 'when the *man* I murdered was such a swine.'

"Ms. Carelli *says* Mark Ransom tried to blackmail her into having sex. But she said that only *after* we found the tape—after Ms. Carelli was committed to a defense built on rape.

"How can we believe Mary Carelli about *anything?*"

Mary's face did not change. But her eyes, fixed on the table in front of her, bespoke her hopelessness and despair. Paget imagined her memories—undressing for Ransom, posing for him naked on the couch—as she heard Marnie Sharpe call her a liar.

"So they offer Marcy Linton," Sharpe went on, "to try to persuade us of what Mary Carelli cannot.

"Without Marcy Linton, Mary Carelli would have no defense at all."

But there could have been Melissa Rappaport, Paget thought, and Lindsay Caldwell. He wondered if Caroline Masters could dismiss them from her thoughts as easily as she had swept them from the case.

Compassion had crept into Sharpe's voice. "None of us who saw her," she said, "will forget Marcy Linton. Nor is there any cause to forgive Mark Ransom for what he did to this young woman. But we are not here to prosecute a dead man for the rape of Marcy Linton."

Sharpe paused again. "Indeed," she went on quietly, "it seems that Mark Ransom had already prosecuted himself. For *that*, Dr. Bass explained to us, is why this man was impotent.

"Impotent," she repeated. "Impotent from the moment he raped Marcy Linton to the day that Ms. Carelli shot him."

Her voice rose for the first time. "That," she said with new assurance, "is the *only* truth Mary Carelli ever told us—that she shot him. And the truth of that shooting is that it was murder."

But the truth of the shooting, Paget knew, lay in the moment that Mark Ransom had pressed Mary Carelli against the wall with his penis in her mouth and watched himself turn soft; the moment when Mary Carelli became the focus of his rage. Assuming, of course, that Mary had finally told the truth.

"Everything else," Sharpe went on, "is false. The story Mary Carelli spun to excuse that shooting is a web of lies. And now, at last, it has hopelessly entangled her.

"That is just. Mr. Paget may use words like 'miscarriage of justice.' But the only result worthy of those words would be to free Mary Carelli on the basis of her testimony."

There was a passion in Sharpe's voice now. She grasped the podium, as if to rein in her emotions. "This is *not* a feminist cause, Your Honor, and Mary Carelli's lies were not an accident," she said. "Mary Carelli told these lies because she is a murderer. We ask the court to enter a finding of probable cause.

"Thank you, Your Honor."

As she turned from the podium, Paget felt the complex skein of his own emotions—fatigue, deep anger at Mary, admiration of Sharpe's effort, disquiet at the hidden injustice of what she had said. And then he saw McKinley Brooks nod toward Sharpe, as one lawyer to another who had done all she could, and done it well.

When Caroline Masters spoke, Paget realized that moments had passed while he sat unmoving in his chair. He felt Mary turn to him in mute appeal, Terri's hand on his arm.

Masters's tone was ironic, but there was puzzlement beneath it. "Mr. Paget," she said, "perhaps you would care to say a few words on Ms. Carelli's behalf."

Paget looked up at her. There were no notes in front of him; he had prepared none.

"Perhaps a few," he said.

Walking to the podium, Paget faced Judge Masters.

It was a strange moment: Caroline Masters must have sensed that she had not yet heard the truth, but Paget alone knew what it was. As if she read his thoughts, the judge said coolly, "What really happened here, Mr. Paget?"

He paused for only a moment. "Mark Ransom abused Mary Carelli," he answered.

The judge leaned forward, as if to scrutinize him. "I admit that Ms. Sharpe can't cover all the bases. It even strikes me that something may have happened in that hotel suite *other* than premeditated murder. But really, Counselor, Ms. Carelli's account is nearly as flawed as Ms. Sharpe suggests. Diaphanous, one might even say."

All at once, Paget felt the hearing move to a new level of reality: the judge was less offended by lies than interested in a truth she had yet to hear. Tell me, she seemed to be saying, why finding for Mary Carelli would be right.

It was just as well, Paget thought, that he had nothing prepared. But it took him a moment to find somewhere to start: he would not lie to Caroline Masters, or ask her to believe the lies that Mary had told in court.

"Mark Ransom beat Mary Carelli," he began. "We know that.

"Mark Ransom beat and raped Marcy Linton. We know that."

Paget paused, looking from Sharpe to Masters. "No one here doubts Ms. Linton. But the prosecution has ignored the striking parallels between Mark Ransom's treatment of Marcy Linton and of Mary Carelli.

"First, he used whatever leverage he had to get them alone—in Ms. Linton's case, the reading of a manuscript; in Ms. Carelli's, the playing of a tape.

"Second, he used alcohol to dull their reactions.

"Third, he used psychological abuse to make them vulnerable."

Paget's gaze fixed on Caroline Masters. "And fourth," he finished quietly, "he used physical abuse. Because that's what excited him."

His voice rose. *"Every one* of these elements had happened to Ms. Linton. *Every one* of them was part of what Ms. Carelli told Inspector Monk. And yet, until this hearing, Mary Carelli had never heard of Marcy Linton."

Caroline Masters folded her hands, gazing fixedly from the bench. Paget had Masters's attention now, he sensed, and that of everyone in the courtroom. Feeling the dense silence behind him, he searched for where to take this: away from Mary, he decided, to the man she killed.

"Marcy Linton," he said quietly, "had told no one. It's a tragedy repeated across this country, countless times a year. We can never know how many women let sexual abuse go unpunished, fearing the shame we visit on them. So that we never know who these men are.

"But now, because Mary Carelli shot Mark Ransom, Marcy Linton came forward. And so at last we know just who and what Mark Ransom was.

"In Mark Ransom's twisted world, there was no room for any woman to be a person, rather than a projection of his fantasies.

"For Mark Ransom, women had no thoughts, no feelings, no *life* apart from his need for them." Quiet scorn entered Paget's voice. "And once one understands that, how fitting it is that his ideal woman had been dead for twenty years.

"For Laura Chase there can be no questioning, no hope, no awareness of all that women have perceived. Nothing, in short, to mar Mark Ransom's image of compliance."

Paget's eyes locked on Caroline Masters. "Mark Ransom died because, in the end, he could not turn Mary Carelli into Laura Chase." Paget paused once more, letting the thought sink in. "And *that* is the deeper truth that George Bass left with us."

Paget nodded to Marnie Sharpe. "Ms. Sharpe called Dr. Bass to testify to impotence. But what he stayed to give us, based on intimate knowledge, was an indelible portrait of the man Mary Carelli encountered in that suite.

"The man," Paget repeated, "whom Marcy Linton has described to us.

"A rapist.

"A man obsessed by Laura Chase.

"A man who derived pleasure from beating women.

"A man who blamed Marcy Linton for his supposed impotence.

"A man determined to reassert himself sexually.

"A man who, armed with the Laura Chase tapes, was searching for a victim in the hope that abuse and fetishes would make him the 'man' he used to be.

"A man who, by the time he fixed on Mary Carelli, had become a sexual psychopath." Paget paused, adding quietly, "A tinderbox, waiting to explode."

Behind the bench, Caroline Masters shifted. It was time, Paget knew, to return to Mary Carelli. "But *that* man," he added quietly, "met the wrong woman. Or, one might say, the right one.

"The only question is whether Mary Carelli acted in self-defense.

"Ms. Sharpe says that Ms. Carelli is unworthy of belief. We can debate the niceties of circumstantial evidence. But all that we can determine, where none of us but Ms. Carelli knows the truth, is all the different theories that trial lawyers can evolve.

"So let us look at the *essence* of what Ms. Carelli says.

"Ms. Carelli says that Mark Ransom beat her. She has the bruises to prove that.

"Ms. Carelli says that Mark Ransom abused her sexually. *We* have Marcy Linton, and Dr. Bass, to say that is the truth.

"That much we *know.*

"Ms. Carelli says that, at some terrible moment of violence and abuse, she shot Mark Ransom out of fear for herself." Paget stood straighter. "Ms. Sharpe would say that we have only Ms. Carelli's word for that. But who among us is the better judge?

"Can we now stand here in this room and pass judgment on *her* judgment at the moment that she killed him? We cannot.

"Mary Carelli faced that moment alone.

"Now Mary Carelli has come before you to claim self-defense. Ms. Sharpe says that Ms. Carelli cannot be believed. But the most credible thing Ms. Carelli says—the central truth of this case—is that Mark Ransom was an abuser of women.

"Because Mary Carelli met him, he changed her life forever. But because *he* met Mary Carelli, hers is the last life Mark Ransom will ever change."

Paget stopped to look at Caroline Masters. "I cannot consider that a tragedy. Except, perhaps, for Mary Carelli."

"Nor, Your Honor, should this court find it to be a crime."

Caroline Masters gave him a querying, troubled look. "The law," she said, "defines what is or is not a crime. And this *is* a court of law, not an outlet for our passions or beliefs. Yours, mine, or anyone's."

Paget nodded. "True, Your Honor. But at its best, this is also a court of justice." He hesitated; the law was against him, and there was no point in evading that. "When this proceeding began, you said that probable cause was *not* a daunting standard. I acknowledge that. And therefore I must acknowledge that as a matter of law, this court can find against Mary Carelli and there is nothing *I* could do."

Paget raised his head. "But that would *not* be justice.

"It would not be just to condemn Mary Carelli to a further trial. Because what we have proven here is that this is *not* a case where the prosecutor can prove guilt beyond a reasonable doubt. They do not have the evidence.

"Instead they rely on the law of probable cause to induce the court to let them go to trial. And there, amidst the passions of a jury trial, they hope to win a conviction they cannot support."

Caroline Masters remained impassive; how was he to reach her as a person, Paget wondered, without offending her as a judge? "This court is bound to apply the law," he said. "But this court is *not* required to measure out the law like some apothecary. For the law is meant to be not a dry prescription but an expression of what is just and moral.

"On *this* evidence, the just result—the moral result—is to let Mary Carelli go free. For in the end, there is too much to say that the Mark Ransom she describes is the man that she encountered, and nothing to say that he was not." Paget paused for the last time, speaking slowly and clearly. "As terrible as it was, what Mark Ransom brought upon himself in that hotel suite was justice. This court cannot improve on it."

Without more, Paget sat down.

Of the next few moments he had only impressions: Caroline Masters's gavel cracking; a softening in Carlo's face; Mary's murmured thanks; Masters leaving the bench; the crowd releasing its tension in a cacophony of sound.

None of it seemed real; he knew only that he believed what he had said. For now, that would have to be enough.

It was Terri, touching his arm, who brought him back. "You can go on now," she said.

He turned to her. For a moment, he watched her face, as if searching for something more to believe in. "To where?" he asked.

SIX

IT HAD BEEN some time since Christopher Paget had thought about Andrea, who once had been his wife.

In the chaos of the courtroom, his bewildered words to Terri had been swallowed by sound. The media had converged before he and Carlo could speak; all that Paget could do was begin pressing toward the hallway, with Mary, Terri, and Carlo carried by the throng that followed. On the steps of the Hall of Justice, Johnny Moore had managed to tell him that he was taking Carlo to school; Paget had time only to suggest that Terri leave with them. Reporters had shouted questions from all sides.

It had seemed wrong that he was not with Carlo. But he was not yet sure what either of them would say, and this was not the place to say it; part of him was simply glad that Johnny could get Carlo away from this. The boy had disappeared in the crush, and Paget and Mary Carelli had faced the cameras alone.

Mary had been uncharacteristically subdued. All that Paget recalled her saying was that she was grateful for what he had done and that the rest was in Judge Masters's hands; she did not proclaim her innocence or even ask for understanding. Then she had disappeared into a limousine, giving Paget a last backward glance, and he was alone with them.

He had said almost nothing; his closing argument, he told them, was what he meant people to remember. He did not add that he himself could hardly remember what he had said. Their faces were a blur.

He had driven home by instinct.

The quiet house had felt deserted, like a place preserved as a museum to some life no longer lived there. Climbing the stairs to his bedroom, he had stopped at the sight of the canopied bed.

Andrea had chosen it. The bed was not to his taste, but when she had gone to Paris, leaving Paget and Carlo in a third-floor flat not suited to a child, she had not taken it. In the semidaze that followed, Paget had kept it; there was a boy to worry about, too many other things to brood on for Paget to replace a bed. The bed had remained until getting rid of it seemed a reaction to pain and disappointment Paget simply wished to put aside; since then, there had been no woman in his life so permanent as to see Andrea's presence in it, or express tastes of her own. The bed had become an artifact.

Now the memory of Andrea was clear and sharp.

Paget stood there in the doorway, staring at the bed until he understood his thoughts.

It was the tape: Mary's voice, telling him that Carlo was not his son, had taken him back to the moment in time when he had decided that the boy needed him, no matter what. Now, pausing in the doorway, he felt himself standing on that threshold again. Time changed for him: Mary Carelli was seven years in the past; Andrea Lo Bianco was his wife again; some other life, now unlived and irretrievable, was still possible for him. Perhaps when Andrea's career was over, and they could look at things anew, they might decide to have a child. There were still times between them that seemed so good.

The moment passed.

He had no idea where Andrea was now; he had let her vanish from his life without a trace. It made him feel shallow and unreal. He had loved her enough to envision a life with her; now she could die without his knowing. He saw her in his mind, a dancer who carried herself so much like Mary, the mother of the son he had not then known.

Except that it was eight years later; Andrea was gone, and Carlo— the boy he now knew well—was not his son at all.

He walked to his dresser, opening the top drawer.

The tapes were inside. It was where he had hidden them, minutes before Carlo had found him downstairs, drinking alone in the darkened library. He still did not know what to do with them.

About this he could not talk to Terri. He could not tell her what he feared: that if the tapes were traced to her, and Paget had destroyed them, Terri would share his culpability. Only by putting Terri at risk could he ensure that Carlo would never hear the tape.

He no longer controlled his life, Paget thought, or even how he felt about it.

He slowly shut the drawer.

Where would he go? he had asked Teresa Peralta.

Paget found himself staring at his calendar. He had always kept it on top of his dresser, to remind him of his schedule, and Carlo's. But he had never flipped it to February; gazing at January, he saw that it was checkered with Carlo's basketball games. Paget had recorded them in December, when the schedule first came out, to remind himself. Now January read like a trail of broken promises; Paget had not seen a game since Carlo's mother shot Ransom.

How would Caroline Masters rule? he wondered.

Tomorrow, at two o'clock, Masters would announce her decision. He did not try to guess what she would say; he knew only that as of today, he had made his final argument as Mary Carelli's lawyer.

Today, February 20th. The first morning he had awakened knowing the truth about himself and Carlo.

He flipped the calendar to February.

February 20th was Carlo's final game.

Had Johnny taken him there? he wondered.

It did not seem likely; how could the boy make himself play basketball? And yet, this morning, he himself had argued Mary's innocence. Every age has its own terrors; often we respond as we are taught. If Paget had made himself go to court, then Carlo, seeing this, might force himself to play. Or perhaps, long ago, the boy had started to respond like Paget. For better or for worse.

Where was he going?

To a basketball game. He had nothing else to do.

Arriving at the game, Paget felt disoriented.

The gym, the red banners with ACADEMY PREP lettered in white, the changing tide of the game itself, were like shadows at the periphery of his mind, the crowd noise like distant signals on a crystal set. But the usual parents were scattered in the bleachers, their faces familiar from the games before Mark Ransom died. Sitting alone, Johnny Moore looked up in amiable surprise.

"Taking the afternoon off?"

"At least." Paget sat down. "Do me a favor, Johnny. If you're planning to kill someone, wait a week or so. And don't murder anyone I know personally."

Moore seemed to know better than to smile. They watched the game in silence.

Amid the red uniforms, Paget saw Carlo.

His face was damp with sweat. He ran down the court to set up for defense, sweeping the thick black hair back from his forehead, glancing at the melee of red and blue uniforms and then up at the time clock. He did not see Paget.

Paget realized that he had been quiet for some moments. Turning to Moore, he asked, "How has he played this year?"

"Well, as I said." Moore kept watching the game. "Carlo's more improved than anyone—he plays hard all the time, really responds to pressure. He's the one on the team who's got real character."

Paget hesitated. "He hasn't said much about it. I figured he wasn't doing well."

Moore shook his head. "He's turned into the player other kids respect. Watching, you'd never know what was happening to his mother—he wouldn't let it show. He just kept getting better."

"I wonder if that's good."

"How would you have him be? Really, Chris, you'd have liked watching him. He loves to play under pressure."

Paget was quiet again. Then, nodding toward the blue uniforms at the other end of the court, he asked, "Who are the bad guys?"

"Woodland Prep." Moore focused his attention on the team in blue. "See the black kid?"

"Uh-huh."

"That's Tony Farrow. He plays a game most of these kids don't even understand." Moore smiled. "It's a shame you missed the *last* Woodland game."

Paget turned to him. "I'm not sure I heard about that."

"Carlo won the game off Farrow." Moore's voice warmed. "Snatched an offensive rebound out of Farrow's hands, got him to buy a fake, slid past him under the basket, and flipped the ball in over his head as the buzzer sounded. It was one for the highlight film."

Where have I been? Paget wondered. Where have *we* been? He lapsed back into silence.

* * *

Most of the first half of the game came to Paget as a collage of images—long periods of introspection, interspersed with sudden moments when Carlo, bursting into action, left an imprint on Paget's retina and brain. The score was not important; Paget was not part of the crowd. It was Carlo the person, not Carlo the player, that registered with Paget. The boy alone kept him from thinking of the past, or Mary Carelli, or what Caroline Masters would decide.

Carlo played harder than anyone.

The game transformed him. He seemed eager to be lost in it, to find himself again in the ebb and flow of bodies; the sudden shifts of emotion; the strategy and errors and spontaneity. His body still did different things at different times, and his shot was not yet consistent. But the still boy with the quick tongue and lazy grin, the one who could seem to occupy an entire couch with no hint that he would ever move, played with an intensity that Paget had not seen. He stole the ball; blocked shots; turned rebounds into baskets; shouted encouragement or advice. He and the black kid, Farrow, seemed to have something going; when Farrow shot an elbow to his ribs, fighting for a rebound, Carlo simply shook it off. But a few plays later, in a melee beneath the basket, Farrow doubled in pain; Carlo emerged from the crush with the ball and a twitch at one side of his mouth which, just for an instant, transformed his stoic face. And then he was off down the court, the first awkward step accelerating into a fast break in which Carlo, passing, sped suddenly past the last defender so that when the ball came back to him he was under the basket alone. He seemed so much faster; when he put the ball in, there was no one within ten feet. The stands erupted.

By what alchemy, Paget wondered, had Carlo made himself this good?

The moments came quicker: Carlo knocking the ball from Farrow's grasp, then launching it down the court into a teammate's hands. Carlo blocking a jump shot so hard that he spiked it to the floor. Carlo sinking a shot of his own, nothing but net. Only Farrow looked better.

Part of Paget could not believe that Carlo had come so far. His mind was still suspended between now and eight years prior; fresh as yesterday was the small dark-haired boy who was afraid to go outside, who snatched vainly at the rubber ball the first time Paget threw it.

But between then and now were a thousand baskets, shot at the hoop Paget had put up in the backyard, first seven feet high, then eight, and finally the full ten. The sound of Carlo's basketball banging on cement still echoed in Paget's ears.

Carlo drove suddenly to the hoop, drawing a foul as the buzzer sounded to end the third quarter.

For the first time, Paget looked at the scoreboard.

Woodland led by a point.

Carlo walked to the foul line. On the opposite side of the gym, the Woodland kids jeered and stomped their feet to rattle him. A red-haired kid with big ears half rose from the Woodland bench and yelled, "Choke."

It made Paget angry. For a moment, he thought of a frightened young boy on a Boston playground, telling Paget that other kids would not play ball with him because he was no good. But Carlo did not seem to hear.

He looked calmly at the basket, the ball in the air. It arced into the basket, barely hitting metal.

Carlo's second shot hit only net. He watched it without expression. Then he turned to the red-haired kid who had jeered him, and gave him the crooked grin that Paget had known for years. But now it was the grin of a competitor, triumphant and without malice. Carlo trotted toward the bench, smiling to himself. Academy led by one.

The boy who was Paget's son, but not his son, was becoming a young man. Paget was no longer sure he knew him.

In the fourth quarter, Carlo felt Tony Farrow taking over.

The game was Carlo's world now. All that he cared about was the next eight minutes. The thought of winning consumed him with a fierce purity.

But Farrow raised his game to where no one else could reach it.

He was six feet two, incredibly quick, completely without nerves, and headed, Carlo was certain, straight for the NBA as soon as he got his driver's license. And he was everywhere. A fall-away jump shot; a drive; a three-point shot; even a tip-in. Mike Stanley, who was guarding Farrow, could do nothing with him. Carlo and Academy kept close with fast breaks, but suddenly Woodland was up by three.

There was one minute left.

Turning to the bench, Carlo saw Coach Mack call a time-out. Carlo glanced up at the clock; fifty-five seconds.

He did not look toward the stands. He knew that his father was not there; he did not want to distract himself by wishing otherwise.

On the way to the bench, Carlo turned to Mike. "Tired?"

Mike shook his head. "It's just that this guy's Jesus Christ."

"Yeah," Carlo said, "I saw the movie. Mind if I try guarding him?"

Mike hesitated, and then looked relieved. "It's fine with me. Just don't tell coach that."

They reached the sideline. Carlo grabbed a towel off the bench and wiped the sweat from his forehead. "What is it?" Coach Mack demanded.

Carlo gave him a level glance. "Let me take Farrow. Mike's knee's acting up."

Mack turned to Mike. "Is that right?"

Mike shifted from foot to foot. "Just a little. Not enough to come out."

"I want to do this," Carlo said. "I really want this guy."

Mack looked from one to the other. "All right," he said to Carlo. "You know what you need to do."

Carlo nodded. The coach no longer barked at him; he had learned that Carlo did not like or need it.

When they ran back onto the floor, Woodland was inbounding the ball, and Carlo was facing Farrow.

A dreamy smile crossed Farrow's round face. "You?" he murmured.

"Uh-huh."

Farrow stood with his back to Carlo, poised to break, staring at the blue-shirted teammate who stood out of bounds at half-court, ready to throw the ball inbounds. Three feet behind Farrow, Carlo tried to keep loose, running through what Woodland might do.

Farrow broke abruptly.

The ball floated to where he should have been. But Carlo had broken too, bumping Farrow with his hip as they sped toward the ball. For two steps, Farrow staggered.

It was enough.

The ball bounced free, and then Carlo got there in full stride. He hurtled toward the basket with three headlong bounces; the quicker Farrow was just fast enough to hack him as the ball left Carlo's hand.

As the ball fell through the basket, Carlo's right wrist went numb.

He winced, grasping it. Beneath the screaming from the stands, Carlo heard the whistle. *"Foul,"* the bearded referee called out. "Blue, number twelve."

Farrow stepped to his place beside the line. There was something almost perfect about him, Carlo decided. Short haircut, large brown eyes, smooth skin, a face of broad planes. Gazing at the basket, Farrow could have been contemplating the moon, with a mild and somewhat dreamy interest.

As Carlo stepped to the foul line, the other ref gave him the ball. He, too, was bearded and middle-aged; before the game, thinking jokes might help him forget his mother's dilemma, Carlo had dubbed the two referees "the Smith Brothers." But nothing was funny now; his wrist hurt too much for him to shoot well, and the joke reminded him of how scared he was for Mary.

The stamping and jeering began again.

The pain from his wrist became nausea in the pit of Carlo's stomach. It was foolish not to have eaten, when last night he had not slept. But today he could do neither.

"Choke," the jug-eared kid yelled again.

Shut it out, Carlo told himself. Shoot as if there were no pain.

He breathed in, once. Then he cradled the ball in his palm, feeling its pebbly surface as he had a thousand times before, eyes focused on the hoop. The jeers became white noise.

He flinched as he shot.

But the ball had already left his hand. The arc was not flawless, merely good enough. It rattled the metal and fell through.

Carlo looked at no one now. He did not think of smiling. There were forty seconds left.

Backpedaling up the court, Carlo held his wrist loosely at his side, keeping three feet between himself and Tony Farrow.

Woodland took its time. The point guard crossed the center line, looking from right to left. They had a set play, Carlo saw. He tried to guess what it was.

The last game, they had set a screen; Carlo had diagnosed it, but Farrow had twisted in the air, sucking Carlo into a two-shot foul. Sooner or later, Carlo knew, the ball would come to Farrow again.

When it did, there were twenty seconds left.

This time, Carlo guessed, Farrow would do something different.

Farrow stood with the ball two feet in front of Carlo. Carlo crouched, hands raised in front of him, knees flexed.

Farrow suddenly drove the lane.

He was at full speed in less than two strides. But Carlo had guessed right again. He was a foot in front of Farrow, blocking his angle to the lane, when Farrow pulled up and shot a fifteen-footer before Carlo could even stop.

The move had the silken perfection of a dance routine, practiced until it involved only muscle memory and the certainty of instinct. The shot was far too good to miss.

Carlo watched it fall through the net.

With fifteen seconds, Woodland led by two.

Coach Mack screamed for time-out. But when Carlo ran to the bench, the coach was under control.

"Nothing you could do," he said to Carlo.

"It's okay," Carlo answered. "They just bought themselves some overtime."

At some point in the season, Coach Mack had learned to smile. "Your wrist okay?"

"Fine." Carlo hesitated. "If it's in the plan, I still want the ball."

Mack nodded. "It's in the plan." He drew the team around him. They leaned forward, faces drawn and intent. "We'll get the ball to Carlo," he said, and gave them the play.

The whistle blew, and then Academy inbounded the ball. Carlo danced in the wing, feinting to keep Farrow off balance, waiting to make his break.

When he broke for the lane with five seconds left, the ball was there for him.

A great pass, perfect timing. But when he spun to drive, Tony Farrow slapped his wrist so hard he heard the sound before he felt it.

The whistle blew.

Carlo doubled over in pain. That sonofabitch Farrow had done it on purpose. "Two shots," the referee called out.

The game was on Carlo's shoulders, where he wanted it. With his wrist hurting the way Farrow wanted it.

Still bent over, Carlo tried to flex his wrist. It felt stiff. He straightened, keeping his face impassive, and walked slowly to the line.

Two shots. He had to make them both.

Carlo knew from experience that the wrist would swell. It would lose all flexibility; he would have to miss practice tomorrow and ice it. Except that there was no more practice; this game was the end of their season. Tomorrow there was only the courtroom, and his mother.

At both sides of his vision, three players lined the key. A blue uniform, then a red, then a blue again, poised to fight for a rebound should Carlo miss. To his right was Tony Farrow. The Woodland kids were stomping again. There were three seconds left.

Forget about it. Just concentrate. Look at nothing but the hoop: screen out the score, the noise, the pain in your wrist. Screen out anything else in your life.

By the time he shot, all he saw was the basket.

Pain ripped through his wrist to his elbow.

The ball bounced on the metal rim, once, then twice more, each time closer to the inside of the rim. The angle of the last bounce was right; the ball rattled within the rim and fell through the net.

The crowd erupted. Carlo never changed expression. But his hand felt like a catcher's mitt. He guessed the truth then; Tony Farrow had fractured his wrist.

One shot to go.

He did not really blame Farrow. He had not meant to break anything. Farrow was just exploiting a weakness, putting the pressure on Carlo by forcing him to shoot fouls with a wrist that hurt. That was the game; people who thought basketball wasn't a contact sport weren't watching hard enough. It was what his father, joking, had once said about law.

What to do about his wrist?

He would have to shoot differently. He could no longer flip the ball with his hand; he must push more with his arm.

The gym was hushed now; it was as if Carlo's first shot had sucked the air out of it. The jeering had stopped.

Just one more.

Carlo straightened at the foul line. He breathed in again, breathed out, felt loose. His vision narrowed to the net.

He held the ball at chin level, cradled in his left palm. Then, with his right hand, he pushed it toward the basket. His eyes stung. But he could see that the trajectory looked decent. Just slightly to the left side of the basket.

It hit the inside left of the rim.

Good, Carlo thought.

The ball bounced, hitting the back of the rim, circling around the edge of the basket. Then it paused, teetering on the rim, and fell to the floor without passing through the net.

There were groans, cheers, a brief scramble where Tony Farrow got the ball. Then the Woodland players gathered in a knot, celebrating.

Carlo bent forward, head down, palms resting on his knees. He had no feeling in his wrist now.

He had lost the game.

Teammates filed by, patting him on the back. The coach put his arm around him. "You're the best we had," he told Carlo. "If I had to lose, I'd want to lose with you."

"Thanks," Carlo said. He did not look up; he needed time to gather himself.

He felt Tony Farrow standing next to him.

Pull yourself together, Carlo.

He looked up. "Your hand okay?" Farrow asked.

"Fine." Carlo shrugged. "It doesn't really matter. Season's over."

Farrow was staring at Carlo's wrist. It had swollen visibly; the skin near his hand seemed discolored. Then Farrow looked at Carlo again, his face solemn. For once, it seemed that someone was home in there. "Man," he told Carlo, "you turned out to be a player."

Carlo nodded. "I figured you didn't want to play alone."

It made Farrow smile. He hesitated a moment, as if to say more, and then extended his left hand.

Carlo shook it.

"See you next season," Farrow said, and was gone.

Next season, Carlo thought. Where would he be? He felt empty.

"Care to go to dinner?" someone asked.

It was his father. His tone was matter-of-fact, as if he had picked up Carlo after practice.

It surprised him. For a moment, Carlo recalled the first time he could remember meeting this man, and he had seemed so tall. It made him feel like a child again. But it was surely still the pain that stung his eyes.

"Better take me to the hospital first," he said.

* * *

The beach looked different than it had the night before.

Terri had expected it to be shadowed by her meeting with Christopher Paget. But they had left no trace. The late-afternoon sun glistened at the water's edge, fuller at high tide. The sound of the waves was deep and lulling.

She sat in a small cove carved into the cliffside, sheltered from the wind. Elena played at her feet. With a child's solemn concentration, she arranged toy people in various formations around pieces of plastic furniture. There seemed, Terri realized, to be a mother, a father, and a little girl; she wished that she could see into Elena's mind. Then Paget broke into her thoughts once more.

He would, she was certain, never again represent Mary Carelli. But Terri thought his final argument had been all that Mary could have asked. Perhaps it was because Terri knew, as others did not, that Paget had spoken to the truth of what Mary had done; perhaps Terri only imagined that he had reached Caroline Masters. But Caroline's last comment, a warning against passion, struck Terri as Caroline's warning to herself.

Terri might be inventing this. Lawyers, their fears unrelieved for days on end, come to read too much into the silences and stray comments of a judge: sometimes, Paget had once quoted Sigmund Freud, a cigar is only a cigar. At least Paget had taken the part he could control to the end. But she was far less sure that the part Paget could not control—the trial of Mary Carelli and the ordeal of the tapes—would end with Caroline Masters. For a moment, she wished that *life* were a tape, which she could fast-forward to tomorrow, so that she would know that the hearing was over.

The tapes.

It scared her now, though she would never say that to Paget. But if he had destroyed them, and they were traced to her, the district attorney might hold her at fault. Paget would try to protect her, Terri knew, but it would hurt her career were the tapes to vanish. And Terri's career, it seemed, was the only security she and Elena had.

She turned back to her daughter.

Elena was talking to her plastic people. "You sit *here*," she insisted, "and Daddy sits there."

"Who are you talking to?" Terri asked.

"You. You're sitting next to Daddy."

"And where do you sit?"

"Right there," Elena said triumphantly, and placed a plastic child between its plastic parents.

A child, Terri thought sadly, ordering the world of adults. Terri had been certain that she had given Elena no sign of her conflicts with Richie; now she searched her mind for times when she had. She found none. But Elena must have some intuition; she had spent an hour at this game of family, far beyond her usual attention span. Terri had seldom seen her so intent.

Let her be, Terri told herself. At least for a while.

Thoughtful, Terri gazed down the beach.

It was a workday afternoon. The beach was not crowded: mothers with children; a couple or two; a few singles who were used to being alone, and so walked or sat by themselves. A shirtless student type threw a Frisbee for his collie to retrieve, his bare skin stretching as he threw, as if there were hardly enough to cover his slender frame. The collie trotted eagerly into the surf, returning with the Frisbee in his mouth; he shook the water from his coat as he ran toward his master. It reminded Terri that Elena kept asking for a dog.

She turned back to her daughter. Elena had moved the figures again; now they sat at a kitchen table. The child was still between her parents.

"Do you like playing that?" she asked.

"Yes." Elena stopped, staring at her plastic family, and then looked up at Terri. "Why are you so mean to Daddy?"

Her daughter's voice was part inquiry and part accusation; there was an eerie certainty in it, as though Elena knew she was speaking an indubitable truth.

Terri was momentarily speechless.

Keep it neutral, she told herself; don't seem defensive or annoyed. Sound as if you're merely seeking information.

"How am I mean to Daddy?" she asked.

Elena did not answer. But her voice still held conviction. "Daddy cries, you know."

"Have you seen him?"

Elena shook her head. "No. He doesn't want to cry in front of me. He does it when he's alone, after you hurt his feelings."

Terri felt herself stiffen. Quite calmly, she asked, "Then how do you know?"

"Because he tells me." Elena's voice held a kind of pride. "When we're alone, and he tucks me in at night, we talk about our feelings."

Terri recognized the note in Elena's voice now: the false wisdom of a child, flattered by the contrived confidences of a manipulative adult. Anger ran through her like a current. When she spoke again, it was without thinking. "Daddy shouldn't say those things to you."

"He *should.*" Elena shook her head, almost angrily. "Daddy says I'm old enough to know things."

She had been foolish, Terri realized. This could not—should not—be resolved between Elena and herself, but between adults with enough compassion to know that, deep inside themselves, children wish to be children.

Terri wanted to confront Richie right away. But it would not do, she realized, to leave abruptly with this conversation fresh in Elena's mind: the child might see the cause and effect.

"Can I play with you?" Terri asked.

All at once, Elena's mood changed. "Okay," she said, and smiled up at her mother.

For a half hour, Terri forced herself to remember that she had come to play with her daughter. They did that, talking about everything and nothing, until the breeze grew too cold for a child.

As they drove home, Terri half listened to Elena. Her mind felt as cold as the breeze had been.

Richie was in the kitchen. At the sight of Elena, he bent to her and flashed an incandescent smile. "How's my sweetheart?"

His voice was almost crooning. Perhaps it was her mood, Terri thought, but something about it made her skin crawl. "Can you put away your toys?" she asked Elena, and watched the little girl scamper down the hallway. She was unusually cooperative, Terri thought; she found herself wondering if, subconsciously, Elena had begun trying to keep her parents happy.

"How was *your* day?" Richie asked. "Court all right?"

"Fine." Terri's voice was cool. "And yours? Or did you spend it crying?"

Richie looked startled, and then tried a puzzled half smile. As he looked at Terri, it died there.

"The funny thing," she said conversationally, "is that you never cry. Sometimes I'd feel better if you did. But the deepest feeling you can dredge up is self-pity, and that's only to manipulate me. Of course, Elena doesn't see that yet."

Failing sun came through the window. It was dusk: facing Richie, Terri felt darkness closing around them. He watched her in silence. "Quit being abusive," he finally said. "People express their emotions in different ways, you know."

"What have you been telling Elena?"

Richie folded his arms; Terri saw the faintest glint of satisfaction in his eyes. "Lainie's a smart little girl, Ter. Not even a parent can keep her from seeing the truth."

There was something frightening, Terri thought, in the way Richie appropriated a five-year-old to corroborate his view of things. "Elena's not some extension of you, Richie. She's her own person."

Richie gave her a knowing smile. "I get it. You've always resented it because Lainie is so much like me, and now you're blaming *me* for that. Well, I'm sorry, Ter—that's just how it is."

Terri stared at him. "What have you been saying to her?" she repeated.

She saw the calculation run through Richie's eyes: how much to say, what spin to put on it. "I'm just being a parent," he said coolly. "I want Lainie to know the difference between real love and false love based on images."

"Oh, and what *is* real love? I'm not sure I'd recognize it."

"Then let me explain it to you." Pausing, Richie spoke with exaggerated patience. "Real love is when people make a commitment to family and carry it out, even through the bad times. It's the opposite of this stage you're in with Christopher Paget, an infatuation with surface instead of substance." There was an edge beneath his monotone. "I feel sorry for you, Ter. If you don't learn to understand yourself, you'll go from crush to crush, never finding the happiness you'd feel from accepting me as I am."

"At least you'd be free of someone who doesn't deserve you." Terri stopped there; what she felt was too deep for sarcasm. "Don't you understand? I never *cared* if you were the world's greatest promoter. That was *your* dream. I just wanted us to live a real life."

He shook his head. "As soon as you got a law job, you changed. All of a sudden you were afraid I'd be a bigger success than you, that you'd look small next to me." He threw his arms open. "Nothing makes you happy. It's like right now. You want me to parent Lainie, and then you complain when I do. I can never win."

Terri shook her head. Softly, she said, "You always win, Richie. But this time I won't let you. Not with Elena."

Richie placed his hands flat on the kitchen counter. "Lainie's not like you, and she'll never see me like you do. She's imaginative, like me. We communicate on levels you don't understand." His voice filled with authority. "It just is, Ter. You should rise above your jealousy and learn to see how good I am for our daughter."

Terri could not answer. All that she could do was let reality sink in—his deep certitude, his irreparable self-involvement. He would always see Elena in terms of his own needs, and if one of his needs was to use Elena to maneuver Terri, he would do that without hesitation, certain it was best for Elena. Perhaps, Terri realized, *that* was the most frightening perception of all. Richie was *not* merely calculating: some unfathomable part of him could make himself believe what he was saying.

"I'm leaving you," Terri said.

Richie stiffened. They stood there watching each other, two still figures in the semidark. The silence felt like a caught breath.

"You can't do that," Richie said at last. He made his voice calm. "Not without counseling. I'll set up an appointment. Six months down the road, we'll see where we are."

It took her a moment to believe what she had already said, another to tell him what else she believed. "You have an uncounselable problem, Richie. And so do I."

Richie looked wounded. "What is so wrong that we can't fix it?"

His voice was suddenly plaintive; it made Terri sad, and sorry for what she had said. But she *had* said it now. "You can't see other people as separate from you, Richie," she said softly. "I can't change it, and I won't fight it."

"You can *help* me, Ter. That's what marriage is about."

His shoulders slumped. He looked so alone, Terri thought, and then she remembered Elena. "No," she answered. "Only *you* can help you. It's too late for us, and I have Elena to think of."

His voice rose. "If you were thinking of Elena, you'd give her an intact family."

Terri felt her throat constrict. "It's all I ever wanted, Richie—a family. But there's a difference between 'intact' and 'healthy.' We're no good for Elena."

The room was dark now. Richie moved closer. "It's not up to you to say what's good. It's up to a judge, and he'll listen to me."

"And what will you tell 'him'?"

"That *I've* been the caretaking parent while you've worked long hours with a man who just may be your lover. That I want Elena." He paused; the smile that followed seemed a reward for his own cleverness. "That I can't provide care for her without sixty percent of your income."

"That's crazy."

His voice filled with triumph. "It's the *law,* Ter. I've checked it out. And even if you get custody, you think it's easy to find a man who wants to raise someone else's kid? You'll be alone."

Terri kept her own voice steady. "I don't love you," she said. "I don't think you're a good father for Elena. I don't think our 'family' is good for Elena. So if I have to be alone, I will. And if I have to fight you for Elena, I'll do that too."

"You'll lose." He paused, words softer. "But don't worry, Ter. Every other weekend, I'll let you see my daughter."

It was near the surface now: the fear that had kept her prisoner here. Some stranger, a man or a woman she did not know, would decide whether Terri could raise Elena and, in deciding, would set the course of Elena's life. Richie would make himself be smooth and plausible; how could Terri explain to a judge how things really were? Somehow she would have to be more determined than Richie in his relentless quest for control. But even the thought made her tired.

She forced herself to speak slowly and evenly. "I'm taking Elena and going to my mother's. We need to decide what to tell her."

Richie moved closer, biting off his words. *"We're* not telling her anything."

"We should. And we should do it together."

He was standing over her now. In the dark, she could barely see his face, and only because it was so near. "We're not telling her anything," he repeated. "And you're not going anywhere."

His voice contained an anger she had never heard before: it quavered with his failure to control her.

She tried to step past him. He moved with her, blocking her way.

Terri felt her own voice shaking. "I am, though. Please, don't make this worse."

"You don't understand, Ter. I'm not letting you do this."

She felt her heart race. All at once, she had to do something. She put her hand on his shoulder, pushing gently so that he would stay where he was, trying to move past him.

"You bitch," he spat out.

She froze as his hand jerked upward in the darkness, poised to hit her. *"Don't,"* she managed.

"Do you still want to leave, Ter?" His hand stayed up, ready to strike unless she shook her head. "Or are you ready to talk?"

Terri was silent. As his hand rose higher, she flinched. *"Don't,"* she cried out again, and turned, running to the kitchen wall.

She heard him move behind her. Hands against the wall, she fumbled for the light switch. When she flicked it on and turned again, Richie was two feet away, his hand still raised, blinking at the light.

Terri was breathing hard. "Do it, Richie. Do it twice. That way the family court won't miss it."

Crimson spread across his face. But his hand did not move.

Terri looked into his face. "At least you weren't abusive, I used to tell myself. Not like my father with my mother." She stopped herself, catching her breath. "Now I know why. Before I ever met you, I was trained to give in. The only difference between you and my father was *me.*"

Richie was silent, flushed, staring.

"But not anymore," Terri finished quietly. "Whether you hit me or not, I'm leaving. And if you *do* hit me, I'll make sure it's the last time you'll ever hit anyone."

He gaped at her, and then anger became another expression— embarrassment, exposure. His hand dropped to his side.

Don't let him see your fear, Terri told herself. She knew that this was not over; with Richie, things were never over until he won. Her only goal was to leave the house with Elena.

Terri made herself stand straighter, as if certain he would not strike. "I'll think of something to tell Elena," she said. And then she walked past him, going to get their daughter, not looking back.

* * *

Carlo gazed at the cast on his wrist. "Guess I can't do homework," he said.

They sat in a grill both had always liked: Paget for its wood and its white tablecloths, reminiscent of old San Francisco; Carlo for its cheeseburgers. Paget sipped his martini. "At least you can keep up with your reading," he answered. "Just flip the pages with your left hand."

Carlo gave him a brief smile. "Sympathetic, aren't you."

"When you're truly maimed, Carlo, get back to me about homework." Paget nodded toward Carlo's empty plate. "I thought you managed that cheeseburger rather neatly."

"I was *hungry*. The emergency room took forever."

It was true enough. In the two hours they had spent waiting there, the traffic in urban tragedy had been harrowing: a battered woman with her face bruised and one eye swollen shut; an elderly man comatose from a hit-and-run; a young Hispanic shot in what Paget guessed was a botched drug deal. Paget and Carlo had watched these horrors in silence; the parade was deadening, and an emergency room was nowhere to talk about what lay between them. A harried doctor had finally looked at Carlo's X rays, sheathed his wrist in a plaster cast, told him to come back in two weeks, and sent them into the night. But the aftershock of the emergency room stayed with them; they had said little about anything, and nothing about Mary. Their brief exchange about Carlo's wrist felt more like reflex than conversation.

They lapsed into silence again. But it seemed that neither wanted to leave; perhaps, Paget thought, both felt that rushing home would underscore their awkwardness and cast them back into the shadow of tomorrow's ruling. What, Paget wondered, was Caroline Masters thinking at this moment? Or, for that matter, Mary Carelli?

He ordered coffee for himself, dessert for Carlo. The boy gazed around the room, toying with his unused spoon. Paget wished he knew what to say. But what he knew, and Carlo did not, felt like a weight. He had not been able to think things through.

Carlo eyed the spoon. Without looking up, he said, "You were great today. It's good you did that for her."

"Honestly, Carlo, I'm not sure who I did it for." He paused. "Remember that first night, when you said I shouldn't take the case?"

"Uh-huh. I didn't think you believed in her."

Paget nodded. "I'm sorry for that. But I did the best I could."

"I know. I was there."

Paget watched his face. "Some pretty tough things were said last night. Some of them by you."

Carlo averted his eyes for a moment. But when he looked up, his gaze was steady. "Before, I was always able to count on you."

"I'm not a robot, Carlo. This involves my feelings as well as yours."

"But you were ready to desert her." Carlo paused, struggling to explain. "It wasn't just about *her*; it was about *you*. If I can't depend on you to be you, what can I depend on?"

"Do you think you were fair?"

"No. I was angry." Carlo hesitated. "Do you think *you* were fair?"

"No. But I think I deserve a break from you." Paget leaned forward. "This case is a strain on me, for reasons you don't understand. But never, ever have I wanted you not to have a mother. What I wanted was for you to be happy and secure."

Carlo's look became more open. "I always have been," he said quietly. "Until now. I don't know what's happening anymore. I don't know what all this is about."

The simple words threw Paget off track. He thought again of a seven-year-old boy with no certain future, nor any sense of being loved. Paget had tried as hard as he could to make the boy sitting in front of him different from the boy he had been; it shook him to think that this might be lost. "It's about your mother and me," Paget answered. "There's too much in the past. At some point, you'll have to accept that I don't feel about her as you do, and that she doesn't feel for *me* what she feels for you." Paget paused. "Just as it's all right with me that *you* love *her*."

"Because any mother is better than no mother?"

"No. Because you and Mary can have something, and I think she wants that very much. If I don't put myself in the way."

Carlo raised his head. "I won't let you."

"Then neither will she." Paget paused. "But I can't be her lawyer, Carlo. If she loses tomorrow, I'll help her find someone else."

After a moment, Carlo nodded his acceptance. Quietly, he asked, "Do you think she *will* lose?"

"Yes. I do."

Carlo took that in. "If she does," he finally said, "it won't be your fault. I had no idea how good you are."

"I never told you?"

"No." Carlo's face remained serious. "After today, I don't think anyone could have done better. It'll help me accept whatever happens."

Paget was quiet a moment. In some small measure, he realized, Carlo had lightened the burden he felt.

"I'm sorry I missed your season," he said at length.

Carlo shrugged. "You can't help that. It's fine."

The last words triggered a memory. They had been watching Mary on television, Paget recalled, emerging from the Hall of Justice on the night Ransom died. How was the game? Paget had finally asked. Fine, Carlo had answered simply. And for the days and weeks since then, Carlo Paget had tried to make things fine.

"You played hard," Paget said. "I was proud of you today."

Carlo looked across at him, as if he had much to say, much more to ask. But all that he said was, "Thanks, Dad."

Two words. Paget did not know why they filled his eyes with tears. "I really do love you, Carlo. Quite a lot."

Carlo gave him a puzzled smile. "It was only a game, Dad. I'll get over it."

Paget managed a smile of his own. "Sometimes parents lack perspective," he said.

It was past ten when they got home, close to eleven when the telephone rang in Paget's bedroom.

It was McKinley Brooks. "We've asked to see Judge Masters tomorrow morning," Brooks said without preface. "Ten o'clock. She requested that I give you notice."

Brooks's voice was somber. "In chambers?" Paget asked.

"No. In open court. We've invited the press."

Paget glanced at the drawer where the tapes were hidden. "What's this about?"

"Can't tell you. You'll have to hear it with everyone else. Assuming you don't know already."

It was Terri; they had traced the tapes, Paget guessed, found her signature. Terri was in trouble, and Brooks intended to make the most of it. "It's too late for games, Mac. If you intend to introduce new evidence, or do anything that would embarrass anyone, you should audition in private."

"It's too late for *that*, Chris. Open court it is, by order of the Honorable Caroline Clark Masters. See you there."

Brooks rang off.

Paget sat on the end of the bed. They would accuse Terri of obstruction, he supposed. And, of course, Paget. For the district attorney, it was a no-lose situation: righteous indignation if Paget had destroyed the tapes, public clamor for their disclosure if he had not. Either would put pressure on Caroline Masters to rule against Mary Carelli. All that it required was indifference to Teresa Peralta—Paget himself, he was sure, had long since ceased to matter.

What Brooks did not know was what the second tape would do to Carlo.

For an instant, Paget wanted to call Terri. But he knew what she would say—destroy the tape for Carlo's sake—and that he would refuse. It was best to spare her a sleepless night.

Paget opened the drawer. Slowly, he took the tapes out, staring at them for a moment. Then he put them in his briefcase.

There was one thing he could do. If Brooks started in on Terri, he could ask for a recess, and give the tapes to Caroline Masters.

He picked up the telephone and called Mary Carelli.

SEVEN

TO PAGET, the courtroom seemed bleak.

It was packed; McKinley Brooks had alerted the press to his last-minute appearance. Brooks sat next to Sharpe at the prosecution table, hands folded across his stomach, wearing the serene expression of someone schooled in self-control. Sharpe seemed less taut than usual; Paget guessed that, this morning, she had no role to play. But there was a gravity to her expression, as if she were about to witness something of moment. Neither looked at Paget or Mary.

Carlo sat behind his mother; Paget had thought of no way to keep him from coming. The boy looked openly worried. Paget had not told him of his suspicions, but the absence of explanation told Carlo enough.

Nor had Paget told Terri. He had waited until this morning even to say they were going back to court; she had looked startled, as if she instantly saw what would happen. Now, sitting next to her, Paget saw the bruise of sleeplessness beneath her eyes: he rebuked himself for how much this case, and all that she had done for Paget and Carlo, already had stolen from her.

Only Mary looked calm.

That was odd, Paget thought. Mary alone knew Paget's suspicions; last night, he had told her of his surmise that Brooks had traced the tapes and of his own desire to surrender them if asked. She had been silent for a time. "You have no choice," she said finally. "If Terri hadn't found them, Brooks would have. You can't very well hang her out to dry."

That had been all. Her expression now was simply resigned; she was caught in a trap of her own making, and would not complain about it. Nor would she let anyone else see what Paget had seen: her feelings were private, and she would go down clinging to them. The rest was out of her hands.

All of them, and the press, waited for Judge Masters.

She was taking her time. That was peculiar; Caroline Masters ran a punctual courtroom. But it was ten minutes past ten. Perhaps, although Paget doubted it, she was relishing a last grand entrance before returning to the obscurity of traffic offenses and petty lawsuits.

"All rise," the courtroom deputy called. "The Municipal Court for the City and County of San Francisco, Judge Caroline Clark Masters presiding, is now in session."

Judge Masters walked to the bench, tented her hands in front of her, and looked directly at Brooks. Her aquiline features held no curiosity: what Paget imagined seeing was challenge and a dash of apprehension. "Well," she said to Brooks, "what is it?"

Brooks stepped forward. "I would like to be heard, Your Honor, on a matter of some importance. I believe it will be worth the court's time."

Masters's expression went opaque. "Of course, Mr. Brooks."

Instinctively, Paget touched the briefcase at his feet, glancing at Terri. When she turned to him, Paget knew that she had guessed as he had.

"I have the tapes," he whispered.

Her eyes widened. "Why?"

"Because it's my responsibility."

She stared at him. "But what about Carlo?"

"I know. But there's nothing for it."

As Brooks stepped to the podium, Paget turned to watch.

"Six weeks ago," Brooks began, "in this city, a prominent woman journalist shot and killed America's most famous writer. His death raised the most fundamental questions: Why are the victims of crime so often forgotten? And how do we treat a woman whose defense—attempted rape—cannot be proven?"

Brooks's voice became reflective. "These are difficult questions," he went on. "The result has been a difficult hearing. Inside the courtroom, it has required this court to make the most delicate judgments, demanded of Ms. Sharpe an extraordinary degree of skill. And outside the courtroom, it has divided men and women of good will.

"As district attorney, I have felt both the pressures of the courtroom and the ambivalence of the community. I have heard the people of this city debate the evidence, question Ms. Carelli's innocence, challenge the sensitivity of my office to the genuine mistreatment too many women face. To them, I have said, 'We believe in women's rights far too fervently to allow them to be abused. For we cannot believe Mary Carelli.'"

Brooks paused, his face becoming almost sad. "But no amount of professionalism in court, no amount of soul-searching at night, has stemmed the unease this case arouses. There are many who question whether the legal process can handle such a case—where the evidence is circumstantial, the issues so emotionally charged, the stakes so high, our belief in justice so fragile. But in the end, our office cannot be dissuaded by fear of the consequences." Brooks paused again. "Political, or legal.

"Whatever passions some people may feel, if the evidence justifies a case, our office must bring it. We did so here. Many have castigated us for that. But now, having listened to the evidence before us, we have the opportunity to restore their faith in our judgment."

Mary's face had turned grim. "He's going to offer up you and Terri," she murmured to Paget. "What better way to show I'm guilty than to point to guilty lawyers."

But Paget had been watching Caroline Masters. "Wait," he whispered.

"We have heard Marcy Linton," Brooks continued. "We have brought forward Dr. Bass. And we have had time to reflect.

"On the current evidence, we must concede that conviction is uncertain. Our only certainty is that far too many people will believe that *any* verdict—including the guilty verdict we seek—is unjust. Thus, even as we have pursued this case in court, we have searched for something that would prove our case and persuade the doubters of its justice." Brooks paused again, glancing at Paget.

"The tapes," Mary whispered.

Paget did not answer. He could only watch, helpless, waiting for Brooks's next words.

"We have found nothing," Brooks said softly. "We now believe there is nothing to find."

Paget stared in surprise. The media people seemed like faces in a frieze.

Only Brooks looked serene. "We therefore move to dismiss the case, and ask the court to discharge Mary Carelli."

The courtroom burst into sound.

Paget could not comprehend. Mary turned to him, lips parted. Only Caroline Masters did not appear surprised.

She cracked the gavel, waiting for silence. Brooks waited calmly at the podium.

"I must concur with you," she told him. "It seems likely that, however it occurred, Mark Ransom mistreated Ms. Carelli. That may not defeat probable cause. But it suggests that a jury should not be asked to find her guilty of murder and, if asked, should not do so. Your decision does you credit." She turned to Sharpe. "As did Ms. Sharpe's performance before this court."

Brooks nodded. "Thank you, Your Honor."

Masters faced Mary Carelli. For a long moment, she seemed to appraise her, and then she spoke the final words. "Case dismissed, Ms. Carelli. You are free to go."

The courtroom stirred again. Quickly, Judge Masters looked from Brooks to Paget. "Mr. Brooks, Mr. Paget, there is one more matter I wish to speak with you about. Ten minutes from now, in chambers."

She cracked her gavel. Paget glanced at Terri; when he looked up again, Caroline Masters had disappeared.

The rest was white noise. Reporters ran for telephones, snatched portables from their briefcases. The cameras zoomed in on Mary Carelli.

She was weeping.

She stood alone, not covering her face. For an instant, she reached toward Paget, pulled back. Then Carlo was there, putting his arms around her. When he turned to murmur thanks to Paget, one arm still around his mother, he was crying as well. Their faces, Paget thought, were so much alike.

He felt a hand on his elbow.

It was Terri. Her face was drawn, and she did not smile. "You did it," she said.

Paget stopped himself from holding her. *"We* did it," he answered. "And you're all right now."

When they filed into chambers—Brooks and Sharpe, Paget and Terri—Caroline Masters asked them to sit.

"You did the right thing," Masters said to Brooks.

Brooks gave her a Delphic smile. "I hope the press sees it that way."

"I'll help them, McKinley. I can talk about this now." She gave a dry smile of her own. "Do you prefer the word 'courageous' or 'sensitive'?"

" 'Courageous,' thank you. 'Sensitive' sounds too effete for a prosecutor."

"I thought as much. I'll stick with 'courageous.' "

Paget felt an undertone in their exchange, something unsaid. But he was still too dazed to sort it out: it seemed that he had lived so long with the Carelli case, and the specter of the tapes, that he could not accept that it was over. He kept the briefcase close to him.

Caroline Masters drew back in her chair. "I have a private concern," she said. "It began in this room, and I'd like it to end here. The matter of the tapes." She turned to Brooks again. "Given that you've dismissed the case, it seems that the two Steinhardt tapes I have—Laura Chase's and Mary Carelli's—are no longer evidence. Would you concur?"

Brooks gave her a quick, knowing glance. "I would."

Masters looked at him for another moment. "There were two things about this case," she continued, "that I found particularly troubling. The first is the pain that it inflicted on Ms. Linton and, prospectively, on Ms. Rappaport and Ms. Caldwell. But Ms. Linton's testimony was the only way Ms. Carelli could make her defense. It's sad, but if the law does not allow corroboration—as in establishing Mark Ransom's sexual pattern—too few sex crimes will ever be proven, and too many women will continue to be abused. So there is no help but for public testimony.

"But that isn't true of these tapes. If I let them out, some other writer will turn a profit on Laura Chase or—after this trial—on Mary Carelli." Masters paused. "I assume, McKinley, that what happens to these tapes is a matter of indifference."

Brooks shrugged. "To *me*. Maybe not to Ms. Steinhardt."

Masters gave a thin smile. "Then perhaps I should ask Ms. Steinhardt whether I should burn them, or simply cut them to shreds. But I won't. What I *will* do is give Ms. Carelli's tape to Mr. Paget. Out of this entire mess, *that's* the justice I'm most certain of."

Paget fought back his surprise. "For one," he said quietly, "I appreciate that."

Masters nodded, then turned to Brooks. "As for the tape involving

Laura Chase and James Colt, I'm leaving it in your custody. I'm sure that everyone can trust your discretion until such niceties as ownership get sorted out."

Brooks smiled. "Of course."

Masters faced Paget again. "Which brings me, Mr. Paget, to the two *missing* tapes: the second Carelli tape and the one regarding Lindsay Caldwell." Masters glanced briefly at Sharpe. "I won't ask if you know where they are—I can't think of any reason for a defense attorney to turn them over. But if there *was* a reason, there isn't anymore. Not after today."

Slowly, Paget nodded. He could think of nothing to say.

Caroline Masters looked at him intently. "I suppose some journalist can argue that by lying, Ms. Carelli brought the 'truth' down on herself. But Lindsay Caldwell deserves better."

"I agree, Your Honor."

"I thought you would." She turned back to Brooks. "I take it you've no further interest in *those* tapes, either?"

"None."

Judge Masters stood abruptly. "Then that concludes our business. You did well, all of you."

They began to file out the door. Paget was the last. When he turned, Caroline Masters was already sitting.

She raised an eyebrow. "Yes?"

"I was just hoping, Your Honor, that I'll see you again."

The thin smile flickered. "In municipal court? I would hope not. For both our sakes." The smile faded. "But there *is* one more thing I'd like to say to you."

This time, Paget smiled. "It's too late to tell me that I'm losing this case."

Caroline Masters did not smile back. "Mary Carelli," she said softly, "is a very lucky woman. That's what I meant to tell you."

Leaving chambers, Paget saw Marnie Sharpe alone at the drinking fountain. He walked over and stood beside her.

"What happened?" he asked.

"We dismissed the case." Pausing, Sharpe fixed him with a level gaze, reading his face. "Or do you mean what *really* happened?"

"Yes."

She turned, glancing down the corridor outside chambers. Brooks and Terri were talking some distance away, waiting for their partners; their faces seemed amiable enough, the look of lawyers whose conflict has been settled. Sharpe shrugged. "I suppose you'd be the last to tell anyone," she finally said. "Perhaps I can give you the condensed version."

"Please." Paget looked at her. "So what *did* happen?"

"Caroline. Yesterday afternoon, she called us."

Some part of Paget had guessed this much, but it still surprised him. "What did she say?"

"That Dr. Bass's testimony had made her rethink excluding Melissa Rappaport and Lindsay Caldwell." Sharpe's voice took on a slight edge. "My mistake, obviously. And that—'probable cause' aside—the case was too murky for Mary Carelli to go to trial. About which, now that it's over, I'm not entirely sure she's wrong."

"And that persuaded Brooks?"

Sharpe smiled without humor. "There was more. Caroline had two choices, she told us. The first was to throw out the case and take the risk of being reversed on probable cause, thereby looking like a bad judge. The second—which she claimed to like better for her own sake— was to reopen the hearing and allow Rappaport and Caldwell to testify. But after *that*, the electorate might return Mac to private practice." Sharpe's voice became a sardonic mimicry of Caroline's. "Of course, she told Brooks, that was sometimes the price of pursuing a case one believed in. But she was giving him a third choice: dismiss the case, and she would help him look like a statesman."

Paget pondered that. "It's not a bad suggestion, you know. Between Linton, Rappaport, and Caldwell, a jury would have hated Ransom. Mac might have ended up wishing Caroline *had* thrown out the case."

Sharpe glanced back over her shoulder; Brooks and Terri were still talking. "He knew that," she said quietly. "And there was something else. The tapes. He didn't want the Laura Chase tape out, given the impact on James Colt's family. That's why he was willing to let Mary's tape go."

"A prudent career move, I would think. What with James Colt junior running for governor."

Sharpe nodded. "Mac could imagine the next D.A. walking over his grave. He spent some time wondering which choice Caroline would make if he refused her, then decided to take her up on it. The right decision, I suppose."

Paget nodded. "If Mac *hadn't* bitten, I wonder which choice she would have made."

"Oh, I always knew—I'd seen her with those women in chambers. I just didn't tell Mac."

"Will you tell *me?* Now that it's over."

Sharpe considered him for a long time. "Caroline was bluffing," she finally answered. "She'd have thrown out the case and taken her chances. But she'd never have put those two women through testifying in public—especially Caldwell."

"You think so?"

"I'm sure so." Pausing, Sharpe gave the wintry smile again. "Caroline said that to kill the case, that's all. She just wanted to be sure about those tapes."

EIGHT

THAT EVENING, Christopher Paget watched himself on television for the last time.

The news began with McKinley Brooks on the courthouse steps, poised and in command, explaining how he had weighed the evidence against the importance of the issues. The story quoted Caroline Masters as calling Brooks's decision "courageous" and "appropriate." As Paget had wished it, his own time on camera was brief: he thanked the district attorney, expressed his admiration of Judge Masters, and was finished.

"As for Ms. Carelli," the newswoman went on, "her comments were uncharacteristically subdued."

Mary appeared on-screen. Her face showed relief but no elation, and she looked too tired to smile. Microphones jabbed at her from every angle. Carlo stood next to her.

"I would like to thank Christopher Paget," she began, "who gave to my defense more than I ever wished to ask."

She paused there; as the camera zoomed in, she seemed to search for words. "I would also like to thank all those who supported me," she finally said. "Especially those women who came forward to testify— Marcy Linton most of all. In a case like this, regrettably, it seems that there is no other way to defend yourself.

"As for me, I'm relieved. I will always think about Mark Ransom's death, but I hope that you will forgive me if I don't wish to talk about it, except for the issues it raises. For me, it's done.

"In three days, I intend to fly back to New York and resume my life." She paused again, voice lower. "But when I do, it will be with special thoughts of my son, Carlo Carelli Paget. Thoughts too private to share, and too deep not to acknowledge. Like his father, he is more than I could have hoped for."

Watching, Paget saw the smile on Carlo's face. Mary glanced at him, then softly finished: "That's all I have to say."

She had been true to her word. The crowd had parted for her; she had stepped into the limousine without looking back.

Now, hearing the doorbell, Paget knew that it was she.

She stood in the doorway. The black limousine was double-parked outside. "Is Carlo ready?" she asked.

"Almost. He's just out of the shower, I think." Paget hesitated. "Would you care to come in?"

"Do you mind?"

Paget looked at her for a moment. Then, slowly, he shook his head. They walked into the library.

Mary studied the palm tree for a moment. "Carlo told me about that tree," she said. "Before, I couldn't imagine why you didn't cut it down."

Paget shrugged. "I was waiting until he went to college."

She turned, studying his face. "Are you going to tell him?"

"No. I'm not."

She paused. "Why?"

Paget looked past her. "Because we put too much time in," he finally said, "believing we were father and son. So now we are."

Her body seemed to relax a fraction. "I don't know what to say to you, Chris."

"Trying would be pointless. Everything you could have said was on that tape." He paused. "I know much more than you ever could have told me. The good, and the bad."

She looked down. "What about Carlo and me? I'll want to see him."

"Then see him. Just arrange it between you and Carlo. You and I are quits with each other, Mary. At last, and as we should be."

Slowly, Mary nodded.

In their silence, Carlo came down the stairs. He smiled at them both, looking happier than he had since Mary had killed Mark Ransom. Perhaps, Paget thought, happier than he had ever been; his mother and father both loved him, and they meant each other no harm.

"You're very handsome," Mary said. "You carry yourself like Chris."

Carlo smiled again. "Can't help *that,*" he told her. "But my friends say I look like you."

"Oh, well," Paget said.

Mary smiled. "Ready for dinner?" she asked her son.

"Always."

They headed for the door, Paget following them, Mary looking fondly up at Carlo. She stopped in the alcove, as if seized by a sudden thought.

"Can I talk to Chris for a second?" she asked Carlo.

"Sure."

Carlo went out to the limousine. Mary looked after him, and then turned to Paget.

"Yes?" he asked.

She hesitated. "Do you remember on the tape, when I told Steinhardt I'd have aborted Carlo if you hadn't bailed me out?"

"Of course."

"That was true." She paused again, and then added softly, "So when you look at Carlo, and think that you see nothing of yourself, remember that."

Later that night, Paget decided to burn the tapes.

He took them to the library. Then he threw logs in the fireplace, lit the kindling. He had time, he reasoned; Carlo and Mary planned to stay out late.

For no particular reason, he started by burning the Lindsay Caldwell tape. Tomorrow, perhaps through Terri, he would find a way to tell Caldwell that her secrets now were her own: what she chose to do with them was hers to decide, just as Paget was deciding for himself. He picked up the first tape of Mary.

He paused for a moment, watching the fire burn. How many times, he thought, had Carlo watched with him, caught by the sinuous dance of flame against darkness. Then he began pulling the tape from its spindle.

When the front door opened, Paget started.

It was Carlo.

He heard his son walk to the library, drawn by the firelight and the crackling logs. By instinct, Paget picked up the second tape. Mary, saying that Carlo was not his son.

The boy stood in the entrance. "What are you doing?" he asked.

There was nothing he could say now, Paget knew, but the truth.

"Burning this tape." Paget paused. "After this, there's one more."

"The one about my mother?"

"No," Paget answered. "The one about *me* and your mother."

Carlo hesitated. "Can you do that?"

"It's not evidence anymore, Carlo. All that's left now is a source of pain. I'm free to do as I wish."

Carlo looked at him steadily. "Then can I hear it? I'm your son, after all."

"You are, Carlo. But you're also becoming an adult. And part of that is accepting that your parents are people apart from you, with their own lives and their own failings." Paget paused. "Yesterday you asked me to help your mother. Today I'm asking you to help us both. By living in the present, and letting us put the past to rest."

Carlo looked at him. It was so strange, Paget thought, to face Carlo with the secret of his birth clutched in one hand, asking as a favor for himself the forbearance that, if only Carlo knew it, would keep the boy's world intact. But he could not tell him: in the end, Carlo's happiness would rest on his compassion for his parents.

"I'll always wonder," Carlo said.

"Try not to. For you, your mother and I are what we are to you today. Nothing else matters." Paget paused again. "Unless, of course, you make it matter."

Carlo looked pensive. "What would *you* do, Dad? If you were me."

Silent, Paget gazed at the second tape. Then he tossed it, underhand, to Carlo. For an instant, the moment reminded him of that first day in Boston, when Paget had thrown this boy a red rubber ball. Except this time, of course, Carlo caught it.

"I'd help me burn this," Paget said.

Carlo gazed at him another moment, then at the tape in his hand. "How long has the first one taken you?" he asked. "You were never very mechanical."

Paget smiled. "It skips generations. My father once built a ship in a bottle."

Carlo hesitated. Then he sat on the rug, Paget sitting next to him. They faced the fireplace, backs against the coffee table, as Carlo and Paget unspooled their tapes.

"I'll bet you planned on doing this without me," Carlo said.

Paget turned to him. "Why *did* you come home early? Nothing wrong, I hope."

"Nope. But my mom and I are doing something this weekend. We got to the end of dinner, and I just wanted to be with you."

"Why?"

Shrugging, Carlo gave Paget a fleeting smile. "Who knows?"

They sat there next to each other in companionable silence, unspooling the tapes of the past. When Carlo was finished, he held the tangle of tape in front of him. Then he stood and silently tossed it into the fire. The tape seemed to wither with the heat, crackling, and then it disappeared in flame.

Together, they watched it burn, and with it, the truth of Carlo's birth. It was right, Paget thought, that this was so. For what Paget had learned from Carlo was that being a parent was not about ties of blood, any more than starting a family can assure love among its members. These bonds are ours to make, Paget knew; we define them, day by day, by who we choose to love and how we choose to love them. And, by these choices, define ourselves.

Paget glanced over at his son. Perhaps, Paget thought, Carlo might have learned as much from the tape. But the lesson of the tape was for Paget to know; Carlo would learn it in his own way. The capacity to love, he already had.

Paget threw the first tape after Carlo's. They watched it vanish in the flame.

"There," Paget said. "It's done."

That night, for the first time in weeks, Paget slept soundly.

In the morning, Carlo went out with Mary. Paget stayed home.

He had a lazy breakfast, avoiding the newspaper. Then he drifted to the deck. There was little on his mind, and that was as he wanted it. It was time, as his friend Larry Colvin once had put it, to let his soul catch up with his body.

The morning sun was bright. A few sailboats flecked the bay; in the foreground, homes of pink and white stucco glistened in the light. Paget found that he liked San Francisco again.

But there was much to get used to. In the measure of his life, he had gained Carlo, and much had been lost. He did not yet know what it all meant. In two years, Carlo would go to college; Paget would be happy for him, and their house would be empty.

The doorbell rang.

It was a reporter, Paget thought, or a delivery. He debated not answering, then went to the door.

It was Terri.

She was dressed in blue jeans and a blouse, and looked wearier than yesterday. Paget smiled at her. "The case is over," he said. "You get to go home. Sleep, even."

She hesitated. "I'm a little at loose ends right now."

Paget nodded. "Sometimes that happens after a trial." He paused for a moment. "I was just out on the deck. Care to join me?"

Terri still seemed hesitant. "Maybe for a while."

Something was wrong, Paget thought. He decided not to ask.

They walked to the deck. Terri went to the railing; she leaned on it with her palms, gazing out at the bay. A light breeze rippled her hair.

She was quiet for some time. Paget watched from behind; she squared her shoulders, staring intently at the water.

"Are you all right?" he asked.

Terri did not turn. "Yes and no," she finally answered.

Paget moved beside her. He stood there, watching with her. When she turned to him, her eyes seemed large and very grave.

"I've left Richie," she said.

The realization washed over him. Terri had not come for his help, or his advice. She had simply come.

"Is this all right?" Terri asked.

He struggled to find words. "I'm forty-five years old," he said at last, "with a teenage son. You're newly separated. And you work for me." His voice softened. "Any counselor in America would tell you I'm a bad idea, and that you just need time to see that."

Terri watched his face. "But how do *you* feel?"

They looked at each other, each afraid to speak. With his next words, Paget knew, she would stay or go.

"This won't be simple," he said at last.

"I know that. I've got a thousand warnings of my own." Terri paused. "But all that we could ever do, Chris, was wonder. Now we can find out."

A moment passed. And then, sudden and warm, the surprise of his good fortune made Paget smile. "You'd make me live in Richie's shadow?"

"Please. As soon as possible."

As her grin cracked, clean and white and sharp, Paget laughed aloud.

"All right," he said. "But first I have a question to ask."

"What?"

"Is *this* what your mother would have done?"

"No-o-o." Terri leaned back, shaking her head slowly, smiling up into his eyes. "This one's for me."

THE FINAL JUDGMENT

FOR ALISON PORTER THOMAS

PART ONE

TWO WOMEN

ONE

TWO DAYS AFTER THE MURDER, listening to Brett Allen's tale of
innocence and confusion, the lawyer wavered between disbelief and
wonder at its richness, so vivid that she could almost picture it as
truth.

The lawyer looked at Brett in silence, taking in the oval face, the
delicate cleft chin, the curly ungroomed hair, the small breasts and
almost too slim body of a late bloomer who, at first glance, looked
younger than twenty-two. But what struck her was the bright green-
ness of the eyes, a gaze so intuitive and direct that it unnerved her.

As Brett described it, the night had been crisp, windless. Moonlight refracted on the still, obsidian waters of the lake and traced the
pines and birches and elms surrounding it. The only sound Brett
heard was the rise and fall of James's breathing.

They were naked. Brett straddled him, as she had when making
love. The cool night chilled her nipples, dried the wetness on her
skin. As she shivered, James, flaccid and unconscious, slid from inside her.

She felt a spurt of anger. And then the nausea returned, mingling the acrid taste of marijuana with the torpor of too much wine.
All at once, the night burst into shards—images without connection, freeze-frames of color amidst a black jumble she could not
remember.

That explained how she had acted with the police, she told her
lawyer—pot and wine, shock and paranoia. Dope was really James's
thing. As Brett said this, her lawyer saw a sheen of tears, as if the
young woman had remembered some fond detail. For days after, as
the lawyer grew to believe that Brett Allen was a murderer, the moment haunted her.

Before the dope, Brett told her, her memory was sound.

James had called her parents' home, where she was staying for the summer. They had talked a little; then, fearing that her mother might listen in, Brett had suggested that they go to the lake, take some cheese and wine. She had a favorite place, and they would be alone.

Whatever James had to say, she sensed, should not be heard by others.

Brett made her excuses. She saw the tight look in her mother's thin face, the cool gray eyes filling with things she did not say. For a moment, Brett was torn between pity and the desire to confront her, and then she decided that this was pointless. She left the house, its dark mass looming behind her.

She drove to the college for James. In the car, he was quiet, intent. His face was a study in black and white—pale skin, dark ringlets of hair, shadows on his sculpted face. One of his acting teachers, with mingled derision and admiration, had once called him "Young Lord Byron." The teacher, Brett pointedly recalled, was a woman.

They drove winding roads, wooded and silent, saw occasional headlights cutting the silver darkness, then the steady glow of a lone car behind them, traveling neither slower nor faster. Abruptly, they turned down a dirt road, hacked so narrow between looming pines that it was pitch black. The car lights behind them passed the trailhead, and vanished.

Hitting the brights, Brett slowed to a crawl, following the headlights as they carved a path between the rough-barked trunks of trees.

Then the path ended.

Brett stopped there. Silent, she opened the trunk of her battered black Jeep, took out the gym bag with the wine and cheese, then tucked a rough woolen blanket under her arm. James followed her into the trees.

Suddenly, there was no sky.

They edged through trunks and branches down a gradually sloping hill, feet sliding on the hardened ground, the result of two dry weeks after a rainy spring. A branch lashed at her face; in the darkness, Brett felt diminished, like some primitive amidst the mysteries of nature.

"Where are we going?" James murmured behind her. "To play Dungeons and Dragons?"

Why was it, Brett wondered, that people whisper in the darkness? She did not answer.

And then they reached the clearing.

A glade of grass, opening to a moonlit lake. She stopped there, looking out.

Behind her, James was quiet again.

"This is yours?" he said at last.

Can you leave this? she felt him ask. But she answered only the question he spoke aloud.

"Yes," she said simply. "It's mine. If I still want it."

She did not mean the lake. It was a mile across and nearly that wide; on the far shore were a few fishing camps and summer houses, unseen in the darkness. But since her birth her family had held the parcel where they stood for Brett. It was a fact as certain as her grandfather's love.

Brett gazed out at the water, postponing by her stillness the moment when they would begin to talk.

She could sense, rather than see, the platform where she had first learned to dive. Yet she could have swum there as surely as in daylight. Just as she could remember standing on the rocky inlet between the glade and the water, holding aloft the rainbow trout, speckled in the sunlight, so that her grandfather could see it.

Turning to James, Brett put down the gym bag and held out the wool blanket so that he could help her spread it on the glade. Laying it down, she could feel the dampness of the grass.

They settled onto the blanket, Brett sitting cross-legged, James lying on his side, head propped on one hand. Woods surrounded them on three sides; in front of them was the smooth black sheen of water. Far across the lake, Brett heard the faint cry of a heron. They were utterly alone.

"What is it?" she asked him.

James brushed the hair back from his forehead. Brett knew this as a temporizing gesture, a sign of hesitancy.

"I want us to go to California," he said at length.

Her voice was level. "I know that."

"I mean soon."

It was hard to read his face. But beneath the casual pose, so characteristic of James, Brett felt his anxiety.

"Why soon?"

He was quiet for a time. But in their year together, Brett had learned the uses of silence. She waited.

"That dope I sold," James said finally. "I never paid for it."

Brett despised James's business. They had fought about it for two months: James was adamant that this was the way for him—left without money or family to speak of—to pay his way through what he had sardonically labeled the "poison ivy league." It was, he promised, temporary.

"Never paid for it . . . ," Brett repeated in a flat voice. "I didn't know your friends gave credit."

"I need the money. *We* need the money. To leave here." James's voice rose. "Sure as hell your family won't give you any. Not for that."

"Why should they?"

"No reason to." His tone softened. "It's just that I had to do something—start a life."

He was trying to make her complicit, Brett knew. "Without asking me?" she shot back. "You're supposed to do what you want, and I'm just supposed to react to it?"

James sat up now, facing her. "I owe a little over thirty-five hundred." He leaned forward in entreaty. "I made almost forty-three selling the stuff. Enough to drive to the Coast and still have first and last months' rent."

Brett knew his dream. He would work part time and look for acting jobs; Brett would break from home and family—the stifling effect she felt of too many years of expectations—and write the books she believed she could. But this image seemed more vivid to James than to her.

"I have a life, James. A real one. And not all of it is with you." She shook her head in impatience. "My parents are *work*, all right—especially my mother. But I have one quarter of school left, and I owe it to them to finish, owe it to myself if I decide to get a master's degree. And my grandfather—who I love a lot, though I understand it's hard for you to get that—has a heart condition. What I do about them, I have to live with. Just like I have to live with *me*. This isn't about you, okay? Or even me writing the Great American Novel." She paused, finishing more quietly: "You never had a family, for bad or good or in between. It's more complex than you think."

James expelled a breath. Taking her hand, he said softly, "You're my family."

It was meant to touch her, Brett knew. But she perceived what James could never admit: that beneath his calculation was the loneliness of a seven-year-old whose mother was dead and his father vanished, his future a series of foster homes that took him in for money.

Conflicted, Brett watched his eyes, searching for the person who lived behind them.

Suddenly, James flinched. He was half standing before she heard the sound.

Underbrush rustling, perhaps the cracking of a branch. James went rigid; in that moment, Brett saw how scared he was.

It was that which raised the gooseflesh on her skin.

"What *was* that?" he said in a low voice.

Watching his face, thin and strained, Brett listened.

Nothing.

Slowly, she turned from him, saw pale branches at the edge of the glade, then darkness.

"Well," she said with a trace of humor, "they say the timber-wolves are coming back from Canada. There are all sorts of animals in the woods at night. Everything but people." When he did not answer, she lowered her voice. "How much trouble is this?"

James clasped her shoulders. "He's been calling me," he said. "My supplier."

"And?"

"He wants his money. I said I didn't have it yet."

Brett felt her eyes close. She was part of a deadline, she realized, that James had created for himself. "Then give him the money, that's all."

She heard him exhale. "Too late. He knows I lied to him."

To Brett, the phrase had an incomplete sound. When she turned to him, he was still looking over her shoulder. "They broke into my apartment, Brett. Last night. The place was torn up, and the sheets slashed."

Brett stared at him. Reflexively, she asked, "Did you call the police?"

He gave her a faint, crooked smile. With a strange mix of bitterness and affection, he said, "You really are the judge's granddaughter, you know."

Her voice rose. "It *can't* be too late, James. All they want is money. What good does it do to hurt you?"

"That's not how it works, Brett. Please believe me."

She shook her head, turning away. "There are too many surprises, too close together. I just can't deal with this. . . ."

Her voice trailed off. He had grown up protecting himself, she thought; he wasn't used to closeness.

Alone, Brett walked to the water's edge.

After a time, she heard his footsteps behind her, then saw his faint reflection in the water next to hers, a slender profile with hands jammed in pockets. He made no move to touch her.

Another part of her, she realized, was listening to the woods behind them.

"What are you going to do?" he asked.

She hunched her shoulders. "I don't know."

"We have to decide."

"You decided without me, James. Now I have to decide what I want. Without you."

His shadow seemed to slump a little. At length, he said, "Then just *be* with me, all right?"

Brett knew what James meant, perhaps before he did. It was James's instinct to see lovemaking as a refuge from his insecurity. So that, taking him inside her, Brett never knew whether he was reaching for her or running from himself.

She turned to him. "Trying to fuck me into submission?"

The crooked smile again. Beneath it Brett saw a flicker of vulnerability—James exposed to himself. "Not really."

She felt a first twinge of guilt. "Good," she said. "Because I'm hungry. And thirsty."

Tentatively, James took her hand. They walked back to the blanket.

They knelt there, James unwrapping the cheese and slicing it with a pocket knife, Brett pouring red wine into a paper cup. There was no sound but their own.

With the second cup of wine, Brett felt the alcoholic glow. A pleasant lassitude crept through her limbs.

She sat between James's legs, back against his chest, in a silent declaration of truce. They shared a cup, James taking it from her hand and placing it back again. Brett was not a drinker; with each sip, the night seemed to close in a little, become a cocoon of warmth. The passing moments were impressions—the rise and fall of crickets chirring, the sheen of water, the rich red taste of wine, the rough-smooth feel of James's face against hers. She tried to push their troubles away, save her decision for the cool, clear morning that would light the lake with silver, then with gold.

"What are you thinking?" he asked.

"I'm just being," she answered, and drained the cup.

James knew not to push her. Silent, he reached around her and filled the empty cup.

"Some grass?" he asked. "I brought a joint."

It was wrong, part of her thought. They should not drift toward lovemaking dulled by dope and wine; whatever happened would have little meaning beyond release. But she needed time to find the answer that might well end them.

When James lit the joint, sucking in the first hit with a low quick breath, she took it from between his fingers.

She did not do this much. The first acrid puff was hot and raw in her throat. But with the second, slower and deeper, she settled in James's arms.

The night changed again. The stars had a diamond clarity, undimmed by clouds or city lights. Brett became lost in them.

They stayed like that, passing the joint back and forth as they finished the bottle of wine. James seemed less a person than a presence; what Brett felt now was a deep immersion in this place—the sky, the water, the rattle of breezes in unseen trees. It was all she wanted.

And then James's hands, tender and tentative, brushed against her breasts.

She wore no bra. Through her T-shirt, she felt her nipples rise beneath his hands, her nerve ends suddenly alive, a pulse of warmth where James had not yet touched. A silent murmur filled her throat.

In this way, at least, he knew her. This way, they worked.

The tips of his fingers touched her nipples now, gently moving. And then she felt the wine and the dope and the shiver of skin exploding in a savage impulse.

She turned to him, balanced on her knees, and raised the T-shirt over her head.

Slowly, as if in a ritual, he untied her sneakers, pushed her to the blanket with one hand cradling her back, then unzipped her jeans and slid them down and off.

That he did not undress said the rest. She lay on her back, watching the stars, as he reached beneath the elastic of her underpants.

Brett opened her legs for him.

James bent his face to her. For an instant, Brett felt it as a silent offering, a plea for closeness. Then all she felt was his face against her thighs, his seeking tongue.

When her hips began to move, she could not help this, nor did she want to. The sounds from her lips were more cry than murmur, becoming quicker, a guide for him. Blood rushed to where his tongue caressed her, swift with the hotness of dope and wanting. Her movements lost all rhythm.

A cry in darkness.

Brett's eyes shut tight as the spasms ran through her body. Only as a tingle reached her fingers did she hear the woman's cries, slower and softer, recognize them as hers.

And then she was still.

She could not seem to move. Beneath the torpor, sex and dope and wine seemed to loop in circuits through her brain.

Awkwardly, Brett got to her knees. She could feel the heat receding from her thighs.

James seemed unreal now, in pieces: eyes wanting her, a hand pulling her close. She felt smoke and alcohol in the pit of her stomach. The night began to spin.

"Jesus," she murmured.

He did not seem to hear; suddenly his movements had the clumsy concentration of drunkenness. As he pulled down his pants, Brett had the jaded, antic vision of a monster she had seen in an old movie, tottering over Tokyo as he swayed from side to side.

She swallowed, fighting sickness and self-disgust. When he held his penis to her face, she shook her head.

Just don't lie down, she told herself.

"Lie back," she murmured.

He did that. Clumsily, she turned from him, crawling naked toward the gym bag.

"Where are you going?" he asked dully.

Mute, she fumbled through the bag and then pulled out a foil square. Crawling back, she held it out to him.

"You're on the pill," he said.

Brett stared at him. "I'll put it on for you."

Watching her face, he said nothing more.

Fragments now: sheathing him in latex, its oily slickness between her fingers. Clambering on her knees to mount him. The blunt feeling of him as he entered her. A fever on her skin, too clammy for passion.

As James moaned, urging himself to climax, she thought of two dogs mating.

She rode him out of stubbornness, fighting sickness. He did not come. Desperate, Brett wrenched him upward with her hands beneath his spine. He flinched beneath her; dimly, she realized that her nails had scraped his skin.

His eyes opened wider. "I love you . . . ," he murmured.

Brett stopped moving. Tenderness overtaking her, she touched his face.

James was asleep.

As she shivered in the sudden cool of night, he slipped from inside her. She stared at him, sick and stupid again, fighting the impulse to lift him by the hair. And then, abruptly, anger became sadness.

There was still goodness in him, she knew, much that had not been ruined. He was tender with her, always. When she grew angry with him, he did not lash back; he watched her, puzzled, trying to comprehend. As if listening for music he could not yet hear.

Gently, she laid his head down, turned it to one side. He slept with a child's innocence.

Lost in dope and darkness, Brett had forgotten the lake was there. And then it struck her: the cool water might clear her head.

Rising, she turned to the water.

It seemed opaque, a glassy rock. Brett clambered naked from the glade across the rocky shore, crying out as the sharp stones cut her bare feet.

A splash, shocking coolness as she hit the water.

Swimming felt hard and slow. Suddenly, she was swathed in blackness, swallowed by the lake. In panic, she flailed to keep from drowning, felt herself go under. . . .

And then, shivering and panting, Brett was lying facedown on the rough wooden planks of the diving platform. She felt surprise, then fright that she could not remember how she got there.

Slowly, like a woman half drowned, Brett turned on her back. Her mouth had the brackish taste of algae and still water. Her heart throbbed in her chest.

Gradually, her breathing eased. She had no thought of swimming back.

Time kept slipping. Brett saw an image from childhood: her mother, calm and sure then, teaching her to dive, her grandfather watching with that air of pleased reserve. Brett stared up at the moon, so seemingly close that she could almost touch the craters on its face.

And then the sense was upon her, primal and instinctive, that they were not alone.

Brett trained her eyes on the water. Distances were lost to her. When she turned to the glade where James lay sleeping, it seemed to move away. The faint moonlight on the grass was like the glow of phosphorus.

A sudden shadow rose from the grass.

Brett sat up. "James . . ."

Startled, the shadow turned. Her voice echoed on the water. "*James* . . ."

Abruptly, the shadow vanished among the shadows of her imaginings. . . .

No.

Brett stood without thinking and dove into the water.

The shock of coolness felt real now. She was less afraid to swim than to stop and look at the glade. She rose from the water's edge, trembling with cold.

The glade was dark and silent. She walked toward the blanket, grass matting beneath her feet.

James was not the shadow. He lay as she had left him, except that he was gazing at the moon.

A sound came from his throat.

Like snoring, Brett thought as she approached. Yet not snoring. In the moonlight, she saw that his mouth was open, heard ragged breaths.

The sound again. A gurgling, Brett thought suddenly. Like the sound of a man whose lungs had filled with water.

James, she thought with horror, was drowning in his own vomit.

With quick, instinctive movements, Brett knelt beside him. As moonlight caught his face, she started CPR.

She felt wetness on his lips, heard her own breath rattle in his throat. Her eyes shut tight. Like a delayed image on the retina, Brett saw his face in the instant before she had placed her mouth to his.

As Brett recoiled, a warm spray rose from his lips, flecking her face and throat and breasts.

His body shivered beneath her in a twitching spasm. His face was speckled, eyes staring at nothing. The last soft spray of blood rose from his severed windpipe.

A knife stuck from his ribs.

Brett made no sound. She stood, trembling, straining to comprehend. Saw the blood on her fingers.

Only then did she realize that she had pulled the knife from his chest.

As her shriek carried across the water, Brett the reasoning human ceased to exist.

All was a nightmare collage: Her hand clutching the knife. His wallet where it had fallen as he undressed. The dark slash through his throat.

She whirled, staring wildly at the woods. The wind, moaning now, was the sound of James dying.

Blindly, Brett ran toward the darkness.

It enveloped her. Branches beat her face and body as she flailed at the darkness with both hands, hacking the leaves from her face. Now the darkness seemed to enter her mind. The flailing became a dream, no moment distinct from the other, the glade behind her no more real than the moon she could not see. Time had no end. And then, in sudden moonlight, the outline of a Jeep appeared.

Brett slowed to a walk. Emerging naked from the trees, she was uncertain of what to believe. Tentative, she rested her hand on the Jeep.

It was real. The keys were still inside.

Brett opened the door, throwing what she had carried on the passenger seat, and turned the ignition.

It worked. Brett locked herself in. She did not know how long she sat there, naked, listening to the low hum of the motor.

She switched on the headlights. When she spun the Jeep around, their beams cut a path between the trunks of trees. Just as before.

Shifting gears, Brett began to drive.

Brett awoke in darkness.

She tasted blood in her mouth, then vomit. Her lip felt swollen.

She was slumped, naked, across the steering wheel. The stench of sickness filled the Jeep. Her stomach felt hollow.

Brett felt a pounding in her head. Stiff-necked, she leaned back in the seat and looked around her.

A wooded roadside. She did not know where she was, how she had gotten there, how long she had been unconscious. She was not sure why she was crying.

A light came toward her.

Brett winced, turning her head. The light filled her windshield.

Behind the flashlight was the shape of a man.

The light circled the hood of her car, moving toward the driver's side. Brett curled sideways, face pressed against the door, arms folded across her chest, eyes and mouth clamped tight.

There was a tap on the window.

No, she thought. *Don't hurt me.*

Fingers digging into her skin, Brett forced her eyes open. The tap of the flashlight stopped. A beam of light crossed her body, captured her hips, a shadow of pubic hair.

As Brett gazed at her own nakedness, a tremor ran through her.

"Open up," a voice demanded.

A young man's voice, Brett thought. She swallowed. "Open up," he said again. "Police."

Police. By instinct, she reached for the window crank, one arm covering her breasts, and lowered the glass between her and the voice.

He was young, with short dark hair and a pale face. Though he wore the jacket of the local police, she did not know him.

He looked startled, embarrassed. "What happened?"

Brett shook her head. Words did not seem to come.

"Sick . . ."

He thrust the flashlight into the car, jabbing the beam here and there. In a taut voice, he asked, "Is someone hurt?"

Sudden images. Straddling James in the night. His staring eyes. A knife in her hand.

"Miss?"

A nightmare. She must be stoned, the terrible pictures a dream. James was home in bed.

Her voice was weak. "Please, take me home. . . ."

His flashlight lit the passenger seat.

A heap of clothes, a wallet. A bloody knife.

"I'm taking you in, miss."

A convulsive sob ripped from Brett's throat. "Why . . . ?"

A moment's pause. "For driving while intoxicated."

The beam moved back to her. Brett saw blood on her hands, speckles of blood on her torso.

She curled, elbows on knees, and vomited.

He gave her his jacket.

Their drive to the station was lost to her. The shotgun in his car, the crackle of a radio, nothing else. When she found herself sitting hunched against the wall of a cinder-block cell, it was like awakening from a blackout. The policeman stood over her.

Looking away from him, she pulled his jacket to midthigh, saw specks of vomit on her legs.

In his hand was James's wallet, opened to his driver's license. Staring from the picture on the laminated card, James looked stiff and frightened.

With terrible vividness, Brett saw the gash in his throat.

The cop's voice was strangely gentle. "I think there's someone hurt out there, needing our help. If we can't find him . . ."

Brett's eyes filled with tears. "Look by the lake," she said dully. "Maybe he's there."

"Heron Lake?"

Swallowing, Brett nodded.

The cop hurried away. Brett heard footsteps on tile, his voice on the telephone. She waited, drained, until the cop returned.

"I'll drive you to the hospital," he said.

A blond, bird-faced woman in a state trooper's uniform was waiting by the emergency entrance.

The cop holding one arm, the trooper the other, Brett was led through the bleak corridors. She passed beneath the fluorescent lights as if sleepwalking.

At the end of a corridor was an empty room.

The trooper took Brett inside. Brett stood there, staring at the room—an examining table, two chairs, a metal cabinet and sink and mirror.

She felt the young cop pause in the doorway. "Is this all right?" he asked.

The trooper nodded. "For waiting, yes. Until they find something."

The cop hesitated, glancing at Brett, and left.

The trooper closed the door behind them, stood facing Brett. "I'm sorry," she said, "but I need to take that jacket off."

Brett clasped it tighter. "Why?"

"Procedures." Without waiting for an answer, she unzipped the jacket and slid it from Brett's shoulders.

Brett shivered again.

"Can I clean up?" she asked.

"No. Not yet."

Brett stared at her. Taking the handcuffs from her belt, the trooper turned one chair to face the cabinet and in the crisp manner of a schoolteacher said, "Sit here, please. I have to cuff you."

Suddenly, Brett was angry. "Tell me why, damn it."

The trooper shot her a level glance. "So that you don't touch yourself."

For that instant, Brett wanted to call her parents, her grandfather. Then the mirror caught her reflection.

Her face was flecked with blood.

Brett walked forward, as if drawn to her image. Dried blood speckled her lips, her throat, her breasts.

Brett sat in the chair.

As she held out her hands, there was blood on her fingertips.

Pulling Brett's arms behind her, the trooper cuffed her to the metal chair.

A plump nurse came. Silent, she took out a needle and punctured Brett's arm. With an odd detachment, Brett watched the plastic tube fill with her own blood. She hardly felt the needle.

The nurse left her with the trooper.

"How long will I be here?" Brett asked.

No answer.

Time passed. Perhaps minutes, perhaps hours.

There was a knock on the door.

Brett turned. The trooper opened the door slightly, speaking through the crack to shield Brett's nakedness.

"What is it?" she asked.

A male voice, new to Brett. "They found him. At Heron Lake."

"Is he all right?" Brett asked.

Whispers now. Closing the door, the trooper handed her some papers.

"This is a search warrant," she said. "For you."

"For what?"

A long, slow look. "He's dead."

Brett began shaking.

Everything changed.

Brett stood there, mute, a magnet for strangers. Another female trooper entered, with a Polaroid, took pictures of Brett's face, her throat and torso, her fingertips.

A knife in her hand . . .

A nurse in a scrub suit snipped a piece of Brett's hair and then, kneeling, clipped from her pubic hair.

The images came quicker now. A shadow, turning . . .

The nurse scraped flecks of blood from Brett's skin onto a piece of plastic.

A soft spray rising from his throat . . .

She turned to the trooper. "I need to see someone."

A quick careful look. "Who?"

"The policeman who brought me here."

The trooper shook her head. "First we have to finish this. Then we'll find him."

At the trooper's signal, a mustached doctor approached from the side. Gently, he led Brett to the examining table, explained that he would take a swab from her vagina.

Brett lay staring at the fluorescent lights. As she opened her legs, Brett remembered the feel of James's tongue.

"It's all right." The doctor's voice was soothing, comfort for a patient. "We're almost done."

Brett stood, unsteady. The trooper held out a jumpsuit. "You can dress now."

Brett did not try to clean herself.

When she was dressed, the nurse took one hand, then the other, slipping a scalpel beneath each fingernail.

James wincing as she scraped his back . . .

She had left him there. For minutes, perhaps hours, she had not told them.

"Please," she pressed, "I need to talk now."

They took her fingerprints and then drove her to the jail.

The sky was purpling with the first thin streak of dawn. Now she recognized the police station.

They led her to a cramped room with two metal desks. The young cop sat at one desk; somehow he had gotten back his jacket. A stranger sat at another, a tape recorder in front of him.

He was stocky and red-faced, with pale-blue eyes and an air of calm authority. He understood she wished to talk. Hoped she wouldn't mind the tape . . .

"You have the right to remain silent . . ."

Brett waited until he finished, and then she began to tell them all she could.

When it was over, she searched their eyes, saw nothing. They led her to the cell again, and she was alone.

Voices came from the next room. "Do you know who her grandfather is?" someone asked.

Only after a time did she see the man standing in front of her cell.

He was tall and almost gangly, his black hair flecked with gray. His work shirt and khakis were wrinkled, and he had not yet shaved. Twin creases elongated his face and made the large brown eyes knowing and a little sad. He seemed kind, somehow familiar.

"Oh, Brett." His voice was soft with melancholy. "What in God's name have you done?"

It was, Brett's lawyer reflected, precisely the question she wished that she could ask. But she was a defense lawyer and could not.

"Who was he?" Brett asked her. "The man at the jail."

The lawyer hesitated, caught in the scene as Brett was describing it, still wondering how much could be believed. But the tall man's face was very real to her.

"It was the prosecutor," she told Brett. "Jackson Watts. Through college, we were friends."

"And now?"

"I don't know." The lawyer paused, then finished. "The last time I saw him was before you were born."

For a moment, Brett looked at her curiously. But she said nothing.

"Tell me," the lawyer inquired. "Did the police ask anything else?"

Brett hesitated. "I think they asked if James had other girlfriends."

The lawyer tilted her head. "To which you answered . . . ?"

"No." Brett's voice was angry now. "No."

TWO

Two DAYS EARLIER, the Honorable Caroline Clark Masters had stretched her tan legs in front of her, wriggled some sand from between her toes, and gazed out at the white-capped blue of Nantucket Sound.

It was summer, and afternoon. Sun glistened on the water; a northeast wind tousled the loose black ringlets of her hair. The ocean was dotted with boats, sailing across the northeast winds to Edgartown. Along the beach, stretching to a faraway point, waves broke onto the tawny sand until they seemed to meet a white mist in the distance, sitting lightly on the water. Caroline's mind flooded with memories.

Perhaps it was the boy. A college kid, really—a distant figure now, growing smaller as he walked the surf.

He had looked, she thought, a little as she remembered David. Not the hair so much. Something about the eyes. Perhaps that was why Caroline, disposed to solitude, had spoken to him.

"Hello."

He stopped on the sand, looking from Caroline to the sprawling house on the bluff behind her. Feeling a little guilty, perhaps, to be walking her private beach.

"Hi." He shifted from foot to foot, dressed only in cutoffs, lean and brown and not bad looking. With a certain awe, he asked, "Is this place yours?"

Caroline smiled, shook her head. "Just renting. For a week."

He took that in, nodding. Yes, Caroline had thought, a certain pensiveness in the eyes, the same gray blue. But not the same quickness.

"I've been wondering about this place," he said. "They say the beach has changed totally, from erosion and storms." He nodded to the rocks and railroad ties behind her, rising from the beach to the bluff. "A few years ago they nearly lost this house, someone told me."

Caroline smiled again. "*Thirty* years ago," she said, "you and I would be standing on the lawn. The owner and his family played croquet there."

"You knew them?"

Caroline nodded. "Yes. I knew them."

As he looked at her more closely, Caroline sensed him calculating her age. Then he turned, pointing to a spit of sand some distance away. "I saw rocks out there, some pilings. Know what that was?"

"A boathouse. But it belonged to the place next door."

"Know what they used it for?"

"Storage, sometimes." There was something else, Caroline saw, the way he tilted his head. "One year, a caretaker lived there."

"Hurricane got it, I guess."

Caroline made her tone dismissive. "I suppose. It was here the last time I was."

The boy was silent, as if reflecting on the transience of things. "I hope you haven't minded my asking these questions."

"Not at all."

He tilted his head again. "Do I know you from somewhere?"

Caroline realized, suddenly, that she was not quite ready to have him leave. Smiling, she decided to flatter him a little. "I think I'd remember you."

"I don't mean it's like we've met." Vaguely flustered, he seemed to peer at her. "Didn't you used to be in the movies or something?"

This tacit reference to her age—which Caroline thought she more than deserved—made her laugh aloud at herself. The grin that came with it had a sardonic quality which was relieved by a dimple on one side of her mouth, a light in her green-flecked brown eyes. "Not that I remember."

The boy stepped closer. "No, really."

Caroline looked up at him, amusement still playing on her mouth. "No," she said firmly. "Really."

Now she watched him, growing smaller, until he vanished.

Forty-five, she thought, scraping the wounds of young womanhood. She did not quite understand this: the events that had defined her had made Caroline Masters a distinctly unsentimental woman.

Yet she had come here. Sometimes it seemed to her that the central events in her life had not happened in New Hampshire, the home of her girlhood, but in this place, Martha's Vineyard, near the water.

She gazed out at the sound. She did not even know whether David was still alive—a man in his forties who thought of her little or, perhaps, with bitterness. She was past all hope of knowing.

Perhaps it was the nomination that had jarred the past from dormancy.

"Is there anything we should know," the President's counsel had asked her, "which might embarrass the White House?"

"No," Caroline had answered. "Nothing."

She had spent twenty years of her life, with rising intensity and ambition, waiting to be asked this question. Perhaps it was inevitable, with the nomination so near her grasp, that she would think about the things that had made her as she was.

The President was down to two choices, Caroline and a fine Hispanic lawyer. At five o'clock, the phone would ring, and Caroline Clark Masters would—or would not—be appointed to the United States Court of Appeals.

A step, though the thought made her superstitious, from the United States Supreme Court.

A giant step, yet perhaps not much farther than the distance she had already come. Caroline had arrived in California at twenty-three, with no friends or family she spoke of. Had put herself through law school, then spent fifteen hard years at the public defender's office, representing murderers and petty drug dealers with more success than the odds allowed; teaching and lecturing and writing articles on criminal justice to spread her reputation; widening her contacts through women's groups and a little politics; yet careful, always, to keep a core of privacy.

And then Caroline was appointed to a minor judgeship, the San Francisco Municipal Court. This much she had planned. But what followed—the Carelli case—was an accident.

The charge was murder. The defendant, Mary Carelli, was a well-known network journalist; the victim was a celebrated novelist. They were alone in a hotel room when, if Carelli could be believed, she had killed him to prevent a rape.

Caroline conducted the preliminary hearing. The medical examiner believed that Carelli's claim of attempted rape did not square with the crime scene or the condition of the body. It was more than enough for a Municipal Court judge to find probable cause for a murder trial in the Superior Court, which—in any other case—would have been Caroline's only job. But then Carelli's lawyer decided to use the preliminary hearing to challenge probable cause, and demanded that the hearing be televised.

For two weeks, Caroline ran the most watched hearing in memory with skill, wit, and, most observers agreed, impeccable fairness. By the end of the hearing Caroline was as much a celebrity as Mary Carelli herself.

Caroline wasted no time. She appeared on television, gave interviews—long on charm and short on biography—to carefully selected journalists. Offers poured in: the one she took, a partnership in a large San Francisco firm, offered her corporate contacts and wider credentials. When the presidency changed hands and the Democrats began dispensing federal judgeships, the people who interested themselves in these things saw the virtue of putting forward a qualified woman who was so widely experienced and so uniquely celebrated. Just as Caroline hoped they would.

The meetings began. First with feminist and other groups whose sympathies Caroline shared. Then with a committee of lawyers who screened candidates for the senior senator from California. Then with the senator herself—a meeting that, after some initial nervousness on Caroline's part, had gone extremely well. The nomination was the President's to make, and the senator was vying with senators of several other states who put forward their preferred candidates. But the senator's letter to the White House had been unusually strong, and the President was in her debt. Caroline permitted herself to hope.

And then, silence.

Months passed. She was convinced that her nomination was slipping away. A law-and-order group wrote the senator, with a copy to the President, opposing her candidacy; a right-to-life organization labeled her "anti-child" and "anti-family." Caroline busied herself in the law, long bike trips, a little hiking.

It really was time, she told herself, to get a dog or something.

And then the senator phoned. "You're still on the list," she told Caroline. "Walter Farris will be calling you—the White House counsel. So be prepared. And call me when it's through."

Farris himself called two days later, a man with a slow, rheumy voice—white-haired and overweight, Caroline knew from his pictures. There were two candidates left, he told her. He had a few questions.

They went over her background. Family history, education, skimming the surface. Simply a lead-in to his final question: *Do you have anything to hide?*

"I think that's where they are," the senator told her later. "The other candidate is a leader in Tucson's Latino community, who is also very qualified, and the senator who recommended him is quite senior on the Senate Finance Committee. If one of you has some problem, it will save the President from having to choose. . . ."

No, Caroline had answered them both, *there was nothing*.

She checked her watch. Three forty-five. In a little more than an hour, Farris would call.

She gazed up at the house. No, she decided, she was not quite ready to go inside.

Jutting from the beach was a narrow wooden dock, stretching out into the ocean until it was deep enough for docking. Caroline walked barefoot across the wooden planks to where she had tied her rented sailboat, pulled a bottled beer from an ice chest in the hull, and sat with her legs dangling over the bow.

She sipped the beer—tart on her tongue, cool in her hand—and idly watched the beads of condensation skitter down the sides of the bottle. The beer was left over from yesterday, when she had packed the ice chest with bread and cheese, beer and mineral water, and set sail in the catboat for Tarpaulin Cove in the Elizabeths, as she once had when she was fourteen. Though Caroline had not sailed the sound for years, she did not need a nautical chart: she remembered each bell and buoy precisely.

The morning of her sail had been clear; the day—water and sky—was vivid shades of blue. Caroline had grinned into the wind. She was a nature sensualist, she knew—sun and sea exhilarated her, rain depressed her. In this, she was like her mother had been.

She sailed for the lighthouse where Tarpaulin Cove lay. Docking the boat, Caroline swam to the beach, where she fell asleep in the sun. Only the lapping of the tide at her feet had awakened her.

As she sailed back, a light skein of fog scudded along the water, and the wind shifted in the Middle Ground. Caroline had fought it a little through the choppy waters, edgy. There had been no real danger. But the pull of memory was strong. . . .

Caroline turned to the house again.

It sat near the bluff, a sprawling clapboard dwelling with views on all sides, an amalgam of Cape architecture and gables, surrounded by roses and a white picket fence. The earliest section had been built in the late 1600s, then hauled by oxen two centuries later from the middle of Edgartown to Eel Pond. Her father had added the rest of the house and, somewhat later, the roses. "They grow well near the water," he had said to the child Caroline. "Like you."

And yet, when she had rented the house from its owners, they had associated the name Masters only with Caroline herself. They did not know her family; Caroline had said simply that she was "familiar with the house."

And every room in it, she did not say, *has memories for me.*

When she climbed the steps to the bluff, entering the house, the grandfather clock read four-twenty.

Forty minutes.

She walked through the alcove past the bedroom where Betty and Larry had stayed that last summer; through the beamed dining room, where their family had dined by candlelight, her father at the head of the table; and then into the sunny bedroom she could only think of as her mother's. Entering the master bath, she imagined a makeup mirror that was no longer there, saw once more her last, enduring image of her mother in life—striking and petite, peering intently at her reflection as she applied mascara with her left hand and imagined the evening ahead. . . .

But the bathroom mirror reflected only Caroline, a woman six years older than the woman in the makeup mirror would ever become. A lawyer, perhaps soon a judge, who looked little like her mother.

Except, Caroline allowed with a slight smile, that she had her mother's vanity.

The rest, to Caroline's regret, seemed to come from her father. The height—at five eight, Caroline was five inches taller than her mother. The auburn-tinted black hair, usually subdued into straightness by brush and dryer. An aquiline face that her Yankee forebears might have described as having "character": a widow's peak, high cheekbones, long nose, full even mouth, her chin cleft and strong.

Every feature would have been a little too emphatic, Caroline thought dryly, if they hadn't invented television; it was the media people who began writing, much to Caroline's public indifference and secret pleasure, about her style and aristocratic good looks. After all, Caroline had thought, it was comfortingly better than "headed straight for menopause, with cellulite lurking around the corner. . . ." Which was not, if you please, a suitable description for a high federal judge.

Four-forty.

Why, Caroline asked herself, was this so very important to her? What would she be if her ambitions turned to dust?

In her heart, she did not wish to know. Her ambition worked for her—it filled her life with interest and challenge. Filled her life, period. Some things should not be tampered with.

Perhaps, Caroline reflected, she had been foolish to come here. Even now, she was impulsive; she had merely learned to stifle her impulses or, at worst, conceal them. Returning here had been an impulse: almost no one but her secretary knew where she was; no one at all knew that this home had once been hers.

Slowly, Caroline walked to the screen porch.

It faced west across the water. Outside, a sea breeze whistled through her father's roses. Near them, on the lawn, was the smooth, flat rock—larger than a table—that her father had ordered hauled there. On his vacations from New Hampshire, he would sit at the rock, facing the water, writing his opinions in longhand. . . .

Nearly five o'clock.

Caroline sat in a wicker chair next to a glass end table with a telephone on top. Lifted the receiver, once and then twice, checking for a dial tone.

Five-ten, then five-fifteen.

Five-sixteen.

The telephone rang.

"Caroline." The rheumy voice sounded far away. "It's Walter Farris."

Caroline composed herself, trying to decipher his tone. "Walter, how are you?"

"Fine. Dandy, actually. Tell me, do you have a moment to speak to the President?"

Caroline gave a startled laugh. "Well, I *was* planning to mow the lawn . . ."

"Just a minute. He's right here."

Caroline felt her face flush. "Caroline," came the familiar soft drawl.

"Mr. President?"

"Walter tells me you want to go on the Appeals Court."

A moment's pause. "I must, Mr. President. I haven't waited this long for a man to call me since the Winter Prom."

A genuine chuckle, a sally enjoyed on two levels.

"Well, Caroline . . . it's yours."

Caroline felt a sigh run through her, and, with it, all pretense of lightness vanished. "It's not easy to tell you, Mr. President, everything this means to me." She paused, voice softening. "I've worked for this since law school. And I'll work even harder to deserve it once I'm there."

"I know you will. Anyhow, Walter wants to speak to you. Do stop by and see us when you come back for the confirmation hearings, okay?" A moment's pause. "Congratulations, Judge Masters. . . ."

"Caroline?" Farris again. "You'll need to rev up for the confirmation hearings. Jennifer Doran from the Justice Department will be in touch, to help you prepare. She's been through it all before. . . ."

Putting down the telephone, Caroline barely remembered how the conversation had ended. There were tears in her eyes.

So strange, Caroline thought, to want something so deeply for so long that you cannot believe you have it . . .

She sat there, tears running down her face now, very glad that no one could see her. At a loss for what to do.

A toast, she thought. A toast to me. She went to the kitchen, buoyant now, and made herself a pitcher of martinis.

The first martini, surgically crisp, went down in two swallows.

To hell with dinner. At a moment like this, anyone gets to be foolish. Tomorrow, no one will know but you.

At seven o'clock, she was still on the porch, watching the ocean fade to gray in evening sunlight. The bitter memories had eased away; for now, at this moment, she had no wish to be elsewhere.

It was dusk when the telephone rang.

She hesitated, trying to arrange her thoughts. A moment passed before she answered the phone.

"Hello."

"Caroline?"

At first, her mind did not quite absorb it. But she felt it on her skin: a voice she had not heard in twenty years, yet more familiar than any other. A voice that belonged to this house.

Caroline stood, suddenly alert. She found that she could not answer.

"Caroline." His voice was older now, perhaps rougher with what this call must be costing him. "There's been trouble here, with Brett. You must come home."

PART TWO

THE RETURN

ONE

THE NEXT MORNING, Caroline Masters flew to Boston, rented a Jeep, and drove north. An hour later, she crossed the state line into New Hampshire and felt herself—leaden and filled with premonitions—drawn from her future into her past.

Twenty-three years ago, she had left this place for good. She remembered little of that; sitting in the back seat behind Betty and her husband, Larry, as they headed toward Martha's Vineyard and their last summer as a family, she had felt no sense of moment. By summer's end, she had sworn never to return.

And now she had done so.

She had called Walter Farris before leaving the island, explaining only that she had a family emergency that might require a few days. He was gracious and understanding; perhaps Caroline had only imagined the faint undertone of caution, the unspoken question— what kind of emergency could be so serious that it distracted her at a time like this, so sensitive that she chose not to explain it. But refusal to explain herself was the defining choice of her adulthood; she was already fighting the superstition—foolish and egocentric, she chastised herself—that by visiting Martha's Vineyard she had reopened the past, which now waited for both Caroline and a girl she did not know.

But still he knew that she would come.

Driving deeper into New Hampshire, she felt him. The scattered farms and small towns were remnants of the long-ago prosperity that had helped make him who he was. Climbing toward the White Mountains—sheer cliffs, winding streams, and plummeting gorges, miles of dense trees broken by granite faces hewn by time and the harshness of weather—Caroline recalled his belief that New England was a place unlike any other, his admonitions on nature and the virtues of winter: how they built resourcefulness and resolve, re-minding man of the challenges ahead and the prudence needed to face them without any help but God's. And she knew, despite all her years and all her efforts, that this man, and this place, had defined the deepest part of her.

Descending from the cloud-swept summit, she drove north and west toward Vermont and into a gray, seeping rain. Yesterday seemed far behind.

The towns had grown sparse, farther apart; the roads were better, some lumber mills seemed to have closed, but little else had changed. It was a place where relationships mattered, Caroline remembered, where lives were private but memories were long, where respect—for a man or for the family he came from—once earned, went deep. For it was not a place where strangers came: the refugees from Massachusetts, the seekers of summer homes, tended to stop short of this corner of New Hampshire. These were the people who had always been there, dwindling a little, their sons or daughters drifting away to look for better jobs, others hanging on. So that life seemed as timeless as the pristine lakes, the rivers, the deep, silent forests.

The country now was undulant valleys, streams, hills rising abruptly against a broad sky. The roads became smaller; at a cross-roads by a shabby church, Caroline turned down a tar-and-gravel road where the arrow pointed to "Resolve Village." A mile short of the town, she left the road, climbing a gravel path through woods that had once been pasture, until she reached the clearing that was still called Masters Hill.

Caroline was only half aware of how slowly she drove. She was more alert to landmarks—the jagged boulder she once had climbed, the distant blue-gray view of Heron Lake—than to the feeling of the places, so familiar and yet from another life. And then, abruptly, she stopped.

Stiff from driving, she stepped into the mist and rain.

On a hillside, cleared from a stand of birch trees, was a white wooden church. The first Masters had built it one hundred fifty years ago, to serve his family and those nearby, and its spires and stained-glass windows were from another time. It was where he had taken first one wife and then another; where Betty and Larry had married, with Caroline as maid of honor; where Caroline herself had once imagined marrying. Caroline had spent most Sunday mornings of her youth here, seated with her parents and her sister in the first row, where the Masters family sat by tradition and by right. She could remember the plain wooden benches and sparse furnishings, the unvarnished services of a religion too established for hysteria. But although she knew that, by long practice, the church would not be locked, Caroline did not enter.

Behind the church was the cemetery where the Masterses lay, generation after generation.

Caroline circled the church and went there, face damp and chill.

Encroaching birches blocked the light, crowded the weathered stones at the cemetery's edge. The granite markers were worn with wind and rain and dirt. A stone—the marker of an infant long lost to memory—had toppled on its face.

At the center were the markers of her own family. On the largest of them, a granite rectangle rising from their midst, were the names of its members: Channing Masters; Elizabeth Brett Masters; then Elizabeth Wells Masters. At the bottom were the words: "Caroline Clark Masters, b. June 17, 1950." Only for Elizabeth Brett Masters did the date of death appear.

In front of this marker was another, set into the ground over the grave of Elizabeth Brett Masters, recording her for posterity as "Beloved wife of Channing and mother of Elizabeth."

Turning, Caroline walked to the edge of the graveyard.

The marker here was dirty, covered with leaves. Kneeling in the rain, Caroline cleared them with cold, clumsy fingertips. Saw the inscription, "Nicole Dessaliers Masters, b. 1925, d. 1964." Then read the stark words which were painful still: "Wife of Channing, mother of Caroline."

Face wet and cold, Caroline stood there, in silent apology for things she had not then known. Only as she left the grave did she notice that the rain had ceased.

A half mile farther, Caroline stopped at the edge of the road. To her right, beyond a wood that gently sloped away, she could spot distant glimpses of the village of Resolve—a spire, a crossroads, white wooden homes from other centuries. And then only woods again. When she was a child, he would describe for her—until she could imagine it—a countryside of farms and stone walls, cross-stitched with the works of men. A time when New England throve, and the Masters who had lived here was a United States senator.

Caroline turned, facing the house where she was born.

Three stories and twenty rooms, it rose majestically to a domed octagonal cupola, from which the Masterses could see for miles. White-painted wood, arched windows, a massiveness unrelieved by ostentation or the fripperies of architectural fashion. The indulgences were inside: twelve-foot ceilings; seven granite fireplaces; a four-story winding staircase; the floating ballroom.

To him, it was a symbol of his birthright and the obligations that imposed: this house could not be abandoned like other houses but must be maintained and passed on, like the life of the Masterses themselves. Yet within the family he could be droll about its origins. The first Masters, Adam, had fallen deeply in love with a young woman from that cosmopolitan oasis Portland, Maine. Intent that she should marry him, Adam had built this home as a monument to his passion, hoping to surprise and dazzle her. A week after its completion, Adam had received his own surprise: a letter from the young woman, breaking their engagement. The home was, her father told Caroline as a child, an enduring monument to how foolish some women can make some men, a folly which every Masters for generations since had borne the cost of heating. To Caroline, it had seemed quite funny, then.

He still bore the cost, of course. The outbuildings—a barn, the attached garage which had once been a stable—were newly painted. Walking the stone path that rose gently up the hill and beneath the shade of ancient trees, Caroline saw that the grounds were well maintained, the water of the small pond near the barn fresh and clear. It seemed much as it was on the day she had last seen it.

She paused, drawing a breath. Then the front door opened; the instant before she saw who it was, Caroline steeled herself. And then Betty appeared in the doorway, hands shoved in the pockets of her khaki pants, gazing across the years at her half-sister.

• • •

Caroline walked toward Betty, studying her face. Comparing her to that last time she had seen her.

Betty stepped onto the covered porch.

"Hello, Caroline."

She's a middle-aged woman, Caroline thought with foolish surprise. Betty wore wire-rimmed glasses, and the brown had faded to a dull sheen in her short-cut gray hair. Age had brought out the gauntness that had waited beneath the surface of the younger Betty's face; the ridged nose was more pronounced; the hollows of her face were deeper, the gray eyes somehow more intent next to the crow's-feet and pale skin. In the years of their fractious sisterhood, Caroline had thought with a teenager's unspoken savagery that Betty looked like the pictures of her mother, who had at once achieved sainthood and cheated an unflattering middle age through the mercy of dying in childbirth. Now, for an instant, the sight of Betty made Caroline sad, for whom she was not sure.

Without preface, Caroline asked, "How is she?"

Betty gave her a sharp look. *How do you suppose she is?* Caroline imagined her thinking. Softly, Caroline said, "You'll remember that I don't know her."

Another swift look, as if Betty had forgotten this, and then a nod of concession. "She's emotional, sometimes willful, but *alive.* The girl of the last two days is a sunken-eyed wreck. At any given moment, she goes from stoic mourning to fear to disbelief."

Caroline nodded. "The marijuana won't have helped. Some part of her may not be sure what really happened."

Another stabbing glance; all at once, her sister looked pinched and afraid. "She didn't *kill* him. . . ."

Silent, Caroline watched Betty realize that she had answered a question Caroline had not asked, then founder in the complexities of their shared past. Stiffly, Betty said, "It was Father's idea to send for you."

Caroline nodded again. "I know that."

Betty seemed to blanch. She was off balance, Caroline saw, searching for the meaning of Caroline's words. Quietly, Caroline said, "We're both out of practice, Betty. And the end was what it was."

Betty looked down, breathed out audibly. But when she looked at Caroline again, it was with a shade less tension. "You look well,

Caroline. But that's no longer a surprise. Not since we saw you on television."

" 'We'?"

A brief glint in Betty's eyes—the hint of jealousy and irony. *So it still matters to you,* Caroline saw her think, and despised herself for her question. For a time, Betty seemed to study her. "You're a famous woman, Caroline. You did that alone—without him, or any of us. Is that what you wanted?"

You know *what I wanted,* Caroline thought with sudden bitterness. With a restraint that took all her effort, she said, "How can you even ask that?"

Betty looked away. After a moment, she said, "Brett's upstairs, Caroline."

Caroline shook her head. "I'm not ready yet. Not for that."

Betty turned to her in surprise. "Then why are you here? Don't you understand that they may charge her with *murder . . .* ?"

Caroline did not bother to explain herself.

"Where is he?" she asked.

TWO

IN A JACKET borrowed from Betty, Caroline climbed the twisting trail up the side of Masters Hill.

It was where, Caroline remembered, he always climbed to think.

"He wasn't expecting you this soon," Betty had told her. "And I couldn't stop him."

It took Caroline a moment to recall that he was well past seventy, another moment to raise her eyebrows.

"Heart trouble," Betty said, as if to a stranger. "An attack last year—mild, but a warning. He won't give up hiking, though, or even talk about it."

Traversing the steep hillside, Caroline remembered when he would take her with him to the top: the child then, and the woman now, could not imagine him as vulnerable.

But she could tell that he hiked seldom now. The trail—once well trod by the Masters family as they followed his tall, lean frame—kept disappearing in underbrush or beneath a carpet of needles: only the thread of Caroline's memory helped her find it again. It rose between thick pine trees at a steep angle, causing her to walk sideways, sometimes slipping or pausing for breath.

She was out of practice, Caroline thought to her disgust. But that was not the reason her temples pounded. Part of it was Betty; a greater part the unseen girl. But the other part lay moments ahead.

She reached a clearing: a granite-face bare cliff weathered by wind and rain. When she was a child, too young to reach the top, she would stop here with her father. Now she paused, half expecting to find him.

No one.

Caroline sat on the rock, resting. From here, the view went on for miles. There were only a few clearings now; nature had reclaimed the land, shrouding abandoned farms and old stone walls as the energy of man moved west, out of sight and mind. As land turned fallow, the Masters family had bought it, with a fortune made first in lumber, then by selling their private railroad line—which once serviced their mills—to the Boston and Maine Railroad. This was not an investment, in the ordinary sense. It was a statement, tinged with unspoken hubris: The Masterses were here to stay, as timeless as the land.

But they were not. Years later, they had sold what land they could; Caroline suspected that the prideful look of the Masters home had cost her father dearly and that, in his heart, Channing Masters feared that he would be the last generation to live and die in that same house. So that Caroline, leaving, had abandoned more than a family.

But he would go with pride, and no one outside the family would read its decline on the face of his home. The place was too much part of him, and he part of it.

This hill remained his property. The entire town could be seen from here, a toy New England village in a clearing. Caroline still recalled when they once sat here and she asked how Resolve had been named. She had imagined some stirring piece of history, a stand against Indians or for independence. But when her father turned, his eyes had the light of humor.

"Resolve," he said, with mock solemnity, "earned its name by seceding from Connaughton Falls. In the storied conflict over total versus partial immersion baptism. Back then, Caroline, New Englanders took their religion to heart."

She saw that he was not teasing. "Which side were we on?"

"The total immersers, of course." As always, his smile for Caroline relieved a somewhat forbidding mien. "We citizens of Resolve brook no half measures."

Even at eight, Caroline heard the ironic undertone. For Judge Channing Masters was Resolve's first citizen, who could speak with confidence for the others.

Later, she understood that Channing—who, as a judge, could not himself serve—helped pick the selectmen, the police chief, the school board, the vestrymen for his church, and, of course, the minister. He never said this to her; it was simply known. It was not a privilege but a duty; his interest was in finding men of probity and judgment. But the men whom Channing Masters picked treated him differently than they did others. Sitting here next to him, it had seemed to Caroline that her father watched over the town.

Caroline doubted that had changed much. In this pocket of New England, time moved slowly. Channing, with his dislike of fashion in thought or dress, found that right. Caroline's mother had not.

Rising, Caroline gazed up the mountainside, and then she resumed her climb.

At the top of the mountain, Caroline found her father sitting on a fallen log.

Channing Masters looked up at her. Caroline saw him fight several emotions at once—pain, thwarted love, instinctive pleasure in seeing her, anger that she should catch him unprepared. His voice, attempting simple gravity, caught the edge of something more.

"Caroline," he said.

She stopped some distance away, preserving space they both seemed to need, fought the numbness seeping through her as she saw the work of time: the piercing eyes looked deep and bruised; harsh lines etched his mouth; the forehead rose to midskull; gray cloaked his hair and mustache, the bushy eyebrows. Age had brought a closeness of skin to bone, and the rawboned frame seemed to stretch his body to a painful thinness. But his jawline was still clean, his black gaze alert and almost fierce. He was as she had imagined him.

She could not bring herself to call him "Father."

"You wanted me here," she said. "So I am."

He gazed at her, as if wishing to open what was closed to him. Quietly, he asked, "What were you doing on Martha's Vineyard, staying in our home?"

"Sailing." She paused. "Why else would I be there?"

Caroline saw him wince at the wall between them. In that moment, she seemed to recover her balance.

She walked to the far end of the log and sat several feet away, gazing out at the sweep of hills and valleys, which seemed less to end than to vanish. When she was ready, she turned to him. "You summoned me here as a lawyer. In every way but that—and perhaps that too—it's the very worst thing for all of us."

Channing turned to her. "Brett is innocent." Suddenly, his voice was stern. "You'll think of me as you like. But she won't be just another case to you."

Caroline studied him. "You may come to wish that she were."

He seemed to consider her meaning. With equal quiet, he answered, "You have better judgment than that."

Caroline felt the familiar weight of childhood, his expectation stated as certainty. "Then I should tell you that I don't know if I'm staying past tomorrow. Let alone if I'll defend her, should it come to that."

His eyes filled with astonishment. "How can you not . . . ?"

"How can *you* not understand?" Pausing, Caroline spoke more softly. "I would have thought you learned from me what emotion does to judgment. I won't visit that on her."

Channing gave her a stoic look. But in his eyes she read both hope and apprehension. "You've met her, then."

Caroline drew a breath. "No. I haven't."

His gaze narrowed. "She's been waiting—"

"And *I'd* like to know what the police know. Before I invite her to tell me whatever story leaps to mind."

His face went hard. "She'd never do that—"

"Frightened people do that," Caroline cut in sardonically. "Even the occasional innocent one. And I'm quite certain that you know far more about what the police know than she does."

A first faint smile at the corner of her father's mouth, remembered pleasure at the cut and thrust of their minds. Then the expression vanished, and he was grave, almost respectful. "Where would you care for me to start?"

"With the first call from Jackson. After he saw that it was Brett they had in custody."

Channing folded his hands in front of him, pensive. "Jackson called around dawn," he said at length. "Betty answered. She was already up, and worried."

"Where did she think Brett was?"

"With *him*, I assume." His voice went flat. "Long ago, Brett became quite sanguine about staying out all night, without feeling the need to explain herself. . . ."

He paused abruptly; only then did Caroline feel the chill smile on her face. Their eyes met, and then her father continued in a subdued tone. "Betty was too shaken to make sense of it. Moments later, I had to call Jackson back. He gave me only the barest details: the body, Brett's condition, the blood and knife and wallet, that she'd made some sort of statement. Then he agreed that we could come for her in exchange for her passport."

"Which puzzles me. Can it be possible that Jackson doubts she killed him? Or is it that he expects she'll make some mistake?"

Her father gave her a sharp look. "Jackson knows our family, knew Brett as a child, though she couldn't quite remember him. He can't easily believe this." He paused. "But, of course, he can tell me nothing."

Caroline cocked her head. "And the chief of police?"

He gave a small shrug. "Told me, as a kindness, that Jackson is waiting for the crime lab results—blood type, fingerprints, and the like—while he checks on this dead boy's background. I believe what bothers Jackson is that Brett waited to tell them what had happened. Or where." His voice turned cold again. "But then James Case had fed her wine or marijuana. Neither of which she was used to."

Caroline found his anger an irritant; it was hard to keep her own thoughts clear. "That's some comfort," she answered in an arid tone. "It also cuts against premeditation."

He stood abruptly, looming over her. His voice filled with anger. "Brett did not *do* this, damn you. She's compassionate to a fault, from stray animals to this stray boy."

Caroline stared up into his face, her own face hard, her tone even. "I once defended a serial killer, who cut his victims' throats and then raped them while they bled to death." Her manner became almost conversational. "After that, he went home and slept with his English spaniel. His biggest fear when they caught him was who would feed the dog."

There was a tremor in his voice now. "This is your own flesh and blood—"

"And I'm a lawyer now. That's why you asked me here, I assume. So spare me the childhood stories, please. This is painful enough." Standing, Caroline faced him. "When we meet, I'll show Brett all the compassion her aunt Caroline should. In the meanwhile, let's return to the problem at hand. For example, have they traced the knife?"

He turned from her, gazing out at the mountains. The rain of midday had become a mist, Caroline saw, settling into the valleys. "Not that I know of," he said at last.

"Did they search the house?"

"Yes."

"And found?"

"Nothing. At least nothing they took."

"What about witnesses?"

He turned back to her. "As I understand it, no one in the area saw anyone come in or go from that trailhead, nor any car or truck. Not even Brett's."

Caroline smiled a little. "Your friend the chief is not exactly a sphinx, is he?" she said, and then her smile faded. "They questioned all of you about the knife, I assume."

"The state police did. I told them I had never seen it." He paused for a moment. "Plainly, they assume Brett brought it there."

Caroline shrugged. "For them to assume otherwise would be to assume that someone happened to be in the neighborhood, decided to butcher James Case in a particularly intimate way, and then left his knife as a calling card. Which assumes a great deal, if you're the police."

Channing stood straighter. "That's not how it happened. Someone followed them."

"Into the woods at night? To my old lot?"

His mouth compressed. "It belongs to Brett now, Caroline, and it's been a long time since you lived in New Hampshire. We don't have random killings here. Someone wanted to kill this boy and waited for a time to do it."

Caroline's head had begun throbbing. She rubbed her temples. "That's a tough sell without some evidence. Brett took him there, to an isolated place, owned by our family. To them, it may mean premeditation—"

"If Brett had not gone swimming, Caroline, she might be dead as well. She's fortunate she startled him—"

"Who, damn it?"

Channing slowly shook his head. "I don't know. Perhaps a vagrant, who picked up the dead boy's wallet and dropped it at the sound of Brett. Perhaps, as she said, it was trouble over drugs."

"Does she know who his supplier is?"

"Of course not."

This time it was Caroline who shook her head. "Professionals don't kill over a few thousand dollars." She paused a moment. "Tell me, is there any evidence that someone was there? Other than Brett's word, that is."

He did not bridle, Caroline noticed; for the moment, he seemed to put anguish aside and accept that they were dealing with facts. "We don't know yet. The crime scene search was done by Jackson's people—the state troopers."

"Who found the body?"

"The Resolve police. Two young patrolmen, checking the trails."

"What do you know about that?"

"Only what the local people told me. The two policemen happened on the body, promptly searched the immediate area. Finding nothing and no one, they called the EMTs and the state police, both of whom came to the scene. The EMTs pronounced Case dead, and the state police called Jackson at his home in Concord. After which he and the Major Crimes Unit got a warrant to search Brett's property and person—with humiliating thoroughness—and then took her statement."

Caroline could see it all. "By which time," she amended, "four or five amateurs had been stumbling all over the crime scene, leaving footprints, handling the body, and generally making a mess. Not to mention, quite possibly, blowing Brett's Miranda warnings."

"True enough." Folding his arms, Channing paused for emphasis. "But the state police are excellent, and so is Jackson Watts. Don't assume that he's still the boy you dated." Another pause. "Or, for that matter, jilted."

Caroline did not rise to this. "How *is* Jackson these days?"

"Smart and unassuming, which is part of his appeal. He's chief of the attorney general's homicide unit, and—prospectively—a judge of the Superior Court. Which, in other circumstances, would please me greatly, as he's a very decent man." His voice became sad, almost valedictory. "In fact, I wish he were already on the bench. As, I'm sure, does he."

He looked ashen, Caroline saw; his thin shoulders had slumped, and the passion had vanished. "Perhaps," she ventured, "Jackson won't handle the case."

Channing slowly shook his head. "He's never owed me anything,

Caroline. Except, perhaps, to remain the man I always knew that he'd become."

Caroline searched his tone for second meanings, a mute reproach. But all she heard was the throbbing in her temples. Almost gently, her father said, "You look tired, Caroline."

I didn't sleep, she almost said. Instead she answered, "The flight, and then the drive, made for a long day. And it's not over yet."

Channing caught the reference. "You'll like her, Caroline." His voice was still soft. "Even under these circumstances."

She rubbed her temples. "Tell me, what was he like—James Case?"

"Very handsome." He paused, then his tone hardened. "But he was one of the unstable ones, weak and selfish, with that narcissistic self-involvement women seem to find so attractive."

Caroline's eyes narrowed. "How often did you meet him?"

"For more than a moment? Twice, perhaps three times."

She looked at him askance. "And you perceived all that," she said in a flat voice. "As well as how he affected Brett."

Channing seemed to blanch. "That's kept you going, all these years, hasn't it? And now it's about to make you a judge."

Caroline felt her face freeze; something in her eyes made her father hold up one hand, for silence. "Whatever your differences, Caroline, Betty has been a good mother. And because of it, Brett is a good person—"

"And one is, after all, only as good as one's mother."

He did not flinch. "You can be cruel, Caroline. But I never felt that. Not then, and not now." His hand fell to the side, and then his voice gentled in entreaty. "You will help her, won't you?"

Caroline gazed at him. "By staying," she finally answered, "or by leaving."

"Stay, Caroline. Please. I'm asking you for peace. Only for a time, and not for me—or Betty. But for her." He stood straight again. "I know my granddaughter, in a way you never can now. Most of all, I know she's innocent."

THREE

AT THE DOOR of the house, Caroline paused, picturing the young woman inside. Silent, Channing Masters opened the door, and Caroline entered her father's house.

She stopped in the living room, hands jammed in her pockets, looking about.

All was as she remembered—the antique furniture, the Chinese carpets, even the smell of things from another time. In the foyer was the grandfather clock, made in the 1850s. Oil paintings of ancestors hung in the living room, portrayed in the heroic convention—a general, a senator, a lumber magnate, a clergyman with beetling eyebrows. Her father's books remained in his library: the original Kipling and Poe, complete editions of Dickens and Henry James, Pliny's letters. It was where he had always read to her.

What was she doing here . . . ?

Slowly, Caroline walked to the dining room.

Her family had eaten every meal at this same polished mahogany table, on china drawn from the beveled-glass cabinet. After Betty had left for Smith, and then Caroline's mother had died, for a few months there had been only the two of them—Channing and his youngest daughter, dining alone, discussing his work or her studies or the news of the day. It was more than conversation, Caroline remembered. It was a tutorial in politics and human nature and how they intersected, with lessons drawn from a scale as large as history—Jefferson, the economics of slavery—or as small as the village of Resolve, the foibles of its affairs and its citizens laid bare by Channing's discerning but not uncharitable eye.

Caroline had basked in it. All that she had wanted then was to settle here as a lawyer, to follow her father's path as far as she could.

On the eve of her departure to boarding school, at Dana Hall, Caroline could feel his loneliness, read the sadness in her father's eyes. Grasping his sleeve, Caroline asked him again if she could stay. He shook his head. "They will attend to your education now," he said. "Better than I or any school nearby. Children do not always live to please their parents, or parents to please themselves. . . ."

It was that, more than anything, that had made her wish to please him.

He was standing next to her, Caroline realized. The house felt empty.

Softly, Caroline asked, "Where is she?"

"Her room's upstairs."

Caroline did not turn. "Which one?"

"Yours."

Alone, Caroline walked to the staircase, still feeling her father's gaze.

She paused, hand on the rail.

Turning her head, Caroline faced the music room, imagined her mother, sitting at a piano that was no longer there.

Even then, before Caroline knew how it would end, her mother had seemed miscast—febrile, high-spirited, too mutable and vivid for this place. Caroline remembered her mother planning trips they somehow never took, until she simply stopped; recalled how her parents began to argue over politics. Nicole had conceived an unreasoning passion for Adlai Stevenson and then John Kennedy, both anathema to her Republican husband. Barely an adolescent, Caroline had sensed this conflict as a metaphor for a conflict too deep to be spoken easily: her mother's desire to leave a life that never quite seemed hers.

She had begun to notice nights when her father grew remote. When her mother, retreating to the music room and the lacquered grand piano, sang Edith Piaf in the breathy French she had never bothered to teach Caroline, that no one in their home could speak or understand.

But even this language, Caroline came to know, was not quite her mother's own. History had left her without family or country, or any home but this.

Even her mother's "La Vie en Rose," Caroline remembered, had the sound of irony. Dark head poised, eyes nearly shut, Nicole Dessaliers Masters would sing with a faint half smile. . . .

Turning from the music room, Caroline slowly climbed the stairs, to Brett's room.

Brett sat facing the window. At first, Caroline could see only her back—the first impression of slimness, brown curls. And then she turned, a quick twist of her body, startled from thought.

Caroline gazed at her for what felt uncomfortably long, though it could only have been seconds. Saw a delicate chin, full, even mouth, slender face and high forehead. Saw that Brett was more than pretty. Saw the smudges above her cheekbones, the hours without sleep. But the green eyes—startlingly alive—gazed at Caroline with uncanny directness.

"You're Caroline, aren't you. My aunt."

Her voice was soft, yet clear. For an instant, Caroline replayed the sound of it. "I'm Caroline, yes." Closing the door, she forced herself to stop looking at Brett, to glance around the room at the mishmash of early womanhood—a red pantsuit slung over a chair; some CDs by the singer Tori Amos; Susan Faludi's *Backlash* on top of a stack of paperbacks. After a moment, she managed to say, "This isn't quite how I remember it."

"This was *your* room, wasn't it."

From birth, Caroline thought, until the day she had left. Every night of her childhood, her father would climb the stairs and kiss her on the forehead. And then there were those much rarer nights, surprising and priceless, when Nicole Masters would read to her, a faint smell of claret on her breath, her lively French-accented English lending each story a touch of the exotic. Turning out the lights, Nicole bent her face to Caroline's. . . .

Caroline found herself staring at Brett.

"What is it?" Brett asked.

Caroline composed an answer. "Nothing, really. Just a foolish memory—my first childhood act of defiance. At night, I used to listen to Red Sox games. After my mother or father would turn off the lights and my radio, I'd sneak a transistor under the covers and keep listening, rapturous to be getting away with it." Caroline smiled faintly. "Looking back, I'm sure he knew. Perhaps was even pleased."

Brett's eyes showed the faint glint of kinship. "Grandfather used to take me to Fenway Park to watch the Red Sox." A quick sideways glance. "Did he take you?"

Caroline nodded. And then remembered, so suddenly that her forgetfulness shocked her, why she had come.

Crossing the room, Caroline sat two feet from Brett.

What happened next surprised her. For close to half her life, Caroline had sat this close to clients accused of rape, or child abuse, or murder by torture or mutilation. The serial killer whom Caroline had described to her father—a pockmarked man with ferret's eyes—would have raped and killed her for the pleasure of it had there not been Plexiglas between them. So that Caroline had learned to stifle certain images. But as Brett gazed back at her, eyes filling with hope and fear, Caroline imagined the blood on her fingertips.

She touched her eyes. "Forgive me if I seem more like a lawyer than an aunt. But we've quite a lot to cover."

Suddenly, Brett looked tense, deflated. Caroline fought back sympathy: she knew too well that the most intense emotions—anguished innocence or the horror of guilt—mimed each other on the faces of her clients.

"Actually," Caroline said, "I'm most interested in whatever you told the police. That's what you have to live with."

Brett sat back. Her voice was taut. "I told them the truth. Just like I'm telling you now."

Brett, Caroline realized, had suddenly perceived the working premises of Caroline Masters the defense lawyer. That Brett was guilty. That she would lie. That Caroline's job was not to learn the truth but to keep it from the prosecution.

"The truth is often useful," Caroline said gently. "But what you told the police is unavoidable. And they do seem to have questions."

Brett swallowed. Gazing back at her, Caroline suddenly imagined a child beneath the woman, frightened and alone. And then Brett Allen reached slowly across Caroline's silence and touched her hand. "Just believe in me," she said. "Please."

Caroline looked down at Brett's fingers, white against the tan of her own skin. She felt the lightness of Brett's fingertips.

By impulse, in the face of years of training, Caroline nodded. "All right," she said. "Tell me everything."

It was dusk when Brett had finished; the quiet room seemed twilit, a filtered gray that soon would fade to darkness. Caroline felt exhausted.

Softly, she asked, "Did anyone know you'd be at the lake?"

"No one." Brett still seemed lost in memory; her response was slow in coming. "It was a last-minute thing. So we could talk in private."

"Because you were worried about being overheard?"

A short nod. "I thought I heard someone picking up another phone. Maybe I just imagined it."

"Someone?"

Brett's voice was toneless. "My mother."

Caroline watched her face. "Not your father? Or your grandfather?"

Brett shook her head. "My dad wasn't home. And Grandfather has his own phone line to his room. That's not something he'd ever do."

Caroline was quiet for a moment. "But your mother would."

"Because of James." Brett turned to the window, added in a lower voice, "My mother hated him. She knew he was dealing."

"You told her?"

"Of course not. But my dad heard rumors, from the campus police." She looked at Caroline again, paused. "You know he teaches there."

Of course, Caroline thought. That was how he lured them back here—a job for a struggling graduate student, a home for his family, a granddaughter to fill the void. And all that Larry had to lose was himself.

"Then your father," Caroline said, "must have had some feelings about James."

"Not like my mom." Anger crossed Brett's face, and vanished, as if she was too weary to sustain it. She finished in a tired monotone. "Mom wanted to give me a perfect world, as if that were even possible. So she was afraid of anyone who threatened that. Even now . . ."

Caroline sat back. In a few concise words, this girl had described the Betty she had known. There was a quick, bitter memory—two decades old—and then Caroline repressed it. She could deal with her private Betty on her own time; Caroline the lawyer had more practical reasons for drawing Brett's attention from her mother.

"This drug dealer," she said. "The one who threatened James. Do you know who he is, or where to find him?"

Brett shook her head. "James knew I hated what he was doing." There was another change in Brett's expression, to stubborn loyalty. "He said he was getting out of it. That he only did it because he had nothing. God knows I wanted to believe it. To believe in him."

Silent, Caroline sorted through her thoughts. The way Brett spoke of James did not suggest murder. Unless, of course, she was a gifted actress. "Did James have roommates?" Caroline asked. "Or friends who might know this dealer?"

"No roommates. Except for me, James pretty much liked being alone."

"Any neighbors?"

Brett hesitated. "I met a guy named Daniel Suarez," she said at length. "He seemed like a good person. But I don't think he and James were close."

"What about women?"

Brett looked startled, then defensive. With an edge, she answered, "We were together."

Pausing, Caroline wondered what had unsettled her: doubts; some problem with James; the need to sanctify a dead lover; or anger that Caroline might question a relationship that had been so sullied by his death that the police might think she murdered him.

"No girlfriends," Caroline repeated. "Just as you told the cops?"

"Not that I know about." Brett folded her arms. "You have to understand how beautiful James was. I don't know what he did before I met him. Or who might have been attracted to him whether or not he cared."

Caroline raised her head, one finger to her lips, contemplating Brett. Softly, she asked, "Is there anything—anything at all—that might lead the police to believe that you had a reason to kill him?"

Brett rose slowly from her chair, wide-eyed. Her voice trembled with sudden anger and emotion. "Do you know, Aunt Caroline, what James looked like when I found him? Because *I* remember it too clearly now." Tears welled in her eyes. "They'd cut his throat. He was choking on his own blood—when I reached for him, his head fell away from his neck, and his blood spattered my face. . . ." For an instant, Brett stopped, and then she stared down at Caroline. "Despite his faults, I loved him. If you can't believe that, or respect that, I don't want you here."

Caroline made herself be still. "What I asked you," she said coolly, "is whether the police might have a reason to believe you killed him."

Brett stood there, alone in her anger. Caroline simply waited. Anything she said or did now might drive Brett away: with an intensity that surprised her, Caroline did not want this.

Brett raised her head. "There is no reason."

"Then sit down, please."

After a moment, Brett sat. Through her exhaustion, she gazed at Caroline with fresh resolve.

Caroline's temples throbbed. "There are things I'll say or ask," she said, "that I won't like and you won't like. Starting with my next question."

Brett squared her shoulders. Something in the gesture made Caroline's heart go out to her. Even as she wondered how much of this girl's volatility—the shifts in mood, the sudden flashes of temper—came from guilt, how much from merely stress and sleeplessness.

"This spurt of blood," Caroline asked softly, "how would you describe it?"

Once more, Brett's eyes widened; but for that, her expression did not change. "It wasn't a spurt."

"But when they photographed you, there was blood on your face and neck and torso."

Still no expression. "Flecks of blood."

Caroline leaned back. "So the spurt—or spray—wasn't heavy."

"No."

Caroline expected Brett to ask why it mattered. But the girl's anger seemed to have depleted her. Even her eyes held no curiosity.

Caroline stood, reaching for the light switch, and turned on the lamp on a nearby end table. Night was falling fast now. As if awakened by Caroline's movement, Brett turned, gazing through the window at the coming darkness.

"That night," Caroline asked, "how much wine did you drink?"

A small shrug. "We shared the bottle."

"Before you smoked the joint?"

Brett still did not turn from the window. "Yes."

"How many times, roughly, had you smoked before that night?"

"In my life?"

"Yes."

"Five or six."

Caroline gave a small smile. "How could you listen to music?"

Another shrug. Her profile in the light-and-shade, Brett seemed distant now, enclosed in glass. After a time, she said, "It made my throat raw, and I felt out of control. I didn't like that."

"Can you describe how it affected you that night?"

Brett seemed to look inward, into some pool of self-doubt. "It's hard to describe," she began, and then her eyes narrowed in concentration. "Have you ever seen a silent movie? It was like that—flickering images, with black spaces in between. I can't remember sound. . . ."

"What do you remember about the cop arresting you?"

Brett's eyes closed. "The knife."

"Where was it?"

"On the seat."

"Where he could see it?"

"Yes."

Caroline leaned forward. "Did the cop who arrested you give you any warnings—right to counsel, the right to remain silent, that any statements would be used against you?"

Brett's brow furrowed. "I don't think so. . . . All that I remember was staring at the knife. Nothing seemed to go together."

"Later, why did you tell them to look for James at the lake?"

"It was the way I just described it—the guy who picked me up said someone might be out there, hurt, and it was like I saw James dying. I was still so confused." Brett looked pale now. "I know how that sounds. . . ."

"Did he give you the warnings then?"

Brett's throat worked; Caroline was not certain that she had heard the question. Then Brett softly answered, "I don't remember warnings then. Later, I do—with the two of them and the tape recorder."

Caroline fell quiet, thoughtful.

Brett turned to her, as if awakened by the silence. "Why does any of this matter?"

She sounded less curious than tired. It was as if Brett had lost her bearings, so that no event had more weight to her than any other.

For a moment, Caroline wondered how much to tell her. But Brett was bright and, beneath the whipsaw of emotions, Caroline sensed her resilience.

"It's a matter of police procedure," Caroline answered. "The first cop probably should have given you the warnings before you told him where to look for James. Which means that a decent lawyer may be able to keep your entire statement out of evidence—"

Brett stood abruptly. "But I want to say what happened—"

"How," Caroline cut in, "do you really know what happened?"

Brett looked startled. "What do you mean?"

"That drugs and alcohol do funny things to memory. What happens is that there are blanks, which you may never fill in. So people end up confusing primary memory—what really happened—with secondary memory. Which is what they *wish* to remember, or *hope* they did. Or simply believe is logical."

In the gloom of the bedroom, Brett began pacing. "It almost sounds like you don't want me to remember."

"What it sounds like," Caroline answered with cool emphasis, "is a warning. Not to remember, with the best of intentions, things that never happened. Because they may hang you for it."

Brett spun on her. "How?"

Caroline stood, walked over to Brett until they were face-to-face, and gently grasped her shoulders. She felt so fragile, Caroline thought. Brett looked up at her in weary surprise; something in Caroline's face seemed to keep her there.

"Brett," Caroline said softly, "you don't know me at all. But I want you to listen to me, please, for a few more minutes, however hard it may be. Because I've been doing things like this since you were a little girl. And whoever handles this case—if there is a case—will need you to think clearly."

Brett gazed up at her. "*You* won't do it?"

"I really shouldn't." The look on Brett's face, fearful and abandoned, made Caroline grasp her tightly. "We're related. I think that makes this harder than we realized. For both of us."

Brett turned away. Gently, Caroline guided her back to the chair. When she sat across from her again, Brett was silent, fighting for composure.

Damn him, Caroline thought. *Damn him.*

Her headache had turned to nausea. Since her father had called, she realized, she had not eaten.

"Let me explain," she said slowly, "what the police case is. Because I already know.

"There are two cases, actually. The first is premeditated murder.

"In that case, you decided to kill James well in advance. But he was much larger and stronger. So you took him to an isolated place—a lake at night—which you knew and he didn't. You brought the knife and told him it was for the bread and cheese. You encouraged him to drink wine and then smoke dope, knowing that it made him sluggish. And it was you, when making love, who got on top of him . . ."

Brett's mouth was half open; she looked stricken. Caroline forced herself to continue. "You never heard the sound of an intruder. The dope dealer story is preposterous. You never went swimming." Caroline paused, took a breath, and finished. "What you did do, before he could reach climax, was cut your lover's throat. . . ."

Pale, Brett shut her eyes.

"Perhaps," Caroline went on, "you didn't count on being spattered with his blood. That's why you made up the story about giving CPR to a man who was semi-decapitated. But you planned the rest of it to look like a robbery. Which is why you took the knife and the wallet, meaning to throw them both away.

"But you were stoned, too, and sickened by what you'd done. You panicked and then ran to the Jeep, crazy to get out. But you only got a little ways past the trailhead when you had to stop and throw up—"

"No!" Brett sat rigid in her chair. "That's not right—"

Caroline made herself finish. "You were caught with the knife and the wallet, with blood all over you. You needed a new story and were in no shape to give one. So you pretended to be so stoned you were a blackout victim, and spent the next eight hours trying to come up with an alibi that covered those facts.

"And after all that, the best you could do is a dope dealer who fol-

lowed James Case to Heron Lake at night so that he could slit his
throat over a few thousand dollars."

Brett curled forward, elbows on her knees.

"So are you really sure about taking the wallet?" Caroline asked
softly. "Maybe James left it in the Jeep. That would certainly be nice.

"It would also be nice if the police were barred from using your
three different statements—'nothing happened'; 'he might be at the
lake'; and 'a drug dealer must have killed him'—and even better if
they aren't allowed to testify that it took eight hours for you to give
the last one. So I would hope very hard that the first cop didn't warn
you." Caroline paused for emphasis. "Because if he blew it, and if
you're *very* lucky, they also won't be able to use the warrant they
got after you sent them to the lake. And that means no blood spatters, no nail samples, and—essentially—no evidence."

Hands to her face, Brett neither moved nor spoke. Quietly, Caroline asked, "Are you listening, Brett?"

Slowly, Brett looked up at her. She was ashen.

"You'd have a clean slate, and all the police would have is you, a
knife, and a body. It's not enough. And even if Jackson Watts thinks
it is, you can decide *then* whether to testify, knowing that whatever
you said before can no longer be used against you.

"That—at worst—is what I want for you."

Brett seemed to gather herself. "It's like you're accusing me."

"Not accusing. Demonstrating."

Brett's voice rose. "I had no reason to do this. . . ."

"No motive." Caroline smiled faintly. "That *is* a problem with
case number one. Which is why *that* case may never come to trial.

"Which brings me to case number two." Pausing, Caroline spoke
to her in a different tone, quiet and compassionate. "Can you stand
any more of this? It's important."

It seemed to bring Brett back to her. "I guess I have to," she
murmured.

Caroline settled back. "Case two," she said, "is manslaughter. But
in some ways, this will be even harder for you to hear."

Brett was still, watching her.

"It's very simple." Caroline's voice was quiet again. "You never
planned to kill him. You got drunk, and then stoned. Quarreled over
something. Lost your temper.

"You weren't rational. In a surreal impulse, you simply cut his throat before you even knew what you had done."

Brett's eyes were open, staring.

Gently, Caroline finished. "You may not even remember killing him. Or, perhaps, don't wish to remember. So you told the police a story you badly need to believe."

Brett averted her eyes. "We never fought—"

"The knife," Caroline interrupted.

Slowly, reluctantly, Brett turned to her. "What about it?"

"The knife is critical. If they can trace it to James, or to you, then the case I just described to you may not be the prosecution theory. It may be your best defense. To a charge of murder one." Caroline's voice became quiet; she reached out, touching Brett's arm. "Before you answer me, Brett, I need to tell you something else.

"You asked me to believe you. I'm offering you something better." Caroline's voice became softer yet. "I don't care what happened. All I care about is that you not be hurt."

Brett sat straighter, her eyes looking straight into Caroline's. With equal softness, she said, "I had no reason to kill him, and I never saw that knife before. I'm innocent."

FOUR

WEARILY DESCENDING the staircase, Caroline was unprepared for Larry.

He turned from the dining room table, a china plate in his hand. As he froze in the candlelight, Caroline saw the young husband she had known, gentle and soft-spoken, beneath the wary gaze of a man of fifty. He was still lean, gray-haired now, the kind aspect of his face tending far less to the amused irony of the graduate student who knew his choice of English lit was feckless but believed that life would somehow reward him for his foolishness, providing the job that he needed and the baby Betty so desperately wanted. For a fleeting moment, Caroline wished that she could stop that summer in midflight, so that she would not now read its end in Larry's face.

"Caro," he said softly.

She merely nodded. There was really nothing to say.

He moved a step closer, still tentative, as if to verify her presence. Caroline gave him no help. He stopped, looking into her face until he seemed to see what was written there.

"Why," Caroline said in a low voice, "did you ever bring her here?"

Larry did not flinch; Caroline saw that he had prepared himself for this. "All that matters, Caroline, is how she is right now."

Through his defensiveness, Caroline heard a trace of rebuke, as though the family that lived here was paying a price Caroline would never know. "Yes," she said coolly. "I'm very sorry for you, of course."

Larry glanced over his shoulder. In an undertone, he said, "Caroline, please . . ."

"The truth, Larry, is that I don't *know* how she is. Only that she's frightened, and smart, and trying to maintain."

The struggle for dispassion, Caroline realized, was costing her: some part of her felt gutted. For a moment, Larry watched her.

"We waited dinner." Larry's tone held a faint apology. "You look pale, Caro. It would be good if you ate something."

Caroline was light-headed from weariness and hunger. Yes, she thought, that was the Larry she remembered—considerate, at pains to empathize. The one she had opened her heart to when she could no longer turn to her own family. She shook her head. "There's been a lot today. . . ."

As if her admission gave him confidence, Larry reached out, his hand resting gently on her shoulder. "Stay," he said. "Please. We've made up a room for you."

Caroline looked into his face. Only then did she realize that Betty watched them from the kitchen door.

Following Caroline's gaze, Larry turned to his wife. To Caroline, Betty's face was an inscrutable mask.

Larry crossed the room to Betty. "I'll help with the pasta." His tone strained for normality. "It'll just be the three of us."

Caroline's mind filled with dark humor, the skewed vision of a television family. *Yes,* she imagined Betty saying chirpily, *Dad's eating in his room tonight. He gets so overexcited whenever he sees Caroline.* She realized that she was studying Betty with a grim half smile.

Betty seemed to stand straighter. At the corner of her eye, Caroline saw Larry give her sister an admonitory gaze, form a few silent words with his lips. They vanished through the kitchen door.

By rote, Caroline sat in the place that had once been hers.

They ate by candlelight, the tradition of Caroline's father and his father before him.

It played tricks on Caroline's memory. The light that danced on the crystal chandelier seemed to come from some other evening; the glow in the beveled mirror from Caroline's childhood. Gazing across the table at her sister, Caroline remembered her father at the head, Betty and Caroline facing each other, Nicole Masters—small and dark and beautiful—at the end opposite her husband. To Caroline now, more sharply than it had then, the image that struck her was of Betty sitting alone, amidst her indifferent stepmother and the half-sister upon whom her father doted. She imagined that Betty's eyes, meeting her own, still held the jealousy and confusion of the girl who—without knowing why—had lost both her mother and her primacy. But now the cost of her own motherhood was etched on Betty's face.

Larry broke the silence. Quietly, he said, "Thank you for coming, Caro."

Caroline turned, slowly, staring at him until his gaze flinched. *I'm sorry,* she imagined him saying. As if to cover this, he murmured, "We know this can't be easy."

What I know, Caroline thought, is that neither of you wants me here. Her sister's face was hard. She made no move to join in Larry's grace note.

Caroline put down her fork. "Perhaps it's best if we try to talk about what happened."

Betty was silent. After a moment, Larry said, "I was gone, Caro. Camping in Vermont." The slightest glance at Betty. "I'd gone to a trout stream, one a friend at the college put me onto."

"By yourself?"

A slow nod, and then he shook his head in wonderment. "I never thought how out of touch it left me. . . ."

Betty's mouth had set, Caroline saw. Caroline picked up her glass of red wine and sipped it, studying Betty over the rim. "But *you* were here," she said.

Betty nodded almost imperceptibly. It was more than the strain of her presence, Caroline realized; both Larry and Betty appeared hollowed out by an event they still could not quite accept. When Larry reached to touch Betty's hand, his wife seemed not to notice.

"Who else was here?" Caroline asked.

Betty stared at Larry's hand as if at a foreign object. "Just Father," she said. "Upstairs."

"When did Brett leave?"

"About eight, I think." A faint note of impatience. "I really don't remember."

"And neither of you went out—you or Father?"

"No."

"Did you know where Brett was going?"

A sharp look. "Of course not."

" 'Of course not'?" Caroline repeated.

Larry's hand tightened on the back of Betty's. "There were strains," he interjected. "Over Brett's relationship to James. Betty bore the brunt of it."

"Meaning . . . ?"

"We fought." Betty's voice was flat. "Over this boy's involvement with drugs—I assume you know about that. Over this boy, period." Betty leaned back, studying Caroline with new frankness. *Did you come here*, the look said, *to judge me?* With an edge, she said, "Being a parent is *hard*, Caroline."

Caroline saw Larry's hand clasp Betty's—a restraining gesture. In her most arid tone, Caroline answered, "So I understand."

A light flush crept across Betty's face. More evenly, she said, "James Case was everything Brett didn't need—self-centered and irresponsible, seeing her only as a convenience. There was failure written all over him. Failure and heartbreak. I didn't want that for her, and I couldn't bear to watch it." Betty slid her hand, slowly and deliberately, from beneath her husband's. "Brett," she resumed with suppressed fervor, "expects the best in people, far more than she should. Instead of a vain young man who aspired to a marginal profession, she saw a damaged boy who could become better if she was only patient. He wanted her to give up everything—"

Betty stopped abruptly, as if she had startled herself.

Larry's anxious gaze moved from Betty to Caroline. But Caroline was silent, her face without expression.

Betty faced her directly, retrieving a look of pride. "What I told her about James," Betty said, "is that she had better hope he never became a success. Because then he would leave her. After he changed her life."

Caroline's throat felt tight. Quietly, she asked, "And what was Brett's answer?"

Betty seemed to study her. "That she was old enough to decide what was best for her. And that she would." Betty's voice grew flinty now. "What she *believes* is that I'm an overprotective mother who can't let go because my obsession with her is all I have in my narrow and limited existence. And what I *know* is that the line between romanticism and self-destruction is one that she has yet to recognize."

Caroline gave her a long, cool look. "Do you really think," she asked, "that she understands herself so incompletely?"

Betty met her eyes. "Do *you* think," she answered, "that she's a murderer?"

Suddenly, Caroline felt off balance. "I don't know," she said. "But then I didn't raise her, did I?"

Caroline heard Larry exhale; saw Betty's mouth open again. Caroline continued in a tone of calm she did not feel. "While you, of course, did. Which leads me to inquire whether you ever listened to her telephone conversations."

Betty stiffened in her chair. "What makes you ask that . . . ?"

"*She* thinks you did. Specifically, that night. When she and James decided to go to Heron Lake."

Betty seemed to blanch. "Why does she say that?"

"Because she heard someone pick up a telephone."

Betty touched her eyes. "No," she said.

"No?"

"No." Betty folded her arms now, staring at the hard gloss of the dining table. "Why would it matter now? To her or to you?"

"To Brett? Because twenty-two-year-olds don't like being spied on, including this one. To me, because I can't help but wonder if you told someone else."

Across the table, Betty froze. Larry placed his hand on Caroline's arm. Voice half anxious, half brusque, he demanded, "Just what is this about, Caroline? The present or the past?"

Caroline did not take her gaze off Betty. "The present, very much so. I'd like to know if either of you knows any way that anyone could have found out where Brett was taking him."

Betty met her eyes. "No," she said succinctly. "I did not spy on my daughter."

Caroline appraised her. "And you have no idea," she inquired, "how anyone else would have known she was there."

"No." A brief pause. "Perhaps James told someone. Perhaps, Caroline, they were simply followed."

Caroline shrugged. "Perhaps."

Betty's voice rose. "*She did not kill him.*"

Deliberately, Caroline picked up the wineglass and drained it. Betty shut her eyes; Caroline felt Larry's gaze. The wine seemed to numb her.

"This knife," Caroline said. "I gather the police asked you about it."

Betty's eyes half opened. Slowly, she nodded.

Caroline turned to Larry. "And you?"

Larry shook his head. "They haven't questioned me yet."

Caroline leaned forward, her gaze sweeping them both. "Because it is *very* important that the knife not be traced to Brett. Or to this house."

Betty stiffened. "You *do* think she killed him."

"I don't think anything," Caroline answered sharply. "But whoever represents Brett can do without surprises. It's quite important that there is nothing that would lead the police to believe Brett brought the knife." Her voice became quiet. "It's not just a matter of you or Father telling the police that you know nothing about a knife, or that no knife is missing. It's a matter of being sure that there is no one in a position to say anything different. Or to be caught in a lie." Caroline paused. "Do you understand, both of you, precisely what I'm saying?"

Betty's mouth was tight. "I understand perfectly. Brett says that she's never seen the knife. You want to be sure that if she's lying, we've thought through whether we can cover it up. Unless we don't know better ourselves."

"In which case," Caroline answered mildly, "you have no problem, do you? . . . Incidentally, what you just said was very foolish. Not the thought so much. But to say it aloud."

Betty stood up from the table, staring down at her sister. "They showed me pictures of the knife, Caroline. And I never saw it before." She looked to Larry and back again. "If you'll excuse me, Brett's alone."

She abruptly left the room.

In Larry's pensive silence, Caroline heard her sister climb the stairs. She reached for the wine bottle, poured some into her glass, then Larry's.

Only then did she turn to him. In the candlelight, his face was lined, his eyes weary and sad and perhaps ashamed. But he did not look away.

"So," Caroline said softly.

Larry exhaled, gazing narrow-eyed at the flickering candle.

Caroline simply waited. Given her emotions, it was best.

"For a long time," he said quietly, "there were no teaching jobs. Finally, I took the only one I could find—at that junior college in Connecticut."

"So I recall from your letter. Something about finding a home, just as you told me you would."

Larry's face tightened. "I know what I said to you. You needn't remind me." He turned to her, finishing in a lower voice. "I wasn't good enough, Caro. I bored them, and they fired me."

"Yes," Caroline answered coolly. "That much I'd worked out."

Larry raised his hands in entreaty. "I had no job—"

"You had a child, and a life." For the first time, Caroline's voice rose. "How could *you* let him do this?"

"It wasn't like that." Larry touched the bridge of his nose. "Your father offered me a job I could believe in—not so hard, coming from someone who's on the board of a college so well endowed by his family that its oldest building is the Channing Library. And Betty wanted—or needed—to be close to him. With you gone, we were all he had—"

"Precisely."

He turned on her. "Damn it, Caroline, I had Brett to care for. I know how you felt, and why, but those feelings weren't mine."

Caroline leaned back, tenting her fingers. "Are they now?"

"Have I paid, do you mean? Would it make you feel better if I said yes?"

"Better? Nothing would. Especially now." Caroline shook her head. "No, the best I can work up is a certain morbid curiosity. About someone I was once quite fond of."

Larry flushed, turned away. When he faced her again, moments later, it was with a look of silent pain, of mute appeal.

"Really," Caroline said. "This is all so unbelievable."

Larry said nothing. Caroline folded her arms, as if against the cold. "So," she said finally, "how *has* it been for you?"

Larry seemed to study his wine. Then he sipped it, eyes still distant, and slowly put it down. "Until this happened to Brett," he said finally, "I would have told you it was mixed. A life of quiet desperation, quietly examined. But just now, I'm coming to see the truth, if the truth about *me* even matters. And it begins to seem much sadder than merely being the son-in-law with tenure."

"How so?"

"Because I'm a spectator in my own life. Although Channing lives upstairs now, this home isn't mine—I'm simply the curator. And, in the ways that are most important, this family isn't mine." He paused, adding softly, "Just as you predicted years ago."

Watching him, Caroline said nothing.

"I should have seen," he said at length, "how it was with Betty. First he loved your mother and then he loved you. Brett was like a present she gave him, because he would never love her for herself."

"Jesus . . ."

"I know, I know. But I didn't then. It's all so complicated. Betty at once worships him and resents him. A lot of the anxiety that has alienated Brett as an adult—the intrusiveness, the overprotectiveness—began because Betty so badly wanted to give Brett the love she spent her childhood pining for. The all-loving, all-embracing parent . . ."

"That's what *I* had, and it nearly ruined me." Caroline paused, finishing in a lower voice. "Perhaps, in a way, it did."

Larry fell quiet, as if unable to respond. "That's the other thing Betty gave him," he said at last. "At some point, I realized she discussed Brett with him more than me. And from the point that Channing retired, when Brett was seven, he always had more time for her." He turned to Caroline. "That's how the chain goes," he finished softly. "From your mother, to you, to Brett."

For a long time, Caroline looked at the china, the oil paintings, the silver snifter on the table. Felt the slow accretion of pain.

"This boy," she said then. "What was he like?"

Larry watched her face. "About as Betty described him, with allowances for her intensity. He was too damaged, I think, not to damage Brett if she stayed with him. What worried me—and what Betty and I could never talk about—was that Betty might affect Brett's otherwise good judgment."

Caroline touched one finger to her mouth. "Could Betty have been spying on her?"

Larry looked embarrassed. "I think she could have, yes. Although she'd feel far too ashamed to admit that, and it would be the last straw for Brett." He paused. "Betty is angry because she's frightened. And frightened people do a great many harmful things. Including trying to control their world until they've made it perfect. The irony is that Betty desperately wanted Brett to stay in New

Hampshire and, in my opinion, made it much more likely that she'd leave this fall, after she graduates, and settle elsewhere." He glanced beyond Caroline, as if to see whether they were still alone, then asked quietly, "Did Brett tell you about the fight?"

"With whom?"

"Between Betty and James. After I found out that he was dealing, James came to the house. Betty answered the door. When I came into the living room, she was asking him to leave." Larry gazed into some middle distance. "Her voice was low and tight—a sign that she's on the edge of losing it altogether, just hanging on. Before I could do much of anything, James did the worst thing he could do. Which was to smile down at her.

"You would have had to see him. He was dark, good looking, and somewhere he'd cultivated a smile that was superior and faintly derisive. So that when he looked down at Betty, his smile was somewhat like that of an anthropologist who'd happened upon a bizarre form of Pygmy."

Larry looked at Caroline now. "It was like a slap in the face," he said softly. "Before I could stop her, Betty whirled, grasped a crystal vase, and threw it at him.

"He didn't even duck. Just moved his head a little, and the crystal shattered on the wall.

"I stepped between them—James still with that quizzical smile, Betty with tears of rage. And then Brett came down the staircase, staring at the rest of us.

" 'Your mother had an accident,' James said carelessly. 'Call me.' And then he turned around and left." Larry paused. "Left a mess on the floor and a mess between my wife and daughter that may take years to fix." His voice grew low and intense. "God, Caroline, how I wish that was still the worst of our problems."

Caroline was silent for a time, caught in the vortex of the scene he had described. "And you couldn't reason with her?"

"Betty?" Larry stared at his lap, as if pondering how much to say. "There've been some problems, Caro. Betty's vulnerable right now, and I don't have much capital in the bank. And Channing felt as she did."

"Yes." Caroline's tone was as chill as her emotions. "Habit is such a hard thing to break."

They sat awhile, quiet again, in the flickering light.

Larry folded his hands. "How was it with him?"

"Father? The same. All the feelings, as fresh as when it happened. Except that instead of being twenty-two, I've spent twenty-two years living with it." She shrugged, foreclosing conversation. "I'm a lawyer now, and I'm here to do a job. If only for a time."

"For a time?"

"Isn't it clear that I shouldn't be Brett's counsel? At least if it comes to a trial."

Larry's face looked drawn now. "Do you think it will?"

"I don't know yet. But I'll try to see Jackson Watts tomorrow. See if I can ferret out what he's thinking."

"Jackson?" Larry shook his head.

Caroline looked at him steadily. "As I said, I shouldn't be counsel."

Larry sat back in his chair. He looked as weary as Caroline felt.

When, she wondered, had his hair become so thin, the lines begun to pull the corners of his mouth, the look of disappointment stolen into his eyes? Once, his smile had been so easy; Caroline had yet to see it today, nor could she imagine smiling herself. His shoulders sagged with the unseen burden of his worry.

"Come on," Caroline said. "I'll help you clear the table."

He looked at her again. And then, as she had wanted, he gave the first faint smile.

Dishes had been their job that summer. Betty was the cook; washing the dishes after dinner, happy in each other's company, Larry and Caroline would argue politics or movies or literature—Larry had admired *Silas Marner;* Caroline had considered George Eliot a life sentence—and watch the setting sun through the window as it spread red across the waters of Nantucket Sound. Five years her senior, with a doctorate in the works, still Larry had taken her seriously, though he had loved to tease and provoke her. One night when they had dried the last dish, finished a particularly hyperbolic argument over George McGovern, Larry had kissed her on the cheek and said, lightly, facetiously, "I married the wrong sister. . . ."

Twenty-three years later, that same Larry suddenly appeared in the eyes of this middle-aged man. "Are you sure . . . ?"

Caroline shrugged. "You have a dishwasher, don't you?"

He gave another slight smile. In silent tandem, they shuttled dishes to the kitchen.

To Caroline, in some ways this was the strangest room in the house; no longer familiar but instead filled with her sister's curios— bright hot pads, an embroidered sampler, some Hummel figurines, a porcelain rooster—the cheerful artifacts of a mother who wished to make a home. Next to her, Larry rinsed dishes and passed them in the rhythm of two decades before. Except that Caroline now placed them in her sister's dishwasher, in the middle of her sister's kitchen.

Caroline took a dish from his hand. "Is that it?" she asked.

"Just about," he said. And then stopped, gazing at her in the track-lit brightness of the kitchen. Almost shyly, as if surprising himself, he said, "You're beautiful, Caro. Still."

Caroline met his eyes, smiling a little. " 'Still,' " she repeated. "Don't you think there's something rather sad about that?"

He shook his head. "For me," he answered, "it's about the only thing that isn't."

Caroline looked down. After a time, she said, "There's something I have to say to you."

"What?"

"I wasn't kidding, Larry. About the knife."

"How do you mean?"

She raised her eyes to his. "We were brought up around guns and knives—hunting knives, fishing knives, whatever. My father had a collection in the stable."

Larry stepped back, as if to look at her. "What are you saying?"

And what are you thinking? Caroline wondered. "That I want to be very sure that knife isn't traceable. And that you're prepared when the police do get around to asking you."

"Caroline." Larry's voice was firm now. "Think a moment. Brett is five feet three. Maybe a hundred ten pounds soaking wet. James's windpipe was cut through—"

"By the time I was ten," Caroline interjected, "I could fillet a fish. So could Betty. With the right knife, newly sharpened, either of us could have cut this boy's throat our first day in junior high school." She touched his arm. "Please, don't delude yourself that there's some easy out here. There isn't."

His mouth was tight. "I don't think I've been quite clear with you. Whatever our problems in this family, we did not raise a murderer. And with whatever reservations, Brett cared for that boy deeply. Even if she didn't, violence is just not in her. No matter how intoxicated."

Caroline looked away. "She has a temper, Larry. I've seen it."

"All you've seen is someone frayed by shock and tragedy." His voice rose. "I mean, wouldn't you be?"

"Of course."

The concession, stated readily and mildly, seemed to drain Larry's anger. "What Brett *is*, Caro, is someone with a lot of grit. Grit and spirit and independence of thought—despite all Betty's protectiveness." He smiled faintly again. "Some days I look at us and wonder just where it came from."

Caroline gazed at Larry, and then she asked the question she would never ask her sister.

"Tell me about her," she said. "Everything."

FIVE

THE NEXT MORNING, Caroline showered, dressed, and drove two pensive hours to Concord, the state capital.

After Larry had shown her to her room, Caroline, too disturbed for sleep, had tried to channel her thoughts toward meeting Jackson Watts. Part of her felt unready; the other part too anxious to wait. At eight-thirty, she had called Jackson's office from the kitchen phone, edgy not only about Brett but about speaking to him at all.

He was in a meeting, his secretary said. Caroline stated her name and business; there was a long delay, Caroline tautly waiting, and then the secretary returned with the bland message that she could come ahead. Filled with anxiety and relief, Caroline was slow to put down the telephone; in that moment, she sensed, perhaps imagined, a soft click on the line.

Eyes narrow, Caroline paused with the receiver in her hand, listening. The house was silent. Returning to the bedroom, she saw no one.

She began getting ready. The night before, Caroline had hung a red dress in the closet, slightly off for her business but all she had. It was not too wrinkled, she noted; when she caught herself applying makeup with extra care, Caroline reproved herself that there was no problem so grave that it would erase her vanity. And then realized, again, how much of this was seeing Jackson Watts.

Her face and body had been so different then; *she* had been so different. It was more than foolish—perverse—to hope that under any circumstances, let alone these, someone she had deeply hurt would still find her attractive. And yet she did.

What was he like now? Caroline wondered. Wondered if he had a wife, or children; and how he had felt when his secretary delivered this morning's message—that Caroline Masters wished to see him, to discuss the murder of James Case.

Carefully, Caroline finished applying her eyeliner. *Whatever else you are,* she admonished herself—*and you may be little else—you still are a professional.*

She picked up her briefcase and left the room.

What, she asked herself, had she heard on the telephone?

She paused on the staircase, trying to place the others' rooms. One flight above her was Brett's room, *her* old room. She could not help but wonder who had chosen that room for her, what Brett's life had been like in this home. For a moment, she imagined Brett as Caroline herself had been, a young girl running down the stairs to go to school, innocent of the past, oblivious to the future, a smile on her lips. . . .

Caroline started toward Brett's room, to see how she was.

No, she told herself. *That is not your role.* This *is—to drive to Concord and see Jackson Watts.* For the next two hours, traveling through sunlight and shadow, Caroline focused her thoughts on the case against Brett Allen.

Concord was little changed. The storefront signs on Main Street were brighter; the brick and stone commercial buildings a shade dingier; the town perhaps was a little poorer. But the side streets were tree-lined and gracious. And there was, of course—as there had been for Caroline the child—the building she still thought of when she heard the word "capitol."

Parking the car, she walked across its grounds. A sweep of green lawn, leafy shade trees, a statue of Daniel Webster. And then, behind it, the sculpted building of granite—a pillared federal design, topped by a gold dome. Another reminder of Channing Masters.

When Caroline was barely nine, her father had brought her here to meet his friend the governor. They had begun by touring the marble corridors, Caroline holding her father's hand, then the intimate Senate gallery, and then the vast and ornate House of Representatives—whose four hundred citizen legislators, Channing explained, made up the third-largest representative body in the Western world, yet selflessly served for two hundred dollars a biennium. After this, they had chatted with Governor Powell—dignified but warm to Caroline, easy yet respectful with Channing—in the governor's spacious reception room, replete with oil portraits of early governors, a hand-carved wooden mantel over a black marble fireplace, fourteen-foot ceilings, a long mahogany table. Sitting with Channing in an overstuffed chair as he talked to the governor about matters she did not yet understand, Caroline felt sure that no man was greater than her father, no state better than New Hampshire. She could not imagine another family, another home. . . .

Her thoughts on Brett now, Caroline walked two more blocks to the old bank building that now housed the attorney general's staff. She took an elevator to the second floor, followed the sign that said "Homicide Division," and asked for Jackson Watts.

The receptionist rang him. Caroline sat in the reception area, legs crossed, arranging her face in a look of distant calm.

A door opened. "Hello, Caroline," a man's voice said, and then she looked up and saw him.

By reflex Caroline almost smiled. The man who stood there was much like the Jackson she remembered—tall and rangy, hair still black, though flecked with gray where it touched the tops of his ears. The ears themselves were still slightly too large, but better now that his face had filled out a bit. His face looked much the same, with the strong cleft jaw, the furrowed cheeks and ridged nose, the luminous brown eyes that were always his best feature. As he studied her, she realized that he was almost handsome now, a handsome Abe Lincoln.

Caroline stood. "Hello, Jackson."

Somewhat awkwardly, she extended her hand, one lawyer to another. His clasp was cool.

"Thank you for seeing me so soon," she said.

A slightly puzzled look. *So soon?* the look said. *It's been twenty-three years since you simply vanished.* But all that he said was, "I'm sure you're worried. Please, come in."

She followed him down a corridor with the stark, slightly Stalinist look of modern government, to a neat rectangular office with files stacked on a faux-wood desk. He sat himself behind it, tie askew and sleeves rolled up, and directed her to sit opposite him. Then silent, he looked at her with an air of puzzlement.

"I've been wondering," Caroline told him, "what to say to you first. When my niece's file is sitting on your desk and you're now the chief of the Homicide Division."

Somehow she had hoped to see some connection in his eyes. But she saw nothing she could read.

"There are a lot of reasons, Caroline, for me to be unhappy about this." He expelled a breath. "Not only do I respect your father a great deal, but I remember meeting Brett when she was eight or nine. . . ." He shrugged; there was nothing he wished to say.

"Let me start over," Caroline said quietly. "How *are* you, Jackson?"

"Fine. Otherwise." Jackson studied her. "The basic facts are these—one teenage daughter I love, one dog, no wife anymore. A fishing camp on Heron Lake, a decent shot at a judgeship, and a certain basic contentment. Surprisingly enough, a lot of my life is pretty much what I expected it to be." Another shrug. "Or maybe that's no surprise to you."

Oh, Jackson, Caroline thought, *it was never that—it was so many things that have nothing to do with you.* Quietly, she said, "I've thought about you a lot. Still do, at times."

He propped his chin on one hand, studying her with a level gaze. "I never heard from you. Not since you wrote that letter from Martha's Vineyard."

Caroline felt a stab of guilt. But it was far too late to apologize, she knew, and she could never explain. "I know," she answered simply. "No one did."

"And now here you are. For Brett."

"Yes."

He leaned back in his chair. "It's a bad case, Caroline."

It took her a moment to catch up with him. Her throat tightened. "Bad? Or just 'looks bad'?"

"Bad." He seemed to hesitate. "I don't have to tell you anything, of course—there've been no charges filed. But the basic facts aren't going to change. I can walk you through what you must already know, or at least guess."

"Please."

"All right." He was crisp now, a prosecutor. "Let's begin with the idea of premeditation. She took him there, to an isolated place, known to her but not to him. And then got him stoned—"

Caroline held up one hand. "Intending to kill him? On her own property? With a knife?"

Jackson considered her. "Her prints were on the knife. And on his throat. No one else's."

"You've finished the lab work, then?"

He paused. "Most of it."

"Because I've never heard of anyone lifting prints off a man's body."

Jackson frowned. "For now, all that I can tell you, Caroline, is that they've done it."

He was not, Caroline sensed, prepared to be pushed. In a muted voice, she asked, "Did the lab find anything else?"

"Yes. His blood was all over her, in a pattern consistent with arterial spurt. Traces of his skin were found beneath her fingernails. And her prints are on the wallet—again, no one else's." He paused. "By now you've met her, Caroline. She's not a fool; even in the worst of circumstances, you can see her mind work. And she seems to have had the presence of mind to take the wallet, the knife, and her clothes—perhaps to make it look like a robbery, or even that she was never there. Yet for hours, she was supposedly too stoned to even tell the police what happened." He shook his head dismissively. "That's a tough one to buy. You could argue pretty easily that she never expected a cop to pick her up and then spent the next several hours adapting. So that we didn't get any real story, such as it was, until close to dawn."

His account was unnervingly like the one Caroline had given Brett. Rather than argue with it, she asked simply, "Do you have the search warrant papers?"

Slowly, Jackson nodded, and drew a file from his drawer.

She read the papers quickly. "According to the arresting officer," she said, "Brett's hair was wet."

"So?"

"So if she was wet, and yet had blood on her, it suggests that she went swimming. Just as she said." She looked up at Jackson. "There's no sign that James was swimming, right?"

Jackson studied her. "Not as I understand it."

"Because I recognize the curly hair he describes here as the family curse—I got it whenever we went swimming, remember? And if Brett went swimming alone, someone else would have had time to kill him. Just as she said." She paused a moment. "Tell me, Jackson, what was her intoxication level?"

"Point one six."

"Impressive."

Jackson tilted his head. "Are you saying that cuts against premeditation?"

"I'm saying that it cuts against your case." Caroline sat straighter now. "You may not like her story, but it explains everything—the blood, the fingerprints, the skin under her nails, even his failure to ejaculate. And there's not a hole in it. Everything that happened could have happened just the way she says it did." Caroline paused for emphasis. "She's either telling the truth or she's an intuitive criminal genius, who not only can plan and carry out the grisly murder of a young man half again her size and twice her strength but can invent the most complex account, covering physical evidence even a criminologist could only guess at, within hours of slashing her boyfriend's throat. All while drunk and stoned. If it weren't for the moral and legal circumstances, I'd be terribly proud of her."

Jackson's eyes opened slightly. His look became wary, yet intent; something about it suggested more than professional pride, perhaps the desire that the woman sitting in front of him never humiliate him again.

"Within eight hours." His voice was clipped now. "More than time enough to sober up."

"I really doubt that." How to say this, Caroline wondered, without being patronizing? "Sorry if I gave my jury argument."

"No, it was interesting. And informative. So *why* do you doubt it?"

"Because drugs are a huge problem in San Francisco, and I was a public defender there. Which means that a lot of my clients were screwed up on drugs and alcohol. Of necessity, I began to take an amateur interest in pharmacology. For one thing, Jackson, the dope these kids smoke now isn't like the pot *we* tried."

A raised eyebrow. "No?"

"No. Today's pot has fifteen percent THC content, three to five times that of our wonder years. If Brett was an amateur doper—and I believe she was—one joint could do things to her that you and I wouldn't even recognize.

"Second, if she drank the wine first—which I also believe—the dope would have had an additive effect. The intoxication is seriously intensified: you get black holes in the memory, some of which never get filled, and there's a kind of surreal dream state, where the images are more like a slide show than real life. So that you doubt your own experience." Caroline paused, then added succinctly, "And an experience this terrible is one that you would very much wish to doubt."

Jackson looked at her skeptically. "And a single joint would account for all that."

"It could account for a lot of things. That she at first tried to administer CPR. That she later had trouble remembering—or believing—that this terrible thing had really happened. And the nausea and vomiting are a typical example of the additive effect, which—like the perceptual problems—are also intensified by orgasm. As you may also recall from your youth."

Suddenly, Jackson looked wary, as if unsure how to answer. *What are you doing?* his expression said. Then a shrug, the barest hint of a smile. "I didn't know what it was. Maybe the earth moving."

What were the rules for this? Caroline wondered. She rushed ahead. "The point is, she wouldn't get over it quickly. The effect lasts not for hours but for days. So that what Brett describes so well—semi-blackout, then flashing on his body, then enough recovery to tell her story—is utterly consistent with the chemistry of memory as affected by drugs. Please, trust me that this is not just defense lawyer's bullshit." She added softly, almost reluctantly, "Which does, however, bring me to Miranda."

"Somehow I thought that it might." His eyes were keen now. "Go ahead. I'm listening."

"You already know, Jackson. In fact, *I* already know when you started calling the shots—when they held Brett at the hospital until they got the warrants to search her person and the property by the lake. That's when they started doing things right. But by then it may have been too late." Caroline kept her voice quiet, respectful. "When they called to tell you they'd picked up this naked, blood-speckled girl with a bloody knife, taken her to jail, and then gotten her to point them to the lake, what did they say about Miranda warnings?"

Jackson's watchful half smile was no smile at all. "You tell me."

"There were none. Which means there's a good chance that Brett's lawyer—whoever that is—could suppress the first statement about where to find James's body and all the evidence based on that; perhaps the body itself and certainly the search of the lake, the search of Brett, and her later statement about the circumstances of James's death." Caroline snapped her fingers. "Gone, just like that. Leaving you with nothing."

Jackson's smile had vanished. "Caroline," he said in a voice of wonderment, "of all the conversations I ever imagined us having, this is not one." His tone became crisper. "You're also wrong. The bloody knife was in plain view, giving the police good reason to feel that someone else might have been hurt. But they didn't know who or what or why, or even whether Brett and whoever else had been attacked by a third party. And no court is going to punish the police for asking if there's a wounded person out there whose life can still be saved. It's called the exigent circumstances doctrine." He leaned forward. "Let me ask you this: Are you willing to advise her to take a lie detector test. Given by one of our people?"

He was very clever, Caroline realized. In a quiet voice, she answered, "I don't believe in them. And a clever police examiner can use a lie test to interrogate her."

You don't believe in her, she saw him think. But it seemed to give him little pleasure. "Then, viewing this as a professional, I must tell you that Brett has real problems. For the reasons you already know, and some that I'm sure you don't.

"Your defense, if you even have one, is that someone followed them to the lake. But look what that requires of your imaginary killer: to start, knowing that she would leave James by himself—after all, who could reasonably expect to hack two able-bodied college students to death? Also knowing that James would be too drunk and/or stoned to defend himself." He gazed at Caroline intently. "*And* knowing how he—or she—could then vanish in the woods without leaving a trace."

Caroline felt a jolt. "Is that what the crime lab people tell you?"

Jackson folded his hands. "When she fled the scene, Brett left a trail behind—trampled brush, broken branches, flecks of James's blood on the leaves. If Brett's story is right, there's no way that the killer wouldn't have left the same trail. So far we've found nothing. . . ."

"That just can't be. The local police were there, and the EMTs. You can't tell me that there aren't footprints all around the lake, and all sorts of signs that the cops—or someone—were thrashing about in the woods. I doubt the crime lab people can tell *who* else might have been there."

Jackson leaned forward. "There seems to be no escape path except for the one Brett left. The killer would have had to have James Case all over him, just as Brett did. But we've got no trail of blood but hers—nothing else, and no one else. And who else are you going to offer me? Some bum, looking to lift the wallet of a college kid? That's not credible." Jackson's voice rose. "This was *personal*, Caroline. The killer butchered this kid like an animal, with a very sharp knife. Name a case you know where someone did that to a stranger."

Caroline looked at him steadily. "Charles Manson, for one. And you've got no reason at all for Brett to kill him. Let alone like that."

Jackson paused, a tacit concession, then parried: "And *you've* got no one else."

"You're forgetting James's supplier."

Jackson raised an eyebrow. "I may not be up on my THC, but I do know there's nothing in this for a petty dealer." He appeared to debate whether to say more. "We searched James's apartment, Caroline. There was no sign of a break-in, let alone torn-up sheets. What Brett told us about someone tearing up his room never happened."

Caroline felt shaken again. "Maybe he lied to her. About the dealer . . ."

Jackson's half smile was melancholy. "So who does that leave us? Just a girl who may have been sufficiently drug-addled when she killed him for you to argue this down to murder two."

Caroline studied him. Softly, she asked, "You haven't tied her to the knife, have you?"

A moment's silence. "No."

"What kind of knife is it?"

"A fishing knife—a Cahill. Quite a fine one." Pausing, Jackson examined her for a time. "As you say, Caroline, you've no rights here. But perhaps you'd like to see it."

"I would, yes."

Reaching into a second drawer, Jackson withdrew a knife in a glassine bag and placed it on the desk.

The knife was finely crafted. Bone handle, long blade, serrated edge. A knife for a fisherman who cared about such things. The blade was encrusted with blood.

Caroline's stomach felt empty. It was a time before she felt Jackson's scrutiny, wondered how long she had gazed at the knife.

Turning over the bag, she saw the serial numbers on the blade, just as she expected.

The blood obscured them. Caroline had to squint; her reading glasses were in the briefcase. But she did not wish Jackson to know what she was doing. Since childhood, it had been her gift to memorize numbers.

Slowly, she passed the bag to Jackson. "A fine one. Just as you said."

He placed the knife on the desk between them, looking into her face. "Is that all?" he asked. "Or is there something else you want to cover?"

"Not now." She hesitated. "Thank you."

Caroline stood. Somehow she felt distant, a bit light-headed.

Jackson rose from behind the desk, hands on hips. "Did I understand that you may not handle this?"

It brought her back a little. She looked at him directly. "If there's no prosecution, it shouldn't really matter."

He did not answer but simply gazed at her, his eyes intent and curious. "I hear you're going to be a federal judge."

"So it seems."

For another moment, he seemed to appraise her. "Well," he said at length, "I'm sorry about this. For Brett, and for everyone involved."

He held out his hand. Caroline took it, clasped it quickly. "Thank you," she said. "I'll let myself out."

She turned and left him there.

She hardly remembered her walk to the car, did not look up at the capitol, or anywhere except in front of her. Getting to the car, she sat there awhile.

Her briefcase was on the seat beside her. She reached inside, found a pen and a piece of paper, and wrote down the serial numbers from the blade of the Cahill knife.

SIX

WHEN CAROLINE RETURNED, she saw no one. It was as she wished. But when she climbed the stairs to the room where her things were, hoping to be alone, there was a message taped to her door.

She stared at Betty's careful script. Bob Carrow had called. From the Manchester *Patriot-Ledger*.

Caroline sat on the bed.

She was not prepared. The one statewide newspaper, the *Patriot-Ledger*, had long dominated New Hampshire; its politics were harshly right-wing—bitterly antagonistic to Democrats, feminists, and judges such as Caroline promised to be—and its stock-in-trade since Caroline's youth had been its crusade for more criminal convictions and longer sentences. There was nothing to gain from returning this call; certainly not for Caroline, whose potential involvement in a criminal matter involving her family—if publicized—would surely get back to the White House. Angry and exhausted, she started to crumple the message into a ball.

Her hand froze. She opened her palm, staring at the crumpled paper.

Who, she wondered, had done this to her?

For there was Brett to consider. If there should be a trial, it would become a major story in such media as New Hampshire had, and never more so than in the *Patriot-Ledger*. For Caroline the defense lawyer, it was important to get her client fair coverage in the press—better than fair, if Caroline could help it. And one did not do that by ignoring the state's largest newspaper.

For another half hour, she thought. About the reasons she had left here. About the twenty years spent trying to become a judge. About a girl she barely knew.

She went to the kitchen to call.

"Bob Carrow."

A voice such as she had heard in countless newsrooms—edgy, eager, aggressive. Part of her despised him.

She made her own tone polite, puzzled, faintly bored. "This is Caroline Masters."

"Oh, yes. Thank you for getting back to me. I hear your niece is Brett Allen."

"Yes." More arid now. "I hear that too."

A hesitation. "She may be charged with murder."

"Really? Who did she kill?"

"Well, James Case . . ."

"Who told you that? Not, I think, the Attorney General's Office." Caroline's tone was firm and even. "This is a young woman who has just lost someone she loved in the most shocking circumstances, including the hideous trauma of finding his body. And no one—no one at all—has any other reason to even *think* about her in connection with his death. Let alone find anything like a motive."

Caroline broke off. Tomorrow, she chastened herself, the police could find something. It was not like her to go too far.

"So you believe she's innocent," Carrow said.

"Of what? Brett might well have been killed herself. In that way—if only that way—she's quite fortunate."

"Then who do you think killed James Case?"

"Someone who wasn't twenty-two and in love with him." Caroline's voice grew quieter. "I hope that Brett can look to you for fairness."

Their talk was over, Caroline's tone suggested. "One more question," Carrow said hastily. "The White House has just announced your nomination to the United States Court of Appeals. Do you feel it's appropriate for a judicial nominee to be involved in a criminal matter?"

At once, Caroline was on edge—where, she wondered, was this coming from. "I think you may misapprehend my role. I've come here as a member of the family."

"But you also visited the Assistant Attorney General this morning, Mr. Watts. What was the purpose of that meeting?"

"To express my family's concern. Including that whoever did this be identified." She permitted herself an edge of irritation. "Think about it, Mr. Carrow. Not only that someone killed my niece's boy-friend but that someone is still out there. Imagine how frightening that is."

A long silence. "Will you be Ms. Allen's lawyer?"

"Lawyer? She doesn't need one. All she needs is her family's sup-port." Caroline paused. "I expect shortly to return to San Francisco and get about the business this tragedy interrupted—preparing for the nomination hearings. About which, of course, I'm very honored. Is there anything else?"

His tone combined politeness and a certain sanctimony. "I know this is a difficult thing. But I really think it would be helpful if Ms. Allen were to speak to us herself."

Caroline drew a long breath. "I think you can understand how lit-tle Brett feels like talking to anyone. So for the moment you'll have to make do with me. But should she ever feel like discussing this—other than with those closest to her—we will surely let you know."

"Okay." He sounded mollified, then eager. "First, if possi-ble—okay?"

"Yes. If possible." She took a breath. "We in this family have great respect for the *Patriot-Ledger*."

"Good." In his own hesitancy, she heard the decision not to push. "Thank you, Ms. Masters."

"Of course."

As he hung up, Caroline found herself listening, once more, for the sound of a second telephone. But there was nothing.

The stable was dim, airy, almost barnlike. The sun came from win-dows high above her, casting shadows in the corners. A white Jeep was parked to one side, dwarfed by the vastness of the space.

The lawyer Caroline knew that she should turn around and leave. Yet she stayed where she was.

At the back of the stable were her father's workbench, his tools, his vise for sawing lumber. Channing Masters believed in self-sufficiency; how many times, his daughter wondered, had she sat with him as he built something, or fixed something, unwilling, she knew, to concede defeat. The standing clock in the foyer was made in the 1850s by a famous clockmaker, Tim Chandler; Caroline still remembered a day when she was seven or so, sitting by her father as he spent half a Sunday with the clock face turned, its complex inner workings exposed, making small adjustments with a jeweler's tools until, suddenly, the heavy chain swayed again, the bell sounded, and she saw the smile of inward pleasure at the corners of her father's eyes.

Caroline walked past the workbench to his gun rack.

Everything was where it had always been—shotguns, for hunting and trapshooting; a revolver; a crossbow; several fly rods. The guns were still cleaned and oiled, their stocks polished; the fly rods and reels were supplied with fishing line. Caroline seemed to recall most of them. Her father cared for his things; out of sentiment and practicality, he preserved what he had, threw little away. He had no taste for the new.

Beside the fly rods was a wooden rack with pegs.

The ten-year-old Caroline had helped him make it, applying lacquer to the wood. She could hardly wait for the lacquer to dry; then they could fix it to the wall and hang his knives there. Later, they had hung them one by one, in leather sheaths.

At the end of the rack, Caroline saw an empty peg. All at once, the stable felt cold and drafty.

Caroline turned, went to the house, and closed the door behind her.

She stood there, leaning against the door. Perhaps she owed Betty and Larry an account of the day—surely she owed that much to Brett. But right now she could not stay here.

She walked to the telephone, reserved a room at the Resolve Inn, and left.

SEVEN

CAROLINE STARTED AWAKE in a strange room, her mind dream-streaked, the window gray with the light just before dawn. It took her a moment to recognize the sparse antiques, the window sash, another to realize that she was in Resolve, the town of her girlhood. She felt adrift; it was as if it had taken twenty years to build a life, and only three days to leave it.

She put on blue jeans and a sweater, went downstairs to the sitting room, and poured coffee into a large mug. After drinking it quickly, black, she drifted out onto the porch and into the main street of town.

On one side was a gradual hill; the other sloped to a rushing creek. The street itself was blacktop now, not gravel, but little else had changed. Caroline took the tree-lined road past white wooden homes from the 1800s, built when the area throve; the spired but austere church where town meetings were held; the yellow one-floor library that, from the sign in front, still kept eccentric hours at the whim of the librarian; the Masonic Hall, its wood frame dingy now, atop a knoll set back from the street. Less out of enthusiasm than from social necessity, Channing Masters had joined the lodge; Caroline still remembered her mother's satirical imaginings of secret Masonic rituals, complete with antlers and women's dresses and blood oaths against non-Masons. Channing had suffered this in silence.

There was only one new structure—a mobile home—and little sign of commerce. The general store was boarded up now, its gas pump closed; Caroline imagined a convenience store and gas station on some more heavily traveled road.

Where the street curved, abruptly crossing a bridge over the creek, she turned back. A faint air of depression hung above the town.

Caroline returned to the room, called Brett, and asked her to go sailing on Lake Winnipesaukee. She was somehow not surprised when Brett said yes.

The air was warm, breezy; Brett handled the tiller of the rented catboat easily, hair curling in the wind. Sailing seemed to change her. On the drive to Winnipesaukee she had been withdrawn. Now there was color in her face, a brightness to her eyes, and her movements were practiced yet instinctive. It was as though, like Caroline herself, physical action freed some part of her. There was a sensual quality Caroline had not seen in her.

With the Vineyard house sold when Brett was an infant, Caroline knew, Channing would have taught his granddaughter to sail on Winnipesaukee. She seemed to know each inlet on the span of blue, to gaze at the forested hills around them with deep familiarity. Caroline guessed that the memories were good; when a sudden gust buffeted the sails, shooting a spray of water over Brett as she tacked, she grinned into the sunlight with sudden, surprising pleasure. Caroline decided to let her sail as long as she wished.

It was not until close to two, after three hours on the water, that Brett and Caroline moored near Woodsman's Cove.

The air was humid now, the sun hot; Caroline drank from a can. "Cheap, watery American beer," she said. "Perfect for a day like this."

They sat across from each other in the stern, gazing out at the water and the hills as the boat rocked fitfully at anchor. Holding her own can of beer, Brett tried to smile. But she seemed to have returned to the realm of fact, and tragedy; there was something muted but alert about her. Caroline waited for her to choose the moment.

"How was it with the prosecutor?" Brett asked at length.

Caroline considered her answer. "He's short two things. Both critical. He can't tie the knife to you or, more important, come up with a reason for you to kill your boyfriend."

"There isn't any," Brett said simply.

To Caroline, she looked fragile again. "Would you have gone to California with him?" she asked.

There was a flicker in Brett's eyes. And then, to Caroline's surprise, she said evenly, "I don't think I would have."

"Was something wrong?"

"Something big." Brett looked at her directly now. "Sometimes it was like I never knew what James was thinking, or planning. He grew up protecting himself—he wasn't used to being close. I could understand that. But it's not a way to live."

Then why did you care for him? Caroline began to ask. But this was not a lawyer's question. She realized that Brett was studying her with new attentiveness.

"Why did you leave?" Brett asked. "Because no one ever talks about it." She paused a moment, as if fearing to be tactless, then added, "Not about you, and not about your mother."

Caroline smiled faintly. "How very New England."

"How very repressed," Brett said flatly. "Until you were all over our television, I hadn't heard your name for years. And then there was Grandfather in his room, watching you run that trial and not saying a word to anyone. And my mother, tight-lipped and short-tempered."

Caroline's shrug was meant to be dismissive. "Sometimes silence is only that. And absence, only absence."

Brett's expression did not waver. "It's not silence, Aunt Caroline. It's something more. For Granddad and my mother."

Perhaps, Caroline thought, Brett was puzzling through her own relationship to this family, looking to Caroline for clues. She smiled briefly. "First you can drop the 'Aunt Caroline'—it sounds like some menopausal dowager in a dreadful Broadway musical. 'Caroline' will do just fine. About our family, I suppose the best real answer is that I wanted to be independent and was absolutely certain that leaving was the only way. How anyone else felt about that I could only guess: I was twenty-two then and—apparently unlike you—didn't give the feelings of others a great deal of thought."

"Where did you go?"

"I spent a year on Martha's Vineyard." Caroline made her tone casual, disinterested. "Then I went to San Francisco, enrolled in law school, and stayed. That's all there is."

"But why San Francisco? Had you ever been there?"

Caroline shook her head. "It just sounded pretty, and it seemed the farthest I could go."

"How did you get by?"

"I worked. And my mother had left me a little money. From a life insurance policy."

Brett studied her for a time, as if torn between curiosity and her sense of Caroline's reticence. Softly, she asked, "I've never even seen a picture of your mother."

Caroline smiled slightly. "That's hardly surprising. She's been dead for thirty years." She paused, disliking her own tone. More gently, she continued: "She was small and dark and very pretty. To a child, quite exotic."

Brett seemed to hesitate, perhaps at the look on Caroline's face. "I'm sorry," she said at last. "But you're both this family mystery. All I know about your mother is that she was French and died in an accident."

Caroline was briefly quiet. But she found it easier to talk about her mother than herself. "French," Caroline amended, "and Jewish. *That* was the first accident, and the one that made all the difference to her."

It was night; Caroline was nine or ten. Her mother had come to say good night. Surprised and pleased, Caroline had asked her to invent a story: lightly, with mock exasperation, Nicole had answered, "But I have no stories tonight."

She had been drinking, Caroline knew. She could tell from her breath, her levity of mood, an ever so slight increase in the difficulty of pronouncing English. Emboldened, Caroline answered, "Then tell me about your family. Your parents and brother."

All Caroline knew for certain was that they were dead. But in the darkness of her bedroom, Caroline felt her mother's silence like a weight on her own chest. Nicole was utterly still.

"Do you really wish to hear, Caroline?"

Her mother's voice was very clear now; the change of mood somehow frightened Caroline. But she could not refuse.

"Yes," she answered. "I do."

The room was quiet. "We lived in Paris," Nicole said at last. "My father taught law at the university. My mother stayed home with my brother Bernard and me." A pause, then a tone of irony. "I remember thinking that she spoke French rather strangely—she was Russian, not a citizen, and came to France in her teens. But at the time, my only feeling was a child's embarrassment.

"She was Jewish, as was my father. But his family was deeply French. Yes, we went to synagogue, observed the holidays, but otherwise I did not feel much different from the children of his faculty friends. Oh, a little different, perhaps—but certainly not threatened." She paused, inquiring softly, "You understand about being Jewish, don't you, Caroline? What happened during the war?"

She nodded. Something beneath her mother's question made Caroline reach for her hand.

Her mother did not seem to notice. "When the Germans invaded," she said quietly, "I was fifteen, and Bernard was twelve. Marshal Pétain became the head of a French puppet government. And *I* began to know what it was to be Jewish. By the time I was seventeen, I was wearing a Star of David. Under race laws passed not by Germans but by our fellow French.

"My father protested the laws as immoral. When he lost his job at the university, a few friends telephoned to express their sympathy. No one came to call.

"We never saw any of them again."

Caroline tried to imagine her mother isolated, her own family—Channing, Nicole, and Betty—ostracized. "What did you do?" she asked.

"My father sold our home and possessions, and we moved to an apartment in the Jewish quarter of Paris. My sharpest memory is of our parents at the table in that darkened room—my father, small and mustached and alert; my brother as dark and bright-eyed as my father. Only my mother seemed gaunt and lost—she was Russian, after all. She had seen it all before.

"Throughout 1942 there were roundups. Foreign Jews taken from their homes by French police or German soldiers, herded to detention points, and then shipped away by rail. To where, we never knew.

"Still I hoped." Nicole paused. "I idolized my father, you see. If he felt hope, then I did. We were French, after all. And what Father believed was that no government of France—even this one—would abandon its own citizens. If only out of pride."

Caroline watched her mother's face in the moonlit room. It was opaque, unfeeling, as if she were reciting by rote a story of which she had grown tired.

"When I was eighteen," she went on, "they sent me to university. As if this act of normality would serve as my protection.

"In a sense, it did.

"One night after class, I found my brother Bernard waiting for me. There was to be a roundup of Jews; a former faculty friend of my father's had heard this and sent word to warn him. So my father asked that I stay with a non-Jewish friend, Catherine.

"I begged Bernard to come with me. But he had to go back." Nicole's tone was quiet with irony. "To let my parents know that he was safe."

Without knowing why, Caroline hugged herself.

Her mother did not see this. She seemed hardly to know that Caroline was there. "I stayed with Catherine that night," she went on. "But the next morning, I could not keep away.

"The section in which we lived went back to medieval times—the streets were narrow and dark, cobblestone. I had turned the corner to the street before I saw a uniformed policeman, French, carrying a suitcase in each hand, and crying. I had never seen a policeman cry before. Behind him, with more policemen, were a straggling line of children and adults, dragging their suitcases with them.

"At the end of the line were my father and mother and brother.

"I waited for them to pass.

"My mother never saw me. She looked straight ahead, one hand in Bernard's, the other in my father's. Tears ran down her face.

"As they passed, my father spotted me at the edge of the street.

"I started to speak, to reach out to him. Quietly, his lips formed the word 'no'; he stared at me a second longer, to ensure that I obeyed, and then snapped his eyes away.

"It was then I understood. My mother was not French, and my father would not leave her. Nor would Bernard.

"I watched until they rounded the corner and disappeared."

Nicole's voice stopped abruptly. In the silent room, Caroline imagined her own parents—Channing and Nicole—vanishing from sight. She found it hard to breathe.

In a muffled voice, she asked, "What happened to you, Mama?"

In the darkness, Nicole seemed to shrug.

"Catherine's father knew someone," she finally answered. "I was sent to Le Chambon, in the Cévennes region. There was a tradition of resistance there—many of the farmers were Protestants, and their ancestors had suffered persecution.

"For the rest of the war I stayed with a farmer family. They were very kind, as were the villagers. But all that time, I dreamed of my parents and Bernard. Wondered how and where they were. Prayed for them in whatever way seemed best.

"After the war, I returned to Paris.

"I worked as a translator for the Americans, badgered everyone I could for records of deportations, even rumors of my family.

"Finally, I learned of them from a kind American legal officer. . . ."

Her mother stopped abruptly. There were tears in her eyes.

Frightened, Caroline clasped her hand. "What, Mama?"

Only then did Nicole look at her. Quite softly, she answered, "Your grandparents died at Auschwitz. As did the boy who would have been your uncle."

By instinct, Caroline reached out to hug her. But Nicole stopped her, staring intently into Caroline's face until her own tears had vanished.

"You are Jewish, Caroline. There is no government, no person, that can ever really be trusted. Please, remember that."

For a long time, Brett said nothing.

They sat in silence, beers cupped in their hands, unnoticed. Brett seemed to study her. At length, she asked, "How was it that she married Grandfather?"

Caroline collected her thoughts. "After his first wife died, having your mother, I think he was a little lost. So he left Betty with an aunt and uncle, and joined the Army Judge Advocate General Corps. In postwar Paris, his job was investigating war crimes by Germans for the Nuremberg tribunal." Caroline finished quietly: "He was the 'kind officer' who told my mother about her parents. After learning that, she must have thought New Hampshire sounded quite safe. And my father had fallen in love with her."

Brett's face filled with sympathy. "Do you think she loved him?"

Caroline gazed past her, at the mountains. "My mother died when I was fourteen," she said simply. "Too young for me to truly know."

Brett's look remained soft, inquiring. "That must have been terrible for you."

More than you will ever guess. "It was hard." A slight smile. "But then fourteen is a difficult age."

Brett was quiet for a time. To Caroline, watching her, it was almost tangible—Brett sorting the missing pieces of her family, wondering what corners of whose hearts she did not yet understand. But Caroline was a stranger to her, and Nicole a marker in a cemetery. Only Channing Masters was real.

"When she died," Brett finally asked, "how was it for Grandfather?"

Caroline grasped the unspoken question: *How was it that you could bring yourself to hurt him?* As to this, at least, Caroline chose the truth.

"Oh," she said quietly, "I'm quite sure it broke his heart."

It was perhaps four; the sunlight slanted gently on the blue waters of the lake. Brett had fallen into a moody silence. But Caroline's story seemed to have distracted her a little from the present. For this much Caroline was grateful.

"Have you ever been married?" Brett asked.

Caroline smiled. "Not even once."

"Doesn't that ever get lonely?"

Caroline considered her. Part of this curiosity must be Brett working out answers for herself: how much, Caroline wondered, does she talk to Betty now? "Not really," she told Brett. "You get used to being your own companion. Of course, there's still this idea that single women are supposed to feel barren, literally and figuratively. Especially," she added with a sardonic twist, "if they compound their misery by being successful."

Brett tilted her head. "Then you never wanted children?"

Caroline shrugged. "As a friend of mine once said, 'I love my children too much already to give them a mother like me.' " She stopped herself; Brett deserved better. "Perhaps I would have liked that, Brett. But the things that you can't help, you put out of your mind. It's better that way."

Brett nodded, watching her more closely. It was clear she would ask nothing more.

There was a first coolness in the air, sun dying. Caroline pulled a windbreaker over her shoulders.

"Once this is over," she asked, "what will you do?"

The question seemed to startle Brett. "I don't know," she said. "Nothing's real to me now. Before, I wanted to write. Short stories, novels."

It might be good, Caroline thought, to get her talking about a future, something outside James Case. "Why writing?"

"Because I seem to have talent—at least my teachers think I do. And getting a straight job, like in a company, is nothing I can see right now. Though I've thought about getting a master's so I can teach writing." Brett's voice warmed. "Writing seems like the only job where what you think and feel really matters."

Caroline nodded. "Have you written much?"

"A lot." A small smile. "I always have. Even when I was small I made stories up all the time—imagining people, places, things I'd never seen in life. My dad used to say I didn't know real from unreal—" Brett glanced quickly at Caroline.

Caroline pretended not to notice. "How did your parents feel?"

Brett was quiet for a moment. "About that they were fine—especially Dad. And Granddad always said a writer needed a place—like Faulkner in Yoknapatawpha County. And that I *had* a place. Right here."

"Well," Caroline said mildly, "it's certainly convenient. For everyone."

Brett smiled a little. "I understood that part of it—wanting me here—all too well. But then my grandfather helped raise me: hiking, or homework, or just talking about books or writing. Most afternoons, when I came home, Granddad would be waiting. To do something, or just to hear about my day." Her smile faded. "I understand that, still, even if it's not convenient. It was like *I* was the one who was left for him."

Caroline felt surprise; without warning, Brett could move from ingenuous to acute. "What do you mean?"

Brett's gaze was direct now. "That my mother was never his favorite, Caroline. *You* were."

"I don't think that's true. I don't think it ever was."

Brett shook her head. "Once, when we were hiking, I asked him about you. He looked so sad that I never asked again." Brett hesitated. "Is that why you came back? For him?"

"The world is not about 'him.'" Caroline paused, softening her tone. "Truth to tell, I came back for you."

Brett looked surprised, then skeptical. "Why?"

"We *are* related, you know." Caroline drew a breath. "I'm a lawyer, and I want to help you. My issues with my family aren't yours."

"I'm sorry—I didn't mean to piss you off."

Caroline waved a hand. "You didn't. Really." Her voice softened to curiosity. "Tell me, though, where your dad fit in all of this."

Brett leaned back. "Dad and you were friends, weren't you?"

"Yes. We were."

Brett nodded. "Dad's an enigma sometimes . . . he more or less left raising me to Mom." Brett's voice became sardonic. "It's a case of the parent with the deepest emotions winning. With the way my mom is, it was no contest—and Dad didn't want the aggravation she'd give him if he tried to make it one." As if ashamed, Brett paused; Caroline felt once more the quicksilver of her emotions. "Really, I shouldn't say that. Dad loves me, I know, and he can be so sweet. It's just that he hates conflict, and I think Mom feels things so intensely that it scares him. Sometimes it seemed like Granddad— who, if anything, intimidates Mom—was more my father than he was."

Caroline remembered Larry of the gentle eyes and slow, warm smile, who first had named her "Caro," who still could talk to her when she and Betty could no longer talk at all. Remembered him holding the infant Brett, gazing from Caroline to the sleeping baby with the wonder of sudden fatherhood. Felt sadness and anger that he had receded to a corner of this girl's life, supplanted by Betty's and Caroline's own father.

"Did you ever rebel?" Caroline asked.

A faint smile, and then Brett's voice became ironic. "Did you see the satellite dish behind the house? *That* was my rebellion. I threatened him—if I couldn't keep up with the outside world, like *Beverly Hills 90210*, I'd go away to boarding school."

Children do not always live to please their parents, he had said as Caroline left for school, *or parents to please themselves.* Softly, Caroline queried, "He didn't send you away to school?"

Neither of them, she realized, had defined "he"; there was no need.

"No," Brett answered in the same tone. "He bought me the dish instead."

"Not much, as rebellions go."

"Don't I know it. I even let them send me to Chase College, where my dad teaches, so I could go for a lot less. My mother implied there was trouble with money, and I couldn't bring myself to ask Grandfather. So instead of being like Mom, going off to Smith, I stayed right in the neighborhood." Brett paused, as if in remembered anger. "Of course, she said to me that James was a rebellion. Especially after they found out about the drug dealing."

Caroline fell quiet, caught between her image of the crosscurrents of her estranged family and her own doubts about Brett's innocence. And then, to her surprise, she saw tears running down Brett's face.

Softly, Caroline asked, "What is it?"

"What you asked me before. About whether I'd have gone with him." Brett paused, fighting to control her voice. "What I didn't tell you was that now I lie awake wishing I *had* gone, no matter how many doubts I had. Just walked to the Jeep with him and started west that night." Brett's eyes shut, and then she finished: "Because we'd have gotten to California today, and James would be alive."

Caroline did not reach her room until eleven.

In the car, Brett had fallen asleep. Caroline had driven steadily, glancing at the girl's face against the headrest. Even had Brett awakened, Caroline could not have brought herself to ask about the knife.

Now she stared at the message in her hand—Walter Farris, from the White House. Next to her on the nightstand, the Manchester *Patriot-Ledger* was opened to an article quoting Caroline. *Why*, she asked herself, *hadn't she called Farris this morning?*

A chill breeze blew about the window sash. Caroline stood, pushing down the window—only a crack now, enough coolness to help her sleep.

Caroline reviewed Brett's expressions, her voice, the way she had said things. Caroline the lawyer knew that no one could read guilt or innocence on the face of a stranger. Another Caroline, whose existence the lawyer scorned, pleaded with her to believe that Brett was truthful—that the Brett she had spent today with could not have sliced her lover's throat to the windpipe, no matter how intoxicated. But there was no way, Jackson Watts had told her, that anyone else had been there.

Tomorrow, she would call Walter Farris. And then, to satisfy both parts of her, she would telephone Jackson Watts and ask if she could see the crime scene, the lot her father once had meant for her.

EIGHT

WHAT CAROLINE HEARD first was the new reserve in Farris's tone.

"I should have called you," Caroline said. "It's just that things have happened so quickly. As you can imagine, it's extremely trying for Brett, and for the family."

"I understand that, Caroline. But what wasn't clear, precisely, is whether you're acting as your niece's lawyer here."

Caroline paused a moment. "More as an aunt . . ."

"Because this meeting with the Attorney General's Office troubles me. Whatever your intention, it could create the appearance that our appointee to the federal bench is trying to use her prospective influence on behalf of a relative. And, even worse, to affect the course of a homicide investigation."

Caroline felt on edge now. "Please know, Walter, that it hardly feels like that from here. As for being a lawyer, I'll continue to practice law until the Senate confirms me. That's standard procedure."

"Of course it is." His voice aspired to patience. "But what *isn't* is to represent a member of your family in a brand-new, potentially high-profile murder case. Even without this nomination, it's hardly wise—you can't help but be emotionally involved, which is what no counsel should be. If your niece needs a lawyer, the best thing you can do is help her find one."

It was, Caroline knew, exactly what she herself would say. "If Brett should be indicted, that's certainly my intention. We're all hoping that she won't be."

"And even if she isn't," Farris retorted, "your confirmation hearing may involve questions none of us wants." His voice became crisp. "We live in a brave new world, Caroline. Republicans control the Senate now, and—although we have great latitude in our appointments—feminist defense lawyers are not the flavor of the year. All we need is someone like Jesse Helms using this 'appearance of impropriety' as an excuse to scuttle you. What I'm saying, to be plain, is that the President has only so much political capital to spend on this. So anything you do up there, other than hold this girl's hand, you do on your own."

"Of course," Caroline said with a calm she did not feel. "And I'll be prudent. As I told the President, this nomination means more to me than I can easily express. As does his confidence." She paused. "And yours."

"I know it does." As if ready to hang up now, Farris tried to sound reassuring. "And this isn't a big story yet. All we want is that it not become one." He paused for emphasis. "All right?"

In the silence of her room, Caroline nodded. "All right."

For a half hour, Caroline lay on the bed and thought.

A faint morning sun came through her window. The town beneath it, familiar from childhood, seemed more alien than yesterday. Yet when she picked up the phone again, it somehow felt inevitable.

"Jackson Watts," he answered crisply.

"It's Caroline," she said without preface. "You didn't happen to tell the *Patriot-Ledger* that I came to see you, did you?"

"No, I didn't. But then that's easy for me. My rule is not to talk to the press, period, unless there's some compelling reason. There isn't here."

Though his tone was not angry, Caroline felt chastised. "Sorry," she said.

"That's all right." A moment's pause. "Is that why you called?"

"Not exactly—"

"Because I've been wanting to talk to you."

It was Caroline's turn for surprise. "About Brett?"

"No." His voice was low, almost reluctant. "About everything *but* Brett."

Caroline sat back on the bed, stretching her legs in front of her. Softly, she asked, "Is that wise?"

"I don't plan to violate any code of ethics, if that's what you mean." Another pause. "When you left my office, Caroline, it felt incomplete. You were suddenly here, and then gone. With little said that wasn't about Brett." His voice changed. "To be reminded of you like that, and be no wiser for it . . ."

Caroline touched her eyes. Then she said, "When. And where?"

"Is that a yes?"

"It's a yes."

"I'll be driving up to my fishing camp tonight. I'm staying for the weekend." He sounded relieved, almost boyish. "So, tomorrow? Maybe I'll take you fishing."

"Fine." Caroline hesitated, then added, "There *was* something else, Jackson."

"What?"

"The crime scene. I'd like to see it. Today, if possible." Her voice was soft. "After all, my father owns it."

Before going to the lake, Caroline made one more phone call.

It was early afternoon when she reached the trailhead. A state trooper was parked there, and the yellow tape across it had already been cut.

"He's here," the trooper told her. "By the lake."

Caroline drove to the end of the trail and parked by his truck.

She sat in her car, looking around her. Then got out and, facing the dense stand of pines that blocked all sign of Heron Lake, took in the dense pungency of wood, needles, decaying leaves.

The smell, Caroline realized, was implanted in her senses. She could not remember being here since the last spring night with Jackson, twenty-three years ago. Her father had bought this land for her; she was to build a cabin, perhaps a home, own a piece of her past forever. She had left that past behind; because of this, in the unfathomable chain of consequence, Brett Allen had brought her lover here, to die.

Slowly, Caroline stepped into the woods.

Dense trees blocked the sun, filtering sunlight as though in a cathedral. Still it was not hard to find the path of Brett's flight—a random zigzag, marked by strips of yellow tape on branches. Caroline took one in her fingers, saw on a leaf the faint streak of purple. It was blood, she was certain, left as Brett ran from the body of James Case.

The woods felt close and cold. Caroline walked more quickly

now. Near the edge of the trees the shafts of sunlight broadened, blue swatches of water appeared among the leaves. She took one deep breath.

Emerging from the woods, Caroline saw him.

He stood by the water, gazing across a mile of lake toward the fishing camp his own father had built in the thirties. He was quite still; what struck Caroline most was how erect he held himself.

She stopped at the edge of the glade. Coolly, she said, "Hello, Father."

He turned to her. Without waiting for his answer, she knelt.

For a strange moment, thinking of Jackson and their first inhibited loving, she recalled the stray guilt-stricken thought—haunting and irrational—that her father might watch them. And then she focused on her task.

The grass seemed matted, Caroline saw. From this she could guess the location of their lovemaking and, perhaps, the body. But it had rained since the night of the murder, and there was no way to be certain.

She felt her father standing over her. "Well?" he asked.

"Jackson's quite impressive." She looked up from the grass into his penetrating black eyes. "He claims there's no sign that anyone else was here."

Channing's eyes narrowed. "No trail of blood?"

"None. Except for Brett's."

Stiffly, he knelt across from Caroline, staring down at the grass. "Of course, they're assuming that *he* was soaked in blood."

" 'He'?"

"The murderer." Channing reached out one hand, as if cradling an imaginary head. "Suppose he knelt at the top of Case's head and then—"

With silent efficiency, Channing drew his free hand slowly across the grass, holding an invisible knife, to cut the throat that was no longer there.

"That's it," he said softly. "He was here. The spurt of blood never touched him."

Caroline felt a chill. Quietly, she said, "Jackson also suggests there were no leaves trampled, no other path of escape."

"Why would there be? Does Brett claim to have heard anything?"

"She didn't mention it."

"All right." Channing's voice was brusque, impatient. "Then he didn't leave through the woods."

He rose, unsteady for a moment, grimacing with distaste for his old age. Curtly, he motioned for Caroline to follow.

Single file, they walked to the edge of the lake, silent. Except when it concerned Brett, Caroline realized, they would say nothing.

He stopped, staring down at a patch of silt in front of him. "This is what I was looking at."

At his feet were boot prints; near them two sets of shoe prints—different sizes, more widely spaced. "The shoe prints are the police, I would guess, running to the water to look for a killer." His voice was quiet. "The boot print might be the killer. Slipping into the water long before."

Still Caroline did not look at him. "Moving along the shore?"

"Yes. Or even to a canoe."

It jolted Caroline from an imagined world, where she almost believed his story, to the reality where she felt grounded. "A canoe? Impossible."

Channing frowned. "We used to canoe from the fishing camp to here." He pointed to the diving platform, his voice rough. "We had picnics there, remember?"

There was a wound beneath the words, Caroline knew. Softly, she said, "I remember perfectly. And if someone else had canoed past us, we would have seen and heard him. As Brett would have."

"Would she? Intoxicated? And at night?"

Caroline shook her head. "I'm sorry, Father. But this makes no sense—a premeditated murder, by a man who paddles silently through the water, confident that a drowsy victim will offer up his throat while his girlfriend goes for a swim. Please don't ask me to sell that to anyone."

He fell silent. Caroline turned from him, gazing along the shoreline as it curled away from them. "No, I like the escape route along the water somewhat better—if only because we don't need to show Jackson any footprints. But how did he get here?"

Grudgingly, her father faced her. "The same way he left, Caroline. Or are you only interested in quarreling with me."

It stung her. "That," she said, "is stupefyingly egocentric. What I'm trying to do is find a defense for Brett. Preferably one that works."

Channing's eyes glinted. "Then *do* try," he snapped.

Caroline looked at him steadily. "That's why I asked you here," she said, and turned from him to face the woods.

After a moment, she walked toward a patch of dirt near the shore, separated from the glade by a thin line of trees and brush. Reaching the spot, she stopped; even after the rain, the mud was packed hard. She felt her father behind her.

"In theory," she said, " 'he' could have waited here—no branches to break, perhaps too hard for footprints. At least it's something one could use to cross-examine their crime lab people."

He was silent for a time. "Then you're back to that, are you? The defense lawyer, trying to fabricate a plausible story for a guilty client."

"Back? I was never there, except perhaps in your own mind." She lowered her voice. "It seems quite plain to everyone but you that I shouldn't handle Brett's case, if there is one. Including, interestingly, my friends in the White House."

"What do you mean?"

Hands thrust in her pockets, Caroline gazed at the lake. In its glassy mirror, clouds skimmed through lapping wavelets, stirred by wind on the surface of the water.

"The White House counsel called today," she said at last. "They'd read a story in the *Patriot-Ledger*."

"Yes." His tone was indifferent now. "I saw it."

"The point is that someone told this reporter about my visit to Jackson." She paused. "It's become a problem for me, Father. That is, if I care to ever become a federal judge."

Channing folded his arms. "*I* had some ambitions once. At least the State Supreme Court, perhaps more. But after your mother died, I forgot them. Because of you."

Caroline heard him. Softly, she asked, "Because of me? Or her?"

Channing seemed to blanch. With equal softness, he inquired, "What do *you* think, Caroline?"

She turned from the look on his face. "In either case," she said coldly, "this is hardly the same thing."

Channing stared at her now. "Isn't it?"

"Not to me. I can't stand more publicity."

"Really." His voice held faint contempt.

She faced him again. Narrow-eyed, he gazed across the water, as if impervious to her concern.

You *told them*, she realized, *to make me choose.* She stood there, caught between doubt and accusation.

Quietly, he said, "What is it?"

Caroline paused, irresolute. But when she decided to speak, the question that came to her was different. "Do you remember the knife I gave you?"

His face froze. "What of it?"

"It's not where you kept it."

His eyes widened and then went cold; in that moment, Caroline knew that he understood the question perfectly. But when he spoke, his voice was soft again.

"There was a time, before I grew used to things, when anything associated with you was painful. A reminder of whatever hope I'd had." His tone became indifferent. "I gave that knife away, Caroline. Years ago."

Caroline hesitated. "Do you remember to whom?"

"No. But then that wasn't the point." His face grew hard. "Are we through here, Caroline?"

Without waiting for her answer, Channing Masters turned and walked back to his truck.

Caroline spent the afternoon alone.

Most of this was stalling, she knew—calling the office, checking her mail, returning messages from friends and clients congratulating her on the nomination. To Caroline's ears, her own gratitude sounded oddly hollow, lines recited by an actress in a play. As if to reassure herself, she told her secretary that she planned to return in four days' time.

Even as she said this, she could not take her mind off Brett.

Her purse was on the bedstand. Putting down the telephone, she reached for it.

Inside was the slip of paper with the serial numbers.

She took it out. A ten-minute hunt through long distance gave her the number for the Cahill Knife Company. Another five minutes, and she was talking to the clerk who might be able to help her.

The woman sounded faintly annoyed. "What was that serial number?"

Slowly, Caroline repeated it.

There was silence. For some reason, perhaps her assessment of Jackson Watts, Caroline had the sense that she was not the first to call. In a cautious voice, the clerk inquired, "What is it that you want, exactly?"

"To see if you can trace the knife. At least to the point of sale."

"And this is for what?"

Caroline hesitated, suddenly tense. "I'm a lawyer," she said slowly. "This knife may end up being evidence. In a criminal case."

"And what is your name?"

Another pause. "Masters. Caroline Masters."

"Uh-huh." More silence. "Well, I don't know about tracking down the point of sale . . ."

"Can you at least try?" To Caroline, her voice sounded oddly pleading. "Even the year of manufacture might help me."

"Tell you what. Give me two or three days, and call back. I may have something then." The clerk paused, as if regretting this. "Tell me, how would the year help?"

"It's a confidential matter, really. But the year could tell me a lot. Please, it's important."

The clerk paused. "Oh, all right," she said.

Politely, Caroline thanked her, and hung up.

NINE

CAROLINE AND JACKSON Watts cruised slowly toward the middle of Heron Lake. Behind the black rubber dinghy, built like a landing craft, the outboard motor made a scudding sound as it beat them through the water. The sky was startlingly blue; sunlight glistened like mica on the shimmering lake. It was a day from Caroline's youth.

They had said little. Jackson had come for her in a green pickup truck with fly rods thrown in the back. They drove to his fishing camp, its spare 1930s rectangle somewhat like her father's own, with a neat and compact kitchen and a view of the lake through trees. He showed her about somewhat awkwardly; Caroline saw a German shepherd sleeping by the stone fireplace and, on the mantel, a framed photograph of a pretty brown-haired girl, perhaps thirteen or so. And then, in a reprise of their past, they had taken the wooden stairs down the hillside to the dinghy, put the two fly rods in, and started up the boat. It was what they once had done when they wished to be with each other and yet feel no pressure to talk until they cared to. There was no one else on the lake.

With a lazy, expert flick of his wrist, Jackson cast a line into the water. Caroline leaned back, arms draped over the sides of the dinghy, taking in the day. Pines and birch and maple trees rose from the shoreline and up steep hillsides, creating the sense of a cocoon around them. The place where James Case had died was too far away to see; Caroline sensed that Jackson would not go near it. The air was cool and still.

Jackson cut the throttle. The dinghy barely moved now; his line floated lazily in the water.

"So you went there," he said finally.

Caroline gazed at the sky. "The 'crime scene,' as it were? Yes. I found the whole thing very strange."

Jackson nodded. "So did I."

They fell quiet again.

He had been so sweet then, Caroline thought. Too eager, of course, but considerate of her; he could not help that it was his first time, any more than Caroline could help that it was hers. Or that, when desire and fulfillment finally met for her, it was not with Jackson Watts.

She watched his face now, two decades later: the crinkles at the corners of his eyes as he watched his line; the hollows beneath the cheekbones, deeper now. Remembering his old smile, quizzical and crooked, Caroline realized that she had yet to see it.

"That letter," she finally said.

His face seemed to tighten. "Yes?"

"I've always felt sorry about it." Her voice was tentative. "Seeing you, I'm more sorry than ever."

He looked at her now. "Why is that?"

"Because I remember how fond of you I was."

Jackson's eyes narrowed in thought, perhaps in remembered pain. "I didn't know what to do with it: 'Don't call, don't write, don't try to see me—I'm never coming back.' I felt helpless." He shrugged. "Helpless, and inadequate."

He spoke the words without emphasis or inflection. But Caroline felt how badly she had hurt him.

She shook her head. "What's so hard for me to explain is that it wasn't about you—which, I know, only makes it worse. Because *how* I did it wasn't kind. But I wasn't a kind person then. Or, perhaps, now."

Jackson turned to her with questioning eyes. "All that you said then was that it was necessary. As if, somehow, you had no choice but to do everything the way you did." He paused, and said in a lower voice, "All these years, I've wondered what it could possibly have been. You didn't just leave *me*—you left a place, a family, a life you had all planned out for yourself."

"Which is why you can believe me, Jackson. It wasn't about you."

He turned from her, gazing at the bright surface of the water. "You know," he said quietly, "I finally asked your father why. When I couldn't stand not knowing anymore."

Caroline felt a tightness in her chest. "And what did he say?"

"That you had your reasons, and that they were your own. And that, in his own mind, there was nothing he could do to ever get you back. It was as if I only reminded him of someone he wanted to forget. After that, I rarely saw him." He faced her again, voice quiet. "What happened to change you, Caroline?"

Caroline gave a deprecating smile. "Please, I don't want to be one of the self-regarding, self-referential singles to whom every tremor of their youth is worthy of a coming-of-age novel. That would be an embarrassment worse than shame."

Jackson did not smile. Simply studied her for a time and then said softly, "You didn't ask for this conversation, Caroline. I did."

Caroline's eyes were grave now. "If talking about my family made any sense, Jackson, I would. But it doesn't. You'll just have to believe me and, I hope, accept my apology. If it's not too late for that."

Jackson seemed to consider her. "No," he said at last. "It's not too late."

In the silence, they looked at each other across the dinghy. "I think I'll toss out a line," Caroline said.

They fished together. To Caroline, the moments had a timeless quality, a ritual shared with a friend, that one could slip into within moments after years apart.

"So you want a judgeship," she said finally.

"Uh-huh." He paused. "Trying cases is a young man's game, I'm beginning to think. And I believe—hope—that I have the right temperament to run a trial." He smiled briefly. "Not like you, of course."

Caroline raised an eyebrow. "Showy, you mean?"

He gave her a first half grin, the one she remembered. "I was thinking of your admirable fairness. And, of course, your erudition. As so admirably displayed on Court TV." He looked at her sideways. "Remember when you decided to be a judge? Tall ambitions for a woman, then. Not to mention for a teenager."

"Yes," she said dryly. "I was much too sure of everything. Including my absolute entitlement to what I wanted."

"Living on Masters Hill," he replied with equal dryness, "would tend to give you that opinion."

Silent, they shared a moment's remembered amusement, a joke of years past. The son of the Congregationalist minister in Connaughton Falls, Jackson had never had much money; while Caroline went to Dana Hall, Jackson attended the local high school, grinding out the grades to get a scholarship to Williams. So that, on Caroline's return each summer, Jackson would gravely inquire about life among the upper classes. But even as a teenager, Jackson seemed remarkably free of envy or rancor—between them, it had been an affectionate game.

"I always wondered," he said after a time, "how much of your ambition for a judgeship came from Channing."

"Then? Perhaps a lot. But a long time ago it became my own ambition. So that I no longer know or care."

He fluttered his line on the water, hoping to attract some imagined trout. "It means a great deal to you, then."

Caroline stared into the distance. "More than I can tell you," she said finally. "So much that even talking about it scares me. Like I'm going to lose it."

His face was solemn now. "This thing with Brett. You're serious about not handling it."

Caroline felt the warmth slip from her. "Yes," she answered. "I'm serious about not handling it."

Quiet, Caroline gazed at him. After a time, she said, "You'd be a fine judge, Jackson. You were always fair. And, it's clear, still are."

Jackson seemed to examine his reel. In that moment, Caroline felt the absence of a woman in his life; then was embarrassed by how little she now knew about him, how little she had asked. Especially when Jackson, in some ways, had continued to care for her.

"Tell me about your marriage," she said.

Jackson reeled some line. "Just like that?"

Caroline smiled. "Not unless you've thought about it. Though I figure you have by now."

"Well, I've worked on my rationalizations, at least." He leaned back against the side of the dinghy. "Carole is one of those people who light up a party—she has a great smile, a ready laugh, and new places and people are a tonic to her. At first, I was charmed: later, I came to believe it was less an attribute than a symptom."

"How do you mean?"

"My version of Carole—polished through many trips to a counselor—is that she's a discontented woman: anything in the future will always be better, because in the present there's always something wrong." He turned to her. "Do you remember saying something like that about your mother?"

Caroline felt a short, painful memory. "I believed that as a teenager. I'm not sure that I do anymore." She forced a wry note into her voice. "But on the subject of your ex-wife, Jackson, you're a qualified adult."

He shrugged. "In any event, we were different. My life pleased me; she thought I was having all the fun. So she decided to go to law school. But once I figured out how to scrape together the money— this was early in our marriage—she decided she despised lawyers. Which I suppose I took somewhat personally." He half sighed. "As it turned out, perhaps I shouldn't have. Carole was just like that—charming her way into a job, finding it dreary, finding another, then quitting that one. Which, I'm afraid, became my fault.

"The weekends were like something from Despair Comics— Carole lolling in bed, and then in her robe till noon, completely affectless. Until we went to some party, and she'd light up like a bulb. The more she smiled at strangers, the more I smoldered in silent anger at what a fraud she was. Which I was too afraid to even say. Because, like so many lawyers when they're not in court, I loathe conflict. At least the kind of conflict where you don't have any rules." He paused, finishing quietly: "She also had a memorably violent temper. I never learned the rules for *that.*"

"What happened?"

Jackson was silent for a time. "In a way, it was such a joke," he said at last. "Like something from *The New Yorker.* I had food poisoning after lunch one day, came home unexpectedly, and found her in bed with her personal trainer. It was absolutely classic Carole, right on the cutting edge—I mean, she was far too trendy to screw the guy next door, or even her therapist." His voice filled with remembered astonishment. "And do you know what I thought? That I hadn't seen her on top like that for years . . ."

Caroline began laughing. "I'm sorry," she managed. "I mean, why not the gardener . . . ?"

"Because we couldn't afford one, what with paying for the trainer. Anyhow, that's when I knew I lacked the energy to try and save the marriage—there was no goodwill left in me." His brief smile did not quite reach his eyes. "So what I was left with was a good story. Which, before today, I've never told to a soul."

Caroline considered him, unsmiling now. "I suppose it felt like a somewhat hollow joke."

" 'Hollow' is a good word. I felt empty—that I had loved her enough to marry her, and then felt nothing. Not even enough to try for our daughter's sake."

Caroline fell quiet.

"Do you know what bothers me now?" Jackson said at last. "Remembering how caught up I was in my own career. That maybe I was so careless that I got Carole—our marriage—all wrong. That at the beginning, when it still mattered, I could have done something. And that *I* was the greatest cause of her unhappiness."

Caroline considered him for a time. "I wasn't there, Jackson. But I would guess not."

Jackson shrugged. "Well," he said, "it's done."

Caroline held her rod in one hand, facing him. "How old was your daughter?"

"Eight. Not a good age." Hand on the tiller, he looped the dinghy in a lazy circle, to keep it away from shore. "She's sixteen now. Which, for us, also seems like not such a good age."

"How so?"

He turned to her. "Really, Caroline, how many bad dinners with divorced men have you suffered through? Listening to these stories about children you don't know and, after you've heard them, don't care to know."

Caroline smiled. "Not nearly enough."

"I'll keep the story brief, then—it's hardly original, so that won't be hard. Carole made Jenny her little confidante, a surrogate adult. I wasn't a strong enough—perhaps a frequent enough—presence to overcome that." He shrugged. "Our relationship is more amiable now. But she *is* sixteen—her priorities are school, friends, boyfriend, and, of necessity, dealing with her mother. Which leaves Dad somewhere down the list, understandably enough." He smiled a little. "Aren't you glad you asked?"

"Yes, actually." Caroline paused. "I've always wondered what I missed, not having children. I suppose it depends on the circumstances."

His smile was more genuine. "It depends on the day. Even so, I wouldn't do without her."

Why? Caroline wondered. For a moment, despite everything, she envied Jackson this feeling. It was not a thought she could express.

They lapsed into silence. Caroline reeled her line in, flicked it again. The instinctive ease of things surprised her. The quiet between them felt deeper, sadder, surer.

There was a sudden jerk on the line.

"Jesus," Caroline said. "A fish."

As the line pulled away, Jackson turned to her, grinning. "That was the idea, wasn't it? Do you remember what to do?"

"Of course," she snapped, and jerked the rod to one side, holding the reel tight. From the side, Jackson watched with amused interest.

Whatever the fish was, Caroline realized, it was strong. She remembered the pitfalls—breaking the line, letting her quarry slip the hook—and as the pole bent with the struggle of the unseen fish, she took in the slack, wondering whether it was bass or trout. "Gently," Jackson murmured.

The line drew closer, shortened in the water. And then the fighting fish broke the surface of the lake. Its colors glistened in the sun.

Caroline grinned. "A trout."

Jackson cut off the motor. The pole bent to the water, Caroline leaning back. A second leap, then a third, as Caroline worked the reel, quickly now.

A sudden jerk of the pole, and then the trout lay at her feet, wide-eyed, sides puffing and trembling with the shock of his defeat, the terrible absence of water.

"A beauty," Jackson said.

Caroline gazed down at the trout. And then, with still expert fingers, she carefully removed the hook.

For a moment, she held the writhing trout in both hands. And then she half stood, tossing him above the water—a glistening flash of rainbow, silver, and then he disappeared.

Together, they watched the ripples spread across the water.

"I'm glad we came," she said.

Jackson smiled a little. After a moment, he asked, "Care for dinner? At the Trout Club, of course. In honor of your humanitarian gesture."

Caroline was quiet for a time. "Yes," she answered. "I would."

TEN

THE TROUT CLUB was a rambling one-story structure from the late nineteenth century, with canoes and kayaks on its beachfront, Adirondack chairs on the lawn, which faced the lake, and behind that, a screened porch with more chairs, lounges, and tables for cocktails and snacks. Caroline's great-grandfather had put up money to help build it: his picture, complete with fierce eyes and a bristling mustache, was on the wall in the front room. Surrounding him were old bamboo fishing rods and photos of long-forgotten members, many of which celebrated the ancient bond between man and fish— triumphant men and the occasional woman from another era, holding aloft a bass or trout or salmon, some of extraordinary size. Caroline had come here since childhood: in her teens she had once remarked, to her father's amusement, that to be on the wall the people had to be as dead as the fish were. Smiling, he had said that he hoped never to see his picture there. "Don't worry," Caroline had answered, "you won't."

She stood in the lobby, quiet now.

"It hasn't changed," she said at last.

Jackson smiled. "This is New England. Reverse ostentation is a way of life."

It was true, of course. It took a kind of genius, Caroline thought, for a place always to seem as if it needed paint.

"Do you want to savor the ambience," Jackson asked, "or would you like a drink outside?"

"Outside, thanks. What are my choices?"

"Scotch. And Scotch."

Caroline smiled. There was no bar; members kept liquor in their private lockers, beer and white wine in a giant refrigerator by the kitchen, maintained on the honor system. There was an ice machine on the porch.

"I'll take Scotch," Caroline said, and picked a canvas chair on the lawn.

Jackson tossed his windbreaker across the back of the chair next to hers, rolled up the sleeves of his cotton work shirt, and went to fetch them drinks.

He came back moments later, with an ice bucket, two dishwasher-scarred milk glasses, and a bottle of Glenlivet. "Good Scotch," Caroline said.

When he filled her glass, she did not complain.

They sat there, quiet again. Caroline took her first sip, felt the whisky glow inside her. Took another, gazing across the lawn at the kayaks and canoes, the lake as it turned gray blue with the sun of an early summer evening.

"Amazing," she said.

"What is?"

"To be here at all."

He turned to her, as if trying to decipher her tone of voice. "Does it seem that strange?"

"Yes. It does." Caroline paused. "I spent a lot of energy leaving."

Jackson was quiet awhile. "Where do you live now?" he asked.

"I have a penthouse." Summoning an image, Caroline found it unnervingly distant. "On Telegraph Hill. Very modern, with glass all around and a roof garden on top. On the right day, I can see not only the bay and the city but miles beyond."

Jackson seemed to imagine this. "Not much like New Hampshire."

"Not at all." She drained her Scotch. "Have you ever been to San Francisco?"

"Once, with Carole. It seemed quite beautiful."

"It is, isn't it." She tried to picture him there, at the opera or a dinner party or eating calamari in the glittering restaurant of the moment; the clearest vision she could manage was of a practical man, looking about him with interest and a certain wry detachment. Somehow New Hampshire seemed very much a part of him.

Thoughtful, Caroline gazed across the lawn.

On the lake, a lone man in a kayak made for shore, stopped paddling, let the kayak drift until it slid onto the rocky beach. He pulled the kayak another few feet and then made purposefully for the club. He was in his sixties, spare, with a white fringe of hair and, Caroline noticed as he approached, bright-blue eyes behind rimless glasses. Seeing Jackson, he smiled and came over.

"Hello, Hugh," Jackson began amiably, and then, as if interrupting himself on the way to introducing Caroline, stopped.

But the man had turned to her. "Hello," he said in a puzzled voice, and then smiled, still hesitant. "Pardon me, but aren't you Caroline? Channing's daughter?"

Caroline summoned her own smile. "That's right."

He extended his hand. "Hugh Askew. President of the Connaughton County Bank—I've done business with Channing for years." He paused. "Sorry for the once-over; except for TV, I'm not sure I'd have known you. I don't think you've been here for a while."

"No. Not for a while."

His smile faded. It struck Caroline that he must know—at least suspect—her business here but was too polite to mention it. Even more so in the presence of Jackson Watts.

"Well," he said in a subdued voice. "Welcome back. I'm sure your dad is very proud of you."

"Thank you."

Briefly, the man nodded to Jackson and went on his way, leaving Caroline self-conscious, her sense of ease diminished.

"Maybe we shouldn't be here," she said quietly.

Jackson gave her a look of concern, then shrugged. "These are not judgmental people, Caroline. And you and I have known each other for years."

She turned to him. "How has it been for you, living here?"

He seemed to contemplate the question. "It's the world I know. Perhaps this says something about me, but it always seemed sufficient. Still does." He sipped his drink. "If I consume enough Scotch, I can probably spin a piece of philosophy that's downright Jeffersonian—that this is the last laboratory of civility, where people are both decent and restrained, where villages run their own affairs and where even politicians can exist without having to lie too much." He smiled again. "But I really *do* need to have been drinking. . . ."

"And where does the *Patriot-Ledger* fit into that theory?"

"Oh, for that I have to drink a lot." His smile faded. "Are we leaving, then? Really, whatever feels comfortable."

What did she want? Caroline wondered. And then realized that Jackson, and then perhaps the Scotch, had dulled her cares for a time.

"Let's stay awhile," she said, and poured them both more whisky.

They ate dinner on the porch. Jackson found a candle, produced a chill bottle of Chardonnay from the refrigerator, and shuttled two warm meals from the kitchen.

"Trout," he said. "The balance of nature continues."

Caroline smiled, finished her third Scotch, and gazed out across the lake.

Dusk was falling; the last light turned to smoke above the sudden blackness of the water. There was the first sound of crickets; against her will, Caroline imagined that night as Brett described it, wondered again how much of it was true. She wanted to ask Jackson about drug dealers, then—for reasons of both tact and tactics—quelled the impulse: if they came up with nothing, it would make the drug-dealer defense less credible. Far better for Brett's lawyer to chastise some detective on the witness stand for his failure to inquire.

"Penny for your thoughts," Jackson said.

"Why?"

"Because you had that sort of veiled, intent look you used to get when we'd argue politics, just before you stuck some rhetorical point in my figurative ear."

Caroline smiled again. "I was thinking of sticking my fork in the literal trout," she answered, and did so.

It was fresh, sautéed in butter—perfect with a little lemon. "This is great," she said. "I haven't had fresh trout in ages."

Jackson poured some wine. Sipping it, oaky on her tongue, Caroline realized that she had well exceeded her self-imposed limit on alcohol. Part of her was troubled by this; the other part was surprised by how good it felt.

"When I asked where you lived," Jackson said, "part of it was whether anyone lives with you."

Caroline shook her head. "Not even a trout."

In a cautious tone, Jackson said, "I read somewhere, I think, that you were never married. . . ."

Caroline gave him a sideways look. As if caught at something, he looked away, and suddenly she began to laugh. "Why don't you just ask me if I'm still straight, Jackson?"

He gave her an astonished look and then put his forehead in his hands and shook his head, like someone detected in the middle of an unpardonable social lapse. "I mean, I did consider all sorts of things. If you could turn your back on me . . ."

Caroline grinned. "You mean, did I go to Martha's Vineyard one summer and become a lesbian?"

He held up his hand. "Please, I surrender. Help me out of this."

Caroline smiled. "Whether gay or straight, single women without obvious attachments get used to it. Although usually from total clods. I'm reminded of Martina Navratilova's great line when some idiot sportswriter asked if she was 'still gay': 'Are you still the alternative?' "

Jackson gave her a sheepish grin. "Sorry. Anyhow, it was only a passing thought, like rabies or Oliver North." His look became curious. "You do sound quite determinedly 'single,' Caroline."

She sipped more wine, considering her answer. It had long been her practice, bordering on superstition, not to say too much about the things she held private. Now, for a night, that felt lonely. She looked across the table at the kind face of Jackson Watts, a friend—with whatever fragility and for however long—reclaimed. So that, in this way at least, one part of her past might still feel warm in the present.

" 'Determinedly'?" Her voice was soft now. "I think perhaps what starts as self-protection, for whatever reason, in the end becomes a habit. So that even if you think you want to do better, you find that your emotional equipment is rusted out. That you're no longer used to intimacy, have no gift for the small compromise." She shrugged. "Perhaps no longer care . . ."

He looked at her gravely. "What do you do, then? Just live alone?"

Perhaps, Caroline thought, it was the wine, the comfort of darkness. Perhaps it was the need to tell him the truth about something. To hope that he would not judge her.

She studied her wineglass. "What I do, Jackson, is a series of small affairs. Sometimes on vacation, just for a night—the longer term seems always to founder on career or children or whatever." Her voice became ironic. "Lately, I seem to have developed a penchant for the long-term married. A couple of them have been good company, and there's no chance they'll become part of my life. Or even, if they're sensible, want to."

It made him quiet. She gazed at the lake, a swath of black beneath a moonlit ridge, then saw him fill her glass and his.

"Well," he said thoughtfully, "we all make do."

When she looked at him, his face was serious but not unkind. He held up his glass and touched it to hers. "To you, Caroline."

She settled back into her chair. Quiet together, they finished their dinner, then the bottle.

When they left, the night was cool and still.

They got into the dinghy, and Jackson started the motor; its low thrum as they crossed was the only sound on the darkened lake.

Caroline sat back, feeling the night air on her face. The glow of wine was receding a little, her sense of time returning; whatever respite she had enjoyed was coming to its end. She watched Jackson pilot them across the water, searching keen-eyed for his camp.

"There," he said.

A moment later, they cruised up to his dock. Jackson jumped out; Caroline tossed him the line, and he hitched it to a spile. Reaching out, he took her hand as she stepped onto the dock.

To her surprise, he did not let go. He looked down at their hands, as if surprised himself, and then let her fingers slip away.

He stuck both his hands in his pockets. "Can I get you something before you leave? Coffee, brandy . . ."

After a moment, Caroline nodded. "Brandy."

"Good." Jackson turned and climbed the stairs up the hillside, Caroline coming after him. A wind stirred the trees, and there was the deep aroma of pine; Caroline remembered sleeping at her father's camp, the comforting sense of woods around her. The stars, she saw, were bright.

They entered the cabin. He went to the fireplace, threw in wood, knelt, spread tinder, and then struck a match. The fire leapt to life. Caroline stood in the kitchen, quiet, watching the first tongues of blue and orange as they rose from the burning log.

Jackson stood, turning to Caroline. "I'll get that brandy now."

He walked through the kitchen without looking at her, opened a cabinet, and reached for two snifters and a bottle of cognac. Carefully, head bent, he poured a measure in both glasses.

Turning, he passed one to Caroline, raised his own glass. "To what, this time?"

Caroline cupped the snifter in both hands. "I don't know, really." She paused for a moment. "I just didn't want to leave without saying something. Like 'thank you.' "

"For what?"

"For forgiving me, a little. For making me feel like you were still a friend."

He gave her a funny look, vulnerable and surprised. Almost under his breath, he said, "Jesus, Caroline . . ."

Her chest tightened. As if without thinking, she went to him, took the brandy from his hand, and put it with hers on the counter.

She turned to him again, hesitant.

"What is it?" he asked.

Caroline took his face in her hands, looking up into his eyes. Her blouse grazed his chest.

Jackson gazed down at her, as if to make certain that he understood. Softly, he said, "I think I remember . . ."

She was still smiling as he kissed her.

His mouth was warm, somehow familiar. She closed her eyes, leaned against him for a while. Silent, gentle, he held her, kissing her hair.

How do we do this? she wondered. Her nerve ends tingled.

Jackson leaned back now. When she looked up at him, his head tilted in inquiry.

Quiet, Caroline nodded.

Slowly, he unbuttoned the top of her blouse.

She looked at him steadily, eyes not moving from his face. When he had finished, she reached behind her, and then her bra fell to the floor.

The rest of it she did herself.

"You're beautiful," he said. "Still."

Smiling a little, she began to undo his shirt.

His body still. Still lean, not quite as taut, but still his. When their skin met, it felt warm to her.

He led her to the fire.

There was a couch there. Still holding her hand, Jackson angled his head toward the couch, inquiring. Caroline shrugged.

They lay together, finding their place.

Jackson kissed her forehead. "I don't have anything," he murmured. "But I'm all right."

"Me too."

Gently, his mouth moved to the hollow of her neck. She slipped beneath him.

He was still careful now, but knowing. Knowing in the touch of his mouth, his hands, his fingertips. Caroline felt her hips move without her thinking. She grasped his neck, suddenly hungry for him, pressing her mouth to his.

When he entered her, it was different.

Caroline thrust against him. They had never had this, then; the warm, confident leisure, the sureness that all would be well. She lost track of anything but the warmth of his body, hers, the slow insistent surge as he moved inside her, she moving with him—quickly now. More quickly . . .

She called his name, and then she exploded with the feel of him.

Fingertips numb, the world dark and close, she clung to him as he came inside her.

Afterward, she lay beside him, not wanting or needing speech. Watching the dance of shadows from the fire.

The seniors league, she thought fondly; what we lose to youth, we make up in grace and comfort. At least so it seemed with Jackson.

Still quiet, she gave him a kiss of tenderness and approval.

He smiled at her. "Better?"

"Better." She kissed him again. "Good old Carole."

It made him laugh. The next time they made love, an hour later, Caroline was on top.

In the morning, she woke in his bed. Her temples throbbed with Scotch and wine.

"Hello," he said.

"Hi."

He propped his head on his elbow, as if gauging her mood. "Are you okay?" he asked after a time. "I didn't turn into a pumpkin, did I?"

She did not smile. "No. Not at all."

He raised an eyebrow. *Talk if you want,* his expression said, *but I won't push you.*

Suddenly, Caroline disliked herself intensely. "Last night," she said, "I was selfish—I liked being with you, and I didn't want it to end. But in the clear light of morning, I'm Brett's semi-lawyer. Who's compounded her ethical confusion by fucking the prosecutor."

His eyes were serious. "Think of me as an ex-boyfriend, Caroline. If that helps."

For Caroline, the reality of Brett had filled the room. "I wish it did."

"Whether or not you represent her?"

Caroline touched her eyes. "I don't know, Jackson. Please, I have to think this all through." She stopped. "That is not, by the way, a reference to Brett's guilt or innocence. But that I even have to tell you that illustrates the problem."

He was quiet now. Caroline sat on the edge of the bed.

"Really," she said quietly. "I think I'd better get back."

"All right."

They dressed in silence.

"Ready?" he asked, and walked briskly to the door.

She stopped him there, a touch on the elbow. He turned to her.

Caroline tried to smile. "What I thought," she said, "is that I'd kiss you goodbye. Here, where no one's watching."

He paused, looking seriously into her eyes.

Slowly and firmly, Caroline kissed him. "I really wish," she said, "that you weren't the prosecutor."

He smiled a little. "I really wish," he answered, "that you had a different niece."

They walked to his truck together.

For the ten minutes to town, they talked about small things. What he would do today. How Resolve had changed. Anything but Brett.

When they stopped in front of the inn, Jackson did not get out.

He leaned on the steering wheel. "I'd like to see you again," he said. "Before you leave."

Caroline touched his hand. "We'll talk, at least."

Slowly, he nodded.

Caroline made herself get out. She was through the door of the inn before his truck disappeared from view—a lawyer again, beginning her day.

ELEVEN

BUT IT WAS several hours before Caroline the lawyer resolved what to do, and another hour until she drove to Chase College, Jackson Watts still too much on her mind.

The campus was wooded, rolling, nestled in hills. A creek, spanned by a covered bridge, meandered past the spired clock tower, brick Gothic buildings, and a wide green commons surrounded by trees. But the building James Case had lived in, a two-story apartment house outside the town, was a remnant of the Eisenhower years. Even the brick was veneer.

Daniel Suarez lived on the second floor. She took the stairs, found room 203, and knocked on the door.

The boy who opened it—he could not have been more than twenty—was tall and slender, with luminous brown eyes and a sensitive, slightly brooding aspect that was somehow quite appealing.

"You're Brett's aunt?" he asked.

"That's right. She mentioned you to me."

He waved her in. To Caroline, the cinder-block room was reminiscent of other, long-ago rooms at Harvard or Radcliffe: clothes thrown about, stacks of books and magazines, stale cooking smells from the kitchen. Even the posters—the Stones and Led Zeppelin— had not changed much.

Caroline found herself smiling faintly at a gray-haired Charlie Watts. "Like them?" Daniel asked.

"Used to," she said carelessly. "Now I'm more into Sheryl Crow and REM. These days, nostalgia hurts."

A glimmer of amusement. "Especially for my dad. He's a real Deadhead."

"Oh, well." Caroline shrugged. "Anyhow, thanks for seeing me."

"Sure. Can I get you anything?"

"Have a Coke?"

"I think so." He went to the kitchen, prowled through the refrigerator, and returned with a cold can of Pepsi.

"Good enough," Caroline said.

She sat in the kitchen. Daniel took a chair across from her, his expression tentative.

"So you saw Brett here," she said.

"Uh-huh." He nodded toward the next apartment. "With James next door, and her over a lot, sometimes we'd borrow things back and forth—milk, food, whatever. Two or three times we'd end up talking."

"What was she like?"

A cautious nod, as if affirming something to himself. "She was really nice, easy to be around, and seemed squared away. You could talk with her about pretty much anything."

"And James?"

Daniel paused, directed a hooded look at the stained rug in front of him. "Different," he said at length. "He was smart, too, and pretty talented, I think. But he seemed more into himself than she was."

"Who were his friends?"

A moment's reflection; whether on the truth, or merely on his answer, Caroline could not tell. "Brett, mostly." His liquid eyes rose to meet Caroline's gaze. "Do the cops really think she killed him?"

"I don't see how they can, in the end." She looked at him closely. "I gather they were here."

His shrug was more a twitch. "Oh, yeah."

"What did they want to know?"

"A lot of the same things. Who James's friends were. Whether I knew Brett. What their relationship was like—"

"And whether he was dealing drugs?"

"That too."

"And what did you tell them?"

"Not to me."

"Did James ever try?"

"No." He paused. "About that stuff, I mind my own business."

His eyes were steady. But Caroline was morally certain that a thorough search of this apartment would produce a bag of marijuana in the sock drawer, and that Daniel Suarez did not wish to say so.

Caroline simply looked at him.

He folded his arms, fidgeting as she tried to hold his gaze. "Why does the drug stuff matter, anyhow?"

The truth, Caroline knew, might drive him further inward. But there was little choice. "Suppose," she asked, "he was in trouble over drugs. Stiffed his supplier, somehow."

Daniel seemed to consider this. "That," he said, "I wouldn't know about."

Their eyes locked. The answer was truthful, Caroline was suddenly sure, just as the tacit admission in its phrasing—that James Case was dealing—had been a deliberate signal. Briefly, she considered the notion that, for dramatic effect, James Case had lied to Brett about his vandalized apartment but not about his problem. And then she had the sudden jarring thought that she could read Daniel Suarez far more easily than she could Brett.

In Caroline's silence, Daniel leaned forward, an unspoken appeal forming in his eyes. "If I could help Brett," he said quietly, "I would."

The best tack, Caroline decided, was to shame him. In a tone of skepticism, she responded. "Oh? And why is that?"

"Because I didn't like the way he treated her. Though I guess she figured she could deal with it."

Caroline felt herself tensing with surprise. Casually, she said, "What do you mean?"

Daniel looked at her hard, and then shrugged. "Maybe Brett didn't know."

"That he mistreated her?" Caroline stopped herself and then, almost against her will, asked, "How could she not know?"

Daniel folded his hands. *So,* his brown gaze said, *you don't know, either.* "There was this girl from school who used to come here—blond. The only name I got was Megan."

" 'Here'?"

"To see James."

"Probably a friend." Caroline paused, affecting a carelessness she did not feel. "How often did she come?"

"A few times." Daniel's voice was soft now. "One morning, she came to my door in James's T-shirt. To borrow milk."

Caroline sat back. It was a moment before she asked, "Did this girl say anything in particular?"

Daniel's face was serious. "It was more how she was—wired, smug, a little in my face. Like she wanted someone to know that she was screwing him. Even me."

Think, Caroline ordered herself. She paused, phrasing her next inquiry with care. "When the police asked about Brett's relationship to James," she said slowly, "what was your answer?"

Their eyes met; the sense of a silent understanding, suddenly shared, ran through Caroline like a shock.

"I told them it was fine." A first, faint smile. "As far as I know, it was."

Caroline was pacing her room when the telephone rang.

She snatched at it. The nasal drone of a secretary announced that the senior senator from California was calling Caroline Masters. There was a click, and then the senator came on the line.

"Caroline?" Her voice was brisk, professional. "Your office said I could find you here. How are you?"

Caroline inhaled. "I've been better, I'm sorry to say. We have something of a family problem."

"That's what I understand." A moment's pause. "Walter Farris called today. To touch base and, I detected, in the hope that I'd underscore his concern. So here I am."

Caroline closed her eyes. "Thank you," she said, although it did not sound quite apt.

"Oh, of course." Pausing, the senator adopted a sympathetic tone. "I'm sure that it must be terrible for you, for all of you. And that you'll want to do everything *appropriate* to help your niece."

Caroline did not miss the inflection. "I will, naturally. But there's only so much I can do."

"I imagine that's true. Hopefully, though, this won't come to anything, and your niece will end up in the clear." Her voice modulated to the casual. "So when will you be able to come back?"

Caroline reflected. "Three or four days, I think."

"Good." Another pause. "After all, a number of us have worked very hard for this nomination. No one more than you."

"Thank you," Caroline said. "I appreciate that."

"Then see you soon," the senator said, and got off.

TWELVE

THE NEXT MORNING, the woman at the front desk called Caroline's room and announced that Mr. Watts was in the parlor.

It surprised her: she was not prepared for him. Distractedly, she checked her hair in the mirror, then went downstairs.

He was seated in a wingback chair. When he saw her, he stood, but he did not give her the smile she half expected. His eyes were somber.

Quietly, she asked, "What is it?"

He glanced toward the front desk. "Let's go outside, all right?"

They went to the porch, sat next to each other on the love seat. Except for a young boy on a bicycle, the street was deserted.

"You were supposed to be back in Concord," she said.

Jackson gave her a sideways look of deep unhappiness. "I should be," he said. "I wish I were."

Caroline felt numb. "Brett," she said softly.

"You'll need to find a lawyer for her, Caroline." He exhaled. "We're getting an arrest warrant. As early as this afternoon."

"For what?"

"Murder one."

Yesterday, Caroline thought, she had awakened with him. "Something happened," she said.

Jackson gave a slow nod. "A new witness contacted the state police yesterday morning. I met with her last night."

Caroline felt a premonition. "What did she say?"

Jackson stood, gazing out at the street. "She claims to be James's lover. According to her, James asked her to go with him to California."

The sentence had an incomplete sound. "And?"

"Brett was obsessively jealous—obsessed with James, period. She watched his apartment for other women." He paused, speaking in a monotone. "One night, James brought this woman home. Her story is that Brett got in with a key and found them in bed together. Then threatened to kill them both."

Caroline rose from the love seat, stood next to him. "Does that really sound right to you?"

Jackson still studied the street. "This woman makes a good impression. She's not an obvious flake."

"Then what took her so long?"

"It hasn't been that long." He turned to Caroline. "How eager would you be to become a principal witness in a very public murder trial?"

Caroline placed her hands on the porch rail. Softly, she said, "I don't see murder one here. Even if you believe this woman."

"If you believe this woman, Caroline, Brett threatened Case well before he was murdered." He lowered his voice. "It's one of two things. Either Brett drove him to the lake with an intent to kill or, high on drugs and wine, she hit a flash point of jealousy and slashed his throat without thinking. Which I imagine will be Brett's lawyer's argument."

Caroline closed her eyes. "What's this girl's name?"

Slowly, Jackson shook his head. "I have to protect her privacy. When Brett's lawyer wants this woman's statement, I'll hand it over at the appropriate time. But not now."

Standing straight, Caroline folded her arms, fought back a sense of helplessness. "And bail?"

Jackson frowned; his voice was a prosecutor's now, well prepared and matter-of-fact. "I'll have to oppose it, and I'll win. In New Hampshire, first-degree murder is virtually nonbailable."

Caroline tried to imagine Brett in jail, found her mind resisting the image. "For God's sake, Jackson, she's no flight risk."

Jackson turned to her. "Really," he said quietly, "there's no point in arguing over this. Please accept that I'm sorry."

"Is that what you came to say?"

He looked at her directly. "I came to make arrangements, for Brett to come in on her own. And, however difficult, to tell you in person."

"What arrangements?"

"We won't arraign Brett until tomorrow afternoon, so that she can have some time with family. As long as a police car follows, I'll let you bring her to the jail at Connaughton Falls, where people can visit easily. And I'll try to keep the press away."

That, Caroline knew, was as decent as he could make this. "Is that it?"

For a moment, he simply looked at her. "That's it."

She nodded. "Thank you."

Jackson began to leave and then stopped close to her, touching her elbow. She stared down at his hand until it fell to his side.

"Goodbye, Caroline." And he walked to his truck and drove away.

Caroline drove to Masters Hill through a light drizzle, not unlike that on the day of her return.

Larry was in the library. Without preface, Caroline demanded, "Is Brett here?"

"She's out for a walk." He studied her expression. "Is something wrong?"

"Go find Betty."

He stood, alarmed now. "Should Channing be here?"

"Just find her, for God's sake."

When Larry returned with her, Betty's face was pale.

"What is it, Caroline?"

"Please, sit down."

They did that. Caroline regarded her sister and brother-in-law; they looked diminished, shrunken, in the overstuffed chairs. Larry struggled to maintain calm; Betty's face was sallow.

Caroline's voice was softer now. "There's no good way to tell you this," she said. "I just saw Jackson. They're charging Brett with first-degree murder."

Betty's lips parted, but she made no sound. "Why?" Larry managed.

"There's a witness—a woman. Her story is that she was involved with James; that Brett found out; and that she threatened to kill them both."

Betty's hands balled into fists. "That's ridiculous. Brett would never threaten anyone." She stopped herself, and Caroline saw the gray eyes move from anger to anxiety. "Who is this woman, Caroline?"

"I don't know." For a moment, Caroline considered asking Larry if he knew a student named Megan, and then did not ask: the risk was too great that Betty—or even Larry—might do something unwise. "Jackson wouldn't say—"

"Because she's a liar."

There was something pitiful, Caroline thought, in Betty's anger. Caroline had seen it before: the look of a mother who has just learned that her child is ensnared in a legal system she cannot control or even comprehend. But always, before, the mother had been a stranger, the child just a client.

Quietly, Caroline said, "Brett's lawyer will find out soon enough."

Larry, Caroline saw, caught her meaning as she spoke. She watched the dawn of comprehension redden Betty's face.

"You won't help her?" she demanded.

Caroline forced herself to be calm. "I didn't think you wanted me to. And I shouldn't. For Brett's sake."

"For Brett's sake." Betty stood, shock and derision mingling in her voice. "Is this what you call selflessness?"

Caroline folded her arms. "Yes," she said coolly. "For lack of a term we can agree on."

Larry crossed the room and took Betty by the arm. "It's Caro's decision. We have to look ahead now."

"What I'd suggest," Caroline said in more even tones, "is someone from in-state, who knows the laws here—written and unwritten. Father will know who's good."

Betty stared at her. "And what will *you* do for her?"

"Other than give her lawyer the best advice I can?" Caroline paused, expelling a breath, and finished in a lower voice. "Go home. For everyone's sake, and for all the reasons I haven't been part of this family for over twenty years."

Caroline watched a range of emotions cross her sister's face—irresolution, dislike, and then so much fear for Brett that it erased all else. "Betty," Caroline said softly, "it's the decent thing for me to do now. That was decided when I decided to leave. No matter what you've done, or how I may feel about it."

Betty sat back in the chair, heavily and gracelessly, face dull with fear and confusion. Larry rested his hand on her leg. Neither looked up at Caroline.

"There is one other thing," Caroline said. "Which, for Brett's sake, I'd very much like to mention."

It took a moment for Larry to raise his head. "Yes?"

"My father had a fishing knife—a bone-handled Cahill that he kept in the garage. Where is it?"

Larry's face clouded. "What are you saying?"

"Betty?" Caroline waited for Betty to look up. "Our father says that he gave it to someone. Years ago."

Betty's upward stare was sharp. "What *are* you saying?"

"That the question may come up." Caroline's tone was neutral. "And that if it does, it would be very much in Brett's interest if the family memory is consistent. Or, at least, that no one gives a careless answer."

Larry's expression grew hard. "Caroline, I have no answer. I leave Channing's things alone—"

"Damn you," Betty burst out. "You think Brett killed him."

Caroline kept her face blank, her voice calm. "I don't 'think' anything. I'm suggesting that *you* think."

Betty's mouth compressed. "Whatever Father says, Caroline, is true. If that's your question."

Caroline watched her for another moment and then spoke to both of them. "I'll tell Brett myself—there are things I need to say to her. I'm sure you won't mind if I wait for her on the porch."

THIRTEEN

CAROLINE FIRST SAW her as a distant, hooded figure in the drizzle, walking with downcast eyes.

Caroline paused, glancing at the sky. And then she rose from the porch and went to meet her on the gravel road. Until she was close enough to hear the crunch of Caroline's footsteps, Brett did not seem to notice her approaching.

She stopped, watching Caroline's face, hands thrust in the pockets of her yellow slicker. "What are you doing, Caroline? Trying for pneumonia?" That she did not smile betrayed her anxiety.

For a long time, Caroline simply looked at her. Quite softly, she said, "Clients lie to lawyers all the time. I should be used to it."

Brett gave her a funny, trapped look, equal parts guilt and surprise. Her lips parted, but no sound emerged.

"No," Caroline went on. "I should put you out of your misery. Who, pray tell, is Megan?"

Brett looked down. Then she stood straighter, facing Caroline, and said, "A woman James was involved with."

Caroline nodded. "So she tells Jackson."

The green eyes locked on Caroline now. "It was over, Caroline."

"Was it? Perhaps you'd care to tell me about that."

Slowly, Brett nodded. When she spoke again, her voice was thick.

"James was so attractive—with him, it was a weakness. This girl, Megan, began looking for him around campus—the library, the student union, after class. Almost like she'd figured out his schedule." Brett's face took on an unsettled look. "There was something creepy about it—"

"And how did James feel?"

Brett began to answer and then looked at Caroline as if one

thought had interrupted another. Quietly, she said, "I'm sorry, Caroline. I wish you weren't so angry with me."

Caroline tilted her head. "Am I?"

"Yes. In that way you seem to have."

In Caroline's silence, Brett's green eyes seemed to fill with challenge and vulnerability. Tersely, Caroline answered, "My emotions, whatever they are, don't matter. Yours do. And his."

Brett folded her arms. After a time, she said, "I think James was attracted to her at first. Something about being stalked was flattering."

"Is that how you saw it—she was 'stalking' him?"

Brett nodded. "I could forgive that much. I mean, he wasn't the aggressor. . . ."

Her voice fell off. Caroline felt the damp in her hair, the wetness on her face. The mist of her breath hung in the air. "What was it," she asked softly, "that was harder to forgive?"

Brett swallowed, looked down, then quickly up at Caroline. "I went to his room one night, to pick up some notes I'd left there. I thought he was going to be out. Instead I found Megan."

"Found?"

"Yes." Brett's voice was toneless. "In bed with him."

"What happened?"

"I just stared at both of them. James looked ashamed and caught, somehow. But she was almost smiling at me, with the strangest glint—like she'd won some contest. I've never hated a woman so much."

All at once, Caroline registered that Brett's reaction to Megan reflected that of Daniel Suarez. Sharply, she asked, "So what did you do?"

Brett exhaled, then said, "I knew I couldn't stay there—I'd scream or cry, make a fool of myself in front of him and this woman. So I pulled the key off my chain, threw it on the bed, and told him in the calmest voice I could, 'If you want to tell me about this, you can call.' " Pausing, her voice was soft with hurt. "Then I left."

"Did you say anything else? To him, or to her?"

"Lots to him. But I never said a word to her. Then, or ever."

"No?"

"No. Why give her the satisfaction?"

"And James?"

"Came to my room that night." Brett shook her head, and then her voice fell. "He promised me it would never happen again, told me she'd just kept after him. And then he seemed to realize that sounded so pathetic that he began to cry. . . ."

"What did you do?"

"Just sat there, I think, shaking my head. I said maybe he had a problem, one I couldn't live with. That I didn't even want to try . . ." Her voice filled with wonder. "He wanted to make love with me."

Despite herself, Caroline gave a short laugh, harsh to her own ears.

Brett looked at her. In a tone of remembered scorn and anger, she said, "I told him not without a rubber."

Caroline placed her hands on her hips. "Which is why," she said, "you brought a rubber that night. And why you weren't going to California."

"Part of it. Yes." She paused. "Maybe other women could live with that kind of doubt. But I don't think I could have."

Caroline looked at her closely. "Why were you even with him?"

Brett seemed to collect herself. "Because he promised me, and because I cared for him enough to try." She looked away. "As far as I know, he kept his word."

Caroline watched her. "How long ago was this?"

"April." Her voice was soft again. "I remember because it was two days before my birthday."

Caroline was quiet for a time. "Did you ever threaten him? Or her?"

"Threaten?" Brett looked at her sharply, and alarm filled her voice. "No. Never. Who says I did?"

"Megan, I think. Though Jackson won't tell me who—"

"That's bullshit."

Caroline simply gazed at her. "You want to know," Brett said quietly, "why I didn't tell you. And why you should believe me now."

It was time, Caroline thought, to tell her. "It hardly matters . . ." she began.

"No," Brett interjected. "I want to explain."

Caroline felt tired. "I already know," she said tonelessly. "Because you thought that you'd look guilty."

"That's part of it." Brett's eyes filled with apprehension. "But there's something else I didn't tell you . . ."

"What?"

"We fought that night." Brett stopped, and then said, "It was over her. . . ."

Facing James in the darkness, Brett shook her head, as if to clear it. "There are too many surprises, too close together. I don't know what I'm doing anymore."

"What do you mean?"

There was pain on his face, and somehow this made her angry. "What do I *mean*? Besides this latest thing?"

James studied Brett with new intensity. "Her? It's over."

She stood straighter. "Do you have any idea how much you hurt me? Do you think me finding you fucking that bitch was something sad that happened to *you*?" Her voice filled with wonder. "Do I even exist for you outside of what you need from me?"

He stretched out his hands. "Brett, please. Will you stop punishing me?"

Her voice went cold. "I didn't punish you enough. That's why you're able to feel so picked on. And why I still feel so much pain and anger that I wake up at night and see you in bed with her."

Her voice carried on the water. James looked around them, as if they might be overheard. More quietly, he said, "I know I hurt you. I saw it on your face. When I started crying that night, ashamed of what I'd done, did you think it was just for me?"

It did not seem to help. Tonelessly, she said, "Who knows."

James came toward her. "I know."

"Well, I don't. I can't. Not yet." She shook her head. "I need time, all right, to know if I can trust you again. And now you tell me I'm out of time. Because of something else I have no say in. Just a little problem involving drugs that has you jumping at every noise in the woods. Or so you tell me . . ."

Turning from him, Brett walked to the water's edge.

After a time, she heard his footsteps behind her, then saw his faint reflection in the water next to hers, a slender profile with hands jammed in his pockets. He made no move to touch her.

"What are you going to do?" he asked.

She hunched her shoulders, helpless. "I don't know. . . ."

Even in the rain, Brett's face was tear-streaked. "I was afraid to tell you," she murmured. "About being so angry at him."

"Because you thought it would look bad?"

Brett shook her head. "Because it was like I'd done something bad." Her voice seemed to fill with superstition. "Like I'd been so angry that it somehow killed him. . . ."

Caroline was suddenly shaken. Carefully, she asked, "Is that what you think happened?"

"No." Brett's voice was fierce now. "But when you said they might think that drugs made me lose my temper, it scared me. Like I could never admit we fought."

Caroline faced her. "Well," she said softly, "you don't have to admit that. Even to your lawyer."

Brett stared at her. Before she could ask, Caroline said, "They've decided to arrest you, Brett. For first-degree murder."

Brett seemed to take a backward step, face filling with shock. "Why?"

"Because of Megan. She claims that you stalked James out of jealousy and threatened both their lives. From where Jackson sits, he may not have much choice."

There were no tears now, no protest. In a dispirited voice, Brett said, "She must truly hate me. . . ."

Caroline gazed at her, trying to decipher the meaning of that. Then she made herself say, "Jackson wants you to come in voluntarily, by tomorrow afternoon. He'll keep you in Connaughton Falls. I think you'll have to stay there."

Brett closed her eyes. "Brett," Caroline said gently, "your parents already know. Before you decide anything, all of you will have to talk this over. I'll try to help find you a lawyer."

Slowly, Brett nodded. There was something in the gesture that Caroline found wrenching; it was as if Brett had lied and thus earned Caroline's abandonment.

Swallowing, she opened her eyes. "Tomorrow," she asked simply, "will you be there?"

Caroline hesitated and then saw the look on Brett's face. "Yes," she said softly. "Of course."

Silent, they turned, hands in their pockets, and walked together to the house.

The next afternoon, when she came for Brett, seemed to Caroline incongruously bright.

Brett was waiting on the porch with a duffel bag. In an awkward clump beside her were her parents and her grandfather.

Channing looked shaken, haunted, and much older; it was as if, Caroline reflected, his own mortality had seeped to the surface of his skin. Betty and Larry were grim, uncertain of what to do or say. Betty had the wounded eyes of someone who has received a shock too heavy and sudden to absorb; she looked at Brett with such inarticulate fear and love that Caroline could not watch it.

Facing Brett, she spoke to her quietly. "We should go."

Brett nodded. As she turned to her family, Caroline edged away. She watched Betty hug her stiffly, kiss her dry-eyed on the cheek, then fold her arms and look at the porch. Saw Larry's wan smile as he clasped Brett's shoulders. And then Channing, the one with tears in his eyes.

His voice was rough, strong. "Don't worry," Caroline heard him say. "I'll have you out soon. Believe that, Brett."

An old man's useless promise, Caroline thought, in a time that has outlasted his power. As if knowing this, Brett pulled her grandfather close.

Awkwardly, the girl turned from them, walked to Caroline, and nodded. As they turned to leave, Betty gazed at Caroline as if she had stolen her child.

In the car, Brett said, "I told them not to come. It would only make things worse."

Caroline nodded. "Did you bring books?"

"Yes." As Caroline started the car, Brett turned to her. "What will this place be like?"

"Somewhat bleak." Caroline tried sounding matter-of-fact. "The good thing is that it's a converted county hospital, so it wasn't designed as a prison. An economy move in the great New Hampshire tradition."

For that moment, the misery in Brett's eyes eased. Calm, Caroline guessed, was what Brett needed. So for the twenty-minute drive, Caroline was calm. It was the longest twenty minutes in her recent memory.

The arraignment itself, quick and quiet, was a blur to Caroline; her clearest impression was of Brett's stoicism. And then, as promised, Jackson let her come with Brett to the county prison.

The converted hospital in Connaughton Falls—a three-story red-brick building from the late 1800s—also served as the police station. Caroline and Brett crossed its shaded grounds, flanked by two police officers, Brett gazing at the windows in the upper floors.

"I'll be up there?" she asked.

"Yes. They'll have a separate cell for you."

Brett's steps slowed. She turned, looking at the sunlit grounds. Caroline waited, hand on the double door, until Brett went inside.

The booking desk waited in a stark green rectangle. Next to the young patrolman at the desk waited Jackson Watts, with a short-haired female trooper. All that he said to Caroline was, "They're ready for her."

The young cop booked her, printed her, input the bare facts of her life on an old computer. Jackson stood in a corner, Caroline close to Brett. The stoic look Brett fought to maintain pierced Caroline's heart.

Was it possible, Caroline wondered, that she had not killed him? Or had Caroline simply crossed the line between lawyer and someone else.

The policeman, she realized, was looking at her. "We're done," he said.

Startled from thought, Caroline turned to Brett. Softly, she said, "It's time now."

It changed something in Brett's face. As if to brace her, Caroline clasped her shoulders. "You'll be all right."

Brett's pleading eyes were her sole answer; by now, Caroline knew that Brett would not ask her to stay. Silent, Brett turned her head.

"It's all right," Caroline murmured again, and pulled her close.

"I didn't kill him. . . ."

She felt so slight, Caroline thought. Over Brett's shoulder, she mouthed to Jackson, "Wait."

He nodded, eyes intent on Caroline.

She held Brett as the girl wept without sound. For this, at least, Caroline had nothing but time.

A few moments passed; Brett seemed to have wept herself out. But it was Caroline, now, who did not know how to leave.

Slowly, Brett looked up at her. Her eyes showed both fear and resolve. "It's okay. . . ."

Caroline felt Jackson watching her, the last monitor of reason. And then, against her will, she took Brett's face in her hands. "I'll stay," she said gently. "Until you don't need a lawyer."

Beyond Brett's expression of surprise and gratitude, Caroline saw Jackson's look of astonishment. When the deputy took Brett away, her eyes were still on Caroline. Jackson watched them both.

Caroline turned and left through the wooden doors.

It was done.

Alone in her room, Caroline did not call Masters Hill. She did not speak to anyone.

On the bed beside her was the number of the Cahill Knife Company.

In what felt like a final loss of will, Caroline reached for the phone.

"Cahill," the operator said.

Caroline read the name she had written, asked for the clerk. When she answered, Caroline sounded quite calm. "This is Caroline Masters. You may remember I called the other day. About a serial number on a Cahill knife."

A moment's silence. Coolly, the clerk told her, "Like I thought, we can't tell you where we shipped it. Not who bought it, or even who sold it to them."

"I understand." Caroline paused. "You thought you might know the year it was made."

"Yes." The voice was more patient now. "I can tell you that much." A brief shuffling of papers, muffled by the phone. "Here it is. From what I've written down, it was made in 1964. Early in the year."

Caroline kept her voice steady. "Nineteen sixty-four."

"That's what I said."

"Thank you," Caroline said politely, and put the phone down.

With an odd detachment, she held her hands in front of her and saw that they were shaking.

PART THREE

SUMMER 1964

ONE

WHEN NICOLE MASTERS proposed to take her to Martha's Vineyard three weeks earlier than planned, Caroline had been surprised.

"It will be the two of us," her mother said with a smile. "A little time, perhaps, before we exile you to boarding school."

Caroline adored her father and would miss him. But she loved the house at Eel Pond, the days spent sailing in the Crosby catboat her father had bought the summer before. And her mother's excitement pleased her. Nicole was often distant, her moods so mutable that Caroline was never quite sure how her mother felt about her, or about Channing himself: as she moved toward young womanhood, Caroline had become preternaturally sensitive to the growing silences between her parents, divining some intricate scheme of cause and effect—in her father's affection for her, Caroline felt her mother's withdrawal.

To Caroline, the signs of this withdrawal were, as so often with her mother, unspoken. Her occasional trips with Channing to New York City—which had seemed Nicole's greatest pleasure—no longer occurred, though Caroline did not know why. Nicole's response was to take less interest in their home and village. She spent long days in her room; with the other women of their class—the wives of lawyers or doctors or bankers—Nicole maintained a polite acquaintance, the by-product of their husbands' prominence, which now lacked all pretense of intimacy. This spring, Caroline had noticed that her mother, who loved small things of beauty, no longer planted the bright flowers she once maintained in the rear garden. With instinctive caution, Caroline did not ask her why.

The trip to Martha's Vineyard happened suddenly. The three of them were at the dinner table; Caroline's father was describing, as if to Caroline alone, how his grandfather had come to have their summer home pulled by oxen to Eel Pond. Across from her husband, Nicole listened with a politeness so unvarying that Caroline could feel the minutes passing in her mother's mind.

As if to compensate, Caroline said to her father, "I can't wait to go back. When will we?"

Her father smiled. "July. Only a month now."

"Perhaps you can go sooner." Her mother had not spoken for some time; as Nicole turned to her, Caroline felt surprise. "I may be able to discard my many obligations, Caroline, and leave early. With your father's consent, of course."

This cool touch of irony made Caroline glance at Channing. But his fathomless gaze was fixed on Nicole. Her look at him was steady; perhaps only Caroline would have felt this as a challenge. In her own discomfort, Caroline said to Channing, "Do you think we could, Father? I could sail the new boat."

For another moment, Channing considered his wife. Then he turned to Caroline with a small, reflective smile. "Of course, Caroline. It was rather a long winter. For both of you."

Watching him, Caroline realized that the thought of having Nicole to herself, away from here, felt like desertion and yet came as a relief. And that her father knew all this.

They left one day after Caroline finished school.

They stopped in Boston, bought some summer dresses, had cocktails and dinner at the Ritz-Carlton. The next day, eyes alight, Nicole presented Caroline with a gold bracelet and her first set of expensive earrings. "We've become so provincial," Nicole said lightly, "that we're both at risk of becoming like the heroines of an English Gothic novel, so earnest and unadorned that no one will read our pages. A tragedy for us and the world alike." By the time they got to Martha's Vineyard, the trip had begun to seem like an escapade, a high-spirited rebellion against a dreariness that only her mother felt.

But Caroline was happy to sustain the mood. One afternoon, they played tennis at the Edgartown Yacht Club and then had dinner at that bastion of Republicanism and plaid pants; after much laughter and perhaps too much champagne, Nicole had wondered aloud why Barry Goldwater had so much compassion for Southern blacks that he would not burden them with the difficulty of voting. If a few heads had turned, Nicole did not care. "These people," she murmured on leaving, "will forever wonder why everyone can't be more like them, while *I* will forever wonder why they wear such foolish clothes."

But beneath this, her mother's feelings were more serious. The island was alive with civil rights ferment—church services, rallies, speeches by young summer residents now working in the South. The next Sunday, a somber Nicole took Caroline to a memorial service for Medgar Evers, the murdered civil rights leader. Though her mother had said nothing, Caroline could not help but wonder whether she was thinking of her own family. When she touched her mother's hand, Nicole squeezed Caroline's fingertips.

Yet much of their time was light, almost airy. When they went to the movies, Nicole chose a Taylor-Burton romance over *The Longest Day*, just as she chose a Beatles album for the record collection. When they played croquet on the lawn above Nantucket Sound, Nicole poured another glass of wine and began changing the rules: their contest became so antic, the antithesis of Channing's geometric game, that Nicole and Caroline forfeited competition to laughter and shared the rest of the wine. But Nicole followed the presidential race with an intensity that brooked no humor: the night the Republican convention shouted down Nelson Rockefeller, she shook her head and murmured, "Frightening. And to think that last year there was Kennedy." Then, a short time later, she said, "Now Americans will have their own racist war."

"What do you mean?"

"Vietnam. So murderous and yet so provincial—to learn nothing from the one thing the French truly have to teach: ethnocentrism."

To Caroline, it was like discovering a stranger, mordant and despairing, who lived below the shifting surface of her mother's moods. Caroline found this sudden window on her mother's soul both exciting and disturbing, as if discerning the distance that Nicole had moved from them, her family, beneath the cover of her silence. Not once in their first days together did Nicole refer to her husband.

It was this realization that most unsettled Caroline. But it did not truly strike her until the night the telephone rang and, as Nicole answered it, Caroline knew that the call was not from Channing Masters.

Perhaps it was a rise in her mother's voice, the slightest change in her slender body, now catlike in its stillness. "Who was that?" Caroline asked.

They sat on the screened porch as sunset spread across the water. Nicole put down her wineglass; the veiled, considering look she gave Caroline seemed imported from New Hampshire, so different was it from their last few days. "Oh," she said casually, "a friend—you remember Paul Nerheim. He hopes to see us sometime."

"All of us?" Caroline asked.

A second's pause, her mother's look keen, then vanishing with a wave of her hand. "I suppose it depends on the time." Her voice became dry. "But I will give you plenty of notice."

So she knows how I feel, Caroline thought. She was not sure that this was a comfort.

Caroline had disliked Paul Nerheim's smile before she sensed her father's feelings.

There was something about it that Caroline did not care for—perhaps, she thought now, the way it seemed to linger on her mother.

"You're very tall," he had said to Caroline. "Like a dancer or an athlete."

It had been the summer before, when Caroline was thirteen. She was not yet used to being taller than Nicole; her breasts had not filled out, and she was afraid of looking too much like her father. Knowing this, her mother had answered, "More like the runway model I could never become," sparing Caroline the necessity of saying anything. As if in sympathy for Caroline, Channing Masters did not smile.

Their family—Channing, Nicole, and Caroline—stood in the entryway of Nerheim's summer home on Martha's Vineyard. Caroline felt their presence as the kind of arbitrary social act peculiar to adults: for some reason, Nerheim had asked them here; someone—her mother, Caroline assumed—had accepted; and Caroline could not understand why anyone had bothered. In a vague way she knew that Nerheim was an investment banker from New York; that he had met her parents on the night when Nicole had inveigled a reluctant Channing into a summer dance in Edgartown; and that

Nerheim was an acquaintance of John F. Kennedy. But what she sensed most keenly was that this man would never be her father's friend.

They even looked different: Nerheim with his even tan, white tennis sweater, gold-coin watch; Channing with his slacks, plain shirt, comfortable hiking shoes. Even Nerheim's thin face, mobile eyes, and lively gestures seemed the opposite of Channing's quiet dignity, his air of watchful judgment. Nicole stood smiling between them, lightly touching Nerheim's arm.

"You were so kind to ask us, Paul. And your 'country place,' as you put it, is lovely."

And it was, in a way. They had taken a twisting dirt road through the woods of Chilmark, close to the unseen bluffs of the Atlantic, which opened unexpectedly to an acre of green manicured lawn, fronting a mansion so eccentric that Caroline found it startling. It was a sprawling, almost gingerbread structure with chimneys, windows, and dormers everywhere, and a glassed-in porch with panes shaped like waves, so that they seemed to flow and ripple across the porch. Nicole contrived to be enchanted.

"This is wonderful," she said. "So many people live as if they're communing with their ancestors."

Caroline glanced at her father, who was studying Nicole with a faint half smile. "This would drive my ancestors crazy," Nerheim said, and gave Nicole a smile of complicity that seemed to exclude Channing. "If I even knew who they were. Come, I'll show you the attic."

Trailing after them, Caroline fell in next to her father.

The attic was made of polished teak, shaped like the prow of a ship. In spite of herself, Caroline was impressed.

"The original owner hired a shipbuilder and then ran out of money," Nerheim explained. "It wasn't finished for years, until I did the rest last summer. A masterpiece of the shipbuilder's art."

"Does it float?" Channing inquired mildly.

Nerheim gave a short laugh. "Perhaps we'll see," he said. "During the next hurricane—"

"But where's the ballroom?" Nicole interjected. "You, Paul, who seem to like dancing so much."

"Oh," he said. "I'll pour some champagne and show you."

Glasses in hand, her parents followed Nerheim across the grass to a carefully laid stone path that meandered artfully through the woods. At its end, a clearing suddenly opened to a clay tennis court.

They stopped by the net. Surrounded by woods, they could not be seen or heard from the house. Nerheim gave a mock bow.

"The ballroom?" Nicole asked.

Nerheim smiled. "Of course."

At a dinner served by two silent servants, Nerheim turned the table talk to the opera season in New York, the symphony, the jazz clubs he knew here or there. Nicole listened appreciatively; her questions sent him on knowing tangents, which, Caroline saw, seemed of interest only to her mother. What inquiries Nerheim addressed to her father seemed so studiedly polite that they underscored Channing's inability to speak to what seemed to engage his wife. To Caroline, Nerheim said almost nothing.

"Can I go for a walk?" she asked before dessert. "I'd like to see the ocean from here."

"Of course," her father answered, excusing her from Nerheim's table without glancing at their host.

Outside, in the cool of early evening, Caroline breathed deeply.

The sun was falling behind the trees. Caroline walked the darkening path through the woods until she reached a fork; she stopped, confused for a moment, and then chose the path which she guessed must lead to water. But the woods were thick and gnarled; it was not until she climbed a steep rise, toward a sudden swatch of evening sky, that she found herself on a sheer cliff above the blue endless sweep of the Atlantic.

The surprise of it caught her in a moment of vertigo, left her pulse racing. Two hundred feet below her was a sandy beach; the orange sandstone cliff, scarred by wind and rain, was so precipitous that it seemed to drop beneath her feet. Down the face of the cliff, stairs crisscrossed to the bottom; beside them were strewn the skeletal remains of other stairs, destroyed by storms.

Caroline sat, gazing across the water.

It was strange. She had always viewed the ocean with a respect close to awe, but never with fear. Yet beneath the gray-blue surface of the water she felt the savage roiling of a storm she could not see, save on the ruined cliffside. It was some time before she rose, a little unsteady, and backed away.

When she returned, the adults were in the living room, still chatting about opera. Her father glanced up from his chair. "Tired?" he asked pleasantly.

To her surprise, Nerheim summoned a look of deep courtesy for Channing, a smile for Caroline that was close to rueful. "She should at least be bored," he said. "I've been so alone lately that I ramble on about whatever interests me, without a care for my guests. My apologies, Caroline."

Caroline did not know what to say. But her mother's expression changed, as if this last remark had engaged her more than what had gone before. "What may seem boredom," she said gently, "is, in Caroline, self-sufficiency. As for us, there is very little opera in Resolve. You are kind to remind us of the larger world."

As he turned to Nicole, Nerheim's smile became warm; perhaps it was only to Caroline that his humility seemed too self-assured. "Thank you, Nicole. I'm sure Resolve has other charms. Next time—and I hope there will be—I'll leave room for you to tell me of them."

Nicole's returning smile was oblique and ambiguous—to Caroline, it could have meant anything, from *Of course, all of us know that we'll never do this again* to *Please give me a few days to consider what Resolve's charms are.* As Channing put down his coffee, contemplating his wife, Caroline sensed an unspoken humiliation.

"I am kind of tired," she said to her mother. "If you don't mind."

"Of course," Nerheim said with a tolerant smile, and rose from the table.

At the door, Nerheim clasped her father's shoulder, one friendly man to another. Knowing that her father disliked being touched by strangers, Caroline winced; Channing's expression did not change. "Channing," Nerheim said, "thank you so much for lending me your family. As I said, I've spent too much time alone."

As Channing extended his hand, the gesture put distance between them. "Thank you," he said with civility. "It was good of you to have us."

The corners of Nerheim's eyes crinkled, and then he turned to Nicole, clasping her hand in both of his. "Nicole," he said. "I hope I see you again. All of you."

Her mother tilted her head; what this suggested to Caroline was that, were it not for Channing, she would have proffered her cheek.

"Oh, you will, Paul." She gave a wry look at their surroundings. "Solitude in such a place must be a trial for you."

Nerheim laughed. "Oh, it is," he said, and released her hand.

The ride home was quiet. Leaving, Channing stopped at the fork in the road, beam lights catching a gnarled tree. "To the left," Nicole said softly. Otherwise, she was silent.

Later, Caroline went to the kitchen for orange juice, heard raised voices from her parents' bedroom. The last voice was her father's.

Despite herself, Caroline crept to the bedroom door.

"The man is cheap and insinuating," she heard her father say. "And you played to him."

"The man is polite, Channing. As was I. For both of us."

"You're my wife." The thick anger in her father's voice was something Caroline had never heard. "You needn't compensate for me. I'm sure that there are other women who can give Paul Nerheim the admiration he so clearly needs."

There was silence. When her mother spoke again, her tone was so quiet and weary that Caroline barely heard. "Admiration," she said softly, "is all that's left to me."

In the darkened hallway, Caroline felt herself flush with the shame of listening. She turned away.

The next day, they left the island, four days earlier than planned. Now, a year later, the memory fell like a shadow between Caroline and Nicole.

"I don't feel like seeing him," Caroline said to her mother.

Nicole finished her wine. "You don't have to," she answered in a careless voice. "I'm not sure that I do, either."

TWO

As the days passed, Nicole Masters seemed restless.

She took less interest in their tennis, did not come up with new excursions, retreated into books. She encouraged Caroline to contact the daughters of other summer people, friends from past years. Yet for two nights running, Nicole walked the beach alone; Caroline watched her, hands in the pockets of her white cardigan sweater, gazing out to sea. Caroline felt a loss.

When her mother returned from the beach on the second night, Caroline was waiting. With new directness, she asked, "Are you all right, Mother?"

Nicole looked startled, as if awakened from her thoughts. "Have I not been?"

Caroline hesitated, afraid to articulate her instincts. "I don't know. . . ."

Nicole gave her a faint smile. Gently, she said, "It's not you, Caroline. If that's what you're sensing."

Caroline felt relief, the tenuous renewal of their bond. "What is it, then?"

Her mother shrugged. "Does 'it' have to be anything? Other than me?" Her voice was dispassionate but not unkind. "I have my moods, that's all. Perhaps you notice them more without your father to distract you. If so, I apologize."

It was less apology than statement of fact; it was as if Nicole had accepted her own apartness, and thus that others should. But Caroline did not wish to.

"I've been thinking—tomorrow, let's go for a day sail." Caroline's voice quickened, as if to impart excitement to her mother. "We'll sail over to Tarpaulin Cove, where Father took me last year—have a picnic on the beach and go swimming. Really, it would be fun for you."

Nicole's smile did not quite hide a sadness in her eyes. "Would it?"

"Sure," Caroline answered. "I'll make the sandwiches and sail the catboat myself. All you have to do is go with me."

Nicole considered her, still smiling a little. "All right, then. You make it hard to argue."

Before Nicole could change her mind, Caroline went to the kitchen and began preparing for their picnic. When the telephone rang, her mother answered it in another room.

Caroline emerged from the kitchen. "The picnic's ready," she said. "Was that Father?"

Nicole seemed to study her. "Your father would have asked for you. But you may call him if you wish."

The tacit rebuke silenced Caroline. She found that she did not want to speak with Channing.

But when morning came, Nicole did not wish to sail.

"I'm sorry, Caroline." Her voice was soft. "I find that I don't feel well."

In her mother's eyes, Caroline saw a silent plea for understanding—of what, she did not know. But Nicole said nothing more.

Caroline's anger burst out unbidden. "It's a beautiful day," she said. "I'm not going to mope around the house all day or hang around that goddamned yacht club, talking about boys."

Nicole looked at her gravely. "Such language, Caroline. But about the 'goddamned yacht club,' I understand. So what do you propose?"

"Sailing. If I have to go by myself, I will."

Nicole glanced down, as if knowing that what Caroline most wanted was a change of heart. Softly, Nicole asked, "Would your father let you do that?"

Caroline folded her arms. "He told me I could last summer. Whenever I felt ready."

"And you are?"

"Yes." Caroline hesitated, still hoping for a sign that Nicole would go with her, saw none. In a flat voice, she finished, "Can I go now, Mother?"

For a long time, Nicole turned to gaze at the weather, eyes hooded. "When would you be back?"

"By six o'clock." Caroline made her voice indifferent. "There's no point in getting back any sooner."

Nicole's eyes were sad again. "All right," she answered. "You can go."

The day was brilliant.

It lightened Caroline's heart, braced her defiance. For a moment, she forgot that her father, knowing the sudden treachery of oceans, never would have let her sail alone. She walked swiftly to the catboat without looking back.

The boat was handsome and beautifully maintained—a twenty-foot Crosby, built in 1909. When her father had first shown it to her, a present for Caroline's thirteenth birthday, she fought back tears of surprise.

"Your birthday is special to me," Channing said gently. "Sail this with the care you deserve."

Warmed by the memory, guilty at her willfulness, Caroline set sail.

The sky was cloudless, the breeze stiff and constant. She did not check the weather.

The sail to Tarpaulin Cove was brisk and sure. Caroline felt a sense of her own mastery. Running before the wind, she headed toward the lighthouse.

At the head of the cove, Caroline moored the catboat, turned to measure the expanse of ocean she had crossed with such ease. On this sparkling day, she still could see the Vineyard.

She would take her time, Caroline told herself, do everything she would have done had her mother not deserted her. She ate her sandwich, drank her Coke, legs dangling over the bow. Only when she had finished did she jump into the bracing water and swim confidently to shore.

The beach was empty, the sand warm. She lay there lost in her own thoughts, the ocean lapping at her legs and feet.

She should not be angry at her mother, Caroline decided. Things that Nicole could not avoid or help had happened well before Caroline was born. Caroline would take the good days as they came, fight the disappointment when her mother slipped away. She wished it seemed that simple for her father.

When at last she looked at the ocean, a long finger of fog crept the line between sky and water.

Caroline sat up, surprised. Knew at once that she must leave long before she had planned.

Forgetting her parents, she swam quickly to the catboat. As she clambered up the stern, the fog was darker, a dense bank rising from the water between Caroline and home.

She set sail toward the fog. The varnished deck of the catboat still glistened in the sunlight; she would sail through the fog, Caroline assured herself, and see the Vineyard through the sunlight on the other side.

Sails creaking, Caroline reached the first seeping mists. The water was suddenly gray, and then fog and solitude closed around her.

Her face was damp and chill. The catboat plowed forward, knifing the water Caroline could scarcely see. But she was on open sea, she told herself; unless someone rammed her, there was little danger.

Suddenly, the fog was no longer sitting on the water but whistling past her, breaking up before her eyes. Startled, Caroline tried to remember what Channing said this meant.

Just before she saw the black line of clouds racing toward her on the horizon, she knew.

A squall.

She had only minutes. Now she remembered clearly what her father had told her—with the thunderstorm would come a driving rain, savage winds from every direction. She saw no sailboats on the water.

For an instant, Caroline was paralyzed. Then the other thing that Channing had said came back: the winds could capsize her. Panicky, she crawled along the ledge toward the bow, one hand over the other, clawing at the handrail. As the storm swept toward her, she loosened the rigging and let the sail drop.

Then the squall hit.

The first wave threw her from the bow, grabbing at the halyard as she fell on her side. She cried out; rain lashed her face. In a moment, the seventy-mile-per-hour winds would be upon her: already the boat bobbed like a cork, waves swamping the cockpit.

Caroline threw herself onto the deck, and then the next wave covered the catboat.

As Caroline grasped the wrought-iron tiller, the surge of water ripped her seaward, turning the boat on its side. Her muscles screamed with pain. There was a quickening surge beneath her, and then the boat righted itself in a spasmodic shiver.

Blinded by seawater, Caroline felt the primal ocean envelop her. The next fierce wave would tear her hands from the tiller and sweep her out to sea.

She clenched the tiller in both hands, eyes stinging with salt and tears from the pelting rain that scoured her face. Through half-open slits she saw the rope swirling in the flooded cockpit.

In her mind, Channing Masters ordered Caroline to lash herself to the tiller.

She grasped at the line with her right hand. The boat knifed into the air. Caroline fell back, head striking the floorboard. The cracking sound filled her ears, and then everything was black and lost and nauseous in the pit of her stomach. With a will of their own, the fingers of one hand still grasped the tiller.

Water pounded her face, seemed to throw the line into her hand. She sat upright; from a great distance, her father's voice told her again to coil the line around her waist and lash her body to the tiller.

In the whirling boat, she snaked the rope between the spokes of the tiller and around her waist. A knot—the work of instinct—and Caroline and the boat were one.

A wall of ocean hit. Caroline wrenched upward, was caught by the rope, ribs cracking against the wheel. She prayed that her knot would hold, that the catboat would not capsize and trap her beneath the ocean, a captive, lungs filling with water until she drowned. A bolt of lightning struck the mast, the roar of thunder deafened her. Caroline shut her eyes and prayed to no one. The boat surged and plummeted at random, wind singing in her ears, rain driving sideways into her face.

And then it stopped.

Caroline opened her eyes.

A last thin darkness passed over her, and then the air was crisp and sparkling. Caroline began to cry.

No, she told herself. With clumsy hands she freed herself. Her head throbbed, her rib cage felt raw.

Then she could not seem to move. It was as if, in some deep trauma, she was helpless.

Straining, she rose from her paralysis and moved haltingly to the rigging. As the sails rose above her, a fresh wind made the canvas crackle and then fill. She could see the Vineyard ahead of her.

Numb, Caroline took the tiller again. Her eyes were swollen with salt.

A second fog was seeping across the sound.

Caroline sailed toward it in the southeast wind. The fog moved slowly, spreading across the water. This time, Caroline sensed, there would be no storm, no sound.

Breathing deeply, she made the most of her last ten minutes in sunlight, and then entered the fog again.

It was different. Silent, still, windless. Her sail flapped and withered on the mast.

Blindly, Caroline drifted with a tide she could only feel.

The tide could sweep her to shore, she knew, break the catboat on the rocks. Through the fog came the haunting toll of the first bell buoy. She was not sure where she was.

Bearings lost, she drifted.

All that she could do was listen to the eerie sound of the buoys slowly clanging, nearer and nearer, until she knew that she was inside them, closer to shore. She sat at the helm in the rear of the cockpit, trying to keep the catboat from the shoals of West Chop, hoping for the breezes that came in midafternoon.

She could sense the cliffs coming closer, feel the choppiness of shallow water. And then—it seemed on schedule—her sails flapped with a gust of wind.

Caroline grasped the tiller. Tilting leeward, the catboat sailed into sunlight, clearing the promontory of West Chop.

It was as though the Vineyard had appeared by magic through a sheer curtain. She could see the mansions of West Chop, the distant masts spiking the harbor at Vineyard Haven. Faint and exhilarated, Caroline grinned as if she would never stop.

She could not wait to tell her mother, to *see* her mother. All memory of anger had been swept away by the storm, the wind, the enormity of survival. The sail home was endless, a blur.

Docking, Caroline forced herself through the rituals of seamanship, bursting with all that she would say to Nicole. Then she hurried stiffly to the house, sore and bruised and filled with love and gratitude.

"Mother," she called out.

The house was silent. "Mom," she called again.

Perhaps she was asleep. Turning, Caroline crept down the hallway to her mother's bedroom. It was only as she turned the knob, too late to stop, that Caroline suddenly knew what she would find.

Next to her mother's face, wide-eyed and startled, the head of Paul Nerheim stared at Caroline.

Their bodies were frozen. Nerheim on his elbows, sheets to his waist; Nicole beneath him, legs apart, the tips of her breasts still touching Nerheim's chest. Their stillness seemed so fragile that Caroline could not move.

"Please." Nicole's eyes were pleading. "Leave us now."

Caroline's legs felt weak beneath her. "My father . . ."

Nicole's eyes shut. *Please.*

Caroline backed slowly from the door.

Wandering to the living room, she slumped in a chair and waited. She did not know whether the nausea she felt was for herself or for her father.

In front of her stood Paul Nerheim.

His hair was mussed, his clothes not right. His voice was soft, tentative. "I'm sorry, Caroline. And so is she."

Caroline simply stared at him.

He shrugged, helpless. "Your mother wants to see you."

Caroline straightened in her chair. With a coldness she did not know was hers, she said, "Get out. Now."

Their eyes met. Slowly, Nerheim nodded, and then he turned and left the house.

THREE

MOMENTS LATER, Nicole appeared.

She was wearing a silk bathrobe and an air of composure that, to Caroline, seemed fragile. Her mother sat across from her, studying her closely, and then Caroline's disarray seemed to register in her eyes.

"What happened to you, Caroline? Your face is bruised."

Caroline folded her arms. She said nothing; it was too late for Nicole's concern, and the idea that she could be so cheaply bought filled her with contempt and anger.

Nicole seemed to know this. "All right," she said softly. "You wish me to explain myself."

Caroline was unsure of this: what she wanted most was for the last half hour to vanish like the nightmare that it seemed. But she had no words to say this.

Nicole crossed her legs, arranging her robe with a distracted air. In the light through the window, her face looked thin and pale. "What I did was wrong," she said at last. "More than anything, because you saw it."

Caroline's voice was cold. "I'm sorry I surprised you, Mother. I know you weren't expecting me."

Her daughter's words seemed to strike Nicole like a slap. Her eyes flew open, and then she sat back, folding her hands. "Do you expect me to flay myself, Caroline? Would that make things better?"

It left Caroline without words again.

"No?" Nicole's voice held gentle irony. "Then perhaps I can trouble you to listen."

Caroline shrugged. But she felt her heart race.

"I did not expect this moment," Nicole continued softly, "and I have no speech prepared. Especially for a daughter who loves her father as much as you love Channing. So if I am tactless, or inartful, please forgive me."

Caroline filled with a kind of dread. Her face was stone.

Pausing, Nicole seemed to swallow. "There is nothing wrong with Channing, Caroline, but that he married me. Perhaps it was his mistake to ask. Certainly, it was my mistake to accept."

Caroline stiffened in her chair. "He gave you a *life*, Mother."

There was a first glint of passion in her mother's eyes. "He gave me *his* life—" She stopped herself abruptly, forced her voice to lower. "I saw a gentle man, Caroline. Perhaps paternalistic, but kind. What I did not see was the frightened man. Frightened of women. Frightened of whatever he could not control—"

"Father's not frightened." Caroline felt her mystification become anger. "People look up to him. Everyone I know."

Slowly, Nicole nodded. "In his world, yes. That is his strength."

Caroline gave her mother a look of cold rejection. Nicole's voice was soft again, as if she was willing herself to ignore the evidence of Caroline's eyes. "I was the choice, Caroline, of a frightened man. Young and rootless, an alien in my own country, shattered by what I had lost. Not just a family, but a world that once made sense to me. I no longer had any world of my own. . . ."

Nicole paused. Her voice was stoic; it did not ask for sympathy. But part of Caroline, just by listening, felt dirty and complicit. She watched her mother in silence.

"Channing," Nicole continued quietly, "believed in his own kindness. But he also believed that I would never defy him, or leave him, or even question him." Nicole looked down. "As a man, or as a lover."

Caroline stiffened, and then Nicole gazed at her directly. "On all counts, Caroline, I have been a disappointment. So perhaps you could say Channing healed me."

Buried in her voice was a trace of bitterness so faint that Caroline could not detect whether it was directed at her father or at Nicole herself. But Caroline seized on it. "Quit trying to turn me against Father." Her voice rose. "You don't deserve him—"

"Don't I?" Nicole burst out. "With his fear, possessiveness, and anger? I would think you would find me more than deserving."

Oddly, the sudden outburst changed the balance between them; Caroline felt her confusion become a chill self-control. "I would never have said that, Mother. Not until I saw you in bed with him. So I guess Father has always understood you better."

Nicole seemed to flinch. "I know," she said in a husky voice, "that I've been no great mother to you. But please take the good from your father without letting him control you. Because the danger is that he will—your life and your thoughts."

At once, Caroline felt the sudden desire to lash out so that her mother would stop. "Damn you," she screamed. "Do you think I need Father to tell me that I just found you fucking Nerheim—"

"Caroline, please." White-faced, Nicole stood. "If this is what we must discuss, at least understand me as a woman. I know you must have begun to feel these things yourself."

Caroline felt herself flush. Pausing, Nicole looked down at her intently. "I have little that is my own, Caroline. But I remain a woman, with a woman's needs." Her voice was calm now. "It is a fact in which, as a man, your father has little interest. Whatever his flaws, Paul Nerheim does. And that, to Channing, is the mirror of his own inadequacy."

The sound of her mother speaking Nerheim's name made this dispassionate shaming of her father unendurable to Caroline. "Don't talk like that. Not about my father," she cried out. "He *saved* you. Do you think what happened to your parents is some kind of excuse? It's like 'They were murdered, so *I* get to hurt anyone I want to hurt—' "

Abruptly, Caroline caught herself. The look on her mother's face was too terrible to watch.

Folding her arms, Caroline looked away. Her mother's voice, soft and clear, seemed to come from far away. "So I've wounded you that badly. . . ."

Caroline could not answer, or even look at her.

There was a long silence, and then she felt Nicole's fingers rest gently on her shoulder. Her voice was softer yet. "I know that you will never tell your father, Caroline. But I won't make you my accomplice. Paul Nerheim will not set foot inside this house again."

Caroline did not answer. It was a moment before she realized that her mother was gone.

Alone, Caroline went to the porch overlooking the water, and wept until she had no tears left.

For the next three days, they barely spoke.

Caroline had no wish to be near her mother, or with friends. She left the house early: on the first day, she willed herself to sail to Tarpaulin Cove and back; for the two days following, she hiked and cycled alone. Nicole made no approach to her.

Caroline did not know, or wish to know, how Nicole Masters spent her days. From their silent dinners, Caroline had the sense of a woman who seemed to have gone somewhere far away, until she would suddenly catch her mother watching her with veiled curiosity. At night, Caroline could hear her pacing the house.

In a week, Caroline knew, Channing Masters was due to join them.

Caroline found the thought unbearable. She could not imagine them dining together, every silence laden with Channing's ignorance, her mother's guilt, and the knowledge that Caroline devoutly wished she could erase. But the only person she could say this to was Nicole.

Finally, Caroline could not stand their silence. On the fourth afternoon, returning from a bike ride, she went to her mother's room.

At the moment Caroline saw Nicole, she froze.

Her mother sat at her dressing table, her fine-boned face reflected in a makeup mirror. With her left hand, she carefully applied eyeliner to the corners of her bright-green eyes.

Caroline's voice was flat. "Going out?"

"Yes." Her mother's expression did not change. "Until midnight or so, perhaps. So you needn't wait up for me."

The moment was strange to Caroline: the irony in her mother's voice; the intent look in her eyes; the light on her face. Nicole did not turn; to Caroline, it was as if her mother was lost to her.

"What are we going to do?" Caroline asked abruptly. "When Father comes."

Nicole moved the eyeliner a fraction, gazing narrow-eyed into the glass. "I haven't considered it. What we always do, I suppose."

To Caroline, this did not ring true; even Nicole's tone had the sound of an evasion. " 'What we always do,' " she said in desperation, "won't be like that for me anymore. I don't think I could stand it."

For the first time, Nicole turned to her, asking softly, "But what can I do, Caroline? Now that you know. Tell him for you? Or simply leave him?" She paused. "Which would mean, once Channing was done with me, that I must leave you as well. For he would never let me take you."

Caroline felt a tremor in her body. "Then don't go out, at least. Please."

Nicole studied her. "I must," she said finally. "At least for tonight."

Caroline could say nothing.

Nicole regarded her and then turned to the mirror, more intently than before. It was as if she did not care to look at Caroline's face.

Caroline drifted to the sun porch.

She gazed out at the waves, swelling, lapping, dying on the beach beneath them. There was something hypnotic about water, Caroline realized; as frightening as the ocean could be, its timelessness soothed her.

Her mother's footsteps sounded on the porch.

Caroline turned, looking into her mother's face. For a moment, Nicole's eyes were soft, and then she bent to kiss Caroline on the cheek.

Caroline froze, silent, neither welcoming nor resisting. Nicole's lips were light, fleeting.

Her mother stood, walked away. To Caroline's surprise, she stopped, turning in the doorway.

"I'm sorry," she said simply, and left.

FOUR

CAROLINE WAITED up for her.

She could not help this, could not sleep. She imagined her mother's evening, prayed that her father would not call. The house was dark and still.

At one o'clock, her mother had not returned.

Caroline went outside, stood on the bluffs, listened to the slow, deep surge of the purple waters against the cliff. The night was black, moonless.

The wind in her face was stiff. Caroline felt a chill; folded her arms against the cold; listened, vainly, for the sound of tires on gravel, the white Porsche that Nicole treasured and Channing found ostentatious.

Nothing.

Caroline tried to envision her mother, found it painful. Perhaps, she told herself, Nicole had drunk a little more than normal, forgotten her promise to return. Perhaps they had made love more than once.

The luminous dial of her wristwatch read one o'clock.

At two, Caroline promised herself, she would do something. What, she did not know; it was as if by setting a deadline she could induce Nicole's return.

Sometimes her mother drank too much.

She said this to herself, curtly and baldly, as she had not before. It made her feel the change in her, the clear-eyed sorrow.

Yet she shrank from calling Nerheim.

Deeply lonely, Caroline returned to the house.

She went to the kitchen. In the pale light, she gazed at the schoolroom-style clock.

She would hate it, Caroline told herself, if her parents ever did this to her, keeping watch. The thought of her parents made her sad again.

Damn Paul Nerheim. He had no right.

Yet at two o'clock, she found that she could not call him.

There was nothing magic about two, she told herself. How would she feel if she interrupted them from lovemaking, like a child with her face pressed against the window? Worse, a child who could not understand the world of adults, who simply needed their attention . . .

Caroline made herself tea.

There was a noise outside. Caroline stood, walked quickly to the front door, cracked it open so that her mother could not see her.

The drive was empty.

Caroline closed the door, leaning against it. Then she went to the kitchen and opened the telephone book.

For long minutes, she stared at Nerheim's number, until she knew it by heart. Then she stood, forcing herself to turn the dial.

"Hello?"

It was Nerheim, dull-voiced, puzzled. Caroline drew a breath. "Is my mother there?"

"Caroline?"

"Yes."

A moment's silence. "She left." Nerheim's voice was clear now. "Hours ago."

Caroline felt her chest constrict. "When?"

"A little before twelve." His tone was oddly kind. "She wanted to get home to you."

Caroline felt her eyes close. Quietly, she said, "She's not here."

Nerheim's silence seemed endless now. When he spoke again, his voice was low; Caroline heard both concern and efficiency. "I'll call the Chilmark police. And the state police."

Caroline was silent; it took her a moment to realize why she did not wish him to do this.

"No," she said. "I will."

An hour later, the telephone rang. Caroline jumped up to snatch it.

"Miss Masters?"

Caroline sagged with disappointment. "Yes?"

The man's voice was quiet and level, with a distinct Massachusetts accent. "This is Sergeant Mannion of the state police. The locals say your mother may be missing. Or at least that you don't know where she is."

"No. No one does."

He seemed to hear the despair in her voice. "They told me she was leaving Windy Gates in Chilmark. Is that right?"

"Yes." Caroline paused. "She was visiting a friend."

"Do you know where else she'd go?"

"No. Just here."

A tentative note entered his voice. "Is your father there?"

"He's in New Hampshire." Defensively, she added, "At our home."

"I see." His voice was careful, neutral. "She hasn't been gone that long—"

"Please," Caroline interrupted. "Can you just look for her? I'm afraid she's had an accident. . . ."

Saying this, Caroline felt her stomach wrench. Wished to tell him, *If it weren't for me, my mother would be home.*

He could not have known this. But when he spoke again, more gently, it was as if he had heard her. "What does she drive?"

"A white Porsche."

Caroline heard the quiet of thought. "All right," he said at last. "I'll look for her. By the time you hear from me, she'll probably be home."

For two hours, the telephone did not ring and no car came. Caroline wandered through the empty house, defenseless against her imaginings. She had never felt so alone.

A little before five, the first thin dawn turned the darkness of the ocean blue gray. Gazing out the window, Caroline realized that night had kept her hopes alive. In the chill light of morning, she knew that her mother would not return.

Caroline heard the spit and crunch of gravel, tires stopping on the drive.

Filled with sudden excitement, she ran to the door. In her mind, Nicole Masters was alive again, stepping from her low-slung Porsche as Caroline opened the door.

When she saw the black patrol car, Caroline froze.

A uniformed man emerged. As he came closer, part of Caroline registered his reddish hair, pink scalded face, mild blue eyes. He was slightly pigeon-toed, she noticed; perhaps that was why he seemed to walk so slowly.

"You're Caroline, aren't you."

It was the voice of the state policeman, softer now. She nodded, numb.

"I'm Frank Mannion." His tone was muted, but his eyes would not leave her face. "There's a car been spotted—a white Porsche. I should call your father now."

Caroline blocked the doorway, as if to keep him from the phone. "Where is it?"

A shadow crossed his face. "On the beach. Below Windy Gates."

Caroline's heart stopped, and then she felt herself shudder. "How . . . ?"

He seemed to inhale. "Caroline," he said, "there's a body near the car. A woman."

She felt her eyes shut, her head bend forward. Heard Mannion say, "Please, let me call your father."

Slowly, eyes still closed, Caroline shook her head.

"Someone should identify her." His voice was still quiet. "And your father should be here for you."

Caroline opened her eyes. "No."

"Caroline, I'm sorry—"

"I won't give you his number." Her voice was tight. "I can't let him find out."

Mannion shook his head. "He has to know . . . ," he began, and then something like comprehension appeared in his eyes.

Quietly, Caroline said, "Take me there."

The ride was impressions. Dawn breaking over the Vineyard, as fresh as creation; the white homes and picket fences of Edgartown; then woods and farmland; telephone poles; stone walls; fields as open as the Scottish moors, rolling toward the sea. As they neared Chilmark, Caroline could feel Mannion's reluctance, the leaden silence between them.

"Did you always live here?" she asked.

She felt his surprise, a moment's hesitancy. "No. I'm new. Until me, they never had state police on the island before."

Caroline was quiet for a time. "Do you like it?"

She felt him turn to her, as if to appraise what she needed. "The islanders aren't so sure about me," he said finally. "They've had their own way all this time. But my wife likes it, and it's good for the kids."

Caroline nodded. "How many do you have?"

"Three."

They turned off the road, down the dirt path toward Windy Gates. Caroline could say nothing more.

Trees enveloped them, thick and ancient and overgrown, hanging over the path so that only patches of morning sun dappled the red clay. Caroline felt the tightening in her chest and throat; with sudden clarity, she imagined her mother the night before, dancing with Paul Nerheim on the tennis court to music no one else could hear, their bodies close, a bucket of chilled champagne nearby. . . .

As they neared the fork in the road—one path leading to Nerheim's estate, the other continuing straight to the water—Mannion slowed the car. His mouth was pressed tight.

Turning, Caroline looked toward the house. Imagined her mother driving down the twisting road, as they had the night Caroline had come with her parents. Saw her mother squinting as the headlights struck the trunks of trees, guiding her on the pitch-dark path until she reached the gnarled tree that marked the fork: toward the ocean, or toward home. Remembered her voice, softly saying to Caroline's father, "Left . . ." Saw her in the darkness alone, this time turning toward the water.

Quietly, Caroline murmured, "She knew the way. . . ."

The look Mannion gave her had a touch of superstition, as if he were afraid to speak. And then they passed the fork, rose slowly upward on the twisting path Caroline had walked until she could go no farther.

They went more slowly now. The twists grew more abrupt; there was a chill on Caroline's skin as the memory came to her, just before they reached it—a final bend to the right, as if to turn a corner, and then a rise breaking from the trees to an open sky. . . .

At the edge of the cliff was an ambulance.

As Mannion stopped the car behind it, Caroline said softly, "They should close this road."

Mannion could not look at her.

They got out. He stood by the car; alone, Caroline walked to where the road simply vanished, like the end of the world.

She inhaled. And then, by an act of will, she gazed down at the beach, two hundred feet below.

What she saw first was the white Porsche. It was upside down near the water, its nose dug into the tawny sand as glistening waves lapped against the hood. Near the car, the small figures of three men walked in a desultory manner, sometimes gazing at the water like lovers of nature who had awaited the dawn. Swallowing, Caroline watched one of the figures break away and slowly cross the sand.

He stopped, gazing down.

A tiny figure lay there in her mother's dress, arms outflung, her black hair strewn across the sand like seaweed washed up by the tide. There were patterns in the sand around her, lines and arcs, darker where the crest of the last wave had touched.

Caroline could not breathe. She felt Frank Mannion behind her.

Slowly, Caroline walked from him to the stairs. Saw her mother as she left the earth, free-falling in darkness.

I sent her here, she thought.

Caroline took the last steps to the stairs.

She descended them with her head bowed, Mannion behind her, not looking at the beach. Perhaps it was not her mother, she told herself in silent prayer; from above, the woman looked too small and frail to be the woman Caroline knew. The stairs behind her groaned beneath Mannion's plodding steps.

She took a tier of stairs, then another and another, until her feet touched sand.

Before her were the scattered ruins of other stairs. She stopped there, looking back up the cliffside. Saw the scarred clay near the bottom where her mother's car first hit.

Cool water lapped at her feet. The tide was rising, she realized; as she turned again, slowly walking toward the body, the first wave swirled her mother's hair away from the white face.

Like an automaton, Caroline walked the last few yards to the body of Nicole Masters.

Her face was china. There was a delicate line of blood from her mouth, and her neck was strangely angled. Otherwise, she seemed untouched. But the spirit that once animated Nicole Masters had left her; to her daughter, this waxen figure in the sand had ceased to be her mother, the woman whose clean profile she had last seen in the mirror, who had kissed her goodbye.

Tearless, Caroline sat by the body. "Leave her," she heard Mannion murmur to the others.

Caroline stayed there, gazing at her mother, wishing to unsay the things that would hurt Nicole no longer.

After a time, she felt Mannion standing next to her.

Caroline did not look up. "That's her," she told him. "My mother."

He knelt by her then, empty hands cupped in front of him. Quietly, he said, "She hit the brakes, Caroline. There were skid marks up above."

Caroline's eyes shut. Only then did the tears run down her cheeks.

"So," Mannion said gently. "You see."

Dully, Caroline nodded. She could not speak.

His voice was still soft. "We need to take her now."

After a moment, Caroline stood. She drew sea air deep into her lungs, gazed up at the cliff from which her mother had come. At its edge, she saw the figure of Paul Nerheim.

Next to Caroline, Mannion said, "I'll call your father."

Caroline still stared at the man above them. "No," she said. "I will."

They buried her mother at Masters Hill, some distance from where her husband would someday lie. The service was brief and spare: no one mentioned that she was French, or Jewish, or how she had come here. The details of her death were unspoken.

But Caroline had spared her father nothing. When he had come for her, he put his arms around her and said in a hoarse, gentle voice, "Fathers protect their daughters, not the other way around. Why did you think I needed that from you?"

Caroline could not answer. When she turned from the look on his face, it was no longer to protect him but to protect herself from the knowledge of her father's pain.

In the days after the funeral, they were alone; at her father's urging, Betty returned to her interrupted tour of Europe. Her father treated Caroline with haunted kindness.

Once, sleepless, she found him in the music room at midnight.

"Do you want to talk?" she asked.

"No, Caroline." His voice was harsh. "Not to you."

In that moment, Caroline felt his solitude, knew that his sternness was directed not at her but at himself. They never spoke of Nicole again.

Nor would he hear of Caroline staying. They had enrolled her in Dana Hall; nothing, Channing insisted, should change their plans. When she thought of leaving him alone, Caroline's heart ached. She wept for her mother where Channing could not see.

In the weeks remaining, they made themselves the semblance of a life.

Channing's birthday fell three days before she left. In secret, Caroline picked a present for him; when the morning of his birthday came, she pressed him to take her fishing on Heron Lake.

There were scattered clouds; sunlight sparkled on the lake, vanished, fell again. Caroline faced her father in the rowboat.

"I love it here," she said. "I wish I weren't leaving."

Channing smiled a little. "You've not leaving, Caroline—this is your home. You're simply going away."

Caroline looked at him: the black hair, deep-set black eyes, strong face on which only Caroline could read hurt. Impulsively, she said, "I wish I could take care of you."

There was a brief wound in his eyes, and then he smiled again. "I'm not nearly old enough, Caroline. You'll have to wait your time."

Caroline felt awkward, knew that she should not have acknowledge what she saw. As if to cover this, she told him, "I've decided what I want to do."

"Oh? And what's that?"

"Be a lawyer. If you're not a judge anymore, I can practice law with you."

He tilted his head. "And after that?"

She hesitated; perhaps it was foolish, but she wanted him to know. "I'd be a judge. Woman or not."

For a long time, he simply looked at her. "Caroline," he said in a soft voice, "that would please me greatly."

Caroline felt a catch in her throat. For a moment, she almost forgot his present.

Awkwardly, she reached into her backpack, pulled out the slim black box with the ribbon she had tied around it.

"What is this?" he asked.

Caroline placed it in his hands. "Happy birthday."

He gazed at the box with a funny half smile. "Shall I open it?"

"That's why I brought it."

Carefully, Channing untied the ribbon. Inside the box was a handsome Cahill fishing knife.

He held it in front of him, admiring the leather sheath, the bone handle, the slender steel blade.

"Caroline . . ." He paused; at first, Caroline thought he could not finish. And then he said, simply, "It's the finest knife I've ever seen."

She tried to smile. "It's so you can fillet a fish without me."

Channing Masters took her hand and covered it in both of his.

At Thanksgiving, when Caroline returned from school, the knife hung on their rack in the old stable. Her father had kept it spotless.

PART FOUR

THE WITNESS

ONE

CAROLINE STOOD at the foot of her mother's grave.

The morning was bright, beginning to warm; only in this corner of the cemetery, shaded by woods, did dew remain on the grass. The edges of Nicole's headstone were covered with moss.

Two days before her father's call, bringing her back to Masters Hill, Caroline had returned to where her mother had died. The trail at Windy Gates was overgrown now, fit only for walking; the stone wall was barely visible beneath a tangle of vines and shrubs. At the end of the path was a wooden barrier, and then sheer cliff. One hundred feet or more had been eroded by time; the cliffside seemed to crumble beneath her feet. Staring over the edge, Caroline had been surprised to see no car, no body, so strong had been her memory. She did not walk the beach.

Turning, Caroline had taken the path to Nerheim's mansion. It was dark and dank and half ruined. There were trucks outside; a rock singer from California had bought it, Caroline had learned, to restore it to its days of pleasure. But the tennis court was overgrown with weeds. . . .

Gazing at her mother's headstone, Caroline heard footsteps behind her.

She did not turn. "What is it?" she asked.

"We need to talk, Caroline."

"Then you could have picked a better time. And place."

Her father was quiet for a moment. "For the twenty years you were away," he answered, "I've come here. The memories, of whatever kind, belong to both of us."

Turning, Caroline walked a few steps, away from the grave, and faced him.

The shock of Brett's arrest was written on his face, and his black eyes had the intensity of fever. "I knew that you would stay, Caroline."

The instinct to escape, the deep imperative to leave this place and this man, returned to Caroline across two decades. She folded her arms. "Is that what you came to tell me?"

The light in his eyes dulled. "Betty says that you're going to Concord, to review the prosecution files. I want to go with you."

"No. Thank you."

He stiffened. "Brett is my granddaughter."

Caroline felt a rush of anger. "Is that what it always comes down to? What's yours?"

"Is this about me, Caroline? Or about you?" His voice mixed pride and desperation. "No one is better equipped to advise you. Are you forgetting—after Nuremberg, I had Jackson's job, then twenty-five years on the bench. I know the law, the lawyers, the judges, all the things that no one ever writes down. If I weren't your father, you'd be begging for my help." He stopped himself, framed his last words with the softness of a plea. "There was a time, Caroline, when you wanted nothing more."

Caroline watched his face. "So that's what this means to you," she said coldly. "Through Brett, you'll win at last. All that she needed to do was kill someone."

A patch of color stained his cheeks. "How can you say that?"

"That she killed him?" Caroline shrugged. "True, I can't be sure. But now that I'm her lawyer, whether or not she murdered this boy is of no particular interest to me. And your feelings about it interest me somewhat less."

Channing walked over to her. For a moment, it seemed that he would reach out to her. His hands were stiff and awkward at his sides.

"Please," he said in a rough voice. "I could die soon. I want to see her vindicated."

Caroline felt suddenly weary. "That won't be easy, Father. You may have to live for a while."

He seemed to slump. "How is she?" he asked softly.

"Under the circumstances? All right. She's frightened, of course, and her moods change. But she seems to have a certain resilience."

Channing looked away. "Do you think she can hold up?"

"Yes. For a time."

Channing turned to her. Quietly, he said, "I know that I've put a lot on you."

"You? I stayed for her."

He did not answer. "This judgeship," he said at length. "Where does it stand?"

The inquiry surprised her. For an instant, she felt her ground slipping from beneath her. "Really, I can't think about it now. . . ."

"I can help, Caroline." His voice gained strength. "Tim Braddock is on the Senate Judiciary Committee, in line for the chairmanship. I could call him. . . ."

Caroline shook her head. "That's the last thing I need. Or want. Can you understand that?"

Momentarily, her father looked more frail. "Yes," he answered with dignity. "I can."

"That part of our life is over, Father." Looking into his face, Caroline drew a breath and then finished: "But if you want to think Brett's problem through with me—without emotion—I'm willing to put all that aside. At least for now."

He raised his head. "Thank you," he said simply, and left her there.

From the photograph, James Case stared up at her.

The fatal slash through his throat was a dark line, and his head twisted at an angle impossible in life. His eyes looked dry, glassy. His face was flecked with blood; from his lips, slightly parted, came a red bubble.

Caroline placed the photograph next to the others on the conference table.

The crime lab technicians had been thorough. There were close to twenty color prints—the stations, Caroline thought, of James Case's agony and death. His nude body sprawled on the blanket. His torso dappled in blood. His flaccid penis sheathed in a condom. The gash in his chest. A shot of his throat so close that Caroline could see his vocal cords.

She could not help but think of Brett. "Your killer," she said, "left no room for chance."

Behind her, Channing studied the photographs with a faint distaste. "Some people," he murmured, "aren't meant to live long lives. How could she have ever slept with him?"

Silent, Caroline turned from him.

They were in a sterile conference room at the state police headquarters in Concord, both reviewing files. Her father let a moment pass. Then, as if nothing had happened, Channing said, "Jackson has no answer for the idea the killer could have come on water. Or along it."

"And who would that have been? The killer, that is."

"Case's supplier. Perhaps even a vagrant."

"I've checked the police reports. No homeless reported in the area—no robberies, either. As for James's angry drug dealer, his break-in story looks bogus." She paused, studying a picture of the dead boy's torso. "No, we're better off keeping bums and dealers a shadowy threat that the police did not take seriously. The more we investigate, the more we prove they shouldn't have."

Channing stood, restless. "You need a suspect, Caroline."

Without answering, Caroline picked up an envelope and removed a sealed glassine bag. Her father's eyes froze.

Wordless, she passed the bag to him.

He held it between his fingers, staring down at the bone-handled Cahill knife. Its hilt was still crusted in blood.

Softly, Caroline asked, "Do you know where Betty was?"

Channing looked up at her face. His face was cold. "At home," he said. "With me."

Their eyes met, and then Caroline gave a slight nod at the bag. "Messy, isn't it. But, as you say, Jackson will never trace the knife to Brett. Given that she's innocent."

Without answering, her father turned and placed the knife back in its envelope.

"So," Caroline said softly. "We can turn our attention to other things." She passed him the photograph of James's torso. "What, for example, is wrong with this picture?"

Distractedly, Channing took it from her and held it in front of his face. "Not much blood," he said at length.

Caroline nodded. "It's too light—he should be blood-soaked from arterial spurt. Particularly if the killer cut his throat from behind James's head, as you suggest, so that he or she didn't absorb the spurt."

Channing studied the picture. "And if Brett were on top of him," he asked, "as the police suggest?"

"Then she'd be blood-soaked, which their own pictures and report show she wasn't. And we can assume she was on top—they lifted her fingerprints from his throat and from the blood on his chest." Caroline paused. "Jackson will disagree, of course. I'm going to need experts."

"A serologist?"

"Possibly. Certainly a criminologist, a forensic pathologist, and a detective. Also—critically—someone who can testify to the effect of drugs and alcohol on memory."

Channing sat down. "How much will all this cost?"

"If we go to trial? A hundred thousand. Perhaps more."

Channing stared at the table. "Caroline," he said slowly. "Except for my pension, I've very little money."

It startled her; she remembered young Caroline Masters, who never wanted for anything. "How can that be?"

He folded his hands in front of him. "It's 'been' for a long time. I just never told you." His voice was tired. "There was a time when I thought you might keep Masters Hill alive. Then you were gone—" Catching himself, he finished with an air of fatalism. "What investments I had grew worse, and Betty and Larry have no money of their own. Leaving us with our home, and what's left of our good name."

The last, Caroline knew, was said without irony. In profile, her father's jawline was set, his face prideful. He did not care to look at her.

"Is that," Caroline asked, "why you didn't send Brett away to prep school? Or college?"

His eyes narrowed. "We did what was best. At whatever cost."

Caroline studied him. Softly, she said, "Aptly put."

Channing stared straight ahead, silent. "If it comes to it," Caroline said at length, "you can mortgage Masters Hill."

His eyes were still. "I already have. And the property values have fallen here. . . ."

It was as if she were tormenting him, Caroline realized.

"All right," she said. "I can raise some money from my place. But I'll need twenty thousand now. From either you or Betty."

"For what?"

"The probable cause hearing." She paused. "I've demanded one from Jackson, and it's in only ten days from now. Assuming I decide to go through with it, I'll require some expert help."

Channing turned to her. "As the defense did in the O. J. Simpson case?"

"Precisely, and for the same reasons. Like Simpson's lawyers, I'll never win—the court will find probable cause. But if the court lets me get away with it, I can examine Jackson's witnesses before they're prepared—like the pathologist and the crime lab people—and lock them into a story."

Channing considered her. "Or," he said pointedly, "encourage Brett to consider a plea bargain when she sees the evidence against her."

Caroline felt herself stiffen. "Of course, I may not succeed in bludgeoning Brett into submission in time to save my judgeship—she's somewhat willful." Her voice was sardonic. "But there are other benefits. Such as winning the battle of pretrial publicity or—better yet—so drowning the public in the evidence against Brett that they no longer find it shocking. As you know, it's somewhat easier to sell reasonable doubt to a jury that's already bored with the worst." She shrugged. "After all, if I have to practice law again, an unexpected victory could keep me in demand. It might even help me cover the expenses of Brett's defense."

Channing flushed. "I won't let you pressure her into a plea—"

"You won't 'permit'? Then you might consider that a life sentence for Brett would run appreciably longer than a life sentence for you." Caroline's words grew softer. "Don't ever tell me, Father, what *you* will or will not permit. Because *I* will do or say whatever I believe to be in Brett's best interests. Including—though I've not quite decided—putting Jackson through this probable cause hearing."

Channing seemed to study her; for a strange moment, Caroline thought she saw the faintest smile cross his face. "I can raise twenty thousand," he said quietly. "In three or four days."

Caroline did not answer. She waited briefly, to clear her head, and then put on her reading glasses.

She had saved the statement of Megan Race for last.

She read it once, for meaning, trying to detach her feelings from the words on the page. The second time, she took careful notes.

When she had finished, Caroline slid it down the table. "Read this."

As if to imitate Caroline, Channing put on horn-rimmed reading glasses. It surprised her; she could not remember that he had ever needed them. He read in silence.

When he was through, Channing put the papers down. His face was pale. "She's lying."

"Why?"

"She has to be." He turned to her. "Without this girl, Jackson lacks a sufficient case. At least if your experts do their job."

"Just so."

Channing looked uneasy. Quietly, he asked, "*She's* why you want a preliminary, isn't she?"

Caroline smiled a little. "Suppose Megan's the obsessive one. Suppose *she* followed them, spied on them." Watching his face, she added with a touch of irony, "Suppose, Father, that she even killed him."

Channing stared at the pages in front of him. "What if she was with friends that night—assuming that you're remotely serious." His voice fell. "Or, more realistically, that her reputation is good."

Caroline's smile grew cold. "Then I'll have to destroy her, won't I? For all our sakes."

TWO

"I'VE GOT everything I need," Jackson told her, "for murder one."

Caroline had found him at his fishing camp. He stood on the pier in a gray morning light, sunlight refracted through a thin layer of clouds. The lake was still.

She put both hands in the pockets of her blue jeans. "Except proof that the knife was hers."

Jackson gave her a look of irony. "They don't register knives, Caroline. I don't have to know where it came from."

Caroline felt her nerves tighten. "You overcharged this one," she persisted. "If you really think this looks like premeditation, then I've a wonderful insanity defense—Brett coolly planning to run naked through the woods, covered in blood, then make her escape still disguised as a hysterical naked woman. All after neatly disposing of the body by leaving it in plain view on her property."

Jackson gave her a look somewhere between compassion and curiosity. Then he sat on the pier, legs over the edge, and motioned for her to join him.

Silent, Caroline sat next to him.

"You're feeling me out," he said softly. "Specifically, you're hoping for manslaughter. With Brett getting out before she turns thirty."

He was good, Caroline thought. Or perhaps, now, she was less good.

"It never hurts," she answered, "to define the real world."

Gazing at the lake, Jackson slowly shook his head. "In your world—San Francisco—real is maybe two hundred murders a year: the prosecution has to plea-bargain, or the system will just break down. But this is New Hampshire, where we have less than forty murders statewide, and the pressure on us is to try them." He looked at her directly. "I won't play games with you, Caroline.

Under our guidelines, manslaughter is out. The best I can do is second-degree murder with a twenty-year minimum."

Caroline sat back, speechless for a moment. "That's absolutely medieval," she said. "She'd be inside until she was forty-two."

Jackson looked defensive. "It's absolutely New Hampshire," he shot back. "And James Case never reached twenty-four. You're expecting me to sell him out."

"Is that what I'm doing?" Abruptly, Caroline turned on him. "Or are you overcompensating?"

"By asking twenty years for a life?" A sudden anger, controlled yet intense, showed in his eyes. He forced himself to finish slowly, softly. "Just what, Caroline, am I compensating for?"

Caroline went silent, regretting her words, unsure of what to say next. She watched his anger die, replaced by the sense that he had withdrawn from her.

"All right." He folded his hands in front of him, staring straight ahead. "If you're referring to my prior relationship to Channing, the other lawyers in my section are no better off—he helped the two senior lawyers get the job and knows the two remaining through Republican politics." His voice became almost casual, as if conveying a minor point of information. "As I said, I haven't spent any real private time with Channing since shortly after you left. It was a little painful for us both.

"Which brings me to you."

He turned to her with a look so cool she found it hurtful. "If I have a problem, it's trying a case with you on the other side. And it's you who shouldn't be here, presuming on whatever there was—or is—between us."

His last words, flat and passionless, hit Caroline like a slap. She forced herself to sound calm. "As it happens, Jackson, that was a very nice day for me. But it has nothing to do with why I came here. Which involves nothing more than seeking fairness for a client."

He crossed his arms. "I offered you a lie test."

"No. For all the reasons I gave before. And because she may well have been too confused by drugs to have any accurate memory."

He raised his eyebrows. "How about one simple question, then. Like 'Did you kill James Case?' What's she going to say—'I don't remember'?" He shrugged at his own question, dismissing its absurdity. "Like it or not, we both know that Brett killed him and that the only question is degree. And you're at once too close to this and too far away: a lawyer from California, who—with all your gifts— knows next to nothing about how things work here."

It stopped her for a moment; the comment came far too close to Caroline's unstated fears. "I can learn, Jackson. With all my gifts . . ."

"Why are you doing this?" he demanded. "I mean, you haven't seen her for twenty years and plainly didn't give a damn—"

"That's not for you to say."

"No?" He shook his head in wonder. "What are you trying to prove here, and to whom? I thought you'd left this place behind—"

"Christ." Caroline leaned back on her palms, staring at him, and finished in a low voice. "Don't try to psychoanalyze me. You don't know enough."

His lips compressed. "Forgive me, Caroline, but there are a lot of very good defense lawyers in this state who don't carry whatever baggage you've returned with and who don't have a judgeship at stake." He paused, tone softer now. "This is already a tragedy for Brett and for her family. I don't want it to be a tragedy for you. Or—and this is my weakness—to be any part of that."

Caroline felt the emotion drain from her. "I promised her," she said simply.

He studied her for a moment. "No manslaughter, Caroline. If you want that, you'll have to try the case."

Slowly, she nodded. "Then count on a hearing, all right?"

He cocked his head. "Is that all?"

"That's all." Caroline got up. "Thank you for your time."

They stood there, silent, looking at each other. Then Caroline smiled a little and turned away. He did not walk with her to the car.

"Megan Race," the detective repeated, and wrote the name at the top of a lined yellow pad.

They sat in the office of Caroline's new local counsel. Carlton Grey, a bespectacled veteran of the local courts, sat at his walnut desk; Caroline and the detective from Concord, Joe Lemieux—dark, ascetic looking, and thirtyish—in guest chairs facing Grey. Lemieux had turned to her.

"What is it you need?" he asked.

"Everything," she answered crisply. "In less than ten days. Where she's from, what jobs she has, what courses she's taken. Her family. Whether she's ever seen a therapist or is seeing one now. What friends she has. And, critically, former boyfriends. That one's a priority."

Lemieux looked curious. "What are we after, exactly?"

"Anything that I can use to destroy her credibility." Caroline paused for emphasis. "She'll have something, Joe. Everyone does."

He nodded, silent.

"Then," Caroline went on, "there's her relationship to the dead boy, James Case."

Carlton Grey leaned forward. "As I understand it, Caroline, you want to know when it ended."

"According to her statement, Megan and James were lovers unto death—so much so that he asked her to go with him to California. But according to Brett, James broke it off in April—two and a half months ago. Did anyone, I wonder, see them together since?"

Lemieux noted this on his pad. He had long fingers, Caroline noted, an air of delicacy. He would not put people on edge. "And the former boyfriends . . . ?" he asked.

"First, were there any. If so, then we'll want to consider approaching them." She looked from Lemieux to Grey and back again. "What would help is for someone to say that she's malicious, spiteful, or—best of all—unbalanced."

Grey nodded. "You need a reason for her to lie."

"Precisely. It would very much help to have it for the probable cause hearing. Whether I use it or not."

"She won't be there," Grey put in. "Jackson would never call her."

Caroline smiled. "But I can subpoena her, can't I? Assuming that the judge lets me."

Grey raised an eyebrow. "You've been reading our statutes."

"Oh, yes, I do that." She still smiled faintly. "It's one of my gifts."

"My niece has asked me to do this," Caroline said slowly. "To my surprise, I find that I can't turn her down."

It was night; she had called Walter Farris at home. At first, she heard only static, a faulty connection. Then Farris said, "That poses a problem."

Caroline forced herself to sound calm. "But should it? There's no realistic question of my using influence here. Really, Walter, in the age of family values, I'd hope that people—including senators— might sympathize a little. What good is twenty years defending strangers if you can't help your own niece?"

The answer, carefully prepared, silenced Farris for a time. When he spoke again, his tone was neutral. "You're quite close, I take it."

Caroline considered her answer. "We've become so," she said, and returned to her carefully wrought appeal. "If it will help things, I'm prepared to write the chairman of the Judiciary Committee, explaining my difficulty, confirming my continuing interest, and expressing the hope that confirmation hearings can be held promptly after completion of the trial."

In the silence, Caroline felt herself tense. At length, Farris asked, "How long might that be?"

Caroline hesitated. "Maybe six months."

"I think that's too long." His voice was brisk. "Once we get near the election, the Republicans can hold things up, see if they can elect a President. You're too obvious a target."

Tense, Caroline forced herself to think swiftly. "Because I'm a woman?" she asked. "Or, as you put it, a feminist? Then that *is* a problem." She made her voice sound tentative, musing. "But I suppose there may be another way to view this—as a chance for the President to remind them that he'll stand by his appointments. Unless there's a better reason than Jesse Helms's displeasure, as you once put it."

Her tone was so mild that Farris could not confront her. "What would you like me to do?" he asked with muted annoyance.

Caroline held her breath. "Just to tell the President," she said, "that I'll do whatever he wishes. After all, I'm the nominee only at his pleasure."

Farris fell quiet again. Caroline could imagine him—cornered, unable to say so, wondering how much of this she had calculated. "All right," he said at last. "I'll run this by him."

Alone in her room, Caroline closed her eyes. "Thank you," she said.

THREE

A WOMAN DEPUTY brought Brett to a stark interview room with
yellow walls and a pressboard table that, to Caroline, seemed passed
on from some county office. Brett sat across from her; the deputy
stepped outside the room, occasionally peering through a wired-
glass rectangle in the metal door. A certain light replaced the dull-
ness in Brett's green eyes.

"Thanks for coming," she said to Caroline. "I've gotten to count
on it."

Caroline smiled. "Oh, it's pure self-indulgence—a place like this
puts my company in a new and attractive light. Quite heady for a
neglectful aunt."

Brett's own smile was slow to come and, when it did, perfunctory;
Caroline could see her imagining endless days like this. "Have you
worked up some sort of routine?" she asked.

"A little." Brett gave a fractional shrug. "It reminds me of something my philosophy prof said once—that life is a way of killing time."

She looked somewhat removed, Caroline thought, almost detached. "What kinds of things do you do?" Caroline asked.

"Yoga, a little reading . . . The people who watch us are nice
enough, and in the cell there's still only me." Brett shifted in her
chair. "A couple of friends came by—high school friends, 'cause the
college people are mostly gone. But they don't know what to say to
me, or me to them." She shrugged again, helpless. "I mean, I can't
tell them about nightmares, or missing James, or this fantasy I have
where we're in California now. It would be too weird for them, you
know." Brett gazed at the table. "It's not their fault, I suppose. Not
many people have this experience. They can't exactly say things like,
'I know how you feel.' "

Brett paused again. "Do you know what's really weird," she went on. "This is the first time I can remember being alone—without Grandfather or my parents, or a roommate, or maybe James. That was another reason I wasn't sure about going with James. It was time for me to be on my own." Her voice filled with wonder. "Now I'm finally alone. . . ."

It was as if, Caroline thought, Brett were musing to herself, in Caroline's presence. She felt a strange intimacy between them.

"There was a time in my life," Caroline said at length, "around your age, when I decided to spend time alone. It lasted for a while—a period of months, actually—and I even wrote a little. And when it was over, I found that I had come to some conclusions about the future I would have, for worse or better. And about the price I'd pay for that."

Brett studied her, curious. And then she simply said, "You're saying that I should do that—take this time to think. And maybe write."

Caroline shrugged. "What else is it good for?"

The fingers of Brett's left hand idly stroked a tendril of brown hair. "All that *I* can think about," she said at last, "is how I got here."

Beneath this statement, uttered with the simplicity of truth, Caroline felt a challenge. *I think about it,* the girl was saying, *because I'm innocent.*

Caroline's own gaze was steady. "Think about whatever comes," she answered softly. "But here you can talk—or write—about anything *but* that. Or James."

Brett's look grew cool. "Because they'll read it."

"Or hear it. And, perhaps, misinterpret it."

Brett sat back, appraising her before she spoke. "Why did you stay here, Caroline? When you don't believe I'm innocent."

Taken by surprise, Caroline flashed on the bloody knife. She kept her own voice calm. "Lawyers don't believe anything. Because belief is pointless. I, and the law, presume your innocence. My job is simply to preserve that presumption."

"That seems so cold."

It was strange, Caroline thought, that a simple word from this girl could hurt her. "Sometimes 'coldness' is merely a point of view. And *you* should presume that some lackey may try to curry favor by reporting something you said. Real or imagined."

Brett folded her arms. "We're in different places, aren't we? And not just now. When you were my age and needed to think, you chose the time and place and subject." Her voice turned bitter. "I'm not free to do any of those things. Unless you get me out of here, I may never be."

Caroline looked down, accepting the rebuke. "What I said was foolish. We're not the same, and this isn't the same. I was only trying to tell you to be careful."

"Fine. And I'll try not to tell anyone that I cut James's throat."

When Caroline looked up, there were tears in Brett's eyes. They regarded each other, silent.

Caroline drew a breath. "There's something else we need to talk about."

Brett seemed to clasp herself tighter. In the pallid fluorescent light, her eyes had a vivid sheen. "Whatever."

Caroline rested her cheek on the fingers of one hand. "I spoke with Jackson," she said slowly. "He won't take manslaughter."

Brett's face hardened. "*I* won't take manslaughter. I already told you that." She leaned forward, looking into Caroline's eyes. "That might sound crazy to someone who only 'presumes' my innocence. But I won't plead guilty to something I didn't do."

After a moment, Caroline shrugged. "Well," she said, "that makes it simple, doesn't it."

Brett stood, pacing. Then, abruptly, she turned on Caroline. "This probable cause hearing you told me about—when is it?"

"Eight days. Assuming we go through with it."

Brett stared down at her. "I want that hearing. And I want to testify."

Caroline pushed her chair back from the table. "No," she said tersely. "Absolutely not."

"Well, I'm going to." Brett's voice rose. "I sit here, day after day, with no one to say I'm innocent. So I'm going to say it."

Caroline kept her own voice quiet, sympathetic. "I understand your feelings—at least as much as I'm able. But my whole purpose in forcing this hearing is to catch Jackson's witnesses unprepared, Megan Race—who refuses to even speak with me—being the most critical of all. I won't let him catch *you* like that."

The mention of Megan seemed to silence Brett, as Caroline had intended. She tried to seize the moment. "Trials are like theater,

Brett. You have to know your lines or, at least, know the play well enough to improvise. I don't have a firm grasp of their evidence yet. And there's not nearly enough time to get you where you need to be."

"Theater?" Brett gave her a look of disbelief and anger. "The truth is the truth, and I'm testifying." Her eyes were bright now. "Whose trial is this? Yours or mine?"

Caroline stood, facing Brett across the table. "This is not negotiable. I refuse to help you commit suicide. Jackson will cut you to shreds before you even figure out that he isn't Jimmy Stewart—"

"Did you hear me, Caroline?"

"Yes." Caroline paused, steeling herself. "Now you hear me. If you insist on this, I quit."

Brett stared at her, lips parted. She was suddenly pale. "Then quit. I'm sick of not controlling my own life."

"This is a poor time to decide *that*," Caroline snapped. "You'll know you've grown up when your first decision isn't quite so stupid." She caught herself. "Don't make the wrong choice for the sake of making one. Please."

Brett's gaze seemed to waver, then her mouth set in a stubborn line. "You can leave now. Grandfather will find me someone else."

With what money? Caroline wanted to say. But the girl she saw stopped her for a moment—vulnerable, with pride and fear fighting for control of her face. "I'll leave," she said at last. "Though not before we do this."

"Do what?"

"Sit down," Caroline said curtly. "I'll be Jackson, and you be you. Just like in that glorious scene in court you so vividly imagine without my interference, a mere eight days from now. And don't forget to write."

Pale, resolute, Brett sat stiffly.

Caroline stood, watching her. "The rules are simple. I ask the questions, you answer within ten seconds. So that your audience can see how forthright you are."

Brett stared at her, defiant. "Not quite so hostile," Caroline said in an advisory tone. "Remember that I'm Jackson and that the truth is the truth."

Brett flushed. "Will you start?"

"All right." Pausing, Caroline could feel her own pulse. "You've described the murder, your own shock and horror, and everyone watching is incredibly sympathetic. Now you're in the police car— all you have to do is explain what you did next."

Caroline saw a first glimmer of uncertainty, perhaps self-doubt.

"When the policeman stopped," Caroline began, "you were naked, correct?"

Mute, Brett nodded.

"You have to speak up for the record. I'd recommend a clear, steady voice."

"Yes." Brett's tone was flinty. "I was naked."

"And covered in blood."

Brett hesitated. "There was blood on me, yes—"

"Eye contact, please—you'll make a bad impression." At once, Caroline slipped back into her role. "Where did you think James was?"

Brett's eyes narrowed, as if straining for memory. "I was stoned."

"But you weren't 'stoned,' were you, when you picked him up?"

Brett squared her shoulders. "No."

"Couldn't you remember *that*?"

"I think so. Yes."

Caroline placed her hands on her hips. "Then did you also 'think' that James had simply vanished?"

"I didn't know." Brett closed her eyes. "I had flashes, like a nightmare."

"There was a bloody wallet in the car, wasn't there?"

Brett's eyes shut. "Yes."

"Did you think *that* was a nightmare?"

Slowly, Brett shook her head. "All I had was fragments. I didn't want to believe them."

"Oh, it's not quite all you had. There was also a bloody knife on the passenger seat, was there not?"

Brett's face was haunted now. "Yes."

"And did you think that had arrived from a dream?"

"No." Brett looked up in silent appeal, as if seeing Caroline and not her tormentor. "You have to understand. Nothing seemed more real to me than any other thing. I couldn't remember what happened."

Silent, Caroline sat across from her. She said, softly, "You mean you can't remember whether or not you killed him?"

"No." Brett's body went rigid. "I couldn't have."

Caroline paused; the pit of her stomach felt hollow now. Quite calmly, she said, " 'Couldn't have'? I thought you couldn't remember."

"I did." Brett's eyes fell. "But later on."

"Eight hours later?"

"I don't know. Whenever it was that my head began to clear."

"Before that, where did you imagine all the blood on you had come from?"

Wearily, Brett shook her head. "I didn't know."

"So that, two hours later, you were only able to recall that James 'might' be at the lake."

"Yes." Brett's voice was husky. "I thought he might be."

Caroline leaned forward. "And why did you think that?"

"Because I remembered taking him there."

"But you *always* remembered, didn't you—just like you remembered picking him up. Because you weren't stoned then."

"I don't know." Brett's voice rose. "Maybe it was the knife in the car."

Slowly, Caroline shook her head. "No, Brett. Because you knew all of this—James, the blood, the knife, the wallet—two hours before, when you were still in your car." Her voice became quiet. "When you told the patrolman absolutely nothing."

Brett touched her eyes. "I didn't remember."

Caroline placed a finger to her lips, contemplating the girl. "Tell me," she said in a tone of mild curiosity, "does your memory always work like that? Where it only comes back to you after hours, or even days."

Brett stared at the table. "It was the drugs. What I wasn't stoned for, I can remember."

Caroline composed herself. "Such as the night you found James in bed?" A lethal pause. "With a naked girl named Megan Race?"

Brett's head fell slightly. "Megan . . ." she began, and stopped.

Caroline leaned forward. With terrible quiet, she asked, "Were you stoned then, Brett?"

"No."

"But when the police asked you about girlfriends, you somehow didn't mention that."

"No." Caroline saw a throbbing in Brett's temple. "I didn't want to think of it. Or remember it."

"I understand." Caroline's voice was gentle now. "Just like you don't want to remember killing James."

A tremor ran through Brett's body. When, at last, Brett raised her head, tears ran down her face. Her silent gaze at Caroline was her last, tenuous show of defiance.

Caroline wanted to comfort her. But all that she said, voice matter-of-fact, was, "Your lines need work."

Brett swallowed, still silent. Caroline waited until she was certain the girl would not be sick, and then went on. "Of course, that was off the top of my head. Jackson will be much better." Her voice was level now. "Unless, of course, I can keep your statements out of evidence—something I mean to set up through the probable cause hearing. In which case, Jackson will never get to ask any of those questions."

Brett could not seem to move or speak; it was as if, Caroline thought, she was staring into the abyss of her own doubt.

Caroline reached for the girl's hand. "Listen to me, Brett." Her voice was soft again, her own. "The only thing I can promise is that you'll get the best that I can give you. And that I won't let anything or anyone—even you—ever get in my way." She paused for a final moment. "Please, let me do this."

Brett looked down at their hands. After a time, she asked, "Can I go now?"

"Of course."

Through the glass window, Caroline watched her leave. Brett's movements were weary, drugged. She did not look back.

Outside, Caroline sat in her car, alone. It was a while before she felt like going anywhere.

Arriving at the inn, she went to her room and called Joe Lemieux. When he answered, she asked her question without preface. "The girl," she demanded. "Do you have her schedule yet?"

FOUR

FROM THE EDGE of the quadrangle, Caroline watched the young blond woman leave her job at the student union and start across the campus with purposeful strides.

Unaware, she walked toward Caroline. There were few people there—a trickle of summer students and their teachers, a group of shirtless boys near Caroline, playing Frisbee in the noonday sun— and the lone figure of the woman somehow seemed apart from them. As she approached, too deep in thought to notice her, Caroline saw that she was pretty—a strong jaw, a snub nose, even features—and that the blond came from a bottle. Her eyes were on the ground in front of her.

Fighting back her tension, Caroline stepped forward. "Megan?"

The woman stopped, eyes flying open, a wary blue-gray. Her gaze narrowed as if she was trying to place the tall woman in front of her on some sliding scale of risk. Comprehension crossed her face; the slight smile that followed, less welcoming than a warning, did not change the guarded look. "You're Brett's lawyer. The woman who called me."

"Yes." Caroline made her tone mild, unthreatening. "Actually, I'm her aunt."

All expression seemed to leave Megan's face. "Who told you to come here? Her father?"

Caroline shook her head. "I asked around, and came on my own—"

"This is like harassment. I already told you, Mr. Watts said not to talk with anyone." Megan placed both hands on her hips. "Look, if you think this has been easy for me . . ."

Caroline held up both hands in front of her, a plea for understanding. "No, I'm sure it's been quite awful for you. Losing someone is bad enough without having to relive it all in court."

Megan stared at Caroline, then folded her arms and looked at the ground again. She pressed her lips together; her eyes closed, and then she slowly shook her head. "It's like she ripped my heart out but my body still keeps moving. . . ."

Megan's voice trailed off. She frowned at the stone path in front of her. "Really," she said in a dubious tone. "I'm not supposed to talk to you."

"But I *need* to talk to you." Caroline paused. "Megan, part of what I need help with is deciding whether Brett should even go to trial. It would be less than honest not to admit that you're the biggest part of that decision."

Megan seemed to stand a little taller; her natural posture, Caroline realized, was straight-backed, athletic. "And you think I can help you."

Beneath the doubt, Caroline sensed a lessening of resistance. "If there's no trial," she said quietly, "wouldn't that be best for everyone?"

Megan's eyes narrowed. "Let me think about it. I'll call Mr. Watts."

"Oh," Caroline said, "you already know what he'll say. If not, I know Jackson, and he loves to try cases—for prosecutors, it's really not the same." She softened her tone again. "While you think about it, there's no harm in not talking with me over coffee, is there? I've been waiting here for a long time, and I wouldn't mind just sitting."

Megan thought a minute and then shrugged. "I guess not."

Together, they started back to the student union. The campus of Chase College was a classic piece of New England—sylvan and quiet, with old brick buildings at its heart. They crossed the white wooden bridge that spanned the brook, lazy with its summer ebb. "Have you liked it here?" Caroline asked. "At least until now?"

"Before James? I don't know. People here are pretty unaware." She gave a sardonic smile. "You know—let's go skiing and drink a lot of beer. Most of them don't know Günter Grass from Kurt Vonnegut." Her smile vanished abruptly, and her voice became almost fierce. "James did."

She had a certain manner, Caroline thought, that suggested they were peers. Instinctively, she decided to pursue it. "It's so hard," Caroline observed, "to really find someone. So many times I feel like what passes for conversation is just making noise, and I end up listening to myself like I were someone else, chattering at a bad cocktail party. It's tough to live on autopilot."

Megan peered at her sideways, as if deciding whether to accord trust. "It's worse at my age," she said finally. "I believe in serious friendships, really intense, with no thoughts held back. But how can you be that way with people who are scared to think?"

"Do you think it gets better," Caroline asked, "just because they're older?"

"I hope so. I mean, I can't stand the idea of dating if all it means is a lot of traffic." Megan stopped, speaking in a lower voice. "At least older men have had a chance to grow up, face a few things about themselves. But James changed all that."

For a time, Caroline chose silence. They got to the door of the student union, a cement Bauhaus structure badly out of keeping with its surroundings. With respectful curiosity, Caroline asked quietly, "Did you ever try that—older guys?"

Megan glanced at her sharply, then nodded. "Except for the sex part, it was better. That was where James had it all."

It was said with a stubborn pride, as if to remind Caroline that James belonged to her and she did not care who heard her; from a nearby table, a boy in glasses looked up from his newspaper. Megan led Caroline to a table at the center of the room.

It was sterile and cavernous, with glass on all sides. Caroline looked around them. "Who was the architect?" she asked in tones of wonder.

Megan waved dismissively. "Awful, isn't it? Like Le Corbusier done by a computer."

They sat, facing each other. Megan flicked back her straight blond bangs, crossed her legs, and sat upright in her chair, looking fixedly at Caroline. "I think architecture is like politics. The nineties aren't about anything, except maybe pushing women back down where they 'belong.' And neither is this building." She gazed about her with a vaguely scornful look. "To me it says two things—'engineer' and 'penis.' There's nothing spiritual about it."

Caroline nodded her understanding, careful not to study Megan too closely; beneath her new animation, Caroline sensed, a warier, second Megan watched her. "Of course," Caroline said, "it's not a spiritual age. The things we used to believe in, we don't anymore, and nothing has taken their place. Not even kindness." She softened her voice. "This meeting is very hard for me, Megan. Because I'm deeply sorry about what happened to James, and to you."

Megan looked down; furrows appeared in her high forehead, and her mouth seemed to quiver. "We were a couple," she murmured, "and then we weren't. Because of her."

Caroline folded her hands. "I don't really know Brett," she admitted. "I'm not close to any of them, actually, and now I have to make sense of this. . . ."

"It makes no sense." Megan's voice was angry now. "Unless you understand what Brett Allen is really like."

Caroline shook her head. "I'm not sure that I do yet, and there isn't much time."

Megan looked up. "Jackson said something about a hearing."

The use of "Jackson," Caroline thought, was the assertion of some new intimacy—adult talking to adult. "In seven days," Caroline said. "But I'm still deciding whether I want one." She paused, as if reluctant, then added, "Brett keeps saying she's innocent—"

"Wouldn't you"—Megan's voice was etched with scorn—"if you'd cut someone's throat?"

"But that's what I have a hard time believing. Even with all the evidence."

"You don't *have* all the evidence." Megan leaned forward, looking intently at Caroline. "She used to threaten us, follow us. She's sick—sick and obsessive."

Caroline inhaled audibly. "It may well be, Megan. But you're the only one who knows that."

"Only because James is dead." Megan grasped Caroline's sleeve. "Don't you sense it by now—there's something feral about her. I see those green eyes in my dreams." Sudden tears appeared. "That's what's so awful—already, I can see her face more clearly than his. Like I'll live with her for the rest of my life."

Caroline lowered her eyes. "This is none of my business," she said softly, "but you have to keep him alive somehow. Have some part of it that stays a part of you."

Megan shook her head. "What can you do when you were with someone so much, looking toward a future, and suddenly all you've got are mental images—the same ones, running over and over, with all the surprises stolen from them?" Her voice caught. "I remember him acting scenes for me, from his play. . . ."

Caroline touched her arm. "I'm sorry . . ."

"We made love all the time, he wanted me all the time. Would ask me to undress for him, to turn around just to see how beautiful I was." She looked at Caroline with sudden vividness. "It wasn't exploitative—just intense, like everything we did. Every moment was so *conscious*."

Caroline looked puzzled. "But what about Brett? Where did she figure in?"

Megan seemed to bristle. "Oh, she was still there—do you know she threatened to kill herself if he ever left her?" Her voice filled with anger. "I wish she had. Instead, she killed James. I guess that was the only part she meant."

"But weren't you afraid?"

"Anyone would be. To have your lover inside you, and then he's suddenly standing at the end of the bed, naked, wrestling with a woman who's trying to scratch your face." Megan shook her head. "After that, we both were careful—it was almost like we went into hiding. Maybe, in a strange way, James was keeping his options open by treating me more like a mistress than a commitment." A faint note of scorn entered her voice—for whom, Caroline was not sure—and then vanished. "But we had what we had. In the end, James decided to be with me."

Megan was bright-eyed now; Caroline felt a sudden warning on her nerve ends. In a tone of bemusement, she asked, "Then why was he with Brett the night he died?"

Megan gave a haunting smile of bitterness and triumph. "Because we'd decided to leave her and this place behind, to go to California. That was the night he was going to tell her." Suddenly, her voice grew quiet. "And when I found out that she'd killed him, I knew that he had."

For a long time, Caroline simply stared at her. She could think of nothing to ask.

It seemed to bring Megan back from anger. "I don't know how you make these decisions," she said evenly. "But whatever you do, don't put these people through a trial. Because their daughter is a murderer." She paused, studying Caroline until compassion seemed to enter her face; lightly, her fingers touched Caroline's wrist, and her voice became almost confiding. "I know that she's your niece, Caroline, and how hard this must be for you to face. But you'll come to see what James did—that beneath that China-doll look is a selfish and demented woman." She paused, finishing quietly, "And to see the one thing James never saw: that, if he left, she'd kill him."

FIVE

BRETT SAT in front of her. The metal door whispered shut, and they were alone.

Brett's eyes were swollen from sleeplessness. She gave Caroline a certain bleak scrutiny; it was as if their conflict yesterday had stripped her of illusion. In a flat voice, she said, "What is it now?"

Caroline placed her arms on the table, struggling to master her emotions.

"I caught up with Megan Race. It's far worse than her statement suggests. According to Megan, she and James were lovers to the end. They'd decided to leave for California. And the night James was to tell you was the night he died."

Brett seemed to have lost the capacity for surprise; the only sign that she had even heard was the stillness of her eyes. Softly, she said, "That never happened. Any of it."

Caroline studied her. "At best," she responded, "you can't know whether he was seeing her or not. And Megan's story is that you stalked them."

A first flash of anger, although Brett's voice was calm. "I didn't need to 'stalk' him. After I found them together, he was with me almost every night."

Brett's self-control, Caroline found, drew her more than protestations. "All night?" she asked.

Brett stared at her now. "I don't go for hit-and-run. If someone wants to make love with me, I want him to stay with me."

Somehow Caroline found this affecting—the remembrance of a code, the reassertion of Brett's pride, in the face of terrible news. "Perhaps Megan's rules were different."

Brett shook her head. "James may have been an actor, but he wasn't a good liar. I could always tell."

It was said with a tinge of fatalism; there was something clear-eyed about Brett, Caroline realized, when she was faced with things she could not change. It was strange that in this moment of extremity—her final acceptance of Brett's guilt—the girl seemed so real to her.

"Then where," Caroline asked, "does the part about California come from?"

For the first time, Brett looked away. "I don't know," she said at last. "Somehow she must have invented it."

"But how? And perhaps more to the point, why?"

Brett looked up again. "I don't know 'how.' But the why is obvious."

"Jealousy?"

Brett stared at her. "*I* was jealous," she said slowly. "But Megan Race is mentally ill."

Caroline sat back. "Because she 'invented' all this . . ."

"Because she invented *me*." Suddenly, Brett looked haunted, as if grasping what she faced. "I cared for James. At times I loved him passionately. But I wasn't obsessed with him—however hard it might have been, I was willing to let him go." Her eyes held a new intensity. "Caroline, when this woman tells you about me, she's talking about herself."

Caroline watched her. "But you don't really know her, do you?"

Brett's body grew taut. "I know her the same way she knows me. Through James."

Caroline leaned forward. "How do you know," she asked softly, "that James *didn't* tell you he was taking her to California? And, please, *think* before you answer."

"I already have, damn it." Brett stood abruptly. "Listen to me. Last night, I couldn't sleep. I just lay there, going over it all, horrified because you'd torn me apart until I felt as if I *had* killed him. But everything you asked me was about how I acted *after* I was stoned, *after* I found him. Because you were right—the things that happened *before* we smoked the dope, I remember perfectly." Her words were a torrent now. "He asked me to go to California, we fought about him screwing Megan and this dope-dealer thing, and then I said I didn't know what I'd do. He was ashamed about Megan, all right? There's no way we both got stoned and then he told me he was taking her to California instead of me. We were making love, not fighting—doesn't that mean anything to you?" She paused, as if interrupted by a sudden thought, and then softened her tone as she gazed down at Caroline. "I know I lied to you about the fight. But I knew I was lying. Just like I know that I'm telling the truth to you now. No matter what you think."

Caroline sat there, silent, staring up at her. There were too many things that she could not say. That she knew about the knife. That, at best, Brett might never know what she had done at the moment of James's death. That Megan Race fit neatly with the evidence. And that the first hard lesson learned by Caroline the lawyer, when Brett was a faceless child in a faraway state, was that given enough time, a guilty person may come to believe the story of her innocence.

As if challenged by Caroline's silence, Brett demanded, "What did *you* think of Megan?"

The question was asked in anger. But beneath it, Caroline felt a plea: Believe in me, not her. And then something came to Caroline, wings beating against the windowpane of her subconscious. It was simple enough: the memory of having loved.

"What I think," she answered finally, "is that Megan never loved him. The James that she describes is a mirror for herself."

It took several hours for Joe Lemieux to return her message, and when he called, from a pay phone, she had fallen asleep from exhaustion.

"Sorry," he said, "but I've been busy on this. Talking to whatever apartment neighbor is willing to talk with me."

Caroline fought for alertness. "And?"

"And most of them aren't college students, so I've had some luck."

"So did I, in a sense. I met Megan today."

"What did you make of her?"

"Quite smart, it's clear. But mercurial, perhaps somewhat narcissistic—she's plainly someone who likes, even needs, attention. Of course, that could describe a lot of people." Caroline paused. "The big questions, in order of importance, are: Did anyone see Megan with James after early April? And can you find any other boyfriends before or after?"

"It's a little thin, on both fronts." Lemieux seemed to organize his thoughts. "She did see Case, all right, and early April doesn't mean anything to her neighbors—they weren't keeping track of her affairs by date. But James's picture has been in all the papers, and the two folks who can remember seeing him at Megan's place think that it was quite a few weeks ago. Which is the same thing that kid Daniel Suarez said. Anyhow, they all agree they hadn't seen them together for over a month. Which gives us at least a couple of weeks before the murder."

"*Her* story is that they were hiding out. Making beautiful love, of course."

"Must have been, is all I can say. 'Cause no one saw them come up for air."

Caroline considered that for a moment. "Keep digging. I need anything that suggests the presence—or absence—of a relationship at any time close to the murder."

"Okay. Now, about the boyfriends, there's even less."

"Less, or nothing?"

"One thing. Months ago, Megan cornered one of her neighbors in the laundry room—a middle-aged lady who wasn't that up for it— and started carrying on about her relationship with an older guy. Something about how much better it was." A note of humor entered Lemieux's voice. "I took awhile to get this lady to admit that 'it' was sex, and that Megan's not very bashful on the subject. Even without meeting her, Megan sounds a little quirky, although even this lady described her as 'charming' and 'vivacious'—just a little too emancipated for her taste."

"The word," Caroline said dryly, "is 'liberated.' Which took place somewhat later than the end of slavery. But I'm wondering if Megan isn't something more."

There was silence. "If you mean unstable," Lemieux said dubiously, "no one seems to think that."

"Does anyone purport to know her?"

"Know her?" Lemieux thought for a moment. "The impression people gave me was that Megan could be pretty voluble. But I don't think they mean the same thing, and I really don't have a handle on how she might be with her peer group."

"No girlfriends visiting?"

"Not that I heard of." Another pause. "Actually, I didn't meet anyone who mentioned being inside her apartment."

"What do you have about her family?"

"A little, and it's not a pretty picture. Her father died in a boating accident when Megan was roughly twelve. Which apparently left her mother so depressed that she became very withdrawn, and stayed there. She's been in and out of institutions."

Caroline was quiet. "Find out more about the mother," she said finally. "Dates of institutionalization, if possible. Also, I'm still interested in any therapy for Megan. And do you think you could get me her class schedule?"

"For what?"

"For ever since she got there."

Lemieux considered this. "Without breaking the law?"

"That would certainly be preferable," Caroline answered in an arid voice. "For both our sakes."

"I agree. Anyhow, I'll see what I can do."

Caroline thanked him, and hung up.

She went to the window. Twilight was settling over the white houses, the rolling countryside. An older couple strolled slowly beneath the window of the inn until they disappeared from view; oddly, it made Caroline wonder how many meals in her lifetime she had eaten by herself.

She should eat something now, Caroline thought without enthusiasm; she felt weak from hunger. She was wondering where to go when the phone rang.

"Hello?"

"Caroline." Betty's voice was strained. "I'd like to see you. Please."

Caroline sat on the edge of the bed. "Can we make it tomorrow?" she asked.

SIX

"THANK YOU for coming," Betty said.

They sat on the porch; the morning was clear but cool, and steam rose from Caroline's cup of black coffee. In profile, her sister was pensive; it was as though the enormity of Brett's problems had dwarfed their estrangement.

"You asked me to," Caroline answered. "So I did."

Betty did not look at her. "I know how much you hate me. You think that I betrayed you—twice."

Caroline suppressed a bitter smile. What was of interest was not Betty's insight—it was hardly that—but the fact that she expressed it. Softly, Caroline answered, "Not just me."

Betty's eyes narrowed; for a moment, Caroline wondered if she had caught her meaning. "For years," Betty said at length, "I told myself that I was acting out of love."

"And now?"

"I know how jealous I was—of you and of him. Of you, I always had been."

Caroline gazed across the gravel road and down the swiftly sloping hill toward the village of Resolve. Remembered those few grades when she and Betty, five years apart, would stand beside the road until the bus came. Together, Caroline thought, and yet separate—sisters, and yet not. "I was only a kid," Caroline said. "No one at all, really."

Betty shook her head. "To me, you were his dark-haired princess, with a beautiful mother who'd taken my mother's place, just like you'd taken mine." Her voice went quiet. "Pathetic, I realize—even then, you didn't think of me at all. But maybe that was the worst of it."

It *was* pathetic, Caroline thought. "If only I'd known the price for it," she answered, "I would have been more sensitive. But then seven-year-olds so seldom are."

Betty turned to her, gray eyes almost accusing. "Do you know how terrible it is to see you now? It's like seeing all my failure and guilt, everything I've done wrong, trying to right what I did then." Her voice softened. "You even blame me for this, don't you?"

So she *had* understood, Caroline thought. She sipped her coffee, coolly studying her sister over the rim. "At the risk of being insensitive yet again, I find that I lack the energy to care. But then we each must form our own ideas about what—and who—is important to us. Especially at a time like this."

Betty turned crimson. "You have a talent for cruelty, Caroline." She paused a moment, and then continued in a halting voice, "I asked you here to talk about Brett, not my feelings. But I thought it might help if first we confronted what happened, as honestly as we could."

Caroline considered her. "What would it help?" she asked quietly. "Sometimes the fact of something overwhelms the reasons for it. Do you think it really matters to me that you didn't intend what happened? Even assuming that it's true."

Betty looked down; in the haggard face of this aging woman, Caroline could see traces of the young Betty she had known—watchful, a little afraid, as if something would be taken from her. It was a measure of all that had happened between them that compassion felt beyond her. "Betty," she said softly, "this does no good. It never will. Perhaps, for both our sakes, we should concentrate on Brett."

Betty closed her eyes. "I did what I thought was best for her, too," she said finally. "And if I hadn't, and she had gone away, perhaps there would never have been someone like James Case."

Caroline said nothing; the knowledge of irony, plain in Betty's eyes, kept her from responding.

"I thought I was being a good mother," Betty continued, "keeping her close, watching over her—everything I used to wish I had a mother to do." She turned to Caroline. "The precious mother that I knew *you* had, and that you and Father loved in common."

Caroline watched her closely. But there was no awareness on her sister's face. *He never told you,* she thought with grim amusement, *just how and why my mother died.* It was as if they had lived in different families, their understanding of each other defined by the one common member, whom, in turn, they had come to see so differently. The thought made Caroline quiet and still.

"Didn't *he*," Caroline asked at length, "also want Brett 'close'?"

Betty straightened in her chair. "We all did. Perhaps I wasn't the best mother, or the wisest. Perhaps I've pushed her away. But I tried." She paused. "This may be cruel of me, Caroline. But you've never had to face the moment where you're holding this baby and suddenly you know that with all your shortcomings and blindnesses, you more than anyone will make her what she becomes." Her voice lowered. "There was only one moment that felt as awesome, and as frightening: the day I sent Brett to kindergarten and it came to me that there was so much in the world which would touch her, and which I couldn't control at all."

Caroline held the coffee cup, cold in her hands, sorting her own emotions. "But that's inevitable," she said softly. "And at some point, when the child is older, the inevitable becomes fitting."

Betty's jawline seemed to tighten. "This world is different than the one we grew up in. The drugs are worse, the random violence is worse, the random sex—rape included—possibly fatal. Who would hurry to push a daughter into *that* world before her judgment is fully formed—"

"But how," Caroline snapped, "does she form it? By being tied to her parents? Or, more accurately, to a rigid old man who's frightened of anything or anyone he can't control—"

Betty spun on her. "Do you think James Case was better? Would you have liked your daughter to be with a worthless, selfish boy who had turned her on to drugs, who had 'promiscuous' written all over his smug face, and who didn't give a damn about anyone but himself? Would you want her to throw her talents and her past away for a promise that had no future?"

Caroline kept her temper in check. "But who makes these decisions?" she asked. "Brett, or you? Because from experience, I can tell you just how well the last works out. . . ."

"And you think *this* worked out?" Betty's own voice was quiet now. "You think Brett made *this* decision, don't you? That she was capable of murder—at least with the help of James's drugs."

Caroline considered her answer. "For someone else to have killed him," she said at last, "he or she would have had to follow them to Heron Lake. Or, at least, to know where they were going."

Betty's eyes met Caroline's. "Are you at least considering that?"

"I'll consider anything that might help. But there's little sign that they were followed—no tire tracks on the trail, no other cars spotted." Caroline watched her sister's face. "As for knowing they'd be at Heron Lake, the question becomes 'who?' And, I suppose, 'how?' "

Betty stood, walking to the edge of the porch. Silent, she gazed out at the distant village. "What about this girl?" she said. "The one that claims James was breaking it off with Brett that night."

"It seems far-fetched to me." Caroline remained in her chair, unable to see Betty's face now. "Did Brett ever talk about her?"

"No. She wouldn't have." The weariness of failure entered Betty's voice. "I still don't even know her name."

Caroline stood, moving next to Betty. "In some ways," she said, "the less you know the better. Because nothing Brett or I can say to you is privileged."

Betty turned to her. "They wouldn't call me to testify against her, would they?"

"As to what?" Caroline put an edge in her voice. "Is there something else I need to know? At least that the police are capable of knowing?"

Quickly, Betty shook her head. "No . . . Of course not. It's just how they can twist things, like the fights we had about James—"

"But how would that hurt Brett?"

"It wouldn't, I suppose." Betty paused. "Except if they tried to make her seem—I don't know—more volatile."

Caroline was quiet for a moment. "I wouldn't worry," she answered. "I doubt that Jackson would want to give the jury too much time with Brett's agonized mother. Regrettably, he has better things to do."

The front door opened behind them. But when Caroline turned, expecting her father, it was Larry who appeared.

His face was grave. "Hello, Caroline."

Betty went to him. "Have you checked Father?"

"Yes. He's up now." Larry turned back to Caroline. "This has been a strain on him. He's usually up at six, but he's seemed so tired.

Still, when it's close to nine, and no one's seen him . . ." He paused, shrugging.

Caroline nodded. "I'm sorry," she said to Larry. "But there's something I need to ask you."

Larry turned to her, his face tired and wary. "What is it?"

"This student—the witness against Brett. Her name is Megan Race. I was wondering if you knew her, or have a faculty friend who does."

"Megan Race?" Larry repeated. He shoved his hands in his pockets, staring down at the porch as Betty watched him intently. "That's the woman James was seeing?"

"Yes."

His eyes seemed to narrow. "Do you know what her major is?"

"Not offhand. Is there any way I could get my hands on her file?"

"No legitimate way . . ."

"I'm not asking you to do that. Just for any information you can come up with."

Larry seemed to exhale. "I'll have to think about it," he said. "Very hard."

When Caroline returned to the inn, there were two messages.

The easiest to return was from Walter Farris. She placed the call, waited on hold for ten minutes, pacing the room. By the time that Farris took her call, she was certain that he would tell her the nomination had been withdrawn.

"Caroline," he said brusquely. "I've spoken to the President."

She felt herself tense. "And?"

"And we reserve the right to withdraw the nomination if this trial goes on too long, or if there's any problem in what you're doing up there. By that I mean any problem as we down here define it." Farris paused for effect. "But, as of now, your nomination is still alive."

Caroline sat down on the bed. "Thank you."

"Thank the President, who has more compassion than I would." His voice grew softer. "Please, Caroline, don't misunderstand this. You're on your own now. Any misstep, and I'll pull the plug myself."

• • •

The second message, from Joe Lemieux, required two calls to his beeper.

"I have her schedule," he said. "No grades, but at least you can see what she was taking. For whatever it might be worth."

"It's a start. We can see what professors might know her, who else might have been in her classes. How did you get it, incidentally?"

"The school's computer system—the student can punch in for class schedule, registration, and a bunch of other stuff." Lemieux laughed softly. "The computer age presents an unlimited potential for invasion of privacy—in this case, all I needed was Megan's student number, which wasn't that hard to come by. But I wouldn't mention this to anyone."

Caroline took a deep breath. "I won't, believe me. And please, check with me before you do anything else like this. I'm not interested in coming up on ethics charges, thank you."

"I understand." He sounded faintly nettled. "Look, do you want this stuff or not?"

Caroline paused for a moment. "Yes," she said. "I want it. But don't fax it over. Drop it off by hand."

She hung up and went to Carlton Grey's office. For the next two hours, she read statute books and talked by phone to experts—a serologist, a criminalist, and a doctor who treated drug and alcohol addiction. So that it was perhaps three-thirty before she returned to the inn and found the manila envelope beneath her door.

Caroline opened it. Megan was a senior now; Caroline reached the first trimester of her junior year before she stopped, staring at the schedule with what she wished were disbelief.

The telephone rang again.

She was slow to answer. "Caroline," Larry said, "there's something I have to tell you."

"Yes," she replied. "I know."

SEVEN

CAROLINE FOUND HIM in his office at the English Department, sitting at his desk. He seemed too distraught to look away.

Caroline sat facing him and then said softly, "You should have told me sooner."

Larry stared at her. "What must you think of me?" he asked with a certain dignity. "I didn't know who the witness was until this morning, and I thought my confession could do without Betty. Given that your presence would complete her humiliation."

Caroline's eyes met his. "She doesn't know?"

"Not to a certainty, and definitely not who." He stood abruptly. "There's something wrong with her."

"Megan, you mean?"

"Of course Megan." His hands gripped the chair. "First getting involved with Case, and now as the key witness against Brett. It's like she's had a plan to destroy my daughter. . . ."

"Somehow, Larry, I doubt she counted on James Case dying."

Larry stiffened. "How do you know Megan didn't kill him? This can't be some coincidence—"

Caroline held up one hand. "I'm not saying that, either. Only that you brought this woman to Brett's doorstep."

He blanched. "But wouldn't that mean Brett's innocent?"

Caroline tilted her head. "No. But what it may mean is that the key witness against her is damaged goods." She paused for a moment. "In addition to whatever it does to your marriage."

Larry's gaze was bleak. "There's no help for that," he said at length. "Like so much else, Caroline, it's far too late."

Slowly, Caroline nodded. "Then tell me about you and Megan. Considering that you're the only one who seems to know her. Besides James Case."

Eyes averted, Larry walked to the door of his office, closing it tight, and then went to the window. He stood there, watching the late-afternoon sun fall softly across the red-brick buildings and rolling campus.

"It's been good here," he said. "All in all."

Caroline studied his slender frame, the sunlight catching the silver in his hair. She said nothing.

Larry seemed to steel himself. "My only excuse, Caro, is that I wasn't looking for her, at least not consciously. This woman came to me."

Caroline considered him. "I don't believe in Kismet. In my experience, people like Megan Race always know who to find."

"Perhaps." Larry turned from the window. "But in the classroom, I was the one they heard. Not like at home."

There was a faint undertone of self-contempt, as if Larry saw both versions of himself—the admired teacher, the deposed husband—as risible. "And Betty?" Caroline asked. "Where was she in all this?"

"Silent, in the great tradition of your family. Which slowly became mine." He faced her again. "In my experience, all those sex manuals miss the point. It isn't a matter of putting tab A in slot B. It's all the things that are unspoken and unresolved." Briefly, Larry looked away. "A kind of gray depression seeps into your soul, almost by stealth. So that you're so taken by how vivid someone like Megan Race can seem that you're blinded to the obvious—that whatever it is she sees in you is not about you.

"At first, she didn't seem that remarkable: a blond girl in the front row, asking questions, listening to your keenest points with her body leaning forward, her face open, straining to get it all. Then you notice the way she'll sit there for a moment when the lecture ends, a thoughtful, almost fond, half smile at the corner of her mouth. Until you begin to look for her and then, in an odd way, to count on her. Without either of you having said a word."

Larry paused for a moment. The sadness in his eyes seemed to go with the creases in his face and neck, the sag of a persona that had lost its vitality with the loss of illusions. "When she started coming to my office," he said quietly, "something inside me knew.

"It all began to fit. The way she moved the conversation from T. S. Eliot to things outside the class. The way she shut the door behind her, showed no interest in having coffee, or being in a public place. The almost reckless candor about herself and, after a few times, her sex life.

"I watched us with a kind of fascination, like a spectator to my own seduction. The married professor, listening with placid interest to the pretty student while she segued from Dylan Thomas to things like, 'I think sex is spiritual, don't you—I mean, a mind that is uninhibited is more sexual than a well-toned body. . . .' " He stopped himself, shaking his head.

"I've met her," Caroline said quietly. "You've developed some gifts as a mimic, Larry. She does have a certain breathless way of speaking."

Larry's eyes shut. "Jesus fucking Christ," he mumbled. "How could I have done this?"

"Because, as with several other things, you didn't see the consequences. At least not all of them."

He turned from her. "I never imagined, Caro, that I was endangering my daughter. Merely that I was risking my marriage and perhaps my job." His voice held a musing bitterness. "Later, I wondered if I didn't have some wish for self-destruction. To end my life, figuratively speaking, as I knew it.

"Whatever, I'd crossed the line. By the time Megan came to my office, to say she wanted an affair with me, I was past surprise.

"I sat there while she proposed the rules, with this strange light in her eyes. We would only meet at her apartment. She would no longer come to my office. She'd never mention my name to anyone. She wouldn't cause trouble in my marriage or take any more of my classes. All that she wanted was time with me." Larry's voice grew quiet again. "When she reached across the desk and placed the key in my hand, I could already imagine us.

"The next afternoon, I went there."

Part of Caroline, the girl who had teased with her sister's husband over twenty years before, had heard enough. But the lawyer Caroline had no good use for her own sensitivities, or the remnants of his pride.

"Please, don't spare me the details," she said. "I need a picture of this woman."

Larry leaned against the wall. As if to himself, he murmured, "I'm late for dinner."

Through the window, the fading light caught the hollows of his face. Caroline did not answer.

"The first time we were alone," Larry said softly, "she asked me to lie on the bed, and watch her.

"There was a full-length mirror on the wall. Slowly, she took off everything, a piece at a time. . . .

"Just before she was naked, she turned to see herself."

Larry paused, shaking his head. "Do you know what I remember? That when our eyes met in the mirror, she mouthed 'I love you.'

"After a moment, she bent over.

"I understood it as she meant me to. When I was inside her, she masturbated until she came. And when *I* came, my eyes still open, she smiled at her own reflection.

" 'I'll do anything you ask me to,' she whispered.

"Suddenly, Caro, I was God. There was nothing I couldn't have from her—nothing. And when we had done whatever I asked, she would tell me that I was the best lover she had ever imagined. . . ."

Larry's voice became tired, empty. " 'Imagined' was the word—I'm sure that my new prowess happened only in her head. But it also happened in mine." He searched for words. "Part of me knew that this 'relationship' was arbitrary, of her own invention. But I was a sexual person again. I felt myself walk taller, smile more easily, a great lover within my secret world. Even as I lay next to Betty, frightened to death . . ."

Caroline watched him steadily. "That was all there was? This meld of *Intermezzo* with *Fatal Attraction*?"

He winced. "No. I also listened to her."

"About what?"

"There were recurring themes. Her social views—which turned out to be some weird hybrid of Camille Paglia and 'the politics of meaning.' Literature, of course: sometimes she'd ask me to read to her." He reflected. "And, more and more frequently, her childhood. Mostly trauma, loneliness . . . Her father was killed in an accident."

Caroline nodded. "Did something strike you about that?"

His eyes narrowed. "Less then than now." He faced her now. "When I broke it off, I gave Brett as a reason. What I remember now is Megan saying that I'd chosen Brett over her." He shook his head, chagrined. "In retrospect, it was like she'd lost a father."

Caroline's eyes changed. "I thought all she wanted was a little piece of your mind. And body."

"At first, yes. There were rules for that too: Monday and Thursday, from three to five-thirty. Until she came to my office by surprise.

"That was the first breach of the rules.

"She was talking before I could protest." Larry stopped, pensive. "What I haven't conveyed to you is any picture of her energy—the excitement, the intimacy with which she looked at you, this incandescent smile. It was like she took you over. . . ."

"Yes. I've seen some of that, too. I sensed a tinge of desperation about it." Caroline considered him. "I assume that she wanted, or needed, something from you."

"To go away for a weekend." In profile, Larry looked ashen, unable now to face her. "And then she slipped a white envelope in my hand and asked me to open it before I answered.

"Inside was a Polaroid picture. One she had taken of herself, in front of the mirror. She had only one hand on the camera. . . ." His voice fell off.

"Yes," Caroline said evenly. "I think I get it. Do go on."

Larry crossed his arms. "There was also a note, making me a promise. The one thing I hadn't dared ask her to do." He paused again. "I don't know whether it was that, or the smile on her face when I looked up.

" 'You see,' she said, 'I know you.' "

Caroline felt a kind of dread. "So you went with her."

"Yes."

"And Betty?"

"When I said I was going camping, she became very quiet." Larry gazed out the window. "I hadn't done that since Brett was small, and Betty has this instinct for anything that threatens her, or hers. The week before I went away, we hardly spoke.

"Megan and I drove to the White Mountains. With every mile, I felt more haunted, less safe. We had hardly pitched the tent before I made her keep her promise. But all that it meant to me was an escape from my own thoughts. . . .

"To Megan, it meant something more.

" 'We're different now,' she told me. 'No boy has ever done that to me. I was waiting for a man.'

"Something in her voice made me cringe. Part of it was the feeling—suddenly quite clear—that she had cast me in a fantasy that was far too comprehensive. But the worst part was the contrast between the 'man' of her imaginings and the real man, filled with the regret and memories of a twenty-five-year marriage, fearful of being caught before he gave that his due." He paused. "And then—and this was eerie—she started asking about Betty."

He shook his head. "I'd had this illusion, Caro, that I'd kept my worlds separate—that all I had to do was spend a few hours in one, and lie a little in the other. And then suddenly Megan wanted to know everything: about how Betty and I met, what she liked, what kind of home we had and what kind of mother she was, what we did in bed together. . . .

"It was so bizarre. I was willing to violate our marriage vows, but to violate our privacy was too great a betrayal." His voice grew quiet again. "It was like whatever there was between us—our disappointments, our failures, our understandings, and even our silences—was Betty's and mine. And that I could never cheapen it to feed this girl's needs."

"And after that?"

Larry turned to her. "Two more weeks, and it was over."

Caroline put a finger to her lips. "Did anything else happen?" she asked.

Silent, Larry nodded. "The whole balance changed," he said finally. "She began to fantasize about her role in my life, to advise me about my career and how to relate to Betty. She even spoke of befriending Brett. . . ." He paused, shaking his head. "I couldn't imagine what Brett would think of her—"

"*I* can," Caroline said coolly. "Tell me, did Megan ever approach her?"

"Not that I know about—if Brett had ever learned about us, I'm sure I'd have gotten more than a piece of her mind. But I felt Megan coming closer to the core of my life." Larry shoved his hands in his pockets. "Just before I broke it off, there were calls close to dinnertime, two nights running. The first one Betty answered; she said whoever it was waited for a moment, and then hung up. I just shrugged it off. But in my heart, I was afraid I knew. . . .

"The next night I made sure to answer.

"We were in the kitchen. When I hurried to the phone, Betty

looked up from the sink. So that she was watching my face when Megan began to speak. . . .

" 'I just wanted to hear your voice,' Megan said.

"Betty had turned to me. " 'I think you have the wrong number,' I managed to say.

" 'Thank you,' Megan whispered, and hung up."

Larry lowered his eyes. "When I put down the phone, Betty watched me for a moment. She didn't ask me anything at all.

"That was when I knew that *she* knew. And that I had to find my way out of this, any way I could.

"For the next two days, until our Monday, I tried to frame my excuses. Something, anything, to dampen the explosion I had begun to fear.

"Megan sat there on the edge of the bed, hands folded in front of her, while I told her. I tried to dwell on the person with whom I thought Megan might sympathize most—Brett." His voice turned harsh. "The whole time I listened to what a fraud I was—this cipher, inflating my role to what a real father might have. But the odd thing is that my story had been true, once—when Brett was six, before I was trapped by tenure, I imagined leaving Betty, the job, the looming omnipresence of your father and that house." His voice softened. "Do you know what stopped me, Caro? That I'd be leaving without Brett. Because they'd never let me have her."

Caroline folded her arms, head bowed. For a moment she could think of nothing to say.

"And Megan?" she asked at length.

"Defied my expectations. There were no tears, or threats, or rage. All that she said, as if she had expected it, was, 'You've chosen your daughter over me.'

"I left as quickly as I could.

"I was on edge for days—jumpy when the phone rang, or the door to my office opened, afraid it would be her.

"There was nothing. Just one sad, simple letter, which, in its own way, frightened me as much. Because it described a relationship that we had never had." He exhaled. "A meeting of souls, she called it."

Caroline looked up at him. "Did you keep the letter?"

"Of course not."

"Because I was hoping that you'd have some proof that any of this ever happened."

Larry stared at her. "I'll have to testify—show how this woman must have said and done these things to get at me. . . ." The thought stopped him, for a moment, and then he finished with calm resolve. "I'll need to tell Betty, of course. As soon as I get home."

Almost absently, Caroline rubbed her temple, still gazing up at Larry. "Did you tell anyone about Megan at the time?"

Larry's eyes widened slightly; with a kind of fascination, Caroline watched as understanding dawned. "No," he said in a flat voice. "I was very careful."

"So no one saw you?"

"I don't think so."

"No gifts, or pictures?" Caroline's voice softened. "Not even a Polaroid?"

Larry flushed. "No."

Caroline sat back. "So now you know, Larry, how Megan expects to get away with this. Because, it appears, *you* did."

Larry lowered himself heavily into his chair. They sat there in the half-light of early evening, silent.

"Why would anyone believe," he said at last, "that I would concoct a story like this, and destroy my marriage in the bargain."

"Oh, I believe you—the whole thing sounds right to me. But the reason you'd 'concoct' this story is simple: to save your daughter by claiming that the key witness against her is acting out of spite. And even your version can't explain Megan's relationship to James, or her quite lethal claim that she was the one James was taking to California." Caroline's voice grew quiet. "For all Jackson Watts knows, Betty may be part of your conspiracy."

Larry's mouth formed a stubborn line. "They'll believe me."

"Will they? Because it's clear that Megan was involved with James—for however long and for whatever reason—and you can't prove that she was ever involved with you." Caroline paused. "When did it end, by the way?"

"Late last fall."

"A nice cold trail, that." Caroline raised an eyebrow. "Then I take it this mythic camp-out with Megan was not the one you were on the night that Case was murdered."

"No." Larry looked away. "Ironically, I really was alone. To think."

Caroline smiled without humor. "Well," she said, "at least you're not Megan's alibi."

Across the desk, she watched as Larry's eyes closed. Softly, he said, "How badly that summer has ended, Caro. For all of us."

For a long while, Caroline was silent. When she spoke again, her voice was gentle. "I'll try to use this without calling you as a witness. Let me speak to Jackson first. If he's afraid Megan is flawed enough, he may dismiss the case while he looks for more. Including more about Megan." Her tone grew quieter still. "So you needn't tell Betty yet, or Brett. I'll let you know if you have to face that."

Larry's eyes opened. "And Channing?"

Caroline sat straighter, and her voice became brittle. "There's been quite enough running to Daddy in our annals, don't you think?" She caught herself, finishing in a level tone: "I refuse, unless I must, to leave this family even worse than I found it. That might be more than even I could bear."

EIGHT

"SO," CAROLINE SAID, "your defendant's father was fucking your prize witness. Who strikes me, by the way, as more than a bit unstable."

Jackson sat next to her on a park bench near the station house. He rolled up his shirtsleeves, expression quite calm, as if she had said nothing at all remarkable. "Too bad," he said finally. "Megan spoke so well of you. Better, it seems, than you do of me."

Caroline gave him a level gaze. "You have to get on this, Jackson, and you know it. The defense has come to you with critical information, which it could have used to sandbag you in court. If you go forward without an inquiry, it's virtual misconduct."

Jackson turned to her. "All right," he said. "What would you have me do?"

Caroline looked at him intently. "For openers, send the Major Crimes Unit to interview Larry and then check out his story—there must be someone, somewhere, to whom Megan said something." She drew a breath. "But if there isn't anyone, I'm asking you to search this girl's apartment."

"A warrant? For what?"

"For anything that would confirm her relationship to Larry. And to explore whether she had any relationship to the victim after April."

Jackson stared at her. "So that's why you came. You want the prosecutor to alienate a prosecution witness by doing what the defense has no power to do—get a search warrant to turn her place upside down." His voice became incredulous. "Tell me, Caroline, have you had any luck with this one in San Francisco?"

"I haven't had this one in San Francisco." Caroline felt herself losing any pretense of dispassion. "Megan has such obvious potential bias that she may have made this whole thing up—"

"Not about going to California," Jackson cut in. "And you damned well know it. Please, don't insult my intelligence."

Caroline folded her hands. "You might be able to explain even that. If you'd simply look in her apartment."

"If I simply treat this girl like a criminal, you mean." His study of her face became lingering and comprehensive. "I know this involves your family. But I've got no basis for doing what you ask."

"Perjury *is* a crime, you know."

"Only if proven." Jackson paused. "Look, I'll talk to Larry myself, without you. I'll also have our people sniff around. And then I'll confront Megan with these charges."

Caroline stood. "With what, damn it? She'll deny it and—like a fool—I will have prepared her for the hearing."

"Not like a fool." His gaze grew pointed. "If you honestly thought you could salvage Brett by destroying Megan Race on cross, you'd have done it in a heartbeat—her parents' marriage be damned. But you don't have anything, do you, and you don't think you're getting anything, either. Unless you have my help." His tone became even. "You're just as well off having me surprise this girl. Because if there's any real problem, you know that I'll act on it."

Caroline considered him. "Yes," she said at length. "That much I do know. But I think I've made a terrible mistake and that you're about to make one too. At whatever cost to Brett."

Jackson stood. "I truly hope not," he answered. "Because this hearing you want so badly is in five days now, and it would be nice if it produced some semblance of the truth. Which, as I continue to believe that you believe, is that Brett Allen killed this boy."

He turned and walked back to his office.

Leaving the car, Caroline faced the stand of trees alone.

It was night, twelve hours since she had driven from Concord, the image of this moment slowly forming in her mind. So that now, entering the trees, she imagined herself as Brett.

Deadwood crackled beneath her feet; branches struck her face, her body. Arms raised for self-protection, she could see almost nothing. Only her senses knew the way.

The darkness seemed interminable. Amidst towering pines, no moonlight came. There was no sound but Caroline.

And then, a first thin light, the trunks of trees appearing.

More swiftly now, Caroline walked to the edge of the stand. Her face was damp with sweat.

In front of her was the glade.

She knelt there, next to where James Case had died, and gazed at the lake.

The moon was crescent, half of what it had been for Brett, and the water was an obsidian sheet. She could not see the platform to which Brett claimed to have swum.

In the woods behind her, something crackled.

Caroline whirled, heart suddenly racing. The woods were black, silent.

She stood there, facing the dark, a chill on her skin.

Slowly, reluctantly, Caroline turned back to the lake.

She was still for a moment, remembering where the platform must be. And then she pulled off her jacket and jeans, and stepped from the glade toward the water. Through her running shorts and tank top, the night air felt cool.

With halting steps, she moved to the shoreline, rocks hurting her feet. Just, she realized, as Brett had described.

The first shock of cold water as she dove jarred her from the thought. She was Caroline now, swimming for the platform her father had built when she was small, borne by a memory that crossed the fissures of her life.

Her strokes were long and smooth, as they had been since she was young. She found that she knew—almost to the moment—when her hand would touch the platform she could not see.

She pulled herself up, sat on the edge, breathing deeply in the cool night air.

The light was better here; on the lake, trees did not block the moon. But the shoreline was a rise in the darkness, formless trees. Only the glade seemed light.

Motionless, she listened.

Nothing.

Slowly, systematically, she scanned the shoreline for movement.

But she saw nothing, heard no one on the water. Felt cold and dampness, the wet tendrils of her hair, her eyes straining for light.

Something had changed.

As she turned, a shadow crossed the glade, silver in moonlight.

Caroline froze. Only when the shadow knelt, still and silent, was she certain it was there.

Caroline dove into the water.

Her strokes were choppy, panicky, as Brett's might have been. Her body strained in the water, nerves tingling as she struggled to shore. Her pulse sounded in her ears.

When she reached the shore and stepped from the water, the shadow was still.

Her breaths were ragged. As she walked toward the glade, grass beneath her feet, the shadow stood to face her.

"Hello, Father," Caroline said.

Channing Masters stepped into the moonlight. His deep-set eyes were shadows.

"You could see me, then."

"Only in the glade. Not before." Caroline paused, to ease her breathing. "Where did you come from?"

"The trail past Mosher's place. It ends perhaps a hundred yards from here."

In the moonlight, she could see that his boots were wet. "And then along the water?"

"Yes. Just as I suggested." His voice was firm. "You couldn't see me, Caroline, or hear me—just as Brett couldn't. Until I reached the glade."

"True. But then your killer, whoever that might be, would have to know the way. And know, somehow, where Brett and James would be."

Silent, Channing sat, staring at the lake. "Just that they would be here," he said finally. "The sign at the head of Mosher Trail says 'Heron Lake.' "

His voice was quieter now. Caroline put on her jacket and knelt on the grass beside him. "Tired?" she asked.

"A little, yes." He still looked at the water. "Do you know what was strange for me, Caroline? That for a moment, as you came toward me in the darkness, your face was like Nicole's."

Caroline folded her arms. Softly, she answered, "I'm no more like her than I ever was. I look at my face, Father, and I see you written there."

He was quiet, still. She stared at the grass in front of her.

"Hasn't it occurred to you," she said at last, "that a knife is the wrong weapon for your killer? How could he, or she, count on slashing two healthy young people at once?"

Slowly, Channing nodded. "He'd use a gun, I think. But suppose he saw that Case was alone, and asleep." His voice became thoughtful. "A knife has the virtue of silence. Which, in turn, could mean escape without detection."

Narrow-eyed, Caroline picked at a blade of grass. "That means bringing a gun *and* the knife. A very nice knife, at that."

When Caroline turned to him, her father would not look at her. "All that I'm saying," he said at last, "is that it's plausible. And that, for a jury, plausible might do."

Caroline said nothing.

He stood up, still gazing at the water. "This Megan. Could she be a suspect? Just as you suggested?"

"A 'plausible' suspect, you mean? As opposed to just a liar?"

Channing hesitated. "Yes."

"I don't know yet." For a moment, Caroline watched him. "But your theory surely needs one. As does Brett, quite desperately."

NINE

CAROLINE PORED OVER her notes and began to outline her examination of the police witnesses—the arresting and interrogating officers, the medical examiner, the crime lab technicians. Carlton Grey's spare office was quiet; the first light of dawn came through the window. It was four days before the hearing.

The press had begun calling. Caroline had been courteous; quietly, she intimated that the hearing would expose deep problems in the prosecutor's case. But Jackson had refused to fuel the stories with any comment of his own. Caroline did not know the status of Megan Race.

She rose from the desk, staring out the window. Brett was facing matters with a new composure; though she was clearly tired and afraid, she treated Caroline with a certain courtesy, as if sensing that self-control was something Caroline needed from her. It was as though they had exchanged roles—Caroline herself was short-tempered, her nerves frayed. She had passed the point of exhaustion without noticing.

When the telephone rang, Caroline flinched.

She turned, saw the phone on an end table she had never noted. She gathered herself, walked across the room, and answered.

"Yes?"

"Caroline?" Jackson said. "I tried the inn, and they said that you were gone. I know it's early, but I also know how concerned you've been."

His tone was so polite that Caroline's hopes began to fade. "This is about Megan, I imagine."

"It is." Jackson spoke quickly, as if his speech was well rehearsed. "If it were simply a matter of Larry's demeanor, I would have found this easier—what he told me sounded persuasive, and seemingly quite painful. I came out wanting to believe him. . . ."

"But?"

"But he couldn't give me any corroborating evidence, and our investigators couldn't find a scrap of it—no one who saw them together, or even heard Megan speak his name outside class. Beyond some vague statement Megan made to a neighbor about the virtues of an older lover, there's nothing that even suggests that Larry might be telling the truth—"

"So give him a lie detector test."

She had said it on impulse. But Jackson's civility was too complete, she realized, to throw her own refusal regarding Brett back at her—sufficient answer in itself.

"Once I do that," he said evenly, "I have to test Megan too. Which transfers the task of assessing witnesses—none of whom are charged with a crime—from the courtroom to a machine, one that a fair number of experts don't accept. We don't run our cases that way and, with respect, I can't start now. Even granting your concern."

Caroline stood straighter. "Quit treating me like I'm some emotional cripple at the deathbed of a relative, all right? I'm a lawyer whose client was indicted because of a witness who may well be a pathological liar."

For the first time, Jackson hesitated. "I've spoken with her, Caroline. Quite angrily—and also quite persuasively—Megan says that Larry was nothing more to her than a moderately interesting professor she had for a single class. And she reminded me, as if I needed it, that her testimony involves a proven relationship with James Case, which was discovered by your client. Another fact that, unless and until Brett testifies, no one has disputed. Not even you."

Caroline was silent for a moment. "Jackson," she said at length, "there's something wrong with Megan Race. Her whole performance the other day was aimed at persuading me to plead Brett guilty. Every instinct I've got tells me she's afraid of testifying."

"Then she's got a poor way of showing it. Because once she came forward, she had to know that testifying is a real possibility. And—assuming Larry's story to be true—that he would be a central subject of any cross-examination—"

"All that she assumed," Caroline interjected, "was that no one would be able to prove it. Which you haven't."

At length he said, "Then that's become your problem, hasn't it."

Caroline's fingers tightened on the telephone. "Please," she said, "get a warrant. Look for calendars, datebooks, scraps of paper—anything with Larry's name on it. Or James's name."

This time Jackson did not hesitate. "I'm sorry, Caroline. I won't harass this witness—not unless you've got something more. Do you?"

Caroline paused. "No. Not yet."

"Then please call me once you do," Jackson said politely, and hung up.

With the office door shut, Caroline listened to Joe Lemieux's report on Megan Race. It was past noon, and Caroline had not eaten.

"There's no therapy we can find," he said in summary. "No history of strange behavior—at least nothing really bizarre."

"What about merely eccentric?"

"Maybe that. She does seem a little short of friends—which may be why she treated that poor neighbor lady, and you, to lectures on her sex life. The one roommate I found said that she sort of glommed onto her, like she was trying to take over her life. The way she put it was that Megan wore her out." Lemieux shrugged. "Since then, Megan's lived alone."

Caroline nodded. "All that fits with Larry's story. There's something obsessive about this girl, Joe. Which is exactly how she described Brett."

"Meaning?"

"That if you're disturbed enough, you project your disturbances onto other people. Megan saw in Brett all the threatening qualities she herself had."

Lemieux frowned; with his thin face and thoughtful eyes, he looked less like a detective than a doctoral student, lost in his own private specialty. "Maybe," he said dubiously. "But if you're right, then Megan's pretty good at maintaining. There's no evidence, for example, that she's ever been in therapy. She was a high school honor student, and she's gotten through three years of college with good grades and no obvious problems—let alone being caught baying at the moon." He looked at Caroline more closely. "There is this, Caroline: You know that job she has at the student union—noon and night?"

"Uh-huh."

"For whatever reason, and for whatever it's worth, she called in sick the night Case was murdered."

Caroline cocked her head. "We can confirm that?"

"With time slips, sure." Lemieux scowled. "The problem, of course, is that there's no good reason to believe that she had any reason to hate the guy, or was anywhere near Heron Lake. Let alone that she walks around with—what was it?—a knife and a gun."

Caroline studied him. Softly, she said, "Anyone can get them, Joe. It's the American way."

"So it is. But you're a long way from putting a gun in this girl's hands. Or even that knife."

Caroline was quiet for a time. "I also wanted her current schedule," she said at last.

Lemieux looked at her hard now. "Can I ask why?"

Caroline shrugged. "Curiosity."

Lemieux's eyes narrowed. In a flat voice, he said, "Same schedule—noon to two serving food, and eight to ten running the coffee bar. Some nights, when it's slow, she closes early."

"Thanks."

Lemieux considered his fingernails. "No luck with the prosecutor?"

"None." Caroline folded her hands in front of her. "What kind of security does Megan's building have?"

Lemieux looked up at her. "It's a fifties apartment," he said slowly, "like the one Case lived in. A buzzer at the front door is all."

For a moment, Caroline was quiet. "Dead bolts?" she inquired.

Lemieux's eyes met hers. With equal quiet, he answered, "I can't do that, Counselor."

Caroline's stomach felt empty. She kept her face expressionless. "You can't tell me if there are dead bolts?"

Lemieux's eyes did not move. "I didn't see dead bolts," he said at last.

At two o'clock, restless, Caroline left the office. She was dressed in jeans and behind the wheel before she knew where she would go.

She drove past Masters Hill, hardly glancing at her father's home, and did not get out until she reached the foot of the trail she had climbed two weeks before—before she had met Brett Allen and be-gun unraveling the self-creation of more than twenty years, until she was no longer sure what it meant to be Caroline Masters.

Slowly and steadily, Caroline traversed the side of the hill, climb-ing between the brush and trees. As she reached the top, she half ex-pected to see her father on the fallen log, surveying Resolve and the country beyond. But Caroline was alone.

Though the day was overcast, she could see great distances—the roofs and spires of the town from which she had driven, mountains undulating westward until the last peaks met the sky. But nothing else was clear to her.

For twenty years, Caroline had lived by the law and its rules. Per-haps not the rules as lay people understood them—Caroline the defense lawyer accepted the hardest truths of justice: That the pre-sumption of innocence must protect the guilty. That when police and prosecutors break the rules, sometimes an evil person must go free. That it was Caroline's job to enforce these rules at whatever cost. Sometimes this had haunted her: police without rules were an injustice waiting to happen, but where was the justice in freeing an incorrigible criminal—a murderer, a rapist, a molester—to harm yet another victim? The fact that she might also have protected the in-nocent was, on certain nights, too theoretical to allow for easy sleep.

But she had always obeyed the rules as she understood them. Just as, she insisted, the police should.

Closing her eyes, she imagined Brett's life.

This was far too easy for her now. Caroline knew Brett's daily routine—loneliness, too little exercise, reading until the words swam in front of her, writing in a diary she must censor to protect her deepest thoughts. And then, in her mind, Caroline followed her through the twenty-year sentence that Jackson Watts, with the pros-ecutor's pitiless sense of duty, demanded as the minimum. Knew the terrible apartness, yet the loss of all her privacy. Felt the absence of friends or lovers or children, the withering of sexuality as twenty-two became thirty-two, and then forty-two. Saw the pallor as Brett at last left prison, her face lined from the passage of empty years, the richness of her youth behind her. All because of a single witness and the darkness of a single night.

All at once, a memory came to Caroline. She was young again, a lawyer for perhaps a year. A client, out on bail, had come to her office. He did not deny his guilt, hoped merely for a lighter sentence. He was scruffy and slight, and wore a slightly aggrieved expression. "They made it so easy," he complained—like so many of her clients, Caroline realized, he blamed a nameless "they" for the actions he had taken. And then, to prove his point, he closed the door to her office, produced a thin plastic credit card, and slid it through the slit near the door handle.

The door seemed to spring open in his hand. "See," he said in an accusatory voice. "No dead bolt."

"Yes," Caroline had answered dryly. "What else can 'they' expect?"

What they could expect, Caroline thought now, was that a judge would honor the law. At whatever cost.

Caroline gazed at the distant town. When she was done, whatever happened, she would ask them to withdraw her nomination.

TEN

CAROLINE SAT in her car, a half block down the twilit street.

Her watch read 7:50. Edgy, she scanned the rearview mirror. No one passed through the front door of the apartment building.

Perhaps, Caroline thought, Megan would not work tonight. She waited, poised between tension and relief.

In the mirror, the door to the building opened.

Caroline did not turn. There was a flash of reflected movement; in the dusk, the figure of a woman was a tiny shadow in a piece of glass. Caroline could not tell who she was.

The passenger window was cracked open. Caroline waited, utterly still, listening for footsteps on the other side of the street. Hoping that twilight and the shade of trees hid her inside the car.

The sound of wooden heels on cement came faintly through the window.

Still Caroline did not turn. Only after another moment did she see the tall, stiff carriage of Megan Race as she passed beneath a tree.

A streetlight came on. Caroline last saw Megan as a shadow, moving from light to darkness, heedless of anything.

Looking about her, Caroline stepped into the silent street.

It was tree-shrouded, empty. Dressed in a light jacket and jeans, Caroline crossed the street. Her running shoes made no sound.

The half block to the apartment seemed vague, unreal. She reached the door with a sense of disbelief.

The building was a sterile rectangle with four floors. Megan was on the fourth, Caroline knew, which increased the difficulty of entrance or escape.

She stood there, irresolute.

This was no good—someone might see her. She fought her imagination: the thing to do was to go one step at a time. Knowing that these moments, however fatal to her spirit, could pass without detection.

Stiffly, Caroline pushed all ten buttons for the second floor.

Silence.

Caroline breathed in, waiting. Then some trusting soul above her pushed the door buzzer, and she was inside.

She stood in a bare lobby—an elevator, a stairwell with a green neon exit sign. Caroline opened the door to the stairwell and then closed it behind her.

The stairs were dark. Soon apartment doors would open on the second floor and tenants would peer into the hall, wondering who had buzzed them. Caroline hurried up the stairs.

At the second floor, she whirled, saw a lone woman in the hallway through the glass window of the exit door. It was only as she reached the fourth floor that she realized this reminded her of Brett, and prison.

Breathing rapidly, Caroline peered through the window. The corridor was empty; there was no sense of the disturbance two floors down. Once in Megan's apartment, Caroline could disappear.

With an air of calm she did not feel, Caroline stepped into the corridor. It was not long, just five doors on each side.

Megan's apartment was on the left.

Don't think, Caroline told herself. *Just do.*

She went to Megan's door.

In the pocket of her jacket was a handkerchief and the thin plastic card that Caroline used to enter her office building after hours. It was the one card that did not bear her name.

Looking over her shoulder, she saw no one. The hollow sound of voices on a television came through the door next to Megan's.

Caroline slipped out the card and placed the handkerchief on the metal doorknob. Her forehead felt damp. No longer would anyone mistake what she was doing; suddenly, she regretted again that wearing gloves would make her conspicuous, that buying them would make her memorable. She slid the card through the crack—

It slipped from her fingers.

Caroline caught her breath. The card hit the tile with a slap and lay at her feet, glistening in the light. Taut, Caroline knew that she could have lost it through the crack.

Quickly, she picked it up.

With every hesitation, the inevitable moment when the next person entered the hallway was that much closer—perhaps the manager, following up the unexplained ringing. Caroline's watch read 8:17.

Slowly, she reinserted the card, eyes narrow. Slipped it above the latch, then at an angle, to catch the indentation of the lock.

Breath held, Caroline slid the card between the lock and the door and pulled gently on the door.

There was a soft click. The knob had moved in her hand.

Opening the door, she slid into Megan's apartment and softly shut the door.

It was pitch dark. It took Caroline a moment of blind fumbling, handkerchief covering her fingertips, to find the switch on the wall.

She stood there, blinking in the light.

The apartment was simple—a living room with a kitchen to one side and, next to that, the door to what must be Megan's bedroom. As Caroline stood there, irresolute, footsteps sounded in the corridor.

She froze.

The footsteps were heavy, a man's. They came closer; for an instant, Caroline imagined that they had stopped at Megan's door. Then the next footstep fell, and another. After a moment, she could not hear them.

For a time, Caroline told herself, she was safe.

Caroline looked around again.

She had expected color, vivid posters, perhaps pictures of Megan herself. But the apartment was bland, impersonal—the furniture looked institutional, the walls were bare cinder block. There was little sense that anyone lived here, Caroline thought—young or old, man or woman.

She went to the bedroom, handkerchief still draped across the fingers of her left hand.

Inside, on the door to Megan's closet, was a full-length mirror.

Just as Larry had described it, the mirror faced the foot of Megan's bed. All at once, Caroline was certain that Larry had told the truth.

Her watch read 8:25.

Swiftly, Caroline went through the drawers of Megan's dresser.

She found nothing but slacks, T-shirts, bras, and underpants—all thrown together in a chaotic mess. Wiping clean the drawer handles, she went to the closet.

It was generous in size, with sliding wood doors. One door was off its tracks; arduously, Caroline pushed it to the side and then peered into the closet.

There were dresses, a parka, boots and shoes. But what stopped Caroline abruptly was a large open box.

On top of the box was a Polaroid camera.

Caroline knelt, carefully putting the camera aside.

Beneath was a spiral notebook. Written on the cover was the name of Larry's course.

Caroline opened the notebook. The notes she read were detailed, less the practical jottings of a college student than something almost reverent, as literal a rendering of lecture upon lecture as the hurried scrawl could make it. But nothing more.

And then Caroline saw the calendar.

It was from the year before. The months of October through November, the time of their affair, had been ripped out as if in rage.

Wedged to the side was a map of the White Mountains.

Caroline opened it. Toward the bottom, circled in pen, was the campsite that Larry had described to her.

For a moment, Caroline was still.

She was right, Caroline now knew—at least about what Megan was, as well as who she had been to Larry. But none of what she had found so far would prove anything in a court of law. Even if she could leave with it.

Carefully, Caroline placed each item back in the box and closed the closet door.

It was 8:43.

Caroline turned, facing the bedroom.

The sole piece of distinctive furniture was a light oak rolltop desk.

There were a few books on its shelf. All dealt with psychology, Caroline saw: the family, dysfunctional or not; only children; the relationship between fathers and daughters. But there were no clues—here or anywhere—to Megan's real family.

Caroline slid open the desk drawer.

Inside were two expensive pens and a red leather-bound journal with a green ribbon coming from between its pages.

The journal fell open in her hands.

The entries were dated from the beginning of Megan's sophomore year. Hurriedly, Caroline began reading. The first pages were an unsettling jumble—vague spiritual yearnings, descriptions of sex acts without names or faces, a paradoxical hostility to men as a group. The entries seemed to gain in extravagance, or vehemence, as Caroline worked toward the middle. And then Caroline turned a page and found the ragged remnant of a ripped-out entry.

The months of September through December were missing.

Without much hope, Caroline resumed in February.

The handwriting seemed jagged now, the sprawl of emotion on the page. But Caroline saw no mention of Larry.

She turned another page and then stopped abruptly.

She read the page, read it again. With trembling fingers, she scanned the entries, until she got to May.

Caroline stopped again, staring at the page.

"Jesus Christ," she said aloud.

Caroline read again, more carefully, sitting cross-legged on the floor. She could feel her heart race.

When she had finished, she sat with the journal in her lap, trying to collect her thoughts.

Her watch read 9:15.

There was no way to copy these pages, return the journal to its drawer as if she had never been here. The only conceivable place to Xerox was the library at Chase College, and there were too many traps: that she would be seen there; that she might not be able to re-enter the building or Megan's apartment; that she would be caught if she tried; that Megan herself could find her. Caroline stared at the journal in her lap.

Whatever the consequences, she could not leave without it.

The time was 9:22.

Fighting her nerves, Caroline systematically reviewed where she had been. Then she put down the journal, went to the living room with her handkerchief in hand, and began to retrace her steps.

At every point—the light switch, the inside knob, the door to Megan's room—Caroline wiped the surface clean of fingerprints.

Sometimes she leaves work early, Lemieux had said.

Hurriedly glancing at her watch, Caroline saw that it was 9:31. There was still much to do.

She went to the bedroom, wiping the dresser drawer handles and then the sliding door to Megan's closet.

The biggest problem, she realized, was the box.

Pulling it from the closet, Caroline wiped all that she could remember touching: the camera; the cover of the notebook; its edges; the corners of the map; the box itself.

As she did this, she listened for sounds. But all she could hear was the faint sound of the television in the apartment next door.

It was 9:51 when Caroline shoved the box back inside with the toe of her shoe.

Turning, she gazed at the journal on the floor.

It was the moment of decision, she knew, the final chance to return the journal to its drawer and leave. She could feel her own hesitancy, the premonition of ill consequence.

Caroline walked across the bedroom and wiped away the final fingerprints on the rolltop desk.

It was 9:54.

Within fifteen minutes, Megan would return.

There was no more time to decide.

Caroline went to the center of the room, picked up the journal, and turned to leave.

There was a sudden sound, the rattle of keys outside the door.

For an instant, Caroline froze. She did not know what saving instinct told her, just before the door opened, to scramble to the wall and switch off the bedroom light.

As Caroline faced the darkened room, Megan closed the door behind her.

Caroline sensed, but could not see, the door to the closet. Her pulse pounded in her ears.

Quickly, Caroline moved forward, hoping not to trip on something. She found the crevice of the closet door as Megan's footsteps crossed the living room, coming closer.

Pushing with one palm, Caroline forced open the reluctant door. As she stepped inside, the door softly squealed, then slid into place.

With crabbed steps, Caroline turned.

Megan's footsteps entered the bedroom.

The light switched on.

Megan stood there, peering about. In profile, she looked wary and unhappy, consumed by secret thoughts.

If she faced the closet, Caroline knew, Megan would see her.

Caroline was utterly still.

Walking to the middle of the room, Megan pulled off her sweatshirt.

With a kind of fascination, Caroline watched—afraid, as Megan slipped off her blue jeans, that she would hang them in the closet.

Megan left them in a heap.

When she was naked, Megan turned to the mirror.

She studied herself intently, critically. And then she tilted her head, eyes opening wider, as if imploring the mirror for compassion. One finger grazed her nipple; she stood there like a statue, caught in her aloneness. Caroline held her breath.

Megan turned from the mirror.

For a moment, she gazed at the floor, pensive. Caroline could see her full face now; all that Megan needed was to look up, and her eyes would meet those of the woman who watched her.

Slowly, Megan turned from the closet and moved toward the dresser, slipping from Caroline's view.

There were only sounds now—a drawer sliding open, hands sifting clothes. And then Megan, wearing a T-shirt, crossed the bedroom and disappeared again.

Caroline hesitated. If she stayed here, Megan would surely find her; even if she did not, Caroline could not chance crossing the bedroom later in the hope that Megan slept.

Megan's footsteps grew lighter.

Please, Caroline begged her, *go to the kitchen.*

Caroline slid from the closet and stole across the bedroom, holding the journal. Her feet made no sound.

At the bedroom door, she peered into the living room.

No one.

As Caroline stepped into the living room, she heard the rattling of silverware.

Caroline tried to remember the layout of the kitchen. The sink and cabinets, she recalled, were on the wall; to use them, Megan could not face the living room.

Caroline took a deep breath and headed, swiftly and silently, for the door.

A few feet farther on, Megan would be able to see her.

Caroline reached the space. As she swiftly turned, half expecting to hear a cry, she saw Megan bend over the sink, a tea bag in her hand.

Soundless, Caroline crossed the living room.

She paused at the door, hearing Megan stir a spoon inside a cup, and took the handkerchief from her pocket.

Fingers draped on the handkerchief, Caroline turned the knob.

The door groaned slightly.

Abruptly, the sounds from the kitchen stopped.

Panicky, Caroline peered into the hallway, saw no one. She slid quickly through the door.

It shut behind her, of its own weight, with a soft click.

Caroline hurried for the stairwell.

She did not care about noise now. Heart racing, she pushed open the door, jerking it closed behind her. Through the glass window, she saw Megan peer into the hallway.

Caroline ran down the stairs, through the alcove, and into the cool night.

The drive was surreal. The mundane became the mirror of Caroline's fears—headlights were police cars; the old man sitting on the porch of the inn had peered at the journal in her hand. She hurried to her room.

She sat on the end of the bed. *Now you know,* she told herself, *how it feels to commit a crime.*

There was nowhere, Caroline knew, that she could hide the journal.

In her briefcase was a flat manila envelope.

As the idea took form, Caroline saw that there was no choice: by now, quite possibly, Megan had called the police.

From the briefcase, Caroline took the Magic Marker she used to red-line pleadings.

On the face of the envelope, she printed her own name. Beneath that she wrote "c/o Betty Allen," the address of Masters Hill, and the words "personal and confidential." Her painstaking block letters were not Caroline's own but those of a child.

She took a roll of stamps from her purse and applied six stamps to the envelope.

For a last moment, she looked at the diary. Then she placed it inside the envelope, licked the flap, and sealed it tight.

When she left her room, descending the stairs, the man no longer sat on the porch. The main street of Resolve was dark and empty.

Alone, Caroline wandered the streets of her childhood. In the quiet, a flash of memory came: Caroline and Jackson Watts in a convertible he had borrowed, careening through the streets on a warm summer night, a six-pack of beer in the back. In that moment, the years vanished, and her life was new again.

But now only Brett's life was new. There was no sound but crickets, the soft fall of each footstep on asphalt.

At the bend in the street was the old general store. As Caroline approached it, she could make out the dark shape of a blue postal box.

Caroline opened the metal lid. For a last minute, she considered her choices. Then she dropped the envelope down the chute, consigning Brett's future, and perhaps her own, to the mercies of the U.S. mail.

There was one more thing to do.

Caroline walked to the bridge. Beneath, she could hear the soft murmur of the brook, see her outline reflected in the moonlight.

She took the Magic Marker from her pocket and gently dropped it in the water. It made no sound at all.

ELEVEN

"I THOUGHT I'd deliver these," Caroline said, "in person."

She had found Jackson on the dock of his fishing camp, repairing an outboard motor. He wiped the grease on his jeans.

"What are they?" he asked.

"Subpoenas—five, actually. For your various people and, of course, for Megan Race. Unless you'd prefer that I serve her myself."

Jackson hesitated. "No. I'll make sure she's there."

Caroline studied him. "Somehow you don't sound confident of that."

Jackson took the subpoenas from her hand. He perused them, eyes narrow, and then gazed at the lake, glistening with midmorning sun.

"Megan called me yesterday," Jackson said at length. "She believes that someone broke into her apartment. The night before last."

Caroline raised her eyebrows. "Believes? Either someone did, or they didn't." Her voice turned arid. "Tell me, is there any sign of a break-in? Or is this a particularly rich chapter in Megan's fantasy life?"

Jackson turned to her. "She thinks you sent someone, Caroline. A professional."

Caroline gave a short laugh. "I didn't 'send' anyone."

Jackson looked at her hard now. "I assumed that, Caroline, even without your saying so. But I couldn't help pondering how intently—and how recently—you were pushing me to search her place."

Caroline considered him. "Why do you even believe her? Is she missing anything?"

Jackson frowned. "I don't know. But whatever she thinks happened seems to have spooked her quite a bit."

"Perhaps it's a guilty conscience. Rather like Lady Macbeth." Caroline smiled faintly. "If Megan starts mumbling 'Out, damned spot,' I'd commence to worry."

Jackson placed his hands on his hips, staring down at the dock. "Caroline," he said softly, "what do you know about this?"

"Is that an accusation?"

Jackson looked at her sideways. "Then let me put it another way," he said at length. "As one professional to another, is there something more that I should know?"

For an instant, Caroline wished to talk with him. But this was now impossible; the impulse died, leaving a residue of sadness. "As you so succinctly told me, Jackson, Megan is my problem now." She paused a moment, and then finished softly, "Just have her there, all right? I'd hate for Megan Race to miss her moment in the sun."

"I have a plan," Caroline said quietly, "to deal with Megan."

Brett tilted her head. "But you won't tell me."

Caroline looked at Brett intently. "You asked me once to believe in you. Now I'm asking you to believe in me—at least that I've done everything I can. And that there's a good reason I can't tell you what that is."

Brett slowly shook her head.

It was strange, Caroline thought, how isolated she felt; it was as if she had crossed into a place she could share with no one. "I don't want you to go to prison, Brett. For that to happen is unacceptable to me."

Something in Brett's face changed, showed a quality of openness.

"I believe that," she said at last. "Maybe it's a choice I've made, like people who decide to believe in God. But I've had endless time to think about you, Caroline. I don't believe that you'll ever think I'm innocent. What I feel instead is this incredible acceptance—as if whether I killed James doesn't matter to you, that all you care about is what happens to me now." Brett considered her for a moment. "Is that how lawyers are?"

Caroline smiled faintly. "That's how defense lawyers are—the last redoubt of unconditional love. Other than your parents, of course."

Brett looked at her. "My poor parents," she said finally. "My father acts as if *he's* guilty, and my mother just sits here, trying to say something when there's nothing to say, helpless when I need help most." Her voice took on a resigned bemusement. "It makes me sad for her, in a way."

Caroline was quiet for a moment, and then shrugged. "She really can't do anything. Except, perhaps, figure out some entertainment for prison visits. Which is harder than you may think."

Brett still watched her. "Why is it," she said at last, "that you dislike her so much?"

"Do I?"

"Of course you do. You talk about her with this awful detachment, like she's a slide under a microscope. It's so much worse than anger."

It's so much deeper than anger, Caroline thought. "Betty and I are different, that's all. Our lives went different places."

Brett gazed steadily at Caroline. "So different that no one can be close to you?"

Caroline felt it again—the strange power Brett had to wound her. "Well," she said dryly, "we just have different gifts." And then Caroline realized how much she had sounded like her mother, Nicole.

"I'm sorry," she said tiredly. "I think I missed the confessional part of the eighties—sometimes I suspect that it does more harm than good. But as to your mother and me, we're the only ones who own the problem." She smiled again. "With luck, you can develop new problems of your very own. Which, of course, is what I live for."

Brett was quiet for a moment. "You sound more optimistic than you have."

Once again, Caroline thought of the knife she would never mention. "I feel better," she said at last. "At least in certain ways."

Pensive, Brett brushed back her hair; something in the distracted gesture interrupted Caroline's own distraction.

"You're left-handed, aren't you?"

Brett gave her a quizzical look. "Why—are you?"

"Not at all." Pausing, Caroline wondered at herself. "It's just something you'd think I'd notice."

For some reason, Brett seemed to find that amusing. As if in condolence, her left hand covered Caroline's. "Don't worry," she said with mock solicitude. "You've had a lot on your mind."

For a moment, they smiled together.

· · ·

For two days, Caroline waited.

She worked in her room, making notes from her memory of Megan's entries. Sometimes she would stop, imagining that the manila envelope had ripped open, that the red journal had become separated and then lost.

The afternoon before the hearing, she drove to Masters Hill, stopping at the cemetery.

The afternoon was clear and bright. Caroline stayed for some time, standing near her mother's marker.

What would you think of all this? she asked.

The cemetery was quiet, still. Smiling faintly at herself, Caroline shook her head.

Leaving, she went to her father's house.

Betty was on the porch.

"Are you all right?" she asked.

Caroline stood awkwardly on the lawn. "I'm fine. . . . All that I want to say is that I'll do the best I can for her. And that nothing's going to distract me."

Slowly, Betty nodded. "I believe that. We all do."

Caroline stared at the grass. *Please,* she thought, *say that it arrived.*

"The hearing starts at nine," she said. "I'd suggest you be there by eight-thirty, sitting in the front row. Suit for you, jacket and tie for Larry—the media, you know."

"Of course." Betty paused, as if at a sudden thought. "There's a package for you. For some reason it came here."

Caroline felt her shoulders slump with weariness and relief. "Can you get it?"

Betty disappeared inside. When she returned, she held the manila envelope, eyeing the childish printing with a wary curiosity.

She handed it to Caroline. "Unopened," she said in a flat voice. "As you can see."

Their eyes met. Caroline said nothing, glanced at the package. "Odd," she murmured. "Thank you."

Turning, she crossed the grassy lawn, feeling the weight of the journal in her hand.

Betty's remark, laden with meaning, had triggered something. It took a moment for Caroline to grasp it—the memory of a summer, so many years before, when another woman had filled a journal with the secrets of her heart.

Walking slowly to her car, Caroline drove away.

PART FIVE

SUMMER 1972

ONE

THE FIRST TIME Caroline saw him was the day before her twenty-second birthday.

The course of her life seemed settled—Harvard Law School in the fall; practice in New Hampshire after that; a tacit understanding with Jackson Watts, with whom she shared such comfort that much between them needed not be said. If there was a certain absence of passion or surprise, Caroline took pride that she was so unlike her mother, the servant of mood and impulse. Caroline knew what her future would be and was content with that.

A part of this contentment was the expectation that, after some suitable time on her own, she might practice law with her father. He had talked of stepping down from the bench at sixty, using his name to draw clients and his experience to counsel Caroline as she spread her own name and reputation. With his network of friendships among Republicans, Channing could advance an ambition of his which was also becoming hers—that some governor a few terms down the road would appoint her to a judgeship. True, Caroline and her father had their differences over politics: Radcliffe and her own maturation had not left Caroline untouched, and her views on Vietnam and the women's movement were at odds with his. But these fissures lacked a personal edge: to Caroline, her father was a man she deeply loved, and their arguments were a form of mental exercise. She felt fortunate to have him.

It was her father, oddly enough, who had encouraged her to summer on the Vineyard.

He had not sold the house. But the remaining Masterses had never returned: for the seven summers since her mother's death, they had rented the house to strangers. Caroline had never spoken of Martha's Vineyard.

And then, to her surprise, her father did.

"What would you do," he asked, the Christmas before her graduation, "if you could spend next summer any way you liked? Go back to Europe?"

Caroline shook her head. "I'd spend it sailing." She thought for a moment. "Maybe I can go to the Caribbean for the summer, work a charter boat, and sail on the side."

Her father sat back in his chair, sipping a glass of wine. "Why don't you go to Martha's Vineyard?" he asked quite casually. "That's where you learned to sail, after all, and you'd have a real home."

Caroline studied him. It came to her that her father wished, by some tacit understanding, to place the past and her mother behind them both forever. But the cost of such a summer—confronting yet dismissing the memory of what had happened—struck Caroline hard.

"I don't know," Caroline said. "I mean, what about making money?"

Her father put down the wineglass. "Caroline," he said, "you've worked hard at Radcliffe. Now you're about to graduate with great distinction and enter a career that will require even more of you. It would please me if you were free from work for one last summer." It was as if his eyes, Caroline thought, were saying what he refused to put into words. "Besides," he finished with new firmness, "Betty and Larry could use a respite from academia, and Larry needs a place to write his thesis. I'm sure that a summer there would please them too."

Of course it would, Caroline reflected—the house holds no memories for them. But to say this seemed both childish and selfish. "Let me think about it, Father."

"Of course." He smiled slightly. "By the way, I'll have your catboat sent there from Winnipesaukee. If you like."

A few weeks later, Caroline decided that she would not run away—that she would take her summer on the Vineyard and enjoy it. None of this was spoken between them.

"I'm pleased," her father said. "I'll come down to visit you, of course. But what's best is how good this will be for you and Betty."

It was, Caroline assumed, a reference to something that she did not think her father cared about—that in the unspoken calculus of her family, the phrase "half-sister" captured her relationship to Betty. Neither Caroline nor Betty had known Betty's mother, Elizabeth Brett; Nicole had treated Betty like the stepdaughter she was. Separated from Caroline by age and looks and temperament, Betty seemed to see her as the interloper whose rapport with their father foreclosed any need for an older sister. Five years after Betty's marriage to Larry Allen, Caroline and her sister were less antagonists than strangers.

"I'm sure it will," Caroline said with indifference.

Curiously, this seemed to be true.

Perhaps the key was Larry. Within days of their arrival on the Vineyard, he and Caroline fell into an easy, joking relationship. Betty did not seem to mind—it was as though Caroline's liking for Larry conferred some approval on her. Which was right, in a sense; Caroline could see how devoted she was to him, how much Betty wished for them both to be happy. And there was about Betty a sort of painful honesty, a lack of pretense or vanity—in looks or manner—which Caroline knew she did not possess. The absence of her father, Caroline realized, might free them to be friends.

To Caroline, the one source of tension in those first weeks was Betty's obsessive desire to have a child.

With the detachment of the cocktail party psychologist, Caroline sensed that Betty needed to lavish on some son or daughter all the care she felt she had missed herself. To say this to Betty would too cruelly expose her deepest insecurities. But Caroline saw it as the source of pressure on Larry: they could not truly afford a child; it was plain that Betty was insisting that they try; and, for whatever reason, no Allen baby was forthcoming. To Caroline, the whole subject hovered in some realm between the painful and the comic, with Larry laboring nightly in the field of Betty, some silent part of him praying that the crops would lie fallow until his tenuous career took root.

"Well," Larry murmured to Caroline one evening, drying the last dish, "back to the salt mines."

He said this good-naturedly enough; with his boyish looks, scoop nose, and nimbus of brown hair, there was an air of blithe optimism about him. So that Caroline grinned before answering, "I just hope you're not overdrawn at the bank."

Larry rolled his eyes in mock exhaustion. "This kid—should she ever be born—will be the only baby in history who allows her parents to sleep *more*."

Caroline raised an eyebrow. " 'She'?"

"Oh, yeah—that's part of the deal. 'No boy sperm need apply.' " Larry smiled again. "Don't stay out late, Caro. For lack of a suitable offspring, Betty and I consider ourselves *in loco parentis*."

"Stay out late?" Caroline asked innocently. "With whom?"

Larry's smile was ambiguous. "I don't know yet," he answered.

The ironic memory that came to Caroline, recalling that particular day, was that it seemed so much like any other.

She was sailing back from Tarpaulin Cove, at peace. Her skills were returning quickly, and the afternoon southeaster was steady and benign. She could not sail this route without remembering her mother. But a little discreet checking had told her that Paul Nerheim no longer owned Windy Gates; it struck her that this summer on the Vineyard, in slow, unnoticed increments, had swollen in contentment.

She missed Jackson and her college friends, of course. But she accepted that her college world was gone, and two of her friends had promised to visit in late August. As for Jackson, she was used to being apart from him, often for weeks or even months. She was, she now knew, something of a loner: unlike many of her friends, she had never lost herself in a man. Nor did she ever plan to.

She first saw him at the end of the Masterses' dock—a slim figure, dark-haired from a distance, his hands in his pockets. Though nothing about him looked familiar, he seemed to be waiting for her.

As she docked, gliding perfectly, she tossed him the line.

"Mind doing that?" she asked.

He caught the line and tied it expertly to the dock. Caroline glanced at him; his head was bowed, and Caroline saw only curly hair as jet black as her own.

"Thanks," she said.

He looked up at her then. With something like shock, she saw a young man in his mid twenties with a trace of the beauty that had belonged to Nicole Dessaliers—long lashes, ridged nose, a face of angles so clean that it was like cut glass. His eyes were a startling blue gray.

She turned, unfurling the sails. When she had finished, he was still there.

"Nice boat," he said.

She stepped on the dock, turning to inspect the catboat. "Do you sail?" she asked.

"A little." He paused. "Where did you go?"

Caroline still did not face him. "To Tarpaulin Cove."

"Have you sailed there before?"

"A few times, seven or eight years ago." She hesitated. "I had a bad sail there once, so it seemed like something I should do again."

Next to her, he nodded. "They say these waters are tricky." Pausing, he seemed to study the ocean. "There was a famous sailor from the Vineyard, Joshua Slocum, who sailed around the world at the end of the last century. Then he came back home, went for a sail on a clear day, and vanished. No one ever saw him again."

Caroline turned to him now, her expression sardonic. "I hadn't heard that one, actually. But it's really inspirational."

He grinned; the smile was crooked and, for Caroline, leavened his prettiness with something boyish and engaging. But it did not change the look in his eyes, observant and a little wary.

He extended his hand. "I'm Scott Johnson. I live at the Rubin place next door, caretaking."

His hand was firm, cool. "Caroline Masters," she said.

He nodded again. "I've seen you." He angled his head toward the house. "Do you come here every summer?"

Caroline looked at him more closely; there was about him some combination of reserve and presumption that did not quite seem to mesh. "Not for years," she said finally.

Scott smiled a little. "The Rubins aren't here much, either. But as Fitzgerald once said, the rich are different." He turned to look at the Masterses' white gabled house, perched on the bluff above the beach, soft with the sun of late afternoon. "It's hard to imagine not wanting to be there. At least whenever you could."

Caroline felt a moment's irritation; how, she wondered, had she gotten involved in this conversation? "My mother died here," she said tersely. "Several years ago, in an accident. My family found other places to go."

He shoved his hands back in his pockets. "Sorry," he said. "Ask too many questions, and sooner or later you'll ask a dumb one. It's just that I saw your place was occupied, then saw you and got curious. I guess I've had too little to think about."

It was a fair enough apology and had the effect, Caroline realized, of making it seem rude to just walk off. "How long have you been here?" she asked.

"Since January. Winters are quiet, I found out."

"You're not from here, then."

"No." He smiled. "I just came, and then answered an ad. Never even been before."

There was a carelessness in the way he spoke, Caroline thought. Yet something about him did not match the feckless image of a rolling stone with nowhere he cared to be and no clear place he wished to go.

"Why the Vineyard?" she asked.

"Seemed like a place to sort things out." He checked his watch. "I'm supposed to call the Rubins now. Give them a report." He smiled again. "The rich *are* different, you know. They expect one to be on time."

Abruptly, he left her there—her curiosity a little piqued.

That night, a windstorm rose suddenly.

It battered the house, rattling the doors and the glass in the windows. Awakening, Caroline thought of the sailboat, imagined it slamming against the dock or drifting out to sea. She had not tied the knot herself.

Restless, she put on blue jeans and a down-filled jacket and went out to check the boat.

The howling wind almost knocked Caroline off balance. But the night was brilliant, the stars bright and close in a black endless sky. The world seemed magical and awesome.

The mast of the catboat spiked above the dock. As Caroline walked toward it, reassured, she saw a still, silent figure at the dock's end.

He was gazing out to sea, his hands in his pockets. The wind seemed not to affect him.

Her footsteps were muffled by the wind sweeping toward her. She stopped by the catboat, about twenty feet from him. Though white-caps thudded against the boat, someone had used a second line to lash it tight to the dock. It hardly moved at all.

"It's safe enough," he said.

He had turned to her; Caroline felt that he had sensed her presence for some moments. "Did *you* secure it?" she asked.

"Yup. I heard the wind and wondered about damage."

It was a sailor's concern, delivered in the impersonal tone of someone who cared more about boats than their owners. The thought dampened Caroline's gratitude. "Thanks," she said.

"Oh, sure."

His face was in shadow, and he came no closer. To Caroline, who owned the dock, it was as if she had invaded his private space. But some courtesy seemed required. "Can I make you a cup of coffee?" she asked. "Seeing how we're up?"

From the stillness of the shadows, he seemed to watch her for a moment. "No," he said. "But thanks yourself."

He began to walk, less toward her than past her. Then he stopped, facing her, and Caroline saw again how beautiful he was.

"The boat'll be fine," he said quietly. "Have a good night, okay?"

Once more, he left her there.

TWO

FOR SEVERAL DAYS, she did not see him.

The weather was poor for sailing, rainy or windless. When a fine morning came—bright and crisp and breezy—Caroline packed a cooler and eagerly left the house.

He sat on the beach near the foot of the dock, a mug of steaming coffee cupped in both hands. It was as if, Caroline thought, he knew she would go sailing. But he did not turn to her.

She stopped beside him. "Hi," she said.

He looked up at her, a hint of humor in the gray-blue eyes. "You're a stone fanatic for sailing, aren't you?"

Caroline heard a certain admiration, or, at least, an understanding. She was not used to this—Jackson, with whom she shared so many things, had no great love of sailing. So that she asked without thinking, "Want to go out?"

His eyes became hooded, as if torn between disinterest in her company and the desire to sail. When, once more, he looked directly up at her, there was a smile at one corner of his mouth. "Think I can take the helm a little?"

Suddenly Caroline thought of her lost solitude, spent making conversation with a stranger. But now it was too late.

"Just remember Joshua Slocum," she said.

He seemed to learn the boat quickly, noting its quirks with interest. He sailed with such skill and confidence that not even a certain modesty, in speech and in movement, could conceal how routine this was for him.

To Caroline, it seemed that she was invisible. For minutes, he would run before the wind, wordless in the bright exhilaration of the day. The sense of his enjoyment gave Caroline silent pleasure.

Just when she thought he had forgotten her altogether, Scott turned to her. "Thanks," he said with a smile. "It's been a while."

Caroline took the helm. "Where did you learn to sail like that?"

"On Lake Erie." Scott's smile broadened. "You've heard about the Great Lakes, right? They noticed those at Radcliffe?"

Caroline felt her annoyance sweep *politesse* aside. "Oh, come off it," she responded. "This middle-class boy meets Daisy Buchanan thing." She softened her voice a little. "It's like bad Fitzgerald. And Fitzgerald was bad enough."

Scott did not answer. But she felt his level, reflective gaze, turning toward the water, as a silent acknowledgment. He never tried it again.

They sailed across the Vineyard Sound to the inlet of Lake Tashmoo, mooring in its sheltered waters. Caroline shared her sandwich and a beer.

"Do you ever go into town?" she asked. "Places like the Black Dog or the Square Rigger?"

"Hanging out with college kids, you mean? Drink beer and listen to music?" Smiling, he shook his head. "Already done that, I'm afraid. For four long years."

Caroline studied him. "You didn't just get out, did you?"

"Oh, no." The smile grew smaller, and the hooded look returned. "No, it's been a while since college."

Something in his tone and manner did not welcome further inquiry. But Caroline found that she did not care. "So what have you been doing?" she asked.

He gave her a sudden look of such directness that Caroline felt she had crossed some invisible line. Softly, he said, "Not much of anything. At least anything that's useful."

She was, Caroline realized, determined not to be buffaloed. She met his gaze, raising her eyebrows in silent inquiry.

After a moment, he seemed to sigh, as though she had cornered him. "I may not look it," he said finally, "but I'm a casualty of our nation's foreign policy. I sacrificed so that others might die."

Caroline's eyes narrowed. "You went to Vietnam?"

Scott smiled slightly. "That's just it. I didn't go to Vietnam. Staying out took all I had to give."

Caroline heard a certain irony, directed at himself. "Let me guess," she said. "You're psychotic, in love with a wonderful guy, and suffering from hay fever."

"Hadn't thought of the last one." Scott slowly shook his head, no longer smiling. "It's such a waste, really. Although all *I* had to waste was time."

"How so?"

Scott seemed to collect his thoughts. "I was sliding through Ohio Presbyterian, secure in the knowledge that the worst form of conscription in my sheltered life was compulsory chapel. 'Cause I could always go to graduate school in something . . .

"But 1968 was a magical year. King and Bobby Kennedy got shot, the Russians invaded Czechoslovakia, and, with his last political breath, LBJ took away our grad school deferments. Enabling the class of '68 to occupy a unique wrinkle in time—the first class to lose their deferments, the last class before the lottery. Which has since saved so many lives that it's put new flesh on the old saying 'Life is a lottery.' "

Caroline thought of Jackson. "I know," she said. "My closest friend got number 301."

He gave her a brief, sharp look. "Well," he said, "your friend's a lucky man. One roommate of mine was killed. Another friend went to jail for draft resistance and had a nervous breakdown. As for me, I was forced to discover my passion for teaching." His voice became ironic. "Kindergarten, in an inner-city school. A meeting of minds."

Caroline shrugged; there was something in his flippancy she did not find attractive. "I guess it got you a deferment."

"Only for a year. My predecessor preempted me by miscarrying. The next September, she was back.

"I briefly considered pregnancy myself. But there was no one I really wanted to make pregnant, and I couldn't act alone. So I fell back on more traditional disabilities."

He gazed out at the ocean, wind ruffling his hair. Caroline's sense of him kept changing; beneath the cynicism, she suspected, lurked some deeper feeling. Abruptly, Scott shrugged. "Anyhow, it worked.

After two years of trying, I was saved by a hiatal hernia. Fortunately, it doesn't affect my sailing."

"Then that's good, isn't it?"

Scott slowly shook his head, seemingly less in disagreement than in bemusement. "It was—it is. But I no longer had a purpose. I'd been trying to beat the draft so long I no longer knew who I was. Or what I wanted."

He fell silent. A cool wind kicked up; a seagull passed overhead, circling above them. Hands on hips, Scott stared at the gull with a small smile of puzzlement.

Watching him, Caroline wondered about what she had heard. People, she reflected, are seldom immobilized unless they want to be, and the reasons they give for not doing something are so often illusory. This one, Caroline sensed, was much smarter than he pretended. And then she made her first judgment of Scott Johnson—no ambition.

Caroline hugged herself. "I'm getting cold," she told him.

He gave her a sideways look, somewhere between amusement and understanding. "Let's go back," he said.

They docked the boat, Caroline tossing him the line. "Have time for a beer?" he asked. "You're buying."

There was one beer left in the cooler. With the same underhand motion, Caroline tossed him the cool brown bottle. He caught it in one hand.

They sat on the dock together, legs dangling over the side, passing the beer back and forth. Caroline felt ready to go in.

"So what are you going to do," he asked, "now that you're out of school? Marry number 301?"

Caroline gave him a sharp look; she had mentioned Jackson only as a "friend." "Why? Is that what I'm supposed to do?"

The corner of his mouth turned up, as if this trace of annoyance amused him. "Only if you want to."

"What I 'want' is to have a career in law."

He tilted his head, interested now. "Why law?"

No one, Caroline realized, had ever asked her that. She was suddenly not quite sure if she had ever asked herself. "My father's a judge," she finally answered. "I've grown up with it."

The answer sounded shallow, inadequate. But Scott, who seemed to have a certain edge, surprised her by not showing this. "What kind of law will you do?" he asked.

Caroline hesitated; she could not yet summon a clear picture. "I'll probably start as a prosecutor. Just for the experience."

Scott turned back to the water. "Well," he answered, "it's nice to know what you want."

This time it was Caroline who left.

THREE

"DID YOU SEE the thing about Eagleton?" Larry asked at dinner.

Caroline poured herself more claret. "What thing?"

"He's admitted to undergoing shock therapy." Larry pulled a wry face. "Nothing major—just a little jolt whenever he got depressed."

"Are you serious?"

"He is," Betty put in. "But it was only two or three times, in the sixties. The press is making a big deal out of it."

Caroline stared at them both. "McGovern's screwed," she said finally. "All the Nixon campaign will have to say is that McGovern wants to put this guy one heartbeat away from the atomic button, and people will wonder what happens the next time Eagleton gets his synapses rewired. I mean, does he wake up all optimistic and decide that Tuesday's a terrific day to nuke the Ukraine? And if McGovern dumps his vice-presidential choice, he looks incompetent." She shook her head. "Politics has gotten so depressing. At least to me."

Larry sat back, wineglass cupped in both hands. "What are Jackson's politics, anyhow? I've never gotten a handle on that."

"That's because Jackson's not big on what he calls extremes." Caroline paused. "When someone works his way through school, politics seems like a luxury. He hasn't had a lot of time for sit-ins."

Larry nodded. "I was just curious, that's all. He and Channing seem to get on so well."

Betty, Caroline noticed, had begun watching Larry closely. "Why shouldn't Father like Jackson?" she inquired.

"No reason," Larry answered, still looking at Caroline. "I like Jackson. Best of all, Caroline likes Jackson."

"Well," Betty said finally, "that makes it unanimous. At least in our family."

Betty's remark was meant to be warm, Caroline knew, perhaps defensive of Caroline herself. But something in the conversation made her edgy; perhaps, she reflected, it was simply the sense that she was a surrogate in some buried argument between Larry and Betty.

"Well," she said dryly, "I'll let you know before I marry Jackson. So we can put it up for a vote."

Larry gave her a keen look. As if in diversion, he said, "I wonder what would have happened if Betty had put *me* up for a vote."

"Simple," Caroline answered with mock imperiousness. "I'd have vetoed you before Father even got his chance. You're far too impoverished to be so obnoxious."

Larry grinned, raising his glass. "To all the little people," he intoned, and then glanced at Betty. "Present and future."

Smiling, Caroline touched her glass to both of theirs. Her sister's smile seemed a little forced.

"What was that about?" Caroline asked Larry afterward.

They were alone in the kitchen, washing dishes. Through the window they could see Betty begin one of her solitary walks on the beach. With dusk descending, she was a lone figure framed against tawny sand, darkening water.

Absently drying a wineglass, Larry watched her. "What was what about?"

"The undercurrent at the dinner table. And I'm not referring to our discussion of Eagleton."

Larry smiled. "Or Jackson?"

"That, either."

Larry was quiet for a time. "Your father has floated a trial balloon," he said at last. "To Betty, if not to me. Help in finding me a teaching job somewhere near him. There's a college or three nearby, and some prep schools."

Caroline turned to him. "How do you feel about that?"

"I'm really not sure. Betty and I've done pretty well with our families at a certain distance." He shrugged. "In fairness to Channing, he's only trying to help. As he put it to Betty, his influence pretty much ends at the state line."

"So what do you think you'll do?"

"Oh, it's way premature." His voice came to life again. "My TA job at Syracuse is going pretty well, I think, and my thesis too. Maybe I can hang on at Syracuse or even find something better."

It was an aspect of Larry that Caroline liked—his optimism, a certain generosity of spirit that seemed to encompass others as well as himself. "I can guess," she ventured, "what Betty is thinking. That you could support a baby."

Slowly, Larry looked away. "Just before we left, Caro, Betty and I went in for a battery of tests. They were pretty thorough—I even got to jerk off in a jar. Which I'm sure was better for the jar than it was for me." He paused. "It took them a while, but they got back to us this morning. Looks like there may be a problem."

Caroline put down her dish. "What, exactly?"

"Low sperm count. Not impossibly low, but definitely substandard." He smiled without humor. "When you made that joke about being 'overdrawn at the bank,' you got it right. I may have fucked myself into a negative balance."

All at once, Caroline felt the pressures bearing down on Larry. "But don't you think that's part of it?" she asked. "If people treated getting pregnant like it was some sort of lab experiment, no one would ever have babies. You and Betty have become this pair of hamsters."

"That's kind of what the doctor said. So my new marching orders are to save myself for prime time." He smiled again. "Betty and I should be free for Scrabble tonight, if you're up for it."

Caroline laughed. "Anything to help. As long as it's all in the family."

"Thanks a million." Larry shook out his towel, wiped another dish. "Anyhow, I figure my count will skyrocket once I get a real job. It's all a question of how many sperm you can afford." He paused, as if at another thought. "This guy next door, Caroline. What's his story?"

Caroline felt her eyes narrow. "How would I know?"

"Well, you did take him sailing the other day. So I thought you two also might have conversed."

Caroline handed him the final dish. "He's late-sixties fallout, that's all. Nowhere to go and nothing to do."

Larry gave the dish a few perfunctory wipes. "Seems like kind of a loner. Nice-looking kid, though."

"He's not a kid, Larry—he's only a couple of years younger than you. It's just that he lacks your driving sense of purpose."

Larry considered her a moment, a smile at one corner of his mouth. "So you did find out something about him."

Caroline gave him a long, cool look. "I don't know what's on your mind. But I know what's on mine—nothing. I was just being charitable." She began drying her hands. "Think you can concentrate on Scrabble now? Because I'm absolutely going to kick your ass."

Larry's smile broadened. "Caro," he said, "you're so beautiful when you're annoyed."

FOUR

IT WAS SEVERAL days before she saw Scott Johnson again, and then only because she refused to let Larry tease her out of every casual impulse.

She had returned from sailing, determinedly alone, dismissing any idea of asking him to join her. The sail had been so good that the memory of his enjoyment made her feel a little selfish. Docking the boat, she paused and then went to find him before she gave this more thought than it was worth.

He lived in the boathouse at the end of the Rubins' narrow pier. From the outside, it was a one-floor layout with a deck that faced the ocean. Beneath her, water slapped at its sturdy cement pilings.

Caroline knocked on the door.

She waited for a moment, restless: perhaps she only imagined soft footfalls inside the boathouse. She had begun looking back toward the Rubins' place when the door opened behind her.

She turned to face him. "Hi," she said.

He peered at her through the half-opened door. Caroline realized that she had prepared herself for his reaction—wariness, or indifference, or even amusement. But what she saw was pure surprise.

"I thought I'd give you one last chance," Caroline went on, "to drink beer with college kids."

The door opened a fraction wider. His expression seemed to go through several changes—hesitancy, puzzlement, distress at being caught off guard. But the last look he gave Caroline told her how alone he was.

"Where?" he asked.

· · ·

The Square Rigger was on the outskirts of Edgartown—a dark, smoky room with a wooden bar and walls, and tables jammed with college students working on the island. Scott seemed to have regained the persona she had seen most often—amused, somehow apart. He took in the ambience and people with a single sweeping glance.

"The future leaders of America," he said, "getting plastered on Budweiser. Somewhere among us may be our forty-third President."

His voice was half sardonic, half bemused. "I don't mind that he's plastered on Bud," Caroline retorted. "I just mind that he's a man."

Scott smiled. "Now that you're here, maybe the odds have evened out a little. Shall we find a table?"

They seized one in the corner, just as the live entertainment came on—two guys and a long-haired blond woman, who appeared, like Scott, to be in their mid twenties. Both men had twelve-string guitars; the woman stepped front and center on a low wooden platform and began to belt out "If I Had a Hammer" in a throaty voice almost as good as it was loud.

"Holy shit," Scott whispered to Caroline. "It's Peter, Paul, and Mary."

With a fractional smile, Caroline braced herself for an evening of sarcasm, beginning to regret that she had roused him from his self-imposed exile. And then she saw the brightness in his eyes.

"Drinks are on me," he said. "What can I get you?"

"Scotch."

He seemed to have no trouble catching the eye of the waitress, a southern-accented brunette with a smile, Caroline told herself, that she could never match this side of a lobotomy. When Miss Congeniality came to the table in record time, to be greeted by a dazzling smile from Scott that Caroline had not known he possessed, she was sure that their service would be excellent.

Gazing down at Scott, the waitress bit her lip, as if reluctant to deliver bad news. "I'm sorry," she said, "but I'm going to have to card y'all. The manager says no exceptions."

Scott pulled a face. "Caught with a minor again," he said, and turned reproachfully to Caroline. "I knew you could never pass for twenty-one."

To Caroline, this burlesque was an abrupt, surprising change of character. She smiled politely and produced her driver's license.

The waitress scrutinized it. "Thank you," she said, and turned expectantly to Scott.

"Scotch," he said firmly. "For both of us."

The waitress hesitated. And then Scott produced a smile more incandescent than the first; forgetful of her duties, the girl smiled into his eyes. Glancing back at him, she went to fill their orders.

Somehow Caroline found this both curious and amusing. "Don't you feel a little embarrassed," she whispered to Scott, "encouraging her like that?"

Scott made himself look innocent. "Who says I was encouraging her?"

"I do. I mean, I was only watching, and *I* felt a little bit encouraged."

Scott's smile, directed at Caroline, became that of a coconspirator. "I'll smile," he said, "and we'll drink. It'll help the music some."

They did that, for one round, and then two more.

The ersatz Peter, Paul, and Mary were not too bad, Caroline thought; Scott watched them faithfully, first with what seemed like courtesy, then with a certain interest and even sympathy. No matter how their waitress smiled, he hardly seemed to notice her.

"It ain't easy," he murmured, "singing to a bunch of drunks. Particularly horny drunks."

The fingers of his right hand, Caroline noticed, had begun keeping the beat.

The room was almost sensual now—the laser voice of the blonde, the thrum of guitars, the smell of smoke and bodies close together, swaying or whispering or smiling at each other. Scott ordered a fourth Scotch. His face was becoming almost careless; he seemed to be partly with Caroline and partly in some other place, perhaps ten other places, bars and parties and student apartments in a time when he had, Caroline found herself guessing, liked himself a little better. On the platform, the blonde was getting into it, twitching and swaying with the beat until each song seemed more sexual than the last.

"I'd love to watch her," Scott murmured wryly, "doing 'Onward Christian Soldiers.' "

His expression was amiable and not unkind. This was not sarcasm, Caroline realized—more an amused acceptance of the singer's humanness that somehow embraced everyone in the room. It struck

Caroline that, unlike many people, Scott might actually become nicer when he drank. The thought surprised her.

When she turned to him again, he was still keeping the rhythm, a half smile on his face. He seemed oblivious to everything but where he was. All at once, Caroline was glad to have invited him.

They stayed until the place closed up.

They found Scott's car in the parking lot, a beat-up VW bug with scrapes in its black paint job.

"Want me to drive?" Caroline asked.

It seemed to interrupt Scott's mood, make him conscious of himself again. He paused to contemplate the question. "I'm okay," he said.

Caroline hesitated. It was not too far to Eel Pond, she told herself, and Scott did not have the truculence of someone from whom she should grab the keys. She got in without argument and buckled her seat belt.

Scott started the car, whistling soundlessly to himself.

They took Beach Road in amiable silence, the shadows of trees by the road vanishing behind them. He was driving a little fast, Caroline thought—not out of control, but braking and accelerating to a kind of inner rhythm, taking the feel of the bar home with him like something he did not care to lose.

The car gained speed.

Caroline felt her tension grow, separate them. She did not need to ask herself the reason.

Five more minutes, she told herself. The road was empty; his driving—if fast—seemed good enough to get them home. It was clear that he knew the road.

She saw him flinch just before the first swirling stab of red flashed in the rearview mirror.

His reaction, she thought, was almost otherworldly. He did not curse or speak or even show emotion; instead there was the sense that he had become someone else again, a sober man, a series of orderly thoughts marching through his brain as he slowed the car to a perfect stop. Only Caroline could see how pale he had become.

The patrol car stopped behind them. Still Scott said nothing.

The beam of a flashlight cut through the rearview mirror.

Narrow-eyed, Scott took a deep breath, straightened in his seat, and then got out to meet the cop. He seemed to have forgotten that Caroline was there.

Instinct told her to get out with him.

The cop was a faceless form behind a flashlight, aimed at Scott's intent eyes and still body. As Caroline circled the car, the cop said evenly, "I'll be needing your license, son."

There was something familiar about the voice, the way the cop's dark figure held itself, heavy in the shoulders. Scott made no move to take out his wallet.

All at once, Caroline thought of the waitress, asking for identification.

The cop's voice was harder now. "Hand over your license, please."

Scott glanced toward the car. Suddenly, Caroline felt a delicate balance, seconds from being broken.

Instinctively, she stepped between them.

The cop's flashlight made her blink. "Hello," she said.

She saw his head tilt, peering at her from behind the beam.

"Caroline? Caroline Masters?"

"Yes," she answered. "I'm Caroline."

The cop stepped forward, face suddenly caught in his own headlights. His voice was hesitant. "I'm Frank Mannion."

The memory came swift and strong; the image of her mother's dark hair, swirling in the water, hit Caroline in the pit of her stomach.

"I remember," she answered quietly.

She saw his shoulders relax. In the light, his face was a little pouchier but still pleasant, his red hair gray at the temples. He took off his patrolman's hat, wiping his forehead, and stood closer to her. His voice became gentle. "I always wondered what happened with you."

"Nothing, really." Her own voice, Caroline was grateful to hear, seemed close to normal. "My father and I made it through, and I'm going to law school next year. Things turned out all right."

Slowly, he nodded. Caroline could feel Scott's gaze; something in his stillness made her throat tight.

"And you?" she asked Mannion. "How did your family adjust to the Vineyard?"

He looked surprised. "You remember that too?"

"I remember everything about that day. Including how nice you were."

Mannion glanced toward Scott, awkwardly shifting his weight. "Well, we're all fine, thanks. My oldest just graduated high school, and soon he's off to Boston College." He interrupted himself. "It's been good here."

Caroline stuck her hands in her pockets. "I'm glad it worked out."

Mannion nodded, and then he seemed to remember Scott. "Mind coming over here?" he asked.

Scott hesitated and then walked toward Mannion. His movements seemed strangely weary—the loss of adrenaline, Caroline thought.

"Do you *have* a license?" Mannion asked.

Scott did not answer. Caroline felt herself tense.

Mannion's tone was soft now, an inquiry. "Son?"

Slowly, Scott slid his wallet from the back pocket of his jeans. He fumbled with it and finally produced a square of paper.

Mannion gazed at it and looked up at Scott. "You're a ways from home," he said at last. "Where you living now?"

Scott's own voice was a murmur. "Eel Pond. I watch the Rubin place."

Mannion appeared to study him. "Then do me a favor, *and* yourself. Don't drive like you've been drinking." He angled his head toward Caroline. "Not with her, or without her, either. Now give me your keys."

As if in a trance, Scott held them out.

Mannion took the keys and gently placed them in Caroline's hand. "Are you all right to drive?" he asked her.

"I'm fine." Caroline felt a surge of relief. "Thank you."

Mannion did not acknowledge this. "Drive carefully, Caroline. And good luck in law school."

Silent, he returned Scott's license and walked back to his car.

Caroline and Scott got inside the VW, not talking. She worked the clutch until she had its feel, and drove cautiously away.

Mannion's patrol car followed them until they reached the turn for Eel Pond. Its headlights flashed past, then the red taillights, and the policeman was gone.

In the passenger seat, Scott touched his eyes.

They passed the Rubins' house, parking at a turnaround above the water. The windshield filled with black ocean, black sky. Caroline could still feel the pounding of her heart.

Softly, Scott asked, "What happened back there?"

"I think I saved your ass." Caroline glanced at him sharply. "From a speeding ticket, at least."

Scott was quiet for a time. "It was something about your mother. The accident you mentioned."

Caroline stared through the windshield. "She was driving." Her voice was flat, emotionless. "When it happened, only the two of us were here. Officer Mannion took me to identify her body."

"And she'd been drinking."

"Yes." Caroline exhaled. "It was eight years ago, all right? I got over it."

Her tone was more curt than she'd intended. "No, it's not all right," he answered. "With you or with me."

His voice was soft with self-disgust. "Do you want to feel sorry for yourself by yourself," Caroline said at last, "or do you feel like making me coffee?"

For a moment, Scott seemed to hesitate. His eyes studied her with an intensity she had not seen before.

"Come on in," he said. "Please."

FIVE

HAND ON THE knob, Scott seemed to hesitate, and then he opened the door.

Inside was a single large room with a hardwood floor and wainscoting and a kitchen along one wall. Glancing around, Caroline saw that the room conveyed no sense of him.

He kept it neat and spare—a couch, a coffee table, a seascape on the wall, everything picked up. The one thing that must be his—and now this did not surprise her—was a battered guitar leaning in one corner.

"Do you play that?" she asked.

"A little." He smiled. "Not well enough to match this evening's entertainment."

Caroline turned to him. "The bar? Or the police?"

"Take your pick," Scott answered, and went to the stove.

He would not explain himself, Caroline realized; perhaps there was nothing to explain. From over his shoulder, Scott asked, "How do you like your coffee?"

"Strong and black. Like for final exams."

Caroline drifted to the window. Beneath them, she heard the ebb and flow of Nantucket Sound; the sensation was not unlike standing on the prow of a ship. She remembered Scott on the night of the storm, gazing out to sea.

"Where do you sleep?" she asked.

He bent over the coffeepot. "On the porch. There's a screen to frustrate bugs, and it gets the breeze at night."

He filled two mugs of coffee. As he gave her one, his hand brushing the back of hers, Caroline's skin tingled. It startled her: the shared tension with the police seemed to have created a current that did not exist before. She was keenly aware of standing close to him.

Caroline turned away. "Can I see the porch?"

His small smile seemed part inquiry, part amusement. "I guess it's all that's left," he answered, and opened a door near the stove. Caroline stepped out onto the shadowed porch.

The steady soughing of the wind and the sea came through the screen. The air was warm and heavy and smelled of salt.

Caroline paused, breathing deeply, and then Scott switched on a lamp.

She turned. Out of the darkness materialized a cot, a nightstand stacked with books, a chair facing the water. There was a pen and what appeared to be a half-finished letter beneath the books, the first two of which, somewhat to Caroline's surprise, were *One Day in the Life of Ivan Denisovich* and Jack Newfield's biography of Robert Kennedy. She found herself wondering just who it was he was writing to.

He waved her to the chair. "Have a seat—I'm used to being horizontal."

She had a sudden image, Scott lying on the bed, and then the few things that were his own seemed to ache with his aloneness. Scott stretched out on the cot, mug cupped in his hands. "I didn't really thank you, did I?"

"For what?"

"For trying to protect me from the law." He seemed to watch her. "Funny work for a future prosecutor."

Caroline shrugged. "It just seemed like too good a night to end with getting busted."

Scott smiled a little. "Except for that, it *was* good. My debut in Vineyard society."

Caroline paused, a question forming, and then decided not to ask it. "Except for your driving," she said wryly, "it was a real success. I even know where you can find a date."

Scott watched her over his smile. "Not interested," he said.

"Oh, well."

There was an awkward silence.

"Speaking of society," Scott said, "who else is over there? So far I've counted a skinny guy who doesn't come out much, and a woman who walks the beach alone. But no one who looks like the patriarch."

This somewhat cavalier summary made Caroline bridle. And it

struck her how much he had seemed to glean from very little—the predominance of her father; her relationship to Jackson.

"The 'skinny guy,'" she answered tartly, "is my very nice brother-in-law, Larry, who's working on a Ph.D. The woman is my sister, Betty—who happens to like nature. As for the 'patriarch,' as you put it, he's coming to inspect his holdings later."

He grinned, refusing to be discouraged. "So what do the three of you do all day?"

"Oh, we perform weird and secret rituals. Play Scrabble, argue about the election." Her tone grew solemn, hushed. "Sometimes Larry and I wash dishes. In the dark . . ."

His grin became a smile, perhaps a little chastened. "Sorry. Families interest me, that's all. I haven't seen mine in a while."

This snippet of biography sounded genuine. Her sense of him kept shifting; at one moment he was flippant, the next, a lonely person with people he seemed to care for.

"What does your family come with?" she asked.

"The all-American package." He gazed at his mug. "Two parents who still like each other. A brother in college who's not too bad. And a sixteen-year-old kid sister, who was born so late that I never got over the fact that she was cute. Still is, unless she's eaten too much junk food."

Beneath the observation, offhand and affectionate, Caroline heard an undertone of regret. "So why don't you go home?" she asked. "You don't have to live in exile just to feel lost."

For an instant he gave her a funny look—vulnerable, caught—and then his gaze grew veiled. "Losing yourself," he said, "is not as simple as you think."

The comment puzzled her. Scott looked away; she found herself studying the unfinished letter on the nightstand, and then the book on Robert Kennedy. She nodded toward the book. "Did you work for him?" she asked.

"Uh-huh. I sacrificed a few weeks of college to the Indiana primary." He seemed to study his mug again. "The night he was shot was the worst thing I've experienced that didn't happen to me personally. Sometimes I wonder how many other people died because of it. Or just lost hope."

Scott was not looking for a response, Caroline saw—he could have been talking to himself. It made her quiet: as wrong as this might be, as lacking in what her father would call perspective, Scott seemed to feel, as Caroline sometimes did, that something irretrievable had been lost.

"I was a little young for that," she said at last. "Later, it hit me that maybe our best leaders are dead and without them all the rest of us are slowly drifting apart."

Gazing at his coffee cup, Scott did not answer. And then he looked up, giving her a faint smile that mingled irony and kinship. "We're a sad pair, aren't we. Nothing to look forward to but the rest of our lives."

"Like sailing trips and graduate school. If you can ever figure out which graduate school you want."

Scott shrugged, silent. Perhaps, Caroline thought, he was simply glad to have backed away from seriousness. But the moment had left something behind that was not there before; once more, she was aware of the ocean sounds, the smell of salt, of him. And that, until tonight, he had pretended to be someone nowhere close to who he was.

As if sensing her thoughts, he shifted subjects again. "Your brother-in-law," he said. "What's his Ph.D. in?"

"English. From Syracuse."

"And Betty?"

"Wants to have a baby."

Scott's look was quizzical. "Is your father paying the freight?"

"Not that I've heard."

"Ouch."

Caroline pondered whether some explanation was more, or less, fair to Betty. "Betty's nice, really. But I think somehow she felt displaced, and now she's got an image of family that goes deeper than for other people." Caroline paused. "The problem is that it's making her a little crazy. Like everyone from here to Mongolia is pregnant except for her."

Scott gave a comic wince, and then inspiration crossed his face. "Wait," he said, got up, and went inside.

He came back with his guitar.

"What's this?" Caroline asked.

He sat on the edge of the bed, assuming a pose of great seriousness. And then, eyes suddenly limpid, he gazed at Caroline and began to sing in a mock-soulful voice.

" 'She's having my ba-by . . .' "

Caroline grinned. "Oh, no . . ."

Scott seemed undeterred. In a parody of blissed-out rapture, he closed his eyes. His features in the pale light looked sculpted, fine.

"She's having my ba-by.
What a lovely way to tell the world she loves me . . ."

Caroline burst out laughing.

With a look of wounded dignity, an artist misunderstood in his own time, Scott sang each heartfelt line.

"Could have swept it from her life but she wouldn't do it . . .
She's having my ba-by."

The lyrics, Caroline thought, were preposterous. What silenced her was how good he was.

Only when he was finished did Scott open his eyes again.

His sudden gaze startled her. "My favorite song," she told him. "It captures my whole worldview."

Scott grinned, giving her a mock bow.

Caroline sat with her elbows resting on her knees, face cupped in her hands, looking at him. Quietly, she said, "You're really good, you know?"

He tried to make a joke of it. "Just good enough to become a bad lounge act. 'Scott Johnson, coming to a Holiday Inn near you.' "

He said it lightly, smiling. And then their eyes met, and they both no longer smiled. In that instant, Caroline sensed that he was more than lost or sad or sweet, felt that something in each of them called to the other, and that he felt it, too.

Caroline did not know what it was. She knew only that—in a fleeting, imperishable moment—something changed for her.

Scott put down the guitar. He stood, gazing at her, silent. There was only a few feet between them.

Walking toward him, Caroline saw nothing but his eyes, felt nothing but her own pulse.

His mouth was warm.

Where had she been? some part of Caroline wondered. Who had she been? Her arms went tight around him.

Slowly, gently, Scott pulled back, forehead resting against hers. Only then did she think of Jackson.

"Jesus," Scott murmured.

So he felt it too. This strange pull, yet the instinct to resist.

Her voice was quiet. "I'd better go."

She went to the door, hardly aware of her own movements. He did not try to stop her.

She turned in the doorway. Scott stood by the bed, gazing at her as if at something he could not have.

As though in consolation, Caroline said, "Tomorrow we'll go sailing, okay?" And then, hearing herself, she softly added, "If you want to."

He watched her, not moving. "I want to," he said at last.

SIX

THEY WENT SAILING the next morning, and the two days after that.

It was different now. There was a new gentleness between them, an unspoken affinity, although, for Caroline, something about Scott remained elusive, just out of reach. At odd moments, she felt them try to read the other's thoughts. But neither crossed their unspoken line. He never touched her.

He was always ready for her company. They hiked in the hills near Menemsha; went to hear Tom Rush sing and play guitar; swam in the freshwater pond at Long Point, the rough surf of the Atlantic a mere hundred feet away. Sometimes it seemed close to effortless; Scott knew the grace of silence, of letting Caroline think her own thoughts. His sarcasm now was sparing, turned solely on himself; he treated Caroline with respect, as if coming too close might harm them. The days fell gently, one upon the other, until time seemed not to matter. There was nothing to tell Jackson.

Perhaps, Caroline later thought, Scott knew more than she did. But for her—almost to the moment when it happened—the night that changed this seemed like any other.

The idea of eating lobster on the beach was hers.

Scott had smiled. "You mean like Faye Dunaway and Steve McQueen in *The Thomas Crown Affair*?"

Caroline shook her head. "Did you ever wonder how they got the lobster pot in his dune buggy? I'm talking take-out lobster. From the Homeport."

Scott rolled his eyes. "Take-out lobster? Where's your New England work ethic?"

"Dead and buried," she answered firmly. "Come on."

They drove to Edgartown for bread and a bottle of chilled wine. Caroline found bread; looking for Scott at the package store, she saw him eyeing the California Chardonnay with a certain practiced leisure, as if such a grave decision should not be rushed.

"Hard to choose?" Caroline said from behind him.

He turned to her, surprised. "Only when you don't know wine," he said, and seemed to pluck a bottle at random. "Let's take a chance on this one."

By some unspoken consensus, Caroline always drove now, taking her time. They reached Menemsha a little before eight.

The fishing village was quaint and quiet—the trawlers were in, the beach was almost deserted, and the sun was slipping beneath the distant line where ocean met a darkening sky. The gentle putt of an outboard motor echoed in the harbor.

All that was open was the Homeport restaurant. People wandered in and out of the wood-frame building, a few tourists on the deck watched the sunset over dinner. Caroline led Scott to the take-out window and ordered two lobster dinners. Patient, he waited with the wine and a woolen blanket tucked beneath his arm until their food was ready, and then they set out to find the right spot on the beach.

There was no hurry. The night felt close and warm; the moon, slowly replacing the sun, cast a first glow on the waves. Caroline felt the luxury of time.

They walked the beach until the lights of Menemsha were far behind, and they were alone.

Scott broke their silence. "I was looking at your catboat the other day. The dinghy's sprung a leak—you should have it fixed pretty soon. And one of the ribs in the hull looks weak."

Caroline smiled at this: among the bonds between them, she sometimes thought, was the proprietary interest he had taken in the catboat. "After I leave," she asked, "would you look after my boat for me? I might decide to keep it here."

Scott stopped, facing the water. "If I'm here," he said at length. "But I don't think I will be."

Caroline turned to him, puzzled by her sadness. Perhaps it was the impermanence of things: as days went by, and the summer grew more precious to her, Scott and the Vineyard had come together in her mind. She could not quite imagine this place without him.

Together, they spread the blanket.

Caroline laid out the bread and the lobster; Scott took a corkscrew to the wine, filled two glasses, and handed one to Caroline. He seemed about to propose a toast, and then looked at her again.

"Is something wrong?" he asked.

Caroline made herself busy with the blanket. "Oh, I don't know," she said at last. "I think in some stupid way I imagined you still here when I came back. Like I'm entitled to arrange every corner of my world just the way I want it."

"And populate it too?"

"I suppose."

Scott studied her. "I guess that happens when things seem good. But they always change. It's a little hard to imagine you, your husband, your kids, and me all going sailing together." He smiled, as if to remove any sting. "For openers, you'll need a bigger boat."

Caroline smiled back. "How many kids do you think I want?"

Scott grinned. "Don't know. Just more than I think I want." He raised his glass. "To population control."

Caroline touched her glass to his and sipped. The wine, she realized, was the best she had ever tasted.

She settled back on her elbows. "So what will you do?"

"I don't have a clue—I just know I can't stay here." He gazed out at the water. "Maybe it's the flip side of what you were saying. That when you go off next month, to begin your real life, the island will seem a little lonely." He gave a dismissive shrug. "There are other places—I'm not that big on nostalgia."

She turned to watch him. There was something very still about him, as if he were holding some moment in his mind. And then, with the sudden realization that she knew parts of him by instinct, came the certainty that he was lying to her but not to himself: that he carried pieces of the past within him, and that this summer would become one.

"Well," she said, "we've got the time we've got. Which hasn't been so bad."

He turned to her, smiling. "Not bad at all. Unless the lobster's cold."

She spread out paper plates and drawn butter. The lobster shells were already cut; all they had to do was eat.

The night was calm, peaceful. The water lapped at their feet; a faint breeze carried the smell of sea and salt. Neither of them spoke, or needed to.

"Remember when you were a kid," he said at last, "and camped out?"

Caroline smiled to herself. It was just right, she realized: the sense of being away from things and yet quite safe, with night closing around you. She knew that Scott required no answer.

All at once, Caroline's senses opened.

She felt everything come together. Felt the breeze on her skin and hair. Saw the moon-streaked ripple on the water, the stars grow bright and close. Felt Scott lying next to her, as lost in the night as she was.

Time seemed to stop.

She did not know how long they lay there, not moving. She knew only what the night had become, and would not have been without him. Until, finally, she found a way to say this.

"Have you ever had a perfect day?"

Scott did not turn. "No," he said at last. "But I've had a perfect hour. Now."

Hesitant, Caroline reached to cover his hand with hers.

He turned to her then, looking into her face. Slowly, he reached out and touched her hair.

There was no mistaking what she saw in his eyes.

"Yes," Caroline heard herself murmur.

He could not seem to move. And then, gently and firmly, Caroline kissed him.

She felt his lips against her face, her neck. Closing her eyes, she held him.

Now it was all feeling. His mouth, slow and unhurried. His lean, hard body against hers. The way his hands seemed to belong wherever they touched. The beating of her own heart.

He slid back from her, and then Caroline felt his fingers on the top button of her blouse.

She opened her eyes.

As he undid the first button, they gazed at each other.

She lay there, silent, as he did this. His eyes did not move until the blouse lay beside them.

Caroline wore no bra.

Gently, she took his head in her hands and cradled it between her breasts.

After a time she felt his mouth on her nipples, her stomach. Felt him unzip her jeans.

She arched her back, helping him.

When she was naked, she lay there uncovered, watching as he undressed. His body was slim, muscular.

He knelt, bowing his head. His mouth grazed her thighs, moving toward the center of her.

Caroline closed her eyes again.

Now it all felt new to her. His tongue. The feel of his body, different from Jackson's, as she opened her legs for him. The wanting as he entered her. The urgency as she moved with him, this strange, blood-rushing need . . .

She could not stop now.

With the first tremor of her body, Caroline cried out his name. For there was no one to hear her but him.

She lay in his arms, weak and shaken, the warm feel of his own release inside her.

Neither spoke. It was as if their minds were absorbing what their bodies already knew.

What does this mean? Caroline wondered. *Anything?*

Or everything?

"Was this just another perfect hour?" she asked.

Silent, Scott pulled her close.

They could not stop.

Sometimes all it needed was for Caroline to look at him. They would go to the boathouse, hardly saying a word, and stand inches apart as they undressed. She spent each night with him.

Each time only fed his hunger for her.

It was as if, some part of Caroline thought, he wished so desperately to talk to her—about what, she was not sure—that he could bear his silence only by making love with her. Sometimes, at night, she would hear him pacing in the next room, so as not to awaken her. Her senses were alive with some unspoken thing.

But when she tried to say this, Scott merely smiled. "I just wish I were that interesting," he said.

She could not bring herself to call Jackson—the thought of lying, or the truth, were both too painful. And the only truth she understood was that she had a lover who could make her feel what Jackson could not.

If wasn't that she did not try to understand: the Caroline who wanted Scott so desperately was not some other person. But her accustomed world seemed far away. In this new world, Caroline was alone: not even Scott—especially not Scott—could help her. Even the world of Martha's Vineyard was divided: quite deliberately, it seemed, Scott deflected any suggestion of spending time with Betty and Larry. His only interest was in Caroline herself.

Why did she want him, Caroline wondered, and what did she want from him?

That Betty and Larry said nothing only increased her isolation: their silence told her that the change in her, her nocturnal comings and goings, were so marked that it made them cautious and confused. Perhaps only her mother, Caroline told herself miserably, might have understood.

And yet with Scott—moment to moment—Caroline felt happy.

One morning, she awakened to find him still asleep, the smile of some pleasant dream playing on his mouth. She watched until he awoke.

"You were smiling," she told him.

The waking Scott smiled again. "Was I? I must have been teaching you how to sail."

She kissed his forehead. "No," she said. "I was teaching you how to drive."

Caroline was still smiling when she crossed the threshold of her father's home.

On the kitchen table was a note in Betty's coiled cursive.

Father called, it said. *When you get the chance, please call him.*

SEVEN

WHEN CAROLINE called her father, his tone was careful, neutral; he asked about her sailing, her plans for the remaining weeks, what she had heard from Jackson. Only at the end did he mention that he was coming earlier than planned—the next day, to be precise.

When Caroline put down the phone, she went to find Betty.

She was sitting on the porch, drinking coffee. Glancing up at Caroline, she studied her expression and then said, "So he told you he's coming early."

Caroline stared at her. "What's this about?"

Betty exhaled. "Caroline, we haven't said a word to him. He's called several times lately, asking to talk to you, and each time one of us covered for you. But Father's not a fool."

"I am twenty-two."

Betty nodded in acknowledgment. "I understand. But you have to imagine this from his point of view—a daughter who's been stable and predictable, with a boyfriend at home, suddenly can't be found at pretty much any hour of the night. Don't you think maybe you'd be a little concerned?"

"It's my life, isn't it?"

Betty's brow knit. "Even Larry and I have worried a little—we don't know this boy at all, you hardly seem to know him except to spend the night with, and even when you're with us now, you're not." Betty paused, voice softening. "Would you mind terribly, Caroline, telling me a little about what's going on?"

Caroline felt her defensiveness die. She sat in the canvas chair next to Betty, gazing at the morning sunlight on the water. "I wish I knew."

Betty sipped her coffee. "Well, he is attractive."

Caroline shook her head. "It's not just sex." She paused, trying to find words. "It's like I know so much more about him than what he tells me."

Betty seemed to reflect. "Has it occurred to you," she said finally, "that maybe there's nothing more to him than what he tells you—a rudderless guy without any deep interests but sailing? And that for reasons you haven't coped with, you're projecting your own needs on someone who's a pretty blank screen?"

Though Betty's voice was not unkind, Caroline found that the words stung. "I don't think I need a shrink, Betty."

"Really." Betty's voice was level and unimpressed. "How are things with Jackson?"

Caroline looked away. "I don't think I can talk about it now."

Betty considered her. "Then let me make one request, as your older sister: that you think about it. And that, while Father's here, you cool things off with Scott a little. There's no point in upsetting Father over something you don't understand yourself."

It was good advice, Caroline knew, and Scott did not disagree.

"Do what you need to do," he said. "Honestly, I understand."

"But we've only got four weeks left. And he's staying for a week."

Scott shrugged. "He's been your father for twenty-two years. And, pretty clearly, the main influence in your life." He took her hand. "I don't expect you to rock that boat, and I really don't want you to. Certainly not on my account."

Why, Caroline wondered, did his understanding make her feel so diminished?

Perhaps, she reflected, it bespoke the limits of her importance to him. Or perhaps it was simply that—like Betty—Scott accepted so easily that Caroline's first obligation was to put Channing Masters at ease.

She did not take Betty's advice.

For the first few days, Caroline spent most of her time with her father, doing many of the things—sailing, hiking, riding rented bikes—that she usually did with Scott. Even in his early fifties, Channing Masters was vigorous and fit, and he took keen pleasure in being outdoors in the company of his youngest daughter, his unspoken favorite. Whatever his concerns were, he kept them to himself, as if the time that Caroline gave him was reassurance enough.

Her occasional absentmindedness seemed not to bother him. He was himself sometimes distracted by memories of Nicole, Caroline sensed; when he lapsed into silence, gazing at the water, Caroline could almost feel the hurt her mother had inflicted on him. As for Caroline, her pretense of normality seemed to satisfy him that nothing was so wrong that she need confront it.

Caroline found that she disliked herself for this. But not nearly as intensely as she missed Scott.

On the third night of her father's visit, she came to the boathouse.

As she approached the porch, Scott startled awake. He sat bolt upright, staring around him. And then she saw him freeze.

"Caroline?" he asked.

His voice was tight. "It's me," she answered.

In the dark, she saw the shadow of his body relax.

She went to the side of his bed, placing the kit that held her diaphragm on the nightstand. "I just missed you," she said.

Gratefully, Scott reached for her.

But it was not the same. Caroline was used to bringing the rhythm of their days to their nights alone; now their lovemaking felt furtive, hurried, something divorced from the rest of her life. Some childish part of her imagined her father breaking in on them: in an odd, chilling moment, she recalled the image of her mother turning to face Caroline as she lay beneath Paul Nerheim.

Scott seemed to sense this. Gently, he said, "It's a little like high school, isn't it? Sneaking down to the family room after the folks have gone to bed."

Caroline lay in the dark, listening to the waves splash beneath them, feeling the cool breeze across her naked skin. "Have you missed me at all?"

Scott was quiet for a time. "Quite a lot, actually." He paused, as if trying for a certain fatalism. "It's just that you've got a father to pacify, and I can't treat that like a tragedy—'Romeo and Juliet at the Beach.' Especially when all that's at stake is your time until law school."

Why, Caroline thought, did she imagine a bitterness buried beneath the offhand realism? And who might he be bitter at?

"What do you want me to do?"

"Nothing." He kissed her neck. "Don't worry about me, Caroline. I've got no need to be a character in your family minidrama. Even if it's a bit part."

In the darkness, she could not see his face.

The next morning, she told her father that she would be sailing with a friend.

Channing raised his eyebrows in pleasant inquiry. "Oh," he asked. "Who?"

"The caretaker from next door. He's quite a good sailor."

"Does he have a name?"

Caroline smiled. "Yes," she said, and went to find Scott.

When Scott opened the door, he did not smile at all.

"How did you explain me?" he asked.

"There's nothing to explain. Are you coming, or am I going out alone?"

Scott gave her an inscrutable look, hesitant, and then took his jacket from the peg beside the door. With a kind of rueful affection, he asked, "Are you familiar with the term 'willful'?"

Why, Caroline wondered, did so many moments—even words— now summon images of her mother? Seeing her expression, Scott's smile vanished.

"I guess you are," he said.

For the next two days, without explaining herself to anyone, Caroline spent time with Scott.

He seemed almost to stand outside their time together, watching her. "Has it occurred to you," he said softly, "that you're using me?"

They were drinking beer beside the boat, after a long day's sail. "Using you for what?" she said.

"To define your own territory."

Caroline gave him a long, level look. Quietly, she said, "When you can think of something better I can use you for, Scott, please let me know."

Their time, Caroline thought with sudden pain, was running out.

That night, she came to him again.

She left before dawn, lost in the feel of him, the chaos of her own thoughts. And then she noticed the dim light on the porch of the Masters house.

She stopped on the beach, gazing up. Her father's shadow stood in the semidark, still and silent, watching her.

For a moment, in unspoken acknowledgment, neither moved.

And then Caroline resumed her walk, crossing the beach and climbing the stairs to the bluff, to face him. She could feel her heart race. But when she reached the bluff, the light was off, and he was gone.

EIGHT

THE NEXT MORNING, at the breakfast table, her father was silent.

Caroline sipped her coffee, trying to look composed. She had not slept.

Larry seemed quite oblivious, chatting on about his thesis. But Betty, Caroline saw, kept looking from her father to her.

When Caroline rose to help clear the dishes, her father raised a hand. "Caroline," he said. "A word with you, please."

Larry glanced at him, newly aware. Betty touched Larry's arm and motioned him to the kitchen.

"Yes?" Caroline said.

Her father folded his hands in front of him. His voice was quite calm. "I couldn't help but notice that you spend a good deal of time with the boy next door, as it were. Before I go, I rather think I'd like to meet him."

Their eyes locked. "Why, Father?"

"Because it seems polite to acknowledge your friends. And because, curiously, Betty and Larry claim not to know him." His gaze grew pointed. "Which strikes me, whoever is at fault, as more than a little uncivilized. Wouldn't you agree?"

Caroline felt cornered; her father knew, or guessed, who was "at fault," and she had no excuse for Scott's reclusiveness. The subtext of the night before lay silently between them.

Caroline shrugged. "All that I can do, Father, is ask. . . ."

"Dinner?" Scott raised his eyebrows. "What are this man and I going to say to each other? And why does it matter to you?"

"Because he knows how it is with us."

Scott shook his head. "But aren't you the one you have to answer to?" he asked.

Caroline crossed her arms. "You'd think you were crossing the Rubicon instead of facing one middle-aged man across the dinner table." She paused, hearing herself, and then said softly, "Sometimes people just do things for other people. Please, don't embarrass me."

Folding his hands, Scott propped them beneath his chin and stared out at the ocean, pensive. "All right," he answered. "If it really means that much to you."

The first hour had a deceptive calm.

To Caroline, Scott seemed another person—respectful to her father; amiable and pleasant to Betty and Larry; attentive to Caroline without overdoing it, so that the impression left was that he valued her. He helped Betty in the kitchen, talked to Larry about academic politics.

He seemed wholly at ease, as if a polite dinner with a privileged family was second nature to him. Caroline saw Larry and Betty warm to him, and him to them. If he minded Channing Masters' inquiries about his background—and Caroline was somehow certain that he did mind—he gave little sign.

With cocktails over, they sat down at the dinner table. "Is it true," Scott was asking Larry, "about publish or perish?"

"Depends on the school." Larry smiled. "Think there's a spot for me at Ohio Presbyterian?"

Scott seemed to reflect. "There should be. My last English course was more like a séance than a seminar. Even the dead dropped out." His voice turned wry. "The professor had published extensively."

From the end of the table, Channing watched him. "Were you an English major?" he asked.

Scott shook his head. "History. Twentieth-century European, mostly. It wasn't very cheerful."

Channing did not smile. "History seldom is. And seldom will be. It's in our nature, I'm afraid."

Caroline turned to her father. "That's rather Hobbesian, isn't it?"

Channing seemed to consider her. "I don't believe in the infinite perfectibility of man, Caroline. If I ever did, I stopped. In Germany."

Caroline looked to Scott. "Father served with the Nuremberg tribunal. As an investigator."

"Out of which," Channing said to Scott, "I came to believe in law. But not in men. People are, in the end, who they are."

Her father's eyes had fixed on Scott. "But men make laws," Caroline interjected. "And write history. Like we're trying to do in Vietnam."

She saw Larry surreptitiously cover his eyes and emit a silent groan. "The *V* word," he murmured.

Channing gave a slight smile and raised his eyebrows at Caroline. "You were saying, Caroline?"

"That if the Vietnamese wrote history, and convened their own tribunal, Nixon and Kissinger might be condemned as war criminals."

Channing frowned. "I think that's much too facile. What our government committed were not crimes of war but acts of war—"

"They bombed civilians, Father. Thousands of them, and for what? To save face in a war we'll never win and now don't even plan to win. Because human beings are only pieces on their geopolitical chessboard."

Channing shook his head. "With respect, Communism is a form of tyranny which has killed at least as many people as the Nazis did. With whom you so blithely compare Messrs. Nixon and Kissinger." His voice became gentle. "Forgive me, Caroline—you're more than entitled to your own ideas. But I hardly think your maternal grandparents, who died at Auschwitz, would grant your comparison. Or even your own mother."

Caroline felt herself flush. Through her shame, she remembered that Nicole had felt much as she now did and that her father knew this. But it was beyond her now to say so.

In the silence, she saw Scott gaze at her with deep surprise, and then compassion. Channing turned to him. "Tell me, Scott, do you have a view on this? Perhaps I've been too harsh."

Caroline saw Scott fold his hands. He paused, gazing at her father quite openly, as if coming to some decision.

"I wouldn't know," he said quietly. "But then I haven't just been trumped with the death of six million Jews. Two of whom were my own grandparents."

Channing looked at him fixedly. To Caroline, everyone else were figures in a painting: Betty with her eyes downcast, Larry quite pale.

"Do you believe," Channing asked softly, "that the Vietnamese are our Jews?"

Scott's faint smile did nothing to his eyes. "What I'm saying," he answered with equal quiet, "is that if the same platoon of Americans had marched into a German village and begun killing and raping everyone in sight until there was pretty much no one left, they wouldn't have put out a record called 'The Battle Hymn of Lieutenant Calley.' They'd have strung him up—"

"And quite legitimately, I'm sure. But it does point out a larger problem with your reference to My Lai." Channing's voice took on a lethal quiet. "Because the young people with, shall we say, the 'finer sensibilities' have claimed the right to select their wars. Sensibilities so fine, in fact, that they left *this* war to those with so few advantages that Vietnam looks like a career opportunity. And to, as you put it, the war criminals. Whom the absence of their moral betters, safely deferred, deprived of so many good examples."

For a moment, the room was silent. "Yes," Scott said. "I'm lucky that I haven't had to die to justify my position. Which leaves me here, free to argue, among the living. Unlike my college roommate, who died there, uselessly."

Channing's face hardened. Then, as if remembering himself, he looked suddenly embarrassed. "Please forgive me, Scott. I've become so used to argument and advocacy that I forget my role as host."

Scott seemed to study him. "No need to apologize," he said. "My dad and I used to do this all the time. Before we stopped speaking."

In the nervous laughter that followed, Caroline saw that her father barely smiled.

"Why haven't you ever told me," Scott asked an hour later, "about your mother?"

Caroline did not face him. "It's not the kind of thing that comes up."

They stood on his deck, hands on the railing, watching the Nantucket Sound at sunset. He turned to her. "But it's important, don't you think?"

She tilted her head. Softly, she asked, "Do I know everything that's important about you?"

He did not answer. Caroline was quiet for a time. "Anyhow," she said, "I'm very sorry. For starting that whole argument about Vietnam."

Scott's eyes narrowed. "That wasn't about Vietnam, Caroline. It was about you. And me and you." He paused for a moment. "Do you really think there's ever a time when your father doesn't know exactly what he's doing? And what he wants?"

She touched his hand. "He's been a good father, Scott. By his own lights, he wants whatever seems best for me."

Scott's hand closed around hers. "I always thought the test of a good parent," he said softly, "was to raise adults."

Withdrawing her hand, Caroline felt herself stiffen. "Are you saying that I'm not one?"

Scott's eyes were still and serious. "What I'm saying," he finally answered, "is that he may force you to choose. But the choice isn't the one he imagines—between him and whatever bad stuff I or anyone else may symbolize for him." He paused, ending quietly. "It'll be between him and *you*."

She found her father on the porch, sipping a brandy. In the dusk, his eyes looked deep-set, shrouded.

Caroline did not sit. "That was unforgivable," she said flatly.

He looked down. "Yes, I suppose it was. Especially when I insisted that he come."

He sounded genuinely contrite. "Why did you do that?" she asked.

"Because I believe that ideas matter. That rigorous thought matters." He looked away. "Perhaps it was more than that, Caroline. I find that being here, I think of Nicole.

"I remember all she went through during the war, and what I thought I meant to her because of that—that I could somehow save her, when her own people could not. And then I think about Paul Nerheim." He paused, finishing softly. "And, in spite of myself, I feel the anger of her betrayal. Which I inflicted on all of you at dinner, without meaning to. It was as if the two of you had cheapened what I felt. For which, of course, I'm quite ashamed."

It was painful for Caroline to hear this, to know how little the years of silent restraint had healed him. She felt her anger deflate, become the sadness of her own memories. There was, she thought, nothing more she could say.

Caroline went to Channing and kissed him on the forehead. "Good night, Father."

She turned to leave.

"Do you want to know what I think?" he asked mildly. "About Scott."

Caroline faced him again. After a moment, she said, "All right."

Her father put down his brandy, as if gathering his thoughts. "There's something wrong with him, Caroline." His tone was still soft, reluctant. "A real person is integrated—they're simply the sum of who they are and what they've done. They don't have to think about it." He looked up at her. "Haven't you noticed this boy thinking? Not so much about his ideas—the passion is real enough. But about who he is. Or pretends to be."

"Just what are you trying to say, Father?"

"I don't know yet." His eyes narrowed. "It's the sense you'll have, perhaps a decade from now, after you've cross-examined a hundred witnesses. You watch their eyes and see that split second of calculation. And you know that they're thinking just a little too hard. Just as this boy spent the first hour of our dinner pretending to be less clever than he is." He paused again. "I don't know where you and Jackson stand. I'm not sure I want to know. But Jackson is a real person, and a fine one."

"Who never disagrees with you." Caroline's voice rose. "Isn't that your trouble with Scott? That he stood up to you?"

"How can you think that? This is about character, not ideas." Her father's gaze grew distant. "I don't want to be intrusive, Caroline. I like to think I haven't been—at least no more than any only parent with basically good intentions. But bad character is a rot, and there is no cure. The only thing you can do is resolve to avoid the taint yourself."

With sudden intuition, Caroline sensed that this conversation, too, was not simply about Scott Johnson, but about her own mother.

"There is no taint," she snapped. "Except in your mind."

Before he could answer, she turned and left the room.

NINE

BUT THE CONFRONTATION with her father ran like a fault line between Caroline and Scott.

With him, she felt joy and passion, yet the undertow of doubt: all her instincts told her that, in some sense she could not identify, Channing Masters was right. Alone in her room, she would add up the discrepancies—between Scott's air of carelessness and his deeply ingrained caution; his supposed unsophistication and his evident worldliness; his studied unsociability and his ease with the few people they had met; his persona of cynical purposelessness and the incisiveness of his mind. Their time was running short, and Caroline might never know him.

Some part of her felt that to penetrate Scott's veneer was dangerous—if there were certain things he did not wish to share, there must be a reason for it. But as each day passed, and Caroline knew only that she wanted to be with him every moment she could, the sense of something between them that they could never say, never reach, ate through her until she feared his silence even more than the reason for it.

"There are things you haven't told me," she said. "Things about you. I want to know why."

They were sitting on the deck after a long day on the water, enjoying wine and cheese and a sunset that stained the wispy clouds orange red. Caroline had broken a pleasant silence; her question, sharp and sudden, so at odds with the mood of their day, startled her.

Yet Scott did not look surprised. With a veiled, wary look, he asked, "Where's this coming from, Caroline? Your father?"

"Quit sparring with me, all right? You're playing at being someone you're not, and I'm supposed to sit on everything I think or feel." She stood, feeling the depth of her anger. "I spend every minute I can with you, like it's life and death, and all I've really been doing is fucking you for the summer. Because I can't reach you."

He put down his wineglass and faced her. "It's you who's going away, Caroline. I don't expect you to drop out of law school. So don't expect me to open up a vein."

Beneath the chill words was an undertone of emotion. Caroline placed both hands on his shoulders, looking up at him. "All the time I'm planning to go on with my life, I feel like you've turned me inside out. Please, doesn't this summer mean anything to you?"

She saw him blanch at her intensity. Suddenly, Caroline felt naked and exposed, without any defense between Scott and her emotions.

"Look at me," Scott said softly.

Slowly, she did that. The tears ran down her face.

Seeing this, his own eyes shut. Caroline saw him swallow. And then his eyes opened; as he touched her face, tracing her tears with his fingertips, he looked at her with a tenderness so open that it was hurtful.

"Why are you doing this?" he asked. "Don't you know by now how much I love you?"

Caroline felt stunned. Mute, she shook her head.

He seemed to slump. "Why do you think I stayed here, Caroline? I should have left weeks ago."

Caroline clasped his shoulders. "Why?"

Shaking his head, Scott put his arms around her. He seemed to hold her with a desperate longing.

"Make love with me," he murmured. "Please."

His voice was hoarse; Caroline felt her body tremble. They went to the bed like children drawn to a flame.

Now they were fumbling, desperate, tearing the clothes from each other, hands and mouths seeking each other's bodies, like two lovers meeting after weeks apart. Yet they had never been like this—lost, heedless, their bodies from the moment he entered her moving with a frenzy so deep that Caroline no longer knew herself.

They cried out together.

Afterwards they lay in the dark. Stunned, defenseless, Caroline pretended to sleep. She felt ripped open.

Beside her, Scott stirred, restless, rose from bed. Caroline said nothing.

She lay in the dark, alone. Scott did not return.

Naked, Caroline stood.

The air was cool. She felt her skin rise, her nipples. Picking through the clothes on the floor, she found his T-shirt and slid it over her head.

He was on the deck, wearing only his jeans, staring out at the water.

She walked behind him. From his stillness, she knew he was aware of her. But he did not move.

"What is it?" she asked.

He turned to her. In the moonlight, she saw him pause.

"My name," he said quietly, "is David Stern."

It was almost as if, Caroline felt, he were talking of someone he had lost. She took both his hands in hers. He gazed down at their fingers, laced together. "The funny thing," he said, "is that I chose Johnson as a joke, because of Lyndon. But Scott was because I always liked Fitzgerald. I guess you and I will never agree on everything."

Caroline stared at him. "But why pretend like this?"

"Haven't you figured it out?" His voice was low and bitter. "I gave myself my own exemption, Caroline. I'm a draft dodger."

It made Caroline quiet; she felt both shaken and relieved. She looked at him, waiting.

"I'm from California, not Ohio," he said at last. "I went to Berkeley and was going to Stanford law." He gazed at the deck. "I was also 1-A.

"I absolutely opposed the war. My father screamed at me about World War II; my mother begged me to go to Canada; my draft counselor told me to work on becoming a conscientious objector.

"Nothing was right.

"I hated the war, and I didn't want to die there. Canada's not my home. And I would have fought in my father's war.

"For two years, I tried for a medical deferment. Until my appeals ran out.

"The only principled thing, I told myself, was to go to jail." He paused and then looked directly at her. "Your father had me pegged. At the last minute, I couldn't face it. The day before I was supposed to report, I just took off."

His tone was laced with self-contempt. As if to encourage him, Caroline squeezed his hands. "My mother gave me some money," he finally said. "My father never knew. One morning, I just lit out with my guitar, a suitcase full of stuff, and a plane ticket to Miami under the name Scott Johnson.

"I picked Miami because I'd never been there." He shook his head. "All I had was two thousand dollars and a California license that said I was David Stern.

"I got myself a crummy room in a hotel that didn't care who I was, and made contact with a draft resisters group I knew about from law school. Some of them had a side business—turning birth certificates for dead people into a new identity. So I gave them some money and waited in my room, working on my interim story."

His voice softened again. "Day by day, what I'd done sank in. . . .

"I was no one anymore. I had no friends. I couldn't tell anyone the truth. I couldn't call my folks or write them—the FBI could tap their phone or read the mail, which happened to that friend of mine who did end up in jail. And I wasn't sure that my dad wouldn't do something stupid, like come look for me, or that my brother or sister wouldn't blow it somehow."

Caroline watched his face. "So they're real. Your family."

"Oh, they're real." He looked at her sharply. "That letter you were looking at, the first time you came over, was to my aunt in Denver. She burns the envelopes and reads them to my mother on the telephone. I can never say where I am."

Caroline tried to imagine herself adrift, cut off from her own family. But David was lost in his memories now. "Before I could get my new ID," he continued, "the FBI busted the people who were working on it.

"I took off before anyone could find me.

"I couldn't rent a car, which would put my name in a computer. So I bought a bus ticket to Boston, the only place I could think of where there are so many students that one more would just blend in. But there were too many people to lie to, and too many people who wanted ID—for jobs, to buy a car, even for drinks. And now I was short of cash and afraid to buy another identity.

"I'd come face-to-face with what a luxury it was to have been David Stern." His voice was soft again. "So I came here—the end of the world, or at least of the United States.

And in none of them, with none of them, had she ever felt as she felt with David Stern.

David.

He was a real person. Beneath the harm he had done himself, he was the person she had sensed he was. For an odd, almost giddy moment, Caroline felt elated. It was possible; *they* were possible.

Because Caroline Masters was in love with David Stern.

Happy and sad, filled with love, terrified by her confusion, Caroline went to him.

He was lying on the bed, staring up at the ceiling.

Quietly, she said, "You have to be David to me, okay? That's at least a start."

He gazed up at her, eyes filled with hope and doubt. "I really do understand," he said. "If you can't go, it's for a good reason."

Caroline stood by the head of the bed, watched him in the moonlight. And then she slowly pulled his T-shirt over her head.

She stood in front of him, not shy. As David looked up from the bed in silence, wanting her, Caroline wished that she could freeze this moment forever.

"I love you, David."

Silent, he reached out to her.

She went to him. Slowly and sweetly, David Stern made love to her.

Afterward, they lay together in the dark.

There were minutes without speaking. And then, still quiet, David ran his fingers down her spine.

Perhaps he wanted her again, Caroline thought. She touched his face.

"Tell me about your mother," he said softly. "Everything."

TEN

I⊤ WAS INSANE.

They would lie there, looking into each other's faces, bodies damp with lovemaking. Caroline could not imagine life without him.

But her life before had been perfectly fine, the steady accretion of steps, one upon the other, down the only path she had ever imagined. The Caroline Masters she had always known was not a woman who lived in a vacuum—she was a New Englander; her father's daughter; a graduate of Radcliffe; a person with a career ahead; even Jackson Watts's girlfriend. Without these things, there *was* no Caroline Masters—there was this passionate creature, defined solely by her love for a man she barely knew, and whose real name felt strange on her lips. Who could not imagine her life *with* him.

It was insane.

She could not sleep, lost her desire for food, felt nauseous in spite of that. There were circles beneath her eyes.

And yet each night she went to David.

She could not decide, and there was no one who could help her.

More deeply than in the months following her death, Caroline missed her mother.

Her father would call, and Jackson. At the times that she was there to answer, Caroline sounded to herself like a chattering stranger. She hardly noticed their reaction.

The only person to whom she could truly speak was David.

In the middle of the night, he listened to her doubts and fears. "Caroline," he told her finally, "if I'd known I'd put you through such hell, I'd never have asked you. I should have just gone away."

He looked so sad that when she left, Caroline was suddenly afraid she would never see him again. So that when she looked out the

"Vineyarders are used to transients. And they leave you alone." He paused. "I scrounged a job, bought a car without registration, and hoped no one would find me until I figured out what to do."

Caroline watched him. "So the night we went to town . . ."

"I'd let myself go out with you, and now you might see my license. How could I know who you might talk to?" David shook his head. "But that was nothing compared to how stupid I was, forgetting myself like that. All your cop friend needed was to put me through a computer or check my registration or even just get curious." His tone turned wondering. "If it weren't for you, I might have ended up in the local can, waiting for some FBI guy from Boston to come around whenever things got slow.

"That was when I knew I had to leave."

In the silence, she touched his face. "Where?"

"Canada." His voice was quiet and sad. "I meant to leave here weeks ago. But every week I made another excuse to stay. Until I knew I'd only leave when you did."

Caroline stepped back from him, trying to absorb it, fingers touching his now. "All those things you told me . . ."

"Were lies, pretty much. Except the part about Bobby Kennedy. Only that it was California, not Indiana. I was there the night they shot him." His voice slowed. "We were going to *win*, Caroline. We were *that* close . . ."

He did not finish the sentence. In the silence, his fingertips curled beneath hers.

It was the smallest of gestures, and it brought his world down on her. The depth of his loss. The fear in which he lived. The weight of her responsibility, suddenly clear, to protect him from whoever, out of carelessness or malice, might choose to turn him in.

"Can't you fix this somehow?" she asked.

His smile seemed knowing but not unkind; it was as if he saw that, in the numbness of first comprehension, she could get no farther than the desire that things be different.

"Short of jail? This is not a forgiving government, or a forgiving time—too many kids far younger than me have gone there and died for most people to feel sorry for a draft dodger. I'm afraid that job's been left to me." He paused for a moment. "And after jail, what would I do? I couldn't practice law here. I don't think I'd even get to vote. I just made a bad decision. And every night I go over it, and over it, and over it. . . .

"I'm tired of it, and sick of myself. At least in Canada there are law schools, and I can be David Stern again. Maybe after a few years I can even figure out who he is now."

It came to her then: his loneliness; his fear of others; his knowledge that—in a moment of fear and indecision—he had damaged himself in some way that would always be part of him. And then, quite softly, he said, "It isn't much to offer you, is it?"

Caroline sat down in a deck chair. "I want a life," David said softly. "I want a life with you. But I can never have one here."

Caroline felt sick. "You're asking me to come with you."

"Yes."

It was as if, Caroline thought, she'd been transported to someone else's life. She had never felt so lost.

He touched her hair. "If I leave here now, not knowing what you'd say, it would be the one thing I could never live with."

Caroline shook her head. "There's just so much . . ."

He withdrew his hand. "I know. You have your father. You have this life. . . ."

"I have the life *you* used to have." Caroline's voice rose. "It's not fair to lay this on my father. Until two years ago, you had my life. Now I find out that most of what you've told me is a lie, that your life as an American is over, and that maybe I can turn mine in and go somewhere I've never been and never cared about. All right, and leave my family behind."

He turned away. "That's why I tried not to fall in love with you. Because loving you isn't fair to either one of us. Certainly not to you . . ."

"Just let me be here, okay? Alone."

He turned to her for a moment. And then, without a word, he stood and left.

It was too much to absorb. For a time, she could only see the places that were part of her and, she had believed, would always be—Masters Hill; the town of Resolve; Harvard Yard; Boston; Heron Lake; the streams and mountains of New Hampshire. And then the faces of her college friends; of Jackson; of Betty and Larry; of Channing Masters, the parent who had been with her, and guided her, since the first dawn of her consciousness.

window the next morning and spotted his curly head as he sat on the corner of his deck, her eyes filled with tears.

There was one week to go, and she was headed for law school like an automaton, spiritless and irresolute.

The morning after Caroline canceled her college friends' visit on the feeblest of excuses, she walked alone on the beach. She felt like a prisoner in her own skin.

Caroline sat on the beach, fighting tears.

Gazing along the edge of the water, she saw the distant figure of her sister, searching for shells.

Instinct told her to get up. But some deep exhausted part of her no longer cared how she appeared. All that she could manage, as Betty approached, was to stop crying.

Silent, her sister sat next to her.

For a time, Betty sifted sand through her fingers, narrowly watching the grains spill on the beach. A cool mist touched their faces.

"Please, Caroline, talk to me."

"There's nothing to say. Really."

Betty was quiet. "Then I have something to tell *you*," she said at last. "I think maybe I'm pregnant."

Caroline turned to her. "How do you feel?"

"Fine, so far." Betty smiled. "But I'm way late."

Forcing a smile of her own, Caroline touched her shoulder. "I hope it's true. Then I get to be 'Aunt Caroline.' "

"You would be, wouldn't you?" The thought seemed to give Betty sudden pleasure, and then her smile faded and she rested her fingers on Caroline's arm. "I know we haven't really been sisters always. But I wish you could talk with me."

Caroline felt too drained to speak. Tears came to her eyes again.

"Please," Betty implored. "You can't go on like this."

For a long time, Caroline stared at the sand. Out of wretchedness and exhaustion, she said, "His name isn't Scott."

The words, raw in Caroline's throat, felt like a betrayal. Betty's lips compressed. "Is he in trouble . . . ?"

Caroline grasped her shoulders. "*I* can't talk about this. *We* can't talk about this."

"What *is* it?" Betty's fingers tightened. "Larry and I are worried sick about you, all right? And so is Father."

Caroline swallowed. "They can't know," she murmured. "Just you."

After a time, Betty nodded.

Caroline felt her eyes shut. "They're after him—he didn't report for induction." She paused and then looked directly at her sister. "He's asked me to go away with him. To Canada."

Betty paled. "My God, Caroline."

The hushed shock in her voice seemed to run through Caroline. Of all people, she thought, Betty might understand. "I know," Caroline said. "It would change my whole life. . . ."

"Then how can you even think about it?"

"Because I've never loved anyone like this. I never even knew I could." Her throat felt tight. "Do you know what that's like?"

Betty gave a first, faint smile. "The feeling you can't get close enough, that he can't get deep enough? That you'd dredge your soul for him?" Her voice sounded husky, rueful. "The world of a new love affair is like insanity. And part of the delusion is that you think you're the only one it ever happened to. . . ."

"I don't think that," Caroline said sharply. "It's just that it's happened to me."

"Just like it happened to me—with Larry." Betty paused. "But he never asked me to throw away my family and everything I knew. And after a few weeks or months, I wouldn't have. Because I was able to put Larry in the context of a life I wanted and see that he was part of a whole. And that—fortunately for me—he fit." Her hands grasped Caroline's shoulders. "You have a whole life planned, Caroline. Scott—or whoever he is—doesn't fit that. And this person whom I'm looking at now isn't you."

"But is it my life," Caroline burst out, "or just the life our father gave me?"

Betty looked astonished. "Is Canada your life?" she retorted, and then her voice softened. "I know he feels like the love of your life. But he isn't—if he were, he wouldn't be asking you to change your life. Because that's not how love is supposed to work. . . ."

"But you have so many rules for things—how love is supposed to work; how families are supposed to work. David's not pushing me—"

"David?"

Caroline hesitated. "Yes."

Somehow this seemed to deflate Betty. Her voice was quiet again. "I'm so sorry, Caroline. I never imagined this happening to you."

Caroline felt her sister's sadness. "What do you mean?"

Betty looked down. "That you always seemed so smart and strong to me—that you'd never need anyone the way I need Larry." She tilted her head. "Here I was wanting to help you, and now it's me who's shaken. I guess even more for Father than for me." She paused, then finished quietly. "*I* can't replace you for him, Caroline. No one can."

It was a hard concession, Caroline knew. Silent, she squeezed her sister's hand.

"Since your mother died," Betty said at last, "he's been so alone. Sometimes I've thought that the hope of practicing law with you is the main thing in his life."

It was as if, Caroline thought, David had numbed her to this painful truth. "I know," she finally answered. "But does that mean I should do it?"

Betty looked at her again. "It hasn't just been Father, Caroline. It's been you. He didn't get you into Harvard Law School—you did." Her voice grew sharper. "You're saying you can't define yourself for Father. How can you define yourself by a decision made by someone who, two months ago, you didn't even know existed. And such a bad decision."

It was nothing more, Caroline silently acknowledged, than she had told herself.

Betty watched her face. Quietly, she said, "Talk to Father, Caroline. It's the least you can do. For him, and for yourself."

Caroline touched her eyes. "I can't," she said miserably.

"David may have a deadline. But you don't. You can go to Canada anytime." Once more, Betty's voice was soft. "Let him go, then talk to Father. Because I couldn't stand to watch what you could do to him."

The thought of Betty, the neglected one, trying to hold the threads of their family brought tears to Caroline's eyes.

"Please," Betty said. "For both your sakes."

Caroline took her sister's hands. "What I do, and how I do it, has to be *my* decision. Please, promise me."

Betty watched her, and then her gaze broke. "All right," she said.

"I'm going to Boston," Caroline said. "To Cambridge, really."

In the darkness, David was quiet. "To see your old stomping grounds? Or your new ones?"

"I don't know yet." She touched his arm. "Part of it's that I can't seem to think here."

He brought her close. A little sadly, he said, "That was the idea."

She flew to Boston the next evening.

In the afternoon, on a crisp, fall-like day, Caroline aimlessly strolled the Harvard campus. She barely saw it.

For a time, she sat on the steps of the law school. Summer students came and went; she could almost have been one of them. But now, Caroline knew quite clearly, she might never be.

She forced herself not to call him.

That night, alone in her hotel room, Caroline slept badly. She had not eaten lunch or dinner.

In the morning, Caroline gazed out her window toward the Public Garden.

It was green and pastoral, a piece of London amidst a much younger city. The skies were darkening, Caroline saw; with the instinct of a sailor, she sensed that the Vineyard was in for stormy weather.

Caroline closed her eyes. In her mind, David sailed the catboat with the wind on his hair, smiling at her across the wheel.

She went to the phone and called him.

The phone rang, and rang again. She did not hang up.

Finally, he answered.

"Hi," she said. "It's me."

"Hi." Her spirits lifted with his voice. "I miss you."

"I miss you, too." Caroline took a breath. "I'm ready to talk about this, okay? I'm flying back this afternoon."

"Shall I pick you up?"

"I'll find you." She paused. "It'll give me that much more time."

There was silence for a moment. Quietly, he said, "Can you give me a preview?"

She sat on the bed. "I think it's better just to talk things through. Okay?"

"Okay."

He was trying to sound stoic. Softly, she said, "I love you, David."

"And I love you, Caroline."

Slowly, Caroline put down the telephone, not knowing that it was the last time she would ever hear him say this.

ELEVEN

CAROLINE FLEW to the Vineyard in a driving rainstorm, which buffeted the twin-engine prop plane. There was the crash of thunder, a sickening jolt; the tiny plane took a brief, vertiginous drop, and then a second bolt of lightning lit the roiling seas below. Caroline gripped the arm of her seat and tried to think of David.

As it dipped for a landing, the plane lurched from side to side. And then the wheels hit the ground, circling to a stop, and the handful of stunned passengers straggled out like refugees into the pelting storm. Caroline was last.

In front of the airport, a wooden outpost that dated from the Second World War, she found a battered taxi. Inside, she shivered; her hair and face were wet, and a sideways rain spattered the windshield like hail. Once she had given her destination, neither Caroline nor the taciturn gray-haired cabbie spoke at all.

She was going straight to the boathouse.

Her life might be about to change, she thought. How foolish to wish for better weather.

The cab turned down the road to Eel Pond.

Caroline tried to compose herself. In the darkness, all that she could see was the cabbie's fleshy neck, the low shrubs and trees of the moorlike fields as the headlights caught them. And then they passed the Rubins' place, and the terrain opened to the bluff above a black, pounding sea.

The cab stopped. Hastily, Caroline fumbled loose some bills from her purse and got out with her suitcase into the rain.

She stood atop the bluff for a moment, gazing at the silhouette of her father's house, perhaps two hundred feet away. A bolt of lightning struck nearby. Caroline started: as the thunder exploded, she imagined in her mind's eye that she had seen the outline of her father's car. But this could not be.

Turning, Caroline ran down the bluff and across the beach.

Her boots labored in the wet, heavy sand; by the time she clambered to the pier, suitcase still in hand, she was panting, half blind from rain. She ran for his door, footsteps hammering the wooden planks.

His light was on, Caroline saw. He was waiting for her.

She sprinted the last four steps and burst through the unlocked door.

She stopped, blinking in the light. David's clothes were pulled from drawers and strewn near his suitcase on the floor.

Caroline turned, stunned and frightened, looking for him.

He stood in the passage to the porch, white-faced. The tension building inside her drove Caroline across the room to him. She clutched the front of his shirt. "What *happened* to you, David?"

He stared down at her. "Your friend came to warn me," he said tersely. "Frank Mannion. He didn't like draft dodgers much, he told me, but he didn't want you hurt anymore." He paused. "The FBI's coming tomorrow, Caroline. Someone turned me in."

Caroline felt herself freeze.

David watched her face. "You were the only one I told. The only one, including my own mother, who even knew that I was here."

Caroline's eyes shut. Silent, she laid her head against his chest. He did not move, or hold her. Quietly, David asked, "Who did you tell?"

Miserably, she whispered, "Only my sister."

Gently, firmly, David pushed her away. When he knelt to close the suitcase, his face was taut and his eyes were narrow slits.

Caroline trembled with cold. "She wouldn't do that."

Snapping the final latch, David looked up. Voice still soft, he answered, "But your father would, wouldn't he?" He paused. "The rich *are* different, after all."

All at once, Caroline went numb. "His car . . ."

"Oh, he's back." His tone was bitter now. "I'm sure to 'inspect his holdings,' as you once put it. Of which you're one."

Tears came to Caroline's eyes, and then the weight of betrayal overwhelmed her—her betrayal of David, Betty's betrayal of her. Her father's . . .

"But I was going *with* you." Her voice filled with anguish. "After we talked, if you still wanted me, I was going *with* you."

David turned pale. "Don't do this. Please. You never would have gone, not really. You're much too tied to all of them."

His voice was flat, final.

Caroline folded her arms, staring at the floor. In a few terrible moments, she realized, her life had changed forever. Despairing, she asked only, "What are you going to do?"

He looked at her and then gave a faint sardonic smile in which, Caroline hoped, she might have seen a glimmer of affection. "Think you can keep a secret?"

"Tell me, damn it."

There was another flash of lightning. David glanced out the window, then said, "I'm stealing your boat."

Caroline stared at him. "That's crazy."

"Is it?" David pulled on his jacket. "The only other ways off this island are the airport and the boat from Vineyard Haven. Both places will be watching for me. The only ticket they'll give me is to prison. And I refuse to go there on account of your family."

Caroline was seized by despair. "You'll never make it. Not in a catboat."

He looked at her steadily. "I've sailed through much worse. And once I do, I'm halfway to Canada. Just a pleasant sail up the coast of Maine."

Wordless, Caroline clutched the front of his jacket, shaking her head.

"I'm taking the boat," he repeated. "You can help me, or say goodbye here."

Caroline fought back tears. In a muffled voice, she said, "I'll help you."

Gently, David removed her hands from his jacket.

He went to the doorway. Standing there, irresolute, Caroline saw his guitar in the corner.

She walked across the room to get it.

Caroline turned to him, guitar in hand. Framed in the doorway, he looked at the guitar, then at her, and a second faint smile crossed his face.

"Let's go," he said.

They walked down the pier in the driving rain, David carrying his suitcase, Caroline his guitar. Not looking at each other, and yet not hurrying. Struggling across the beach, they left twin trails of footprints.

At the end of the Masterses' dock, the catboat bobbed in the storm. Caroline stopped abruptly.

"I never fixed the dinghy," she said. "Or the rib."

"I know."

David paused for a moment, gazing at the boat, and then kept walking.

Slowly, she followed him. Beneath the wind and rain, his footsteps sounded hollow.

Turning, David looked at her, and then he tossed his suitcase onto the catboat.

As Caroline leapt onto the boat, guitar in hand, the rain came down in sheets.

She went below. Carefully, she placed his guitar in one corner.

Above, David had begun to unfurl the canvas. His curly hair was rain-soaked.

Caroline went to help him, a catch in her throat. Together, they raised the sail aloft, flapping in the punishing wind.

Numb, Caroline moved from one task to the next. Just as they had done in so many days of summer—silent, knowing their routine so well that there was no need to speak.

In the rain, Caroline's tears were nothing.

David had turned to her. Softly, he said, "I think we're ready, Caroline."

She could not seem to move.

He came to her then, taking her face in his hands. "No," he said. "You can't."

The boat lurched violently beneath them. Tears ran down Caroline's face.

David placed both hands on her waist and looked intently into her eyes. It was as if, Caroline thought for a moment, he wanted to remember them.

Perhaps he would change his mind.

Gently, he lifted her over the side and placed her on the dock. She started to reach out, realized she could no longer touch him.

"Think you can toss me the line?" he asked.

Caroline knelt, freeing the line from the spile that secured it. For a last moment, she held it in her hand. And then, underhand, she tossed it to him as he had asked.

"Please," she said, "at least let me know that you've made it. Somehow."

Silent, he gazed at her and seemed to force a smile. "Don't worry. I'll remember Joshua Slocum."

Wind flapped in the sails above him. David gave her a last long look and then turned quickly to his task.

Caroline watched, hands in her pockets, as the catboat slipped into the storm.

Soon it began to merge with the dark. Caroline strained to see him. He was a slim figure at the helm; perhaps in her imagination, in the last moment before he vanished, David turned to wave.

As far as Caroline knew, they never found him. She never heard from him again.

Later, when she came to California, Caroline tried to find his parents. But she could not. Perhaps it was best; she was not sure what she would have said.

She made her own life. At odd times, Caroline the defense lawyer imagined a man named David Stern, in Canada. She hoped he had forgiven her, for she had so much to tell him.

PART SIX

THE HEARING

ONE

AMIDST A THRONG of reporters, Caroline Masters ascended the steps of the Connaughton County Courthouse.

The crowd—the outthrust microphones, the cameras, the reporters jockeying for position—was largely Caroline's doing. Two days before the hearing, she had told the *Patriot-Ledger* that she would expose weaknesses in the prosecution case and singled out Megan Race by name. She repeated this challenge on television, to ensure that Megan would not miss it. Now the hearing had become an event, its centerpiece Megan's testimony, perhaps three days away.

"Do you expect to vindicate Brett Allen?" a woman reporter called out.

Caroline paused, gazing straight into a hand-held camera. She had sacrificed sleep to preparation, and the circles beneath her eyes had required more work than usual. But in her sleekly tailored blue suit, with her hair freshly cut, she looked crisp and in command.

"What I intend," Caroline answered, "is to show that the prosecution case against Brett Allen should not satisfy anyone who comes to this courthouse with an open mind. I hope the prosecution meets that description."

Caroline turned away, making this challenge to Jackson her sound bite of the morning. It also hid her own discomfort; after all, she thought grimly, only she could guess the origin of the murder weapon, only she knew that Brett and James Case had quarreled in the moments before his death. Her stomach felt hollow.

At the top of the courthouse steps she turned, waiting for her family.

Dressed in a three-piece suit, Channing Masters was a figure of judicial rectitude, head held high as he climbed the stairs toward Caroline. Betty clasped one elbow, Larry the other; their faces, as

Caroline had schooled them, were open and hopeful. They met Caroline, forming the tableau of a family come to seek justice for its youngest member.

Minutes before, Jackson had arrived.

With a certain restraint, he said only that what mattered was the evidence. As for Megan Race, she was in virtual seclusion: two nights before, a television camera had caught her leaving the apartment, straight-backed and angry. She would not speak at all.

The previous day, Jackson had appeared at the inn unannounced.

They had gone to her room. In a voice much colder than usual, Jackson asked, "What have you done to Megan Race?"

With feigned indifference, Caroline had answered, "What does Megan think I've done?"

Jackson gazed at her across the room. His eyes looked puffy; Caroline knew that he was as tired as she was.

"She wants me to investigate you," he said finally. "She still thinks someone broke into her apartment."

Caroline sat back. "Any more proof of a break-in?"

Jackson hesitated. "No. Not that we can see."

"Then it never happened, did it? Just like a drug dealer never broke into James's apartment . . ."

"Don't play games with me. Megan's jumpy as a cat now—you did something to intimidate her."

"Maybe she's trying to intimidate *me*. Or maybe you are." Caroline's voice was brittle with strain. "If you want to investigate me, go ahead. But not until this hearing's over."

Jackson folded his arms. "Save it for the cameras, Caroline. I've been watching you ratchet up the pressure on this girl for the last two days. If you've got some reason to believe she's not reliable, tell me."

"I already did," Caroline snapped. "And yet you insist on calling her."

"She denies any relationship to Larry." Jackson stood, hands on hips. "Look, if you've got something else, tell me. But don't try to set me up."

Rubbing the bridge of her nose, Caroline was silent. "This is a capital case," she said at last. "It's about Brett, not you and me, and you've chosen to base it on Megan Race. I'm entitled to cross-examine her without giving you a preview."

"You did do something, didn't you?" Jackson's tone was sharp now. "Hasn't it occurred to you that whatever it is will come out too? What about your judgeship?"

Caroline looked at him wearily. *And what about* your *judgeship,* she wanted to ask; all at once, she understood what public embarrassment might do to him as well. It made her sorry for them both.

"I'm a defense lawyer," she answered. "Brett comes first."

"Just what do you plan?" her father had asked.

They sat in Carlton Grey's office a few hours after Jackson's visit. Perhaps it was fatigue; Caroline felt the full weight of her memories, the deep despairing wish never to have returned. It took an act of will to address her father as a lawyer.

"Several things," she said. "First, to show that the physical evidence, in which Jackson put such stock, is ambiguous. I've been over this with our experts—on serology, on drugs, on pathology, and on forensics—until the lab reports are swimming before my eyes."

"Yes." Her father's tone was suddenly gentle. "You look tired."

Caroline did not want sympathy. In a flat voice, she said, "I've had a lot on my mind."

Channing was quiet for a moment. "Being tired is no good," he said finally. "For you or for Brett. And from the way you've dealt with the press, you've staked a lot on this."

"Yes," Caroline said with some asperity. "I've considered that."

Channing turned to the window. The office was shadowed, but outside it was brilliant summer; in the half-light, the skin of Channing's face had the translucent look of parchment. "You're still my daughter," he answered softly, "and Brett is my granddaughter."

There was nothing Caroline wished to say.

After a time, Channing spoke as if her silence had never happened. "Judge Towle is a friend, Caroline. He's hardly pro-defendant, but he does have a certain libertarian streak. I think he'll give you latitude in showing that Brett was too intoxicated for the police to question, or that they didn't warn her properly."

Caroline raised an eyebrow. "Even if it means that everything—her statement and the warrants to search her person and the property—goes out the window? Leaving Jackson with next to nothing?"

Channing shrugged. "As a district judge, Fred Towle won't have to make that ruling—the Superior Court judge will, if Fred otherwise finds probable cause. But I believe that Fred will let you call Jackson's principal witnesses and tie them down on that and other points."

Caroline raised an eyebrow. "Even though under New Hampshire law I'm not allowed to ferret out Jackson's case? After all, in theory, the sole purpose of this hearing is to establish probable cause."

"Fred may find that a hard line to draw."

Watching him, Caroline found herself wondering if her father had spoken to Judge Towle: the integrity of New Hampshire judges was a matter of great pride, but Channing Masters had helped Towle secure his judgeship. And who could know what might be said in some passing conversation over bourbon at the Trout Club.

"I hope you're right," Caroline said at length. "I want the sworn testimony of Jackson's witnesses before they're as well prepared as Jackson will have them at trial. If we can show how drunk Brett really was, the pressure will build for Jackson to knock the charge down to manslaughter."

Channing's mouth compressed. "She's not guilty, Caroline."

"Oh, I know. You've already said that."

Channing straightened in his chair. "You may have become so jaded that guilt or innocence doesn't matter. But it should." His voice turned hard. "Now that you've made this hearing such an event—for reasons I don't completely follow—nothing will do but that you destroy Jackson's case if Fred Towle lets you try. Because if you don't do Jackson real damage, Brett will be worse off than ever. Not simply because you'll have lost the battle of publicity, with the attendant effect on prospective jurors. But because we'll have given away to Jackson, and his witnesses, your best lines of attack at trial."

Caroline frowned; she knew all too well the perils of the decision she had made. "This isn't helping me. Assuming that's what you came for."

Her father folded his hands in front of him. "Caroline," he said at last, "what will you do about Megan Race?"

His voice mingled apology and concern; more than antagonism,

Caroline found, this made her edgy. She did not want to feel the burden of her father's sleepless nights.

"I'm going to destroy her, Father. Just as you suggest." She smiled faintly. "After all, how do I know that *she* didn't kill him? How do Jackson and the police know, when, as I intend to show, they were so quick to latch onto Brett that they never even looked for the real killer?"

Her father studied her. "You still believe she's guilty."

Caroline no longer smiled. "We're all guilty," she said quietly. "Brett no more than the rest of us."

Her father gave her a complex look of inquiry and comprehension. "And you won't tell me what you mean to do to Megan."

Caroline folded her hands in front of her. "No," she answered. "Over the years I've learned to keep my own counsel."

Her father blanched and then looked down. After a time, he said, "You never will forgive me, will you."

It took Caroline long to answer, but when she did, her voice was steady. "All these years, and you've learned nothing. You think that feelings are an elective—that I elect to feel this way to hurt you. But all that I elected was to survive." Her tone grew quiet. "You say you look at me and see my mother. But when I look at you, it's David's face I see. No matter how hard I try."

He gazed up at her, stricken. Softly, she finished: "That is far more painful to me than I can ever tell you, Father. And it will never change."

With her father beside her, Caroline entered the courtroom.

She faced him, pausing a moment. And then, for the press who watched them—for Brett—she touched him on the shoulder, then Larry, and turned to Betty.

Betty looked away. To cover this, Caroline clasped her shoulders, and kissed her softly on the cheek. Her lips barely touched her sister's skin.

Turning, Caroline drew a breath and walked to the defense table.

The courtroom was small and plain, with the American and the New Hampshire flag at each side of the judge's bench. The press began to cluster in the back, and the slow gathering of a courtroom reaching critical mass began—Jackson shuffling papers at the prosecution table; a bailiff coming through the judge's door at the back of the room, the court reporter sitting at her machine in front of the raised bench where Judge Towle would sit. The murmur of onlookers grew quieter.

Caroline folded her hands beneath the table. At the back of the courtroom, a second door opened, and then Brett appeared with a deputy.

She wore the simple blue dress Caroline had selected for her, and her hair was pulled back from her face. The effect was demure; Brett's eyes seemed to widen at the courtroom, and her bright green gaze sought out Caroline. And then she smiled a little and came to her directly.

Feeling strangely light, Caroline stood. This was what she was here for.

Brett gazed up at her. "Hi," she said.

Her voice was close to normal. "Are you all right?" Caroline asked.

Brett smiled again. "Anything to get out of there."

The joke did not quite work; for a moment, Caroline wished that she could hug her.

"Well," she said in her calmest tone, "I'll see what I can do."

They sat together. Caroline squeezed Brett's hand beneath the table. Then Carlton Grey joined them, and she let go.

"All rise," the bailiff called out.

District Judge Frederick Towle appeared. He was plump and brown-haired, no older than Caroline and no taller. He took his time, his round, amiable face solemn and a little abstracted, as if he was aware of being watched. Assuming the bench, he looked at Jackson.

Jackson did not look happy. Caroline knew why: at seven-thirty that morning, Judge Towle had brought the lawyers in to take care of preliminary motions. Carlton Grey had moved Caroline's admission for the purposes of the case; graciously, Judge Towle had welcomed her back to New Hampshire, and then he set the rules for the hearing. His sole purpose, he went on, was to determine whether the prosecution had probable cause to pursue a charge of murder in the first degree: Jackson would be allowed to put on hearsay evidence, asking the police to testify as to knowledge gained from other witnesses. But after argument from Caroline, Towle ruled that Jackson could not show probable cause solely through the lead investigator. Instead he must himself call four of the prosecution witnesses whom Caroline had subpoenaed—the arresting officer; the lead investigator; the medical examiner; and Megan Race.

Jackson had protested vigorously—this, he said, would present the defense discovery not permitted by New Hampshire law. But Towle held his ground: the purpose was not discovery, he responded, but establishing probable cause in a matter that relied on the credibility of Megan Race and on medical evidence—including photographs—too complex for hearsay testimony from lay witnesses. Jackson had looked astonished; watching, Caroline could feel her father's presence, though he was nowhere near the courtroom.

Now, still facing Jackson, Towle nodded. "Mr. Watts," he said, and the hearing began.

TWO

WATCHING JACKSON RISE, Caroline wondered if this would be her last appearance in a courtroom. The sense of emptiness frightened her—who would she be if not a judge or lawyer. And then she felt Brett beside her.

Get a grip, Caroline told herself. What Brett needed now was for Caroline to be as good as she ever had been.

Passing before the cramped spectator section, jammed with media, a young policeman in uniform took the stand.

Officer Jack Mann of the Resolve police was much as Brett had described him: stocky, well built, barely in his twenties. His brown hair was cut short on the sides, Marine-style, emphasizing his square chin and prominent nose. But his face seemed hardly written on, and his eyes were guileless: the effect was of someone decent, striving to fill his role and almost painfully sincere. Caroline could see why Brett had trusted him.

Jackson stood near the witness box in his prosecutor's outfit: navy-blue suit, white shirt, subdued tie. The sober spokesman of law and order, soberly examining its first line of defense.

Quickly, Jackson disposed of the preliminaries and got to the critical facts. "That night," he asked, "when did you first encounter Brett Allen?"

"I saw her Jeep." Mann glanced quickly at Brett. "It was stopped by the side of the county road, with the headlights on. I thought someone might be needing help."

Next to Caroline, Brett sat with her head bowed. She made herself look up at Mann; in Caroline's line of vision were two young profiles—Brett gazing at the policeman; Mann facing Jackson.

"So you stopped?" Jackson asked.

"Yessir. And went to the car."

Jackson shoved his hands in his pockets. "And what did you find?"

"At first I couldn't see anyone. So I went to the driver's-side window with my flashlight."

"And?"

Mann stared straight ahead now. "There was a naked woman inside. She was hunched down behind the wheel, face pressed against the car door." His voice carried the memory of puzzlement. "Sort of curled up in the fetal position, like she was trying to hide."

Brett's face reddened. Caroline touched her arm.

"I called to her through the window," Mann went on. "After about the third time, she opened it." He paused a moment. "She tried to cover herself. But I could see the blood and vomit on her."

"Did she say anything?"

"Only that she was sick. I could smell it too—along with marijuana and maybe wine."

Caroline glanced about. An odd decorousness had settled over the courtroom: Judge Towle studied nothing in particular, and reporters soberly scribbled notes. But Betty and Larry were rigid in profile, and her father's stare was fixed.

Caroline turned back to Jackson.

He was moving closer to Mann. "Did she tell you how she'd gotten that way?"

"No."

"Nothing about a boyfriend?"

"No."

Eyebrow raised, Jackson skipped a beat. "Or a murder?"

"Nothing like that, sir. She didn't say anything about him."

On Brett's eyes was the sudden film of doubt—all at once, Caroline sensed that Brett herself was not sure of what had happened. She wondered if this was better, or worse, than the settled knowledge of one's guilt.

"Did you search the car?" Jackson asked Mann.

"No, sir—I didn't have a warrant. But there were certain items on the passenger seat, in plain view."

The young cop's voice was stiff now—he wanted to show how well he had stuck to the rules. As if to affirm this, Jackson nodded before asking, "What were those items?"

"A wallet and a knife." Mann's voice lowered. "The knife had blood on it. From the looks of it, the blood hadn't dried yet."

The process had begun, Caroline thought: the slow accretion of fact upon fact to establish Brett's guilt. Brett herself was still, attentive.

"Did you ask her about that?"

"I asked if anyone was hurt."

"And what did she answer?"

"I don't remember, exactly. But what it amounted to was 'no.'"

"And how was her demeanor?"

"It was like she was so scared she was numb. But her eyes followed me—I could see she understood my questions. When I asked her name, she told me."

"And what did you do then?"

"Told her I was taking her in, for DWI." Mann's voice turned defensive. "I didn't know what else had happened, but it was pretty clear she was drunk or maybe stoned."

The next question, Caroline knew, was critical. Jackson paused before asking it, and each word was slow and distinct.

"At the time you arrested Ms. Allen, Officer Mann, did you believe that a homicide had been committed?"

Mann fidgeted in his chair, but his voice was firm. "I had no idea what had happened, except that there was blood in the car, and someone might be hurt. At first, I thought it might be *her* blood. But she wasn't telling me a thing."

"So you took her to the station in Resolve."

"Yessir. I gave her my jacket and drove her in. Then I booked her for DWI and put her in a cell."

"What did you do then?"

"I went through the wallet and found a driver's license with a man's picture and a name—James Case. That was the first time I was sure the wallet wasn't hers."

Jackson nodded. "Did that concern you?"

"Yessir." Mann's shoulders hunched together, and his forehead creased; with a certain detachment, Caroline watched the young policeman gather himself to give the answer he and Jackson had rehearsed. "I was worried that someone might be hurt somewhere and needing help. I mean, that's one of the reasons you take this job—to help protect people. You have to consider all sorts of things, like maybe there's a killer out there who might hurt someone again if we didn't find him, who even might hurt Ms. Allen. But the first thing was this guy on the driver's license, and was *he* hurt and still out there."

It might even be true, Caroline thought; at least Mann was young enough to believe it. Next to her, Brett stared at the table.

Caroline whispered, "Keep looking at him. No matter what."

Brett did that. But she could not look at Caroline.

"So at the time," Jackson was asking, "your concern was public safety?"

"Yessir. And maybe saving a life."

"And you did not believe that a homicide had been committed, or that Ms. Allen had committed it?"

For the first time, Caroline rose to address Judge Towle. "Objection," she said in a calm, clear voice. "To both questions, actually. I don't want to interrupt Mr. Watts's testimony, but he shouldn't be telling our nominal witness what his answers should be. After all, these proceedings should have at least some spontaneity."

Towle's owlish look at Caroline said that he understood perfectly: that Jackson, unsure of his witness, was steering him through a trap Caroline wished to spring—that he had waited too long to read Brett her rights for a charge of murder. And that Caroline must cut this off.

"Sustained." Towle turned to Jackson. "Let's have this in Officer Mann's own words. And thoughts, if possible."

Jackson looked unruffled; his question had already provided Mann with the answer, and Caroline's objection had underscored how central it was. "Did you show the license to Ms. Allen?" he asked.

"Yessir."

"And what, if anything, did you say to her?"

"What I just said—that I was afraid someone out there might be hurt, might get worse if we couldn't help him."

Jackson nodded in approval. "And did she answer you?"

"She did. She told me to look out by Heron Lake." Turning to Brett, he finished quietly, "When they found him, his throat had been cut with a knife."

Brett's face was white. Beneath the table, Caroline touched her knee.

Jackson let a moment pass. "Between the time of Ms. Allen's statement and the time James Case was found dead, what did you do?"

Slowly, Mann's gaze returned to Jackson. "I called the state police. At their instructions, I took her to Connaughton County Hospital and then drove back to the station."

"And when did you next see her?"

"After they'd found the body, and we'd called the Major Crimes Unit of the state police. They called from the hospital and said she wanted to see me."

"What did you do?"

"Waited for Sergeant Summers from Major Crimes in Concord. When he got there, he had them put her in a room with both of us."

"And at that time, did you give Ms. Allen her Miranda warnings?"

"Sergeant Summers did. It's all on tape."

"And how did she seem to you?"

"Pale and upset. But sober—anxious to talk."

"Did she seem to understand her rights?"

"Yessir. On the tape, she says that doesn't matter—that she wants to talk."

Jackson paused a moment. "How long," he asked slowly, "had it been since you picked her up?"

"It was nearly six. I'd picked her up at approximately eleven-thirty."

"Did she seem coherent?"

"Yessir."

Jackson nodded. "We'll introduce the tape through Sergeant Summers. But could you describe the essence of her statement as to how James Case had died?"

Mann nodded. "She told us that someone else had killed him. And that she found him like that."

"And in the course of her statement, did you ask Ms. Allen about her relationship to Mr. Case?"

"Yessir."

"And what did she say?"

"He was her boyfriend."

All at once, Caroline could see what was coming. She had an

objection—that the tape spoke for itself. But to raise this would only make things worse.

Pausing, Jackson gave Mann a long, considering look. "And did you then ask her if Mr. Case was involved with any other women?"

"Yessir.

"And what did she answer?"

As he turned to Brett, Caroline saw the girl brace herself. "Ms. Allen said, 'Of course not.' " Pausing, Mann seemed bemused. "It was the only time she sounded angry."

Caroline felt the implications in the pit of her stomach: that Brett was sober enough to lie. And that she had needed to lie about Megan Race because she needed to lie about everything.

In an involuntary reflex, Brett looked down.

Turning to Caroline, Jackson said with grave politeness, "Your witness, Counsel."

THREE

WALKING TOWARD the witness, Caroline took a moment to gather herself. She saw her family watching her, her father's grim inspection. Most of all, she felt Brett waiting behind her.

"Let's take this from the beginning," she said. "You found Brett Allen in her Jeep, by the side of the road. Naked."

Mann gave her a wary look. "That's right."

"Spattered with blood."

"Yes."

"Specked with vomit."

"Yes."

"And, it seems fair to say, disoriented."

Mann shook his head. "I don't know if I could say that."

Caroline appraised him. *Take it slow,* she told herself. Quietly, she asked, "You had no doubt she was intoxicated, right?"

"Not really, no."

"And what did you base that on?"

"Like I said, I thought I could smell wine and marijuana. Plus she'd thrown up."

"Is that all?"

Mann leaned back in the witness stand. "I think so, yes."

Caroline raised an eyebrow. "She was naked, wasn't she?"

"Yes."

"How many other naked drivers have you arrested?"

Mann hesitated, and then shrugged. "None."

"And yet you testified that at the time you picked her up for DWI, she seemed to understand you. Was that based on anything she said?"

"No."

"Because she didn't respond at all, did she?"

"Not that I remember."

Caroline moved closer. In a flat voice, she said, "Indeed, after you told her you were taking her in, the next thing she did—the very next thing—was throw up."

Pausing, Mann looked troubled. "She did that, yes."

"And on the way to the station she said nothing, correct?"

"Correct."

"So your entire basis for believing that this naked, blood-spattered, nauseous, and intoxicated young woman was nonetheless not 'disoriented' was that she could tell you her name. Oh, and that her eyes 'followed' you when you asked questions."

Mann glanced toward Jackson. "I guess so," he said at length.

"But how do you know that she understood you?"

Mann's brow furrowed. "I can't *know* that."

"Or even that she knew what had happened to her?"

Mann glanced at Brett. "She told us she did later. She gave a whole statement about what happened."

It was a good answer. Caroline felt it break her rhythm; in that moment, she knew why Jackson had let this go.

She drew a breath. Quietly, she asked, "Have you ever been intoxicated, Officer Mann?"

Jackson was on his feet at once. "Objection, Your Honor. Officer Mann's personal experience in this regard—if any—is irrelevant to Ms. Allen's conduct here."

Caroline faced Judge Towle. "Your Honor, Officer Mann has offered an opinion—at least a surmise—on Ms. Allen's state of mind from the moment of arrest until she finished her statement. Unless he has a medical background, that opinion is based solely on practical experience. Perhaps including his own."

Towle propped his chin on one hand, glancing quickly toward Channing Masters. Almost absently, he said, "I'll allow it."

"Have you?" Caroline asked Mann.

Mann flushed. "I would say so, yes. A few times—always whiskey."

"Ever get so drunk that you didn't know where you were?"

Mann looked down; a painful attempt at honesty seemed to tighten his face. "Once. After a bachelor party."

"And do you remember everything that happened that night?"

"Most of it . . ." His voice trailed off, and he looked at Caroline with sudden comprehension.

Quietly, she finished for him. "But not until later."

He nodded slowly. "That's right. And not everything."

That last comment, Caroline realized, was far too close too home.

"At the time you arrested Ms. Allen," she asked abruptly, "was her hair wet?"

Mann blinked, surprised. "I think so, yes."

"On what do you base that?"

Mann thought for a time. "Like I said, I gave her my jacket. When I put it over her shoulders, her hair felt wet." He scrutinized Brett briefly. "Her hair was curlier and tighter than it looks to me now."

Caroline paused. "So that later, when she gave her statement, there was at least one part you believed. When Brett told you she'd gone swimming."

"I guess so, yes."

"That must have been before James Case was killed, correct?"

Mann hesitated, and then spread his hands. "How would I know?"

"Because when you arrested her, Officer Mann, her face and neck and torso and hair all were flecked with blood."

Mann looked surprised. "That's true. . . ."

"So that it's quite possible that—just as she told you—Brett Allen was in the middle of Heron Lake at the time James Case was killed."

There was a first murmur from the press. Instantly, Jackson rose to object. "Your honor," he said. "That may be counsel's argument. But how and when Ms. Allen's hair got wet is well beyond the knowledge of this witness."

That, Caroline knew, was utterly correct. "Not so," she answered tartly. "Not when there was blood on Ms. Allen's skin and in her ad-mittedly wet hair."

Towle permitted himself a smile. "It's not the 'wet' part Mr. Watts objects to. It's the 'lake' part. Objection sustained."

Caroline did not argue; she had made her point. Turning back to Mann, she asked, "Would you characterize the blood spatter on Ms. Allen's skin and hair as heavy?"

Mann seemed to search his memory. "No, I wouldn't say 'heavy.' "

"Then how would you describe it?"

Mann folded his hands, glancing again at Jackson. "It was more like spray—dots and a few drops."

"So the surface of her skin was hardly blood-soaked."

Mann shook his head. "It was more like a spray on her face, and then spots on her breasts and stomach. Pretty far apart."

Caroline wondered for an instant how hearing this felt to Brett. And then Jackson was up again. "Your Honor, we have photographs of the spray pattern on Ms. Allen. I suggest that these exhibits are the best evidence of what Ms. Masters is trying to elicit here."

Caroline still faced Judge Towle. "With a few more questions, Your Honor, I believe that I can demonstrate that Mr. Watts's pictures are not 'best evidence' of anything. May I proceed?"

Towle nodded briskly. "Go ahead, Ms. Masters. But quickly— otherwise, I'm inclined to agree with Mr. Watts."

Caroline faced Mann again. "You gave Ms. Allen your jacket, correct?"

"Yes."

"And she zipped it up?"

Mann hesitated. "*I* did, actually."

"And she wore it to the jail."

"Yes."

"How much of Ms. Allen would you say the jacket covered?"

Mann looked down. "Maybe to midthigh."

"And did Ms. Allen pull the jacket down around her, trying to cover herself?"

Mann seemed to flush. "I remember that. Yes."

"So that, inevitably, the jacket touched her skin?"

Mann looked down. In a slow, reluctant voice, he said, "When I got the jacket back, there were spots of blood on it. So I'd have to say yes."

Caroline felt briefly sorry for him; for perhaps the first time in his life, Mann was learning what the most thoughtful—or thoughtless— act might become in the hands of a defense lawyer. "Did you send your jacket to the cleaners, Officer Mann?"

"Yes."

"And you never discussed this with the medical examiner or anyone from the state police?"

Mann raised his head. "No, ma'am," he said formally. "I did not."

"All right. Then let's move to your conversation with Ms. Allen after you got to jail. You did not advise Ms. Allen of her rights—such as the right to counsel and against self-incrimination."

Mann's face hardened. "That's right," he said firmly. "We didn't even have a body, ma'am. All I was after was protecting public safety and maybe finding someone who'd been hurt."

Caroline placed both hands on her hips. "And how did you think this unknown person might have gotten hurt?"

Mann gave a fractional shrug. "I didn't know."

"Maybe with the knife? After all, it was bloody, and there were no stab wounds you could see on Ms. Allen." Caroline paused. "And you'd pretty much seen everything."

Mann flushed again. "I thought it was possible that it was the knife, yes."

"Possible? Except for the knife and the blood on Ms. Allen, you had no reason to wonder if anyone had been 'hurt,' correct?"

"I guess not."

Caroline mustered an incredulous look. "And how did you think that this person had gotten 'hurt'? By falling on the knife?"

Jackson stood at once. "Objection, Your Honor. There's no reason for counsel to badger this witness. If she has a question, let her ask it straight out."

"I accept that, Your Honor." Caroline turned to Mann again. "My apologies," she said quietly. "But in all candor, didn't you consider the possibility that this unknown person had been 'hurt' by Brett Allen?"

Folding his hands again, Mann took a long time to answer. Caroline became aware of the dampness of her palms. Then, in a soft voice, Mann said, "Yes, ma'am, I suppose I did. But all it was was speculation."

"So when you asked Ms. Allen if someone was hurt out there, you'd considered the possibility that Ms. Allen might have committed an act of violence?"

Mann drew a silent breath. "Yes."

"And after Ms. Allen told you that you might want to look at Heron Lake, you called the state police."

"Yes."

"With whom did you speak?"

"Sergeant Summers. The one who came here after we found the body."

"And what did you tell him?"

Mann hesitated. "That we might have some sort of actual or attempted homicide. Maybe involving someone named James Case."

Caroline nodded. "Did you tell Sergeant Summers about Brett, the knife, the wallet, and the blood? To get his advice on what to do?"

"Yes."

"And when Sergeant Summers told you to take her to Connaughton County Hospital, it was to preserve the evidence on her body, right?"

"Yes."

"Until you could get a warrant to search her person."

Mann's voice was softer now. "Yes."

"Because she was a potential suspect, correct?"

"Objection." Quickly, Jackson moved forward; for the first time, he looked angry. "What Officer Mann may have said or been told after Ms. Allen's initial statement is irrelevant to what he thought before. Ms. Masters is trying to turn good police work into something sinister."

Ignoring him, Caroline faced Judge Towle. "Not at all, Your Honor. Officer Mann is entitled to take reasonable measures to find a theoretically wounded person, including inquiries of Ms. Allen. But without Miranda warnings, Mr. Watts is not entitled to use the statement of an intoxicated, disoriented young woman in police custody as evidence for a charge of murder. Or as a basis for warrants to gather yet more evidence—dubious as the evidence may be."

Towle held up a hand, gazing from Jackson to Caroline. "That question," he said to them both, "will be resolved by the Superior Court should this court find probable cause. It's not the purpose of this proceeding. But while we're here, I'll allow Ms. Masters to ask the questions, as they may also relate to probable cause."

"Thank you, Your Honor." Caroline glanced at her father. His gaze was inward, his face quite composed; perhaps Caroline alone could have read the satisfaction in his face. She turned to Mann again.

"The question, Officer Mann, was whether, at the time you sent

Ms. Allen to the hospital at Connaughton Falls, she was a potential suspect in some possible crime of violence."

Mann's jaw worked. "Yes."

"Based on her statement regarding where to look for James Case."

Mann hesitated, formulating his answer. "That," he said, "and the knife and blood and wallet."

"But without Ms. Allen's statement, you wouldn't have known where to look, would you?"

Mann's face had closed now. "Not right away."

Caroline tilted her head. "Prior to Ms. Allen's initial statement, did you test her for intoxication?"

"No."

"How did she seem to you?"

Mann glanced at Brett again; his expression softened a bit. "Slow. Kind of stunned."

"Did she have a hard time speaking?"

"A little."

"Have you ever arrested someone who was under the influence of marijuana?"

"Yes."

"Was Ms. Allen's demeanor like that?"

Mann paused. "She seemed to have a hard time remembering words, and her speech was slurred."

Caroline moved closer. "Tell me, Officer Mann—about how long was it from your arrest of Ms. Allen until she arrived at Connaughton County Hospital?"

"Maybe two hours."

"And was she then tested for intoxication?"

"Yes."

"Did you see the results?"

"Yes."

"Was Ms. Allen intoxicated?"

Mann folded his hands. "According to the report, Ms. Allen was at nearly twice the legal limit."

"So that it's fair to say that she was intoxicated the whole time she was with you?"

"I would say so."

Caroline nodded, satisfied. Not only was it clear that Brett had been intoxicated at the moment of the murder, but if the Superior

Court followed the law, what Brett said before her trip to the hospital might be kept out of evidence. Even the evidence obtained through the two search warrants, secured because of her initial statement, could possibly be suppressed.

It was time to address Brett's final statement.

"What is your understanding, Officer Mann, as to when Ms. Allen was tested for intoxication?"

Mann's eyes narrowed. "Pretty quickly, from the report. Maybe thirty minutes after getting there."

"So about two o'clock?"

"I'd have to see the report again. But I think that's pretty close."

"And you and Officer Summers started questioning her around six-fifteen, correct? At least according to the tape."

"Yes."

"And before that, Sergeant Summers read Ms. Allen her Miranda rights?"

"True."

"Did you also retest her for intoxication?"

Mann hesitated. "We did not."

Caroline made herself sound puzzled. "So you don't know whether she was still intoxicated?"

Mann frowned. "She was a whole lot different by then—coherent, eager to talk." His voice rose. "Before we questioned her, we called Dr. Pumphrey at the hospital—the one who tested her. He said that by four hours the effect should have worn off."

"But the doctor didn't see her before questioning, right?"

"No."

"Or test her?"

"No."

"Do you know when Ms. Allen had last eaten?"

"No."

"Or slept?"

"No."

"Did you give her any food?"

For a moment, Mann looked chastened. "No."

"Are you familiar with a chemical known as THC?"

Another pause. "I know it's in marijuana."

"Do you know how it affects memory?"

"Not really, no."

"Or how long it stays in the bloodstream?"

"No."

"Or the extent to which the potency of marijuana may be affected by the prior use of alcohol, followed by sexual intercourse?"

Mann's mouth formed a stubborn line. "I'm not a doctor, ma'am."

But Caroline's expert was, and he was prepared to say at trial that Brett could not have been sober and that her memory was inevitably confused. Quietly, Caroline responded, "I appreciate that, Officer Mann. Thank you."

Mann looked toward Towle, as if hopeful that this was over. His demeanor was different now—less conviction and idealism, stubbornness seeming to alternate with confusion. Still, Caroline was not quite done.

"Tell me," she asked, "during the time you spent with Ms. Allen, did you form an impression as to whether she was right- or left-handed?"

Mann leaned back in his chair. "Left-handed," he said finally.

"And on what do you base that?"

"I remember she was always brushing the hair back from her face, like she was nervous or distracted. She'd use her left hand."

Caroline nodded. "Thank you, Officer Mann. No further questions."

FOUR

"YOU'RE REALLY GOOD," Brett said.

Caroline felt anything but good; the adrenaline of the courtroom had evanesced, leaving only weariness and a certain vague depression. But Caroline did not believe in false modesty, and it was better to place more pressure on herself if it helped Brett through the hearing.

"Yes," she answered. "I am. And I did better than I'd expected."

They sat at a beat-up desk in a spare room at the Connaughton County Courthouse; court was adjourned for the day, and an officer waited outside to deliver Brett back to prison. But they needed to talk, Caroline knew, though perhaps Brett just needed time.

Brett was quiet for a moment. "I felt a little sorry for him, though. The cop."

"Maybe he wanted to help you, in a way. Or maybe he'll just learn to lie next time. In San Francisco, he already would have."

Brett considered her. "Is that hard for you? Embarrassing someone like that?"

Caroline shrugged. "You just don't think about it. Lawyers can't—if I did, where would *you* be?"

Brett looked curious. "It's like you can turn your feelings off. Like flicking a switch."

It was odd, Caroline reflected, how little she minded this girl's probing now. "Is that so interesting?" she asked.

"It's not *usual*. At least not for a woman." Brett shook her head, as if bemused. "You're so unlike my mother it's ridiculous."

"We had different mothers. Genes count for a lot." For the first time, Caroline smiled. "You don't have to understand everything, Brett. Or everyone."

Looking at Caroline, Brett's face became softer. "It's just so childish. Three weeks ago, I didn't even know you. And now I depend on you completely, and I'm so damned scared."

How best to answer? Caroline wondered. "Being on trial does that to people," she said quietly. "It's part of the reason I am the way I am. Or, at least, try to appear that way to you."

Brett tilted her head, as if to see her from a different angle. "Who worries about you, Caroline?"

Caroline gave a wry smile. "Why should anyone? I'm only the lawyer here."

Brett studied the desk. "Someday," she said, "I hope we can just be friends."

Caroline smiled again. "That's why I'm trying to spring you, of course. Because you've never come to San Francisco."

Brett's face seemed to relax, and Caroline watched her imagine a place she had seen only in pictures. At another time, Caroline would have been content to sit quietly in her company. But there was far too much to do.

"There's something we've never really gone over," Caroline said at last. "That telephone call to James. Just before you went to the lake."

Torn from fantasy, Brett looked down again; the memory led to a vortex of confusion, Caroline could see—or, perhaps, guilt. In a quiet voice, Brett asked, "Why is that important now?"

But Caroline could not answer. "Just humor me," she said.

Hours later, Caroline cracked open the window of her room. The air of a fresh summer night felt cool on her skin.

She could not sleep yet.

On her desk, next to a mug of coffee, were police reports and transcripts of interviews—of Brett, Betty, Larry, her father, Megan Race. On top of that was Megan's diary.

She sat at the desk, reading the entries yet again.

Even as she studied them, mentally extracting her cross-examination from Megan's coiled script, this invasion made Caroline queasy. Too clearly, she remembered her own diary. Could recall across the years the entries after David vanished, in the months she stayed on at Martha's Vineyard, estranged from her family, hoping still to hear from him: a litany of loss, longing, guilt, regret, rage—at her father, at Betty, and, most of all, at herself. Until the hope faded and, with resignation and resolve, Caroline forced herself to imagine a new life. The diary stopped one page from the end.

The day before she left for California, Caroline had burned it.

Rising now, she returned to the window. Saw again the church, the white frame houses, the rolling hills. A snapshot from her memory.

She had never thought to return here. Never thought that the decision she had once believed essential to that new life might, in the end, undo it.

She had lied to Brett. With a longing as deep as it was pointless, Caroline wished that she could talk to someone. But it could not, in fairness, be this girl. And, in open court, Caroline would ruin what remained of her friendship with the other person who might understand.

Three mornings from now, Megan Race would take the stand.

Caroline returned to the desk and began making notes.

FIVE

CAROLINE'S FIRST IMAGE of the morning was Jackson, bending over the rail between lawyer and spectator, murmuring to her father. The moment was awkward, formal: a civil handshake; a few words from Jackson; her father's slight nod; Larry and Betty pretending not to notice. And then Judge Towle assumed the bench, and Jackson called Sergeant Kenton Summers.

From his first moments on the stand, Caroline saw that Summers would be difficult: as Jackson quickly established, he had sixteen years' experience with the state police and an expertise in forensics, and had been lead investigator in twenty-seven homicides. The experience of court was stamped on his ruddy face—in the heavy lids, the calm cobalt eyes, a certain absence of expression. With his chestnut hair and still youthful face, Summers could not be much over forty, but he had the air of someone who was beyond surprise or anger. He gazed at the tape machine in front of Jackson.

"Prior to your interrogation," Jackson was asking, "how would you describe Ms. Allen's behavior?"

Before responding, Summers seemed to consider each response; it was a trick, Caroline sensed, to cover those moments when he was truly surprised. Now, quietly, he answered, "She was sober, coherent, and clearly followed our questions. As the tape will show."

As if on cue, Jackson punched a button, and the tape began playing.

Summers' voice filled the courtroom, calmly reciting the Miranda warnings. Next to Caroline, Brett listened, intent and pale, as she waived her rights. She sounded quite lucid.

Save for Brett's voice, the policeman's soft questions, the courtroom was silent.

As she approached the facts of the murder, Brett's tone moved from hesitancy to dread. Perhaps only Caroline heard the pause as Brett recounted her conversation with James, omitting their fight. But while Brett listened to herself describe finding the body, voice trembling with a surprise and horror that seemed quite genuine, anyone could see the convulsion of her throat. And then the tape reached her incontrovertible lie.

"Did James have other girlfriends?" Summer asked.

"No." Brett's voice was shocked and angry. "There's no way."

Listening, Brett was still. *When?* Caroline wrote on her pad, and then the tape ended.

Someone coughed, and Jackson spoke again. "Did you begin by placing credence in Ms. Allen's statement?" he asked.

Summers nodded. "It was the only clear account we had. In fact, one of our main objectives was attempting to confirm what she told us."

It was clever, Caroline saw: Jackson would use Summers to show how much they had wished to believe Brett's story. "Could you describe your efforts?" Jackson asked.

"To start, there was the crime scene. We used six investigators, including two from the crime lab, to cordon off two hundred square feet around where the body was. Then we divided the area into ten-foot sections. For one week, we went through each section inch by inch."

"What did you find?"

"That we could follow Ms. Allen's path from the body clearly— there were broken branches, trampled underbrush, specks of blood on the leaves. But we found no such signs of a second person. With as much blood as Mr. Case lost, it would be almost impossible for the killer to leave the scene without traces of blood on leaves or shrubbery."

Judge Towle watched Summers intently. "Did you take other steps," Jackson asked, "to explore Ms. Allen's claim of an unknown killer?"

"We did." Raising a thick hand, Summers ticked them off. "We talked to neighbors and other people in the area, looking for sightings of strange people or vehicles anywhere near the lake. We found none.

"We checked for reports of vagrants or break-ins, searched for signs that anyone had been living in the woods recently. Again, nothing.

"We looked for evidence that James Case, as Ms. Allen claimed, was in trouble with some unknown drug dealer. But we found no evidence of a break-in at his apartment, or any stolen money.

"We interviewed his neighbors, his landlord—anyone we could find who knew him. And we came up with no one who, as far as we could tell, had any motive to do what someone had done to this boy." Summers paused. "Which was cut his throat so deeply that his head was more off than on."

This last was delivered with such matter-of-fact authority that, even for Caroline, it took a moment to register. "And on what basis," Jackson asked calmly, "did you conclude that it was Ms. Allen who had done this?"

Summers stroked his chin. "To start, there was the physical evidence. Other than Officer Mann's, the only prints on the knife were Ms. Allen's.

"We found her fingerprints on the neck of the victim—but no one else's except the EMTs.

"Her prints were on the wallet—again, no others.

"The only path from the scene, leaving traces of the victim's blood, was hers.

"The only hairs on the victim's body were from Ms. Allen's head and pubic area.

"There were no signs of a struggle, and the only marks on his body—other than knife wounds—were scratches on his back. Which were accounted for when we found traces of his skin beneath Ms. Allen's fingernails.

"A search of Ms. Allen showed the victim's blood spattered on her hair and body, and established that they had had sexual intercourse." For the first time, Summers looked directly at Judge Towle. "And yet the victim had never climaxed."

"Were there other factors?" Jackson asked.

Pausing, Summers frowned. "The nature of the homicide. In my experience, drug dealers don't go around killing other drug dealers with knives. Too dangerous."

This was right, Caroline knew; next to her, she saw Brett's eyes shut. "This had the look of a very personal killing," Summers continued. "Driven by passion and anger, and not done by a stranger."

"Keep looking at him," Caroline whispered to Brett, and stood. "Move to strike," she snapped. "This witness's opinions on what the mode of death must mean are the sheerest speculation, as in all the business regarding the mode of investigation. And, as I once pointed out to Mr. Watts, neither Charles Manson nor his friends knew the people they butchered."

Jackson faced Judge Towle. "Your Honor," he said, "this is not a jury trial, and the court is fully capable of weighing any piece of testimony in assessing probable cause. Moreover, we are about to show that the nature of the killing seems consistent with the motive for the killing."

"I'll hear it," Towle said promptly. "Overruled." But when Caroline sat down, Brett was composed again.

At once, Jackson turned to Summers. "You'll recall, Sergeant Summers, that Ms. Allen told you James Case had asked her to go to California, and that—at least as far as she knew—the victim had no other romantic involvements. Did there come a time when another witness came forward to shed light on that statement?"

"There did." Pausing, Summers seemed to draw the courtroom closer: as reporters paused, pencils over pads, Towle leaned forward. Next to Caroline, Brett seemed not to breathe. "A student at Chase College," Summers went on, "who told us that she and the victim had a continuing and intimate relationship, and that he had asked her to go with him to California. And that he had promised to break this to Ms. Allen on the night he was murdered."

There was a stirring in the courtroom. With a cold, channeled anger, Caroline resolved to make Jackson pay for this. "Were you able to confirm that such a relationship existed?" he asked.

"Yes. Through neighbors." Summers faced the judge again. "And according to our witness, Ms. Allen knew about it."

Amidst the sound of stirring, Jackson nodded. "Based on this new information, what—if anything—did you conclude?"

"Conclude? Nothing. But it was a motive, jealousy and anger, and it helped make sense of how Ms. Allen acted." Summers gathered himself. "In my view, Ms. Allen used wine and marijuana to place James Case in a position of extreme vulnerability—sexual intercourse. And then cut his throat before he climaxed." His voice was soft, uninflected. "Which may also explain why she took his wallet afterward. Because her imaginary drug dealer, the one that she invented, wanted back his money."

SIX

SUMMERS' EYES were pale-blue chips, Caroline thought—opaque and unimpressed.

"You placed considerable emphasis," Caroline began, "on Brett's taped statement. But her initial statement was made to Officer Mann, wasn't it? When she suggested the police look at Heron Lake."

"Yes. That's why Officer Mann called me."

"Did he express concern that there had been an act of violence?"

"Yes."

"After which you told him to take Ms. Allen to the hospital?"

"Yes."

"So that the police could get a warrant to search her?"

"If it seemed justified."

"And did you subsequently determine that a warrant to search her person was justified?"

"Yes."

"Because you found Mr. Case's body?"

"Yes."

Caroline paused. "Based on Ms. Allen's prior statement?"

A first stubbornness in the blue eyes, the instinct to resist. "We would have found him," he said finally. "It might have helped us find him quicker."

It was a good answer: Summers understood the trap—that much of the evidence against Brett was based on her initial statement—and was trying to avoid it. Caroline made herself look puzzled. "The location of the body is fairly inaccessible, isn't it?"

"Yes."

"Making it unlikely you would have found it before daylight."

Slight hesitation. "Maybe."

"By which time you were questioning Ms. Allen for the second time."

"Yes."

"After you'd already obtained a warrant from Judge Deane, at three a.m., and searched her body."

Once more, the minimal answer. "Yes."

"And searched Mr. Case."

"Yes."

"And Brett Allen's property."

"As best we could, in the dark."

"Searches based on a warrant application which cited Ms. Allen's statement and the body, correct?"

Summers frowned. "Yes."

"And you understood that Brett Allen's statement—the one to Officer Mann—was obtained without Miranda warnings?"

Summers sat back. "When Officer Mann called, that was what he told me, yes."

"During that conversation, did you and Officer Mann discuss whether he should interrogate Ms. Allen further?"

Summers' lids dropped slightly. "Yes," he said at length.

Caroline felt a moment's relief: at least they were honest. "And did you," she ventured, "advise Officer Mann not to question her?"

Summers folded his hands. "At that time, yes."

"For what reason?"

Summers considered her. "It was a matter of experience."

"And intoxication?"

"That too."

"So that you were concerned not only that Ms. Allen hadn't been Mirandized but that she was too intoxicated to make sense."

Summers shrugged, a slow shifting of shoulders. "I wouldn't say concerned. When in doubt, it's better to test someone."

"And, when tested, Ms. Allen proved to be intoxicated, correct?"

"As of roughly two o'clock."

"And at six o'clock, when you interrogated Ms. Allen, what was that based on?"

Summers gave her a level gaze. "Her request."

It was a splendid answer, and quite wounding. Caroline stood very still. "I meant the interrogation," she said evenly. "It was based, was it not, on finding the body, searching Ms. Allen, and searching her property?"

Summers hesitated. "In the main."

"All of which was based on her initial statement to Officer Mann, telling him where to look?"

A longer pause: Summers knew quite well that, if Caroline was lucky, she could suppress almost every piece of evidence obtained through the initial statement. "We would have questioned her," he said, "as soon as she was sober—body or no body. Which we'd have found in daylight. But she came to us."

Another damaging answer. "Sober?" Caroline shot back.

"Sober."

"According to whom?"

"Dr. Pumphrey."

"Who never saw her, correct?"

For the first time, Caroline watched Summers fight himself: he wanted to argue with her but was too experienced to do so. Watts, he knew, would handle this. "Dr. Pumphrey saw her at the hospital," Summers answered. "At six o'clock, I just described her to him."

"So the people who did see Brett at six were you and Officer Mann?"

"Yes."

"And you, like Officer Mann, cannot offer a medical opinion as to her sobriety?"

"No. Just an eyeball opinion . . ."

"On the effect of THC on memory?"

"No."

"Or personality?"

"No."

Caroline put her hands on her hips. "Do you also have no medical opinion on whether marijuana and alcohol can have the effect of inducing what is commonly known as paranoia?"

Annoyance, she saw, expressed itself through a certain deadness in Summers' eyes. "No," he said tersely.

Caroline paused a moment. "So based on your assumption that Ms. Allen was functioning normally, if she gave you any information you perceived to be misleading, you thought this was deliberate?"

"Not necessarily." Summers' voice rose slightly. "After all, she *had* been intoxicated. . . ."

"Precisely. But now she was a suspect, right? Had to be, or you wouldn't have given her Miranda warnings."

Summers folded his hands again. "If someone is even potentially a suspect, we'll warn them."

"Perhaps you," Caroline retorted. "But not Officer Mann."

"Objection," Jackson said. "Asked and answered."

"Sustained." Towle glanced at Caroline. "Your point is taken, Counsel. Move on."

In the moment Caroline took to compose her thoughts, she was aware of everyone around her and everything at stake—for her and, most of all, for Brett. And then, as at other moments of her life, a blessed calm came over her.

"Isn't it true," she asked, "that from the minute you first questioned her, Brett Allen was your prime suspect?"

Summers shook his head. "Prime, no. An obvious possibility, sure. As I said, we looked for others—like this drug dealer."

"But you dismissed that, right?"

"No evidence—no money in his apartment, no sign of a break-in."

Caroline looked bemused. "Does it seem logical to you that someone who wanted to hide stolen drug money would stick it in his apartment?"

"Objection," Jackson interjected. "Calls for speculation."

"No more so than that drug dealers are too genteel to cut throats." Caroline turned to Judge Towle. "I'm calling on Sergeant Summers' extensive knowledge of the drug culture, Your Honor. As did Mr. Watts."

Towle smiled faintly. "Overruled," he said, and looked to Summers.

"It is speculation," Summers answered finally. "But no, your own apartment might not be the best place to hide money."

Caroline paused a moment. "It is also true, is it not, that Mr. Case's door lacks a dead bolt?"

Summers gave her a long, hard look. "That's right."

"And based on your knowledge of the criminal element, one desiring to enter an apartment can take a mold and have a key designed, correct?"

"Yes."

Caroline could feel Jackson's gaze now; her pulse was rapid. "Or even, with sufficient skill, enter by using a credit card?"

Summers put a finger to his mouth, tapping it lightly, still appraising Caroline. "True," he said at length.

"After which, to the extent the apartment was disordered, James Case could simply have cleaned it up. If not the intruder himself."

"I suppose so."

Motionless, Jackson stared at the table. "Now," Caroline went on, "can you say whether or to what extent James Case was dealing drugs? Because, among other reasons, it's something college kids don't chat with cops about."

"Sometimes," Summers retorted quickly. "But there's no evidence that this drug dealer ever existed, let alone found his way to an isolated spot in time to murder James Case with a knife. The physical evidence all points to Ms. Allen."

It was the answer Caroline had hoped for. "Let's take that evidence, then. You say, for example, that you found Brett's fingerprint on the victim's neck. Would you call that print important?"

A small shrug. "It's one among many pieces of evidence. I wouldn't want to classify it."

"Isn't it true that, at least in the reported literature, no one has ever lifted a print off the body of a man?"

Summers emitted a soundless sigh, as if reaching for calm. "I wouldn't know."

"Are you personally aware of any?"

"No."

"Because, among other reasons, the hair and roughness of a man's skin make lifting prints more difficult."

"True. But in this case, Ms. Allen left a print on the skin surrounding the wound. Where there was blood to reflect a print."

"That's hardly surprising, is it—she says she touched him *after* his throat was cut. Tell me, didn't you find other prints in the blood?"

Summers considered her with chilly eyes. "One. It belonged to an EMT who was called to the scene."

Caroline raised an eyebrow. "Is he a suspect?"

"No."

"And, in truth, there are no prints on the skin other than those found in the victim's blood?"

"No. There are not."

Caroline nodded. "Brett's prints on the knife are also found in a deposit of blood, are they not?"

"Yes."

"As are Officer Mann's?"

Summers tapped his lips again and then, quite consciously, placed both hands in his lap. "Yes."

"Who made them, just as Ms. Allen did, by touching the bloody knife?"

"Yes."

Caroline tilted her head. "Are there any clean prints on the knife? Ones not imprinted in blood?"

"Not that we found, no. . . ."

"Nor," Caroline pursued softly, "can you link that knife to Brett Allen."

"No."

"What about the wallet? Was Ms. Allen's print there found on a deposit of blood?"

Another pause. "Yes."

"Any clean prints?"

"No."

"Not even James Case's? It *was* his wallet."

"No." Summers examined his hands. "Leather usually won't take a print."

"Then all this could have happened just the way Brett told you, correct? She found the body, tried to administer CPR, and got blood on her hands." She paused. "And, therefore, left bloody prints on the victim's neck, the knife, and the wallet. Just like the EMT and Officer Mann."

"Whose prints we can explain." Looking up, Summers finished in a chill voice. "There are no other prints, Ms. Masters."

"And a thousand possible reasons why." Jackson, Caroline saw, had remained quite still. "For example, might the killer have worn gloves?"

Summers assumed a certain calm again. "Counselor," he said patiently, "there's not many ways to tell if someone was wearing gloves."

"Precisely. But if Brett had her hands on the knife, about to slice Mr. Case's windpipe, wouldn't she have left at least one clean print on the handle of the knife?"

"The handle's bone. Not an easy print, either."

"But the sole print Brett Allen left on the hilt is a bloody one, correct? Clearly made sometime after Mr. Case's throat was cut."

Summers lowered his eyelids, studying her closely. "That's true."

"So it couldn't be the prints that caused you to opine that Brett Allen must be a murderer."

"Not in themselves, no." Summers' patience sounded strained. "You have to look at the totality of the evidence."

"Let's do that, Sergeant. Pick a piece—any piece."

"Is that a question?" Jackson interjected.

Caroline ignored him. "All right," she said to Summers. "I believe you mentioned Mr. Case's failure to ejaculate."

Summers nodded. "I did."

"And what did the tests show regarding Mr. Case's level of intoxication?"

"That he was intoxicated."

Caroline smiled slightly. "In your observation, does intoxication in the adult male sometimes lead to, shall we say, incomplete sexual performance? Or is impotence inevitably the result of death?"

From the back of the courtroom, someone coughed, suppressing laughter. "Maybe," Summers said mildly, "I should leave that one for the medical examiner."

"But you don't insist, do you, that violent death is the only explanation for Mr. Case's failure to ejaculate?"

A first grim glint of humor. "No."

"And, in your pantheon of evidence, would you say that this failure is more or less important than *your* purported failure to find evidence of an escape path other than Brett Allen's?"

Summers hesitated. "Less."

"Much less?"

"I would say so."

"We'll get to that in a minute, then. But let me ask you this: Do you have any reason to quarrel with Officer Mann's belief that Ms. Allen's hair was wet?"

"I've got nothing on that, one way or the other."

"So you also have no belief as to whether Ms. Allen went swimming?"

"No."

Caroline raised an eyebrow. "The police photographs do show a bare footprint by the beach, do they not?"

Slowly, Summers nodded. "One. But it could be anyone's."

"And did you attempt to determine whether the print might be Ms. Allen's?"

"Not specifically, no."

"Wouldn't that have tended to confirm Ms. Allen's claim that she went swimming? And thus was nowhere near Mr. Case at the moment of his death?"

"Objection," Jackson called out. "Compound. And either question calls for speculation."

"Only because the job wasn't done," Caroline shot back. "Which makes this whole proceeding speculative. I'm entitled to show that—contrary to the prosecution claim—no one pretzeled himself to believe Brett Allen."

Towle looked from Jackson to Summers, and then nodded. "Overruled," he said.

Summers shifted in his chair. "It might have," he said finally. "But there's no way to tell."

"Not now there isn't." Caroline crossed her arms. "According to the police photographs, wasn't there also an unidentified boot print twenty feet further down the lake? Along the water toward Mosher Trail?"

Summers frowned. "Again, it could have been anyone's. The police were there and the EMTs."

"Any of them wearing boots?"

"I don't know." A trace of asperity. "For all we know, it could have been some fisherman."

"Or the murderer?"

Summers threw up his hands. "Because of one print, maybe forty feet from the body? There's no reason to connect the two."

Caroline folded her arms. "Describe for me, if you will, the terrain between the body and that footprint."

Summers went quiet; the pauses were no longer feigned. Caroline's throat felt tight. "Grass," Summers said at last, "near the body. Then small rock along the shore."

"No way to get footprints off grass, correct?"

A reluctant nod. "We couldn't have."

"And the rocks on the shore were knocked about?"

"True. But it could have been the police, or anyone." Another pause, then a concession. "No way to get prints there, either."

"So that it was possible for someone to walk from the body, all the way to the muck that captured this boot print, without leaving any other print?"

Summers seemed to appraise her. "A theoretical possibility, yes. But there was also no sign of blood."

"And no branches or bushes to leave blood on, correct?"

Another pause. "That's right. But there was grass and rocks."

Caroline looked astonished. "Grass and rocks? Is it your belief that this 'theoretical' killer crawled away from the scene?"

Summers nodded. "I don't believe in this killer at all, Counsel—"

"Answer the question, please. Why would a killer who—in your version—was sitting on James Case's chest have blood on the soles of his feet?"

Summers folded his arms. "I wouldn't know."

"A judicious answer." Caroline cocked her head. "Did you also consider whether the killer might have other means of approaching the lake? Along the water, for example, or even by boat?"

Summers looked annoyed and then visibly reached for calm. "We didn't consider helicopter, Counselor. But we did consider other means of approaching the lake than by going through Ms. Allen's property. And in no instance did any resident report seeing an unknown person or vehicle."

"Let's take an example, then. Mosher Trail is the next-closest path to the crime scene, true?"

"I would say so, yes."

"And it goes to the edge of the water?"

"Yes."

"Did you attempt to determine whether there were fresh vehicle tracks or footprints?"

Summers gave her a level stare. "The ground was packed hard—dried mud from spring—and that trail's pretty well traveled. So there was no way to tell who might have come there, or when."

"So that, again, it would be possible for a killer to walk or drive to the end of Mosher Trail, walk along the water, and approach the place where James Case was lying. All without leaving footprints."

"I suppose so. Assuming that no one had seen this person."

"It was night, wasn't it?"

"Of course."

"All right," Caroline said equably. "Have we adequately reviewed the 'physical evidence' that you say points to Brett Allen's guilt—the knife, the wallet, the fingerprints, the supposed lack of an exit path, and Mr. Case's lamentable failure to ejaculate?"

Summers' mouth and eyes seemed smaller now. "You can't compartmentalize it like that. Among other things, there's the pattern of blood on Ms. Allen and the victim, as attested to by the medical examiner."

"Oh," Caroline said carelessly, "we'll take that up with him. But tell me, Sergeant Summers, when did you and Mr. Watts receive the ME's report?"

"About four days after the incident."

"By which time you already had the lab results."

"Yes."

"You didn't run right out and arrest her, did you?"

"No. We didn't."

"So when, relative to that report, did you determine to charge Brett Allen?"

Another faint smile, a small acknowledgment that Summers knew where she was going. "About five days after."

"Really?" Caroline made herself sound curious. "What happened in those five days to make your case so compelling?"

Summers paused for a moment. "We had time to put it all together—"

"Come now, Sergeant Summers. Wasn't that when your witness came forward? Mr. Case's supposed lover—Megan Race?"

Summers' mouth opened, then shut. In that moment, it was plain to Caroline that Summers knew to be careful on the subject of Megan, but that neither he nor Jackson knew why. "Yes," he said tersely.

"Who claimed, among other things, that the night James Case died, he was to tell Brett that he and Megan were taking off for California?"

"I said that this morning."

Caroline cocked her head. "James sure had a funny way of getting his message across, didn't he? Of course, maybe that's why he couldn't climax—the guilt was just too much."

"Is that a question?" Rising, Jackson gave Caroline a look of annoyance. "Because if it's a statement, perhaps Ms. Masters should leave it to the only living person who was there."

Jackson, she could see, was at the limit of his patience; the challenge for Brett to testify showed that she had damaged him. "There were two people," she answered mildly. "Brett and the killer."

For an instant, Jackson gazed at her, eyes steady now. Softly, he repeated, "Do you have a question, Caroline?"

He had broken her rhythm, Caroline knew, and now her concentration. "Yes," Towle interjected. "Please find a question to ask."

Caroline nodded to Jackson and then turned back to Summers. "From the evidence at the scene—including a condom—does it appear that they were having consensual sex?"

"It does."

"And is there anything to support your theory that this was Brett's idea? Or is that just theoretical?"

"I'd have to say it's theoretical. . . ."

"Indeed, Sergeant Summers, is there anyone other than Megan Race to say that Mr. Case meant to leave with her at all?"

Summers paused. "They *were* seen together, Ms. Masters."

"That wasn't my question, Sergeant. But I'll take your answer and ask this—is there any evidence that Ms. Race and the victim were seen together after early April?"

Summers considered her. "We didn't specifically ask that, counselor."

"Do you have an answer?"

"No." Summers paused; suddenly, he looked relieved. "But how would Ms. Race know to talk to us about the same subject Ms. Allen did—that he had asked her to go to California but somehow wound up dead?"

From the stand, Summers seemed to watch her face for signs of alarm. But Caroline simply smiled. "So you considered it important that Ms. Race knew the victim wished to go to California?"

Summers paused; it was as if, Caroline thought, he sensed the trap but could not see it. "Yes," he said at length.

"And this enhanced her credibility."

A curt nod. "To me."

"As well as, according to this morning's testimony, providing you with a motive? A promise to drop a bomb on Brett that would surely make her angry?"

"Yes."

"Indeed, for you, it explained why Brett Allen had killed him."

Summers gave her a look of veiled defiance. "I already said that."

"Is it also fair to say, then, that Megan Race is a critical part of the case against Brett Allen?"

"There's lots of other evidence," Summers began, and stopped himself. "But she's a significant witness."

Briefly, Caroline imagined Larry behind her; when she turned, glancing at him, he looked away. Turning back to Summers, she asked, "In fact, didn't the appearance of Ms. Race cause the decision to charge Ms. Allen with the crime?"

"Calls for speculation," Jackson said evenly, and turned to Caroline. "As Ms. Masters knows, it wasn't his decision."

Towle nodded. "Sustained."

But Caroline was already facing Summers. "Prior to charging Ms. Allen with murder, did Mr. Watts ask your opinion?"

A reluctant nod, late in coming. "Yes."

"And what did you tell him?"

"That we had enough to charge her."

Caroline touched a finger to her lips. "And before Ms. Race came forward, did you express an opinion to Mr. Watts on whether to charge Ms. Allen?"

For the first time, Summers glanced at Jackson. "I did."

"And what was that opinion?"

"That we should keep looking."

Silent, Caroline considered him; she could see Summers hope that she would be satisfied with this concession of Megan's importance. But Caroline was not quite done. "How long was it," she asked, "between the time Mr. Case was killed and the time that Megan Race first came to you?"

"About six days."

"Didn't you suggest to Mr. Watts that this was curious? After all, according to Ms. Race, they were so in love that they were going away together."

Almost absently, Summers glanced at his cuff. "We discussed it, yes. But according to Ms. Race, she was afraid of what Ms. Allen might do."

"Did you accept that?"

A small shrug, watchful eyes: Caroline imagined him wondering why she had not raised the affair with Larry. "I'm not Ms. Race," he said.

Caroline let him sit there for a moment. "Isn't the major reason you believed Ms. Race that, in your view, Brett Allen lied to you about her very existence?"

Summers leaned forward to answer, as if she had thrown him a life raft, and then his head snapped back and his glacial eyes turned faintly puzzled, probing her for a motive. "Could you repeat that?" he asked.

Moving closer, Caroline said curtly, "Did you believe Megan Race because you thought Brett had lied about her?"

Summers hesitated, then came to a decision. "That was a factor, yes."

Caroline smiled down at him. "But according to the tape, you didn't ask Brett about James's past involvements, did you?"

Summers put one arm on the rail and propped his chin in his hand, ostentatiously weary of a hair-splitting lawyer. "Not explicitly," he said, and then added, "I guess I expected her to answer the question reasonably."

Caroline's smile turned sardonic. "Because you assumed that Megan's alleged relationship with the victim continued to his death?"

"Yes."

"Then perhaps you should have made that assumption clear to Ms. Allen." Caroline paused a moment. "Before you suggested indicting her for lying to you."

Summers flushed. "I know *that's* not a question," Jackson snapped.

Caroline turned to him. "Do you? Then I have none."

Facing Summers, she thanked him and sat down. As with her first, her last image of that day in court involved Jackson and her father, now both facing her—Jackson's look of wariness; Channing's cool, appraising eyes.

Turning from them, she focused on Brett's smile for her, filled with relief and gratitude.

SEVEN

CAROLINE CUT HERSELF another piece of Gruyère, washed it down with a deep red Chianti, raw in her throat.

"Thanks for bringing this," she said. "And for the information about Megan's mother."

Joe Lemieux smiled. "Was your day productive? Or just long?"

Caroline did not answer; perhaps the hardest part, she thought, was pretending to everyone—herself included—that she felt nothing. She sipped more wine. "That may depend," she said at last. "What else have you got?"

They sat in Carlton Grey's office. It was nine o'clock, and Caroline's lamp cast shadows in the corners. Lemieux shifted in his chair.

"I can't say for sure. It's already been three weeks since this guy was murdered, and now no one remembers seeing her. But then they've got no reason to—that night was nothing special to them." Lemieux seemed to watch her. "All I can really tell you, Counsel, is what we knew before—that she called in sick to her boss at the student union."

Caroline shrugged. "Keep looking, then."

"I have been. No one near the lake remembers seeing her, or her blue Honda." Pausing, Lemieux made a steeple of his fingers. "Are you serious about trying to place her there, or will it do if no one saw her?"

Caroline considered him. "Near the lake is better, obviously."

"Because all it takes is for her to be watching TV with a friend, and you're out of luck." He gazed at her with curiosity. "Unless you believe . . ."

Caroline gave him a wintry smile. "I don't know what I believe. But then, in my job, it's not essential." Abruptly, her smile vanished, and she asked in a quiet voice, "Did you show them *all* the pictures?"

Lemieux looked at her hard now. "Every one of them."

"Is there anyone we missed?"

Lemieux studied the tips of his fingers. Softly, he said, "You *are* serious."

Caroline simply stared at him.

"There's a gas station left," Lemieux told her. "By the head of Mosher Trail. The kid who works nights took off for Florida the next day, to see his mother. He won't be back till two nights from now. Thursday."

Caroline reflected. "She'll take the stand on Thursday, I think. I'll try to keep her there until Friday. Somehow I doubt that will be too hard."

Lemieux's eyes asked a silent question. "I'd better get going," he said at length.

Caroline leaned back in her chair. "By the way," she asked, "is Megan right- or left-handed? I never noticed."

Lemieux gave her a faint, puzzled smile. "Right, I think."

Caroline nodded. "Good."

EIGHT

DR. JACK CORN, the medical examiner, had lank gray-blond hair, wire-rim glasses, and the amiable half smile of a small-town banker. Little about this mild appearance suggested that—as Caroline well knew—he was a nationally recognized pathologist who had brought the New Hampshire Medical Examiner's Office to a place of professional esteem. His manner was courteous, his voice soft and faintly midwestern.

Methodically, he took Jackson from his appearance at the crime scene through the trip to the morgue in Concord—Corn and two assistants assessing and photographing the body; inspecting it for trace evidence; measuring the width and depth of the wounds; taking blood samples; searching for prints on the body. The reality of this, Caroline knew, was not pleasant; it was part of Corn's gift to make the process sound clinical, thorough, and scientific. Which it clearly was.

"And in the course of these procedures," Jackson was asking, "did you determine the cause of death?"

Corn nodded slowly. "The victim died from a deep wound to the throat, severing the jugular vein, the carotid artery, and the victim's airway. As a result, the airways were filled. So that, quite literally, Mr. Case drowned in his own blood."

Next to Caroline, Brett folded her hands on the table, took a deep breath, and kept on looking at the witness. "Could you describe," Jackson said, "the nature of such a death?"

Corn's face had lost its semi-smile. "It would not be instantaneous, Mr. Watts. There would be a gurgling sound, perhaps with the victim thrashing in agony, for as long as three or four minutes. What Mr. Case would have experienced was the quite horrific knowledge that he was drowning and that there was nothing he could do."

Caroline saw Brett's eyes shut. Jackson moved forward. "This gurgling sound, Dr. Corn—what would account for that?"

"Asphyxia. The victim would be unable to speak. Instead he would suffer what we call agonal breaths, spewing blood from his mouth for approximately ten to fifteen seconds." Corn paused, as if imagining the moment. "Eventually, he would suffer hypovolemic shock: the absence of sufficient blood to the brain. I should add that with respect to movement, there does not seem to have been much. But then the wound was so grave that Mr. Case's head was partially severed."

Touching Brett's arm, Caroline felt a spasm pass through her. Caroline's fingers tightened around her wrist.

"Was there also, Dr. Corn, a second wound?"

"There were three, actually. I believe that the first in time was also a throat wound, but much shallower, from which we concluded that the fatal wound was a second and more successful effort to sever the victim's throat. The last wound, we believe, was the stab wound near the heart."

Corn's narrative, calm and uninflected, somehow conveyed the picture of a determined killer, a butchering both intimate and passionate. "And did you determine the type of wound?" Jackson asked.

Corn folded his hands. "It was a knife wound. From the tearing of the skin, it appeared that the knife had a serrated edge. From that, and from our measurements, we determined that the wounds were consistent with the Cahill fishing knife found in Ms. Allen's possession."

"And did you photograph the body and the wounds?"

"My assistant did. Yes."

Jackson produced a sheaf of photographs from an envelope on the prosecution table. Reluctantly, he turned to Caroline, glancing at Brett as he did so. "Would you care to review these again, Ms. Masters?"

Briefly, Caroline turned to Brett. She had her own copies. But it had been Caroline's judgment that seeing the photographs would only haunt Brett's nights. "Don't look," she whispered. "There's no point to it." Pale, Brett nodded and turned away.

"Yes," Caroline said evenly. "Thank you."

Looking down at Caroline, Jackson hesitated. Then he handed her the photographs and went back to his table.

Caroline took them one at a time.

By agreement, they were premarked for identification: the first, prosecution exhibit number twenty-seven, was an overhead shot that captured the staring eyes of a man for whom death was the end of agony.

Next to her, Caroline felt Brett flinch. Caroline wondered if this was the horror of discovery, or of memory.

"Don't" she murmured. "They get no better."

Caroline reviewed the photographs as quickly as she could. "Thank you," she said to Jackson.

Taking the exhibits, Jackson shot a quick, opaque glance at Brett. In that moment, Caroline saw in close-up the deepening lines at the edges of his eyes, the bruises of weariness.

Within minutes, a blond assistant from Jackson's office had pinned the photographs to a bulletin board. Even from a distance, Caroline could see the spatters of blood on James's face, the gash in his throat.

Glancing at her family, Caroline saw Betty and Larry looking down; only her father, face impassive, seemed to study the photographs. Next to her, Caroline heard the slow intake of breath. "It was dark," Brett murmured. "I couldn't see him."

Caroline turned to her. Staring at the pictures, Brett's face had filled with something close to awe. "How could someone do that . . . ?"

Jackson stepped forward. "Dr. Corn," he asked, "were these the photographs taken as part of your autopsy of Mr. Case?"

"They were."

"And are they consistent with your opinion with respect to the cause of death?"

"Yes." Corn left the witness stand and stood before the photographs; Caroline saw the judge's gaze, intent and narrow, follow him. "For example, Exhibit Twenty-seven shows the pattern of blood on the victim's face—large spots in some areas, spatters in others. For lack of a more felicitous description, the airway wound sustained by Mr. Case creates a pattern similar to a can of spray paint that is running low, where spurts and spatters alternate with the degree of pressure." Pausing, Corn adjusted his glasses, and then he concluded: "After a time, ten to fifteen seconds, the pressure subsides altogether. But this pattern was already here."

Caroline knew what was coming now. Within moments—a few brief exchanges between Jackson and Towle—a second bulletin board of premarked exhibits stood near the first. Next to Caroline, Brett was still.

In the photographs where Brett's eyes showed, they were dull with shock. Her breasts and face and torso were flecked with blood.

"I'm sorry," Caroline said softly. "But there's no help for this."

Brett's eyes had frozen. Perhaps, Caroline thought, it was simply humiliation; more likely, it was the shock of seeing the masks of James's dead face, her shocked one, twinned by specks of blood. Even Judge Towle seemed transfixed by the imagery.

"Did you also," Jackson asked Corn, "examine the pattern of blood on Ms. Allen's face, neck, arms, and body?"

"I did."

"And are these photographs consistent or inconsistent with the conclusion that Ms. Allen killed Mr. Case?"

"In my opinion, they are consistent."

Brett stared at Corn, her body rigid with anger. But Jackson sounded quite calm; it was as if, Caroline thought, he preferred this case in someone else's hands. "And on what, Dr. Corn, do you base that opinion?"

"The pattern of blood." Pausing, Corn pointed to a photograph of Brett's neck. "The pattern in Exhibit Thirty-nine, for example, is consistent with the spraying from the first infliction of the wound. It's the spray I would expect when, in the alternating force of pressure, it lessens."

"Could it also be consistent with the administration of CPR, which Ms. Allen claims to have attempted?"

"Not in my view. For instance, there's no contact pattern of blood on Ms. Allen's mouth, as one might reasonably expect. And, while CPR might possibly cause the pinpoint spray one sees in Exhibit Thirty-seven, it would not account for the teardrop pattern on Ms. Allen's stomach. As shown by Exhibit Thirty-nine, for example." Corn turned to the judge, as if conducting a seminar for one. "You'll notice the teardrop pattern of the spatters here: slender at the bottom, much wider at the top. That would not be caused by CPR on

the victim after the immediate spurt from his wound had abated—
it's much too heavy. But it could be consistent with the agonal
breaths of the first few seconds."

He was quite impressive, Caroline thought. "It's all right," she
murmured to Brett, and scrawled a note—*cast-off pattern?*—on the
pad in front of her.

Jackson's voice was firm now. "Are there other factors which are
consistent with the commission of a homicide by Ms. Allen?"

"There are." Corn turned to the picture of James's stomach. "As
I understand the prosecution theory, Ms. Allen cut the victim's
throat while sitting astride his torso, perhaps during intercourse.
You will note from the photographs of Mr. Case's chest that there is
a void—a distinct lessening of spatter—on the area of his chest and
stomach. Suggesting that the spray was blocked by Ms. Allen's chest
and stomach."

Watching, Judge Towle seemed to nod. "In sum," Jackson said,
"the pattern on both Mr. Case and Ms. Allen is consistent with the
belief that she cut his throat and then stabbed him?"

"It is."

Slowly, Jackson turned to Brett, eyes a little melancholy. "How
could a woman as slight as Ms. Allen inflict such grievous wounds?"

Facing Brett, Corn's expression was somber. "Quite easily."

"On what do you base that?"

"The murder weapon, to begin with. The blade was razor sharp."
Pausing, Corn retreated to the professorial. "A number of years ago,
a famous pathologist, Bernard Knight, established that it takes just a
little over one pound of force to stick a sharpened knife into the human body. Which, when one thinks about it, we know from our
own experience. After all, how much force does it take for a nurse to
give you a flu shot?" Folding his hands, Corn finished quietly. "The
knife was quite a fine one, and it was well maintained. With a knife
like that, Mr. Watts, a woman like Brett Allen would have no trouble
killing this boy at all."

NINE

Walking toward Corn and the bloody photographs, Caroline took her time. Her face was as serene as she could make it.

"Are you familiar," she asked, "with Ms. Allen's account of the murder?"

Corn gazed at her, neither welcoming nor defensive. "I believe so, yes."

"Specifically, that she and Mr. Case had wine and marijuana. That afterward, while making love, Mr. Case passed out. That she went swimming. That she saw a shadow over Mr. Case. That when she returned, she heard a gurgling sound. That in the belief that Mr. Case might be choking in his own vomit, she got on his chest and administered CPR. That this caused blood to spray on her face. And that, in horror and shock, she pulled out the knife she discovered in his chest." Abruptly, Caroline's voice softened. "You *are* aware of all that, aren't you?"

Corn folded his hands; the effect was of someone bracing himself. "Yes, Ms. Masters. I am."

"Well, what's wrong with that? From your review of the medical evidence, couldn't it have happened just as she says?"

Corn frowned. "I don't believe so."

"But it is consistent with the lack of struggle, is it not?"

"It could be."

"And with the agonal breaths you describe."

"Possibly."

Caroline put her hands on her hips. "By the way, you're not asserting here that Brett Allen did kill Mr. Case, are you? Only that she could have."

"Yes. Who killed this man is beyond my province."

"And the entire reason that you prefer Mr. Watts's story to Ms. Allen's is that, in your view, the spatter on Ms. Allen is inconsistent with CPR?"

Corn pursed his lips, forming a small *o*. "It's the totality of the circumstances. But sticking to the spatter pattern, it's at least two things. First, the appearance that the blood on Ms. Allen's torso accounts for the void on Mr. Case's. Second, the fact that the teardrop pattern of some spatter on Ms. Allen is inconsistent with what CPR would cause."

Caroline nodded. "All right, Dr. Corn. Let's take CPR first. You're not saying that all the blood on Ms. Allen is inconsistent with CPR?"

"No. CPR could have caused a brief spray from Mr. Case's throat, resulting in the light spattering found on Ms. Allen's face. But it could not, in my opinion, explain the teardrop spatter."

Caroline looked puzzled. "But as you described the fatal wound, at least in its first seconds, a spray would alternate with a spewing pattern—almost a gushing. Correct?"

"Yes."

Turning to the first bulletin board, Caroline gazed for a moment at James's dead, staring eyes. "Indeed, on Exhibit Twenty-three, the streaks of blood on Mr. Case's face reflect that spewing effect."

"That's true."

Walking to the second board, Caroline stood next to a picture of Brett's face. "But there is no such pattern on Ms. Allen's face, is there?"

Corn paused. "There is not. But that could be the result of distance."

Caroline turned to him. "Forgive my indelicacy, Doctor, but does 'spray' travel farther than 'spew'?"

"Not necessarily. But you're assuming that, through those first seconds, Ms. Allen kept her face equidistant from Mr. Case's throat." Corn examined the board. "I also point out Exhibits Thirty-five and Thirty-six—the heavier spatter on Ms. Allen's breasts and stomach."

For a moment, Caroline simply looked at him. With a hint of asperity, she asked, "Are you familiar with the term 'cast-off pattern'?"

"Of course."

"Could you define it for us?"

Corn gave her a glance of oblique annoyance. "It's the blood spatter made by the entry of a sharp object into the human body."

"Or exit?"

"That too."

"What are the characteristics of a cast-off pattern?"

For a moment, Corn gazed at the photographs of Brett. "It can have a teardrop effect," he conceded. "As you see on Ms. Allen."

"And can that effect result from the *withdrawal* of a knife?"

"It's possible. Yes."

"So that it's also possible that the medium-velocity splash pattern on Ms. Allen's face resulted from her administration of CPR, and the teardrop pattern on her torso from the withdrawal of the knife?" Here Caroline paused for emphasis. "And not from the agonal breaths you ascribe to Mr. Case?"

Turning to Caroline, Corn seemed to study her with the interest of a professional. "Yes," he said at length. "That's also possible."

"Which leaves Mr. Watts only with the void in the pattern of blood on Mr. Case's chest."

Corn's small brown eyes were watchful. "If you're referring to the pattern of blood and not to the prosecution's entire case."

Caroline nodded briefly. "You've already told us that the void would have been caused by the murderer sitting astride Mr. Case. From the pattern of blood on the victim's face, what pattern would you expect on the murderer?"

Corn removed his glasses, polishing them with a handkerchief. "Hard to say, Ms. Masters. Again, it might depend on distance."

Turning, Caroline pointed to the spray on Brett's shoulders and breasts. "Wouldn't you expect a pattern heavier than this?"

Corn studied the photograph. "All that I can tell you," he finally answered, "is that it's possible. . . ."

"So that it's also possible that the killer, not Brett, absorbed a heavy spray of blood. Thus creating the void on Mr. Case's chest and leaving Ms. Allen with the far lighter spray caused by CPR?"

"Again, that's possible. But what about the absence of a contact pattern on Ms. Allen's mouth?"

Caroline raised her eyebrows. "Do you happen to know, Dr. Corn, how long it was between the murder and the time these pictures were taken?"

"In my understanding, about two hours."

"More than long enough, in other words, for Ms. Allen to lick her lips. Or, as we know she did, to vomit and then wipe her mouth."

"I suppose so." Rising, Corn walked to the second bulletin board. "But as we talk, Ms. Masters, I should note the existence of a spurt of blood on Ms. Allen's neck. Which is neither spray nor teardrop, but similar to the kind of spewing pattern I might expect from an agonal breath."

"One spot?" Caroline stood next to him. "Are you familiar with Officer Mann's testimony that he lent Ms. Allen his jacket?"

"Yes."

"And could the single spot you note be a smear? Caused by contact between the jacket and Ms. Allen's skin?"

Narrow-eyed, Corn considered the photograph. "Yes," he said tersely. "At this point, I can't tell."

Turning, Corn headed for the witness stand. "While you're here," Caroline interjected, "there's something else I'd like to ask you. About this picture."

Corn turned back to her. "Yes?"

Caroline rested her index finger beneath a smudge mark on James Case's neck. "What's that?"

Corn studied the mark. "On the body," he said dryly, "it looked like a bruise. Left by a finger, perhaps."

"Could you lift a print?"

"We could not." Corn's voice remained dry. "As I believe you pointed out yesterday to Sergeant Summers, that's quite difficult on the body of a male. At least in the absence of blood."

Towle, Caroline noticed, was leaning forward from the bench. Quietly, she asked, "Could it also be difficult, Dr. Corn, because the person who made this mark was wearing gloves?"

Corn angled his head. "Impossible to say. At least from this."

"Then hang on." Quickly, Caroline walked back to the defense table and produced a photograph from her briefcase. "Subject to proof," she said to Towle, "this is a blowup of the area on Mr. Case's neck. With the court's permission, I'd like to ask Dr. Corn about it now, rather than recalling him."

Towle looked toward Jackson. "Mr. Watts?"

Jackson stepped forward, took the photograph from Caroline,

and studied it for what seemed quite long. When he gave it back to her, his expression was blank. "Subject to proof," he said to Towle.

"Thank you," Caroline responded, and gave the photograph to Corn. Standing next to him, she indicated with a finger a faint line at one edge of the bruise.

If he's honest, her expert had told her, *the ME can't say no. At least not for sure.*

"Do you see that line?" Caroline asked.

Slowly, Corn nodded. "I see it, yes."

"Could it have been made by the seam of a leather glove?"

For a long moment, Corn squinted, silent. "Yes," he said at last. "That's possible."

"And yet we know, from her fingerprints in Mr. Case's blood, that Ms. Allen was not wearing gloves."

Corn appeared troubled now; though whether by doubt, or by being cornered, Caroline could not tell. "We know that, yes."

He looked up at Caroline, expecting her to drive the point home. Instead she passed the photograph to Judge Towle, and said simply, "Thank you, Dr. Corn. You may sit down now."

Corn gave her a brief, querying glance, and then resumed the stand.

Standing in front of him, Caroline permitted a moment's silence. "Are you quite certain," she asked, "that whoever killed Mr. Case did so while sitting astride him?"

A look of surprise, and then renewed confidence. "Yes. I am."

"And why is that?"

"There are several reasons. The void on Mr. Case's chest, the angle of the chest wound—suggesting a thrust down and in—and the presence of spray on the grass behind him all suggest as much."

Caroline nodded. "All right, then. Could you demonstrate the motion with which you believe the murderer slashed the victim's throat?"

Corn hesitated for a moment. And then he raised his right arm and cocked his wrist; with a blunt downward-slashing motion, he cut James Case's imaginary throat. "Like so," he said. "That would be the motion."

"Thank you." As if puzzled, Caroline paused. "But shouldn't you have used your left hand? Assuming, that is, that you were imitating Brett Allen."

Corn looked surprised and then gave her a slight smile. "I guess so."

"And the reason you agree with me?"

"Her fingerprints on the hilt of the knife—the ones in the victim's blood—were made with her left hand."

"Just so." Caroline moved to the bulletin board again, standing next to the photograph of the gashes in the dead man's neck. "You measured the depth of the victim's neck wounds, correct?"

"Yes."

"And was the depth of the wound uniform?"

"Of course not. As you would expect, it was deepest at mid-thrust."

"But were the wounds deeper at one end than the other?"

At the edge of her vision, Caroline saw Jackson stir. "As I remember," Corn answered, "they were deeper on the right side."

Caroline nodded. "Tell me, Dr. Corn, are you familiar with a phenomenon known as the tailing effect?"

A brief pause. "Yes."

"And could you describe it to us?"

Corn glanced at Jackson and then faced Caroline again. "As a very general rule, the blade of a knife is presumed to enter the throat more deeply—assuming a horizontal slash wound—than it exits."

"And here, in both cases, the right-side wound was deeper."

"Yes."

Pausing, Caroline folded her arms. "And what, assuming the tailing effect, does that suggest about the person who killed James Case?"

"Objection." Quickly, Jackson came to the bench. "The question not only calls for speculation but piles one piece of speculation on the other. Starting with the motion with which the murderer wielded the knife."

"With which," Caroline retorted, "Mr. Watts was perfectly content—as long as the killer was Ms. Allen, sitting on the victim's chest. Which is also the foundation for my seeking Dr. Corn's expert opinion."

Nodding, Towle turned to Jackson. "I'm going to allow it, Mr. Watts. And weigh it for myself." He turned to Corn. "You may answer, Dr. Corn."

Corn looked steadily at Caroline. "It is speculative. But if I'm correct about how the wounds were inflicted, and the tailing effect holds true, the murderer is more likely to be right-handed."

Behind her, Caroline felt a stirring in the courtroom. "Thank you," she said crisply. "I have nothing more."

TEN

"So," Jackson said, "are you going to offer us the real killer? Or do you prefer a nameless phantom?"

Caroline shrugged. "I don't know yet."

It was six o'clock, and they stood beneath the trees on the lawn of the Connaughton County Courthouse. The press had gone to file their stories—that Caroline had called for Jackson to dismiss the case. Brett had returned to prison, and the rest of Caroline's family to Masters Hill. So that now it was only the two of them, in the light of early evening.

Caroline kicked off her shoes.

Jackson was in an edgy humor, she decided—he treated her with a mixture of familiarity and distrust, and his tone was sardonic. But he had approached her for a reason, and she could guess what it was.

Caroline breathed in deeply, face raised to the failing sun, waiting out his silence. "It's weird," she said. "Being locked up like this all day. You forget there's a world."

Hands in his pockets, Jackson looked around them. Connaughton Falls was in the heart of the valley that embraced Resolve, and the vista of hills and forests was familiar to them both from childhood. "Did you ever miss this?" he asked.

"Some. Because I knew I'd never come back."

Jackson glanced at her sideways. "Well, you're back," he said finally. "And you're the best I've seen. There's capable—like me—and then there's something more."

His tone was one of detachment; because he could acknowledge her gifts, this said, he was also smart enough to beat her. "You make it sound," Caroline replied, "as if Brett's defense is a matter of talent. Perhaps you should consider that it may be something more."

Jackson turned to her. "Brett's defense so far, Caroline, is possibility upon surmise, 'could be' upon 'should be' upon 'might be.' What impresses me is your ability to assimilate what is obviously a slough of expert advice, all in ten days, and find some black hole in each witness's testimony from which to extract yet one more 'possibility.' "

Caroline shook her head. "The holes are there, and the possibilities are real. Your problem—your witnesses' problem—is that when Megan Race came along with a motive, she made all of you assume too much. So that you believed you had the practical equivalent of a locked-door killing: no other suspects need apply."

Jackson shoved his hands in his pockets. "Yes," he said sharply. "Megan. Tomorrow's witness."

This did not call for an answer, and Caroline gave him none.

After a time, Jackson took off his suit jacket, unknotted his tie, and sat with his back against a tree. "So who is Megan the biggest problem for? Brett, or me, or you?"

Caroline sat next to him, gazing out at the lawn. "One of *us*," she answered quietly. "Brett's not even in the running."

"And you won't tell me anything."

"I can't. For Brett's sake. Unless you dismiss the case for good."

"Which I can't, as you damned well know. Not without reason."

Caroline shrugged. "So there we are."

Jackson turned to her. Softly, he said, "Even if an inch-by-inch survey of Megan's apartment turns up funny fingerprints?"

Caroline's face closed. "If I understand you," she answered coolly, "you're assuming a conflict between Brett's interests and mine. Or, perhaps, my ambitions."

Jackson shook his head. "I'm trying to understand *you*, Caroline. And I can't."

Caroline tented her fingers, placed them in her lap. "Then perhaps it will help," she said at last, "to know that I've put ambition aside. You're now the only one of us who still wishes to become a judge."

His silent gaze was without comprehension: it was as if Caroline watched them both, trapped in a moment only she understood. By instinct, she touched his arm. "I'd have taken anyone else for a prosecutor, Jackson. But that's really all I can say to you."

He gazed at her hand. "Because of Brett?"

"Yes."

Slowly, Jackson slid his arm from beneath her fingers. "Then let's set aside Megan and discuss where we are right now."

Caroline felt awkward. And then she felt the reflex of her adulthood: the withdrawal of feeling in exchange for thought. "You want to offer me manslaughter," she said.

Jackson smiled without humor. "How did you ever guess?"

"Is there a recommended sentence that goes with it?"

"Ten years." His smile vanished. "It's open for one day only, Caroline. Let me know before court tomorrow."

Caroline felt herself go cold. "I thought this wasn't about your star witness. And whatever I may have in store for her."

Jackson's eyes narrowed. "And I thought *you* had no conflict." He paused for a moment. "I don't know what you've got for Megan. But it can't change the case we've built already, and Fred Towle isn't going to bounce me. Because your questions have been about reasonable doubt, not probable cause. And you'll have to offer a New Hampshire jury more than some song and dance about a right-handed drug dealer in gloves who paddled in by canoe while Brett was swimming, cut James's throat, and paddled out again. In the end, it just won't wash."

This, Caroline feared, might be true. "Then why the offer?"

"Because between intoxication and jealousy, I expect you can entice a jury to believe that Brett acted without thought. That might even be a just result. But what you can't guarantee her is ten years." Jackson's voice became soft again. "Out by age thirty-two, Caroline, with the rest of her life back. Not much of a price for what we saw in those pictures."

"Those pictures," Caroline retorted, "may never get into evidence—at least not the ones of Brett. Because most of what you have is a direct result of her first statement to Mann, which I'll suppress for sure. That makes a whole lot else—the pictures, the search of Brett's person and property, her second statement—the proverbial fruit of the poisonous tree."

Jackson rested his arms on his knees, regarding her quite calmly. "I can tell you what'll happen. You'll get Brett's first statement tossed and, if you're very lucky, the second. But all the physical evidence resulting from finding the body comes in because we would have found him without her help. And at trial, Brett will have to tell her story, anyhow, and give me or my successor a shot at cross-examination. Because no reasonable jury will forgive her for not explaining herself in the face of all the evidence."

Caroline stared at him. "Or your successor?" she repeated.

"That's right. I find that I'm not enjoying this case quite the way I should."

Caroline sat back. Was this distaste or prudence? she wondered; the deeper stress she sensed in him could be dislike of what he was doing, fear of losing a judgeship, or the ascendancy of doubt over zeal that comes with middle age. From her own experience, it was probably all of these.

"Back in high school," she said at last, "could you have imagined this conversation?"

Jackson gave the small, lopsided smile that had hardly changed since then. "Even if I could have, Caroline, I couldn't have guessed how it would feel."

Caroline became quiet, without quite knowing why. Then it came to her: this was likely the last civil conversation she would have with Jackson Watts.

Turning, she gazed at the lawn, the trees, the deepening shadows. "I'll talk to Brett," she said. "But if you're still calling Megan, I'd have her ready to go."

Tonight, everything about Brett—the vivid green eyes, the coils of brown hair, the quick movement of her hands—seemed to quiver with suppressed anxiety. She looked far more real than Caroline felt, standing on the precipice of doubt. So that Brett's long silence startled her.

"I must not be explaining this well," Caroline said.

"You explained it fine." Brett's gaze was steady and penetrating. "Ten years and out. I'm just trying to read what you're not saying."

Caroline felt one thought intersecting with another. And then she remembered the moment in a famous murder case, in which a celebrity was accused of cruelly butchering his wife, when Caroline had known that he was guilty—the day two months after the killing that the accused, prompted by his public relations expert, had offered a reward for the "real" murderer of the beloved mother of his two young children. "I was wondering," Caroline said at last, "what you would say if I asked who you think murdered James. A drug dealer?"

"No. I don't believe that now." Brett's eyes did not waver. "Any more than you do."

Surprised, Caroline hesitated. "Then *who*?"

"That's what scares me." For a moment, Brett was quiet. "All day I looked at those pictures. I've thought about them ever since." Her words became low, intense. "There's memory, and then there's the things you just know. That's nothing I could ever have done to him. I don't know anyone who could."

In the bare yellow room, Caroline studied her: the moment carried echoes of other talks in other rooms, risks being bartered for years. And yet it was so different.

"But what do *you* think, Caroline?" Brett's voice became ironic. "I get so hung up on being innocent I forget that you're my lawyer."

Inwardly, Caroline winced. "Perhaps I'm not as detached as I should be."

Torn from her own concerns, Brett gave her a brief, curious look, and then her voice grew softer. "The last three days have been horrible. Sometimes it's hard to imagine how anyone else feels about it. Or to care much, either."

"No reason to. But is my advice so important to you?"

"Yes." Brett's voice was quiet. "Now, it is."

Caroline inhaled. "I wouldn't take Jackson's deal."

Brett's eyes probed hers. "Why?"

"Because any capable defense lawyer can get this deal later—even Jackson's case screams manslaughter." Pausing, Caroline felt the weight of her last words. "Of course, that's easy for me to say. Take ten years now, and you'll cap your risk forever. No more trial, or waiting, or fear. You just start serving your time, hoping that when you get out you'll still have some sort of life—a career, kids, who knows. And maybe Jackson's successor will be a real hardass, and you'll never get this deal again." Finishing, Caroline felt shaken. "But I can't tell you to do this, Brett. Because—although it scares me to say so—I think that I can make things better for you."

Brett looked at her in hope and doubt. After a time, she asked softly, "Because of Megan?"

For a long moment, Caroline was silent. "Yes," she answered. "At least because of Megan."

ELEVEN

THERE ARE DAYS in the courtroom that have a deeper texture, Caroline thought. Sometimes this is felt only by the lawyers; at other times, those watching know it also. But Megan Race brought with her something more: the sense that, for her, this was a defining moment.

She seemed conscious of everything—the reporters, the Masters family, the import of her testimony—in the way that an actress, pretending to ignore her audience, shows her awareness through her bearing, the specificity of her gestures, the inflection of a word, a telling stillness. From the time that she walked to the stand, tall and straight and proud, Megan drew a particular quiet.

Caroline was quite certain that she alone felt the potential for the rarest of courtroom events, a psychic meltdown that would not be pleasant to watch. But this was merely the smallest reason, among several, that made her wish this morning had never come.

She had told Jackson privately, and briefly, in a corner of the lobby. "Brett can't do it," Caroline said. "Among other things, she insists she's innocent."

Jackson looked at her in silence; he seemed as subdued as Caroline felt. "Can I ask what you advised her?" he said at length.

"The same, I'm afraid." Caroline shrugged. "So there we are."

For another moment, Jackson watched her. "I keep trying to understand you," he said. "You can't seriously believe her, can you?"

"I've begun to actively consider it, Jackson. As should you." Caroline paused. "I really wish we could talk about Megan. But it's not in Brett's interests."

Jackson smiled without humor. "Oh, well," he said, and turned to enter court. To Caroline, watching, the moment was sadder than he imagined.

Now, sitting next to Brett, she knew why she had come.

Brett, of course, understood none of this. Her focus was on Megan: she watched her with a cool anger that, to Caroline, was bracing.

"What kind of person," Brett murmured, "gets pleasure out of this?"

That was it, Caroline thought, and Brett had caught it: there was a narcissism about Megan, and the courtroom fed it. Worried about Caroline as she might be, Megan would not, in the end, be able to hold back.

"Prepare yourself for a long morning," Caroline murmured to Brett. "But after that, things will get better."

Head raised, eyes straight ahead, Megan swore to tell the truth.

For a last moment, Caroline turned to watch her family. Her father had fixed Megan with a gelid stare, as if she were an insect. Somehow Caroline found this more chilling than anger; perhaps it was the memory of her first horrified awareness, the night that David had vanished, of the way Channing Masters could dismiss the claim of another human being to any shred of sympathy. For all that she was like him, Caroline thought, this was the difference that had made her a defense lawyer; that made her, in this way at least, Nicole Dessaliers' daughter.

As if by reflex, Caroline glanced at her sister.

Betty, she thought grimly, lacked her father's resources: her face was pale, distorted by fear and anger. The anger, Caroline knew, was far deeper yet no more complex than the outrage of a mother whose child is picked on by a bully. But it was the fear that never left her—that whatever Betty most valued would be taken from her, for reasons she could not comprehend. It was fortunate that she did not know that it was Larry, by violating her trust, who had helped place Brett at risk; not even Caroline could take pleasure in what this would do to Betty.

Next to her, Larry clasped Betty's hand, unable to look at Megan. With a certain lack of charity, Caroline made sure that he saw her. It was not until his gaze broke that Caroline turned away.

Damn all of you, she thought.

Beneath the table, she touched Brett's hand, and felt the girl's fingertips close around hers. Softly, Caroline said, "Don't worry."

On the stand, Megan was a portrait of grief and dignity.

She wore a suit, blue and severe, such as one would wear to a job interview. Which was how Jackson treated her first moments in the public eye.

"And what, to this point, is your grade point average at Chase?"

Megan folded her hands. "Three point seven," she said. "Straight A's would be a four point."

Her air, Caroline thought, was a touch supercilious. Quickly, Jackson moved to the most appealing part: that Megan, a high school honor student, was at Chase on partial scholarship; that her father had died when she was twelve; that she worked to help pay for school. With a certain fascination, Caroline watched Jackson gild Megan's character, wondering if he suspected that the one detail of importance was the loss of Megan's father.

"And you and your mother are close?" Jackson was asking.

"Very. Since Dad died, it was just the two of us. But his dream was that I go to college, and we've dedicated ourselves to that." She paused, looking down. "Until now, going to Chase was his dream come true."

"Here we go," Caroline murmured.

Jackson paused, as if permitting Megan to regain her bearings. "Are you acquainted with the defendant, Brett Allen?"

For the first time, Megan turned to Brett; her quick glance at Caroline was both surreptitious and defiant. "Yes," she said. "I am."

Her answer was given with a catch in her throat. So far, Caroline acknowledged, Megan showed close to perfect pitch. "Don't take your eyes off her," Caroline whispered to Brett. "Make her feel you."

"And do you know any other members of her family?" Jackson asked.

At the edge of Caroline's view, Larry looked down. "Her father." Megan folded her hands. "But only as a professor for one class, or to visit his office if I had a question."

"And what grade did you receive?"

"An A."

"Do you have any animosity toward any member of the Allen family?"

Megan raised her chin, displaying a long, elegant neck. Her blond hair, Caroline noted, had been carefully trimmed, so that it barely touched her shoulders. "Only one," she said at last. "Brett Allen."

It was a good answer, Caroline thought; whatever else, Megan had been carefully coached.

"Can you tell us, Ms. Race, the reason for this animosity?"

Her eyes seemed to widen in shock, suddenly recalled, at the loss she had suffered. In a quiet voice, she said, "Because James Case and I were in love."

It was a demure answer, Caroline thought, reflecting Jackson's advice. His own voice softened to match Megan's. "And how long was that relationship?"

Megan raised her chin again. "It began in February. And continued until the day he died."

"And your relationship was an intimate one?"

"Yes. It was very intense." Megan's voice took on an assertive pride. "Physically and emotionally."

Brett's jawline tightened. But what Caroline felt was a *frisson* of unease; what she heard was not Megan's claim of intimacy but the need for it, the sad secret of the young woman whom Caroline had witnessed in a lonely, unguarded moment, touching herself in the mirror.

As if she had read her thoughts, Megan turned to Caroline. Caroline smiled faintly. When Jackson spoke again, Megan seemed to flinch.

"How often did you see each other?" Jackson asked.

A hesitancy, distracted. "At least twice a week."

"Why not more often?"

"I have to work at night, as well as study—my scholarship depends on maintaining a certain GPA, and it doesn't cover everything." Megan's voice fell. "And James was trying to make up his mind."

"About what?"

Megan touched her collarbone; to Caroline, the gesture had a certain widowed sensuality, the feel of a lover recalled. "Between Brett," she answered softly, "and what he had found with me."

Brett's face showed anger and distaste; for all that she appeared volatile, Caroline sensed that she had the New Englander's dislike for self-dramatization. But Caroline's second thought went deeper than reason could justify—that Brett seemed too real for there to be a second Brett, waiting beneath the first to be summoned by drugs or wine.

"So, in your understanding, James was involved with Brett at the time you began dating?"

"Yes." Megan's voice became sententious and a little sad. "He was obviously looking for a way out. But like a lot of men, he had this misplaced sense of guilt."

Caroline did not bother to stand. "I wonder, Your Honor, if we might stick to what Mr. Case did, as opposed to how Ms. Race cares to imagine him. Assuming that she knows the difference."

Caroline's tone, while mild, was so unsympathetic that Jackson—clearly expecting Caroline to tread more carefully—gave her a look of genuine surprise which was mirrored in Towle's raised eyebrows. "Well," Towle observed, "it's probably best to let events speak for themselves." He turned to Megan, adding courteously, "If you could, Ms. Race."

But Megan was staring at Caroline, and the prideful look had become rigid. *You can't take it,* Caroline thought, *can you?* "Thank you, Your Honor," she said to Towle, but never took her eyes off Megan.

"In any event," Jackson said promptly, "there came a time when James was seeing both you and Ms. Allen?"

Megan's head snapped back toward Jackson. "Yes. There was."

"And was Ms. Allen aware of this?"

"Yes."

"How did you know this?"

Briefly, Megan looked unsettled. "At first, I almost couldn't believe it, what James said—that she was following us."

It was nicely done, Caroline thought: a bizarre story that, in retrospect, had become horrifying because of James's death. This time Caroline stood. "Move to strike," she said. "Ms. Race's account of James's supposed knowledge is clearly hearsay."

"Of course it is," Jackson retorted. "But it's admissible under a standard exception—that it is offered not for the truth of the assertion but to describe Mr. Case's state of mind—"

"Then what good is it to you?" Caroline snapped.

"Because, among other things, it helps explain Mr. Case's later conduct toward both Ms. Race and Ms. Allen."

Towle nodded, and turned to Caroline. "I'm going to allow it, Ms. Masters."

Caroline sat down. As she had expected, the smallest reinforcement lent Megan a sense of triumph; her eyes seemed to glint, and she looked briefly, imperiously, around the courtroom. And then, head bowed, Megan slipped back into her role.

"Did there come a time," Jackson asked her, "that you gained personal knowledge that Brett Allen was following you?"

A slight, reluctant nod. "Yes."

"And when was that?"

Megan looked into a middle distance; once more, there was the glaze of shock remembered. "She burst into James's apartment and found us together."

Next to her, Caroline saw Brett grip the edge of the table. "What were the circumstances?" Jackson asked.

Megan's eyes half shut; her voice was a curious mix of reticence and pride. "We were making love. In James's bed."

"That's a relief," Caroline whispered. But Brett did not seem to hear her. She had the concerned look that Caroline had seen before—someone trapped in a courtroom, listening to a version of her life she could not challenge, reduced to wondering how her reaction appeared to others.

Silent, Caroline touched Brett's hand.

"I know this is difficult," Jackson said, "but could you describe what happened?"

Megan paused, looking away. "James was on top of me. So that I was the one who saw her first."

"Go on."

She shook her head, as if in disbelief remembered. "Brett's eyes were wide and staring. And then she got this kind of crazy smile, but filled with hate.

"I think I screamed then—I'm not sure. What I remember is James's eyes becoming frightened, and then him turning to face her.

"At first, she was after *me*. Calling me a bitch and trying to scratch his face so she could get to me." As if by reflex, Megan touched her face. "I was so stunned that all I did was pull the sheet up over me. . . ."

Brett's fingertips, pressed against the table, were white. "Our time's coming," Caroline whispered.

"But James was wonderful." Pausing, Megan shook her head. "I don't know how he did it, but somehow he got his arms around her so she couldn't move. She was wriggling, struggling . . ." Her voice fell off.

"Yes?"

"And then she leaned back, spit in his face, and told him, 'I'll kill you for this.' "

Thinking of Brett, Caroline felt her stomach clench.

Megan raised her head. "I'll never forget it," she said with new clarity. "James with her saliva on his face, her eyes so green and scary. And then, very softly, she said it again. To be sure he didn't miss it.

" '*I'll kill you.*' "

Megan touched her forehead. "Suddenly, she was gone."

The last words, slightly tremulous, carried their own resonance: Brett was not gone, the words said. Because she *had* killed him.

"It's all right," Caroline murmured.

But Jackson let the moment linger—in Towle's subdued, unhappy look, in the reporter, writing furiously, who could not take her eyes off Megan. And, most of all, in Megan herself—so suddenly still, so clearly elsewhere. It was easy to see how she had stolen Jackson's case.

Gently, he asked, "How did that affect your relationship with James?"

"He kept on seeing her." Megan sounded drained now, reciting a tragedy she knew by heart but whose end she could not change. "She'd threatened to kill herself, you see."

Brett leaned forward. "Jesus . . ."

"Objection." Caroline stood again. "Once more, hearsay. And whose state of mind are we talking about now?"

"The victim's," Jackson said curtly. "As my next question will show."

Towle nodded. "Go ahead."

Jackson turned to Megan. She waited there, her posture patient, courteous, dispirited: to Caroline, her manner was meant to suggest that she was not taking revenge but keeping faith with a man she loved.

"Did this affect, Ms. Race, the way you and James went about seeing each other?"

Slowly, Megan nodded. "What James said was that he wanted to be rid of her but that he felt so responsible. I think he really believed that if he broke off with her, Brett might harm herself." Megan steepled her hands in front of her. "So we entered this phase which seemed endless to me then and now seems so short—where I was almost like James's mistress, a secret who couldn't be known, and we spent our nights alone at my place.

"We saw absolutely no one—it was like we were safe within our secret. Part of me hated it. But now I remember how he read me poetry, or acted out scenes for a play, and I realize we'd discovered that we needed no one else. That what we had, emotionally and as lovers, was enough to turn my small apartment into a world." Her head rose again. "We didn't need anyone."

Yes, Caroline thought, this is who I expected. For the first time, Jackson looked faintly disconcerted. "But you stayed together," he said.

"Oh, yes. Sometimes I thought I was being foolish." Megan gave a faint, fond smile. "But then at the end, I knew I had been right to wait.

"The night before he died, James came to me.

"We made love, beautiful love. It had such a desperate quality that part of me was afraid of losing him. That he had come to say that we were over, and it hurt him so much that he needed, one last time, to be as close to me as he could be."

Caroline saw Brett wince; the description must sound enough like James to her to make her wonder if this was true. The tragedy of Megan, Caroline thought, was a certain ruined sensitivity; her comprehension of others was uncanny, but incomplete. So that her version of these final days had the feel of reality.

Megan turned to Brett now. "But I was wrong," she said softly. "James had come to ask me to go away with him. To California."

Brett's lips parted, silent. "What did you say?" Jackson asked softly.

"That I loved him. But that I had an obligation to my mother, and to my father's memory. And that before I tried to pull all that together, he needed to put *us* together." Her voice grew firm. "To go to Brett. To tell her what he had asked me and that he would never see her again."

"And what did he say?"

"That he would." Megan's stare at Brett was accusing now, but her voice was soft. "The night he died, Mr. Watts, was the night he promised to tell her."

Suddenly, Brett's face was less angry than wounded—as if doubting, as Caroline once had made her doubt, the truth of her own memory. Jackson seemed to approach Megan with diffidence, reluctant to interrupt her grief. "And where were you that night?"

"Alone in my apartment." Megan's eyes filled with sudden tears. "Waiting for James, with a bottle of champagne. You see, after he told her the truth, James was coming to me. . . ."

Megan could not seem to go on.

"Perfect," Caroline murmured.

TWELVE

CAROLINE STOOD, a half smile on her face, gazing at Megan in silence. Megan seemed to square her shoulders, waiting for Caroline to come forward. But Caroline did not move from the defense table.

"Hello, Megan."

Caroline's greeting, soft and a little sad, seemed to straighten Megan in her chair. Warily, she answered, "Hello."

For Caroline, there was no sound, no audience, no one else but the girl in front of her. "This incident you described, when Brett found you and James in bed together. When did it occur?"

Megan folded her hands. "April."

"And how often did you see James after that?"

Megan's mouth tightened. "As I said, once or twice a week. At my apartment."

"Did the two of you ever socialize with anyone else?"

"No. We needed time alone."

"Or go anywhere?"

"No." Megan's voice was harsh. "I already testified that James was worried about what Brett might do."

Caroline tilted her head. "Were you frightened?"

A delayed nod. "I couldn't help it."

"Did you ever talk to anyone about it?"

"James. Of course."

"Anyone else?"

A slight pause. "No. It was very painful, and emotional."

Caroline nodded her understanding. "Is it fair to say that, at least to this point, James was the love of your life?"

Megan raised her head, prideful again. "Yes, it is."

"Then would you also say that when he died, he was the person you were closest to?"

"Yes," Megan said promptly, and then amended this. "Except for my mother."

Caroline nodded again. "How many times a week do you talk to your mother?"

Megan paused a moment. "Two or three times a week. Sometimes more, sometimes less."

"Did you ever mention James to her?"

Megan's eyes narrowed. "What do you mean?"

"I mean his *existence*."

Megan seemed to flush. "Of course."

"How many times?"

Megan hesitated. In a quiet voice, she answered, "Two or three."

"Two or three? What did you tell her about him?"

Megan's mouth compressed. "I don't remember, exactly. I'm sure she knew that I was seeing him."

"Not that you were in love with him?"

Megan gave her a long stare of annoyance. "I really don't remember what I said. My mother and I talk about a lot of things."

"You must. Did they happen to include that Brett had threatened James?"

Megan hesitated. "I don't think so."

"Or was following you?"

"I don't remember."

Caroline raised an eyebrow. "After this incident in April, did you mention James to your mother at all?"

For the first time, Megan looked toward Jackson. "I'm over here," Caroline said softly. "And Mr. Watts can't help you. Because he knows exactly why I'm asking these questions."

Jackson rose at once, to buy his witness time. "Rather than lecture the witness, Ms. Masters, perhaps you can repeat the question."

Caroline did not look at him. "Megan," she asked quietly, "after Brett found you in bed with James, did you ever again mention James to your mother?"

Megan gazed at her lap. "I don't remember. As I said, the place I was in with James was embarrassing."

"Didn't you think your mother could help?"

Megan frowned. "I didn't want to upset her."

Caroline looked astonished. "Surely you must have talked

to *someone* about him. Given how important James was in your life."

Megan hesitated. "I really don't remember. Being with James was more important than talking about him."

Caroline was quiet for a moment. "So am I correct in understanding that after this incident in April, you never mentioned James Case to anyone?"

Megan gave Caroline a quick, hostile look. "I don't remember."

"After April, did anyone *see* you together?"

"I don't know."

"Did you and James ever leave your apartment?"

"No."

"Did you ever invite people over when he was there?"

"No."

"When did he come over? Weekends, or weekdays?"

Megan's face was stiff. "Weekdays. At night."

"Any particular nights?"

"No. Just when he could, and I could."

"What did you do, exactly?"

"That's private." Megan's voice was brittle now. "I don't see why I have to answer private questions."

Caroline's voice remained quiet. In the precise same tone, she asked again, "What did you do, exactly?"

Glancing at Jackson, Megan seemed to gather herself. "We made love. We were just with each other, and it was beautiful."

"Did you talk?"

"Of course."

"What about?"

"Everything. We were each other's best friends."

Pausing, Caroline felt the door shut on her compassion, the complete and deadly coldness come into her again. In a voice of bored politeness, she asked, "Where was James from?"

Megan put her hands on the rail of the witness stand. "I don't remember, exactly."

"Where did his parents live?"

"I don't remember."

"Do you know where he was born?"

"No."

"Or whether he had brothers and sisters?"

"No."

Caroline looked curious. "Would you describe James as a closed personality?"

Megan mustered the prideful look. "Maybe with other people. Not with me."

"Did he happen to mention to you that he was an orphan?"

Megan's fingers, Caroline noted, clasped the edge of the rail. "No."

"Or that he had lived in a series of foster homes?"

"No."

Next to her, Caroline saw Brett's eyes widen with surprise that Megan knew so little. "Well," Caroline said softly, "I'm sure those subjects were painful for him. Tell me, then, where were you and James planning to live in California?"

Megan glanced at Jackson Watts. "We hadn't gotten that far," she said at last. "The first thing was for him to break it off with her."

"Did *James* at least have things narrowed down? Like, for example, which city you'd live in?"

Megan sat back, rigid. "Why are you asking all this? It's like harassment." Swiftly, she turned, glaring from the judge to Jackson. "Do I have to answer this?"

Towle took off his glasses, gazing at her narrowly. "Oh, yes," he said quietly. "You do."

Jackson, Caroline saw, was gazing sharply at his witness. "Which city?" Caroline snapped.

Megan turned abruptly, lips parted. Then she said, "We hadn't decided yet."

"What were you going to do there?"

"If I went? Finish school, of course." Her voice became scornful. "But I wasn't sure I'd throw everything over for a man."

"That would be a big decision, wouldn't it? Did you happen to discuss it with your mother?"

"No. Like I said, it hadn't gone that far." She paused, modulating her voice to sorrow. "And then James was dead."

"And you were waiting for him, at your apartment. With a bottle of champagne."

"Yes." It was as if Megan found the question, and her answer, reassuring. "Yes," she repeated, and then tears welled in her eyes.

"When James didn't appear, what did you do?"

Megan shook her head. "I kept calling him, all night. . . ."

"Oh? Did you happen to leave a message on his machine?"

Megan's eyes shut. "I don't remember. I mean, it was so awful . . ."

Slowly, Caroline reached beneath the table and took out her briefcase. She laid it in front of her on the table, releasing the latches with a soft click.

At the sound, Megan's eyes flew open. She stared at the briefcase, then at Caroline. "Tell me," Caroline asked softly, "how did you learn that James was dead?"

Megan looked disoriented. "On the radio."

"What did you do?"

Megan went pale. "I cried."

"Did you call anyone?"

"No. I couldn't."

"Or tell anyone?"

"No."

Caroline paused a moment. "Not even your mother?"

"No."

"When *did* you tell her James was dead?"

"I don't remember."

Quietly, Caroline asked, "Do you happen to remember when James was buried? Or where?"

The hush in the courtroom had become a pained collective silence. Megan's voice seemed to tremble. "I couldn't stand—"

"Did you make any effort to find out?"

"I don't remember."

"Or if there was a memorial service?"

Eyes averted, Megan shook her head. "No," she said in a shrill voice. "Don't you understand how painful this was—"

"Who did you think had killed him?" Caroline snapped.

Megan hesitated. "It had to be Brett."

Caroline crossed her arms. "Knowing that must have been awfully hard to live with."

"Yes."

"Unbearable, in fact."

Megan still looked away. "Yes."

"So when did you go to the police?"

Megan put one finger on her mouth, face frozen.

Caroline's voice rose. "When did you go to the police?"

Megan shook her head. "I don't remember."

"Was it six days after James was found?"

Megan looked up. "I was *afraid* of her."

"Brett?"

"Yes."

"Because she might stalk you?"

"Yes."

Caroline rested one hand on the table. "Did you ever *see* Brett stalking you?"

"Yes." Megan's voice was angry now. "I did."

"Tell me how she did it."

Megan swallowed. "She crept up into the shrubbery beneath my apartment." Her voice quavered. "We could see her in the bushes, staring up at us. . . ."

"What did you do?"

"Nothing. James said she had this violent temper. . . ."

"Didn't you call the police?"

Megan flinched. "No."

"Or ask your mother for advice?"

"No."

Caroline was in another zone now; the questions came swift and sure, one upon the other. "So let me see if I understand you, Megan. James Case and you were lovers, yes?"

"Yes."

"Brett threatened to kill him."

"Yes."

"And to kill herself."

"That's what James said."

"And she stalked you?"

"Yes."

"Hid outside your building."

"I just told you that."

"And so, for over two months, you and James never left the apartment?"

"Yes."

"But in the end, James chose you."

"Yes." Megan clamped the arms of the witness stand. "He chose me."

"And asked you to go to California."

"Yes."

"And on the night of his death, you waited for him to tell Brett Allen and then come to you."

Megan clasped her hands together, gathering herself again. "Yes," she said softly. "I did."

Caroline waited for a moment. "And yet," she said with equal quiet, "you never told anyone about any of this. Until the day you went to Mr. Watts and accused Brett Allen of murder."

For a time, Megan simply watched her. "No." Her voice was barely audible. "I could never talk about it."

"Not even to your mother."

"No."

Caroline paused, then asked, softly, "Despite all those telephone calls you made to her . . . what was it, at least two or three a week?"

From the stand, Megan seemed to stare at her in desperation, as if trying to read her mind. "I don't remember now. I already said that."

"Do you remember whether you called your mother collect or put it on your own phone bill?"

"Objection," she heard Jackson say. "This is not only irrelevant, it's petty harassment."

"Hardly," Caroline said to Towle. "It goes directly to this witness's credibility on crucial matters. As I'll show in a moment."

Towle nodded, grim-faced. "Go ahead, Ms. Masters."

Caroline turned to Megan. "Collect or not," she snapped.

Megan hesitated, hunched back in her chair. "Collect, I think."

"Oh? And who was there to accept your calls?"

Megan's mouth fell open and then closed again.

"It could hardly be your mother," Caroline asked, "could it?"

Megan stared at her, new tears in her eyes. "What do you mean?"

Caroline moved closer. Softly, she said, "That she's been institutionalized for depression and doesn't speak to anyone. And hasn't for the last five months."

Megan's face was ashen. "Did you hear me?" Caroline demanded.

Megan flinched. "Yes," she said dully. "She hasn't been well."

"So these conversations with your mother—the ones you told us about under oath—never happened. Were, in fact, fabrications."

Megan's jawline set. "I was protecting her privacy. . . ."

Pausing. Caroline let the stillness of the courtroom build. From the bench, Towle looked at Megan with open disdain. "So," Caroline continued calmly, "the only thing that *is* true is that you never talked to anyone about James Case. Ever, at any time."

Megan looked down. "I can't remember now."

Eyes still on Megan, Caroline opened the lid of her briefcase. Almost casually, she asked, "Did you ever *write* about him?"

Megan stared at the briefcase, as if transfixed. In a hushed voice, she asked, "What do you mean?"

Slowly, Caroline reached inside the briefcase and removed the red journal. She stood it on one end, beneath her fingertips, and looked once more at Megan.

Megan's face seemed to crumble. But except for the fingers of one hand, brought suddenly to her collarbone, she did not move.

Softly, Caroline asked again, "Did you ever write about your relationship to James Case?"

Megan's fingers pressed against her chest, and then she spun, looking about for Jackson. "I'd like a recess. . . ."

Caroline watched her. "Answer the question, please. Then you can have all the time you want."

Megan stood, voice shrill. "I won't put up with this. . . ."

"Because you're a compulsive liar," Caroline said with cutting coldness. "I know it, you know it, and—in five minutes—everyone in this room will know it."

Hurriedly, Jackson stepped forward, his own voice taut. "The witness has been on for most of the day, Your Honor. If she's tired, or upset, no one's served by making her go longer. We can start again tomorrow."

Towle looked at Megan, staring from the witness stand, and then at Caroline herself. "Counsel?"

Caroline's eyes still did not move from Megan. Quietly, she said, "As soon as she admits she lied, I'll be through with Ms. Race for the day. All that she has to say is 'I made up everything I told you.' It won't even take that long."

"No." Megan's look at Jackson mingled fear and betrayal. "I want to talk with Mr. Watts."

Towle studied her with something like distaste, and then turned to Caroline. "It seems to me, Ms. Masters, that this witness should be allowed to consider her own position. Quite carefully. As should Mr. Watts."

Caroline gave Megan a silent look of pity and contempt. "Tomorrow morning then, Your Honor. I think I can remember my last question. As, I'm quite sure, will Ms. Race."

Towle looked from Caroline to Megan. "Very well," he said. "Court is adjourned until nine o'clock a.m."

There was sudden movement—people stirring, a cacophony of voices. Jackson quickly went to Megan and shepherded her past Caroline. Her face was streaked with tears.

Turning to Caroline, Jackson said tersely, "I want to see you, Caroline. Five minutes."

"Take your time," Caroline answered calmly. "I think Megan has something to tell you."

Megan could not look at her. Abruptly, Jackson led her away.

Brett stared at the journal. "What is it?"

"A kind of diary." Caroline kept her voice low. "She lied about almost everything, and it's all in here. James dumped her after you caught them together. She started following you and James, hiding beneath his window. The only way she knew about California is that she went to him, begging for another chance." Caroline turned to her. "James said he wanted to leave with you. What you remember, at least about that, is how things were."

Brett slowly shook her head. "How did you get it?" she said at last.

Through her weariness and worry, Caroline smiled a little. "That's what Jackson wants to know."

Jackson shut the journal and slammed it down. "What in God's name are you doing?" he demanded.

Caroline shrugged. "Exposing perjury. She really is quite mad, you know."

In the spare office Caroline and Brett had used, Jackson stared at her across the tarnished desk. "You could have come to me with this."

"I could have. But would you have dismissed the case with prejudice? I doubt that, somehow."

"So instead you let me put on a lying witness and just watch me do it, waiting to destroy her. So that the prosecution seems like such a travesty that we look bad if we even consider pursuing it."

"You will." Caroline's voice was steely now. "Once I'm finished with Megan."

"Sorry. She's so hysterical now that she's incoherent. I'm withdrawing her as a witness—"

"Too late. She's under subpoena, and she's mine. By noon tomorrow, that girl's going to be far more than a pathetic liar. She'll be the best murder suspect you've ever overlooked."

Softly, Jackson answered, "Not unless you use this diary."

"Which I've every intention of doing."

Jackson shook his head. "You've already destroyed her," he said. "Use that diary tomorrow, and you destroy yourself. Megan saved you by imploding."

Caroline was silent for a moment. "My story is that it came to me in the mail. Which Betty can confirm."

Jackson's face was stained with anger. "Don't insult me, Caroline. You mailed it to yourself. Though Betty may not know that."

"So file a case. But first you have to finish *this* one." Caroline paused for emphasis. "I want her back, tomorrow morning. Or I want the case against Brett dismissed with prejudice."

Jackson's mouth set. "I can't do that. Megan may be a liar, but that doesn't make Brett innocent. So you'll have to make a public fool of me. And risk your reputation and maybe your career." His eyes were keen. "You did it yourself, didn't you? Broke in with a credit card and searched until you found this thing."

Caroline stood. "I told you about Larry. I asked you to check Megan out. Asked—no, begged—you to search her place. But you didn't want to *offend* her. Because she was such an *important* witness . . ."

"She looked credible, damn it."

Caroline waved a hand, contemptuous. "Sorry. I'd forgotten that I'm morally disqualified from throwing this back at you."

"Fuck you, Caroline. You withheld evidence and used it to set me up. Even though, for you, it's a suicide mission. You should have brought this to me the day that you first had it." Jackson caught himself, looked at her hard again. "There's something else to this, isn't there?"

Caroline stood. "Just have her here tomorrow," she said, and left.

THIRTEEN

CAROLINE REMOVED THE envelope from beneath the seat of her car and spread the sheaf of pictures in her lap.

Joe Lemieux had done well, she thought. Satisfied, she rearranged them: from the top, a close-up of Megan Race gazed up at her, as vivid as in life. And then Caroline replaced them in the envelope.

It was dusk, a little past eight, and Caroline was alone.

Tomorrow would be bad for all of them—Jackson, Megan, Caroline herself. And then, after that, they would each live with the consequences. But that was for tomorrow; before finishing with Megan, there was one more thing to do.

She could have sent Lemieux. But the defense of Brett possessed her now; this was not a task she wished to delegate. She smiled mirthlessly, remembering the young Caroline, the impatient, sometimes impetuous lawyer who did her own investigation. This was far more than that, she knew—more, even, than Brett. Every instinct Caroline had said that she should do this alone.

She turned on the ignition and left Resolve behind.

The road to Heron Lake was, she guessed, much as it had been for Brett that night—winding, tree-shrouded, dusk becoming a film of gray, then darkness. Caroline's headlights cut the dark; a first moon, brightening silver, appeared in the break of trees above the road.

Passing the dirt road to Brett's lot, Caroline slowed but did not turn.

The road became darker, narrower. Perhaps a quarter mile farther, Caroline saw the neon sign of a gas station and convenience store. The successor, no doubt, of the Resolve General Store.

A few yards past it was the head of Mosher Trail.

Caroline turned there.

The road had several switchbacks, twisting among the trees; for a strange, disturbing moment, Caroline remembered the road at Windy Gates; her mother. Then the road opened, and she found herself on a gentle slope of dirt and rock, gazing at Heron Lake.

Caroline got out.

The moon was yellow now, its pale light moving slowly in the water. She walked to the edge.

There was a soft wind; water lapped gently at Caroline's feet. In the swirls of time, it seemed not so very different from some summer night with Jackson, when she had been younger than Brett was now.

Turning, Caroline gazed toward the lot that had once been hers. She could see, in the curve of the lake, a shadow between the lake and trees, the soft grass of the glade.

Perhaps she hoped for too much, or feared too much. There were too many pieces missing. But, standing here, it was not hard to imagine someone silently walking the shallows of the water's edge, moving toward two lovers in the grass.

There were still too many pieces missing, and one that was not—a knife. Unless, in the dark recesses of her memory, she had confused one knife with another.

Megan could have followed them. Assuming that she knew the lake, she might even have found them.

There was a chill in the air, Caroline thought.

She returned to the car, checking the photographs once more. Then she left the lakeside, driving slowly to the trailhead, until she saw the neon light of the gas station.

The building was white and the fluorescent lighting from within gave it a bright, unearthly glow. When Caroline pulled up to the gas tank, a slender man in a baseball cap came out from the store and walked over to her window. He stepped beneath the light above the gas tanks, and Caroline saw that he was barely out of his teens, with a goatee and a ponytail that somehow only made him look younger.

"Fill it up?" he asked.

"Thanks."

He went to the tank and inserted the hose, and then began cleaning her front window with a squeegee.

Caroline stuck her head out the driver's side. "There was something I wanted to ask you."

With a flick of the wrist, he erased a squashed bug. "Sure."

Caroline propped her head on her chin. "I'm a lawyer, working on the murder that happened out at Heron Lake. You've heard about that?"

He stopped, curious. "A little. I just got back last night—been in Florida, seeing my mother." He paused a moment. "Who you working for?"

"Brett Allen, the defendant, who's about your age. I don't think she did it, and I've been trying to figure out if someone in the area saw anything that might help."

Slowly, he nodded. "Yeah, my boss said there was a guy out here the other day. I guess the night this other guy was killed was the last night I was on. Before vacation." He peered more closely at Caroline. "What you looking for?"

"Anything." Caroline made herself sound bemused, a woman at sea. "Like a car, or a person you'd never seen before. Or maybe someone turning down Mosher Trail."

"Boy." His show of teeth was reflexive, the surprise of someone asked to find significance in a mundane night three weeks in the past. "I mean, I was just sort of shuffling between the tanks and in there, thinking more about vacation than anything else. I wasn't really watching the trail."

The nozzle of the hose clicked off. The boy went back, gave the nozzle a final squeeze, and replaced the hose on the tank. Caroline gave him her credit card and watched him walk to the building.

He returned with a charge slip and a pen. Neatly, Caroline wrote her name and said in a hopeful voice, "Maybe pictures would help. Think you could look at some?"

He paused, reluctant to be involved in this, and then his better nature seemed to overtake him. "Okay," he said. "Sure."

Slowly, Caroline took the pictures from the envelope. Pausing, she reshuffled them. "Let's try vehicles first," she said.

"Okay."

She flicked on the inner light of the car and handed him three photographs.

The boy leaned inside, squinting at the black-and-white blowups.

He went through the pictures, once, then twice. He paused at the last one. "Where was this taken?" he asked.

"The Connaughton County Courthouse."

He exhaled softly, puffing out his cheeks. "Because I've seen this van before. Or one like it, anyhow."

Caroline kept her voice calm. "When?"

"That night. When the driver stopped for gas."

"Man or woman?"

The boy hesitated. "Woman. I'm pretty sure."

Don't react, Caroline told herself. *Think of all the witnesses who get things wrong.* "Is there some reason you remember her?"

Silently, the boy nodded. "I remember she seemed upset." His eyes narrowed with the effort of memory. "I'm pretty sure it was the one in the van."

Caroline tilted her head. "Upset . . ."

"Yeah. I always like to do a good job on the windows. But this one, she told me to stop, like she didn't have time, and her voice was real sharp."

What did she look like? Caroline wanted to ask. She stopped herself. "Could you recognize her from a picture?"

The boy turned to her. "Is this important?"

Caroline picked up the remaining photographs. "It could be. Yes."

The boy scrutinized her another moment and took the pictures from her hand, leaning back through the window into the light.

He shuffled the first picture, then another, then another.

At the fourth one, he stopped.

"What is it?"

The boy's mouth closed, then opened again. "That's her."

Caroline's throat constricted. "You're sure?"

"Yeah. I mean, she looks upset in this picture. Like she did that night."

Caroline sat back in her seat. "After that, did you see where she went?"

Her voice, she thought, sounded calm enough. But the boy looked at her with new suspicion. "Will I have to testify or something?"

"I don't know. I hope not."

Pausing, he gazed at the picture. "Well, I don't know where she went, or what direction. But I'd have to say I remember her."

In the shadows of the car, Caroline collected herself. "If you wouldn't mind, I'd prefer that you not mention this to anyone. After all, it may be nothing."

He looked relieved. "No problem."

"Thanks. I'll let you know what happens."

"Sure." He handed back the picture. "Have a nice night, okay?"

Caroline placed the picture on the seat beside her. "Okay."

Slowly, he turned and walked to the gas station. It was a moment before Caroline started the car.

She drove past Mosher Trail, out of sight of the gas station, and stopped by the side of the road.

She sat in darkness, forcing herself to think. But nothing could dull the ache of guilt and memory, sickness and anger. She could not look at the photograph of Betty.

FOURTEEN

WHEN CAROLINE ARRIVED at Masters Hill, there was a dim glow from the first-floor windows. The upper floors were dark.

The air was quiet, still. When Caroline stepped on the porch, her footsteps sounded hollow.

Softly, she knocked on the door.

Caroline heard a stirring inside, the rattle of a latch. The door opened slightly.

Betty peered at her through the crack. She looked startled. "Caroline."

Caroline watched her for a moment. "Who else is home?"

"Just Larry." Betty's voice was tight. "What is it?"

"We need to talk."

Betty hesitated, glancing over her shoulder. "Larry's trying to sleep now. Today upset him terribly."

"Come outside, then. We won't need him for this."

Still Betty did not move; the tone of Caroline's voice seemed to stop her. Then, reluctant, she stepped out onto the porch.

Caroline walked away from the door. She heard Betty slowly follow her.

"Do you think," Betty asked, "that you can discredit this despicable woman?"

Caroline turned to her. "Which one?"

In the half-light, Betty seemed to blink. Caroline felt a terrible calm come over her. "Actually," she said, "I'm calling you as a witness tomorrow. I think that will help Brett more."

Betty stiffened. "Why?"

Caroline ignored this. "When we discussed the possibility, you seemed concerned. So I thought it might help if we went over a few questions."

Betty became still again. "What are they?"

Caroline moved toward her. When she stopped, their faces were two feet apart. Quietly, Caroline asked, "Why have you been lying to me?"

Betty's eyes widened. "Lying . . ."

"You knew that Brett would take him to the lake that night. Because you listened on the upstairs telephone." Caroline's voice was chill with withheld anger. "By the way, I'd suggest not lying to me now. Or on the stand tomorrow. There's only so much nostalgia I can take."

Betty took one step back, wordless.

"Open your mouth, Betty. And see if it can make a sound. Something like, 'Yes, Caroline. I'm an eavesdropper.' "

Betty did not move now. "Caroline," she said tautly, "you don't know what you're doing."

"Oh, I've known for years now." Caroline's tone was quiet still. "Did you listen to her, Betty?"

"Yes." Betty stood straighter. "Because I love her. I've loved her all these years you were away."

Caroline felt her fists clench. "What did you overhear, damn you? That he wanted her to go to California?"

"Yes." Betty's voice rose in anger. "And that he was in trouble over drugs—"

"And," Caroline cut in, "that there'd been a girl named Megan. You lied about that too, didn't you?"

Betty walked to the corner of the porch.

Caroline's voice became soft again. "How long after that did you leave the house?"

In the darkness, Betty's profile was still.

Caroline moved closer. "You left the house, damn it. Just tell me when."

Slowly, Betty turned to Caroline. With something close to calm, she asked, "How do you know that?"

"Because you stopped at the gas station," Caroline paused. "That wasn't very smart, Betty."

Betty seemed to slump. She looked thin and tired; Caroline had a stark, pitiless image of Betty as an old woman.

"I wasn't planning this," Betty said at last. "Any of it."

The admission, so simply stated, drained the anger within Caroline. Suddenly, all she felt was a horror so deep that she wished to erase it. "My God, Betty." She heard the tremor in her own voice. "My God."

Betty's look became pleading. Tonelessly, she asked, "So you understand now?"

"Understand?" Caroline stared at her. "How can anyone understand that?"

Betty came toward her, then stopped abruptly, shock filling her eyes. "That's what you think of me, Caroline? *That's* who you think I am?" Her voice was thick. "A woman so deranged she'd kill Brett's boyfriend, then let *her* be blamed for it?"

Caroline could only stare at her.

Betty grasped her collar. "You're the one who's sick, Caroline—poisoned with guilt and hatred and years of being alone—"

With an awful deliberation, Caroline slapped her sister across her face.

There was a sharp crack; Betty's muffled shriek. Caroline felt a numbness in her wrist, tears in her eyes. Betty stared at her, hand pressed to her cheek.

In a flat voice, Caroline said, "What were you doing there?"

Betty turned from her. After a time, she murmured, "I was coming back from Father's fishing camp."

"Why?"

Betty touched her eyes. "Because he was so upset. He wanted to be alone."

Caroline felt a tightness in her chest. She raised a hand, as if to steady herself. "You told him."

"Yes." Betty's expression mingled shame with pride. "Larry was gone, Caroline. I needed to talk to someone."

Caroline felt herself shiver. It was a moment before she could speak. "Do you have any idea," she asked, "what you may have done? *Again?*"

Betty folded her arms, as if against the cold. "Father and I couldn't tell anyone. If the police had known that Brett and James had been fighting over Megan . . ."

She looked away.

Caroline felt a terrible rush of comprehension. "You think Brett killed him. That you protected her by lying . . ."

Betty looked at her steadily now. But she would not, could not, answer.

"What fools we are." Pausing, Caroline shook her head. "Brett didn't kill anyone."

Betty swallowed. "Who, then?"

Caroline felt a wave of nausea. "My God, Betty. Have you forgotten who it was that taught us to fillet a fish?"

In the silence, Betty's eyes shut.

"Where is he?" Caroline demanded.

"At his fishing camp." When Betty opened her eyes, her voice was shaking. "I'll go with you. It's better if we talk to him together."

Caroline made herself stand straight again. "No," she answered softly. "This is mine to do. After all, I *am* Brett's mother."

In the wind and rain, the roiling sea at her back, Caroline had slowly crossed the beach.

She was numb; in her mind, David fought the storm, not knowing the thing that—in the guilt of her betrayal—Caroline could not bring herself to tell him. Mechanically, she went to the boathouse for her suitcase.

The boathouse was stark, empty. She looked vainly about for any sign of him; all that was left were two paperbacks he had forgotten. Unlatching her suitcase, she tucked them in a corner. She would save them for him or, if he wrote to her, send them back.

And then the anguish came over her again—a half hour ago they had faced each other in his room, and now he was gone, and all she had of him was an untold secret.

Turning, she stepped outside and shut the door softly behind her.

Her father's house was dark. She climbed the stairs from the beach, knowing only that she could not tell him that David was gone. And then, in her misery, Caroline saw how she must buy her lover time.

She opened the door and walked silently through the house.

Her father was in the night-shadowed porch. As she stood in the doorway, she saw him pacing distractedly, now and then gazing out to sea.

"Hello, Father."

He started. "Caroline," he said, and then hesitancy entered his voice, and Caroline knew for certain that her father had betrayed them. "Where have you been?" he asked.

"Boston. You knew that."

"But you're drenched."

Caroline did not answer. She fought the impulse to scream at him, to tell him what he had done. But for David's sake, she could not.

Drawing herself up, she said in a calm voice, "I came back to tell you something."

In the dim light, she saw the wariness in his deep-set eyes and knew what he expected—that she had come to say she was in love with David and was going away with him. Cautiously, he asked, "What is it?"

"I'm pregnant, Father."

"Pregnant?" His voice was hollow, appalled. "Are you quite sure?"

"Yes. That's why I went to Boston. To see my doctor."

Her voice sounded civil, Caroline thought, if unapologetic. But her father was quite still; what he knew, and how he felt, kept him from coming close to her. "You can't have this baby, Caroline." His tone was soft now. "Surely that must be clear."

Caroline raised her hand. "What I'm going to do, Father, is go to bed. In the morning, after I've thought more, I'll go see Scott. We're the ones who must decide."

Her father seemed to blanch. With a satisfaction born of hatred, Caroline saw the terrible emotion cross his face—the knowledge that he had turned in the father of his daughter's child, that David would go to prison. And then, most contemptible of all, Caroline read the hope that she would never know who had betrayed them.

"Caroline." His voice was rough. "We must talk about this. Now."

"I'm sorry, Father. Not now. I seem to be more tired these days."

"But you're my daughter . . ."

"I know," Caroline said softly. And then, for David's sake, she crossed the room and kissed her father on the cheek. "I know."

She could not sleep that night. The windows of her bedroom rattled with waves of rain and howling wind; her mind fought back terrified imaginings, willed David through the storm. The life that he had left inside her seemed barely real.

In the morning, drawn and nauseous, Caroline forced herself to dress.

Her stomach was still flat, she saw. But her body had the first swelling of water retained, and she found that she no longer liked coffee. That, and the sickness, were the small intimations of this living thing that only her sister had craved.

Larry and Betty were in the kitchen. From their expressions—the edgy wariness they had lately assumed for meetings between Channing and the new and unpredictable Caroline—she surmised that Channing had told them nothing.

Yes, she thought, that would be like him. An abortion, then Harvard, and life goes on as it was. With no one but the two of them, and David, ever knowing the truth.

Larry gave her a quizzical smile, Betty a more cautious one. "How are you?" Larry asked.

But it was Betty whom Caroline looked at. "Pregnant," she said.

Betty's mouth fell open. Almost conversationally, Caroline said, "If you're not feeling nauseous, Betty, it's probably a false alarm. Take it from me."

Betty half stood. Ignoring this, Caroline walked past them and out into the rear yard.

The morning was sparkling, with that crisp purity of wind and sky that follows a fierce storm. Perfect for sailing, Caroline thought.

Her father was staring at the empty mooring.

Quiet, Caroline came up behind him. "Oh, yes," she said. "David's gone."

He turned to her: it was a moment before the shock suffused his face. "Last night," she said in a tight voice, "was the hardest thing I'd ever done. But that's almost over for me now. Because this is the last time you and I are ever speaking."

"Caroline." He reached out for her, anguish in his face. "Please . . ."

"You made my decision for me. I shouldn't be with David, so you decided to have him sent to jail, letting me think it was just bad luck." She paused, breathing hard now. "Well, you've lost me now. And you know the part I hate most? You don't feel sorry for David. You feel sorry for you. . . ."

"Caroline." Channing drew his hands back, fought for dignity. "You don't know what it is to love a child."

"No. But I know the difference between love and ownership." Caroline fought to control her temper; suddenly what she felt was deeper, and surer, than anger. "But if you love me, Father, please don't hope for forgiveness. Hope, for my sake, that David Stern is still alive."

She turned and left him there.

That fall, she stayed alone on the Vineyard.

Her father had given up. She felt him, alone in New Hampshire, waiting out her anger and disaffection. But what he would have known were they still speaking was that Caroline no longer cared.

A life was growing inside her.

Part of this, Caroline admitted to herself with ruthless honesty, was deeply irrational—that the life was part of David, who might already be lost. Were he here, to end this baby might have been possible; perhaps to bear his child was a deep, even twisted, act of anger and revenge. But she could not live with the thought of having killed him and then his child as well.

For that was the crux of it. Caroline had no rules for what other women must do; her rule for society was that women must decide. But she was too unsparing with herself to deny that the decision was to take, or not take, a life. For David, for the child, and, most of all, for herself, Caroline could not do this.

And so, by default, the child remained inside her. Until the choice was only whether to keep it or give it away.

Even as she hoped against hope to hear from David, Caroline began, at last, to imagine a future on her own.

She knew what she would do without the child—move as far from New Hampshire as was possible, put herself through law school, stand on her own. Become the kind of lawyer that Caroline Masters—and no one else—would come to believe she should be. But as hard as it was to imagine life with this baby, it was as hard to imagine the strangers who would become its parents; in that bleak winter on the Vineyard, Caroline had far too much time to consider what a parent might do to a child.

One morning, with a crisp frost on the ground, Larry appeared at the door.

He gave her a small, embarrassed smile. "I've come to visit you."

To her surprise, Caroline realized she was glad to see him. She felt grateful that her bitterness had not yet tarnished Larry.

"Come on in," she said. "These days, I don't have too much company. None, in fact."

He shot a wry glance at her stomach. "One," he amended. "But I guess he—or she—isn't talking yet."

Caroline smiled. "No. But she's walking a little."

Impulsively, Larry stepped forward and put his arms around her. "I'm glad to see you, Caro. No one quite knows what to do."

She pressed her face against his shoulder. "I don't, either," she murmured. "Not about this baby."

For a while, she just let him hold her. It was strange, she thought, that this made her feel like crying.

"Caro," he said softly. "I'm so sorry."

"I know. I know. . . ."

At last, she led him to the porch, still holding his hand.

They sat together on the couch. The seascape before them was stark and gray, and smudges of frost remained on the grass. Caroline hugged herself.

"Have you ever heard from him?" Larry asked.

Caroline shook her head. "Either he's dead or he's unwilling to forgive me. I hope it's the last."

Larry fell silent. "Are you thinking of keeping it?" he said after a time.

"I don't know. I shouldn't, really. But if I don't, it's like throwing a life into the lottery. How do I know who this baby gets?" She turned to him. "It's not enough that someone wants a child. Look how much my father wanted me."

Larry looked away, as if gathering himself. "I don't know how else to say this, Caroline, but to say it. I want you to think about something."

All at once, Caroline knew why he had come. Coldly, she said, "What is it?"

Larry could not face her now. "We'll never have a baby, Caro. The problem's not just me, it turns out. It's Betty too. . . ."

Caroline stood abruptly. "Never. It's better for our relationship, Larry, if I just pretend to be speechless. But I can't believe that you—the only one I still care about—would come to me for *this*." Her voice rose. "Really, what fucking vultures all of you are. But *you* . . ."

Larry looked at her now. Quietly, he said, "Who else could ask you, Caroline? And who else would you want for this baby's father?"

Caroline drew a breath, staring at him. "You may hate Betty," Larry went on, "until the day you die. Although I've got to tell you, for her sake, that she's heartsick and ashamed. But I'm not asking this for her sake. I'm asking for the baby's sake, and mine. . . ."

"This baby thing was Betty's idea, remember?"

"Was," Larry retorted. "Until I knew we couldn't have one. And knew you were." He walked over to Caroline, clasped both her shoulders, and looked into her face. "Whatever you may think of her, Betty will love this child. And I'll be there to make sure everything goes right. I'll be the father, Caroline. Would you rather trust a stranger?"

Caroline turned from him, walked back to the couch. "This is just too much," she said.

Silent, Larry watched her.

Caroline sat with her elbows on her knees, face cradled in both hands, staring at the brick floor. "It's not just Betty," she said at last. "It's my father."

"Your father's not adopting anyone."

Caroline looked fiercely up at him. "My father adopts *lives*. If you're not careful, yours will be one of them." Her voice turned slow and cold. "I will not have this child living the life my father sets for her. If it just were you, Larry, this might be possible. But I look at all of you, and I don't believe it *is* possible."

Larry sat beside her. Finally, he said, "What would you want from me?"

My God, Caroline thought; for a moment, she had imagined this baby with Larry—with her own home and a father who could separate her life from his. "What I would want," she said in a low voice, "is for you to live away from him—different town, different state. So that he never, ever runs anyone's life again."

Larry gazed out at the water. "I can do that," he said at last. "One way or another."

Slowly, Caroline turned to him. To her own surprise, she said, "Then I'll think about it. Now, please, leave me alone."

Two days after the baby was born, Larry came to the hospital.

He was alone; Caroline had not had to ask this. With bemusement and wonder, he looked at the baby she held.

"God," he said. "All that hair. I didn't know babies came with hair."

"Neither did I."

Looking down, Caroline studied the little girl's face. It was red, still swollen from birth, but she had the most remarkable eyes. Squinting, the baby stretched an arm, as if reaching out for her. It was strange, Caroline thought, how easy it was for a mother to impose meaning on a baby's simplest reflexes.

"Would you like to hold her?" she asked Larry.

Awkwardly, Larry reached out. Cradling the baby in both hands, Caroline slid her into his arms.

He sat back in the visitor's chair, smiling into the baby's unseeing eyes, until the image of that moment imprinted itself in Caroline's mind, to remain forever—sun streaming through the hospital window, lighting the baby's face and hair as Larry rested his cheek against hers. "She smells good," Larry murmured. "New."

"I know."

Larry sat there, holding the baby, until Caroline saw that he could not bring himself to do what must be done. Softly, she said, "I'm all packed, Larry. There's nothing more for me to do here."

Slowly, he looked up at her. "Okay, then."

Caroline stood. "I'll carry her."

"You're all right to do that?"

"Uh-huh."

For the last time, Caroline took the baby in her arms. She kissed her head and then, because she could not help herself, smelled her skin again.

The first few steps were strange; Caroline still felt wounded, and her stomach seemed a shapeless flap of skin. In time, she supposed, she would be herself again.

As they walked through the corridor, Larry took her arm.

The nurse at the reception desk smiled at them. "Going home?"

Caroline nodded. "Going home."

The nurse brought out a form to sign. Passing the baby to Larry, Caroline could not look at either one of them.

Wordless, she signed the papers.

The nurse patted her hand. "Enjoy her," she said.

"Oh," Caroline said, "I'm sure I will." Turning, she saw that, now, Larry could not look at her.

Outside the Vineyard Hospital, it was a clear, cool April day. Caroline stopped for a moment, blinking in the light.

"My car's over here," Larry said.

They walked there. Betty was waiting across the sound, in Woods Hole, Caroline knew; Larry would drive the baby to the ferry, and within two hours, the three of them would be together.

But Larry did not know how to leave.

"I don't want to hear from you," Caroline said. "I don't want to know about any of you. Just, please, take good care of her."

Baby in his arms, Larry looked at her steadily. "We will," he said. "*I* will."

There was a catch in Caroline's throat. Softly, she asked, "What will you name her?"

"I don't know yet." He tried to smile. "To me, she looks like Baby Allen."

Caroline gazed at the baby in his arms. At that instant, the little girl opened her eyes.

"To me," Caroline said, "she looks like my mother."

Slowly, Larry nodded. "Can I give you a ride?" he asked.

"No. Thanks. I'll call a cab."

With the baby in his arms, Larry came to Caroline and kissed her on the forehead. She could feel the child's small body graze her arm.

"Go, *now*," she said.

Without answering, Larry put the baby in the car and got inside. As they left, Caroline turned away.

Out of kindness and anger and self-preservation, Caroline did what she thought a birth mother should do. She moved to California, entered law school. She never saw her daughter again.

She had made her own life, and Brett had paid for it.

PART SEVEN

THE FINAL JUDGMENT

ONE

FOR THE FIRST time in twenty-three years, Caroline approached the wooden door of her father's rustic fishing camp, his retreat from the world.

In the cool, still darkness, her childhood came back to her—the soughing of pine boughs in a fitful wind; camping beneath a star-filled sky; eating their catch by the light of a flame in the old stone fireplace. She still knew how the inside would look to her.

Heart pounding, she knocked on the door.

There was silence. And then, with an old man's impatience, her father jerked the latch.

"Caroline."

He seemed to blink a little, perhaps with surprise, perhaps to adjust his eyes to the light. He wore a robe and slippers; seeing her, he drew himself up, an attempt at dignity. He seemed unsure of whether to ask her in.

"I was sleeping," he said. "As you can see."

Caroline did not answer. Channing hesitated for a moment and then, with a look that mingled resolve and reticence, opened the door.

The living room was not quite as she remembered it. The familiar things remained—the fly rods, the shelf of books on fishing and nature, the pastoral painting of a lake in England—and the sense of order was the same. What startled her was the only photograph, placed carefully on the bookshelf: Caroline at perhaps sixteen, head raised in laughter, hair forming a windblown wave. Caroline recalled the moment precisely: she had just caught a trout and thrown it back. But what she had not seen then was that, captured in that random instant, she looked uncannily like her mother. Uncannily like Brett.

Caroline stared at it.

Her father's eyes followed her. "I had little else of you," he said.

Slowly, Caroline turned to him. "Only Brett," she answered. "And the knife."

He looked pale, she thought. Then he moved his shoulders, steadying himself. "Yes," he said at last. "I could never bring myself to throw it out."

For the briefest moment, he glanced to his side; on a wooden standing desk, Caroline saw a gray revolver. Her heart still thudded in her chest.

"You followed the shore," she said in a low voice. "Just as you described for me."

With silent dignity, Channing Masters raised his head and looked into Caroline's eyes. His own gaze did not waver.

In that moment, Caroline felt the crushing weight of what she had recoiled from accepting. Sickness rose to her throat. She could not finish. His expression, raw and wounded as he looked at her, was the mirror of her own horror.

"You lost my mother." Her voice was slow, unsteady. "And then you lost me. To other men, you thought. You couldn't let another man take Brett—"

"Damn you, Caroline." Her father's face hardened. "It's all about that summer for you, isn't it—an evil and possessive man doing in young Lochinvar. I didn't mean for your David to do what he did, though I was willing to accept the consequences as if I had. But don't confuse your trauma with this one, or *that* boy with this one. James Case was narcissistic, manipulative, bent on involving Brett with drugs—"

"So you decided to save her. Just as you saved me."

"Don't judge me," her father snapped. "Just where were *you*, Caroline, when Brett was growing up? Following your own ambitions in California, ignoring your daughter and your family. You were even less to Brett than Nicole was to you." Channing made himself stand straighter. "That night, I didn't know what I would do. I knew only that this involvement with James must end, and that no one else could end it—not Betty, and surely not Larry. And so I took the knife and gun, and when I saw them, I saw what I must do."

His eyes were distant, as if that first sighting were more vivid than this moment. His voice filled with sadness and anger. "I saw her drinking with him, smoking marijuana, throwing herself away. This beautiful girl, doing gutter things with her body, while this gutter boy invited her to share his gutter life—"

"My God." A tremor ran through her words. "Do you know what you've done to her? You are truly insane."

Channing's face became closed, implacable. "The doctor gives me a year to live, Caroline. Perhaps two." He paused. "There's a certain freedom in that, I find. A certain clarity of thought and purpose. And a distinct lack of sentiment.

"My life—this life we had—is almost at an end. All that remains of it is Brett. Watching from those bushes, I saw that, with what little life was left to me, I might save the rest of hers."

Caroline felt something in his manner change her. He was calm now, almost detached; she would force herself to be no less. A stillness of heart and mind came over her.

Softly, Caroline said, "Then tell me what happened. Because, it seems, saving Brett has fallen to me at last."

The night was dark, shadowed; listening to his sparing words, recalling Brett's passionate ones, Caroline could see it clearly now.

Kneeling behind the bushes, her father watched them. Two silhouettes in the moonlight: the man's head between her legs, the silver-black outline of the woman, softly crying out.

Was that how it had been, he wondered—Nicole and Paul; Caroline and her lover? Part of him wished to look away. But he could not stop watching. The night felt cold to him; the old man's joints ached.

In the moonlight, Brett mounted James.

She moved with a rhythmic frenzy. Beneath her, the man's body became still.

Brett stared down at him. Clumsily, she disengaged her pelvis. And then, to her grandfather's revulsion, knelt to kiss James on the face.

Perhaps it was seeing her at that moment—slavish and lost—that decided him.

Slowly, he took the revolver from his belt.

The air was cool on his face. His fingers felt arthritic, stublike in the leather gloves. The sharp pain in his knees brought tears to his eyes.

Awkwardly, Brett stood, naked against the blackness of the lake.

She paused for a moment. Then, impulsively, she ran toward the water. Channing heard the first splash, her feet and ankles in the shallows, then the awkward slap as she hit the surface of the lake.

Painfully, Channing stood.

He was frightened for her; she seemed too impaired to swim. And then he saw the next, long strokes, as they fell into the rhythm he had taught her, taking her to the platform where they once had sunned themselves.

She had left the two of them alone.

Slowly, Channing put the revolver in his belt.

From the water, the sound of Brett's swimming stopped. There was a splash, the skim of water on her skin as she climbed onto the platform. Even with the lake as a backdrop, Channing could barely see her now—a slightly deeper shadow amidst a moonlit square of boards and nails.

Stiffly, Channing stepped from behind the bushes.

The boy lay on the blanket, arms flung to the sides, like a soldier who had died where he had fallen. Channing's feet were silent in the grass.

Kneeling on the blanket, Channing winced. The only sounds were the hollow crack of cartilage and bone, then the susurrus, barely heard, of James's breathing.

Channing looked into his face.

James's skin was smooth, his lips, slightly parted, were regular and full. As he slept, his look of arrogance slept as well.

But when he awoke, Channing knew, he would envelop Brett in his selfishness and need.

In an act of will, Channing took from its sheath the knife that Caroline had given him.

For a moment, Channing paused, knife held over the boy's sleeping face. In the back of his mind, Channing heard the crickets, felt Brett a hundred feet away.

He breathed in once, closing his eyes. And then, knife angled above James's bare neck, he felt the trembling hesitation of his hand. . . .

Now.

He slashed downward. Numb with age, halt with indecision, his hand betrayed him.

James's eyes flew open. A thin ribbon of blood appeared in a shallow wound.

My God, my God.

"No," James gasped.

Channing's gloves clasped his throat. Beneath him, James's naked body struggled to free itself from sleep and shock and horror. Channing's heart raced.

His second stroke was swift and sure.

With sickening suddenness, Channing felt the warm spurt of blood on his face and shirt, saw James's eyes, staring up at his in terror and recognition.

Another spurt of blood half blinded him. With a spastic twitch, James reached for Channing's arm.

Channing drove the knife into his heart.

The arm fell back. The first terrible gurgling issued from James's throat.

Channing recoiled in horror.

"James . . ."

Brett, calling across the water. Reeling, Channing stood.

On the blanket below him, James writhed in shock and agony. The sound was of someone drowning.

"James . . ."

Behind him, Channing heard the splash of Brett's panicky dive.

Throat filled with bile and revulsion, Channing stumbled into the darkness before Brett could see who he was, the thing that he had done.

TWO

"Brett," Caroline said quietly. "Yes, there was that, wasn't there."

In the half-light of his old lamp, Channing's face seemed bloodless; his voice was ashen now. "I knew it would be terrible for her, as that moment was for me. But it was done. I never thought that she'd be blamed for it. The fingerprints, the mouth-to-mouth, the blood spatter. Taking the knife and wallet. How could I have imagined all those things?" He paused. "I couldn't even imagine how it would be to kill a man like that."

Caroline fought back pity and repugnance. "Could you imagine," she asked coldly, "how it is to be charged with a murder you didn't commit?"

Channing turned from the look on Caroline's face. "I didn't want her to know. And, yes, I did not want to have our family—me—associated with this boy's death." He paused, voice quiet with shame. "I thought, knowing she was innocent, that they never would indict her. And when they did, that it would never stand. As to that, at least, I was right."

Caroline shook her head, numb. "What perversity made you call *me*?"

Channing seemed to reach within himself. "Because I knew you'd feel responsible for her. After all, you'd chosen to have her, then to leave her. And because, even from a distance, I could see how gifted you were." He turned to her again. "I know how this will sound to you—the way saying it sounds to me. But through all the misery of the last four days, I found a certain pleasure in watching you." His voice grew softer yet. "You're a remarkable lawyer, Caroline. But then I always knew you would be."

Caroline felt the words in the pit of her stomach. "Then you must have thought I'd find you out. Perhaps hoped I would."

He shook his head, and then a rueful pride crept into his voice. "I knew that it was possible. But I never thought you'd recall that knife; I thought I was the only one who remembered your gift, like yesterday." There was life in his eyes now. "I believed that you had put everything about those years, and our life together, out of your mind. That all you wished to remember was the last summer."

For a moment, Caroline could not speak. But when she did, her voice was chill. "Wasn't part of the pleasure to match wits with me, Father? To re-enact the murder for me and wait to see if I was apt enough to respond to your instruction?"

Channing flushed. "How can you think that? What I told you was for Brett's sake. She was my responsibility. . . ."

"For *Brett's* sake." Caroline's voice cracked with anger. "I don't know how to describe what you've put her through."

Channing stared at her. Then he turned and went to his bedroom.

Even before he returned, Caroline braced herself.

Inside the clear plastic bag he held was a bloodstained shirt and pants. Taped to it was a letter.

In Caroline's silence, he handed her the bag. "Read it," he said.

Caroline stared through the plastic. The spurts of blood, dried thickly on the blue work shirt, were as she knew they must be.

"Read it," he repeated roughly.

Caroline laid down the bag. Fumbling, she opened the envelope. The letter was addressed to her.

Swallowing, she made herself read. The voice, she thought, could be no one else's.

The prose was flat, unemotional. In persuasive detail, with little feeling, it explained how he had killed James Case. The letter gave his reasons, but asked no sympathy. Its only excuses were for Brett.

Silent, Caroline looked up at him.

"The original is in my safe-deposit box," he said. "In case I was suddenly taken."

"And if you weren't . . . ?" She let the question die there.

Her father stood taller. "Then I was prepared to go to Jackson—to go, in fact, if you failed at this hearing. But it seemed you were on the verge of discrediting that wretched Megan."

"And look at how you let Brett suffer, waiting."

"Three weeks isn't that long to live with something." Channing's face was stoic now. "I know. I've lived with that last summer for twenty-three years."

Caroline stared at him. "Lived with *what* . . . ?"

Her father paused. And then, with quiet simplicity, he said, "Your David is dead, Caroline."

Caroline felt herself step backward, heart pounding like an anvil in her chest. "How can you know that?"

"He was lost on the sound that night." Her father paused, forcing himself to look at her. "They found the catboat near Tarpaulin Cove, broken to pieces on the rocks."

Caroline folded her arms, bent her head. She rocked on her heels, back and forth, to keep herself from writhing. "You knew." Her voice was choked. "All along, you *knew*. . . ."

Channing touched his forehead. "For three days, Caroline, I hoped—even prayed—that he had somehow gotten through it. I never meant for that to happen." Slowly, he shook his head, as if reliving the moment of knowledge. "And then the Coast Guard called.

"The boat was registered to me, you see. They didn't associate it with David. So I simply told them the boat had slipped its moorings. . . ."

"Why?"

"To keep you from knowing." Channing's face was etched with pain. Softly, he finished, "I didn't want to lose you, Caroline."

Helpless, Caroline turned from him. It was as if she could not breathe.

"You know everything now." Her father's voice was lifeless. "I'll come to Jackson tomorrow. Please go."

In front of her, Caroline saw the books, the picture of a laughing girl, the gun. Through an act of will, she faced her father again.

His face was a ghost of what it once had been. Only his eyes, suddenly moist, remained alive to her.

"Caroline . . . ," he tried, and for that moment she remembered all there was between them: the hikes, long days on the lake, the death of her mother, talks across the dinner table, their plans for her future, the lawyer she would be. The loss of David. The ways in which, for all the years since and against her will, he still defined who Caroline Masters was.

Whatever he had meant to say, it seemed that he could not.

"You came home again, Caroline. At last, and for whatever reason." His voice became thick. "Now, please, leave me here."

Caroline steeled herself. For a last moment, she looked into his face. And then, unable to answer, nodded.

Blindly, she walked past him, into the night.

She stopped there, a few feet from his door, and then the effort of composure overtook her.

Caroline held her head up. In deep breaths, she inhaled the pine-scented air.

Still she did not leave. She stood there, listening. The night was cool and quiet.

Through the half-open door, Caroline heard a hollow pop.

Her eyes shut. In the aching, awful silence, she could not bring herself to move.

But there was no one else. As she had said to Betty, this was hers to do.

Slowly, Caroline turned and walked back through the door.

She stopped, stiff and silent. No sound came from her throat.

Her father had been kind, she saw. His face and head were intact; the wound, fresh blood still spreading, had been to the heart.

The gun lay by his hand, near the letter and the bag of clothes. His eyes stared up at her, unseeing. They would never see her again.

Caroline knelt, and closed them.

As she did this, she looked into his face. Within moments, she knew, the humanity would leave him, and his body would have the waxen otherness of death. But there was color in his face yet, and his skin was still warm.

Slowly, she removed her hand.

She stayed one more moment, the beating of a heart. And then she stood, turning away, and went to call Jackson. She never looked at her father again.

THREE

A FEW YARDS from her, the headlights stopped. The motor cut off. A car door slammed, and then Caroline heard the crunch of footsteps on gravel.

In the darkness, Jackson stood in front of her. There was something unready about him, as if he was still startled from sleep. But his eyes were quite clear.

"He's in there," Caroline said.

Jackson did not move. Silent, he watched her face.

"Please," she told him. "Just take care of this for me. I can't do it, anymore."

But Jackson did not leave her; perhaps he knew that some part of her did not wish him to leave. He took both her wrists, and asked, "What has all this been about?"

"Too many things." Caroline paused, then looked into his face. "Brett's my daughter, Jackson."

His eyes were still. Softly, he murmured, "Sweet Jesus Christ."

He did not let go of her wrists.

When the EMTs came, the two of them had not moved. Behind the ambulance was the flashing light of a police car.

All at once, Caroline thought of Brett. "Go ahead," she told him. "You'll need to see what he left. Before they screw it up."

He looked at her, understanding now, and slowly nodded.

Motionless, Caroline heard him enter the cabin. Stood there as the EMTs and police, barely noticing her, rushed past in the driveway.

Below the cabin, she remembered, was a bench that faced the lake.

Taking the steps her father had built, Caroline went there. She sat gazing at the lake, a sheet of glass on the windless night.

There was little sound, only voices from the cabin, sometimes

Jackson's. Caroline wished that she could feel something. But all she felt was emptiness, her emotions at bay.

He was dead, she told herself, and Brett was free. Why did she feel nothing?

It was a moment before she heard Jackson Watts behind her. "I've called the state police," he said. "I'm getting you out of here. They can do the rest."

She did not look up. "There are others to call," she answered. "Betty . . ."

"She can wait."

Caroline did not argue.

The drive to Jackson's fishing camp was perhaps ten minutes. Caroline sat in the passenger seat; Jackson glanced over from time to time, but said nothing. Entering his cabin, Caroline saw the fireplace, registered that they had once made love here. It seemed years ago.

Jackson led her to the screened porch. She sat on a couch; through a clearing in the trees, the lake was a dark oval. Caroline stared at it, unseeing.

"Do you want something?" he asked.

"No. Thank you."

Sitting in a corner of the couch, Jackson did not touch her. The one sensation Caroline had was of her separateness.

"You can talk to me," he said at last. "Or you can go on the way I think you must have, for years."

Caroline did not look at him; even speaking was an effort. "I'm not sure I know how," she answered. "I don't even know where to start."

"Anywhere, Caroline. The first thing that comes to you."

She was too weary for defenses; in silent answer, against her will, Caroline's mind broke free. The first startling image that came to her—black hair swirling in the water—constricted her chest.

"My mother," she heard herself say, and then she could not finish.

Caroline felt his arms around her. "Tell me."

In a monotone, before she could stop to think, Caroline told him everything.

Her mother, and how she had died. Falling in love with David.

Her sister's betrayal, and then her father's. How Brett had come to be born, and given up. Why Caroline had returned.

And then, because he must know, the events of the last three weeks. The missing knife. Breaking into Megan's apartment. The pattern, half fact and half intuition, through which she had divined her father's guilt. Their last confrontation. The moment, twenty-three years late, when she learned that David was dead.

When she had finished, Caroline could not look at him.

"Do you know what Father told me?" she asked dully. "That he was afraid of losing me."

She felt Jackson's arms close tighter. "Well," he said at last, "you didn't lose me. Just misplaced me for a while."

Caroline felt something move inside her. She turned to him, looking into his worn, kind face, and then quite suddenly, helpless to prevent this, she began crying, convulsively and uncontrollably, as she never had since the night that David had vanished.

Jackson simply held her.

The first light broke on the lake.

Exhausted, Caroline lay on the couch in Jackson's arms. It was, she thought, cruelly like a normal day.

"What are you thinking?" she asked.

He was quiet for a moment. "That you were right not to tell me, in a way. I could never have understood, then."

"And now?"

"I think so, yes."

If only, Caroline thought, she could stay here with him. And then the image of her father came to her again.

As if knowing this, Jackson said, "We have things to do this morning. Starting with Fred Towle, who's expecting us in court."

Through her weariness, Caroline felt the lawyer part of her stir again. She sat up. "How should we handle that?"

"I will." Jackson slid away, facing her. "I'll tell Fred that your father's dead. And that I'm dismissing the case without prejudice. . . ."

"Without prejudice?"

"It's all I can do, Caroline. Until we've had an autopsy and completed our inquiry. I won't tell Fred or the media what's happened until you and I have worked out what to say. But I'll make sure

Brett's kicked loose this morning." Jackson paused, and then finished evenly. "Your job is to explain all this to her. At least as much as you care to."

Silent, Caroline nodded.

Jackson watched her. Then, quietly, he asked, "Does Brett think that she's their daughter?"

Caroline looked away. "Yes."

Walking to the edge of the porch, he stood there, gazing at the lake, hands in his pockets. "Do you mean to tell her the truth?"

Somewhere in her subconscious, Caroline realized, she had asked this of herself. "I don't know, Jackson. I'm in no shape to do that now. Or even to decide about it."

Jackson turned to her, studying her face. "But our world goes on, doesn't it? Perhaps today, that's a mercy."

Caroline thought of Betty. For a moment, she felt too weary to stand.

Slowly, she walked to Jackson's telephone, to tell Betty that their father was dead.

FOUR

CAROLINE'S CAR WAS still at her father's camp. Jackson made telephone calls, arranged for its release; when he dropped her there, the yellow tape marking the scene had been cut at the head of the driveway, and a trooper was waiting. Her father's body was gone; for Caroline, the false cheer of morning had a bleak, pitiless quality.

She turned to Jackson. "Thank you."

He nodded but did not touch her. They were professionals once more.

"Call me," he said. "After you've seen Brett. Among other things, we'll need to work on a statement."

"Sure."

She sounded all right, Caroline thought, and she would need to be. But watching Jackson leave, she felt alone.

She walked to her car, got in. Sat there, gazing through the windshield at her father's cabin. And then she remembered the photographs.

They were still on the car seat. Numb, she looked at them again, the faces she had asked Joe Lemieux to capture as they entered the courthouse.

Megan. Betty. Larry. Her father . . .

He was climbing the courthouse steps, stiff-gaited, refusing to look down. Gaze straight ahead, the last effort of an old man's dignity.

Caroline's eyes filled with tears again.

Brett, she knew, should never see these. Before she started the car, Caroline placed the photographs beneath the seat.

. . .

When the woman trooper brought her to the booking area, Brett looked stunned. Her first steps toward Caroline were tentative.

For a moment, Caroline could not speak. The reality had hit her; the young woman in front of her, David's daughter, had been given back her life.

"It's over," Caroline said. "You're free."

At Brett's first, uncertain smile, Caroline looked away.

"What happened?" Brett asked.

Caroline took her hand. "Let's go outside."

As they left, Brett looked over her shoulder. In the sunlight, the large brick building appeared bland, even benign. But its shadow, Caroline suspected, would never quite leave either of them.

Brett turned back to her. "How did you do this?" she asked.

Silent, Caroline walked ahead of her, and sat on the grass. Brett stopped, looking down at her; Caroline could see her own expression register in the girl's green eyes. She knelt, still watching Caroline.

Caroline drew a breath. "Your grandfather is dead. He shot himself."

Brett's face seemed to twitch. And then it fixed in a queer, hurt look, the struggle to absorb and understand. "James . . ."

"Yes. Father killed him."

It was a day, Caroline thought, for tears.

When Brett's came, they were silent. Even as they ran down her face, her eyes remained on Caroline, as if searching for a reason.

It's been too much, Caroline thought. She took Brett's hands in hers. And to her surprise, Brett asked, "Tell me how it happened."

Caroline considered her, and then, without emphasis or inflection, told her as much as seemed right.

"He wouldn't have left you here," she finished. "But he couldn't face you, either."

Brett winced; Caroline imagined her remembering the moment she found James dying. A moment now much farther from healing, or even comprehension.

As if aware of this, Brett's thoughts flickered to Caroline. "You found Grandfather."

"Yes."

"My God . . ."

"I'm all right." Caroline paused, correcting herself. "No. I'm not all right. But I wanted to tell you myself."

The answer seemed to push Brett's thoughts back to herself. Where, Caroline thought, they should be. She did not want this girl's compassion, much less when it was not for the truth. It was enough that Caroline was here.

Arms folded, Brett stared at the grass between them. "I loved Grandfather," she said at last. Beneath the pain in her voice, Caroline heard the fear of something too enormous to bear. "I'm sorry . . . I don't know what to do. About him, or any of this."

Caroline felt the words pierce her. It was a while before she spoke. "Some things—terrible things—are like that. There's no lesson to be learned, no explanation that will help. Sometimes no explanation, period. In the end, all you're left with is yourself. And, if you're lucky, the understanding of a friend or two."

Tears filled Brett's eyes again. "You're talking about you, too."

Caroline hesitated, and then she nodded. "I'm not even sure when I'll next sleep through the night. But I've been here before, so I know the way back. Perhaps I can help."

Brett reached out for Caroline's hands again; her fingers, curled in her mother's, felt warm. "Can we stay here?" she said at last. "I don't want to see them yet. Or anyone."

Caroline looked at her, filling with a silent ache. David is dead, she wanted to tell her, your father is dead. But she could not. At least for now, for better or for worse, Brett had a father, the one whom Caroline had given her. Caroline did not know how to replace him with a memory that was hers alone.

"I'll stay with you," she answered. "As long as you want."

FIVE

Jackson had been right, Caroline thought: today the law's demands were a kindness.

She had driven Brett to Masters Hill. Larry and Betty waited on the porch; dropping Brett off, Caroline did not go in. As Brett looked back at her, Caroline had the irrational, bitter sense of having deserted her once more. Then Betty pulled Brett into her arms, and Caroline drove away.

Now she worked with Jackson at Carlton Grey's office. Again, Jackson was the consummate professional. His press release required little editing.

Retired Judge Channing Masters, it said, was an apparent suicide. A preliminary inquiry had uncovered substantial evidence—including a written confession—to suggest that he had killed James Case. Pending full investigation, the indictment against Brett Allen was dismissed. A more complete statement would be forthcoming as the facts were known.

Caroline's statement was equally terse. It confirmed that Channing Masters was dead. On her family's behalf, she expressed understanding that the evidence had led to a mistaken judgment, and thanked the Attorney General's Office for Brett's prompt release. Except to state relief at Brett's exoneration and sadness over the circumstances of Judge Masters' death, the family would have no further comment. Now, or ever.

Jackson read it. "Very gracious. At least to me."

"Of course."

He pushed his chair back, gazing at her across the desk. "I'll do the press," he said. "Go hide."

• • •

Afternoon became evening, and then night. Caroline stayed in her room, not hungry, unable to sleep. Betty was dealing with the prosaic details of a nonprosaic death: scheduling a service, arranging a burial, trying to fathom what a clergyman might say. As she should be, Brett was with them; like Caroline, they were not answering any but the most pressing messages; unlike Caroline, they could retreat into the circle of family. There was nothing for Caroline to do.

Far too tired to sift her own thoughts, she lay there, far from sleep.

There was a knock on the door.

What could it be? Caroline wondered. She had refused to answer any calls from the press; one after another, slips of paper had appeared beneath the door, to be filed in her wastebasket until the moment—if ever—that further comment was helpful to Brett.

Gingerly, Caroline opened the door.

It was the night manager, a shy man with a cowlick and a look of perpetual bemusement. "It's another telephone call," he said. "This man says he's the President. Problem is, the man sounds like the President."

For a moment, Caroline did not know what to say. "I'd like to hear this," she answered. "Put him through."

A minute later, the telephone rang in her room.

"Caroline?"

"Mr. President?"

"Well, I'm glad I reached you." His voice, Caroline realized as he paused, was a mixture of warmth and discomfort. "They brought me a wire report, not long ago. It's obvious you've suffered a tragedy, and we wanted you to know how much we sympathize. About your father, and about how you must be feeling." Another pause. "It's not too early to call, is it? This must just be sinking in."

Caroline found herself strangely touched. "No. It's not too early. Actually, this is a help to me."

"Then there's something else I ought to say, for whatever little it's worth in circumstances like these. That you were right to believe in your niece, and stand by her no matter what." His voice grew quieter. "They say a lot of us ought to be disqualified from office for wanting it too much. I don't know about that. But the choice you made reflects well on you, as a person and a prospective judge. And it's sure not any disqualification."

All at once, the irony of this came over her. There was never any choice but to stand by Brett; not knowing that, the President admired her for something she could not help. But she was far too tired, and too grateful for the misperception, to say this.

She simply thanked him, and got off.

Two nights later, her life in suspension, Caroline ate with Jackson at his fishing camp. It slowly dawned on her that he had remained here, taking a few vacation days, because of her. But she did not know how to acknowledge this.

Caroline ate a juicy piece of T-bone steak, washed it down with Cabernet. "I just couldn't tell him," she said.

It continued a conversation dropped before dinner. But Jackson, looking at her over his wineglass, knew at once that she meant the President. "I expect," he answered, "that you didn't really want to."

Caroline felt defensive. "As I said before the hearing, I've stopped wanting to be a judge. After all this, why on earth should it matter to me?"

Jackson gazed at the fire. "Over the years, Caroline, you became someone. You don't stop being that person just because you've had to face the reasons for it."

Who would she be, Caroline remembered asking herself, if not a judge or a lawyer? "It's not just that. Or even the time it will take to process what my father did. It's that I broke into Megan's apartment." Her voice turned flat. "That's not the kind of thing that judge-type people do."

Jackson gazed at the fire. "Megan perjured herself," he said at last. "Who'd believe her?"

"No," Caroline said sharply. "I can't lie about that."

Jackson turned to her now. With great calm, he answered, "You'll never have to. I've made it very clear to your friend Megan that whether she's indicted for perjury is wholly up to me. And that I don't expect to see her charging anyone else with any crimes—whether in the courts or in the media." He paused. "She's left college, Caroline, and dropped out of sight. All she wants to do is avoid what last humiliation she can. She's not a problem for you, anymore. And never will be." He smiled a little. "After all, I have her diary now."

Caroline frowned. "I don't want you to salvage me. Please don't try. . . ."

"You were trying to salvage your daughter, for Christ sake. People do worse every day—I did worse, in this case, without breaking a single law. Which has led to some sobering midnight thoughts. But I very much doubt I'll let them keep me from a judgeship."

Caroline shook her head. "You misjudged a witness, Jackson. I broke the law. On the Court of Appeals I'd have to review case after case of other people who broke it, many of whom offer up the most sympathetic of reasons. How can I do that, knowing what I know?"

"Because it would be so colossally stupid not to. You're a brilliant lawyer and, more to the point, a compassionate one. Nothing about this experience makes either of those less true."

Caroline stood abruptly, walking to the fire. For a time, she watched the flames, flickering orange blue. "Right now," she said at last, "what I do with Brett seems a little more important."

She felt Jackson step behind her. "What do you want to do?"

"Want?" She turned to him with sudden intensity, felt the depth of her desire and need. "Every fiber in me wants her for my daughter. I'm so damned sick of lies. But it's much more than that." She looked at him intently now, tears coming to her eyes. "I want her in my life, Jackson. The other day, watching Betty put her arms around her, I was so damned scared of losing her again."

He looked at her with sympathy and something that, in her despair, she could not quite identify. "How would Brett take it, I wonder?"

"I don't know—all right, I think, in time. But the one sure way to keep her is to tell her who I am. If anyone knows the power of parenthood, I do." With sickening suddenness, Caroline heard herself, and then her voice became almost pleading. "She's still a young woman, and I could help her. Before, I never believed that. But now I've been with her, and I know I could. How can I just walk off and leave her again?"

Jackson gave her a considering look. He did not reach for her. "As I just told you," he said at last, "you're a compassionate person. Whatever it is, I'm sure you'll know what's right to do."

SIX

THREE MORNINGS LATER, when they buried her father, Caroline still did not know.

The service was at the chapel at Masters Hill. The family sat in its pew—Larry at the end, Brett between Caroline and Betty. None of them said much; before the service began, Brett touched Caroline's hand. She looked tired but composed.

"Are you all right?" Caroline asked.

Brett could not quite answer. "He was my grandfather," she said simply.

The pews were almost filled. Caroline knew many of the faces: people too decent to stay away or to forget who Channing Masters had been to them. Caroline felt the passing of a time. Many who came were old; Channing had been retired for over a decade, and most of his works—large and small—were now a matter of memory. He would surely be the last of them to be buried on Masters Hill.

The service itself was spare and decorous—a soft-spoken minister whom Caroline did not know, simple words from the Old Testament, an expression of hope and redemption. Caroline listened fitfully; she had left this to Betty and Larry. As little as she believed in an afterlife, she believed even less in public pieties, the rituals by which the living, seeking to comfort themselves, obscure the truth about the dead and the act of dying. Her mother's funeral had been enough: Caroline would bury her father, and David, in whatever way her heart might find.

Still, she went to the graveside.

They buried him next to Betty's mother, Elizabeth Brett. What might have happened, Caroline wondered, if Elizabeth had lived? There might have been sons to slake her father's needs; Nicole Dessaliers might still live, an old woman in Paris. Surely there would have been no Caroline, no Brett, and her father would have died as he had meant to, in the fullness of time. And then the earth had covered him, and the four of them were alone.

They stood facing each other, standing around the fresh-turned dirt, Brett between Betty and Larry. What memories of him did they have together? Caroline wondered; in that moment, what she must do became clear to her. Though perhaps she had always known.

She looked at Brett, then at Larry. "Leave us here," she asked.

They knew what she meant. Larry nodded, and turned to Brett. Caroline watched them leave, side by side, walking to their house beneath the cool gray sky.

Caroline faced Betty across their father's grave. "I won't tell her," she said at last.

Betty's gaze was steady, stoic. "Why, Caroline? When it's so clear to me that you want to."

Caroline nodded. "I do, very much. But no one should have to re-interpret her entire life at the age of twenty-two. That's what you, and Father, made *me* do. I can't bring myself to do the same to Brett." Caroline's voice filled with emotion. "Though there have been times, understanding what was done to limit her, that I've quite forgotten how selfish that would be."

Betty reddened. "Yes. It would be selfish."

"But there's a price," Caroline went on. "When she was born, I let her go. I can do it again. As long as you do, too."

"What do you mean?"

"That it's time for Brett to leave here. Leave you, if she wishes. Which, when she comes to terms with this, I'm very sure she will."

Silent, Betty gazed at their father's grave, and then nodded. "If she does, I won't try to keep her. *Now.*"

Caroline regarded her. "Then I doubt you'll see me again. Except, I hope, on Brett's occasions—a wedding, perhaps a baby. But you needn't have me on your conscience, Betty. I think that, now, I'll be able to let you go." She paused a moment; in the distance, she could see Brett and her father. "As for Larry, tell him that perhaps I always knew what he would do, and shut my eyes. It was all too much for me, then."

Betty seemed to look at her across the years, a graying woman who long ago, and at great cost, had gained for herself a daughter.

"Can you really live without telling her?" she asked. "You won't look at her, or someday her child, and need for her to know?"

Caroline shook her head. "I've become a very disciplined person, Betty. You should know that much by now." Caroline paused for a moment, and then told her sister the rest of it. "It's enough that I came back for her," she finished softly. "Brett will never be my daughter. But, for me, I've earned the right to feel like her mother."

SEVEN

ALONE, CAROLINE STOOD by her mother's grave, where Betty had left her.

Well, Caroline said silently, *it's over now. I've done the best I could.*

In the quiet, a few birds calling, she felt someone behind her.

Turning, Caroline saw her daughter, waiting for her.

"Do you mind?" Brett asked. "My mother said you might be here."

"No. I meant to see you before I left." Caroline paused. "To say how sorry I am that you have to live with this."

Brett stepped closer now, hands in her pockets, seeming to avoid the sight of Channing's grave. "I've loved Grandfather all my life. And then he kills someone I care for. How could he have thought that was out of love for me?"

How best to answer? Caroline wondered. "He was old, Brett. Something happened to him."

Brett gave a short, dissatisfied shake of the head. "He wasn't old when you left here. Was that over a boy?"

Her face, Caroline thought, was so very much like Nicole's. Except that the mouth and chin were David's. "Yes," she answered simply. "It was."

Brett regarded her in silence. "I'm too old to need protecting, Caroline. From whatever this is about."

"I know that. But I'm protecting me. And I've got enough to deal with just sorting through this for myself." Pausing, Caroline searched for a truth that might be helpful. "Your grandfather was a troubled man. I don't know why; he wouldn't, couldn't, talk about himself . . . his own parents, his own hurts, anything. But there was something damaged about him: although he badly wanted to, he didn't know how to love my mother, or your mother, or me, or you, or how to give us what we needed. Because whatever it was he needed kept him from knowing. So that, in the end, all of us were damaged too. You least of all.

"You're young, Brett. You've got a whole life, and now it's yours. There's nothing about you to keep you from living it fully."

Brett seemed to watch her. "I'd never met you," she said at last. "But ever since you got here, I could sense you weren't going to let anything worse happen to me. At least if you could help it."

Caroline gazed back at her, the daughter she loved in secret, standing near the headstone of her grandmother Nicole. It made Caroline want to smile, though she did not know why. "I wasn't," she answered. "It didn't matter what you'd done. Though it rather pleases me that it was nothing."

Brett tilted her head. "Was that because of Grandfather? Things you thought we had in common?"

"Perhaps at the start. But, in the end, it was because of you."

Brett hesitated, and then she touched Caroline's sleeve. "Will I see you again?"

Caroline smiled. "Maybe you'll come to see me. I'd like that, very much."

"Would you?"

"Oh, yes. After all, you've never been to San Francisco."

Brett smiled at this; for an instant, Caroline wanted to hold her, to tell her how she truly felt. Then she saw the fresh grave of her father, and knew once more that the final judgment was hers to make, the wounds of silence hers to bear.

For a last time, Caroline studied her daughter's face.

"I'm ready to leave here," she said. "Are you?"

Brett was quiet for a moment. "Yes," she answered, "I am."

EIGHT

"So you're leaving tomorrow," Jackson said.

"Uh-huh. By six o'clock, I'll be in San Francisco." Caroline's voice softened. "It's time, Jackson. Before I make some terrible mistake."

They sat at the end of Jackson's boat dock, each drinking a can of beer and watching the last light of evening fade on Heron Lake. Quietly, Jackson said, "You did the right thing, you know."

Caroline turned to him. "Did I?"

"Sure." He smiled a little. "Besides, who ever said you'd be such a great mother? Was yours?"

Caroline gave him a cool look. "That hurts a bit, you know. But no, she wasn't particularly. In some ways, I suppose, I was my own mother."

Jackson had stopped smiling. "Then I take it all back." He fell quiet for a moment. "You're a good person, Caroline. To me, you grasped what seems important here: that your father's silence hurt you, but that—at least for now—yours is a kindness. And that there are no rules for this kind of thing, merely the hope of empathy."

She faced him now, sitting cross-legged on the dock. "You're the only person I've told all this. Perhaps the only one I'll ever tell."

He gazed at her a moment, accepting this. "Then that makes me indispensable, doesn't it? Or maybe just inconvenient."

Caroline shook her head. "No," she said. "You've helped me a lot. You know that."

The look that Jackson gave her was tentative, inquiring. "Because I've wondered, after all this settles in, whether you'd ever want to see me again. Or whether, for your own sake, it would be easier to do what you did before."

For a long time, Caroline was quiet. "It's gone too far for that, I think. Although I guess I'd like it better if, like Brett, you came to San Francisco." Caroline smiled. "Of course, you'll save hotel fare if you stay with me. I hear civil servants in New Hampshire don't make much money. Even judges." She touched his hand, finishing quietly: "I do care for you, Jackson. More than I ever knew."

After a moment, Jackson smiled again. "Then do me a favor, okay?"

"What's that?"

"Take the judgeship, Caroline. You don't have to give up everything. And it may make you better company."

In that moment, looking at Jackson, Caroline saw that this was more than kindness. He was asking her to accept the gift of his generosity. To accept it for herself.

Perhaps she could, Caroline thought. Perhaps she could accept who she was: the daughter of Channing and Nicole, mother in silence to Brett. Flawed, with a life she did not yet understand, but learning still. She could feel Jackson watching her.

That night, Caroline stayed with him.

The next morning Caroline Clark Masters, soon to be a judge of the United States Court of Appeals, flew back to San Francisco to prepare for her confirmation hearings. Her niece, Brett, drove her to the airport.

ACKNOWLEDGMENTS

As usual, my task was made easier by a number of friends, old and new.

In San Francisco, I consulted Assistant District Attorney Bill Fazio; defense attorneys Hugh Anthony Levine and Jim Collins; medical examiner Boyd Stephens; homicide inspector Napoleon Hendrix; and private investigator Hal Lipset. And once again, Assistant District Attorney Al Giannini advised me and reviewed the manuscript. For three books now, their help has been invaluable.

Readers devoted to New Hampshire will recognize that Masters Hill and the town of Resolve are fictional locations: a small community in New Hampshire seemed too particular a place to fairly depict here. I hope that I have nonetheless captured the flavor and legal milieu of this unique region. My dear friend and fellow writer Maynard Thomson helped impart to me his deep love and appreciation for the state. Others generous with their time include Assistant Attorney General Janice Rundles; County Attorney Lincoln Soldati; Jennifer Soldati of the New Hampshire Trial Lawyers Association; attorney and writer John Davis; defense attorneys Bob Stein and Paul Maggiotto; Kathy Deschenaux of the office of the New Hampshire Medical Examiner; and Sergeant Kevin Babcock of the New Hampshire State Police. I owe all of them a great debt for whatever success I have achieved; any errors, or simplifications for narrative purposes, are mine.

Special mention should be made of the late Dr. Roger Fossum, chief medical examiner for the State of New Hampshire. In the time that I spent with Roger, I quickly came to appreciate the professionalism, intelligence, humanity, and good humor that endeared him to his many friends.

Martha's Vineyard has a unique charm and history. William Marks—environmentalist, publisher, and writer—was extraordinarily generous in sharing the history of the island, suggestions for locating specific scenes, and advice on sailing. The Vineyard portions of the novel would have been far different without him. Thanks also go to George Manter, a former chief of police of West Tisbury, who helped fill in several gaps in island history. In addition, John